Known to millions of readers for such novels as *Lady Chatterley's Lover*, *Women in Love*, and *The Fox*, D. H. Lawrence was an even greater artist in the shorter forms of fiction—the novella and the short story.

A Modern Lover is a comprehensive new collection of twenty-two of his finest stories. Selected from the more than fifty short stories and novellas he published, they span his entire career and include his most famous shorter works—"The Prussian Officer," "The Princess." "The Rocking Horse Winner," "The Woman Who Rode Away"—stories that place him with Chekov among the great masters of the short story form.

Above all, these stories reflect the ideas—the obsessions—of Lawrence's creative life: the struggle for dominance between the possessive woman and the male; the acceptance of the body's sexuality; the recognition that the spontaneous promptings of desire are stifled and crushed in modern technological society; and the belief that powerful tides of sexual attraction in men and women are the source of health and of life.

WITH A FOREWORD BY JULIAN MOYNAHAN
Professor of English, Rutgers University

A MODERN LOVER
and other stories
by

D. H. Lawrence

with a foreword by
Julian Moynahan

BALLANTINE BOOKS • NEW YORK

Contents

Foreword ix

A Modern Lover 1

New Eve and Old Adam 25

The Prussian Officer 51

Daughters of the Vicar 75

The Shades of Spring 131

The White Stocking 148

Odour of Chrysanthemums 173

England, My England 195

Tickets, Please 229

The Blind Man 243

Monkey Nuts 264

You Touched Me 279

Samson and Delilah 298

The Horse Dealer's Daughter 316

The Princess 335

Sun 379

The Woman Who Rode Away 398

The Lovely Lady 437

Rawdon's Roof 457

The Rocking-Horse Winner 469

The Blue Moccasins 486

Things 504

Foreword

SOME WRITERS are better than others at bringing out the truth about the life, inner and outer, of a whole people living together at a particular time and in a particular place. They make us believe in what they saw. No amount of subsequent cultural, social and demographic change ever quite manages to cover up or make irrelevant to the present and future their inspired testimony.

One goes to Mark Twain to recover the life of mid-nineteenth-century middle America and to Thoreau for the life of New England villages and farms in its autumnal, postpuritan phase. The rural England of the eighteenth-century squirearchy and yeomanry is alive in the novels of Fielding, the early industrial megalopolis of London is animate in the novels of Dickens, and the whole strange transition of American life from the town and the farm to the city, the urban neighborhood and the plant is expressed in the novels Dreiser was writing forty to fifty years ago. Quite possibly the most recent non-fiction books of Norman Mailer, books like *Armies of the Night*, have this same knack, this same fidelity, in rendering the life of a people in a period of acute cultural and social crisis, although, because we as readers are in the midst of this crisis, we cannot be absolutely sure until a few more years have elapsed.

Notice that this quality of fidelity has little to do with objectivity, "realism," universal scope, possession of vast accumulations of data. The books of Twain and Fielding are full of comic distortion and fantasy, and even Dreiser's massively documented novels are full of ill-founded, essentially subjective notions of fate, "chemisms" and Darwinian determinism. Thoreau was a poet and mystic who did most of his observing locally and on foot and whose library consisted largely of 750 unsold copies of his first book, *A Week on the Concord and the Merrimac*. Dickens' London is the city of a great fantasist and caricaturist, not that of a literary urban sociologist or realist. But if you go to the middle of New York State, to the factory towns of the Mohawk River valley and the lakes nearby, you will find yourself reentering a world in which Dreiser's Clyde Griffiths, with his pathetic and ultimately murderous dreams of material success and luxury, still haunts the air. If you go to modern, traffic-snarled London you will find, around the first or second corner off High Holborn or Mile End Road, the old weird London of Dickens still palpably present. And if you go to the Mississippi River valley some part of you at least will find itself vibrating to rhythms and tones of life which Twain first plucked from the air in the town of Hannibal, Missouri, and orchestrated in books like *Pudd'nhead Wilson* and *Huckleberry Finn*.

It seems from what I have said that any truth about the life of people, about human beings and their habitations, which is first grasped and expressed with fidelity by a writer somehow tuned in to, in touch with, fundamental aspects of this life will become a permanent truth, surviving any amount of subsequent historic change. I believe that this is so. The best writers of the sort I am talking about don't merely record but rather create the full human environment in which we as readers are privileged to live, and what passed centuries ago is still present and vital in their ever-living work: therefore also present in us as conscious, sentient persons and present in the world or the parts of a world which these writers truly saw and brought for the first time permanently into view.

D. H. Lawrence was this sort of writer and the first world he brought to view was the life of the ordinary English as they lived it in the first few decades of this century. This was the England of grimy brick and slate industrial villages and towns, of a still beautiful and ample rural establishment surrounding, yet constantly diminished by, an aggressive and powerful industrial establishment and by the congestion of a growing population, an England of class barriers, extremes of wealth and poverty, of power and powerlessness. Born a sickly child in a coal miner's household in the Midlands he saw ordinary English life from the inside and saw in particular—this is his fundamental note—how the crowding, the want, the ugliness, the mechanical and routinized patterns of work, personal relations and even recreation which a rich, acquisitive, production-oriented society imposed on all but the most privileged combined to stultify and devitalize men and women, separating them from one another, destroying the possibility of a vital human community, alienating each man from his own most basic and creative instincts for living.

Lawrence's indictment of the culture of industrialism was not new. The case had been made before as early as Ruskin and goes on being made. What was new was his genius for making poignantly evident through vivid but never merely realistic stories and novels the conditions creating human alienation and a visionary prospect of escape from those conditions. His artistic career became a search for what he once called "life kindled into vividness," and it carried him far beyond England, to Italy and Sicily, to the Orient and Australia, to the American southwest, generally to places that were remote enough from the centers of machine civilization to have perserved some naive spontaneous life.

Nevertheless, and even though Lawrence is the least insular of modern British writers, the center of his created world is England. One enters the long gray estuary of the Solent and disembarks at Southhampton. Perhaps one takes the train north from London through the red-brick factory districts and endless rows of brick row houses and suburban villas encroaching on more and more green pasture, tillage, woodland and shaggy common. Perhaps one gets off in a colliery or pottery or factory town, noticing that the chill air is full of noxious particles, and escapes into a pub where men speak of football, complain stupidly of the colored immigrants, or exchange bromides with barmaids wearing tight slacks or mini-miniskirts. With a few trifling changes it is still Lawrence's milieu, the milieu he put on the literary map, and, sadly enough, it is still unredeemed by Lawrence's vision. But perhaps on that same journey one notices something else: the way late sunlight slants across a plowed field, a certain ring in the laughter of a child, some unquenchable energy in the way a gaunt housewife strides along a market street. There is something in the air—a sort of glimmer, possibly an odor of chrysanthemums.

Let us consider Lawrence's superb early story, "An Odour of Chrysanthemums," for its fidelity to the life lived by ordinary people and for its vision of a remote yet real possibility of rekindling life to vividness. It is a story of entrapment, of the lives of working people trapped within the industrial system, but it finally locates in those lives irreducible human elements which define the characters' worth and dignity beyond the contingencies of any class or system.

The opening paragraph (see p. 73) establishes a tension which is expressed everywhere in Lawrence's work but always most movingly in the setting of his own native Midlands. Its principle of composition is simple contrast, the whole suffused in an atmosphere of diminishment and decline. We see colt against locomotive engine, jolting wagon against flying birds, pit bank against pond, black headstocks against late afternoon light; we hear the jolting, spasmodic clank of machinery against evening quiet; we sense the contrast between the bound, repetitive motion of lift machinery and locomotive wheels and the free movement in flight of animals and birds. These arrayed contrasts between machinery and a natural setting, embodying a tension between the necessity of human survival which called the industrial system into existence and the instinct of all living things to maintain themselves freely in being, are disturbed by one anomalous feature. A woman stands motionless, hemmed in between track and hedge, neither free to take flight like the animals, nor bound into a steely pattern of mechanical motion like the locomotive. She disappears immediately from the scene but the anomaly of this human entrapment remains and becomes the central motive of the story.

The drab cottage of Elizabeth Bates, clutched by its bony vine and with its long garden containing a few apple trees and some ragged chrysanthemums, presses up against the cinder roadbed of the line. The mother is tall, straight, handsome and fruitful, and she is also tense, unhappy and exhausted because of her miner husband's evening visits to the pub, with the worrisome inroads they make on the scanty housekeeping allowance. The family atmosphere, established by the scene of the supper and the talk between the children and the mother, is warm and close, and would normally include the father, whose prolonged absence on this particular evening disturbs all three.

Yet this atmosphere is also suffused with a parmanent tension. Elizabeth's inevitable anger at her husband's fecklessness, like the miner's drinking bouts, continues from day to day, and the children react anxiously to both these disturbing features of the shared life of the family. Finally, the husband, although we never see him alive, is a figure of anomaly. On the one hand his life is bound in with the motions of the machine through the rigid patterns of a work schedule; and perhaps the machine principle has even invaded his "free" time, since the drinking habits of workmen are at least partially determined by the over-fatigue and boredom consequent on heavy industrial labor. On the other hand, his mother remembers the warm laugh, perfect health and high animal spirits of his childhood. His wife has laid her "living flesh" against his and out of these conjunctions have come children and a child as yet unborn—new life that is unbound, unpredictable, alive with possibility.

In the story's central scene—the laying out of the miner's body by Elizabeth and her mother-in-law—we seem to pass beyond these contradictions:

> "You must help me now," she whispered to the old woman. Together they stripped the man.
> When they arose, saw him lying in the naive dignity of death, the women stood arrested in fear and respect. For a few moments they remained still, looking down, the old mother whimpering. Elizabeth felt countermanded. She saw him, how utterly inviolable he lay in himself. She had nothing to do with him. She could not accept it. Stooping, she laid her hand on him, in claim. He was still warm, for the mine was hot where he had died. . . . Elizabeth embraced the body of her husband, with cheek and lips.

She seemed to be listening, inquiring, trying to get some connection. But she could not. She was driven away. He was impregnable.

In this moving scene Elizabeth, and the reader, seem to recover an ultimate true vision of the fundamental, living reality of a man. But it is illusory. He *has* been violated. His warmth is from the mine. He is dead. Yet the image of this inviolable reality lingers, and tortures the wife in her grief as she reflects that she had never known him, or he known her. They had denied each other fundamentally. "And this had been her life and his life. She was grateful to death, which restored the truth."

The story's image of life in the industrial age is that of a sickly, late-blooming flower growing beside a rail line and appearing first in association with pregnancy—Elizabeth puts chrysanthemums in the band of her apron—finally in association with death. But we must be careful about this change. The flower is sickly, yet it has grown by itself until picked and will grow again. The miner's death restores the truth which the anomalous and alienating features of the industrial system have covered up. With perfect control and compassion Lawrence describes a waste of life in order to affirm life and discriminates the point from which civilizaiton must begin to reconstruct itself if we wish to recover a true vision of ourselves, one another, and the world. And this point is a deep recognition of the naive, inviolable, impregnable dignity of an ordinary workman laid out on the floor of a miner's cottage, his life wasted "accidentally," the lives of his family blighted, his cooling body prepared for burial.

II

Impressed by the exact knowledge Lawrence displayed of the routines of a mining community and by the story's brevity and apparent objectivity Ford Madox Ford, then editor of *The English Review,* immediately accepted "An odour of Chrysanthemums" for publication when it was submitted to him in 1911. Ford admired above all fiction in the manner of Flaubertian realism: stories should be products of painstaking,

impersonal craftsmanship; every detail must make a func-
tional contribution to a unified rendering of a subject or
theme, and the personal opinions and temperament of the
author must never come between the reader and the rendering. This in fact was not Lawrence's way with a story, as Ford
soon found out. It is important for us to understand how
energetically and explicitly Lawrence took issue with the as-
sumptions and techniques of the Flaubertian mode of prose
realism which, on the whole, have dominated twentieth-
century fiction from the early stories of Joyce to the latest
well-made *New Yorker* piece of today. As early as 1913
Lawrence writes disparagingly of Thomas Mann as the "last
sick sufferer from the complaint of Flaubert":

> while he has a rhythm in style, yet his work has none of the
> rhythm of a living thing, the rise of a poppy, then the after up-
> lift of the bud, the shedding of the calyx and the spreading wide
> of the petals, the falling of the flower and the pride of the seed-
> head. There is an unexpectedness in this such as does not come
> from . . . carefully plotted developments. Even *Madame Bovary*
> seems to me dead in respect to the living rhythm of the whole work.
> ("German Books—Thomas Mann," *Phoenix*: *The Posthumous Papers
> of D. H. Lawrence*, London, 1936, p. 313.)

What is most important here is Lawrence's insistence that
there are qualities and aspects of life, a certain vital rhythm,
a certain "pride" and "unexpectedness" which the fine stylistic
and technical calculations of a deliberated fictional method
are powerless to render.

He continued the argument into the years of his maturity
and it was based, not on caprice and ignorance, but on wide
thoughtful reading in the works of the great continental real-
ists, French, Russian, Italian and German, more often than
not in the original languages. Perhaps the clearest statement of
Lawrence's anti-Flaubertian position comes in the two intro-
ductory essays he wrote for his own translation of *Mastro-don
Gesualdo*, a novel by the great nineteenth-century Sicilian
writer Giovanni Verga. Here he attacks Flaubert and his
school for making a fetish of self-effacement ("self-effacement
is, of course, self-conscious and any form of emotional self-
consciousness hinders a first rate artist") and for the tightness

of their plotting and construction when so much of the meaning of life has nothing to do with tightness:

> As a matter of fact, we need more looseness. We need an apparent formlessness, definite form is mechanical. We need more easy transition from mood to mood and from deed to deed. A great deal of the meaning of life and art lies in the apparently dull spaces, the pauses, the unimportant passages. They are truly passages, the places of passing over.

("Preface to *Mastro-don Gesualdo*," *Phoenix*, p. 248.)

This is not an argument in favor of a weltering subjectivity, but for a loosening and opening up of form which will enable the writer to express subtle, perhaps inarticulate and inchoate shifts of consciousness and feeling that are not the less important for being totally unexpected when they occur. After the young doctor prevents Mabel Pervin in "The Horse Dealer's Daughter" from drowning herself in the pond he does what he is professionally trained to do by undressing her, wrapping her in blankets and warming her back to consciousness with whisky and a blazing fire. What happens after that —his slow, agonized recognition that he must say yes to her pathetic and naive question, "Do you love me then?"—comes as a total surprise, to him and to the reader, but it is also a surprise that is fully believable. One believes because the scene leading to the doctor's change of heart is a masterly, "indefinite" exposure of true states of feeling and awareness in both these shy and deeply shocked people. It is "true to life" in ways which the "tight" procedures of an objective realism are quite unable to grasp and express.

Lawrence also criticizes the school of realism for its submissiveness and abjectness. It sees too little in man's life that is creative and dynamic and takes the heart out of the human creature by pretending that we are in fact much less free and sovereign than we have it in us to become:

> Realism is just one of the arbitrary views man takes of man. It sees us all as little ant-like creatures toiling against the odds of circumstance, and doomed to misery. It is a kind of aeroplane view. It becomes the popular outlook, and so today we actually are, millions of us, little ant-like creatures toiling against the odds of circumstance and doomed to misery; until we take a

different view of ourselves. For man always becomes what he
passionately thinks he is; since he is capable of becoming almost
anything.
(*"Introduction to Mastro-don Gesualdo," Phoenix II: Uncollected
Prose Works by D. H. Lawrence,* London, 1968, p. 280.)

A capability of becoming almost anything, this based on
man's capacity for thinking passionately about the human
enterprise. Lawrence is, after all, the most hopeful and future-
oriented of modern writers. His call for looseness and open-
ness in fictional form is part of his impassioned vision of freedom for modern man: the freeing of instinct from its cultural
prison, the freeing of the human community from its bondage to outworn customs, from conventional religious beliefs
gone stale and dead, from all creeds and ideologies, including
literary ones, which teach that man is tied or doomed by
odds of present circumstance or the accumulated errors and
failures of his historic past.

Let it be said, however, that there is a rhythm of destruction in Lawrence's work to balance the emphasis on creative
becoming. Whatever is disintegrated or moribund receives
short shrift in the novels and stories. Characters like Egbert
in "England, My England," who cannot "come to grips with
life," come swiftly enough to ignoble death and there will
always be readers who are shocked by Lawrence's apparent
callousness in finishing such people off. But Egbert chooses
his fate, step by step. Until the very end he could choose
otherwise, could choose to move back from the brink and
begin to get in touch. Getting in touch is painful—witness
the insane confusion of Bertie when he is touched by Maurice
in "The Blind Man." And so Egbert, shrinking from that pain,
lacking "the robust, sap-like faith which keeps man going,"
gives himself to death on a Flanders battlefield.

Stories like "England, My England" risk more and in sur-
mounting that risk achieve more than any number of stories
by lesser writers who limit themselves to telling us what we
already know—even when it isn't true. But Lawrence can go
wrong and it is up to the reader to fight back when he does.
Reading Lawrence is always a battle—he intended it that
way—and my battle with "The Woman Who Rode Away,"

conducted over may years, convinces me that this is one place
where he went wrong. The lonely white woman goes to her
death robbed of her power to choose—she is captive *and*
drugged!—and she is heaped, scapegoat-fashion, with sins
of the white race that are never coherently defined. The
Indians are an idle bullying lot—one wonders when they ever
do any work. They are just as stereotyped as the redskins who
spend their lives biting the dust in the average movie western.
The story is full of beautiful scenic and stylistic effects. The
opening pages, which describe the woman's extraordinary condition of spiritual and psychological isolation, are unforget-
table. But finally there is a failure, precisely, of passion and
hope. The story misses the revelation at which it aimed.

Still, it is good to have it in the collection, to remind us that
Lawrence, like all great writers, worked constantly in a zone
of danger, snatching success again and again out of the very
jaws of defeat. His perpetual antagonists were despair and
anger. He wanted too much and hoped for too much out of
human kind. His was bound to be a self-lacerating sort of mission and when he died at the age of forty-five, prey to several
deadly organic diseases, he had quite literally written himself
to death in the pursuit of life. Yet how little of that exhaustion
and agony are reflected in the shapely, vital stories he composed during the relatively brief span—it was only two decades—of his mature working life. Lawrence was self-effacing
in the best, if not necessarily the Flaubertian sense. His advice was "trust the tale, not the artist." That is just what
the reader, encountering for the first or hundredth time the
animated, luminous images of his story-telling art, can almost
invariably do.

III

The present collection represents most sides of Lawrence's
story-telling career, from the earliest tales when he was drawing on first-hand knowledge of the lives of working people
in the Nottinghamshire-Derbyshire border areas of the Midlands, to the last stories when he was writing in a rather more
brittle, ironic manner about the rich and comfortable, yet

neurotic and capricious English upper and middle classes.
These latter stories were also based on first-hand knowledge,
for his early fame as a writer after the publication of *Sons and
Lovers* had brought him, as literary fame in England usually
does, into contact with the cultivated, educated coteries
whose center is London and the southern counties and
whose friendly acclaim frequently smothers the artists they
so generously, if patronizingly, admire. Lawrence escaped
this fate by refusing to forget his working-class origins, by
declining to become a literary house pet of the Bloomsbury
group and its bourgeois allies, and by leaving England for
a year or so before the First World War and more or less
for good after the Armistice.

Lawrence's tie to the working-class milieu was and remained, I think, a bond of love, but the love is open-eyed,
taking note of and rejecting qualities of meanness and drab-
ness in the living arrangements of ordinary people. He is not
in love with their poverty and puritancial inhibitions but believes they may be able to run the spiritual risks attendant
on a deep renewal of life quite simply because they have so
little security to lose. The strayed husband and the innkeeper
wife of "Samson and Delilah" wrestle each other into reconciliation when all the marriage counselors and family solicitors
of middle-class England might have been impotent to give
them useful advice, supposing they could have afforded such
services. The women in "An Odour of Chrysanthemums" and
"The Horse Dealer's Daughter" come to a deep if painful
recognition of truth only because the exposed circumstances
of their lives force them into wincing contact with what would
otherwise have remained covered up forever.

Money buys the leisure and cosmetics to forestall and then
hide the ravages of middle age. It buys power that can be
wielded over younger, poorer people. It buys "things" which
can be spread around to cover up the truth of life including
that physical truth called "change of life." Lawrence's middle-
aged, middle-class vampires in stories like "The Lovely Lady,"
"Rawdon's Roof" and "The Blue Moccasins" are handled
rather pitilessly and may represent in part the overpaying of
a debt of resentment he felt he owed his former Taos, New

Mexico hostess, Mrs. Mabel Evans Dodge Sterne Luhan. Nevertheless, his revelation of the domestic power politics and emotional bullying that can go on in the "best" households—he had broached this theme as early as "Daughters of the Vicar" and would bring it to a final rich climax in his opus posthumous, *The Virgin and the Gipsy*—is perfectly compelling and supplies a counterpoise to his many explorations into the family affairs of the working and lower middle classes.

More puzzling and ambiguous is Lawrence's relation to the displaced WASP Americans and English of stories like "Sun," "The Princess," and "The Woman Who Rode Away." Having himself followed the path of voluntary exile he knew the condition of rootlessness by looking into his own soul and by observing all too acutely many of the idle, monied people he lived among in Capri, Sicily, New Mexico and southern France after the War. There may be some self-hatred in his portrait of the icy and destructive "princess" Dollie Urquhart, but Lawrence after all had his art and his splendid wife Frieda to keep him occupied and loosened up. Certainly no heroine or hero in Lawrence receives a richer reward than the invalid Juliet in "Sun," when she is wooed back to health and fruitfulness by the sun god himself. The invalid Lawrence, pursuing the sun life-long and never getting close enough to save his life, may have written this story in "compensation" as they say but it seems to me like a free act of splendid generosity.

Of the stories reprinted in this volume I should say that the principal masterpieces are "The Prussian Officer," "Daughters of the Vicar," "An Odour of Chrysanthemums," "England, My England," "The Horse Dealer's Daughter," perhaps "The Princess" and "Sun" (in its restored version) and certainly "The Rocking-Horse Winner." The great successes occur in the early, middle and late phases of Lawrence's career, are composed in a number of extraordinarily distinct creative idioms, and are flanked by numerous stories—"The White Stocking," "The Blind Man" and "You Touched Me," for instance—which miss inclusion in the front rank by inches. This impression of creative abundance is greatly strengthened if one considers that the present editors have had to pass over another twenty-six stories which are given in the standard three-volume edition of Lawrence's complete short stories and that from this group one could probably select another seven or eight works of the first rank, none of which would merely embroider on the achieved technique and invention of any previous Lawrence story.

"The Prussian Officer," a tale of violation rendered in a style of now icy, now molten, now "electrical" brilliance, continues after more than fifty years and all the horrifying revelations of the totalitarian military and concentration-camp systems, to strike home with the force of revelation. It moves in an area between parable and allegory on the one hand and a studied realism on the other. It makes its effects felt from both extremes and from all the points in between. We remember that Lawrence admired the fluent allegorical stories of Hawthorne and wonder whether the timid New Englander would even have had the nerve to accept this fierce and masculine prose poem of mutual disintegration as a tribute properly due him from a great modern disciple.

"Daughters of the Vicar" uses quite a different idiom—it is much less violent and highly colored, much more subdued and apparently prosaic—to bring the destinies of the Lindley family at Aldecross out of the shadows of genteel respectability, genteel Christianity and genteel ill-health. To evoke only the opening pages, what is new here is Lawrence's fully concrete and penetrating sense of relationships among actions ordinary in themselves, suppressions of impulses to act, and downright refusals to act that lead on to certain consequences definable as "losing hold on life," and "going dead." Halfway between the specified actions performed, suppressed or thwarted, and the full consequences occur expressions like "going quiet" and "becoming neutral" which acquire a full and blighting precision in the context of the Lindley lives. It is all pitched quite low and is non-analytical in the sense of psychological analysis, and one reads on feeling that never before has any writer gotten so deep into the moral and spiritual morass of what we call "private life" without surrendering either his sympathy *or* his detachment *or* the full precision of an objective—but never impersonal!—style.

"The Rocking-Horse Winner," which is also about violation—in this case the violation of a child's life by his parents' money obsessions—uses still another idiom, opening like a folk tale, winning the reader's belief in the boy's magical powers as a handicapper by never losing touch with the tone of naïveté of narrative fable—until it all comes down, like a house of cards, a house of money rather, in the awful closing exchanges which return us in fear and trembling to what is called, with something less than complete accuracy, the "real world."

> "I never told you, mother, that if I can ride my horse and *get there,* then I'm absolutely sure—oh, absolutely! Mother, did I ever tell you? I *am* lucky!"
>
> "No, you never did," said his mother.
>
> But the boy died in the night.
>
> And even as he lay dead, his mother heard her brother's voice saying to her: "My God, Hester, you're eighty-odd thousand to the good, and a poor devil of a son to the bad. But poor devil, poor devil, he's best gone out of a life where he rides his rocking-horse to find a winner."

IV

Lawrence's ways of writing a story are not very imitable. Without the animating power of his vision the would-be disciple is apt to produce overblown lyricism, realism run to seed in lushness, hapless parody, or soft-core pornography. The modern realistic story, with its managed point of view and spare use of what Ford called "telling details" is, on the contrary, perfectly imitable. It can even be taught in creative-writing classes, as the late Frank O'Connor used to teach students in the Harvard Summer School to write Hemingway stories, Chekhov stories and O'Connor stories. Has Lawrence then any followers? And what is the extent of his influence on writers coming after him?

I think the answer is that Lawrence had had few close followers—the American novelist and short-story writer Sherwood Anderson tried to strike the Laurentian note in some of his later work and the results were disastrous—but that his influence has been inescapable and pervasive. He has shown all later writers something fundamental: new forms can be generated through the freeing of feeling, yet this is a process requiring a very arduous discipline, the discipline of utter emotional honesty. Like all lessons offered by the masters it may take more than a lifetime to grasp. Nevertheless, writers as far apart as Saul Bellow and George Orwell, Bernard Malamud and the Australian Patrick White, William Faulkner and Norman Mailer, Flannery O'Connor and Tillie Olsen, could not have moved as freely and adventurously in their artistic pursuits as they did and do had not Lawrence preceded them with his major breakthrough.

The literary future belongs to the young and the unborn. If they forget Lawrence they will be forgetting more than they can ever learn.

JULIAN MOYNAHAN
Rutgers University
New Brunswick, New Jersey

A MODERN LOVER

A Modern Lover

I

THE ROAD was heavy with mud. It was labour to move along it. The old, wide way, forsaken and grown over with grass, used not to be so bad. The farm traffic from Coney Grey must have cut it up. The young man crossed carefully again to the strip of grass on the other side.

It was a dreary, out-of-doors track, saved only by low fragments of fence and occasional bushes from the desolation of the large spaces of arable and of grassland on either side, where only the unopposed wind and the great clouds mattered, where even the little grasses bent to one another indifferent of any traveller. The abandoned road used to seem clean and firm. Cyril Mersham stopped to look round and to bring back old winters to the scene, over the ribbed red land and the purple wood. The surface of the field seemed suddenly to lift and break. Something had startled the peewits, and the fallow flickered over with pink gleams of birds white-breasting the sunset. Then the plovers turned, and were gone in the dusk behind.

Darkness was issuing out of the earth, and clinging to the trunks of the elms which rose like weird statues, lessening down the wayside. Mersham laboured forwards, the earth sucking and smacking at his feet. In front the Coney Grey farm was piled in shadow on the road. He came near to it, and saw the turnips heaped in a fabulous heap up the side of the barn, a buttress that rose almost to the eaves, and stretched out towards the cart-ruts in the road. Also, the pale breasts of the turnips got the sunset, and they were innumerable orange glimmers piled in the dusk. The two labourers who were pulping at the foot of the mound stood shadow-like to watch as he passed, breathing the sharp scent of turnips.

1

It was all very wonderful and glamorous here, in the old places that had seemed so ordinary. Three-quarters of the scarlet sun was settling among the branches of the elm in front, right ahead where he would come soon. But when he arrived at the brow where the hill swooped downwards, where the broad road ended suddenly, the sun had vanished from the space before him, and the evening star was white where the night urged up against the retreating, rose-coloured billow of day. Mersham passed through the stile and sat upon the remnant of the thorn tree on the brink of the valley. All the wide space before him was full of a mist of rose, nearly to his feet. The large ponds where hidden, the farms, the fields, the far-off coal-mine, under the rosy outpouring of twilight. Between him and the spaces of Leicestershire and the hills of Derbyshire, between him and all the South Country which he had fled, was the splendid rose-red strand of sunset, and the white star keeping guard.

Here, on the lee-shore of day, was the only purple showing of the woods and the great hedge below him; and the roof of the farm below him, with a film of smoke rising up. Unreal, like a dream which wastes a sleep with unrest, was the South and its hurrying to and fro. Here, on the farther shore of the sunset, with the flushed tide at his feet, and the large star flashing with strange laughter, did he himself naked walk with lifted arms into the quiet flood of life.

What was it he wanted, sought in the slowly-lapsing tide of days? Two years he had been in the large city in the south. There always his soul had moved among the faces that swayed on the thousand currents in that node of tides, hovering and wheeling and flying low over the faces of the multitude like a sea-gull over the waters, stooping now and again, and taking a fragment of life—a look, a contour, a movement—to feed upon. Of many people, his friends, he had asked that they would kindle again the smouldering embers of their experience; he had blown the low fires gently with his breath, and had leaned his face towards their glow, and had breathed in the words that rose like fumes from the revived embers, till he was sick with the strong drug of sufferings and ecstasies and sensations, and the dreams that ensued. But most folk had choked out the fires of their fiercer experience with rubble of sentimentality and stupid fear, and rarely could he feel the hot destruction of Life fighting out its way.

Surely, surely somebody could give him enough of the philtre of life to stop the craving which tortured him hither and thither, enough to satisfy for a while, to intoxicate him till he could laugh the crystalline laughter of the star, and bathe in the retreating flood of twilight like a naked boy in the surf, clasping the waves and beating them and answering their wild clawings with laughter sometimes, and sometimes gasps of pain.

He rose and stretched himself. The mist was lying in the valley like a flock of folded sheep; Orion had strode into the sky, and the Twins were playing towards the West. He shivered, stumbled down the path, and crossed the orchard, passing among the dark trees as if among people he knew.

II

He came into the yard. It was exceedingly, painfully muddy. He felt a disgust of his own feet, which were cold, and numbed, and heavy.

The window of the house was uncurtained, and shone like a yellow moon, with only a large leaf or two of ivy, and a cord of honeysuckle hanging across it. There seemed a throng of figures moving about the fire. Another light gleamed mysteriously among the out-buildings. He heard a voice in the cow-shed, and the impatient movement of a cow, and the rhythm of milk in the bucket.

He hesitated in the darkness of the porch; then he entered without knocking. A girl was opposite him, coming out of the dairy doorway with a loaf of bread. She started, and they stood a moment looking at each other across the room. They advanced to each other; he took her hand, plunged overhead, as it were, for a moment in her great brown eyes. Then he let her go, and looked aside, saying some words of greeting. He had not kissed her; he realised that when he heard her voice:

"When did you come?"

She was bent over the table, cutting bread-and-butter. What was it in her bowed, submissive pose, in the dark, small head with its black hair twining and hiding her face, that made him wince and shrink and close over his soul that had been open like a foolhardy flower to the night? Perhaps it was her very submission, which trammelled him, throwing the responsibility of her wholly on him, making him shrink from the burden of her.

Her brothers were home from the pit. They were two well-built lads of twenty and twenty-one. The coal-dust over their faces was like a mask, making them inscrutable, hiding any glow of greeting, making them strangers. He could only see their eyes wake with a sudden smile, which sank almost immediately, and they turned aside. The mother was kneeling at a big brown stew-jar in front of the open oven. She did not rise, but gave him her hand, saying: "Cyril! How are you?" Her large dark eyes wavered and left him. She continued with the spoon in the jar.

His disappointment rose as water suddenly heaves up the side of a ship. A sense of dreariness revived, a feeling, too, of the cold wet mud that he had struggled through.

These were the people who, a few months before, would look up in one fine broad glow of welcome whenever he entered the door, even if he came daily. Three years before, their lives would draw together into one flame, and whole evenings long would flare with magnificent mirth, and with play. They had known each other's lightest and deepest feelings. Now, when he came back to them after a long absence, they withdrew, turned aside. He sat down on the sofa under the window, deeply chagrined. His heart closed tight like a fir-cone, which had been open and full of naked seeds when he came to them.

They asked him questions of the South. They were starved for news, they said, in that God-forsaken hole.

"It is such a treat to hear a bit of news from outside," said the mother.

News! He smiled, and talked, plucking for them the leaves from off his tree: leaves of easy speech. He smiled, rather bitterly, as he slowly reeled off his news, almost mechanical-ly. Yet he knew—and that was the irony of it—that they did not want his 'records'; they wanted the timorous buds of his hopes, and the unknown fruits of his experience, full of the taste of tears and what sunshine of gladness had gone to their ripening. But they asked for his 'news', and, because of some subtle perversity, he gave them what they begged, not what they wanted, not what he desired most sincerely to give them.

Gradually he exhausted his store of talk, that he had thought was limitless. Muriel moved about all the time, laying the table and listening, only looking now and again across the barren garden of his talk into his windows. But he hardened his heart and turned his head from her. The boys had stripped to their waists, and had knelt on the hearth-rug and washed themselves in a large tin bowl, the mother sponging and drying their backs. Now they stood wiping themselves, the firelight bright and rosy on their fine torsos, their heavy arms swelling and sinking with life. They seemed to cherish the firelight on their bodies. Benjamin, the young-er, leaned his breast to the warmth, and threw back his head, showing his teeth in a voluptuous little smile. Mersham watched them, as he had watched the peewits and the sunset.

Then they sat down to their dinners, and the room was dim with the steam of food. Presently the father and the eldest brother were in from the cow-sheds, and all assembled at table. The conversation went haltingly; a little badinage on Mersham's part, a few questions on politics from the father. Then there grew an acute, fine feeling of discord. Mersham, particularly sensitive, reacted. He became extremely attentive to the others at table, and to his own manner of eating. He used English that was exquisitely accurate, pronounced with the Southern accent, very different from the heavily-sounded speech of the home folk. His nicety contrasted the more with their rough, country habit. They became shy and awkward, fumbling for something to say. The boys ate their dinners hastily, shovelling up the mass as a man shovels gravel. The eldest son clambered roughly with a great hand at the plate of bread-and-butter. Mersham tried to shut his eyes. He kept up all the time a brilliant tea-talk that they failed to appreciate in that atmosphere. It was evident to him; without forming the idea, he felt how irrevocably he was removing them from him, though he had loved them. The irony of the situation appealed to him, and added brightness and subtlety to his wit. Muriel, who had studied him so thoroughly, confusedly understood. She hung her head over her plate, and ate little. Now and again she would look up at him, toying all the time with her knife—though it was a family for ugly hands—and would address him some barren question. He always answered the question, but he invariably disregarded her look of earnestness, lapped in his unbreakable armour of light irony. He acknowledged, however, her power in the flicker of irritation that accompanied his reply. She quickly hid her face again.

They did not linger at tea, as in the old days. The men rose, with an "Ah well!" and went about their farm-work. One of the lads lay sprawling for sleep on the sofa; the other lighted a cigarette and sat with his arms on his knees, blinking into the fire. Neither of them ever wore a coat in the house, and their shirt-sleeves and their thick bare necks irritated the stranger still further by accentuating his strangeness. The men came tramping in and out to the boiler. The kitchen was full of bustle, of the carrying of steaming water, and of draughts. It seemed like a place out of doors. Mersham shrank up in his corner, and pretended to read the *Daily News*. He was ignored, like an owl sitting in the stalls of cattle.

"Go in the parlour, Cyril. Why don't you? It's comfortable there."

Muriel turned to him with this reproach, this remonstrance, almost chiding him. She was keenly aware of his discomfort, and of his painful discord with his surroundings. He rose without a word and obeyed her.

III

The parlour was a long, low room with red colourings. A bunch of mistletoe hung from the beam, and thickly-berried holly was over the pictures—over the little gilt-blazed water-colours that he hated so much because he had done them in his 'teens, and nothing is so hateful as the self one has left. He dropped in the tapestried chair called the Countess, and thought of the changes which this room had seen in him. There, by that hearth, they had threshed the harvest of their youth's experience, gradually burning the chaff of sentimentality and false romance that covered the real grain of life. How infinitely far away, now, seemed *Jane Eyre* and George Eliot. These had marked the beginning. He smiled as he traced the graph onwards, plotting the points with Carlyle and Ruskin, Schopenhauer and Darwin and Huxley, Omar Khayyam, the Russians, Ibsen and Balzac; then Guy de Maupassant and *Madame Bovary*. They had parted in the midst of *Madame Bovary*. Since then had come only Nietzsche and William James. They had not done so badly, he thought, during those years which now he was apt to despise a little, because of their dreadful strenuousness, and because of their later deadly, unrelieved seriousness. He wanted her to come in and talk about the old times. He crossed to the other side of the fire and lay in the big horse-hair chair, which pricked the back of his head. He looked about, and stuffed behind him the limp green cushions that were always sweating down.

It was a week after Christmas. He guessed they had kept up the holly and mistletoe for him. The two photographs of himself still occupied the post of honour on the mantelpiece; but between them was a stranger. He wondered who the fellow could be; good-looking he seemed to be; but a bit of a clown beside the radiant, subtle photos of himself. He smiled broadly at his own arrogance. Then he remembered that Muriel and her people were leaving the farm come Lady-day. Immediately, in valediction, he began to call up the old days, when they had romped and played so boisterously, dances, and wild charades, and all mad games. He was just telling himself that those were the days, the days of unconscious, ecstatic fun, and he was smiling at himself over his information, when she entered.

She came in, hesitating. Seeing him sprawling in his old

abandonment, she closed the door softly. For a moment or two she sat, her elbows on her knees, her chin in her hands, sucking her little finger, and withdrawing it from her lips with a little pop, looking all the while in the fire. She was waiting for him, knowing all the time he would not begin. She was trying to feel him, as it were. She wanted to assure herself of him after so many months. She dared not look at him directly. Like all brooding, constitutionally earnest souls, she gave herself away unwisely, and was defenceless when she found herself pushed back, rejected so often with contempt.

"Why didn't you tell me you were coming?" she asked at last.

"I wanted to have exactly one of the old tea-times, and evenings."

"Ay!" she answered with hopeless bitterness. She was a dreadful pessimist. People had handled her so brutally, and had cheaply thrown away her most sacred intimacies.

He laughed, and looked at her kindly.

"Ah, well, if I'd thought about it I should have known this was what to expect. It's my own fault."

"Nay," she answered, still bitterly; "it's not your fault. It's ours. You bring us to a certain point, and when you go away, we lose it all again, and receive you like creatures who have never known you."

"Never mind," he said easily. "If it is so, it is! How are you?"

She turned and looked full at him. She was very handsome; heavily moulded, coloured richly. He looked back smiling into her big, brown, serious eyes.

"Oh, I'm very well," she answered, with puzzled irony. "How are you?"

"Me? You tell me. What do you think of me?"

"What do I think?" She laughed a little nervous laugh and shook her head. "I don't know. Why—you look well—and very much of a gentleman."

"Ah—and you are sorry?"

"No—No, I am not! No! Only you're different, you see."

"Ah, the pity! I shall never be as nice as I was at twenty-one, shall I?" He glanced at his photo on the mantelpiece, and smiled, gently chaffing her.

"Well—you're different—it isn't that you're not so nice, but different. I always think you're like that, really."

She too glanced at the photo, which had been called the portrait of an intellectual prig, but which was really that of a sensitive, alert, exquisite boy. The subject of the portrait lay smiling at her. Then he turned voluptuously, like a cat spread out in the chair.

"And this is the last of it all——!"

She looked up at him, startled and pitiful.

"Of this phase, I mean," he continued, indicating with his eyes the room, the surroundings. "Of Crossleigh Bank, I mean, and this part of our lives."

"Ay!" she said, bowing her head, and putting into the exclamation all her depth of sadness and regret. He laughed.

"Aren't you glad?" he asked.

She looked up, startled, a little shocked.

"Good-bye's a fine word," he explained. "It means you're going to have a change, and a change is what you, of all people, want."

Her expression altered as she listened.

"It's true," she said. "I do."

"So you ought to say to yourself, 'What a treat! I'm going to say good-bye directly to the most painful phase of my life.' You make up your mind it shall be the most painful, by refusing to be hurt so much in the future. There you are! 'Men at most times are masters of their fates,' etcetera."

She pondered his method of reasoning, and turned to him with a little laughter that was full of pleading and yearning.

"Well," he said, lying, amiably smiling, "isn't that so?—and aren't you glad?"

"Yes!" she nodded. "I am—very glad."

He twinkled playfully at her, and asked, in a soft voice:

"Then what do you want?"

"Yes," she replied, a little breathlessly. "What do I?" She looked at him with a rash challenge that pricked him.

"Nay," he said, evading her, "do you even ask me that?"

She veiled her eyes, and said, meekly in excuse:

"It's a long time since I asked you anything, isn't it?"

"Ay! I never thought of it. Whom have you asked in the interim?"

"Whom have I asked?"—she arched her brows and laughed a monosyllable of scorn.

"No one, of course!" he said, smiling. "The world asks questions of you, you ask questions of me, and I go to some oracle in the dark, don't I?"

She laughed with him.

"No!" he said, suddenly serious. "Supposing you must answer me a big question—something I can never find out by myself?"

He lay out indolently in the chair and began smiling again. She turned to look with intensity at him, her hair's fine foliage all loose round her face, her dark eyes haunted with doubt, her finger at her lips. A slight perplexity flickered over his eyes.

"At any rate," he said, "you have something to give me."

She continued to look at him with dark, absorbing eyes. He probed her with his regard. Then he seemed to withdraw, and his pupils dilated with thought.

"You see," he said, "life's no good but to live—and you can't live your life by yourself. You must have a flint and a steel, both, to make the spark fly. Supposing you be my flint, my white flint, to spurt out red fire for me?"

"But how do you mean?" she asked breathlessly.

"You see," he continued, thinking aloud as usual: "thought—that's not life. It's like washing and combing and carding and weaving the fleece that the year of life has produced. Now I think—we've carded and woven to the end of our bundle—nearly. We've got to begin again—you and me—living together, see? Not speculating and poetising together—see?"

She did not cease to gaze absorbedly at him.

"Yes?" she whispered, urging him on.

"You see—I've come back to you—to you——" He waited for her.

"But," she said huskily, "I don't understand."

He looked at her with aggressive frankness, putting aside all her confusions.

"Fibber!" he said gently.

"But——" she turned in her chair from him—"but not clearly."

He frowned slightly:

"Nay, you should be able by now to use the algebra of speech. Must I count up on your fingers for you what I mean, unit by unit, in bald arithmetic?"

"No—no!" she cried, justifying herself; "but how can I understand—the change in you? You used to say—you couldn't.—Quite opposite."

He lifted his head as if taking in her meaning.

"Ah, yes, I have changed. I forget. I suppose I must have changed in myself. I'm older—I'm twenty-six. I used to shrink from the thought of having to kiss you, didn't I?" He smiled very brightly, and added, in a soft voice: "Well—I don't, now."

She flushed darkly and hid her face from him.

"Not," he continued, with slow, brutal candour—"not that I know any more than I did then—what love is—as you know it—but—I think you're beautiful—and we know each other so well—as we know nobody else, don't we? And so we . . ."

His voice died away, and they sat in a tense silence, listening to the noise outside, for the dog was barking loudly. They heard a voice speaking and quieting him. Cyril Mersham listened He heard the clatter of the barn door latch, and a slurring ring of a bicycle-bell brushing the wall.

"Who is it?" he asked, unsuspecting.

She looked at him, and confessed with her eyes, guiltily, beseeching. He understood immediately.

"Good Lord!—Him?" He looked at the photo on the mantelpiece. She nodded with her usual despair, her finger between her lips again. Mersham took some moments to adjust himself to the new situation.

"Well!—so *he's* in my place! Why didn't you tell me?"

"How could I?—he's not. Besides—you never would have a place." She hid her face.

"No," he drawled, thinking deeply. "I wouldn't. It's my fault, altogether." Then he smiled, and said whimsically: "But I thought you kept an old pair of my gloves in the chair beside you."

"So I did, so I did!" she justified herself again with extreme bitterness, "till you asked me for them. You told me to—to take another man—and I did as you told me—as usual."

"Did I tell you?—did I tell you? I suppose I must. I suppose I am a fool. And do you like him?"

She laughed aloud, with scorn and bitterness.

"He's very good—and he's very fond of me."

"Naturally!" said Mersham, smiling and becoming ironical. "And how firmly is he fixed?"

IV

She was mortified, and would not answer him. The question for him now was how much did this intruder count. He looked, and saw she wore no ring—but perhaps she had taken it off for his coming. He began diligently to calculate what attitude he might take. He had looked for many women to wake his love, but he had been always disappointed. So he had kept himself virtuous, and waited. Now he would wait no longer. No woman and he could ever understand each other so well as he and Muriel whom he had fiercely educated into womanhood along with his own struggling towards a manhood of independent outlook. They had breathed the same air of thought, they had been beaten with the same storms of doubt and disillusionment, they had expanded together in days of pure poetry. They had grown so; spiritually, or rather psychically, as he preferred to say, they were married; and now he found himself thinking of the way she moved about the house.

The outer door had opened and a man had entered the kitchen, greeting the family cordially, and without any formality. He had the throaty, penetrating voice of a tenor singer, and it came distinctly over the vibrating rumble of the men's talking. He spoke good, easy English. The boys asked him about the 'iron-men' and the electric haulage, and he answered them with rough technicalities, so Mersham concluded he was a working electrician in the mine. They continued to talk casually for some time, though there was a false note of secondary interest in it all. Then Benjamin came forward and broke the check, saying, with a dash of braggart taunting:

"Muriel's in th' parlour, Tom, if you want her."

"Oh, is she? I saw a light in; I thought she might be." He affected indifference, as if he were kept thus at every visit. Then he added, with a touch of impatience, and of the proprietor's interest: "What is she doing?"

"She's talking. Cyril Mersham's come from London."

"What!—is *he* here?"

Mersham sat listening, smiling. Muriel saw his eyelids lift. She had run up her flag of challenge taut, but continually she slackened towards him with tenderness. Now her flag flew out bravely. She rose, and went to the door.

"Hello!" she said, greeting the stranger with a little song of welcome in one word, such as girls use when they become aware of the presence of their sweetheart.

"You've got a visitor, I hear," he answered.

"Yes. Come along, come in!"

She spoke softly, with much gentle caressing.

He was a handsome man, well set-up, rather shorter than Mersham. The latter rose indolently, and held out his hand, smiling curiously into the beautiful, generous blue eyes of the other.

"Cyril—Mr. Vickers."

Tom Vickers crushed Mersham's hand, and answered his steady, smiling regard with a warm expansion of feeling, then bent his head, slightly confused.

"Sit here, will you?" said Mersham, languidly indicating the arm-chair.

"No, no, thanks, I won't. I shall do here, thanks." Tom Vickers took a chair and placed it in front of the fire. He was confusedly charmed with Mersham's natural frankness and courtesy.

"If I'm not intruding," he added, as he sat down.

"No, of course not!" said Muriel, in her wonderfully soft,

fond tones—the indulgent tone of a woman who will sacrifice anything to love.

"Couldn't!" added Mersham lazily. "We're always a public meeting, Muriel and I. Aren't we, Miel? We're discussing affinities, that ancient topic. You'll do for an audience. We agree so beastly well, we two. We always did. It's her fault. Does she treat you so badly?"

The other was rather bewildered. Out of it all he dimly gathered that he was suggested as the present lover of Muriel, while Mersham referred to himself as the one discarded. So he smiled, reassured.

"How—badly?" he asked.

"Agreeing with you on every point?"

"No, I can't say she does that," said Vickers, smiling, and looking with little warm glances at her.

"Why, we never disagree, you know!" she remonstrated, in the same deep indulgent tone.

"I see," Mersham said languidly, and yet keeping his wits keenly to the point. "*You* agree with everything *she* says. Lord, how interesting!"

Muriel arched her eyelids with a fine flare of intelligence across at him, and laughed.

"Something like that," answered the other man, also indulgently, as became a healthy male towards one who lay limply in a chair and said clever nothings in a lazy drawl. Mersham noted the fine limbs, the solid, large thighs, and the thick wrists. He was classifying his rival among the men of handsome, healthy animalism, and good intelligence, who are children in simplicity, who can add two and two, but never xy and yx. His contours, his movements, his repose were, strictly, lovable. "But," said Mersham to himself, "if I were blind, or sorrowful, or very tired, I should not want him. He is one of the men, as George Moore says, whom his wife would hate after a few years for the very way he walked across the floor. I can imagine him with a family of children, a fine father. But unless he had a domestic wife——"

Muriel had begun to make talk to him.

"Did you cycle?" she asked, in that irritating private tone

so common to lovers, a tone that makes a third person an impertinence.

"Yes—I was rather late," he replied, in the same caressing manner. The sense did not matter, the caress was everything.

"Didn't you find it very muddy?"

"Well, I did—but not any worse than yesterday."

Mersham sprawled his length in the chair, his eyelids almost shut, his fine white hands hanging over the arms of the chair like dead-white stoats from a bough. He was wondering how long Muriel would endure to indulge her sweetheart thus. Soon she began to talk second-hand to Mersham. They were speaking of Tom's landlady.

"You don't care for her, do you?" she asked, laughing insinuatingly, since the shadow of his dislike for other women heightened the radiance of his affection for her.

"Well, I can't say that I love her."

"How is it you always fall out with your landladies after six months? You must be a wretch to live with."

"Nay, I don't know that I am. But they're all alike; they're jam and cakes at first, but after a bit they're dry bread."

He spoke with solemnity, as if he uttered a universal truth. Mersham's eyelids flickered now and again. Muriel turned to him:

"Mr. Vickers doesn't like lodgings," she said.

Mersham understood that Vickers therefore wanted to marry her; he also understood that as the pretendant tired of his landladies, so his wife and he would probably weary one another. He looked this intelligence at Muriel, and drawled:

"Doesn't he? Lodgings are ideal. A good lodger can always boss the show, and have his own way. It's the time of his life."

"I don't think!" laughed Vickers."

"It's true," drawled Mersham torpidly, giving his words the effect of droll irony. "You're evidently not a good lodger. You only need to sympathise with a landlady—against her husband generally—and she'll move heaven and earth for you."

"Ah!" laughed Muriel, glancing at Mersham. "Tom doesn't

believe in sympathising with women—especially married women."

"I don't!" said Tom emphatically, "—it's dangerous."

"You leave it to the husband," said Mersham.

"I do that! I don't want 'em coming to me with their troubles. I should never know the end."

"Wise of you. Poor woman! So you'll broach your barrel of sympathy for your wife, eh, and for nobody else?"

"That's it. Isn't that right?"

"Oh, quite. Your wife will be a privileged person. Sort of home-brewed beer to drink *ad infinitum*? Quite all right, that!"

"There's nothing better," said Tom, laughing.

"Except a change," said Mersham. "Now, I'm like a cup of tea to a woman."

Muriel laughed aloud at this preposterous cynicism, and knitted her brows to bid him cease playing ball with bombs.

"A fresh cup each time. Women never weary of tea. Muriel, I can see you having a rich time. Sort of long after-supper drowse with a good husband."

"Very delightful!" said Muriel sarcastically.

"If she's got a good husband, what more can she want?" asked Tom, keeping the tone of banter, but really serious and somewhat resentful.

"A lodger—to make things interesting."

"Why," said Muriel, intervening, "do women like you so?"

Mersham looked up at her, quietly, smiling into her eyes. She was really perplexed. She wanted to know what he put in the pan to make the balance go down so heavily on his side. He had, as usual, to answer her seriously and truthfully, so he said: "Because I can make them believe that black is green or purple—which it is, in reality." Then, smiling broadly as she wakened again with admiration for him, he added: "But you're trying to make me conceited, Miel—to stain my virgin modesty."

Muriel glanced up at him with softness and understanding, and laughed low. Tom gave a guffaw at the notion of Mersham's virgin modesty. Muriel's brow wrinkled with irritation, and she turned from her sweetheart to look in the fire.

V

Mersham, all unconsciously, had now developed the situation to the climax he desired. He was sure that Vickers would not count seriously in Muriel's movement towards himself. So he turned away, uninterested.

The talk drifted for some time, after which he suddenly bethought himself:

"I say, Mr. Vickers, will you sing for us? You do sing, don't you?"

"Well—nothing to speak of," replied the other modestly, wondering at Mersham's sudden change of interest. He looked at Muriel.

"Very well," she answered him, indulging him now like a child. "But——" she turned to Mersham—"but do you, really?"

"Yes, of course. Play some of the old songs. Do you play any better?"

She began "Honour and Arms."

"No, not that!" cried Mersham. "Something quiet—'Sois triste et sois belle'." He smiled gently at her, suggestively. "Try 'Du bist wie eine Blume,' or 'Pur dicesti'."

Vickers sang well, though without much imagination. But the songs they sang were the old songs that Mersham had taught Muriel years before, and she played with one of his memories in her heart. At the end of the first song, she turned and found him looking at her, and they met again in the poetry of the past.

"Daffodils," he said softly, his eyes full of memories.

She dilated, quivered with emotion, in response. They had sat on the rim of the hill, where the wild daffodils stood up to the sky, and there he had taught her, singing line by line: "Du bist wie eine Blume." He had no voice, but a very accurate ear.

The evening wore on to ten o'clock. The lads came through the room on their way to bed. The house was asleep save the father, who sat alone in the kitchen, reading *The Octopus*. They went in to supper.

Mersham had roused himself and was talking well. Muriel stimulated him, always, and turned him to talk of art and philosophy—abstract things that she loved, of which only he had ever spoken to her, of which only he could speak, she believed, with such beauty. He used quaint turns of speech, contradicted himself waywardly, then said something sad and whimsical, all in a wistful, irresponsible manner so that even the men leaned indulgent and deferential to him.

"Life," he said, and he was always urging this on Muriel in one form or another, "life is beautiful, so long as it is consuming you. When it is rushing through you, destroying you, life is glorious. It is best to roar away, like a fire with a great draught, white-hot to the last bit. It's when you burn a slow fire and save fuel that life's not worth having."

"You believe in a short life and a merry," said the father.

"Needn't be either short or merry. Grief is part of the fire of life—and suffering—they're the root of the flame of joy, as they say. No! With life, we're like the man who was so anxious to provide for his old age that he died at thirty from inanition."

"That's what we're not likely to do," laughed Tom.

"Oh, I don't know. You live most intensely in human contact—and that's what we shrink from, poor timid creatures, from giving our souls to somebody to touch; for they, bungling fools, will generally paw it with dirty hands."

Muriel looked at him with dark eyes of grateful understanding. She herself had been much pawed, brutally, by her brothers. But, then, she had been foolish in offering herself.

"And," concluded Mersham, "you are washed with the whitest fire of life—when you take a woman you love—and understand."

Perhaps Mersham did not know what he was doing. Yet his whole talk lifted Muriel as in a net, like a sea-maiden out of the waters, and placed her in his arms, to breathe his thin, rare atmosphere. She looked at him, and was certain of his pure earnestness, and believed implicitly he could not do wrong.

Vickers believed otherwise. He would have expressed his opinion, whatever it might be, in an: "Oh, ay, he's got plenty to say, and he'll keep on saying it—but, hang it all . . . !"

For Vickers was an old-fashioned, inarticulate lover; such as has been found the brief joy and the unending disappointment of a woman's life. At last he found he must go, as Mersham would not precede him. Muriel did not kiss him good-bye, nor did she offer to go out with him to his bicycle. He was angry at this, but more angry with the girl than with the man. He felt that she was fooling about, 'showing off' before the stranger. Mersham was a stranger to him, and so, in his idea, to Muriel. Both young men went out of the house together, and down the rough brick track to the barn. Mersham made whimsical little jokes: "I wish my feet weren't so fastidious. They dither when they go in a soft spot like a girl who's touched a toad. Hark at that poor old wretch—she sounds as if she'd got whooping-cough."

"A cow is not coughing when she makes that row," said Vickers.

"Pretending, is she?—to get some Owbridge's? Don't blame her. I guess she's got chilblains, at any rate. Do cows have chilblains, poor devils?"

Vickers laughed and felt he must take this man into his protection. "Mind," he said, as they entered the barn, which was very dark. "Mind your forehead against this beam." He put one hand on the beam, and stretched out the other to feel for Mersham. "Thanks," said the latter gratefully. He knew the position of the beam to an inch, however dark the barn, but he allowed Vickers to guide him past it. He rather enjoyed being taken into Tom's protection.

Vickers carefully struck a match, bowing over the ruddy core of light and illuminating himself like some beautiful lantern in the midst of the high darkness of the barn. For some moments he bent over his bicycle-lamp, trimming and adjusting the wick, and his face, gathering all the light on its ruddy beauty, seemed luminous and wonderful. Mersham could see the down on his cheeks above the razor-line, and the full lips in shadow beneath the moustache, and the brush of the eyebrows between the light.

"After all," said Mersham, "he's very beautiful; she's a fool to give him up."

Tom shut the lamp with a snap, and carefully crushed the match under his foot. Then he took the pump from the bicycle, and crouched on his heels in the dimness, inflating the tyre. The swift, unerring, untiring stroke of the pump, the light balance and the fine elastic adjustment of the man's body to his movements pleased Mersham.

"She could have," he was saying to himself, "some glorious hours with this man—yet she'd rather have me, because I can make her sad and set her wondering."

But to the man he was saying:

"You know, love isn't the twin-soul business. With you, for instance, women are like apples on a tree. You can have one that you can reach. Those that look best are overhead, but it's no good bothering with them. So you stretch up, perhaps you pull down a bough and just get your fingers round a good one. Then it swings back and you feel wild and you say your heart's broken. But there are plenty of apples as good for you no higher than your chest."

Vickers smiled, and thought there was something in it— generally; but for himself, it was nothing.

They went out of the barn to the yard gate. He watched the young man swing over his saddle and vanish, calling "Good-night."

"*Sic transit*," he murmured—meaning Tom Vickers, and beautiful lustihood that is unconscious like a blossom.

Mersham went slowly in the house. Muriel was clearing away the supper things, and laying the table again for the men's breakfasts. But she was waiting for him as clearly as if she had stood watching in the doorway. She looked up at him, and instinctively he lifted his face toward her as if to kiss her. They smiled, and she went on with her work.

The father rose, stretching his burly form, and yawning. Mersham put on his overcoat.

"You will come a little way with me?" he said. She answered him with her eyes. The father stood, large and silent, on the hearth-rug. His sleepy, mazed disapproval had no more effect than a little breeze which might blow against them. She smiled brightly at her lover, like a child, as she pinned on her hat.

It was very dark outside in the starlight. He groaned heavily, and swore with extravagance as he went ankle-deep in mud.

"See, you should follow me. Come here," she commanded, delighted to have him in charge.

"Give me your hand," he said, and they went hand-in-hand over the rough places. The fields were open, and the night went up to the magnificent stars. The wood was very dark, and wet; they leaned forward and stepped stealthily, and gripped each other's hands fast with a delightful sense of adventure. When they stood and looked up a moment, they did not know how the stars were scattered among the treetops till he found the three jewels of Orion right in front.

There was a strangeness everywhere, as if all things had ventured out alive to play in the night, as they do in fairytales; the trees, the many stars, the dark spaces, and the mysterious waters below uniting in some magnificent game.

They emerged from the wood on to the bare hillside. She came down from the wood-fence into his arms, and he kissed her, and they laughed low together. Then they went on across the wild meadows where there was no path.

"Why don't you like him?" he asked playfully.

"Need you ask?" she said simply.

"Yes. Because he's heaps nicer than I am."

She laughed a full laugh of amusement.

"He is! Look! He's like summer, brown and full of warmth. Think how splendid and fierce he'd be——"

"Why do you talk about him?" she said.

"Because I want you to know what you're losing—and you won't till you see him in my terms. He is very desirable—I should choose him in preference to me—for myself."

"Should you?" she laughed. "But," she added with soft certainly, "you don't understand."

"No—I don't. I suppose it's love; your sort, which is beyond me. I shall never be blindly in love, shall I?"

"I begin to think you never will," she answered, not very sadly. "You won't be blindly anything."

"The voice of love!" he laughed; and then: "No, if you pull your flowers to pieces, and find how they pollinate, and where are the ovaries, you don't go in blind ecstasies over to them. But they mean more to you; they are intimate, like friends of your heart, not like wonderful, dazing fairies."

"Ay!" she assented, musing over it with the gladness of understanding him. "And then?"

Softly, almost without words, she urged him to the point.

"Well," he said, "you think I'm a wonderful, magical person, don't you?—and I'm not—I'm not as good, in the long run, as your Tom, who thinks you are a wonderful, magical person."

She laughed and clung to him as they walked. He continued, very carefully and gently: "Now, I don't imagine for a moment that you are princessy or angelic or wonderful. You often make me thundering mad because you're an ass . . ."

She laughed low with shame and humiliation.

"Nevertheless—I come from the south to you—because— well, with you I can be just as I feel, conceited or idiotic, without being afraid to be myself . . ." He broke off suddenly. "I don't think I've tried to make myself out to you—any bigger or better than I am?" he asked her wistfully.

"No," she answered, in beautiful, deep assurance. "No! That's where it is. You have always been so honest. You are more honest than anybody ever——" She did not finish, being deeply moved. He was silent for some time, then he continued, as if he must see the question to the end with her:

"But, you know—I do like you not to wear corsets. I like to see you move inside your dress."

She laughed, half shame, half pleasure.

"I wondered if you'd notice," she said.

"I did—directly." There was a space of silence, after which he resumed: "You see—we would marry tomorrow—but I can't keep myself. I am in debt——"

She came close to him, and took his arm.

"—And what's the good of letting the years go, and the beauty of one's youth——?"

"No," she admitted, very slowly and softly, shaking her head.

"So—well!—you understand, don't you? And if you're willing—you'll come to me, won't you?—just naturally, as you used to come and go to church with me?—and it won't be—it won't be me coaxing you—reluctant? Will it?"

They had halted in front of a stile which they would have to climb. She turned to him in silence, and put up her face to him. He took her in his arms, and kissed her, and felt the night mist with which his moustache was drenched, and he bent his head and rubbed his face on her shoulder, and then pressed his lips on her neck. For a while they stood in silence, clasped together. Then he heard her voice, muffled in his shoulder, saying:

"But—but, you know—it's much harder for the woman—it means something so different for a woman."

"One can be wise," he answered, slowly and gently. "One need not blunder into calamities."

She was silent for a time. Then she spoke again.

"Yes, but—if it should be—you see—I couldn't bear it."

He let her go, and they drew apart, and the embrace no longer choked them from speaking. He recognised the woman defensive, playing the coward against her own inclinations, and even against her knowledge.

"If—if!" he exclaimed sharply, so that she shrank with a little fear. "There need be no ifs—need there?"

"I don't know," she replied, reproachfully, very quietly.

"If I say so——" he said, angry with her mistrust. Then he climbed the stile, and she followed.

"But you *do* know," he exclaimed. "I have given you books——"

"Yes, but——"

"But what?" He was getting really angry.

"It's so different for a woman—you don't know."

He did not answer this. They stumbled together over the mole-hills, under the oak trees.

"And look—how we should have to be—creeping together in the dark——"

This stung him; at once, it was as if the glamour went out of life. It was as if she had tipped over the fine vessel that held the wine of his desire, and had emptied him of all his vitality. He had played a difficult, deeply-moving part all night, and now the lights suddenly switched out, and there was left only weariness. He was silent, tired, very tired, bodily and spiritually. They walked across the wide, dark meadow with sunken heads. Suddenly she caught his arm.

"Don't be cold with me!" she cried.

He bent and kissed in acknowledgment the lips she offered him for love.

"No," he said drearily; "no, it is not coldness—only—I have lost hold—for to-night." He spoke with difficulty. It was hard to find a word to say. They stood together, apart, under the old thorn tree for some minutes, neither speaking. Then he climbed the fence, and stood on the highway above the meadow.

At parting also he had not kissed her. He stood a moment and looked at her. The water in a little brook under the hedge was running, chuckling with extraordinary loudness: away on Nethermere they heard the sad, haunting cry of the wild-fowl from the North. The stars still twinkled intensely. He was too spent to think of anything to say; she was too overcome with grief and fear and a little resentment. He looked down at the pale blotch of her face upturned from the low meadow beyond the fence. The thorn boughs tangled above her, drooping behind her like the roof of a hut. Beyond was the great width of the darkness. He felt unable to gather his energy to say anything vital.

"Good-bye," he said. "I'm going back—on Saturday. But— you'll write to me. Good-bye."

He turned to go. He saw her white uplifted face vanish, and her dark form bend under the boughs of the tree, and go out into the great darkness. She did not say good-bye.

New Eve and Old Adam

I

"AFTER ALL," she said, with a little laugh, "I can't see it was so wonderful of you to hurry home to me, if you are so cross when you do come."

"You would rather I stayed away?" he asked.

"I wouldn't mind."

"You would rather I had stayed a day or two in Paris—or a night or two."

She burst in to a jeering "pouf!" of laughter.

"You!" she cried. "You and Parisian Nights' Entertainment! What a fool you would look."

"Still," he said, "I could try."

"You *would*!" she mocked. "You would go dribbling up to a woman. 'Please take me—my wife is so unkind to me!' "

He drank his tea in silence. They had been married a year. They had married quickly, for love. And during the last three months there had gone on almost continuously that battle between them which so many married people fight, without knowing why. Now it had begun again. He felt the physical sickness rising in him. Somewhere down in his belly the big, feverish pulse began to beat, where was the inflamed place caused by the conflict between them.

She was a beautiful woman of about thirty, fair, luxuriant, with proud shoulders and a face borne up by a fierce, native vitality. Her green eyes had a curiously puzzled contraction just now. She sat leaning on the table against the tea-tray, absorbed. It was as if she battled with herself in him. Her green dress reflected in the silver, against the red of the firelight. Leaning abstractedly forward, she pulled some primroses from the bowl, and threaded them at intervals in the plait which bound round her head in the peasant fashion. So,

25

with her little starred fillet of flowers, there was something of the Gretchen about her. But her eyes retained the curious half-smile.

Suddenly her face lowered gloomily. She sank her beautiful arms, laying them on the table. Then she sat almost sullenly, as if she would not give in. He was looking away out of the window. With a quick movement she glanced down at her hands. She took off her wedding-ring, reached to the bowl for a long flower-stalk, and shook the ring glittering round and round upon it, regarding the spinning gold, and spinning it as if she would spurn it. Yet there was something about her of a fretful, naughty child as she did so.

The man sat by the fire, tired, but tense. His body seemed so utterly still because of the tension in which it was held. His limbs, thin and vigorous, lay braced like a listening thing, always vivid for action, yet held perfectly still. His face was set and expressionless. The wife was all the time, in spite of herself, conscious of him, as if the cheek that was turned toward him had a sense which perceived him. They were both rendered elemental, like impersonal forces, by the battle and the suffering.

She rose and went to the window. Their flat was the fourth, the top storey of a large house. Above the high-ridged, handsome red roof opposite was an assembly of telegraph wires, a square, squat framework, towards which hosts of wires sped from four directions, arriving in darkly-stretched lines out of the white sky. High up, at a great height, a seagull sailed. There was a noise of traffic from the town beyond.

Then, from behind the ridge of the house-roof opposite a man climbed up into the tower of wires, belted himself amid the netted sky, and began to work, absorbedly. Another man, half-hidden by the roof-ridge, stretched up to him with a wire. The man in the sky reached down to receive it. The other, having delivered, sank out of sight. The solitary man worked absorbedly. Then he seemed drawn away from his task. He looked round almost furtively, from his lonely height, the space pressing on him. His eyes met those of the beautiful woman who stood in her afternoon-gown, with flowers in her hair, at the window.

"I like you," she said, in her normal voice.

Her husband, in the room with her, looked round slowly and asked:

"Whom do you like?"

Receiving no answer, he resumed his tense stillness.

She remained watching at the window, above the small, quiet street of large houses. The man, suspended there in the sky, looked across at her and she at him. The city was far below. Her eyes and his met across the lofty space. Then, crouching together again into his forgetfulness, he hid himself in his work. He would not look again. Presently he climbed down, and the tower of wires was empty against the sky.

The woman glanced at the little park at the end of the clear, grey street. The diminished, dark-blue form of a soldier was seen passing between the green stretches of grass, his spurs giving the faintest glitter to his walk.

Then she turned hesitating from the window, as if drawn by her husband. He was sitting still motionless, and detached from her, hard; held absolutely away from her by his will. She wavered, then went and crouched on the hearth-rug at his feet, laying her head on his knee.

"Don't be horrid with me!" she pleaded, in a caressing, languid, impersonal voice. He shut his teeth hard, and his lips parted slightly with pain.

"You know you love me," she continued, in the same heavy, sing-song way. He breathed hard, but kept still.

"Don't you?" she said, slowly, and she put her arms round his waist, under his coat, drawing him to her. It was as if flames of fire were running under his skin.

"I have never denied it," he said woodenly.

"Yes," she pleaded, in the same heavy, toneless voice. "Yes. You are always trying to deny it." She was rubbing her cheek against his knee, softly. Then she gave a little laugh, and shook her head. "But it's no good." She looked up at him. There was a curious light in his eyes, of subtle victory. "It's no good, my love, is it?"

His heart ran hot. He knew it was no good trying to deny

he loved her. But he saw her eyes, and his will remained set and hard. She looked away into the fire.

"You hate it that you have to love me," she said, in a pensive voice through which the triumph flickered faintly. "You hate it that you love me—and it is petty and mean of you. You hate it that you had to hurry back to me from Paris."

Her voice had become again quite impersonal, as if she were talking to herself.

"At any rate," he said, "it is your triumph."

She gave a sudden, bitter-contemptuous laugh.

"Ha!" she said. "What is triumph to me, you fool? You can have your triumph. I should be only too glad to give it you."

"And I to take it."

"Then take it," she cried, in hostility. "I offer it you often enough."

"But you never mean to part with it."

"It is a lie. It is you, you, who are too paltry to take a woman. How often do I fling myself at you——"

"Then don't—don't."

"Ha!—and if I don't—I get nothing out of you. Self! self! that is all you are."

His face remained set and expressionless. She looked up at him. Suddenly she drew him to her again, and hid her face against him.

"Don't kick me off, Pietro, when I come to you," she pleaded.

"You *don't* come to me," he answered stubbornly.

She lifted her head a few inches away from him and seemed to listen, or to think.

"What do I do, then," she asked, for the first time quietly.

"You treat me as if I were a piece of cake, for you to eat when you wanted."

She rose from him with a mocking cry of scorn, that yet had something hollow in its sound.

"Treat you like a piece of cake, do I!" she cried. "I, who have done all I have for you!"

There was a knock, and the maid entered with a telegram. He tore it open.

"No answer," he said, and the maid softly closed the door.

"I suppose it is for you," he said, bitingly, rising and handing her the slip of paper. She read it, laughed, then read it again, aloud:

" 'Meet me Marble Arch 7:30—theatre—Richard.' Who is Richard?" she asked, looking at her husband rather interested. He shook his head.

"Nobody of mine," he said. "Who is he?"

"I haven't the faintest notion," she said, flippantly.

"But," and his eyes went bullying, "you *must* know."

She suddenly became quiet, and jeering, took up his challenge.

"Why must I know?" she asked.

"Because it isn't for me, therefore it must be for you."

"And couldn't it be for anybody else?" she sneered.

" 'Moest, 14 Merrilies Street,' " he read, decisively.

For a second she was puzzled into earnestness.

"Pah, you fool," she said, turning aside. "Think of your own friends," and she flung the telegram away.

"It is not for me," he said, stiffly and finally.

"Then it is for the man in the moon—I should think *his* name is Moest," she added, with a pouf of laughter against him.

"Do you mean to say you know nothing about it?" he asked.

"Do you mean to say," she mocked, mouthing the words, and sneering; "Yes, I do mean to say, poor little man."

He suddenly went hard with disgust.

"Then, I simply don't believe you," he said coldly.

"Oh—don't you believe me!" she jeered, mocking the touch of sententiousness in his voice. "What a calamity. The poor man doesn't believe!"

"It couldn't possibly be any acquaintance of mine," he said slowly.

"Then hold your tongue!" she cried harshly. "I've heard enough of it."

He was silent, and soon she went out of the room. In a few minutes he heard her in the drawing-room, improvising furiously. It was a sound that maddened him: something yearning, yearning, striving, and something perverse, that counteracted the yearning. Her music was always working up towards a certain culmination, but never reaching it, falling away in a jangle. How he hated it. He lit a cigarette, and went across to the sideboard for a whisky and soda. Then she began to sing. She had a good voice, but she could not keep time. As a rule it made his heart warm with tenderness for her, hearing her ramble through the songs in her own fashion, making Brahms sound so different by altering his time. But today he hated her for it. Why the devil couldn't she submit to the natural laws of the stuff!

In about fifteen minutes she entered, laughing. She laughed as she closed the door, and as she came to him where he sat.

"Oh," she said, "you silly thing, you silly thing! Aren't you a stupid clown?"

She crouched between his knees and put her arms round him. She was smiling into his face, her green eyes looking into his, were bright and wide. But somewhere in them, as he looked back, was a little twist that could not come loose to him, a little cast, that was like an aversion from him, a strain of hate for him. The hot waves of blood flushed over his body, and his heart seemed to dissolve under her caresses. But at last, after many months, he knew her well enough. He knew that curious little strain in her eyes, which was waiting for him to submit to her, and then would spurn him again. He resisted her while ever it was there.

"Why don't you let yourself love me?" she asked, pleading, but a touch of mockery in her voice. His jaw set hard.

"Is it because you are afraid?"

He heard the slight sneer.

"Of what?" he asked.

"Afraid to trust yourself?"

There was silence. It made him furious that she could sit there caressing him and yet sneer at him.

"What *have* I done with myself?" he asked.

"Carefully saved yourself from giving all to me, for fear you might lose something."

"Why should I lose anything?" he asked.

And they were both silent. She rose at last and went away from him to get a cigarette. The silver box flashed red with firelight in her hands. She struck a match, bungled, threw the stick aside, lit another.

"What did you come running back for?" she asked, insolently, talking with half-shut lips because of the cigarette. "I told you I wanted peace. I've had none for a year. And for the last three months you've done nothing but try to destroy me."

"You have not gone frail on it," he answered sarcastically.

"Nevertheless," she said, "I am ill inside me. I am sick of you—sick. You make an eternal demand, and you give nothing back. You leave one empty." She puffed the cigarette in feminine fashion, then suddenly she struck her forehead with a wild gesture. "I have a ghastly, empty feeling in my head," she said. "I feel I simply *must* have rest—I must."

The rage went through his veins like flame.

"From your labours?" he asked, sarcastically, suppressing himself.

"From you—from *you*?" she cried, thrusting forward her head at him. "You, who use a woman's soul up, with your rotten life. I suppose it is partly your health, and you can't help it," she added, more mildly. "But I simply can't stick it—I simply can't, and that is all."

She shook her cigarette carelessly in the direction of the fire. The ash fell on the beautiful Asiatic rug. She glanced at it, but did not trouble. He sat, hard with rage.

"May I ask how I use you up, as you say?" he asked.

She was silent a moment, trying to get her feeling into words. Then she shook her hand at him passionately, and took the cigarette from her mouth.

"By—by following me about—by not leaving me *alone*. You give me no peace—*I* don't know what you do, but it is something ghastly."

Again the hard stroke of rage went down his mind.

"It is very vague," he said.

"I know," she cried. "I can't put it into words—but there it is. You—you don't love. I pour myself out to you, and then—there's nothing there—you simply aren't there."

He was silent for some time. His jaw had set hard with fury and hate.

"We have come to the incomprehensible," he said. "And now, what about Richard?"

It had grown nearly dark in the room. She sat silent for a moment. Then she took the cigarette from her mouth and looked at it.

"I'm going to meet him," her voice, mocking, answered out of the twilight.

His head went molten, and he could scarcely breathe.

"Who is he?" he asked, though he did not believe the affair to be anything at all, even if there were a Richard.

"I'll introduce him to you when I know him a little better," she said. He waited.

"But who is he?"

"I tell you, I'll introduce him to you later."

There was a pause.

"Shall I come with you?"

"It would be like you," she answered, with a sneer.

The maid came in, softly, to draw the curtains and turn on the light. The husband and wife sat silent.

"I suppose," he said, when the door was closed again, "you are wanting a Richard for a rest?"

She took his sarcasm simply as a statement.

"I am," she said. "A simple, warm man who would love me without all these reservations and difficulties. That is just what I do want."

"Well, you have your own independence," he said.

"Ha," she laughed. "You needn't tell me that. It would take more than you to rob me of my independence."

"I meant your own income," he answered quietly, while his heart was plunging with bitterness and rage.

"Well," she said, "I will go and dress."

He remained without moving, in his chair. The pain of this was almost too much. For some moments the great, inflamed pulse struck through his body. It died gradually down, and he went dull. He had not wanted to separate from her at this point of their union: they would probably, if they parted in such a crisis, never come together again. But if she insisted,

well then, it would have to be. He would go away for a
month. He could easily make business in Italy. And when he
came back, they could patch up some sort of domestic
arrangement, as most other folk had to do.

He felt dull and heavy inside, and without the energy for
anything. The thought of having to pack and take a train to
Milan appalled him; it would mean such an effort of will. But
it would have to be done, and so he must do it. It was no use
his waiting at home. He might stay in town a night, at his
brother-in-law's, and go away the next day. It were better to
give her a little time to come to herself. She was really
impulsive. And he did not really want to go away from her.

He was still sitting thinking, when she came downstairs.
She was in costume and furs and toque. There was a radiant,
half-wistful, half-perverse look about her. She was a beautiful woman, her bright, fair face set among the black furs.

"Will you give me some money?" she said. "There isn't
any."

He took two sovereigns, which she put in her little black
purse. She would go without a word of reconciliation. It
made his heart set hard again.

"You would like me to go away for a month?" he said,
calmly.

"Yes," she answered, stubbornly.

"All right, then, I will. I must stop in town for to-morrow,
but I will sleep at Edmund's."

"You could do that, couldn't you?" she said, accepting his
suggestion, a little bit hesitating.

"If you want me to."

"I'm so *tired*!" she lamented.

But there was exasperation and hate in the last word, too.

"Very well," he answered.

She finished buttoning her glove.

"You'll go, then?" she said suddenly, brightly, turning to
depart. "Good-bye."

He hated her for the flippant insult of her leave-taking.

"I shall be at Edmund's to-morrow," he said.

"You will write to me from Italy, won't you?"

He would not answer the unnecessary question.

"Have you taken the dead primroses out of your hair?" he asked.

"I haven't," she said.

And she unpinned her hat.

"Richard *would* think me cracked," she said, picking out the crumpled, creamy fragments. She strewed the withered flowers carelessly on the table, set her hat straight.

"Do you *want* me to go?" he asked, again, rather yearning.

She knitted her brows. It irked her to resist the appeal. Yet she had in her breast a hard, repellent feeling for him. She had loved him, too. She had loved him dearly. And—he had not seemed to realise her. So that now she *did* want to be free of him for a while. Yet the love, the passion she had had for him clung about her. But she did want, first and primarily, to be free of him again.

"Yes," she said, half pleading.

"Very well," he answered.

She came across to him, and put her arms round his neck. Her hat-pin caught his head, but he moved, and she did not notice.

"You don't mind very much, do you, my love?" she said caressingly.

"I mind all the world, and all I am," he said.

She rose from him, fretted, miserable, and yet determined.

"I *must* have some rest," she repeated.

He knew that cry. She had had it, on occasions, for two months now. He had cursed her, and refused either to go away or to let her go. Now he knew it was no use.

"All right," he said. "Go and get it from Richard."

"Yes." She hesitated. "Good-bye," she called, and was gone.

He heard her cab whirr away. He had no idea whither she was gone—but probably to Madge, her friend.

He went upstairs to pack. Their bedroom made him suffer. She used to say, at first, that she would give up anything rather than her sleeping with him. And still they were always together. A kind of blind helplessness drove them to one another, even when, after he had taken her, they only felt more apart than ever. It had seemed to her that he had been mechanical and barren with her. She felt a horrible feeling of aversion from him, inside her, even while physically she still desired him. His body had always a kind of fascination for her. But had hers for him? He seemed, often, just to have served her, or to have obeyed some impersonal instinct for which she was the only outlet, in his loving her. So at last she rose against him, to cast him off. He seemed to follow her so, to draw her life into his. It made her feel she would go mad. For he seemed to do it just blindly, without having any notion of her herself. It was as if she were sucked out of herself by some non-human force. As for him, he seemed only like an instrument for his work, his business, not like a person at all. Sometimes she thought he was a big fountain-pen which was always sucking at her blood for ink.

He could not understand anything of this. He loved her—he could not bear to be away from her. He tried to realise her and to give her what she wanted. But he could not understand. He could not understand her accusations against him. Physically, he knew, she loved him, or had loved him, and was satisfied by him. He also knew that she would have loved another man nearly as well. And for the rest, he was only himself. He could not understand what she said about his using her and giving her nothing in return. Perhaps he did not think of her, as a separate person from himself, sufficiently. But then he did not see, he could not see that she had any real personal life, separate from himself. He tried to think of her in every possible way, and to give her what she wanted. But it was no good; she was never at peace. And lately there had been growing a breach between them. They had never come together without his realising it, afterwards. Now he must submit, and go away.

And her quilted dressing-gown—it was a little bit torn, like most of her things—and her pearl-backed mirror, with one of the pieces of pearl missing—all her untidy, flimsy, lovable things hurt him as he went about the bedroom, and made his heart go hard with hate, in the midst of his love.

II

Instead of going to his brother-in-law's, he went to an hotel for the night. It was not till he stood in the lift, with the attendant at his side, that he began to realise that he was only a mile or so away from his own home, and yet farther away than any miles could make him. It was about nine o'clock. He hated his bedroom. It was comfortable, and not ostentatious; its only fault was the neutrality necessary to an hotel apartment. He looked round. There was one semi-erotic Florentine picture of a lady with cat's eyes, over the bed. It was not bad. The only other ornament on the walls was the notice of hours and prices of meals and rooms. The couch sat correctly before the correct little table, on which the writing-sachet and inkstand stood mechanically. Down below, the quiet street was half illuminated, the people passed sparsely, like stunted shadows. And of all times of the night, it was a quarter-past nine. He thought he would go to bed. Then he looked at the white-and-glazed doors which shut him off from the bath. He would bathe, to pass the time away. In the bath-closet everything was so comfortable and white and warm—too warm; the level, unvarying heat of the atmo-sphere, from which there was no escape anywhere, seemed so hideously hotel-like; this central-heating forced a unity into the great building, making it more than ever like an enor-mous box with incubating cells. He loathed it. But at any rate the bath-closet was human, white and business-like and lux-urious.

He was trying, with the voluptuous warm water, and the exciting thrill of the shower-bath, to bring back the life into his dazed body. Since she had begun to hate him, he had gradually lost that physical pride and pleasure in his own physique which the first months of married life had given him. His body had gone meaningless to him again, almost as if it were not there. It had wakened up, there had been the physical glow and satisfaction about his movements of a creature which rejoices in itself; a glow which comes on a man who loves and is loved passionately and successfully.

Now this was going again. All the life was accumulating in his mental consciousness, and his body felt like a piece of waste. He was not aware of this. It was instinct which made him want to bathe. But that, too, was a failure. He went under the shower-spray with his mind occupied by business, of some care of affairs, taking the tingling water almost without knowing it, stepping out mechanically, as a man going through a barren routine. He was dry again, and looking out of the window, without having experienced anything during the last hour.

Then he remembered that she did not know his address. He scribbled a note and rang to have it posted.

As soon as he had turned out the light, and there was nothing left for his mental consciousness to flourish amongst, it dropped, and it was dark inside him as without. It was his blood, and the elemental male in it, that now rose from him; unknown instincts suffocated him, and he could not bear it, that he was shut in this great, warm building. He wanted to be outside, with space springing from him. But, again, the reasonable being in him knew it was ridiculous, and he remained staring at the dark, having the horrible sensation of a roof low down over him; whilst that dark, unknown being, which lived below all his consciousness in the eternal gloom of his blood, heaved and raged blindly against him.

It was not his thoughts that represented him. They spun like straws or the iridescence of oil on a dark stream. He thought of her, sketchily, spending an evening of light amusement with the symbolical Richard. That did not mean much to him. He did not really speculate about Richard. He had the dark, powerful sense of her, how she wanted to get away from him and from the deep, underneath intimacy which had gradually come between them, back to the easy, everyday life where one knows nothing of the underneath, so that it takes its way apart from the consciousness. She did not want to have the deeper part of herself in direct contact with or under the influence of any other intrinsic being. She wanted, in the deepest sense, to be free of him. She could not bear the close, basic intimacy into which she had been drawn. She wanted her life for herself. It was true, her strongest desire

had been previously to know the contact through the whole
of her being, down to the very bottom. Now it troubled her.
She wanted to disengage his roots. Above, in the open, she
would live. But she must live perfectly free of herself, and
not, at her source, be connected with anybody. She was using
this symbolical Richard as a spade to dig him away from her.
And he felt like a thing whose roots are all straining on their
hold, and whose elemental life, that blind source, surges
backwards and forwards darkly, in a chaos, like something
which is threatened with spilling out of its own vessel.

This tremendous swaying of the most elemental part of
him continued through the hours, accomplishing his being,
whilst superficially he thought of the journey, of the Italian
he would speak, how he had left his coat in the train, and the
rascally official interpreter had tried to give him twenty lire
for a sovereign—how the man in the hat-shop in the Strand
had given him the wrong change—of the new shape in hats,
and the new felt—and so on. Underneath it all, like the sea
under a pleasure pier, his elemental, physical soul was heaving in great waves through his blood and his tissue, the sob,
the silent light, the slightly-washing fall away again. So his
blood, out of whose darkness everything rose, being moved to
its depth by her revulsion, heaved and swung towards its own
rest, surging blindly to its own re-settling.

Without knowing it, he suffered that night almost more
than he had ever suffered during his life. But it was all below
his consciousness. It was his life itself at storm, not his mind
and his will engaged at all.

In the morning he got up, thin and quiet, without much
movement anywhere, only with some of the clearing after-
storm. His body felt like a clean, empty shell. His mind was
limpidly clear. He went through the business of the toilet
with a certain accuracy, and at breakfast, in the restaurant,
there was about him that air of neutral correctness which
makes men seem so unreal.

At lunch, there was a telegram for him. It was like her to
telegraph.

"Come to tea, my dear love."

As he read it, there was a great heave of resistance in him.

But then he faltered. With his consciousness, he remembered how impulsive and eager she was when she dashed off her telegram, and he relaxed. It went without saying that he would go.

III

When he stood in the lift going up to his own flat, he was almost blind with the hurt of it all. They had loved each other so much in his first home. The parlour-maid opened to him, and he smiled at her affectionately. In the golden-brown and cream-coloured hall—Paula would have nothing heavy or sombre about her—a bush of rose-coloured azaleas shone, and a little tub of lilies twinkled naïvely.

She did not come out to meet him.

"Tea is in the drawing-room," the maid said, and he went in while she was hanging up his coat. It was a big room, with a sense of space, and a spread of whitey carpet almost the colour of unpolished marble—and grey and pink border; of pink roses on big white cushions, pretty Dresden china, and deep chintz-covered chairs and sofas which looked as if they were used freely. It was a room where one could roll in soft fresh-comfort, a room which had not much breakable in it, and which seemed, in the dusky spring evening, fuller of light than the streets outside.

Paula rose, looking queenly and rather radiant, as she held out her hand. A young man whom Peter scarcely noticed rose on the other side of the hearth.

"I expected you an hour ago," she said, looking into her husband's eyes. But though she looked at him, she did not see him. And he sank his head.

"This is another Moest," she said, presenting the stranger. "He knows Richard, too."

The young man, a German of about thirty, with a clean-shaven æsthetic face, long black hair brushed back a little wearily or bewildered from his brow, and inclined to fall in an odd loose strand again, so that he nervously put it back with his fine hand, looked at Moest and bowed. He had a finely-cut face, but his dark-blue eyes were strained, as if he did not quite know where he was. He sat down again, and his pleasant figure took a self-conscious attitude, of a man whose business it was to say things that should be listened to. He was not conceited or affected—naturally sensitive and rather naïve; but he could only move in an atmosphere of literature and literary ideas; yet he seemed to know there was something else, vaguely, and he felt rather at a loss. He waited for the conversation to move his way, as, inert, an insect waits for the sun to set it flying.

"Another Moest," Paula was pronouncing emphatically. "Actually another Moest, of whom we have never heard, and under the same roof with us."

The stranger laughed, his lips moving nervously over his teeth.

"You are in this house?" Peter asked, surprised.

The young man shifted in his chair, dropped his head, looked up again.

"Yes," he said, meeting Moest's eyes as if he were somewhat dazzled. "I am staying with the Lauriers, on the second floor."

He spoke English slowly, with a quaint, musical quality in his voice, and a certain rhythmic enunciation.

"I see; and the telegram was for you?" said the host.

"Yes," replied the stranger, with a nervous little laugh.

"My husband," broke in Paula, evidently repeating to the German what she had said before, for Peter's benefit this time, "was quite convinced I had an *affaire*"—she pronounced it in the French fashion—"with this terrible Richard."

The German gave his little laugh, and moved, painfully self-conscious, in his chair.

"Yes," he said, glancing at Moest.

"Did you spend a night of virtuous indignation?" Paula laughed to her husband, "imagining my perfidy?"

"I did not," said her husband. "Were you at Madge's?"

"No," she said. Then, turning to her guest: "Who is Richard, Mr. Moest?"

"Richard," began the German, word by word, "is my cousin." He glanced quickly at Paula, to see if he were understood. She rustled her skirts, and arranged herself comfortably, lying, or almost squatting, on the sofa by the fire. "He lives in Hampstead."

"And what is he like?" she asked, with eager interest.

The German gave his little laugh. Then he moved his fingers across his brow, in his dazed fashion. Then he looked, with his beautiful blue eyes, at his beautiful hostess.

"I——" He laughed again nervously. "He is a man whose parts—are not very much—very well known to me. You see," he broke forth, and it was evident he was now conversing to an imaginary audience—"I cannot easily express myself in English. I—I never have talked it. I shall speak, because I know nothing of modern England, a kind of Renaissance English."

"How lovely!" cried Paula. "But if you would rather, speak German. We shall understand sufficiently."

"I would rather hear some Renaissance English," said Moest.

Paula was quite happy with the new stranger. She listened to descriptions of Richard, shifting animatedly on her sofa. She wore a new dress, of a rich red-tile colour, glossy and long and soft, and she had threaded daisies, like buttons, in the braided plait of her hair. Her husband hated her for these familiarities. But she was beautiful too, and warm-hearted. Only, through all her warmth and kindliness, lay, he said, at the bottom, an almost feline selfishness, a coldness.

She was playing to the stranger—nay, she was not playing, she was really occupied by him. The young man was the favourite disciple of the most famous present-day German poet and *Meister*. He himself was occupied in translating Shakespeare. Having been always a poetic disciple, he had never come into touch with life save through literature, and for him, since he was a rather fine-hearted young man, with a human need to live, this was a tragedy. Paula was not long in discovering what ailed him, and she was eager to come to his rescue.

It pleased her, nevertheless, to have her husband sitting by, watching her. She forgot to give tea to anyone. Moest and the German both helped themselves, and the former attended also to his wife's cup. He sat rather in the background, listening, and waiting. She had made a fool of him with her talk to this stranger of "Richard;" lightly and flippantly she had made a fool of him. He minded, but was used to it. Now she had absorbed herself in this dazed, starved, literature-bewildered young German, who was, moreover, really lova-ble, evidently a gentleman. And she was seeing in him her mission—"just as," said Moest bitterly to himself, "she saw her mission in me, a year ago. She is no woman. She's got a big heart for everybody, but it must be like a common-room; she's got no private, sacred heart, except perhaps for herself, where there's no room for a man in it."

At length the stranger rose to go, promising to come again.

"Isn't he adorable?" cried Paula, as her husband returned to the drawing-room. "I think he is simply adorable."

"Yes!" said Moest.

"He called this morning to ask about the telegram. But, poor devil, isn't it a shame what they've done to him?"

"What who have done to him?" her husband asked coldly, jealous.

"Those literary creatures. They take a young fellow like that, and stick him up among the literary gods, like a mantel-piece ornament, and there he has to sit, being a minor ornament, while all his youth is gone. It is criminal."

"He should get off the mantelpiece, then," said Moest.

But inside him his heart was black with rage against her. What had she, after all, to do with this young man, when he himself was being smashed up by her? He loathed her pity and her kindliness, which was like a charitable institution. There was no core to the woman. She was full of generosity and bigness and kindness, but there was no heart in her, no security, no place for one single man. He began to under-stand now sirens and sphinxes and the other Greek fabulous female things. They had not been created by fancy, but out of bitter necessity of the man's human heart to express itself.

"Ha!" she laughed, half contemptuous. "Did *you* get off your miserable, starved isolation by yourself?—you didn't. You had to be fetched down, and I had to do it."

"Out of your usual charity," he said.

"But you can sneer at another man's difficulties," she said.

"Your name ought to be Panacea, not Paula," he replied.

He felt furious and dead against her. He could even look at her without the tenderness coming. And he was glad. He hated her. She seemed unaware. Very well; let her be so.

"Oh, but he makes me so miserable, to see him!" she cried. "Self-conscious, can't get into contact with anybody, living a false literary life like a man who takes poetry as a drug.— One *ought* to help him."

She was really earnest and distressed.

"Out of the frying-pan into the fire," he said.

"I'd rather be in the fire any day, than in a frying-pan," she said, abstractedly, with a little shudder. She never troubled to see the meaning of her husband's sarcasms.

They remained silent. The maid came in for the tray, and to ask him if he would be in to dinner. He waited for his wife to answer. She sat with her chin in her hands, brooding over the young German, and did not hear. The rage flashed up in his heart. He would have liked to smash her out of this false absorption.

"No," he said to the maid. "I think not. Are you at home for dinner, Paula?"

"Yes," she said.

And he knew by her tone, easy and abstracted, that she intended him to stay, too. But she did not trouble to say anything.

At last, after some time, she asked:

"What did you do?"

"Nothing—went to bed early," he replied.

"Did you sleep well?"

"Yes, thank you."

And he recognised the ludicrous civilities of married people, and he wanted to go. She was silent for a time. Then she asked, and her voice had gone still and grave:

"Why don't you ask me what I did?"

"Because I don't care—you just went to somebody's for dinner."

"Why don't you care what I do? Isn't it your place to care?"

"About the things you do to spite me?—no!"

"Ha!" she mocked. "I did nothing to spite you. I was in deadly earnest."

"Even with your Richard?"

"Yes," she cried. "There *might* have been a Richard. What did you care!"

"In that case you'd have been a liar and worse, so why should I care about you then?"

"You *don't* care about me," she said, sullenly.

"You say what you please," he answered.

She was silent for some time.

"And did you do absolutely nothing last night?" she asked.

"I had a bath and went to bed."

Then she pondered.

"No," she said, "you don't care for me."

He did not trouble to answer. Softly, a little china clock rang six.

"I shall go to Italy in the morning," he said.

"Yes."

"And," he said, slowly, forcing the words out, "I shall stay at the Aquila Nera at Milan—you know my address."

"Yes," she answered.

"I shall be away about a month. Meanwhile you can rest."

"Yes," she said, in her throat, with a little contempt of him and his stiffness. He, in spite of himself, was breathing heavily. He knew that this parting was the real separation of their souls, marked the point beyond which they could go no farther, but accepted the marriage as a comparative failure. And he had built all his life on his marriage. She accused him of not loving her. He gripped the arms of his chair. Was there something in it? Did he only want the attributes which went along with her, the peace of heart which a man has in living to one woman, even if the love between them be not complete; the singleness and unity in his life that made it easy; the fixed establishment of himself as a married man with a home; the feeling that he belonged somewhere, that one woman existed—not was paid but *existed*—really to take care of him; was it these things he wanted, and not her? But he wanted her for these purposes—her, and nobody else. But was that not enough for her? Perhaps he wronged her—it was possible. What she said against him was in earnest. And what she said in earnest he had to believe, in the long run, since it was the utterance of her being. He felt miserable and tired.

When he looked at her, across the gathering twilight of the room, she was staring into the fire and biting her finger-nail, restlessly, restlessly, without knowing. And all his limbs went suddenly weak, as he realised that she suffered too, that something was gnawing at her. Something in the look of her, the crouching, dogged, wondering look made him faint with tenderness for her.

"Don't bite your finger-nails," he said quietly, and, obediently, she took her hand from her mouth. His heart was beating quickly. He could feel the atmosphere of the room changing. It had stood aloof, the room, like something placed round him, like a great box. Now everything got softer, as if it partook of the atmosphere, of which he partook himself, and they were all one.

His mind reverted to her accusations, and his heart beat like a caged thing against what he could not understand. She said he did not love her. But he knew that in his way, he did. In his way—but was his way wrong? His way was himself, he thought, struggling. Was there something wrong, something missing in his nature, that he could not love? He struggled madly, as if he were in a mesh, and could not get out. He did not want to believe that he was deficient in his nature. Wherein was he deficient? It was nothing physical. She said he would not come out of himself, that he was no good to her, because he could not get outside himself. What did she mean? Not outside himself! It seemed like some acrobatic feat, some slippery, contortionist trick. No, he could not understand. His heart flashed hot with resentment. She did nothing but find fault with him. What did she care about him, really, when she could taunt him with not being able to take a light woman when he was in Paris? Though his heart, forced to do her justice, knew that for this she loved him, really.

But it was too complicated and difficult, and already, as they sat thinking, it had gone wrong between them and things felt twisted, horribly twisted, so that he could not breathe. He must go. He could dine at the hotel and go to the theatre.

"Well," he said casually, "I must go. I think I shall go and see 'The Black Sheep'."

She did not answer. Then she turned and looked at him with a queer, half-bewildered, half-perverse smile that seemed conscious of pain. Her eyes, shining rather dilated and triumphant, and yet with something heavily yearning behind them, looked at him. He could not understand, and, between her appeal and her defiant triumph, he felt as if his chest was crushed so that he could not breathe.

"My love," she said, in a little singing, abstract fashion, her lips somehow sipping towards him, her eyes shining dilated; and yet he felt as if he were not in it, himself.

His heart was a flame that prevented his breathing. He gripped the chair like a man who is going to be put under torture.

"What?" he said, staring back at her.

"Oh, my love!" she said softly, with a little, intense laugh on her face, that made him pant. And she slipped from her sofa and came across to him quickly, and put her hand hesitating on his hair. The blood struck like flame across his consciousness, and the hurt was keen like joy, like the releasing of something that hurts as the pressure is relaxed and the movement comes, before the peace. Afraid, his fingers touched her hand, and she sank swiftly between his knees, and put her face on his breast. He held her head hard against his chest, and again and again the flame went down his blood, as he felt her round, small, nut of a head between his hands pressing into his chest where the hurt had been bruised in so deep. His wrists quivered as he pressed her head to him, as he felt the deadness going out of him; the real life released, flowing into his body again. How hard he had shut it off, against her, when she hated him. He was breathing heavily with relief, blindly pressing her head against him. He believed in her again.

She looked up, laughing, childish, inviting him with her lips. He bent to kiss her, and as his eyes closed, he saw hers were shut. The feeling of restoration was almost unbearable.

"Do you love me?" she whispered, in a little ecstasy.

He did not answer, except with the quick tightening of his arms, clutching her a little closer against him. And he loved the silkiness of her hair, and its natural scent. And it hurt him that the daisies she had threaded in should begin to wither. He resented their hurting her by their dying.

He had not understood. But the trouble had gone off. He was quiet, and he watched her from out of his sensitive stillness, a little bit dimly, unable to recover. She was loving to him, protective, and bright, laughing like a glad child too.

"We must tell Maud I shall be in to dinner," he said.

That was like him—always aware of the practical side of the case, and the appearances. She laughed a little bit ironically. Why should she have to take her arm from round him, just to tell Maud he would be in to dinner?

"I'll go," she said.

He drew the curtains and turned on the light in the big lamp that stood in a corner. The room was dim, and palely warm. He loved it dearly.

His wife, when she came back, as soon as she had closed the door, lifted her arms to him in a little ecstasy, coming to him. They clasped each other closer, body to body. And the intensity of his feeling was so fierce, he felt himself going dim, fusing into something soft and plastic between her hands. And this connection with her was bigger than life or death. And at the bottom of his heart was a sob.

She was gay and winsome at the dinner. Like lovers, they were just deliciously waiting for the night to come up. But there remained in him always the slightly broken feeling which the night before had left.

"And you won't go to Italy," she said, as if it were an understood thing.

She gave him the best things to eat, and was solicitous for his welfare—which was not usual with her. It gave him deep, shy pleasure. He remembered a verse she was often quoting as one she loved. He did not know it for himself:

> "On my breasts I warm thy foot-soles;
> Wine I pour, and dress thy meats;
> Humbly, when my lord disposes,
> Lie with him on perfumed sheets."

She said it to him sometimes, looking up at him from the pillow. But it never seemed real to him. She might, in her sudden passion, put his feet between her breasts. But he never felt like a lord, never more pained and insignificant than at those times. As a little girl she must have subjected herself before her dolls. And he was something like her lordliest plaything. He liked that too. If only . . .

Then, seeing some frightened little way of looking at him which she had, the pure pain came back. He loved her, and it would never be peace between them; she would never belong to him, as a wife. She would take him and reject him, like a mistress. And perhaps for that reason he would love her all the more; it might be so.

But then, he forgot. Whatever was or was not, now she loved him. And whatever came after, this evening he was the lord. What matter if he were deposed to-morrow, and she hated him!

Her eyes, wide and candid, were staring at him a little bit wondering, a little bit forlorn. She knew he had not quite come back. He held her close to him.

"My love," she murmured consolingly. "My love."

And she put her fingers through his hair, arranging it in little, loose curves, playing with it and forgetting everything else. He loved that dearly, to feel the light lift and touch—touch of her finger-tips making his hair, as she said, like an Apollo's. She lifted his face to see how he looked, and, with a little laugh of love, kissed him. And he loved to be made much of by her. But he had the dim, hurting sense that she would not love him to-morrow, that it was only her great need to love that exalted him to-night. He *knew* he was no king; he did not feel a king, even when she was crowning and kissing him.

"Do you love me?" she asked, playfully whispering.

He held her fast and kissed her, while the blood hurt in his heart-chambers.

"You know," he answered, with a struggle.

Later, when he lay holding her with a passion intense like pain, the words blurted from him:

"Flesh of my flesh. Paula!—Will you——?"

"Yes, my love," she answered consolingly.

He bit his mouth with pain. For him it was almost an agony of appeal.

"But, Paula—I mean it—flesh of my flesh—a wife?"

She tightened her arms round him without answering. And he knew, and she knew, that she put him off like that.

IV

Two months later, she was writing to him in Italy: "Your idea of your woman is that she is an expansion, no, a *rib* of yourself, without any existence of her own. That I am a being by myself is more than you can grasp. I wish I could absolutely submerge myself in a man—and *so I do*. I *always* loved you . . .

"You will say 'I was patient.' Do you call that patient, hanging on for your needs, as you have done? The innermost life you have *always* had of me, and you held yourself aloof because you were afraid.

"The unpardonable thing was you told me you loved me.— Your *feelings* have hated me these three months, which did not prevent you from taking my love and every breath from me.—Underneath you undermined me, in some subtle, corrupt way that I did not see because I believed you, when you told me you loved me . . .

"The insult of the way you took me these last three months I shall never forgive you. I honestly *did* give myself, and always in vain and rebuffed. The strain of it all has driven me quite mad.

"You say I am a tragédienne, but I don't do any of your

perverse undermining tricks. You are always luring one into the open like a clever enemy, but you keep safely under cover all the time.

"This practically means, for me, that life is over, my belief in life—I hope it will recover, but it never could do so with you . . ."

To which he answered; "If I kept under cover it is funny, for there isn't any cover now.—And you can hope, pretty easily, for your own recovery apart from me. For my side, without you, I am done . . . But you lie to yourself. You *wouldn't* love *me*, and you won't be able to love anybody else—except yourself."

The Prussian Officer

I

THEY HAD marched more than thirty kilometres since dawn, along the white, hot road where occasional thickets of trees threw a moment of shade, then out into the glare again. On either hand, the valley, wide and shallow, glittered with heat; dark-green patches of rye, pale young corn, fallow and meadow and black pine woods spread in a dull, hot diagram under a glistening sky. But right in front the mountains ranged across, pale blue and very still, snow gleaming gently out of the deep atmosphere. And towards the mountains, on and on, the regiment marched between the rye-fields and the meadows, between the scraggy fruit trees set regularly on either side the high road. The burnished, dark-green rye threw off a suffocating heat, the mountains drew gradually nearer and more distinct. While the feet of the soldiers grew hotter, sweat ran through their hair under their helmets, and their knapsacks could burn no more in contact with their shoulders, but seemed instead to give off a cold, prickly sensation.

He walked on and on in silence, staring at the mountains ahead, that rose sheer out of the land, and stood fold behind fold, half earth, half heaven, the heaven, the barrier with slits of soft snow, in the pale, bluish peaks.

He could now walk almost without pain. At the start, he had determined not to limp. It had made him sick to take the first steps, and during the first mile or so, he had compressed his breath, and the cold drops of sweat had stood on his forehead. But he had walked it off. What were they after all but bruises! He had looked at them, as he was getting up: deep bruises on the backs of his thighs. And since he had made his first step in the morning, he had been conscious of them, till now he had a tight, hot place in his chest, with suppressing the pain, and holding himself in. There seemed no air when he breathed. But he walked almost lightly.

The Captain's hand had trembled at taking his coffee at dawn: his orderly saw it again. And he saw the fine figure of the Captain wheeling on horseback at the farmhouse ahead, a handsome figure in pale-blue uniform with facings of scarlet, and the metal gleaming on the black helmet and the sword-scabbard, and dark streaks of sweat coming on the silky bay horse. The orderly felt he was connected with that figure moving so suddenly on horseback: he followed it like a shadow, mute and inevitable and damned by it. And the officer was always aware of the tramp of the company behind, the march of his orderly among the men.

The Captain was a tall man of about forty, grey at the temples. He had a handsome, finely-knit figure, and was one of the best horsemen in the West. His orderly, having to rub him down, admired the amazing riding muscles of his loins.

For the rest, the orderly scarcely noticed the officer any more than he noticed himself. It was rarely he saw his master's face: he did not look at it. The Captain had reddish-brown, stiff hair, that he wore short upon his skull. His moustache was also cut short and bristly over a full, brutal mouth. His face was rather rugged, the cheeks thin. Perhaps the man was the more handsome for the deep lines in his face, the irritable tension of his brow, which gave him the look of a man who fights with life. His fair eyebrows stood bushy over light-blue eyes that were always flashing with cold fire.

He was a Prussian aristocrat, haughty and overbearing. But his mother had been a Polish countess. Having made too many gambling debts when he was young, he had ruined his prospects in the Army, and remained an infantry captain. He had never married: his position did not allow of it, and no woman had ever moved him to it. His time he spent riding— occasionally he rode one of his own horses at the races—and at the officers' club. Now and then he took himself a mis-tress. But after such an event, he returned to duty with his brow still more tense, his eyes still more hostile and irritable.

With the men, however, he was merely impersonal, though a devil when roused; so that, on the whole, they feared him, but had no great aversion from him. They accepted him as the inevitable.

To his orderly he was at first cold and just and indifferent: he did not fuss over trifles. So that his servant knew practically nothing about him, except just what orders he would give, and how he wanted them obeyed. That was quite simple. Then the change gradually came.

The orderly was a youth of about twenty-two, of medium height, and well built. He had strong, heavy limbs, was swarthy, with a soft, black, young moustache. There was something altogether warm and young about him. He had firmly marked eyebrows over dark, expressionless eyes, that seemed never to have thought, only to have received life direct through his senses, and acted straight from instinct.

Gradually the officer had become aware of his servant's young vigorous, unconscious presence about him. He could not get away from the sense of the youth's person, while he was in attendance. It was like a warm flame upon the older man's tense, rigid body, that had become almost unliving, fixed. There was something so free and self-contained about him, and something in the young fellow's movement, that made the officer aware of him. And this irritated the Prussian. He did not choose to be touched into life by his servant. He might easily have changed his man, but he did not. He now very rarely looked direct at his orderly, but kept his face averted, as if to avoid seeing him. And yet as the young soldier moved unthinking about the apartment, the elder watched him, and would notice the movement of his strong young shoulders under the blue cloth, the bend of his neck. And it irritated him. To see the soldier's young, brown, shapely peasant's hand grasp the loaf or the wine-bottle sent a flash of hate or of anger through the elder man's blood. It was not that the youth was clumsy: it was rather the blind, instinctive sureness of movement of an unhampered young animal that irritated the officer to such a degree.

Once, when a bottle of wine had gone over, and the red gushed out on to the tablecloth, the officer had started up with an oath, and his eyes, bluey like fire, had held those of the confused youth for a moment. It was a shock for the young soldier. He felt something sink deeper, deeper into his soul, where nothing had ever gone before. It left him rather blank and wondering. Some of his natural completeness in himself was gone, a little uneasiness took its place. And from that time an undiscovered feeling had held between the two men.

Henceforward the orderly was afraid of really meeting his master. His subconsciousness remembered those steely blue eyes and the harsh brows, and did not intend to meet them again. So he always stared past his master, and avoided him. Also, in a little anxiety, he waited for the three months to have gone, when his time would be up. He began to feel a constraint in the Captain's presence, and the soldier even more than the officer wanted to be left alone, in his neutrality as servant.

He had served the Captain for more than a year, and knew his duty. This he performed easily, as if it were natural to him. The officer and his commands he took for granted, as he took the sun and the rain, and he served as a matter of course. It did not implicate him personally.

But now if he were going to be forced into a personal interchange with his master he would be like a wild thing caught, he felt he must get away.

But the influence of the young soldier's being had penetrated through the officer's stiffened discipline, and perturbed the man in him. He, however, was a gentleman, with long, fine hands and cultivated movements, and was not going to allow such a thing as the stirring of his innate self. He was a man of passionate temper, who had always kept himself suppressed. Occasionally there had been a duel, an outburst before the soldiers. He knew himself to be always on the point of breaking out. But he kept himself hard to the idea of the Service. Whereas the young soldier seemed to live out his warm, full nature, to give it off in his very movements, which had a certain zest, such as wild animals have in free movement. And this irritated the officer more and more.

In spite of himself, the Captain could not regain his neu-

trality of feeling towards his orderly. Nor could he leave the
man alone. In spite of himself, he watched him, gave him
sharp orders, tried to take up as much of his time as possible.
Sometimes he flew into a rage with the young soldier, and
bullied him. Then the orderly shut himself off, as it were out
of earshot, and waited, with sullen, flushed face, for the end
of the noise. The words never pierced to his intelligence, he
made himself, protectively, impervious to the feelings of his
master.

He had a scar on his left thumb, a deep seam going across
the knuckle. The officer had long suffered from it, and
wanted to do something to it. Still it was there, ugly and
brutal on the young, brown hand. At last the Captain's
reserve gave way. One day, as the orderly was smoothing out
the tablecloth, the officer pinned down his thumb with a
pencil, asking:

"How did you come by that?"

The young man winced and drew back at attention.

"A wood axe, Herr Hauptmann," he answered.

The officer waited for further explanation. None came.
The orderly went about his duties. The elder man was sullenly angry. His servant avoided him. And the next day he had
to use all his will-power to avoid seeing the scarred thumb.
He wanted to get hold of it and—— A hot flame ran in his
blood.

He knew his servant would soon be free, and would be
glad. As yet, the soldier had held himself off from the elder
man. The Captain grew madly irritable. He could not rest
when the soldier was away, and when he was present, he
glared at him with tormented eyes. He hated those fine, black
brows over the unmeaning, dark eyes, he was infuriated by
the free movement of the handsome limbs, which no military
discipline could make stiff. And he became harsh and cruelly
bullying, using contempt and satire. The young soldier only
grew more mute and expressionless.

"What cattle were you bred by, that you can't keep
straight eyes? Look me in the eyes when I speak to you."

And the soldier turned his dark eyes to the other's face,
but there was no sight in them: he stared with the slightest

possible cast, holding back his sight, perceiving the blue of his master's eyes, but receiving no look from them. And the elder man went pale, and his reddish eyebrows twitched. He gave his order, barrenly.

Once he flung a heavy military glove into the young soldier's face. Then he had the satisfaction of seeing the black eyes flare up into his own, like a blaze when straw is thrown on a fire. And he had laughed with a little tremor and a sneer.

But there were only two months more. The youth instinctively tried to keep himself intact: he tried to serve the officer as if the latter were an abstract authority and not a man. All his instinct was to avoid personal contact, even definite hate. But in spite of himself the hate grew, responsive to the officer's passion. However, he put it in the background. When he had left the Army he could dare acknowledge it. By nature he was active, and had many friends. He thought what amazing good fellows they were. But, without knowing it, he was alone. Now this solitariness was intensified. It would carry him through his term. But the officer seemed to be going irritably insane, and the youth was deeply frightened.

The soldier had a sweetheart, a girl from the mountains, independent and primitive. The two walked together, rather silently. He went with her, not to talk, but to have his arm round her, and for the physical contact. This eased him, made it easier for him to ignore the Captain; for he could rest with her held fast against his chest. And she, in some unspoken fashion, was there for him. They loved each other.

The Captain perceived it, and was mad with irritation. He kept the young man engaged all the evenings long, and took pleasure in the dark look that came on his face. Occasionally, the eyes of the two men met, those of the younger sullen and dark, doggedly unalterable, those of the elder sneering with restless contempt.

The officer tried hard not to admit the passion that had got hold of him. He would not know that his feeling for his orderly was anything but that of a man incensed by his stupid, perverse servant. So, keeping quite justified and conventional in his consciousness, he let the other thing run on. His nerves, however, were suffering. At last he slung the end of a belt in his servant's face. When he saw the youth start back, the pain-tears in his eyes and the blood on his mouth, he had felt at once a thrill of deep pleasure and of shame.

But this, he acknowledged to himself, was a thing he had never done before. The fellow was too exasperating. His own nerves must be going to pieces. He went away for some days with a woman.

It was a mockery of pleasure. He simply did not want the woman. But he stayed on for his time. At the end of it, he came back in an agony of irritation, torment, and misery. He rode all the evening, then came straight in to supper. His orderly was out. The officer sat with his long, fine hands lying on the table, perfectly still, and all his blood seemed to be corroding.

At last his servant entered. He watched the strong, easy young figure, the fine eyebrows, the thick black hair. In a week's time the youth had got back his old well-being. The hands of the officer twitched and seemed to be full of mad flame. The young man stood at attention, unmoving, shut off.

The meal went in silence. But the orderly seemed eager. He made a clatter with the dishes.

"Are you in a hurry?" asked the officer, watching the intent, warm face of his servant. The other did not reply.

"Will you answer my question?" said the Captain.

"Yes, sir," replied the orderly, standing with his pile of deep Army plates. The Captain waited, looked at him, then asked again:

"Are you in a hurry?"

"Yes, sir," came the answer, that sent a flash through the listener.

"For what?"

"I was going out, sir."

"I want you this evening."

There was a moment's hesitation. The officer had a curious stiffness of countenance.

"Yes, sir," replied the servant, in his throat.

"I want you to-morrow evening also—in fact you may consider your evenings occupied, unless I give you leave."

The mouth with the young moustache set close.

"Yes, sir," answered the orderly, loosening his lips for a moment.

He again turned to the door.

"And why have you a piece of pencil in your ear?"

The orderly hesitated, then continued on his way without answering. He set the plates in a pile outside the door, took the stump of pencil from his ear, and put it in his pocket. He had been copying a verse for his sweetheart's birthday card. He returned to finish clearing the table. The officer's eyes were dancing, he had a little, eager smile.

"Why have you a piece of pencil in your ear?" he asked.

The orderly took his hands full of dishes. His master was standing near the great green stove, a little smile on his face, his chin thrust forward. When the young soldier saw him his heart suddenly ran hot. He felt blind. Instead of answering, he turned dazedly to the door. As he was crouching to set down the dishes, he was pitched forward by a kick from behind. The pots went in a stream down the stairs, he clung to the pillar of the banisters. And as he was rising he was kicked heavily again and again, so that he clung sickly to the post for some moments. His master had gone swiftly into the room and closed the door. The maid-servant downstairs looked up the staircase and made a mocking face at the crockery disaster.

The officer's heart was plunging. He poured himself a glass of wine, part of which he spilled on the floor, and gulped the remainder, leaning against the cool, green stove. He heard his man collecting the dish from the stairs. Pale, as if intoxicated, he waited. The servant entered again. The Captain's heart gave a pang, as of pleasure, seeing the young fellow bewildered and uncertain on his feet with pain.

"Schöner!" he said.

The soldier was a little slower in coming to attention.

"Yes, sir!"

The youth stood before him, with pathetic young

moustache, and fine eyebrows very distinct on his forehead of dark marble.

"I asked you a question."

"Yes, sir."

The officer's tone bit like acid.

"Why had you a pencil in your ear?"

Again the servant's heart ran hot, and he could not breathe. With dark, strained eyes, he looked at the officer, as if fascinated. And he stood there sturdily planted, unconscious. The withering smile came into the Captain's eyes, and he lifted his foot.

"I forgot it—sir," panted the soldier, his dark eyes fixed on the other man's dancing blue ones.

"What was it doing there?"

He saw the young man's breast heaving as he made an effort for words.

"I had been writing."

"Writing what?"

Again the soldier looked him up and down. The officer could hear him panting. The smile came into the blue eyes. The soldier worked his dry throat, but could not speak. Suddenly the smile lit like a flame on the officer's face, and a kick came heavily against the orderly's thigh. The youth moved sideways. His face went dead, with two black, staring eyes.

"Well?' said the officer.

The orderly's mouth had gone dry, and his tongue rubbed in it as on dry brown-paper. He worked his throat. The officer raised his foot. The servant went stiff.

"Some poetry, sir," came the crackling, unrecognisable sound of his voice.

"Poetry, what poetry?" asked the Captain, with a sickly smile.

Again there was the working in the throat. The Captain's heart had suddenly gone down heavily, and he stood sick and tired.

"For my girl, sir," he heard the dry, inhuman sound.

"Oh!" he said, turning away. "Clear the table."

"Click!" went the soldier's throat; then again, "click!" and then the half-articulate:

"Yes, sir."

The young soldier was gone, looking old, and walking heavily.

The officer, left alone, held himself rigid, to prevent himself from thinking. His instinct warned him that he must not think. Deep inside him was the intense gratification of his passion, still working powerfully. Then there was a counteraction, a horrible breaking down of something inside him, a whole agony of reaction. He stood there for an hour motionless, a chaos of sensations, but rigid with a will to keep blank his consciousness, to prevent his mind grasping. And he held himself so until the worst of the stress had passed, when he began to drink, drank himself to an intoxication, till he slept obliterated. When he woke in the morning he was shaken to the base of his nature. But he had fought off the realisation of what he had done. He had prevented his mind from taking it in, had suppressed it along with his instincts, and the conscious man had nothing to do with it. He felt only as after a bout of intoxication, weak, but the affair itself all dim and not to be recovered. Of the drunkenness of his passion he successfully refused remembrance. And when his orderly appeared with coffee, the officer assumed the same self he had had the morning before. He refused the event of the past night—denied it had ever been—and was successful in his denial. He had not done any such thing—not he himself. Whatever there might be lay at the door of a stupid insubordinate servant.

The orderly had gone about in a stupor all the evening. He drank some beer because he was parched, but not much, the alcohol made his feeling come back, and he could not bear it. He was dulled, as if nine-tenths of the ordinary man in him were inert. He crawled about disfigured. Still, when he thought of the kicks, he went sick, and when he thought of the threat of more kicking, in the room afterwards, his heart went hot and faint, and he panted, remembering the one that had come. He had been forced to say: "For my girl." He was much too done even to want to cry. His mouth hung slightly open, like an idiot's. He felt vacant, and wasted. So, he wandered at his work, painfully, and very slowly and clumsily, fumbling blindly with the brushes, and finding it difficult, when he sat down, to summon the energy to move again. His limbs, his jaw, were slack and nerveless. But he was very tired. He got to bed at last, and slept inert, relaxed, in a sleep that was rather stupor than slumber, a dead night of stupefaction shot through with gleams of anguish.

In the morning were the manœuvres. But he woke even before the bugle sounded. The painful ache in his chest, the dryness of his throat, the awful steady feeling of misery made his eyes come awake and dreary at once. He knew, without thinking, what had happened. And he knew that the day had come again, when he must go on with his round. The last bit of darkness was being pushed out of the room. He would have to move his inert body and go on. He was so young, and had known so little trouble, that he was bewildered. He only wished it would stay night, so that he could lie still, covered up by the darkness. And yet nothing would prevent the day from coming, nothing would save him from having to get up and saddle the Captain's horse, and make the Captain's coffee. It was there, inevitable. And then, he thought, it was impossible. Yet they would not leave him free. He must go and take the coffee to the Captain. He was too stunned to understand it. He only knew it was inevitable—inevitable, however long he lay inert.

At last, after heaving at himself, for he seemed to be a mass of inertia, he got up. But he had to force every one of his movements from behind, with his will. He felt lost, and dazed, and helpless. Then he clutched hold of the bed, the pain was so keen. And looking at his thighs he saw the darker bruises on his swarthy flesh, and he knew that if he pressed one of his fingers on one of the bruises, he would faint. But he did not want to faint—he did not want anybody to know. No one should ever know. It was between him and the Captain. There were only the two people in the world now—himself and the Captain.

Slowly, economically, he got dressed and forced himself to walk. Everything was obscure, except just what he had his hands on. But he managed to get through his work. The very pain revived his dull senses. The worst remained yet. He took the tray and went up to the Captain's room. The officer, pale and heavy, sat at the table. The orderly, as he saluted, felt himself put out of existence. He stood still for a moment submitting to his own nullification—then he gathered himself, seemed to regain himself, and then the Captain began to grow vague, unreal, and the younger soldier's heart beat up. He clung to this situation—that the Captain did not exist—so that he himself might live. But when he saw his officer's hand tremble as he took the coffee, he felt everything falling shattered. And he went away, feeling as if he himself were coming to pieces, disintegrated. And when the Captain was there on horseback, giving orders, while he himself stood, with rifle and knapsack, sick with pain, he felt as if he must shut his eyes—as if he must shut his eyes on everything. It was only the long agony of marching with a parched throat that filled him with one single, sleep-heavy intention: to save himself.

II

He was getting used even to his parched throat. That the snowy peaks were radiant among the sky, that the whity-green glacier-river twisted through its pale shoals, in the valley below, seemed almost supernatural. But he was going mad with fever and thirst. He plodded on uncomplaining. He did not want to speak, not to anybody. There were two gulls, like flakes of water and snow, over the river. The scent of green rye soaked in sunshine came like a sickness. And the march continued, monotonously, almost like a bad sleep.

At the next farmhouse, which stood low and broad near the high roads, tubs of water had been put out. The soldiers clustered round to drink. They took off their helmets, and the steam mounted from their wet hair. The Captain sat on horseback, watching. He needed to see his orderly. His helmet threw a dark shadow over his light, fierce eyes, but his moustache and mouth and chin were distinct in the sunshine. The orderly must move under the presence of the figure of the horseman. It was not that he was afraid, or cowed. It was as if he was disembowelled, made empty, like an empty shell. He felt himself as nothing, a shadow creeping under the sunshine. And, thirsty as he was, he could scarcely drink, feeling the Captain near him. He would not take off his helmet to wipe his wet hair. He wanted to stay in shadow, not to be forced into consciousness. Starting, he saw the light heel of the officer prick the belly of the horse; the Captain cantered away, and he himself could relapse into vacancy.

Nothing, however, could give him back his living place in the hot, bright morning. He felt like a gap among it all. Whereas the Captain was prouder, overriding. A hot flash went through the young servant's body. The Captain was firmer and prouder with life, he himself was empty as a shadow. Again the flash went through him, dazing him out. But his heart ran a little firmer.

The company turned up the hill, to make a loop for the return. Below, from among the trees, the farm-bell clanged. He saw the labourers, mowing bare-foot at the thick grass, leave off their work and go downhill, their scythes hanging over their shoulders, like long, bright claws curving down behind them. They seemed like dream-people, as if they had no relation to himself. He felt as in a blackish dream: as if all the other things were there and had form, but he himself was only a consciousness, a gap that could think and perceive.

The soldiers were tramping silently up the glaring hill-side. Gradually his head began to revolve, slowly, rhythmically. Sometimes it was dark before his eyes, as if he saw this world through a smoked glass, frail shadows and unreal. It gave him a pain in his head to walk.

The air was too scented, it gave no breath. All the lush green-stuff seemed to be issuing its sap, till the air was deathly, sickly with the smell of greenness. There was the perfume of clover, like pure honey and bees. Then there grew a faint acrid tang—they were near the beeches; and then a queer clattering noise, and a suffocating, hideous smell; they were passing a flock of sheep, a shepherd in a black smock, holding his crook. Why should the sheep huddle

together under this fierce sun? He felt that the shepherd
would not see him, though he could see the shepherd.

At last there was a halt. They stacked rifles in a conical
stack, put down their kit in a scattered circle around it, and
dispersed a little, sitting on a small knoll high on the hillside.
The chatter began. The soldiers were steaming with heat, but
were lively. He sat still, seeing the blue mountains rising upon
the land, twenty kilometres away. There was a blue fold in
the ranges, then out of that, at the foot, the broad, pale bed
of the river, stretches of whity-green water between pinkish-
grey shoals among the dark pine woods. There it was, spread
out a long way off. And it semed to come downhill, the
river. There was a raft being steered, a mile away. It was a
strange country. Nearer, a red-roofed, broad farm with white
base and square dots of windows crouched beside the wall of
beech foliage on the wood's edge. There were long strips of
rye and clover and pale green corn. And just at his feet,
below the knoll, was a darkish bog, where globe flowers
stood breathless still on their slim stalks. And some of the
pale gold bubbles were burst, and a broken fragment hung in
the air. He thought he was going to sleep.

Suddenly something moved into this coloured mirage before his eyes. The Captain, a small, light-blue and scarlet
figure, was trotting evenly between the strips of corn, along
the level brow of the hill. And the man making flag-signals
was coming on. Proud and sure moved the horseman's figure,
the quick, bright thing, in which was concentrated all the
light of this morning, which for the rest lay fragile, shining
shadow. Submissive, apathetic, the young soldier sat and
stared. But as the horse slowed to a walk, coming up the last
steep path, the great flash flared over the body and soul of
the orderly. He sat waiting. The back of his head felt as if it
were weighted with a heavy piece of fire. He did not want to
eat. His hands trembled slightly as he moved them. Meanwhile the officer on horseback was approaching slowly and
proudly. The tension grew in the orderly's soul. Then again,
seeing the Captain ease himself on the saddle, the flash blazed
through him.

The Captain looked at the patch of light blue and scarlet,

and dark head, scattered closely on the hill-side. It pleased him. The command pleased him. And he was feeling proud. His orderly was among them in common subjection. The officer rose a little on his stirrups to look. The young soldier sat with averted, dumb face. The Captain relaxed on his seat. His slim-legged, beautiful horse, brown as a beech nut, walked proudly uphill. The Captain passed into the zone of the company's atmosphere: a hot smell of men, of sweat, of leather. He knew it very well. After a word with the lieutenant, he went a few paces higher, and sat there, a dominant figure, his sweat-marked horse swishing its tail, while he looked down on his men, on his orderly, a nonentity among the crowd.

The young soldier's heart was like fire in his chest, and he breathed with difficulty. The officer, looking downhill, saw three of the young soldiers, two pails of water between them, staggering across a sunny green field. A table had been set up under a tree, and there the slim lieutenant stood, importantly busy. Then the Captain summoned himself to an act of courage. He called his orderly.

The flame leapt into the young soldier's throat as he heard the command, and he rose blindly, stifled. He saluted, standing below the officer. He did not look up. But there was the flicker in the Captain's voice.

"Go to the inn and fetch me . . ." the officer gave his commands. "Quick!" he added.

At the last word, the heart of the servant leapt with a flash, and he felt the strength come over his body. But he turned in mechanical obedience, and set off at a heavy run downhill, looking almost like a bear, his trousers bagging over his military boots. And the officer watched this blind, plunging run all the way.

But it was only the outside of the orderly's body that was obeying so humbly and mechanically. Inside had gradually accumulated a core into which all the energy of that young life was compact and concentrated. He executed his commission, and plodded quickly back uphill. There was a pain in his head as he walked that made him twist his features unknowingly. But hard there in the centre of his chest was himself, himself, firm, and not to be plucked to pieces.

The Captain had gone up into the wood. The orderly plodded through the hot, powerfully smelling zone of the company's atmosphere. He had a curious mass of energy inside him now. The Captain was less real than himself. He approached the green entrance to the wood. There, in the half-shade, he saw the horse standing, the sunshine and the flickering shadow of leaves dancing over his brown body. There was a clearing where timber had lately been felled. Here, in the gold-green shade beside the brilliant cup of sunshine, stood two figures, blue and pink, the bits of pink showing out plainly. The Captain was talking to his lieutenant.

The orderly stood on the edge of the bright clearing, where great trunks of trees, stripped and glistening, lay stretched like naked, brown-skinned bodies. Chips of wood littered the trampled floor, like splashed light, and the bases of the felled trees stood here and there, with their raw, level tops. Beyond was the brilliant, sunlit green of a beech.

"Then I will ride forward," the orderly heard his Captain say. The lieutenant saluted and strode away. He himself went forward. A hot flash passed through his belly, as he tramped towards his officer.

The Captain watched the rather heavy figure of the young soldier stumble forward, and his veins, too, ran hot. This was to be man to man between them. He yielded before the solid, stumbling figure with bent head. The orderly stooped and put the food on a level-sawn tree-base. The Captain watched the glistening, sun-inflamed, naked hands. He wanted to speak to the young soldier, but could not. The servant propped a bottle against his thigh, pressed open the cork, and poured out the beer into the mug. He kept his head bent. The Captain accepted the mug.

"Hot!" he said, as if amiably.

The flame sprang out of the orderly's heart, nearly suffocating him.

"Yes, sir," he replied, between shut teeth.

And he heard the sound of the Captain's drinking, and he

clenched his fists, such a strong torment came into his wrists. Then came the faint clang of the closing of the pot-lid. He looked up. The Captain was watching him. He glanced swiftly away. Then he saw the officer stoop and take a piece of bread from the tree-base. Again the flash of flame went through the young soldier, seeing the stiff body stoop beneath him, and his hands jerked. He looked away. He could feel the officer was nervous. The bread fell as it was being broken. The officer ate the other piece. The two men stood tense and still, the master laboriously chewing his bread, the servant staring with averted face, his fist clenched.

Then the young soldier started. The officer had pressed open the lid of the mug again. The orderly watched the lip of the mug, and the white hand that clenched the handle, as if he were fascinated. It was raised. The youth followed it with his eyes. And then he saw the thin, strong throat of the elder man moving up and down as he drank, the strong jaw working. And the instinct which had been jerking at the young man's wrists suddenly jerked free. He jumped, feeling as if it were rent in two by a strong flame.

The spur of the officer caught in a tree root, he went down backwards with a crash, the middle of his back thudding sickeningly against a sharp-edged tree-base, the pot flying away. And in a second the orderly, with serious, earnest young face, and underlip between his teeth, had got his knee in the officer's chest and was pressing the chin backward over the farther edge of the tree-stump, pressing, with all his heart behind in a passion of relief, the tension of his wrists exquisite with relief. And with the base of his palms he shoved at the chin, with all his might. And it was pleasant, too, to have that chin, that hard jaw already slightly rough with beard, in his hands. He did not relax one hair's breadth, but, all the force of all his blood exulting in his thrust, he shoved back the head of the other man, till there was a little "cluck" and a crunching sensation. Then he felt as if his head went to vapour. Heavy convulsions shook the body of the officer, frightening and horrifying the young soldier. Yet it pleased him, too, to repress them. It pleased him to keep his hands pressing back the chin, to feel the chest of the other man yield in expiration to the weight of his strong, young knees, to feel the hard twitchings of the prostrate body jerking his own whole frame, which was pressed down on it.

But it went still. He could look into the nostrils of the other man, the eyes he could scarcely see. How curiously the mouth was pushed out, exaggerating the full lips, and the moustache bristling up from them. Then, with a start, he noticed the nostrils gradually filled with blood. The red brimmed, hesitated, ran over, and went in a thin trickle down the face to the eyes.

It shocked and distressed him. Slowly, he got up. The body twitched and sprawled there, inert. He stood and looked at it in silence. It was a pity *it* was broken. It represented more than the thing which had kicked and bullied him. He was afraid to look at the eyes. They were hideous now, only the whites showing, and the blood running to them. The face of the orderly was drawn with horror at the sight. Well, it was so. In his heart he was satisfied. He had hated the face of the Captain. It was extinguished now. There was a heavy relief in the orderly's soul. That was as it should be. But he could not bear to see the long, military body lying broken over the tree-base, the fine fingers crisped. He wanted to hide it away.

Quickly, busily, he gathered it up, and pushed it under the felled tree trunks, which rested their beautiful, smooth length either end on the logs. The face was horrible with blood. He covered it with the helmet. Then he pushed the limbs straight and decent, and brushed the dead leaves off the fine cloth of the uniform. So, it lay quite still in the shadow under there. A little strip of sunshine ran along the breast, from a chink between the logs. The orderly sat by it for a few moments. Here his own life also ended.

Then, through his daze, he heard the lieutenant, in a loud voice, explaining to the men outside the wood, that they were to suppose the bridge on the river below was held by the enemy. Now they were to march to the attack in such and such a manner. The lieutenant had no gift of expression. The orderly, listening from habit, got muddled. And when the lieutenant began it all again he ceased to hear.

He knew he must go. He stood up. It surprised him that

the leaves were glittering in the sun, and the chips of wood reflecting white from the ground. For him a change had come over the world. But for the rest it had not—all seemed the same. Only he had left it. And he could not go back. It was his duty to return with the beer-pot and the bottle. He could not. He had left all that. The lieutenant was still hoarsely explaining. He must go, or they would overtake him. And he could not bear contact with anyone now.

He drew his fingers over his eyes, trying to find out where he was. Then he turned away. He saw the horse standing in the path. He went up to it and mounted. It hurt him to sit in the saddle. The pain of keeping his seat occupied him as they cantered through the wood. He would not have minded anything, but he could not get away from the sense of being divided from the others. The path led out of the trees. On the edge of the wood he pulled up and stood watching. There in the spacious sunshine of the valley soldiers were moving in a little swarm. Every now and then, a man harrowing on a strip of fallow shouted to his oxen, at the turn. The village and the white-towered church was small in the sunshine. And he no longer belonged to it—he sat there, beyond, like a man outside in the dark. He had gone out from everyday life into the unknown and he could not, he even did not want to go back.

Turning from the sun-blazing valley, he rode deep into the wood. Tree trunks, like people standing grey and still, took no notice as he went. A doe, herself a moving bit of sunshine and shadow, went running through the flecked shade. There were bright green rents in the foliage. Then it was all pine wood, dark and cool. And he was sick with pain, and had an intolerable great pulse in his head, and he was sick. He had never been ill in his life. He felt lost, quite dazed with all this.

Trying to get down from the horse, he fell, astonished at the pain and his lack of balance. The horse shifted uneasily. He jerked its bridle and sent it cantering jerkily away. It was his last connection with the rest of things.

But he only wanted to lie down and not be disturbed. Stumbling through the trees, he came on a quiet place where beeches and pine trees grew on a slope. Immediately he had lain down and closed his eyes, his consciousness went racing on without him. A big pulse of sickness beat in him as if it throbbed through the whole earth. He was burning with dry heat. But he was too busy, too tearingly active in the incoherent race of delirium to observe.

III

He came to with a start. His mouth was dry and hard, his heart beat heavily, but he had not the energy to get up. His heart beat heavily. Where was he?—the barracks—at home? There was something knocking. And, making an effort, he looked round—trees, and litter of greenery, and reddish, bright, still pieces of sunshine on the floor. He did not believe he was himself, he did not believe what he saw. Something was knocking. He made a struggle towards consciousness, but relapsed. Then he struggled again. And gradually his surroundings fell into relationship with himself. He knew, and a great pang of fear went through his heart. Somebody was knocking. He could see the heavy, black rags of a fir tree overhead. Then everything went black. Yet he did not believe he had closed his eyes. He had not. Out of the blackness sight slowly emerged again. And someone was knocking. Quickly, he saw the blood-disfigured face of his Captain, which he hated. And he held himself still with horror. Yet, deep inside him, he knew that it was so, the Captain should be dead. But the physical delirium got hold of him. Someone was knocking. He lay perfectly still, as if dead, with fear. And he went unconscious.

When he opened his eyes again he started, seeing something creeping swiftly up a tree trunk. It was a little bird. And the bird was whistling overhead. Tap-tap-tap—it was the small, quick bird rapping the tree trunk with its beak, as if its head were a little round hammer. He watched it curiously. It shifted sharply, in its creeping fashion. Then, like a mouse, it slid down the bare trunk. Its swift creeping sent a flash of revulsion through him. He raised his head. It felt a great weight. Then, the little bird ran out of the shadow across a still patch of sunshine, its little head bobbing swiftly, its white legs twinkling brightly for a moment. How neat it was in its build, so compact, with piece of white on its wings. There were several of them. They were so pretty—but they crept like swift, erratic mice, running here and there among the beech-mast.

He lay down again exhausted, and his consciousness lapsed. He had a horror of the little creeping birds. All his blood seemed to be darting and creeping in his head. And yet he could not move.

He came to with a further ache of exhaustion. There was the pain in his head, and the horrible sickness, and his inability to move. He had never been ill in his life. He did not know where he was or what he was. Probably he had got sunstroke. Or what else?—he had silenced the Captain for ever—some time ago—oh, a long time ago. There had been blood on his face, and his eyes had turned upwards. It was all right, somehow. It was peace. But now he had got beyond himself. He had never been here before. Was it life, or not life? He was by himself. They were in a big, bright place, those others, and he was outside. The town, all the country, a big bright place of light: and he was outside, here, in the darkened open beyond, where each thing existed alone. But they would all have to come out there sometime, those others. Little, and left behind him, they all were. There had been father and mother and sweetheart. What did they all matter? This was the open land.

He sat up. Something scuffled. It was a little brown squirrel running in lovely undulating bounds over the floor, its red tail completing the undulation of its body—and then, as it sat up, furling and unfurling. He watched it, pleased. It ran on again, friskily, enjoying itself. It flew wildly at another squirrel, and they were chasing each other, and making little scolding, chattering noises. The soldier wanted to speak to them. But only a hoarse sound came out of his throat. The squirrels burst away—they flew up the trees. And then he saw the one peeping round at him, half-way up a tree trunk. A start of fear went through him, though in so far as he was conscious, he was amused. It still stayed, its little keen face

staring at him half-way up the tree trunk, its little ears
pricked up, its clawey little hands clinging to the bark, its
white breast reared. He started from it in panic.

Struggling to his feet, he lurched away. He went on walking, walking, looking for something—for a drink. His brain
felt hot and inflamed for want of water. He stumbled on.
Then he did not know anything. He went unconscious as he
walked. Yet he stumbled on, his mouth open.

When, to his dumb wonder, he opened his eyes on the
world again, he no longer tried to remember what it was.
There was thick, golden light behind golden-green glitterings,
and tall, grey-purple shafts, and darknesses farther off, surrounding him, growing deeper. He was conscious of a sense
of arrival. He was amid the reality, on the real, dark bottom.
But there was the thirst burning in his brain. He felt lighter,
not so heavy. He supposed it was newness. The air was
muttering with thunder. He thought he was walking wonderfully swiftly and was coming straight to relief—or was it to
water?

Suddenly he stood still with fear. There was a tremendous
flare of gold, immense—just a few dark trunks like bars
between him and it. All the young level wheat was burnished
gold glaring on its silky green. A woman, full-skirted, a black
cloth on her head for head-dress, was passing like a block of
shadow through the glistening, green corn, into the full glare.
There was a farm, too, pale blue in shadow, and the timber
black. And there was a church spire, nearly fused away in
the gold. The woman moved on, away from him. He had no
language with which to speak to her. She was the bright,
solid unreality. She would make a noise of words that would
confuse him, and her eyes would look at him without seeing
him. She was crossing there to the other side. He stood
against a tree.

When at last he turned, looking down the long, bare grove
whose flat bed was already filling dark, he saw the mountains
in a wonder-light, not far away, and radiant. Behind the soft,
grey ridge of the nearest range the farther mountains stood
golden and pale grey, the snow all radiant like pure, soft
gold. So still, gleaming in the sky, fashioned pure out of the

ore of the sky, they shone in their silence. He stood and looked at them, his face illuminated. And like the golden, lustrous gleaming of the snow he felt his own thirst bright in him. He stood and gazed, leaning against a tree. And then everything slid away into space.

During the night the lightning fluttered perpetually, making the whole sky white. He must have walked again. The world hung livid round him for moments, fields a level sheen of grey-green light, trees in dark bulk, and the range of clouds black across a white sky. Then the darkness fell like a shutter, and the night was whole. A faint flutter of a half-revealed world, that could not quite leap out of the darkness!—Then there again stood a sweep of pallor for the land, dark shapes looming, a range of clouds hanging overhead. The world was a ghostly shadow, thrown for a moment upon the pure darkness, which returned ever whole and complete.

And the mere delirium of sickness and fever went on inside him—his brain opening and shutting like the night—then sometimes convulsions of terror from something with great eyes that stared round a tree—then the long agony of the march, and the sun decomposing his blood—then the pang of hate for the Captain, followed by a pang of tenderness and ease. But everything was distorted, born of an ache and resolving into an ache.

In the morning he came definitely awake. Then his brain flamed with the sole horror of thirstiness! The sun was on his face, the dew was steaming from his wet clothes. Like one possessed, he got up. There, straight in front of him, blue and cool and tender, the mountains ranged across the pale edge of the morning sky. He wanted them—he wanted them alone—he wanted to leave himself and be identified with them. They did not move, they were still and soft, with white, gentle markings of snow. He stood still, mad with suffering, his hands crisping and clutching. Then he was twisting in a paroxysm on the grass.

He lay still, in a kind of dream of anguish. His thirst seemed to have separated itself from him, and to stand apart, a single demand. Then the pain he felt was another single self. Then there was the clog of his body, another separate thing. He was divided among all kinds of separate things. There was some strange, agonised connection between them, but they were drawing farther apart. Then they would all split. The sun, drilling down on him, was drilling through the bond. Then they would all fall, fall through the everlasting lapse of space. Then again, his consciousness reasserted itself. He roused on to his elbow and stared at the gleaming mountains. There they ranked, all still and wonderful between earth and heaven. He stared till his eyes went black, and the mountains, as they stood in their beauty, so clean and cool, seemed to have it, that which was lost in him.

IV

When the soldiers found him, three hours later, he was lying with his face over his arm, his black hair giving off heat under the sun. But he was still alive. Seeing the open, black mouth the young soldiers dropped him in horror.

He died in the hospital at night, without having seen again.

The doctors saw the bruises on his legs, behind, and were silent.

The bodies of the two men lay together, side by side, in the mortuary, the one white and slender, but laid rigidly at rest, the other looking as if every moment it must rouse into life again, so young and unused, from a slumber.

Daughters of the Vicar

I

MR. LINDLEY was first vicar of Aldecross. The cottages of this tiny hamlet had nestled in peace since their beginning, and the country folk had crossed the lanes and farm-land, two or three miles, to the parish church at Greymeed, on the bright Sunday mornings.

But when the pits were sunk, blank rows of dwellings started up beside the high roads, and a new population, skimmed from the floating scum of workmen, was filled in, the cottages and the country people almost obliterated.

To suit the convenience of these new collier-inhabitants, a church must be built at Aldecross. There was not too much money. And so the little building crouched like a humped stone-and-mortar mouse, with two little turrets at the west corners for ears, in the fields near the cottages and the apple trees, as far as possible from the dwellings down the high road. It had an uncertain, timid look about it. And so they planted big-leaved ivy, to hide its shrinking newness. So that now the little church stands buried in its greenery, stranded and sleeping among the fields, while the brick houses elbow nearer and nearer, threatening to crush it down. It is already obsolete.

The Reverend Ernest Lindley, aged twenty-seven, and newly married, came from his curacy in Suffolk to take charge of his church. He was just an ordinary young man, who had been to Cambridge and taken orders. His wife was a self-assured young woman, daughter of a Cambridgeshire rector. Her father had spent the whole of his thousand a year, so that Mrs. Lindley had nothing of her own. Thus the young married people came to Aldecross to live on a stipend of about a hundred and twenty pounds, and to keep up a superior position.

They were not very well received by the new, raw, disaffected population of colliers. Being accustomed to farm labourers, Mr. Lindley had considered himself as belonging indisputably to the upper or ordering classes. He had to be humble to the county families, but still, he was of their kind, whilst the common people were something different. He had no doubts of himself.

He found, however, that the collier population refused to accept this arrangement. They had no use for him in their lives, and they told him so, callously. The women merely said: "they were throng," or else: "Oh, it's no good you coming here, we're Chapel." The men were quite good-humoured so long as he did not touch them too nigh, they were cheerfully contemptuous of him, with a preconceived contempt he was powerless against.

At last, passing from indignation to silent resentment, even, if he dared have acknowledged it, to conscious hatred of the majority of his flock, and unconscious hatred of himself, he had confined his activities to a narrow round of cottages, and he had to submit. He had no particular character, having always depended on his position in society to give him position among men. Now he was so poor, he had no social standing even among the common vulgar tradespeople of the district, and he had not the nature nor the wish to make his society agreeable to them, nor the strength to impose himself where he would have liked to be recognised. He dragged on, pale and miserable and neutral.

At first his wife raged with mortification. She took on airs and used a high hand. But her income was too small, the wrestling with tradesmen's bills was too pitiful, she only met with general, callous ridicule when she tried to be impressive.

Wounded to the quick of her pride, she found herself isolated in an indifferent, callous population. She raged indoors and out. But soon she learned that she must pay too heavily for her outdoor rages, and then she only raged within the walls of the rectory. There her feeling was so strong that she frightened herself. She saw herself hating her husband,

and she knew that, unless she were careful, she would smash her form of life and bring catastrophe upon him and upon herself. So in very fear she went quiet. She hid, bitter and beaten by fear, behind the only shelter she had in the world, her gloomy, poor parsonage.

Children were born one every year; almost mechanically, she continued to perform her maternal duty, which was forced upon her. Gradually, broken by the suppressing of her violent anger and misery and disgust, she became an invalid and took to her couch.

The children grew up healthy, but unwarmed and rather rigid. Their father and mother educated them at home, made them very proud and very genteel, put them definitely and cruelly in the upper classes, apart from the vulgar around them. So they lived quite isolated. They were good-looking, and had that curiously clean, semi-transparent look of the genteel, isolated and poor.

Gradually Mr. and Mrs. Lindley lost all hold on life, and spent their hours, weeks and years merely haggling to make ends meet, and bitterly repressing and pruning their children into gentility, urging them to ambition, weighting them with duty. On Sunday morning the whole family, except the mother, went down the lane to church, the long-legged girls in skimpy frocks, the boys in black coats and long, grey, unfitting trousers. They passed by their father's parishioners with mute clear faces, childish mouths closed in pride that was like a doom to them, and childish eyes already unseeing. Miss Mary, the eldest, was the leader. She was a long, slim thing with a fine profile and a proud, pure look of submission to a high fate. Miss Louisa, the second, was short and plump and obstinate-looking. She had more enemies than ideals. She looked after the lesser children, Miss Mary after the elder. The collier children watched the pale, distinguished procession of the vicar's family pass mutely by, and they were impressed by the air of gentility and distance, they made mock of the trousers of the small sons, they felt inferior in themselves, and hate stirred their hearts.

In her time, Miss Mary received as governess a few little daughters of tradesmen; Miss Louisa managed the house and

went among her father's church-goers, giving lessons on the
piano to the colliers' daughters at thirteen shillings for twenty-six lessons.

II

One winter morning, when his daughter Mary was about
twenty years old, Mr. Lindley, a thin, unobtrusive figure in
his black overcoat and his wideawake, went down into Aldecross with a packet of white papers under his arm. He was
delivering the parish almanacs.

A rather pale, neutral man of middle age, he waited while
the train thumped over the level-crossing, going up to the pit
which rattled busily just along the line. A wooden-legged man
hobbled to open the gate, Mr. Lindley passed on. Just at his
left hand, below the road and the railway, was the red roof
of a cottage, showing through the bare twigs of apple trees.
Mr. Lindley passed round the low wall, and descended the
worn steps that led from the highway down to the cottage
which crouched darkly and quietly away below the rumble of
passing trains and the clank of coal-cars, in a quiet little
underworld of its own. Snowdrops with tight-shut buds were
hanging very still under the bare currant bushes.

The clergyman was just going to knock when he heard a
clinking noise, and turning saw through the open door of a
black shed just behind him an elderly woman in a black lace
cap stooping among reddish big cans, pouring a very bright
liquid into a tundish. There was a smell of paraffin. The
woman put down her can, took the tundish and laid it on a
shelf, then rose with a tin bottle. Her eyes met those of the
clergyman.

"Oh, is it you, Mr. Lin'ley!" she said, in a complaining
tone. "Go in."

The minister entered the house. In the hot kitchen sat a
big, elderly man with a great grey beard, taking snuff. He
grunted in a deep, muttering voice, telling the minister to sit
down, and then took no more notice of him, but stared
vacantly into the fire. Mr. Lindley waited.

The woman came in, the ribbons of her black lace cap, or

bonnet, hanging on her shawl. She was of medium stature, everything about her was tidy. She went up a step out of the kitchen, carrying the paraffin-tin. Feet were heard entering the room up the step. It was a little haberdashery shop, with parcels on the shelves of the walls, a big, old-fashioned sewing-machine with tailor's work lying round it, in the open space. The woman went behind the counter, gave the child who had entered the paraffin-bottle, and took from her a jug.

"My mother says shall yer put it down," said the child, and she was gone. The woman wrote in a book, then came into the kitchen with her jug. The husband, a very large man, rose and brought more coal to the already hot fire. He moved slowly and sluggishly. Already he was going dead; being a tailor, his large form had become an encumbrance to him. In his youth he had been a great dancer and boxer. Now he was taciturn, and inert. The minister had nothing to say, so he sought for his phrases. But John Durant took no notice, existing silent and dull.

Mrs. Durant spread the cloth. Her husband poured himself beer into a mug, and began to smoke and drink.

"Shall you have some?" he growled through his beard at the clergyman, looking slowly from the man to the jug, capable of this one idea.

"No, thank you," replied Mr. Lindley, though he would have liked some beer. He must set the example in a drinking parish.

"We need a drop to keep us going," said Mrs. Durant.

She had rather a complaining manner. The clergyman sat on uncomfortably while she laid the table for the half-past ten lunch. Her husband drew up to eat. She remained in her little round arm-chair by the fire.

She was a woman who would have liked to be easy in her life, but to whose lot had fallen a rough and turbulent family, and a slothful husband who did not care what became of himself or anybody. So, her rather good-looking square face was peevish, she had that air of having been compelled all her life to serve unwillingly, and to control where she did not want to control. There was about her, too, that masterful aplomb of a woman who has brought up and ruled her sons:

but even them she had ruled unwillingly. She had enjoyed managing her little haberdashery shop, riding in the carrier's cart to Nottingham, going through the big warehouses to buy her goods. But the fret of managing her sons she did not like. Only she loved her youngest boy, because he was her last, and she saw herself free.

This was one of the houses the clergyman visited occasionally. Mrs. Durant, as part of her regulation, had brought up all her sons in the Church. Not that she had any religion. Only, it was what she was used to. Mr. Durant was without religion. He read the fervently evangelical *Life of John Wesley* with a curious pleasure, getting from it a satisfaction as from the warmth of the fire, or a glass of brandy. But he cared no more about John Wesley, in fact, than about John Milton, of whom he had never heard.

Mrs. Durant took her chair to the table.

"I don't feel like eating," she sighed.

"Why—aren't you well?" asked the clergyman, patronising. "It isn't that," she sighed. She sat with shut, straight mouth. "I don't know what's going to become of us."

But the clergyman had ground himself down so long that he could not easily sympathise.

"Have you any trouble?" he asked.

"Ay, have I any trouble!" cried the elderly woman. "I shall end my days in the workhouse."

The minister waited unmoved. What could she know of poverty in her little house of plenty!

"I hope not," he said.

"And the one lad as I wanted to keep by me——" she lamented.

The minister listened without sympathy, quite neutral.

"And the lad as would have been a support to my old age! What is going to become of us?" she said.

The clergyman, justly, did not believe in the cry of poverty, but wondered what had become of the son.

"Has anything happened to Alfred?" he asked.

"We've got word he's gone for a Queen's sailor," she said sharply.

"He has joined the Navy!" exclaimed Mr. Lindley. "I think

he could scarcely have done better—to serve his Queen and country on the sea . . ."

"He is wanted to serve *me*," she cried. "And I wanted my lad at home."

Alfred was her baby, her last, whom she had allowed herself the luxury of spoiling.

"You will miss him," said Mr. Lindley, "that is certain. But this is no regrettable step for him to have taken—on the contrary."

"That's easy for you to say, Mr. Lindley," she replied tartly. "Do you think I want my lad climbing ropes at another man's bidding, like a monkey——"

"There is no *dishonour*, surely, in serving in the Navy?"

"Dishonour this dishonour that," cried the angry old woman. "He goes and makes a slave of himself, and he'll rue it."

Her angry, scornful impatience nettled the clergyman, and silenced him for some moments.

"I do not see," he retorted at last, white at the gills and inadequate, "that the Queen's service is any more to be called slavery than working in a mine."

"At home he was at home, and his own master. *I* know he'll find a difference."

"It may be the making of him," said the clergyman. "It will take him away from bad companionship and drink."

Some of the Durants' sons were notorious drinkers, and Alfred was not quite steady.

"And why indeed shouldn't he have his glass?" cried the mother. "He picks no man's pocket to pay for it!"

The clergyman stiffened at what he thought was an allusion to his own profession, and his unpaid bills.

"With all due consideration, I am glad to hear he has joined the Navy," he said.

"Me with my old age coming on, and his father working very little! I'd thank you to be glad about something else besides that, Mr. Lindley."

The woman began to cry. Her husband, quite impassive, finished his lunch of meat-pie, and drank some beer. Then he turned to the fire, as if there were no one in the room but himself.

"I shall respect all men who serve God and their country on the sea, Mrs. Durant," said the clergyman stubbornly.

"That is very well, when they're not your sons who are doing the dirty work. It makes a difference," she replied tartly.

"I should be proud if one of my sons were to enter the Navy."

"Ay—well—we're not all of us made alike——"

The minister rose. He put down a large folded paper.

"I've brought the almanac," he said.

Mrs. Durant unfolded it.

"I do like a bit of colour in things," she said, petulantly.

The clergyman did not reply.

"There's that envelope for the organist's fund——" said the old woman, and rising, she took the thing from the mantelpiece, went into the shop, and returned sealing it up.

"Which is all I can afford," she said.

Mr. Lindley took his departure, in his pocket the envelope containing Mrs. Durant's offering for Miss Louisa's services. He went from door to door delivering the almanacs, in dull routine. Jaded with the monotony of the business, and with the repeated effort of greeting half-known people, he felt barren and rather irritable. At last he returned home.

In the dining-room was a small fire. Mrs. Lindley, growing very stout, lay on her couch. The vicar carved the cold mutton: Miss Louisa, short and plump and rather flushed, came in from the kitchen; Miss Mary, dark, with a beautiful white brow and grey eyes, served the vegetables; the children chattered a little, but not exuberantly. The very air seemed starved.

"I went to the Durants," said the vicar, as he served out small portions of mutton; "it appears Alfred has run away to join the Navy."

"Do him good," came the rough voice of the invalid.

Miss Louisa, attending to the youngest child, looked up in protest.

"Why has he done that?" asked Mary's low, musical voice.

"He wanted some excitement, I suppose," said the vicar. "Shall we say grace?"

The children were arranged, all bent their heads, grace was pronounced, at the last word every face was being raised to go on with the interesting subject.

"He's just done the right thing, for once," came the rather deep voice of the mother; "save him from becoming a drunken sot, like the rest of them."

"They're not *all* drunken, mama," said Miss Louisa, stubbornly.

"It's no fault of their upbringing if they're not. Walter Durant is a standing disgrace."

"As I told Mrs. Durant," said the vicar, eating hungrily, "it is the best thing he could have done. It will take him away from temptation during the most dangerous years of his life—how old is he—nineteen?"

"Twenty," said Miss Louisa.

"Twenty!" repeated the vicar. "It will give him wholesome discipline and set before him some sort. of standard of duty and honour—nothing could have been better for him. But——"

"We shall miss him from the choir," said Miss Louisa, as if taking opposite sides to her parents.

"That is as it may be," said the vicar. "I prefer to know he is safe in the Navy than running the risk of getting into bad ways here."

"Was he getting into bad ways?" asked the stubborn Miss Louisa.

"You know, Louisa, he wasn't quite what he used to be," said Miss Mary gently and steadily. Miss Louisa shut her rather heavy jaw sulkily. She wanted to deny it, but she knew it was true.

For her he had been a laughing, warm lad, with something kindly and something rich about him. He had made her feel warm. It seemed the days would be colder since he had gone.

"Quite the best thing he could do," said the mother with emphasis.

"I think so," said the vicar. "But his mother was almost abusive because I suggested it."

He spoke in an injured tone.

"What does she care for her children's welfare?" said the invalid. "Their wages is all her concern."

"I suppose she wanted him at home with her," said Miss Louisa.

"Yes, she did—at the expense of his learning to be a drunkard like the rest of them," retorted her mother.

"George Durant doesn't drink," defended her daughter.

"Because he got burned so badly when he was nineteen— in the pit—and that frightened him. The Navy is a better remedy than that, at least."

"Certainly," said the vicar. "Certainly."

And to this Miss Louisa agreed. Yet she could not but feel angry that he had gone away for so many years. She herself was only nineteen.

III

It happened when Miss Mary was twenty-three years old that Mr. Lindley was very ill. The family was exceedingly poor at the time, such a lot of money was needed, so little was forthcoming. Neither Miss Mary nor Miss Louisa had suitors. What chance had they? They met no eligible young men in Aldecross. And what they earned was a mere drop in a void. The girls' hearts were chilled and hardened with fear of this perpetual, cold penury, this narrow struggle, this horrible nothingness of their lives.

A clergyman had to be found for the church work. It so happened the son of an old friend of Mr. Lindley's was waiting three months before taking up his duties. He would come and officiate, for nothing. The young clergyman was keenly expected. He was not more than twenty-seven, a Master of Arts of Oxford, had written his thesis on Roman Law. He came of an old Cambridgeshire family, had some private means, was going to take a church in Northampton-shire with a good stipend, and was not married. Mrs. Lindley incurred new debts, and scarcely regretted her husband's illness.

But when Mr. Massy came there was a shock of disappointment in the house. They had expected a young man with a pipe and a deep voice, but with better manners than Sidney, the eldest of the Lindleys. There arrived instead a small, *chétif* man, scarcely larger than a boy of twelve, spectacled, timid in the extreme, without a word to utter at first; yet with a certain inhuman self-sureness.

"What a little abortion!" was Mrs. Lindley's exclamation to herself on first seeing him, in his buttoned-up clerical coat. And for the first time for many days she was profoundly thankful to God that all her children were decent specimens.

He had not normal powers of perception. They soon saw that he lacked the full range of human feelings, but had rather a strong philosophical mind, from which he lived. His body was almost unthinkable, in intellect he was something definite. The conversation at once took a balanced, abstract tone when he participated. There was no spontaneous exclamation, no violent assertion or expression of personal conviction, but all cold, reasonable assertion. This was very hard on Mrs. Lindley. The little man would look at her, after one of her pronouncements, and then give, in his thin voice, his own calculated version, so that she felt as if she were tumbling into thin air through a hole in the flimsy floor on which their conversation stood. It was she who felt a fool. Soon she was reduced to a hardy silence.

Still, at the back of her mind, she remembered that he was an unattached gentleman, who would shortly have an income altogether of six or seven hundred a year. What did the man matter, if there were pecuniary ease! The man was a trifle thrown in. After twenty-two years her sentimentality was ground away, and only the millstone of poverty mattered to her. So she supported the little man as a representative of a decent income.

His most irritating habit was that of a sneering little giggle, all on his own, which came when he perceived or related some illogical absurdity on the part of another person. It was the only form of humour he had. Stupidity in thinking seemed to him exquisitely funny. But any novel was unintelligibly meaningless and dull, and to an Irish sort of humour he listened curiously, examining it like mathematics, or else simply not hearing. In normal human relationship he was not there. Quite unable to take part in simple everyday talk, he padded silently round the house, or sat in the dining-room looking nervously from side to side, always apart in a cold, rarefied little world of his own. Sometimes he made an ironic remark, that did not seem humanly relevant, or he gave his little laugh, like a sneer. He had to defend himself and his own insufficiency. And he answered questions grudgingly, with a yes or no, because he did not see their import and was nervous. It seemed to Miss Louisa he scarcely distinguished one person from another, but he liked to be near to her, or to Miss Mary, for some sort of contact which stimulated him unknown.

Apart from all this, he was the most admirable workman. He was unremittingly shy, but perfect in his sense of duty: as far as he could conceive Christianity, he was a perfect Christian. Nothing that he realised he could do for anyone did he leave undone, although he was so incapable of coming into contact with another being that he could not proffer help. Now he attended assiduously to the sick man, investigated all the affairs of the parish or the church which Mr. Lindley had in control, straightened out accounts, made lists of the sick and needy, padded round with help and to see what he could do. He heard of Mrs. Lindley's anxiety about her sons, and began to investigate means of sending them to Cambridge. His kindness almost frightened Miss Mary. She honoured it so, and yet she shrank from it. For, in it all Mr. Massy seemed to have no sense of any person, any human being whom he was helping: he only realised a kind of mathematical working out, solving of given situations, a calculated well-doing. And it was as if he had accepted the Christian tenets as axioms. His religion consisted in what his scrupulous, abstract mind approved of.

Seeing his acts, Miss Mary must respect and honour him. In consequence she must serve him. To this she had to force herself, shuddering and yet desirous, but he did not perceive it. She accompanied him on his visiting in the parish, and whilst she was cold with admiration for him, often she was touched with pity for the little padding figure with bent shoulders, buttoned up to the chin in his overcoat. She was a handsome, calm girl, tall, with a beautiful repose. Her clothes were poor, and she wore a black silk scarf, having no furs. But she was a lady. As the people saw her walking down Aldecross beside Mr. Massy they said:

"My word, Miss Mary's got a catch. Did you ever see such a sickly little shrimp!"

She knew they were talking so, and it made her heart grow hot against them, and she drew herself as it were protectively towards the little man beside her. At any rate, she could see and give honour to his genuine goodness.

He could not walk fast, or far.

"You have not been well?" she asked, in her dignified way.

"I have an internal trouble."

He was not aware of her slight shudder. There was silence, whilst she bowed to recover her composure, to resume her gentle manner towards him.

He was fond of Miss Mary. She had made it a rule of hospitality that he should always be escorted by herself or by her sister on his visits in the parish, which were not many. But some mornings she was engaged. Then Miss Louisa took her place. It was no good Miss Louisa's trying to adopt to Mr. Massy an attitude of queenly service. She was unable to regard him save with aversion. When she saw him from behind, thin and bent-shouldered, looking like sickly lad of thirteen, she disliked him exceedingly, and felt a desire to put him out of existence. And yet a deeper justice in Mary made Louisa humble before her sister.

They were going to see Mr. Durant, who was paralysed and not expected to live. Miss Louisa was crudely ashamed at being admitted to the cottage in company with the little clergyman.

Mrs. Durant was, however, much quieter in the face of her real trouble.

"How is Mr. Durant?" asked Louisa.

"He is no different—and we don't expect him to be," was the reply. The little clergyman stood looking on.

They went upstairs. The three stood for some time looking at the bed, at the grey head of the old man on the pillow, the grey beard over the sheet. Miss Louisa was shocked and afraid.

"It is so dreadful," she said, with a shudder.

"It is how I always thought it would be," replied Mrs. Durant.

Then Miss Louisa was afraid of her. The two women were uneasy, waiting for Mr. Massy to say something. He stood, small and bent, too nervous to speak.

"Has he any understanding?" he asked at length.

"Maybe," said Mrs. Durant. "Can you hear, John?" she asked loudly. The dull blue eyes of the inert man looked at her feebly.

"Yes, he understands," said Mrs. Durant to Mr. Massy. Except for the dull look in his eyes, the sick man lay as if dead. The three stood in silence. Miss Louisa was obstinate but heavy-hearted under the load of unlivingness. It was Mr. Massy who kept her there in discipline. His non-human will dominated them all.

They they heard a sound below, a man's footsteps, and a man's voice called subduedly:

"Are you upstairs, mother?"

Mrs. Durant started and moved to the door. But already a quick, firm step was running up the stairs.

"I'm a bit early, mother," a troubled voice said, and on the landing they saw the form of the sailor. His mother came and clung to him. She was suddenly aware that she needed something to hold on to. He put his arms round her, and bent over her, kissing her.

"He's not gone, mother?" he asked anxiously, struggling to control his voice.

Miss Louisa looked away from the mother and son who stood together in the gloom on the landing. She could not bear it that she and Mr. Massy should be there. The latter stood nervously, as if ill at ease before the emotion that was running. He was a witness nervous, unwilling, but dispassionate. To Miss Louisa's hot heart it seemed all, all wrong that they should be there.

Mrs. Durant entered the bedroom, her face wet.

"There's Miss Louise and the vicar," she said, out of voice and quavering.

Her son, red-faced and slender, drew himself up to salute. But Miss Louisa held out her hand. Then she saw his hazel eyes recognise her for a moment, and his small white teeth showed in a glimpse of the greeting she used to love. She was covered with confusion. He went round to the bed; his boots clicked on the plaster floor, he bowed with dignity.

"How are you, dad?" he said, laying his hand on the sheet, faltering. But the old man stared fixedly and unseeing. The son stood perfectly still for a few minutes, then slowly recoiled. Miss Louisa saw the fine outline of his breast, under the sailor's blue blouse, as his chest began to heave.

"He doesn't know me," he said, turning to his mother. He gradually went white.

"No, my boy!" cried the mother, pitiful, lifting her face. And suddenly she put her face against his shoulder, he was stooping down to her, holding her against him, and she cried aloud for a moment or two. Miss Louisa saw his sides heaving, and heard the sharp hiss of his breath. She turned away, tears streaming down her face. The father lay inert upon the white bed, Mr. Massy looked queer and obliterated, so little now that the sailor with his sun-burned skin was in the room. He stood waiting. Miss Louisa wanted to die, she wanted to have done. She dared not turn round again to look.

"Shall I offer a prayer?" came the frail voice of the clergyman, and all kneeled down.

Miss Louisa was frightened of the inert man upon the bed. Then he felt a flash of fear of Mr. Massy, hearing his thin, detached voice. And then, calmed, she looked up. On the far side of the bed were the head of the mother and son, the one in the black lace cap, with the small white nape of the neck beneath, the other, with brown, sun-scorched hair too close and wiry to allow of a parting, and neck tanned firm, bowed as if unwillingly. The great grey beard of the old man did not move, the prayer continued. Mr. Massy prayed with a pure lucidity that they all might conform to the higher Will. He was like something that dominated the bowed heads, something dispassionate that governed them inexorably. Miss Louisa was afraid of him. And she was bound, during the course of the prayer, to have a little reverence for him. It was like a foretaste of inexorable, cold death, a taste of pure justice.

That evening she talked to Mary of the visit. Her heart, her veins were possessed by the thought of Alfred Durant as he held his mother in his arms; then the break in his voice, as she remembered it again and again, was like a flame through her; and she wanted to see his face more distinctly in her mind, ruddy with the sun, and his golden-brown eyes, kind and careless, strained now with a natural fear, the fine nose tanned hard by the sun, the mouth that could not help smiling at her. And it went through her with pride, to think of his figure, a fine jet of life.

"He is a handsome lad," said she to Miss Mary, as if he had not been a year older than herself. Underneath was the deeper dread, almost hatred, of the inhuman being of Mr. Massy. She felt she must protect herself and Alfred from him.

"When I felt Mr. Massy there," she said, "I almost hated him. What right had he to be there!"

"Surely he has all right," said Miss Mary after a pause. "He is *really* a Christian."

"He seems to me nearly an imbecile," said Miss Louisa.

Miss Mary, quiet and beautiful, was silent for a moment:

"Oh, no," she said. "Not *imbecile*——"

"Well then—he reminds me of a six months' child—or a five months' child—as if he didn't have time to get developed enough before he was born."

"Yes," said Miss Mary, slowly. "There is something lacking. But there is something wonderful in him: and he is really *good*——"

"Yes," said Miss Louisa, "it doesn't seem right that he should be. What right has *that* to be called goodness!"

"But it *is* goodness," persisted Mary. Then she added, with a laugh: "And come, you wouldn't deny that as well."

There was a doggedness in her voice. She went about very quietly. In her soul, she knew what was going to happen. She knew that Mr. Massy was stronger than she, and that she must submit to what he was. Her physical self was prouder, stronger than he, her physical self disliked and despised him. But she was in the grip of his moral, mental being. And she felt the days allotted out to her. And her family watched.

IV

A few days after, old Mr. Durant died. Miss Louisa saw Alfred once more, but he was stiff before her now, treating her not like a person, but as if she were some sort of will in command and he a separate, distinct will waiting in front of her. She had never felt such utter steel-plate separation from anyone. It puzzled her and frightened her. What had become of him? And she hated the military discipline—she was antagonistic to it. Now he was not himself. He was the will which obeys set over against the will which commands. She hesitated over accepting this. He had put himself out of her range. He had ranked himself inferior, subordinate to her. And that was how he could get away from her, that was how he would avoid all connection with her: by fronting her impersonally from the opposite camp, by taking up the abstract position of an inferior.

She went brooding steadily and sullenly over this, brooding and brooding. Her fierce, obstinate heart could not give way. It clung to its own rights. Sometimes she dismissed him. Why should he, her inferior, trouble her?

Then she relapsed to him, and almost hated him. It was his way of getting out of it. She felt the cowardice of it, his calmly placing her in a superior class, and placing himself inaccessibly apart, in an inferior, as if she, the sentient woman who was fond of him, did not count. But she was not going to submit. Dogged in her heart she held on to him.

V

In six months' time Miss Mary had married Mr. Massy. There had been no love-making, nobody had made any remark. But everybody was tense and callous with expectation. When one day Mr. Massy asked for Mary's hand, Mr. Lindley started and trembled from the thin, abstract voice of the little man. Mr. Massy was very nervous, but so curiously absolute.

"I shall be very glad," said the vicar, "but of course the decision lies with Mary herself." And his still feeble hand shook as he moved a Bible on his desk.

The small man, keeping fixedly to his idea, padded out of the room to find Miss Mary. He sat a long time by her, while she made some conversation, before he had readiness to speak. She was afraid of what was coming, and sat stiff in apprehension. She felt as if her body would rise and fling him aside. But her spirit quivered and waited. Almost in expectation she waited, almost wanting him. And then she knew he would speak.

"I have already asked Mr. Lindley," said the clergyman, while suddenly she looked with aversion at his little knees, "if he would consent to my proposal." He was aware of his own disadvantage, but his will was set.

She went cold as she sat, and impervious, almost as if she had become stone. He waited a moment nervously. He would not persuade her. He himself never even heard persuasion, but pursued his own course. He looked at her, sure of himself, unsure of her, and said:

"Will you become my wife, Mary?"

Still her heart was hard and cold. She sat proudly.

"I should like to speak to mama first," she said.

"Very well," replied Mr. Massy. And in a moment he padded away.

Mary went to her mother. She was cold and reserved.

"Mr. Massy has asked me to marry him, mama," she said.

Mrs. Lindley went on staring at her book. She was cramped in her feeling.

"Well, and what did you say?"

They were both keeping calm and cold.

"I said I would speak to you before answering him."

This was equivalent to a question. Mrs. Lindley did not want to reply to it. She shifted her heavy form irritably on the couch. Miss Mary sat calm and straight, with closed mouth.

"Your father thinks it would not be a bad match," said the mother, as if casually.

Nothing more was said. Everybody remained cold and shut-off. Miss Mary did not speak to Miss Louisa, the Reverend Ernest Lindley kept out of sight.

At evening Miss Mary accepted Mr. Massy.

"Yes, I will marry you," she said, with even a little movement of tenderness towards him. He was embarrassed, but satisfied. She could see him making some movement towards her, could feel the male in him, something cold and triumphant, asserting itself. She sat rigid, and waited.

When Miss Louisa knew, she was silent with bitter anger against everybody, even against Mary. She felt her faith wounded. Did the real things to her not matter after all? She wanted to get away. She thought of Mr. Massy. He had some curious power, some unanswerable right. He was a will that they could not controvert. Suddenly a flush started in her. If he had come to her she would have flipped him out of the room. He was never going to touch *her*. And she was glad. She was glad that her blood would rise and exterminate the little man, if he came too near to her, no matter how her judgment was paralysed by him, no matter how he moved in abstract goodness. She thought she was perverse to be glad, but glad she was. "I would just flip him out of the room," she said, and she derived great satisfaction from the open statement. Nevertheless, perhaps she ought still to feel that Mary, on her plane, was a higher being than herself. But then Mary was Mary, and she was Louisa, and that also was inalterable.

Mary, in marrying him, tried to become a pure reason such as he was, without feeling or impulse. She shut herself up, she shut herself rigid against the agonies of shame and the terror of violation which came at first. She *would* not feel, and she *would* not feel. She was a pure will acquiescing to him. She elected a certain kind of fate. She would be good and purely just, she would live in a higher freedom than she had ever known, she would be free of mundane care, she was a pure will towards right. She had sold herself, but she had a new freedom. She had got rid of her body. She had sold a lower thing, her body, for a higher thing, her freedom from material things. She considered that she paid for all she got from her husband. So, in kind of independence, she moved proud and free. She had paid with her body; that was henceforth out of consideration. She was glad to be rid of it. She had bought her position in the world—that henceforth was taken for granted. There remained only the direction of her activity towards charity and high-minded living.

She could scarcely bear other people to be present with her and her husband. Her private life was her shame. But then, she could keep it hidden. She lived almost isolated in the rectory of the tiny village miles from the railway. She suffered as if it were an insult to her own flesh, seeing the repulsion which some people felt for her husband, or the special manner they had of treating him, as if he were a "case". But most people were uneasy before him, which restored her pride.

If she had let herself, she would have hated him, hated his padding round the house, his thin voice devoid of human understanding, his bent little shoulders and rather incomplete face that reminded her of an abortion. But rigorously she kept her position. She took care of him and was just to him. There was also a deep, craven fear of him, something slave-like.

There was not much fault to be found with his behaviour. He was scrupulously just and kind according to his lights. But the male in him was cold and self-complete, and utterly domineering. Weak, insufficient little thing as he was, she had not expected this of him. It was something in the bargain she had not understood. It made her hold her head, to keep still. She knew, vaguely, that she was murdering herself. After all, her body was not quite so easy to get rid of. And this manner of disposing of it—ah, sometimes she felt she must rise and bring about death, lift her hand for utter denial of every-thing, by a general destruction.

He was almost unaware of the conditions about him. He did not fuss in the domestic way, she did as she liked in the house. Indeed, she was a great deal free of him. He would sit obliterated for hours. He was kind, and almost anxiously considerate. But when he considered he was right, his will was just blindly male, like a cold machine. And on most points he was logically right, or he had with him the right of the creed they both accepted. It was so. There was nothing for her to go against.

Then she found herself with child, and felt for the first time horror, afraid before God and man. This also she had to go through—it was the right. When the child arrived, it was a bonny, healthy lad. Her heart hurt in her body, as she took the baby between her hands. The flesh that was trampled and silent in her must speak again in the boy. After all, she had to live—it was not so simple after all. Nothing was finished completely. She looked and looked at the baby, and almost hated it, and suffered an anguish of love for it. She hated it because it made her live again in the flesh, when she *could* not live in the flesh, she could not. She wanted to trample her flesh down, down, extinct, to live in the mind. And now there was this child. It was too cruel, too racking. For she must love the child. Her purpose was broken in two again. She had to become amorphous, purposeless, without real being. As a mother, she was a fragmentary, ignoble thing.

Mr. Massy, blind to everything else in the way of human feeling, became obsessed by the idea of his child. When it arrived, suddenly it filled the whole world of feeling for him. It was his obsession, his terror was for its safety and well-being. It was something new, as if he himself had been born a naked infant, conscious of his own exposure, and full of apprehension. He who had never been aware of anyone else, all his life, now was aware of nothing but the child. Not that he ever played with it, or kissed it, or tended it. He did nothing for it. But it dominated him, it filled, and at the same time emptied his mind. The world was all baby for him.

This his wife must also bear, his question: "What is the reason that he cries?"—his reminder, at the first sound: "Mary, that is the child,"—his restlessness if the feeding-time were five minutes past. She had bargained for this—now she must stand by her bargain.

VI

Miss Louisa, at home in the dingy vicarage, had suffered a great deal over her sister's wedding. Having once begun to cry out against it, during the engagement, she had been silenced by Mary's quiet: "I don't agree with you about him, Louisa, I *want* to marry him." Then Miss Louisa had been angry deep in her heart, and therefore silent. This dangerous state started the change in her. Her own revulsion made her recoil from the hitherto undoubted Mary.

"I'd beg the streets barefoot first," said Miss Louisa, thinking of Mr. Massy.

But evidently Mary could perform a different heroism. So she, Louisa the practical, suddenly felt that Mary, her ideal, was questionable after all. How could she be pure—one cannot be dirty in act and spiritual in being. Louisa distrusted Mary's high spirituality. It was no longer genuine for her. And if Mary were spiritual and misguided, why did not her father protect her? Because of the money. He disliked the whole affair, but he backed away, because of the money. And the mother frankly did not care: her daughters could do as they liked. Her mother's pronouncement:

"Whatever happens to *him*, Mary is safe for life,"—so evidently and shallowly a calculation, incensed Louisa.

"I'd rather be safe in the workhouse," she cried.

"Your father will see to that," replied her mother brutally. This speech, in its directness, so injured Miss Louisa that she hated her mother deep, deep in her heart, and almost hated herself. It was a long time resolving itself out, this hate. But it worked and worked, and at last the young woman said:

"They are wrong—they are all wrong. They have ground out their souls for what isn't worth anything, and there isn't a grain of love in them anywhere. And I *will* have love. They want us to deny it. They've never found it, so they want to say it doesn't exist. But I *will* have it. I *will* love—it is my birthright. I will love the man I marry—that is all I care about."

So Miss Louisa stood isolated from everybody. She and

Mary had parted over Mr. Massy. In Louisa's eyes, Mary was degraded, married to Mr. Massy. She could not bear to think of her lofty, spiritual sister degraded in the body like this. Mary was wrong, wrong, wrong: she was not superior, she was flawed, incomplete. The two sisters stood apart. They still loved each other, they would love each other as long as they lived. But they had parted ways. A new solitariness came over the obstinate Louisa, and her heavy jaw set stubbornly. She was going on her own way. But which way? She was quite alone, with a blank world before her. How could she be said to have any way? Yet she had her fixed will to love, to have the man she loved.

VII

When her boy was three years old, Mary had another baby, a girl. The three years had gone by monotonously. They might have been an eternity, they might have been brief as a sleep. She did not know. Only, there was always a weight on top of her, something that pressed down her life. The only thing that had happened was that Mr. Massy had had an operation. He was always exceedingly fragile. His wife had soon learned to attend to him mechanically, as part of her duty.

But this third year, after the baby girl had been born, Mary felt oppressed and depressed. Christmas drew near: the gloomy, unleavened Christmas of the rectory, where all the days were of the same dark fabric. And Mary was afraid. It was as if the darkness were coming upon her.

"Edward, I should like to go home for Christmas," she said, and a certain terror filled her as she spoke.

"But you can't leave baby," said her husband, blinking.

"We can all go."

He thought, and stared in his collective fashion.

"Why do you wish to go?" he asked.

"Because I need a change. A change would do me good, and it would be good for the milk."

He heard the will in his wife's voice, and was at a loss. Her language was unintelligible to him. But somehow he felt that

Mary was set upon it. And while she was breeding, either about to have a child, or nursing, he regarded her as a special sort of being.

"Wouldn't it hurt baby to take her by the train?" he said.

"No," replied the mother, "why should it?"

They went. When they were in the train it began to snow. From the window of his first-class carriage the little clergyman watched the big flakes sweep by, like a blind drawn across the country. He was obsessed by thought of the baby, and afraid of the draughts of the carriage.

"Sit right in the corner," he said to his wife, "and hold baby close back."

She moved at his bidding, and stared out of the window. His eternal presence was like an iron weight on her brain. But she was going partially to escape for a few days.

"Sit on the other side, Jack," said the father. "It is less draughty. Come to this window."

He watched the boy in anxiety. But his children were the only beings in the world who took not the slightest notice of him.

"Look, mother, look!" cried the boy. "They fly right in my face"—he meant the snowflakes.

"Come into this corner," repeated his father, out of another world.

"He's jumped on this one's back, mother, an' they're riding to the bottom!" cried the boy, jumping with glee.

"Tell him to come on this side," the little man bade his wife.

"Jack, kneel on this cushion," said the mother, putting her white hand on the place.

The boy slid over in silence to the place she indicated, waited still for a moment, then almost deliberately, stridently cried:

"Look at all those in the corner, mother, making a heap," and he pointed to the cluster of snowflakes with finger pressed dramatically on the pane, and he turned to his mother a bit ostentatiously.

"All in a heap!" she said.

He had seen her face, and had her response, and he was

somewhat assured. Vaguely uneasy, he was reassured if he could win her attention.

They arrived at the vicarage at half-past two, not having had lunch.

"How are you, Edward?" said Mr. Lindley, trying on his side to be fatherly. But he was always in a false position with his son-in-law, frustrated before him, therefore, as much as possible, he shut his eyes and ears to him. The vicar was looking thin and pale and ill-nourished. He had gone quite grey. He was, however, still haughty; but, since the growing-up of his children, it was a brittle haughtiness, that might break at any moment and leave the vicar only an impoverished, pitiable figure. Mrs. Lindley took all the notice of her daughter, and of the children. She ignored her son-in-law. Miss Louisa was clucking and laughing and rejoicing over the baby. Mr. Massy stood aside, a bent, persistent little figure.

"Oh a pretty!—a little pretty! oh a cold little pretty come in a railway train!" Miss Louisa was cooing to the infant, crouching on the hearth-rug, opening the white woollen wraps and exposing the child to the fireglow.

"Mary," said the little clergyman, "I think it would be better to give baby a warm bath; she may take cold."

"I think it is not necessary," said the mother, coming and closing her hand judiciously over the rosy feet and hands of the mite. "She is not chilly."

"Not a bit," cried Miss Louisa. "She's not caught cold."

"I'll go and bring her flannels," said Mr. Massy, with one idea.

"I can bath her in the kitchen then," said Mary, in an altered, cold tone.

"You can't, the girl is scrubbing there," said Miss Louisa. "Besides, she doesn't want a bath at this time of day."

"She'd better have one," said Mary, quietly, out of submission. Miss Louisa's gorge rose, and she was silent. When the little man padded down with the flannels on his arm, Mrs. Lindley asked:

"Hadn't *you* better take a hot bath, Edward?"

But the sarcasm was lost on the little clergyman. He was absorbed in the preparations round the baby.

The room was dull and threadbare, and the snow outside seemed fairy-like by comparison, so white on the lawn and tufted on the bushes. Indoors the heavy pictures hung obscurely on the walls, everything was dingy with gloom.

Except in the fireglow, where they had laid the bath on the hearth. Mrs. Massey, her black hair always smoothly coiled and queenly, kneeled by the bath, wearing a rubber apron, and holding the kicking child. Her husband stood holding the towels and the flannels to warm. Louisa, too cross to share in the joy of the baby's bath, was laying the table. The boy was hanging on the door-knob, wrestling with it to get out. His father looked round.

"Come away from the door, Jack," he said ineffectually. Jack tugged harder at the knob as if he did not hear. Mr. Massy blinked at him.

"He must come away from the door, Mary," he said. "There will be a draught if it is opened."

"Jack, come away from the door, dear," said the mother, dexterously turning the shiny wet baby on to her towelled knee, then glancing round: "Go and tell Auntie Louisa about the train."

Louisa, also afraid to open the door, was watching the scene on the hearth. Mr. Massy stood holding the baby's flannel, as if assisting at some ceremonial. If everybody had not been subduedly angry, it would have been ridiculous.

"I want to see out of the window," Jack said. His father turned hastily.

"Do *you* mind lifting him on to a chair, Louisa," said Mary hastily. The father was too delicate.

When the baby was flannelled, Mr. Massy went upstairs and returned with four pillows, which he set in the fender to warm. Then he stood watching the mother feed her child, obsessed by the idea of his infant.

Louisa went on with her preparations for the meal. She could not have told why she was so sullenly angry. Mrs. Lindley, as usual, lay silently watching.

Mary carried her child upstairs, followed by her husband with the pillows. After a while he came down again.

"What is Mary doing? Why doesn't she come down to eat?" asked Mrs. Lindley.

"She is staying with baby. The room is rather cold. I will ask the girl to put in a fire." He was going absorbedly to the door.

"But Mary has had nothing to eat. It is *she* who will catch cold," said the mother, exasperated.

Mr. Massy seemed as if he did not hear. Yet he looked at his mother-in-law, and answered:

"I will take her something."

He went out. Mrs. Lindley shifted on her couch with anger. Miss Louisa glowered. But no one said anything, because of the money that came to the vicarage from Mr. Massy.

Louisa went upstairs. Her sister was sitting by the bed, reading a scrap of paper.

"Won't you come down and eat?" the younger asked.

"In a moment or two," Mary replied, in a quiet, reserved voice, that forbade anyone to approach her.

It was this that made Miss Louisa most furious. She went downstairs, and announced to her mother:

"I am going out. I may not be home to tea."

VIII

No one remarked on her exit. She put on her fur hat, that the village people knew so well, and the old Norfolk jacket. Louisa was short and plump and plain. She had her mother's heavy jaw, her father's proud brow, and her own grey, brooding eyes that were very beautiful when she smiled. It was true, as the people said, that she looked sulky. Her chief attraction was her glistening, heavy, deep-blonde hair, which shone and gleamed with a richness that was not entirely foreign to her.

"Where am I going?" she said to herself, when she got outside in the snow. She did not hesitate, however, but by mechanical walking found herself descending the hill towards Old Aldecross. In the valley that was black with trees, the colliery breathed in stertorous pants, sending out high conical columns of steam that remained upright, whiter than the snow on the hills, yet shadowy, in the dead air. Louisa would not acknowledge to herself whither she was making her way, till she came to the railway crossing. Then the bunches of snow in the twigs of the apple tree that leaned towards the fence told her she must go and see Mrs. Durant. The tree was in Mrs. Durant's garden.

Alfred was now at home again, living with his mother in the cottage below the road. From the highway hedge, by the railway crossing, the snowy garden sheered down steeply, like the side of a hole, then dropped straight in a wall. In this depth the house was snug, its chimney just level with the road. Miss Louisa descended the stone stairs, and stood below in the little back-yard, in the dimness and the semi-secrecy. A big tree leaned overhead, above the paraffin-hut. Louisa felt secure from all the world down there. She knocked at the open door, then looked round. The tongue of garden narrowing in from the quarry bed was white with snow: she thought of the thick fringes of snowdrops it would show beneath the currant bushes in a month's time. The ragged fringe of pinks hanging over the garden brim behind her was whitened now with snowflakes, that in summer held white blossom to Louisa's face. It was pleasant, she thought, to gather flowers that stooped to one's face from above.

She knocked again. Peeping in, she saw the scarlet glow of the kitchen, red firelight falling on the brick floor and on the bright chintz cushions. It was alive and bright as a peep-show. She crossed the scullery, where still an almanac hung. There was no one about. "Mrs. Durant," called Louisa softly, "Mrs. Durant."

She went up the brick step into the front room, that still had its little shop counter and its bundle of goods, and she called from the stair-foot. Then she knew Mrs. Durant was out.

She went into the yard, to follow the old woman's footsteps up the garden path.

She emerged from the bushes and raspberry canes. There was the whole quarry bed, a wide garden white and dimmed, brindled with dark bushes, lying half submerged. On the left, overhead, the little colliery train rumbled by. Right away at the back was a mass of trees.

Louisa followed the open path, looking from right to left, and then she gave a cry of concern. The old woman was sitting rocking slightly among the ragged snowy cabbages. Louisa ran to her, found her whimpering with little, involuntary cries.

"Whatever have you done?" cried Louisa, kneeling in the snow.

"I've—I've— I was pulling a brussel-sprout stalk—and—oh-h!—something tore inside me. I've had a pain," the old woman wept from shock and suffering, gasping between her whimpers,—"I've had a pain there—a long time—and now—oh—oh!" She panted, pressed her hand on her side, leaned as if she would faint, looking yellow against the snow. Louisa supported her.

"Do you think you could walk now?" she asked.

"Yes," gasped the old woman.

Louisa helped her to her feet.

"Get the cabbage—I want it for Alfred's dinner," panted Mrs. Durant. Louisa picked up the stalk of brussel-sprouts, and with difficulty got the old woman indoors. She gave her brandy, laid her on the couch, saying:

"I'm going to send for a doctor—wait just a minute."

The young woman ran up the steps to the public-house a few yards away. The landlady was astonished to see Miss Louisa.

"Will you send for a doctor at once to Mrs. Durant," she said, with some of her father in her commanding tone.

"Is something the matter?" fluttered the landlady in concern.

Louisa, glancing out up the road, saw the grocer's cart driving to Eastwood. She ran and stopped the man, and told him.

Mrs. Durant lay on the sofa, her face turned away, when the young woman came back.

"Let me put you to bed," Louisa said. Mrs. Durant did not resist.

Louisa knew the ways of the working people. In the

bottom drawer of the dresser she found dusters and flannels. With the old pit-flannel she snatched out the oven shelves, wrapped them up, and put them in the bed. From the son's bed she took a blanket, and, running down, set it before the fire. Having undressed the little old woman, Louisa carried her upstairs.

"You'll drop me, you'll drop me!" cried Mrs. Durant.

Louisa did not answer, but bore her burden quickly. She could not light a fire, because there was no fire-place in the bedroom. And the floor was plaster. So she fetched the lamp, and stood it lighted in one corner.

"It will air the room," she said.

"Yes," moaned the old woman.

Louisa ran with more hot flannels, replacing those from the oven shelves. Then she made a bran-bag and laid it on the woman's side. There was a big lump on the side of the abdomen.

"I've felt it coming a long time," moaned the old lady, when the pain was easier, "but I've not said anything; I didn't want to upset our Alfred."

Louisa did not see why "our Alfred" should be spared.

"What time is it?" came the plaintive voice.

"A quarter to four."

"Oh!" wailed the old lady, "he'll be here in half an hour, and no dinner ready for him."

"Let me do it," said Louisa, gently.

"There's that cabbage—and you'll find the meat in the pantry—and there's an apple-pie you can hot up. But *don't you* do it——!"

"Who will, then?" asked Louisa.

"I don't know," moaned the sick woman, unable to consider.

Louisa did it. The doctor came and gave serious examination. He looked very grave.

"What is it, doctor?" asked the old lady, looking up at him with old, pathetic eyes in which already hope was dead.

"I think you've torn the skin in which a tumour hangs," he replied.

"Ay!" she murmured, and she turned away.

"You see, she may die any minute—and it *may* be swaled away," said the old doctor to Louisa.

The young woman went upstairs again.

"He says the lump may be swaled away, and you may get quite well again," she said.

"Ay!" murmured the old lady. It did not deceive her. Presently she asked:

"Is there a good fire?"

"I think so," answered Louisa.

"He'll want a good fire," the mother said. Louisa attended to it.

Since the death of Durant, the widow had come to church occasionally, and Louisa had been friendly to her. In the girl's heart the purpose was fixed. No man had affected her as Alfred Durant had done, and to that she kept. In her heart, she adhered to him. A natural sympathy existed between her and his rather hard, materialistic mother.

Alfred was the most lovable of the old woman's sons. He had grown up like the rest, however, headstrong and blind to everything but his own will. Like the other boys, he had insisted on going into the pit as soon as he left school, because that was the only way speedily to become a man, level with all the other men. This was a great chagrin to his mother, who would have liked to have this last of her sons a gentleman.

But still he remained constant to her. His feeling for her was deep and unexpressed. He noticed when she was tired, or when she had a new night-cap. And he bought little things for her occasionally. She was not wise enough to see how much he lived by her.

At the bottom he did not satisfy her, he did not seem manly enough. He liked to read books occasionally, and better still he liked to play the piccolo. It amused her to see his head nod over the instrument as he made an effort to get the right note. It made her fond of him, with tenderness, almost pity, but not with respect. She wanted a man to be fixed, going his own way without knowledge of women. Whereas she knew Alfred depended on her. He sang in the choir because he liked singing. In the summer he worked in the garden, attended to the fowls and pigs. He kept pigeons. He played on Saturday in the cricket or football team. But to her he did not seem the man, the independent man her other boys had been. He was her baby—and whilst she loved him for it, she was a little bit contemptuous of him.

There grew up a little hostility between them. Then he began to drink, as the others had done; but not in their blind, oblivious way. He was a little self-conscious over it. She saw this, and she pitied it in him. She loved him most, but she was not satisfied with him because he was not free of her. He could not quite go his own way.

Then at twenty he ran away and served his time in the Navy. This had made a man of him. He had hated it bitterly, the service, the subordination. For years he fought with himself under the military discipline, for his own self-respect, struggling through blind anger and shame and a cramping sense of inferiority. Out of humiliation and self-hatred he rose into a sort of inner freedom. And his love for his mother, whom he idealised, remained the fact of hope and of belief.

He came home again, nearly thirty years old, but naïve and inexperienced as a boy, only with a silence about him that was new: a sort of dumb humility before life, a fear of living. He was almost quite chaste. A strong sensitiveness had kept him from women. Sexual talk was all very well among men, but somehow it had no application to living women. There were two things for him, the *idea* of women, with which he sometimes debauched himself, and real women, before whom he felt a deep uneasiness, and a need to draw away. He shrank and defended himself from the approach of any woman. And then he felt ashamed. In his innermost soul he felt he was not a man, he was less than the normal man. In Genoa he went with an under-officer to a drinking-house where the cheaper sort of girl came in to look for lovers. He sat there with his glass, the girls looked at him, but they never came to him. He knew that if they did come he could only pay for food and drink for them, because he felt a pity for them, and was anxious lest they lacked good necessities. He could not have gone with one of them; he knew it, and was ashamed, looking with curious envy at the swaggering, easy-passionate Italian whose body went to a woman by instinctive impersonal attraction. They were men, he was not a man. He sat feeling short, feeling like a leper. And he went away imagining sexual scenes between himself and a woman, walking wrapt in this indulgence. But when the ready woman presented herself, the very fact that she was a palpable woman made it impossible for him to touch her. And this incapacity was like a core of rottenness in him.

So several times he went, drunk, with his companions, to the licensed prostitute-houses abroad. But the sordid insignificance of the experience appalled him. It had not been anything really: it meant nothing. He felt as if he were, not physically, but spiritually impotent: not actually impotent, but intrinsically so.

He came home with this secret, never changing burden of his unknown, unbestowed self torturing him. His Navy training left him in perfect physical condition. He was sensible of, and proud of his body. He bathed and used dumb-bells, and kept himself fit. He played cricket and football. He read books and began to hold fixed ideas which he got from the Fabians. He played his piccolo, and was considered an expert. But at the bottom of his soul was always this canker of shame and incompleteness: he was miserable beneath all his healthy cheerfulness, he was uneasy and felt despicable among all his confidence and superiority of ideas. He would have changed with any mere brute, just to be free of himself, to be free of this shame of self-consciousness. He saw some collier lurching straight forward without misgiving, pursuing his own satisfactions, and he envied him. Anything, he would have given for this spontaneity and this blind stupidity which went to its own satisfaction direct.

IX

He was not unhappy in the pit. He was admired by the men, and well enough liked. It was only he himself who felt the difference between himself and the others. He seemed to hide his own stigma. But he was never sure that the others did not really despise him for a ninny, as being less a man than they were. Only he pretended to be more manly, and was surprised by the ease with which they were deceived. And, being naturally cheerful, he was happy at work. He was sure of himself there. Naked to the waist, hot and grimy with labour, they squatted on their heels for a few minutes and talked, seeing each other dimly by the light of the safety lamps, while the black coal rose jutting round them, and the props of wood stood like little pillars in the low, black, very dark temple. Then the pony came and the gang-lad with a message from Number 7, or with a bottle of water from the horse-trough or some news of the world above. The day passed pleasantly enough. There was an ease, a go-as-you-please about the day underground, a delightful camaraderie of men shut off alone from the rest of the world, in a dangerous place, and a variety of labour, holing, loading, timbering, and a glamour of mystery and adventure in the atmosphere, that made the pit not unattractive to him when he had again got over his anguish of desire for the open air and the sea.

This day there was much to do and Durant was not in humour to talk. He went on working in silence through the afternoon.

"Loose-all" came, and they tramped to the bottom. The white-washed underground office shone brightly. Men were putting out their lamps. They sat in dozens round the bottom of the shaft, down which black, heavy drops of water fell continuously into the sump. The electric lights shone away down the main underground road.

"Is it raining?" asked Durant.

"Snowing," said the old man, and the younger was pleased. He liked to go up when it was snowing.

"It'll just come right for Christmas?" said the old man.

"Ay," replied Durant.

"A green Christmas, a fat churchyard," said the other sententiously.

Durant laughed, showing his small, rather pointed teeth.

The cage came down, a dozen men lined on. Durant noticed tufts of snow on the perforated, arched roof of the chain, and he was pleased. He wondered how it liked its excursion underground. But already it was getting soppy with black water.

He liked things about him. There was a little smile on his face. But underlying it was the curious consciousness he felt in himself.

The upper world came almost with a flash, because of the glimmer of snow. Hurrying along the bank, giving up his lamp at the office, he smiled to feel the open about him again, all glimmering round him with snow. The hills on either hand were pale blue in the dusk, and the hedges looked savage and dark. The snow was trampled between the railway lines. But far ahead, beyond the black figures of miners moving home, it became smooth again, spreading right up to the dark wall of the coppice.

To the west there was a pinkness, and a big star hovered half revealed. Below, the lights of the pit came out crisp and yellow among the darkness of the buildings, and the lights of Old Aldecross twinkled in rows down the bluish twilight.

Durant walked glad with life among the miners, who were all talking animatedly because of the snow. He liked their company, he liked the white dusky world. It gave him a little thrill to stop at the garden gate and see the light of home down below, shining on the silent blue snow.

X

By the big gate of the railway, in the fence, was a little gate, that he kept locked. As he unfastened it, he watched the kitchen light that shone on to the bushes and the snow outside. It was a candle burning till night set in, he thought to himself. He slid down the steep path to the level below. He liked making the first marks in the smooth snow. Then he came through the bushes to the house. The two women heard his heavy boots ring outside on the scraper, and his voice as he opened the door:

"How much worth of oil do you reckon to save by that candle, mother?" He liked a good light from the lamp.

He had just put down his bottle and snap-bag and was

hanging his coat behind the scullery door, when Miss Louisa came upon him. He was startled, but he smiled.

His eyes began to laugh—then his face went suddenly straight, and he was afraid.

"Your mother's had an accident," she said.

"How?" he exclaimed.

"In the garden," she answered. He hesitated with his coat in his hands. Then he hung it up and turned to the kitchen.

"Is she in bed?" he asked.

"Yes," said Miss Louisa, who found it hard to deceive him. He was silent. He went into the kitchen, sat down heavily in his father's old chair, and began to pull off his boots. His head was small, rather finely shapen. His brown hair, close and crisp, would look jolly whatever happened. He wore heavy, moleskin trousers that gave off the stale, exhausted scent of the pit. Having put on his slippers, he carried his boots into the scullery.

"What is it?" he asked, afraid.

"Something internal," she replied.

He went upstairs. His mother kept herself calm for his coming. Louisa felt his tread shake the plaster floor of the bedroom above.

"What have you done?" he asked.

"It's nothing, my lad," said the old woman, rather hard. "It's nothing. You needn't fret, my boy, it's nothing more the matter with me than I had yesterday, or last week. The doctor said I'd done nothing serious."

"What were you doing?" asked her son.

"I was pulling up a cabbage, and I suppose I pulled too hard; for, oh—there was such a pain——"

Her son looked at her quickly. She hardened herself.

"But who doesn't have a sudden pain sometimes, my boy? We all do."

"And what's it done?"

"I don't know," she said, "but I don't suppose it's anything."

The big lamp in the corner was screened with a dark green screen, so that he could scarcely see her face. He was strung tight with apprehension and many emotions. Then his brow knitted.

"What did you go pulling your inside out at cabbages for," he asked, "and the ground frozen? You'd go on dragging and dragging, if you killed yourself."

"Somebody's got to get them," she said.

"You needn't do yourself harm."

But they had reached futility.

Miss Louisa could hear plainly downstairs. Her heart sank. It seemed so hopeless between them.

"Are you sure it's nothing much, mother?" he asked, appealing, after a little silence.

"Ay, it's nothing," said the old woman, rather bitter.

"I don't want you to—to—to be badly—you know."

"Go an' get your dinner," she said. She knew she was going to die: moreover, the pain was torture just then. "They're only cosseting me up a bit because I'm an old woman. Miss Louisa's *very* good—and she'll have got your dinner ready, so you'd better go and eat it."

He felt stupid and ashamed. His mother put him off. He had to turn away. The pain burned in his bowels. He went downstairs. The mother was glad he was gone, so that she could moan with pain.

He had resumed the old habit of eating before he washed himself. Miss Louisa served his dinner. It was strange and exciting to her. She was strung up tense, trying to understand him and his mother. She watched him as he sat. He was turned away from his food, looking in the fire. Her soul watched him, trying to see what he was. His black face and arms were uncouth, he was foreign. His face was masked black with coal-dust. She could not see him, she could not know him. The brown eyebrows, the steady eyes, the coarse, small moustache above the closed mouth—these were the only familiar indications. What was he, as he sat there in his pit-dirt? She could not see him, and it hurt her.

She ran upstairs, presently coming down with flannels and the bran-bag, to heat them, because the pain was on again.

He was half-way through his dinner. He put down the fork, suddenly nauseated.

"They will soothe the wrench," she said. He watched, useless and left out.

"Is she bad?" he asked.

"I think she is," she answered.

It was useless for him to stir or comment. Louisa was busy. She went upstairs. The poor old woman was in a white, cold sweat of pain. Louisa's face was sullen with suffering as she went about to relieve her. Then she sat and waited. The pain passed gradually, the old woman sank into a state of coma. Louisa still sat silent by the bed. She heard the sound of water downstairs. Then came the voice of the old mother, faint but unrelaxing:

"Alfred's washing himself—he'll want his back washing——"

Louisa listened anxiously, wondering what the sick woman wanted.

"He can't bear if his back isn't washed——" the old woman persisted, in a cruel attention to his needs. Louisa rose and wiped the sweat from the yellowish brow.

"I will go down," she said soothingly.

"If you would," murmured the sick woman.

Louisa waited a moment. Mrs. Durant closed her eyes, having discharged her duty. The young woman went downstair. Herself, or the man, what did they matter? Only the suffering woman must be considered.

Alfred was kneeling on the hearth-rug, stripped to the waist, washing himself in a large panchion of earthenware. He did so every evening, when he had eaten his dinner; his brothers had done so before him. But Miss Louisa was strange in the house.

He was mechanically rubbing the white lather on his head, with a repeated, unconscious movement, his hand every now and then passing over his neck. Louisa watched. She had to brace herself to this also. He bent his head into the water, washed it free of soap, and pressed the water out of his eyes.

"Your mother said you would want your back washing," she said.

Curious how it hurt her to take part in their fixed routine of life! Louisa felt the almost repulsive intimacy being forced upon her. It was all so common, so like herding. She lost her own distinctness.

He ducked his face round, looking up at her in what was a very comical way. She had to harden herself.

"How funny he looks with his face upside down," she thought. After all, there was a difference between her and the common people. The water in which his arms were plunged was quite black, the soap-froth was darkish. She could scarcely conceive him as human. Mechanically, under the influence of habit, he groped in black water, fished out soap and flannel, and handed them backward to Louisa. Then he remained rigid and submissive, his two arms thrust straight in the panchion, supporting the weight of his shoulders. His skin was beautifully white and unblemished, of an opaque, solid whiteness. Gradually Louisa saw it: this also was what he was. It fascinated her. Her feelings of separateness passed away: she ceased to draw back from contact with him and his mother. There was this living centre. Her heart ran hot. She had reached some goal in this beautiful, clear, male body. She loved him in a white, impersonal heat. But the sun-burnt, reddish neck and ears: they were more personal, more curious. A tenderness rose in her, she loved even his queer ears. A person—an intimate being he was to her. She put down the towel and went upstairs again, troubled in her heart. She had only seen one human being in her life—and that was Mary. All the rest were strangers. Now her soul was going to open, she was going to see another. She felt strange and pregnant.

"He'll be more comfortable," murmured the sick woman abstractedly, as Louisa entered the room. The latter did not answer. Her own heart was heavy with its own responsibility. Mrs. Durant lay silent awhile, then she murmured plaintively:

"You mustn't mind, Miss Louisa."

"Why should I?" replied Louisa, deeply moved.

"It's what we're used to," said the old woman.

And Louisa felt herself excluded again from their life. She sat in pain, with the tears of disappointment distilling in her heart. Was that all?

Alfred came upstairs. He was clean, and in his shirt-sleeves. He looked a workman now. Louisa felt that she and he were foreigners, moving in different lives. It dulled her again. Oh, if she could only find some fixed relations, something sure and abiding.

"How do you feel?" he said to his mother.

"It's a bit better," she replied wearily, impersonally. This strange putting herself aside, this abstracting herself and answering him only what she thought good for him to hear, made the relations between mother and son poignant and cramping to Miss Louisa. It made the man so ineffectual, so nothing. Louisa groped as if she had lost him. The mother was real and positive—he was not very actual. It puzzled and chilled the young woman.

"I'd better fetch Mrs. Harrison?" he said, waiting for his mother to decide.

"I suppose we shall have to have somebody," she replied.

Miss Louisa stood by, afraid to interfere in their business. They did not include her in their lives, they felt she had nothing to do with them, except as a help from outside. She was quite external to them. She felt hurt and powerless against this unconscious difference. But something patient and unyielding in her made her say:

"I will stay and do the nursing: you can't be left."

The other two were shy, and at a loss for an answer.

"We s'll manage to get somebody," said the old woman wearily. She did not care very much what happened, now.

"I will stay until to-morrow, in any case," said Louisa. "Then we can see."

"I'm sure you've no right to trouble yourself," moaned the old woman. But she must leave herself in any hands.

Miss Louisa felt glad that she was admitted, even in an official capacity. She wanted to share their lives. At home they would need her, now Mary had come. But they must manage without her.

"I must write a note to the vicarage," she said.

Alfred Durant looked at her inquiringly, for her service. He had always that intelligent readiness to serve, since he had been in the Navy. But there was a simple independence in his willingness, which she loved. She felt nevertheless it was hard to get at him. He was so deferential, quick to take the slightest suggestion of an order from her, implicitly, that she could not get at the man in him.

He looked at her very keenly. She noticed his eyes were golden brown, with a very small pupil, the kind of eyes that can see a long way off. He stood alert, at military attention. His face was still rather weather-reddened.

"Do you want pen and paper?" he asked, with deferential suggestion to a superior, which was more difficult for her than reserve.

"Yes, please," she said.

He turned and went downstairs. He seemed to her so self-contained, so utterly sure in his movement. How was she to approach him? For he would take not one step towards her. He would only put himself entirely and impersonally at her service, glad to serve her, but keeping himself quite removed from her. She could see he felt real joy in doing anything for her, but any recognition would confuse him and hurt him. Strange it was to her, to have a man going about the house in his shirt-sleeves, his waistcoat unbuttoned, his throat bare, waiting on her. He moved well, as if he had plenty of life to spare. She was attracted by his completeness. And yet, when all was ready, and there was nothing more for him to do, she quivered, meeting his questioning look.

As she sat writing, he placed another candle near her. The rather dense light fell in two places on the overfoldings of her hair till it glistened heavy and bright, like a dense golden plumage folded up. Then the nape of her neck was very white, with one down and pointed wisps of gold. He watched it as if it were a vision, losing himself. She was all that was beyond him, of revelation and exquisiteness. All that was ideal and beyond him, she was that—and he was lost to himself in looking at her. She had no connection with him. He did not approach her. She was there like a wonderful distance. But it was a treat, having her in the house. Even with this anguish for his mother tightening about him, he was sensible of the wonder of living this evening. The candles glistened on her hair, and seemed to fascinate him. He felt a little awe of her, and a sense of uplifting, that he and she and his mother should be together for a time, in the strange, unknown atmosphere. And, when he got out of the house, he was afraid. He saw the stars above ringing with one brightness, the snow beneath just visible, and a new night was gathering round him. He was afraid almost with obliteration. What was this new night ringing about him, and what was he? He could not recognise himself nor any of his surroundings. He was afraid to think of his mother. And yet his chest was conscious of her, and of what was happening to her. He could not escape from her, she carried him with her into an unformed, unknown chaos.

XI

He went up the road in an agony, not knowing what it was all about, but feeling as if a red-hot iron were gripped round his chest. Without thinking, he shook two or three tears on to the snow. Yet in his mind he did not believe his mother would die. He was in the grip of some greater consciousness. As he sat in the hall of the vicarage, waiting whilst Mary put things for Louisa into a bag, he wondered why he had been so upset. He felt abashed and humbled by the big house, he felt again as if he were one of the rank and file. When Miss Mary spoke to him, he almost saluted.

"An honest man," thought Mary. And the patronage was applied as salve to her own sickness. She had station, so she could patronise: it was almost all that was left to her. But she could not have lived without having a certain position. She could never have trusted herself outside a definite place, nor respected herself except as a woman of superior class.

As Alfred came to the latch-gate, he felt the grief at his heart again, and saw the new heavens. He stood a moment looking northward to the Plough climbing up the right, and at the far glimmer of snow in distant fields. Then his grief came on like physical pain. He held tight to the gate, biting his mouth, whispering "Mother!" It was a fierce, cutting, physical pain of grief, that came on in bouts, as his mother's pain came on in bouts, and was so acute he could scarcely keep erect. He did not know where it came from, the pain, nor why. It had nothing to do with his thoughts. Almost it had nothing to do with him. Only it gripped him and he must submit. The whole tide of his soul, gathering in its unknown towards this expansion into death, carried him with it helplessly, all the fritter of his thought and consciousness caught up as nothing, the heave passing on towards its breaking, taking him farther than he had ever been. When the young man had regained himself, he went indoors, and there he was almost gay. It seemed to excite him. He felt in high spirits: he made whimsical fun of things. He sat on one side of his mother's bed, Louisa on the other, and a certain gaiety seized them all. But the night and the dread was coming on.

Alfred kissed his mother and went to bed. When he was half undressed the knowledge of his mother came upon him, and the suffering seized him in its grip like two hands, in agony. He lay on the bed screwed up tight. It lasted so long, and exhausted him so much, that he fell asleep, without having the energy to get up and finish undressing. He awoke after midnight to find himself stone cold. He undressed and got into bed, and was soon asleep again.

At a quarter to six he woke, and instantly remembered. Having pulled on his trousers and lighted a candle, he went into his mother's room. He put his hand before the candle flame so that no light fell on the bed.

"Mother!" he whispered.

"Yes," was the reply.

There was a hesitation.

"Should I go to work?"

He waited, his heart was beating heavily.

"I think I'd go, my lad."

His heart went down in a kind of despair.

"You want me to?"

He let his hand down from the candle flame. The light fell on the bed. There he saw Louisa lying looking up at him. Her eyes were upon him. She quickly shut her eyes and half buried her face in the pillow, her back turned to him. He saw the rough hair like bright vapour about her round head, and the two plaits flung coiled among the bedclothes. It gave him a shock. He stood almost himself, determined. Louisa cowered down. He looked, and met his mother's eyes. Then he gave way again, and ceased to be sure, ceased to be himself.

"Yes, go to work, my boy," said the mother.

"All right," replied he, kissing her. His heart was down at despair, and bitter. He went away.

"Alfred!" cried his mother faintly.

He came back with beating heart.

"What, mother?"

"You'll always do what's right, Alfred?" the mother asked, beside herself in terror now he was leaving her. He was too terrified and bewildered to know what she meant.

"Yes," he said.

She turned her cheek to him. He kissed her, then went away in bitter despair. He went to work.

XII

By midday his mother was dead. The word met him at the pit-mouth. As he had known, inwardly, it was not a shock to him, and yet he trembled. He went home quite calmly, feeling only heavy in his breathing.

Miss Louisa was still at the house. She had seen to everything possible. Very succinctly, she informed him of what he needed to know. But there was one point of anxiety for her.

"You *did* half expect it—it's not come as a blow to you?" she asked, looking up at him. Her eyes were dark and calm and searching. She too felt lost. He was so dark and inchoate.

"I suppose—yes," he said stupidly. He looked aside, unable to endure her eyes on him.

"I could not bear to think you might not have guessed," she said.

He did not answer.

He felt it a great strain to have her near him at this time. He wanted to be alone. As soon as the relatives began to arrive, Louisa departed and came no more. While everything was arranging, and a crowd was in the house, whilst he had business to settle, he went well enough, with only those uncontrollable paroxysms of grief. For the rest he was superficial. By himself, he endured the fierce, almost insane bursts of grief which passed again and left him calm, almost clear, just wondering. He had not known before that everything could break down, that he himself could break down, and all be a great chaos, very vast and wonderful. It seemed as if life in him had burst its bounds, and he was lost in a great, bewildering flood, immense and unpeopled. He himself was broken and spilled out amid it all. He could only breathe panting in silence. Then the anguish came on again.

When all the people had gone from the Quarry Cottage, leaving the young man alone with an elderly housekeeper, then the long trial began. The snow had thawed and frozen, a fresh fall had whitened the grey, this then began to thaw. The world was a place of loose grey slosh. Alfred had nothing to do in the evenings. He was a man whose life had been filled up with small activities. Without knowing it, he had been centralised, polarised in his mother. It was she who had kept him. Even now, when the old housekeeper had left him, he might still have gone on in his old way. But the force and balance of his life was lacking. He sat pretending to read, all the time holding his fists clenched, and holding himself in, enduring he did not know what. He walked the black and sodden miles of field-paths, till he was tired out: but all this was only running away from whence he must return. At work he was all right. If it had been summer he might have escaped by working in the garden till bedtime. But now, there was no escape, no relief, no help. He, perhaps, was made for action rather than for understanding; for doing than for being. He was shocked out of his activities, like a swimmer who forgets to swim.

For a week, he had the force to endure this suffocation and struggle, then he began to get exhausted, and knew it must come out. The instinct of self-preservation became strongest. But there was the question: Where was he to go? The public-house really meant nothing to him, it was no good going there. He began to think of emigration. In another country he would be all right. He wrote to the emigration offices.

On the Sunday after the funeral, when all the Durant

people had attended church, Alfred had seen Miss Louisa, impassive and reserved, sitting with Miss Mary, who was proud and very distant, and with the other Lindleys, who were people removed. Alfred saw them as people remote. He did not think about it. They had nothing to do with his life. After service Louisa had come to him and shaken hands.

"My sister would like you to come to supper one evening, if you would be so good."

He looked at Miss Mary, who bowed. Out of kindness, Mary had proposed this to Louisa, disapproving of her even as she did so. But she did not examine herself closely.

"Yes," said Durant awkwardly, "I'll come if you want me." But he vaguely felt that it was misplaced.

"You'll come to-morrow evening, then, about half-past six."

He went. Miss Louisa was very kind to him. There could be no music, because of the babies. He sat with his fists clenched on his thighs, very quiet and unmoved, lapsing, among all those people, into a kind of muse or daze. There was nothing between him and them. They knew it as well as he. But he remained very steady in himself, and the evening passed slowly. Mrs. Lindley called him "young man".

"Will you sit here, young man?"

He sat there. One name was as good as another. What had they to do with him?

Mr. Lindley kept a special tone for him, kind, indulgent, but patronising. Durant took it all without criticism or offence, just submitting. But he did not want to eat—that troubled him, to have to eat in their presence. He knew he was out of place. But it was his duty to stay yet awhile. He answered precisely, in monosyllables.

When he left he winced with confusion. He was glad it was finished. He got away as quickly as possible. And he wanted still more intensely to go right away, to Canada.

Miss Louisa suffered in her soul, indignant with all of them, with him too, but quite unable to say why she was indignant.

XIII

Two evenings after, Louisa tapped at the door of the Quarry Cottage, at half-past six. He had finished dinner, the woman had washed up and gone away, but still he sat in his pit-dirt. He was going later to the New Inn. He had begun to go there because he must go somewhere. The mere contact with other men was necessary to him, the noise, the warmth, the forgetful flight of the hours. But still he did not move. He sat alone in the empty house till it began to grow on him like something unnatural.

He was in his pit-dirt when he opened the door.

"I have been wanting to call—I thought I would," she said, and she went to the sofa. He wondered why she wouldn't use his mother's round arm-chair. Yet something stirred in him, like anger, when the housekeeper placed herself in it.

"I ought to have been washed by now," he said, glancing at the clock, which was adorned with butterflies and cherries, and the name of "T. Brooks, Mansfield". He laid his black hands along his mottled dirty arms. Louisa looked at him. There was the reserve, and the simple neutrality towards her, which she dreaded in him. It made it impossible for her to approach him.

"I am afraid," she said, "that I wasn't kind in asking you to supper."

"I'm not used to it," he said, smiling with his mouth, showing the interspaced white teeth. His eyes, however, were steady and unseeing.

"It's not *that,*" she said hastily. Her repose was exquisite and her dark grey eyes rich with understanding. He felt afraid of her as she sat there, as he began to grow conscious of her.

"How do you get on alone?" she asked.

He glanced away to the fire.

"Oh——" he answered, shifting uneasily, not finishing his answer.

Her face settled heavily.

"How close it is in this room. You have such immense fires. I will take off my coat," she said.

He watched her take off her hat and coat. She wore a cream cashmir blouse embroidered with gold silks. It seemed to him a very fine garment, fitting her throat and wrists close. It gave him a feeling of pleasure and cleanness and relief from himself.

"What were you thinking about, that you didn't get washed?" she asked, half intimately. He laughed, turning aside his head. The whites of his eyes showed very distinct in his black face.

"Oh," he said, "I couldn't tell you."

There was a pause.

"Are you going to keep this house on?" she asked.

He stirred in his chair, under the question.

"I hardly know," he said. "I'm very likely going to Canada."

Her spirit became very quiet and attentive.

"What for?" she asked.

Again he shifted restlessly on his seat.

"Well,"—he said slowly—"to try the life."

"But which life?"

"There's various things—farming or lumbering or mining. I don't mind much what it is."

"And is that what you want?"

He did not think in these times, so he could not answer.

"I don't know," he said, "till I've tried."

She saw him drawing away from her for ever.

"Aren't you sorry to leave this house and garden?" she asked.

"I don't know," he answered reluctantly. "I suppose our Fred would come in—that's what he's wanting."

"You don't want to settle down?" she asked.

He was leaning forward on the arms of his chair. He turned to her. Her face was pale and set. It looked heavy and impassive, her hair shone richer as she grew white. She was to him something steady and immovable and eternal presented to him. His heart was hot in an anguish of suspense. Sharp twitches of fear and pain were in his limbs. He turned his whole body away from her. The silence was unendurable. He could not bear her to sit there any more. It made his heart get hot and stifled in his breast.

"Were you going out to-night?" she asked.

"Only to the New Inn," he said.

Again there was silence.

She reached for her hat. Nothing else was suggested to her. She *had* to go. He sat waiting for her to be gone, for relief. And she knew that if she went out of that house as she was, she went out a failure. Yet she continued to pin on her hat; in a moment she would have to go. Something was carrying her.

Then suddenly a sharp pang, like lightning, seared her from head to foot, and she was beyond herself.

"Do you want me to go?" she asked, controlled, yet speaking out of a fiery anguish, as if the words were spoken from her without her intervention.

He went white under his dirt.

"Why?" he asked, turning to her in fear, compelled.

"Do you want me to go?" she repeated.

"Why?" he asked again.

"Because I wanted to stay with you," she said, suffocated, with her lungs full of fire.

His face worked, he hung forward a little, suspended, staring straight into her eyes, in torment, in an agony of chaos, unable to collect himself. And as if turned to stone, she looked back into his eyes. The souls were exposed bare for a few moments. It was agony. They could not bear it. He dropped his head, whilst his body jerked with little sharp twitchings.

She turned away for her coat. Her soul had gone dead in her. Her hands trembled, but she could not feel any more. She drew on her coat. There was a cruel suspense in the room. The moment had come for her to go. He lifted his head. His eyes were like agate, expressionless, save for the black points of torture. They held her, she had no will, no life any more. She felt broken.

"Don't you want me?" she said helplessly.

A spasm of torture crossed his eyes, which held her fixed.

"I—I——" he began, but he could not speak. Something drew him from his chair to her. She stood motionless, spell-bound, like a creature given up as prey. He put his hand tentatively, uncertainly, on her arm. The expression of his face was strange and inhuman. She stood utterly motionless. Then clumsily he put his arms round her, and took her, cruelly, blindly, straining her till she nearly lost consciousness, till he himself had almost fallen.

Then, gradually, as he held her gripped, and his brain reeled round, and he felt himself falling, falling from himself, and whilst she, yielded up, swooned to a kind of death of herself, a moment of utter darkness came over him, and they began to wake up again as if from a long sleep. He was himself.

After a while his arms slackened, she loosened herself a little, and put her arms round him, as he held her. So they held each other close, and hid each against the other for assurance, helpless in speech. And it was ever her hands that trembled more closely upon him, drawing him nearer into her, with love.

And at last she drew back her face and looked up at him, her eyes wet, and shining with light. His heart, which saw, was silent with fear. He was with her. She saw his face all sombre and inscrutable, and he seemed eternal to her. And all the echo of pain came back into the rarity of bliss, and all her tears came up.

"I love you," she said, her lips drawn to sobbing. He put down his head against her, unable to hear her, unable to bear the sudden coming of the peace and passion that almost broke his heart. They stood together in silence whilst the thing moved away a little.

At last she wanted to see him. She looked up. His eyes were strange and glowing, with a tiny black pupil. Strange, they were, and powerful over her. And his mouth came to hers, and slowly her eyelids closed, as his mouth sought hers closer and closer, and took possession of her.

They were silent for a long time, too much mixed up with passion and grief and death to do anything but hold each other in pain and kiss with long, hurting kisses wherein fear was transfused into desire. At last she disengaged herself. He felt as if his heart were hurt, but glad, and he scarcely dared look at her.

"I'm glad," she said also.

He held her hands in passionate gratitude and desire. He had not yet the presence of mind to say anything. He was dazed with relief.

"I ought to go," she said.

He looked at her. He could not grasp the thought of her going, he knew he could never be separated from her any more. Yet he dared not assert himself. He held her hands tight.

"Your face is black," she said.

He laughed.

"Yours is a bit smudged," he said.

They were afraid of each other, afraid to talk. He could only keep her near to him. After a while she wanted to wash her face. He brought her some warm water, standing by and watching her. There was something he wanted to say, that he dared not. He watched her wiping her face, and making tidy her hair.

"They'll see your blouse is dirty," he said.

She looked at her sleeves and laughed for joy.

He was sharp with pride.

"What shall you do?" he asked.

"How?" she said.

He was awkward at a reply.

"About me," he said.

"What do you want me to do?" she laughed.

He put his hand out slowly to her. What did it matter!

"But make yourself clean," she said.

XIV

As they went up the hill, the night seemed dense with the unknown. They kept close together, feeling as if the darkness were alive and full of knowledge, all around them. In silence they walked up the hill. At first the street lamps went their way. Several people passed them. He was more shy than she, and would have let her go had she loosened in the least. But she held firm.

Then they came into the true darkness, between the fields. They did not want to speak, feeling closer together in silence. So they arrived at the vicarage gate. They stood under the naked horse-chestnut tree.

"I wish you didn't have to go," he said.

She laughed a quick little laugh.

"Come to-morrow," she said, in a low tone, "and ask father."

She felt his hand close on hers.

She gave the same sorrowful little laugh of sympathy. Then she kissed him, sending him home.

At home, the old grief came on in another paroxysm, obliterating Louisa, obliterating even his mother for whom the stress was raging like a burst of fever in a wound. But something was sound in his heart.

XV

The next evening he dressed to go to the vicarage, feeling it was to be done, not imagining what it would be like. He would not take this seriously. He was sure of Louisa, and this marriage was like fate to him. It filled him also with a blessed feeling of fatality. He was not responsible, neither had her people anything really to do with it.

They ushered him into the little study, which was fireless. By and by the vicar came in. His voice was cold and hostile as he said:

"What can I do for you, young man?"

He knew already, without asking.

Durant looked up at him, again like a sailor before a superior. He had the subordinate manner. Yet his spirit was clear.

"I wanted, Mr. Lindley——" he began respectfully, then all the colour suddenly left his face. It seemed now a violation to say what he had to say. What was he doing there? But he stood on, because it had to be done. He held firmly to his own independence and self-respect. He must not be indecisive. He must put himself aside: the matter was bigger than just his personal self. He must not feel. This was his highest duty.

"You wanted——" said the vicar.

Durant's mouth was dry, but he answered with steadiness:

"Miss Louisa—Louisa—promised to marry me——"

"You asked Miss Louisa if she would marry you—yes ——" corrected the vicar. Durant reflected he had not asked her this:

"If she would marry me, sir. I hope you—don't mind."

He smiled. He was a good-looking man, and the vicar could not help seeing it.

"And my daughter was willing to marry you?" said Mr. Lindley.

"Yes," said Durant seriously. It was pain to him, nevertheless. He felt the natural hostility between himself and the elder man.

"Will you come this way?" said the vicar. He led into the dining-room, where were Mary, Louisa, and Mrs. Lindley. Mr. Massy sat in a corner with a lamp.

"This young man has come on your account, Louisa?" said Mr. Lindley.

"Yes," said Louisa, her eyes on Durant, who stood erect, in discipline. He dared not look at her, but he was aware of her.

"You don't want to marry a collier, you little fool," cried Mrs. Lindley harshly. She lay obese and helpless upon the couch, swathed in a loose dove-grey gown.

"Oh, hush, Mother," cried Mary, with quiet intensity and pride.

"What means have you to support a wife?" demanded the vicar's wife roughly.

"I!" Durant replied, starting. "I think I can earn enough."

"Well, and how much?" came the rough voice.

"Seven and six a day," replied the young man.

"And will it get to be any more?"

"I hope so."

"And are you going to live in that poky little house?"

"I think so," said Durant, "if it's all right."

He took small offence, only was upset, because they would not think him good enough. He knew that, in their sense, he was not.

"Then she's a fool, I tell you, if she marries you," cried the mother roughly, casting her decision.

"After all, mama, it is Louisa's affair," said Mary distinctly, "and we must remember——"

"As she makes her bed, she must lie—but she'll repent it," interrupted Mrs. Lindley.

"And after all," said Mr. Lindley, "Louisa cannot quite hold herself free to act entirely without consideration for her family."

"What do you want, Papa?" asked Louisa sharply.

"I mean that if you marry this man, it will make my position very difficult for me, particularly if you stay in this parish. If you were moving quite away, it would be simpler. But living here in a collier's cottage, under my nose, as it were—it would be almost unseemly. I have my position to maintain, and a position which may not be taken lightly."

"Come over here, young man," cried the mother, in her rough voice, "and let us look at you."

Durant, flushing, went over and stood—not quite at attention, so that he did not know what to do with his hands. Miss Louisa was angry to see him standing there, obedient and acquiescent. He ought to show himself a man.

"Can't you take her away and live out of sight?" said the mother. "You'd both of you be better off."

"Yes, we can go away," he said.

"Do you want to?" asked Miss Mary clearly.

He faced round. Mary looked very stately and impressive. He flushed.

"I do if it's going to be a trouble to anybody," he said.

"For yourself, you would rather stay?" said Mary.

"It's my home," he said, "and that's the house I was born in."

"Then"—Mary turned clearly to her parents, "I really don't see how you can make the conditions, papa. He has his own rights, and if Louisa wants to marry him——"

"Louisa, Louisa!" cried the father impatiently. "I cannot

understand why Louisa should not behave in the normal way. I cannot see why she should only think of herself, and leave her family out of count. The thing is enough in itself, and she ought to try to ameliorate it as much as possible. And if——"

"But I love the man, papa," said Louisa.

"And I hope you love your parents, and I hope you want to spare them as much of the—the loss of prestige as possible."

"We *can* go away to live," said Louisa, her face breaking to tears. At last she was really hurt.

"Oh yes, easily," Durant replied hastily, pale, distressed.

There was dead silence in the room.

"I think it would really be better," murmured the vicar, mollified.

"Very likely it would," said the rough-voiced invalid.

"Though I think we ought to apologise for asking such a thing," said Mary haughtily.

"No," said Durant. "It will be best all round." He was glad there was no more bother.

"And shall we put up the banns here or go to the registrar?" he asked clearly, like a challenge.

"We will go to the registrar," replied Louisa decidedly.

Again there was a dead silence in the room.

"Well, if you will have your own way, you must go your own way," said the mother emphatically.

All the time Mr. Massy had sat obscure and unnoticed in a corner of the room. At this juncture he got up, saying:

"There is baby, Mary."

Mary rose and went out of the room, stately; her little husband padded after her. Durant watched the fragile, small man go, wondering.

"And where," asked the vicar, almost genial, "do you think you will go when you are married?"

Durant started.

"I was thinking of emigrating," he said.

"To Canada? Or where?"

"I think to Canada."

"Yes, that would be very good."

Again there was a pause.

"We shan't see much of you then, as a son-in-law," said the mother, roughly but amicably.

"Not much," he said.

Then he took his leave. Louisa went with him to the gate. She stood before him in distress.

"You won't mind them, will you?" she said humbly.

"I don't mind them, if they don't mind me!" he said. Then he stooped and kissed her.

"Let us be married soon," she murmured, in tears.

"All right," he said. "I'll go to-morrow to Barford."

The Shades of Spring

It was a mile nearer through the wood. Mechanically, Syson turned up by the forge and lifted the field-gate. The blacksmith and his mate stood still, watching the trespasser. But Syson looked too much a gentleman to be accosted. They let him go on in silence across the small field to the wood.

There was not the least difference between this morning and those of the bright springs, six or eight years back. White and sandy-gold fowls still scratched round the gate, littering the earth and the field with feathers and scratched-up rubbish. Between the two thick holly bushes in the wood-hedge was the hidden gap, whose fence one climbed to get into the wood; the bars were scored just the same by the keeper's boots. He was back in the eternal.

Syson was extraordinarily glad. Like an uneasy spirit he had returned to the country of his past, and he found it waiting for him, unaltered. The hazel still spread glad little hands downwards, the bluebells here were still wan and few, among the lush grass and in shade of the bushes.

The path through the wood, on the very brow of a slope, ran winding easily for a time. All around were twiggy oaks, just issuing their gold, and floor spaces diapered with woodruff, with patches of dog-mercury and tufts of hyacinth. Two fallen trees still lay across the track. Syson jolted down a steep, rough slope, and came again upon the open land, this time looking north as through a great window in the wood. He stayed to gaze over the level fields of the hill-top, at the village which strewed the bare upland as if it had tumbled off the passing wagons of industry, and been forsaken. There was a stiff, modern, grey little church, and blocks and rows of red dwellings lying at random; at the back, the twinkling headstocks of the pit, and the looming pit-hill. All was naked and out-of-doors, not a tree! It was quite unaltered.

Syson turned, satisfied, to follow the path that sheered downhill into the wood. He was curiously elated, feeling himself back in an enduring vision. He started. A keeper was standing a few yards in front, barring the way.

"Where might you be going this road, sir?" asked the man. The tone of his question had a challenging twang. Syson looked at the fellow with an impersonal, observant gaze. It was a young man of four- or five-and-twenty, ruddy and well favoured. His dark blue eyes now stared aggressively at the intruder. His black moustache, very thick, was cropped short over a small, rather soft mouth. In every other respect the fellow was manly and good-looking. He stood just above middle height; the strong forward thrust of his chest, and the perfect ease of his erect, self-sufficient body, gave one the feeling that he was taut with animal life, like the thick jet of a fountain balanced in itself. He stood with the butt of his gun on the ground, looking uncertainly and questioningly at Syson. The dark, restless eyes of the trespasser, examining the man and penetrating into him without heeding his office, troubled the keeper and made him flush.

"Where is Naylor? Have you got his job?" Syson asked.

"You're not from the House, are you?" inquired the keeper. It could not be, since everyone was away.

"No, I'm not from the House," the other replied. It seemed to amuse him.

"Then might I ask where you were making for?" said the keeper, nettled.

"Where I am making for?" Syson repeated. "I am going to Willey-Water Farm."

"This isn't the road."

"I think so. Down this path, past the well, and out by the white gate."

"But that's not the public road."

"I suppose not. I used to come so often, in Naylor's time, I had forgotten. Where is he, by the way?"

"Crippled with rheumatism," the keeper answered reluctantly.

"Is he?" Syson exclaimed in pain.

"And who might you be?" asked the keeper, with a new intonation.

"John Adderley Syson; I used to live in Cordy Lane."

"Used to court Hilda Millership?"

Syson's eyes opened with a pained smile. He nodded. There was an awkward silence.

"And you—who are you?" asked Syson.

"Arthur Pilbeam—Naylor's my uncle," said the other.

"You live here in Nuttall?"

"I'm lodgin' at my uncle's—at Naylor's."

"I see!"

"Did you say you was goin' down to Willey-Water?" asked the keeper.

"Yes."

There was a pause of some moments, before the keeper blurted: "*I'm* courtin' Hilda Millership."

The young fellow looked at the intruder with a stubborn defiance, almost pathetic. Syson opened new eyes.

"Are you?" he said, astonished. The keeper flushed dark.

"She and me are keeping company," he said.

"I didn't know!" said Syson. The other man waited uncomfortably.

"What, is the thing settled?" asked the intruder.

"How, settled?" retorted the other sulkily.

"Are you going to get married soon, and all that?"

The keeper stared in silence for some moments, impotent.

"I suppose so," he said, full of resentment.

"Ah!" Syson watched closely.

"I'm married myself," he added, after a time.

"You are?" said the other incredulously.

Syson laughed in his brilliant, unhappy way.

"This last fifteen moñths," he said.

The keeper gazed at him with wide, wondering eyes, apparently thinking back, and trying to make things out.

"Why, didn't you know?" asked Syson.

"No, I didn't," said the other sulkily.

There was silence for a moment.

"Ah well!" said Syson, "I will go on. I suppose I may." The

keeper stood in silent opposition. The two men hesitated in
the open, grassy space, set round with small sheaves of sturdy
bluebells; a little open platform on the brow of the hill. Syson
took a few indecisive steps forward, then stopped.

"I say, how beautiful!" he cried.

He had come in full view of the downslope. The wide path
ran from his feet like a river, and it was full of bluebells,
save for a green winding thread down the centre, where the
keeper walked. Like a stream the path opened into azure
shallows at the levels, and there were pools of bluebells, with
still the green thread winding through, like a thin current of
ice-water through blue lakes. And from under the twig-purple
of the bushes swam the shadowed blue, as if the flowers lay
in flood water over the woodland.

"Ah, isn't it lovely!" Syson exclaimed; this was his past, the
country he had abandoned, and it hurt him to see it so
beautiful. Wood-pigeons cooed overhead, and the air was full
of the brightness of birds singing.

"If you're married, what do you keep writing to her for,
and sending her poetry books and things?" asked the keeper.
Syson stared at him, taken aback and humiliated. Then he
began to smile.

"Well," he said, "I did not know about you . . ."

Again the keeper flushed darkly.

"But if you are married——" he charged.

"I am," answered the other cynically.

Then, looking down the blue, beautiful path, Syson felt his
own humiliation. "What right *have* I to hang on to her?" he
thought, bitterly self-contemptuous.

"She knows I'm married and all that," he said.

"But you keep sending her books," challenged the keeper.

Syson, silenced, looked at the other man quizzically, half
pitying. Then he turned.

"Good day," he said, and was gone. Now, everything
irritated him: the two sallows, one all gold and perfume and
murmur, one silver-green and bristly, reminded him that here
he had taught her about pollination. What a fool he was!
What god-forsaken folly it all was!

"Ah well," he said to himself; "the poor devil seems to

have a grudge against me. I'll do my best for him." He grinned to himself, in a very bad temper.

II

The farm was less than a hundred yards from the wood's edge. The wall of trees formed the fourth side to the open quadrangle. The house faced the wood. With tangled emotions, Syson noted the plum blossom falling on the profuse, coloured primroses, which he himself had brought here and set. How they had increased! There were thick tufts of scarlet, and pink, and pale purple primroses under the plum trees. He saw somebody glance at him through the kitchen window, heard men's voices.

The door opened suddenly: very womanly she had grown! He felt himself going pale.

"You?—Addy!" she exclaimed, and stood motionless.

"Who?" called the farmer's voice. Men's low voices answered. Those low voices, curious and almost jeering, roused the tormented spirit in the visitor. Smiling brilliantly at her, he waited.

"Myself—why not?" he said.

The flush burned very deep on her cheek and throat.

"We are just finishing dinner," she said.

"Then I will stay outside." He made a motion to show that he would sit on the red earthenware pipkin that stood near the door among the daffodils, and contained the drinking-water.

"Oh no, come in," she said hurriedly. He followed her. In the doorway, he glanced swiftly over the family, and bowed. Everyone was confused. The farmer, his wife, and the four sons sat at the coarsely laid dinner-table, the men with arms bare to the elbows.

"I am sorry I come at lunch-time," said Syson.

"Hello, Addy!" said the farmer, assuming the old form of address, but his tone cold. "How are you?"

And he shook hands.

"Shall you have a bit?" he invited the young visitor, but taking for granted the offer would be refused. He assumed that Syson was become too refined to eat so roughly. The young man winced at the imputation.

"Have you had any dinner?" asked the daughter.

"No," replied Syson. "It is too early. I shall be back at half-past one."

"You call it lunch, don't you?" asked the eldest son, almost ironical. He had once been an intimate friend of this young man.

"We'll give Addy something when we've finished," said the mother, an invalid, deprecating.

"No—don't trouble. I don't want to give you any trouble," said Syson.

"You could allus live on fresh air an' scenery," laughed the youngest son, a lad of nineteen.

Syson went round the buildings, and into the orchard at the back of the house, where daffodils all along the hedgerow swung like yellow, ruffled birds on their perches. He loved the place extraordinarily, the hills ranging round, with bear-skin woods covering their giant shoulders, and small red farms like brooches clasping their garments; the blue streak of water in the valley, the bareness of the home pasture, the sound of myriad-threaded bird-singing, which went mostly unheard. To his last day, he would dream of this place, when he felt the sun on his face, or saw the small handfuls of snow between the winter twigs, or smelt the coming of spring.

Hilda was very womanly. In her presence he felt constrained. She was twenty-nine, as he was, but she seemed to him much older. He felt foolish, almost unreal beside her. She was so static. As he was fingering some shed plum blossom on a low bough, she came to the back door to shake the tablecloth. Fowls raced from the stack-yard, birds rustled from the trees. Her dark hair was gathered up in a coil like a crown on her head. She was very straight, distant in her bearing. As she folded the cloth, she looked away over the hills.

Presently Syson returned indoors. She had prepared eggs and curd cheese, stewed gooseberries and cream.

"Since you will dine to-night," she said, "I have only given you a light lunch."

"It is awfully nice," he said. "You keep a real idyllic atmosphere—your belt of straw and ivy buds."

Still they hurt each other.

He was uneasy before her. Her brief, sure speech, her distant bearing, were unfamiliar to him. He admired again her grey-black eyebrows, and her lashes. Their eyes met. He saw, in the beautiful grey and black of her glances, tears and a strange light, and at the back of all, calm acceptance of herself, and triumph over him.

He felt himself shrinking. With an effort he kept up the ironic manner.

She sent him into the parlour while she washed the dishes. The long low room was refurnished from the Abbey sale, with chairs upholstered in claret-coloured rep, many years old, and an oval table of polished walnut, and another piano, handsome, though still antique. In spite of the strangeness, he was pleased. Opening a high cupboard let into the thickness of the wall, he found it full of his books, his old lesson-books, and volumes of verse he had sent her, English and German. The daffodils in the white window-bottoms shone across the room, he could almost feel their rays. The old glamour caught him again. His youthful water-colours on the wall no longer made him grin; he remembered how fervently he had tried to paint for her, twelve years before.

She entered, wiping a dish, and he saw again the bright, kernel-white beauty of her arms.

"You are quite spendid here," he said, and their eyes met.

"Do you like it?" she asked. It was the old, low, husky tone of intimacy. He felt a quick change beginning in his blood. It was the old, delicious sublimation, the thinning, almost the vaporising of himself, as if his spirit were to be liberated.

"Aye," he nodded, smiling at her like a boy again. She bowed her head.

"This was the countess's chair," she said in low tones. "I found her scissors down here between the padding."

"Did you? Where are they?"

Quickly, with a lilt in her movement, she fetched her

workbasket, and together they examined the long-shanked old scissors.

"What a ballad of dead ladies!" he said, laughing, as he fitted his fingers into the round loops of the countess's scissors.

"I knew you could use them," she said, with certainty. He looked at his fingers, and at the scissors. She meant his fingers were fine enough for the small-looped scissors.

"That is something to be said for me," he laughed, putting the scissors aside. She turned to the window. He noticed the fine, fair down on her cheeks and her upper lip, and her soft, white neck, like the throat of a nettle flower, and her forearms, bright as newly blanched kernels. He was looking at her with new eyes, and she was a different person to him. He did not know her. But he could regard her objectively now.

"Shall we go out awhile?" she asked.

"Yes!" he answered. But the predominant emotion, that troubled the excitement and perplexity of his heart, was fear, fear of that which he saw. There was about her the same manner, the same intonation in her voice, now as then, but she was not what he had known her to be. He knew quite well what she had been for him. And gradually he was realising that she was something quite other, and always had been.

She put no covering on her head, merely took off her apron, saying: "We will go by the larches." As they passed the old orchard, she called him in to show him a blue-tit's nest in one of the apple trees, and a sycock's in the hedge. He rather wondered at her surety, at a certain hardness like arrogance hidden under her humility.

"Look at the apple buds," she said, and he then perceived myriads of little scarlet balls among the drooping boughs. Watching his face, her eyes went hard. She saw the scales were fallen from him, and at last he was going to see her as she was. It was the thing she had most dreaded in the past, and most needed, for her soul's sake. Now he was going to see her as she was. He would not love her, and he would know he never could have loved her. The old illusion gone, they were strangers, crude and entire. But he would give her her due—she would have her due from him.

She was brilliant as he had not known her. She showed him nests: a jenny wren's in a low bush.

"See this jinty's!" she exclaimed.

He was surprised to hear her use the local name. She reached carefully through the thorns, and put her finger in the nest's round door.

"Five!" she said. "Tiny little things."

She showed him nests of robins, and chaffinches, and linnets, and buntings; of a wagtail beside the water.

"And if we go down, nearer the lake, I will show you a kingfisher's. . . ."

"Among the young fir trees," she said, "there's a throstle's or a blackie's on nearly every bough, every ledge. The first day, when I had seen them all, I felt as if I mustn't go in the wood. It seemed a city of birds: and in the morning, hearing them all, I thought of the noisy market. I was afraid to go in my own wood."

She was using the language they had both of them invented. Now it was all her own. He had done with it. She did not mind his silence, but was always dominant, letting him see her wood. As they came along a marshy path where forget-me-nots were opening in a rich blue drift: "We know all the birds, but there are many flowers we can't find out," she said. It was half an appeal to him, who had known the names of things.

She looked dreamily across to the open fields that slept in the sun.

"I have a lover as well, you know," she said, with assurance, yet dropping again almost into the intimate tone.

This woke in him the spirit to fight her.

"I think I met him. He is good-looking—also in Arcady."

Without answering, she turned into a dark path that led uphill, where the trees and undergrowth were very thick.

"They did well," she said at length, "to have various altars to various gods, in old days."

"Ah yes!" he agreed. "To whom is the new one?"

"There are no old ones," she said. "I was always looking for this."

"And whose is it?" he asked.

"I don't know," she said, looking full at him.

"I'm very glad, for your sake," he said, "that you are satisfied."

"Aye—but the man doesn't matter so much," she said. There was a pause.

"No!" he exclaimed, astonished, yet recognising her as her real self.

"It is one's self that matters," she said. "Whether one is being one's own self and serving one's own God."

There was silence, during which he pondered. The path was almost flowerless, gloomy. At the side, his heels sank into soft clay.

III

"I," she said, very slowly, "I was married the same night as you."

He looked at her.

"Not legally, of course," she replied. "But—actually."

"To the keeper?" he said, not knowing what else to say.

She turned to him.

"You thought I could not?" she said. But the flush was deep in her cheek and throat, for all her assurance.

Still he would not say anything.

"You see"—she was making an effort to explain—"*I* had to understand also."

"And what does it amount to, this *understanding*?" he asked.

"A very great deal—does it not to you?" she replied. "One is free."

"And you are not disappointed?"

"Far from it!" Her tone was deep and sincere.

"You love him?"

"Yes, I love him."

"Good!" he said.

This silenced her for a while.

"Here, among his things, I love him," she said.

His conceit would not let him be silent.

"It needs this setting?" he asked.

"It does," she cried. "You were always making me to be not myself."

He laughed shortly.

"But is it a matter of surroundings?" he said. He had considered her all spirit.

"I am like a plant," she replied. "I can only grow in my own soil."

They came to a place where the undergrowth shrank away, leaving a bare, brown space, pillared with the brick-red and purplish trunks of pine trees. On the fringe, hung the sombre green of elder trees, with flat flowers in bud, and below were bright, unfurling pennons of fern. In the midst of the bare space stood a keeper's log hut. Pheasant-coops were lying about, some occupied by a clucking hen, some empty.

Hilda walked over the brown pine-needles to the hut, took a key from among the eaves, and opened the door. It was a bare wooden place with a carpenter's bench and form, carpenter's tools, an axe, snares, traps, some skins pegged down, everything in order. Hilda closed the door. Syson examined the weird flat coats of wild animals, that were pegged down to be cured. She turned some knotch in the side wall, and disclosed a second, small apartment.

"How romantic!" said Syson.

"Yes. He is very curious—he has some of a wild animal's cunning—in a nice sense—and he is inventive, and thoughtful—but not beyond a certain point."

She pulled back a dark green curtain. The apartment was occupied almost entirely by a large couch of heather and bracken, on which was spread an ample rabbit-skin rug. On the floor were patchwork rugs of cat-skin, and a red calf-skin, while hanging from the wall were other furs. Hilda took down one, which she put on. It was a cloak of rabbit-skin and of white fur, with a hood, apparently of the skin of stoats. She laughed at Syson from out of this barbaric mantle, saying:

"What do you think of it?"

"Ah——! I congratulate you on your man," he replied.

"And look!" she said.

In a little jar on a shelf were some sprays, frail and white, of the first honeysuckle.

"They will scent the place at night."

He looked round curiously.

"Where does he come short, then?" he asked. She gazed at him for a few moments. Then, turning aside:

"The stars aren't the same with him," she said. "You could make them flash and quiver, and the forget-me-nots come up at me like phosphorescence. You could make things *wonderful*. I have found it out—it is true. But I have them all for myself, now."

He laughed, saying:

"After all, stars and forget-me-nots are only luxuries. You ought to make poetry."

"Aye," she assented. "But I have them all now."

Again he laughed bitterly at her.

She turned swiftly. He was leaning against the small window of the tiny, obscure room, and was watching her, who stood in the doorway, still cloaked in her mantle. His cap was removed, so she saw his face and head distinctly in the dim room. His black, straight, glossy hair was brushed clean back from his brow. His black eyes were watching her, and his face, that was clear and cream, and perfectly smooth, was flickering.

"We are very different," she said bitterly.

Again he laughed.

"I see you disapprove of me," he said.

"I disapprove of what you have become," she said.

"You think we might"—he glanced at the hut—"have been like this—you and I?"

She shook her head.

"You! No; never! You plucked a thing and looked at it till you had found out all you wanted to know about it, then you threw it away," she said.

"Did I?" he asked. "And could your way never have been my way? I suppose not."

"Why should it?" she said. "I am a separate being."

"But surely two people sometimes go the same way," he said.

"You took me away from myself," she said.

He knew he had mistaken her, had taken her for something she was not. That was his fault, not hers.

"And did you always know?" he asked.

"No—you never let me know. You bullied me. I couldn't help myself. I was glad when you left me, really."

"I know you were," he said. But his face went paler, almost deathly luminous.

"Yet," he said, "it was you who sent me the way I have gone."

"I!" she exclaimed, in pride.

"You *would* have me take the Grammar School scholarship—and you would have me foster poor little Botell's fervent attachment to me, till he couldn't live without me—and because Botell was rich and influential. You triumphed in the wine-merchant's offer to send me to Cambridge, to befriend his only child. You wanted me to rise in the world. And all the time you were sending me away from you—every new success of mine put a separation between us, and more for you than for me. You never wanted to come with me: you wanted just to send me to see what it was like. I believe you even wanted me to marry a lady. You wanted to triumph over society in me."

"And I am responsible," she said, with sarcasm.

"I distinguished myself to satisfy you," he replied.

"Ah!" she cried, "you always wanted change, change, like a child."

"Very well! And I am a success, and I know it, and I do some good work. But—I thought you were different. What right have you to a man?"

"What do you want?" she said, looking at him with wide, fearful eyes.

He looked back at her, his eyes pointed, like weapons.

"Why, nothing," he laughed shortly.

There was a rattling at the outer latch, and the keeper entered. The woman glanced round, but remained standing, fur-cloaked, in the inner doorway. Syson did not move.

The other man entered, saw, and turned away without speaking. The two also were silent.

Pilbeam attended to his skins.

"I must go," said Syson.

"Yes," she replied.

"Then I give you 'To our vast and varying fortunes.' " He lifted his hand in pledge.

" 'To our vast and varying fortunes,' " she answered gravely, and speaking in cold tones.

"Arthur!" she said.

The keeper pretended not to hear. Syson, watching keenly, began to smile. The woman drew herself up.

"Arthur!" she said again, with a curious upward inflection, which warned the two men that her soul was trembling on a dangerous crisis.

The keeper slowly put down his tool and came to her.

"Yes," he said.

"I wanted to introduce you," she said, trembling.

"I've met him a'ready," said the keeper.

"Have you? It is Addy, Mr. Syson, whom you know about. —This is Arthur, Mr. Pilbeam," she added, turning to Syson. The latter held out his hand to the keeper, and they shook hands in silence.

"I'm glad to have met you," said Syson. "We drop our correspondence, Hilda?"

"Why need we?" she asked.

The two men stood at a loss.

"*Is* there no need?" said Syson.

Still she was silent.

"It is as you will," she said.

They went all three together down the gloomy path.

" 'Qu'il était bleu, le ciel, et grand l'espoir,' " quoted Syson, not knowing what to say.

"What do you mean?" she said. "Besides, *we* can't walk in *our* wild oats—we never sowed any."

Syson looked at her. He was startled to see his young love, his nun, his Botticelli angel, so revealed. It was he who had been the fool. He and she were more separate than any two strangers could be. She only wanted to keep up a correspondence with him—and he, of course, wanted it kept up, so that he could write to her, like Dante to some Beatrice who had never existed save in the man's own brain.

At the bottom of the path she left him. He went along with the keeper, towards the open, towards the gate that closed on the wood. The two men walked almost like friends. They did not broach the subject of their thoughts.

.   .   .   .   .

Instead of going straight to the high-road gate, Syson went along the woods' edge, where the brook spread out in a little bog, and under the alder trees, among the reeds, great yellow stools and bosses of marigolds shone. Threads of brown water trickled by, touched with gold from the flowers. Suddenly there was a blue flash in the air, as a kingfisher passed.

Syson was extraordinarily moved. He climbed the bank to the gorse bushes, whose sparks of blossom had not yet gathered into a flame. Lying on the dry brown turf, he discovered sprigs of tiny purple milkwort and pink spots of lousewort. What a wonderful world it was—marvellous, for ever new. He felt as if it were underground, like the fields of monotone hell, notwithstanding. Inside his breast was a pain like a wound. He remembered the poem of William Morris, where in the Chapel of Lyonesse a knight lay wounded, with the truncheon of a spear deep in his breast, lying always as dead, yet did not die, while day after day the coloured sunlight dipped from the painted window across the chancel, and passed away. He knew now it never had been true, that which was between him and her, not for a moment. The truth had stood apart all the time.

Syson turned over. The air was full of the sound of larks, as if the sunshine above were condensing and falling in a shower. Amid this bright sound, voices sounded small and distinct.

"But if he's married, an' quite willing to drop it off, what has ter against it?" said the man's voice.

"I don't want to talk about it now. I want to be alone."

Syson looked through the bushes. Hilda was standing in the wood, near the gate. The man was in the field, loitering by the hedge, and playing with the bees as they settled on the white bramble flowers.

There was silence for a while, in which Syson imagined her will among the brightness of the larks. Suddenly the keeper exclaimed "Ah!" and swore. He was gripping at the sleeve of his coat, near the shoulder. Then he pulled off his jacket, threw it on the ground, and absorbedly rolled up his shirt-sleeves right to the shoulder.

"Ah!" he said vindictively, as he picked out the bee and flung it away. He twisted his fine, bright arm, peering awkwardly over his shoulder.

"What is it?" asked Hilda.

"A bee—crawled up my sleeve," he answered.

"Come here to me," she said.

The keeper went to her, like a sulky boy. She took his arm in her hands.

"Here it is—and the sting left in—poor bee!"

She picked out the sting, put her mouth to his arm, and sucked away the drop of poison. As she looked at the red mark her mouth had made, and at his arm, she said, laughing:

"That is the reddest kiss you will ever have."

When Syson next looked up, at the sound of voices, he saw in the shadow the keeper with his mouth on the throat of his beloved, whose head was thrown back, and whose hair had fallen, so that one rough rope of dark brown hair hung across his bare arm.

"No," the woman answered. "I am not upset because he's gone. You won't understand. . . ."

Syson could not distinguish what the man said. Hilda replied, clear and distinct:

"You know I love you. He has gone quite out of my life—don't trouble about him. . . ." He kissed her, murmuring. She laughed hollowly.

"Yes," she said, indulgent. "We will be married, we will be married. But not just yet." He spoke to her again. Syson heard nothing for a time. Then she said:

"You must go home now, dear—you will get no sleep."

Again was heard the murmur of the keeper's voice, troubled by fear and passion.

"But why should we be married at once?" she said. "What more would you have, by being married? It is most beautiful as it is."

At last he pulled on his coat and departed. She stood at the gate, not watching him, but looking over the sunny country.

When at last she had gone, Syson also departed, going back to town.

The White Stocking

I

"I'M GETTING up, Teddilinks," said Mrs. Whiston, and she sprang out of bed briskly.

"What the Hanover's got you?" asked Whiston.

"Nothing. Can't I get up?" she replied animatedly.

It was about seven oclock, scarcely light yet in the cold bedroom. Whiston lay still and looked at his wife. She was a pretty little thing, with her fleecy, short black hair all tousled. He watched her as she dressed quickly, flicking her small, delightful limbs, throwing her clothes about her. Her slovenliness and untidiness did not trouble him. When she picked up the edge of her petticoat, ripped off a torn string of white lace, and flung it on the dressing-table, her careless abandon made his spirit glow. She stood before the mirror and roughly scrambled together her profuse little mane of hair. He watched the quickness and softness of her young shoulders, calmly, like a husband, and appreciatively.

"Rise up," she cried, turning to him with a quick wave of her arm—"and shine forth."

They had been married two years. But still, when she had gone out of the room, he felt as if all his light and warmth were taken away, he became aware of the raw, cold morning. So he rose himself, wondering casually what had roused her so early. Usually she lay in bed as late as she could.

Whiston fastened a belt round his loins and went downstairs in shirt and trousers. He heard her singing in her snatchy fashion. The stairs creaked under his weight. He passed down the narrow little passage, which she called a hall, of the seven and sixpenny house which was his first home.

He was a shapely young fellow of about twenty-eight,

sleepy now and easy with well-being. He heard the water drumming into the kettle, and she began to whistle. He loved the quick way she dodged the supper cups under the tap to wash them for breakfast. She looked an untidy minx, but she was quick and handy enough.

"Teddilinks," she cried.

"What?"

"Light a fire, quick."

She wore an old, sack-like dressing-jacket of black silk pinned across her breast. But one of the sleeves, coming unfastened, showed some delightful pink upper-arm.

"Why don't you sew your sleeve up?" he said, suffering from the sight of the exposed soft flesh.

"Where?" she cried, peering round. "Nuisance," she said, seeing the gap, then with light fingers went on drying the cups.

The kitchen was of fair size, but gloomy. Whiston poked out the dead ashes.

Suddenly a thud was heard at the door down the passage.

"I'll go," cried Mrs. Whiston, and she was gone down the hall.

The postman was a ruddy-faced man who had been a soldier. He smiled broadly, handing her some packages.

"They've not forgot you," he said impudently.

"No—lucky for them," she said, with a toss of the head. But she was interested only in her envelopes this morning. The postman waited inquisitively, smiling in an ingratiating fashion. She slowly, abstractedly, as if she did not know anyone was there, closed the door in his face, continuing to look at the addresses on her letters.

She tore open the thin envelope. There was a long, hideous, cartoon valentine. She smiled briefly and dropped it on the floor. Struggling with the string of a packet, she opened a white cardboard box, and there lay a white silk handkerchief packed neatly under the paper lace of the box, and her initial, worked in heliotrope, fully displayed. She smiled pleasantly, and gently put the box aside. The third envelope contained another white packet—apparently a cotton handkerchief neatly folded. She shook it out. It was a long white stocking, but there was a little weight in the toe. Quickly, she thrust down her arm, wriggling her fingers into the toe of the stocking, and brought out a small box. She peeped inside the box, then hastily opened a door on her left hand, and went into the little cold sitting-room. She had her lower lip caught earnestly between her teeth.

With a little flash of triumph, she lifted a pair of pearl earrings from the small box, and she went to the mirror. There, earnestly, she began to hook them through her ears, looking at herself sideways in the glass. Curiously concentrated and intent she seemed as she fingered the lobes of her ears, her head bent on one side.

Then the pearl ear-rings dangled under her rosy, small ears. She shook her head sharply, to see the swing of the drops. They went chill against her neck, in little, sharp touches. Then she stood still to look at herself, bridling her head in the dignified fashion. Then she simpered at herself. Catching her own eye, she could not help winking at herself and laughing.

She turned to look at the box. There was a scrap of paper with this posy:

> "Pears may be fair, but thou art fairer.
> Wear these for me, and I'll love the wearer."

She made a grimace and a grin. But she was drawn to the mirror again, to look at her ear-rings.

Whiston had made the fire burn, so he came to look for her. When she heard him, she started round quickly, guiltily. She was watching him with intent blue eyes when he appeared.

He did not see much, in his morning-drowsy warmth. He gave her, as ever, a feeling of warmth and slowness. His eyes were very blue, very kind, his manner simple.

"What ha' you got?" he asked.

"Valentines," she said briskly, ostentatiously turning to show him the silk handkerchief. She thrust it under his nose. "Smell how good," she said.

"Who's that from?" he replied, without smelling.

"It's a valentine," she cried. "How do I know who it's from?"

"I'll bet you know," he said.

"Ted!—I don't!" she cried, beginning to shake her head, then stopping because of the ear-rings.

He stood still a moment, displeased.

"They've no right to send you valentines now," he said.

"Ted!—Why not? You're not jealous, are you? I haven't the least idea who it's from. Look—there's my initial"—she pointed with an emphatic finger at the heliotrope embroidery——

"E for Elsie,
Nice little gelsie,"

she sang.

"Get out," he said. "You know who it's from."

"Truth, I don't," she cried.

He looked round, and saw the white stocking lying on a chair.

"Is this another?" he said.

"No, that's a sample," she said. "There's only a comic." And she fetched in the long cartoon.

He stretched it out and looked at it solemnly.

"Fools!" he said, and went out of the room.

She flew upstairs and took off the ear-rings. When she returned, he was crouched before the fire blowing the coals. The skin of his face was flushed, and slightly pitted, as if he had had small-pox. But his neck was white and smooth and goodly. She hung her arms around his neck as he crouched there, and clung to him. He balanced on his toes.

"This fire's a slow-coach," he said.

"And who else is a slow-coach?" she said.

"One of us two, I know," he said, and he rose carefully. She remained clinging round his neck, so that she was lifted off her feet.

"Ha!—swing me," she cried.

He lowered his head, and she hung in the air, swinging from his neck, laughing. Then she slipped off.

"The kettle is singing," she sang, flying for the teapot. He bent down again to blow the fire. The veins in his neck stood out, his shirt collar seemed too tight.

> "Doctor Wyer,
> Blow the fire,
> Puff! puff! puff!"

she sang, laughing.

He smiled at her.

She was so glad because of her pearl ear-rings.

Over the breakfast she grew serious. He did not notice. She became portentous in her gravity. Almost it penetrated through his steady good-humour to irritate him.

"Teddy!" she said at last.

"What?" he asked.

"I told you a lie," she said, humbly tragic.

His soul stirred uneasily.

"Oh aye?" he said casually.

She was not satisfied. He ought to be more moved.

"Yes," she said.

He cut a piece of bread.

"Was it a good one?" he asked.

She was piqued. Then she considered—*was* it a good one? Then she laughed.

"No," she said, "it wasn't up to much."

"Ah!" he said easily, but with a steady strength of fondness for her in his tone. "Get it out then."

It became a little more difficult.

"You know that white stocking," she said earnestly. "I told you a lie. It wasn't a sample. It was a valentine."

A little frown came on his brow.

"Then what did you invent it as a sample for?" he said. But he knew this weakness of hers. The touch of anger in his voice frightened her.

"I was afraid you'd be cross," she said pathetically.

"I'll bet you were vastly afraid," he said.

"I *was*, Teddy."

There was a pause. He was resolving one or two things in his mind.

"And who sent it?" he asked.

"I can guess," she said, "though there wasn't a word with it—except——"

She ran to the sitting-room and returned with a slip of paper.

"Pearls may be fair, but thou art fairer.
Wear these for me, and I'll love the wearer."

He read it twice, then a dull red flush came on his face.

"And *who* do you guess it is?" he asked, with a ringing of anger in his voice.

"I suspect it's Sam Adams," she said, with a little virtuous indignation.

Whiston was silent for a moment.

"Fool!" he said. "An' what's it got to do with pearls?—and how can he say 'wear these for me' when there's only one? He hasn't got the brain to invent a proper verse."

He screwed the slip of paper into a ball and flung it into the fire.

"I suppose he thinks it'll make a pair with the one last year," she said.

"Why, did he send one then?"

"Yes. I thought you'd be wild if you knew."

His jaw set rather sullenly.

Presently he rose, and went to wash himself, rolling back his sleeves and pulling open his shirt at the breast. It was as if his fine, clear-cut temples and steady eyes were degraded by the lower, rather brutal part of his face. But she loved it. As she whisked about, clearing the table, she loved the way in which he stood washing himself. He was such a man. She liked to see his neck glistening with water as he swilled it. It amused her and pleased her and thrilled her. He was so sure, so permanent, he had her so utterly in his power. It gave her a delightful, mischievous sense of liberty. Within his grasp, she could dart about excitingly.

He turned round to her, his face red from the cold water, his eyes fresh and very blue.

"You haven't been seeing anything of him, have you?" he asked roughly.

"Yes," she answered, after a moment, as if caught guilty. "He got into the tram with me, and he asked me to drink a coffee and a Benedictine in the Royal."

"You've got it off fine and glib," he said sullenly. "And did you?"

"Yes," she replied, with the air of a traitor before the rack.

The blood came up into his neck and face, he stood motionless, dangerous.

"It was cold, and it was such fun to go into the Royal," she said.

"You'd go off with a nigger for a packet of chocolate," he said, in anger and contempt, and some bitterness. Queer how he drew away from her, cut her off from him.

"Ted—how beastly!" she cried. "You know quite well——" She caught her lip, flushed, and the tears came to her eyes.

He turned away, to put on his neck-tie. She went about her work, making a queer pathetic little mouth, down which occasionally dripped a tear.

He was ready to go. With his hat jammed down on his head, and his overcoat buttoned up to his chin, he came to kiss her. He would be miserable all the day if he went without. She allowed herself to be kissed. Her cheek was wet under his lip, and his heart burned. She hurt him so deeply. And she felt aggrieved, and did not quite forgive him.

In a moment she went upstairs to her ear-rings. Sweet they looked nestling in the little drawer—sweet! She examined them with voluptuous pleasure, she threaded them in her ears, she looked at herself, she posed and postured and smiled and looked sad and tragic and winning and appealing, all in turn before the mirror. And she was happy, and very pretty.

She wore her ear-rings all morning, in the house. She was self-conscious, and quite brilliantly winsome, when the baker came, wondering if he would notice. All the tradesmen left her door with a glow in them, feeling elated, and unconsciously favouring the delightful little creature, though there had been nothing to notice in her behaviour.

She was stimulated all the day. She did not think about her husband. He was the permanent basis from which she took these giddly little flights into nowhere. At night, like chickens and curses, she would come home to him, to roost.

Meanwhile Whiston, a traveller and confidential support of a small firm, hastened about his work, his heart all the while anxious for her, yearning for surety, and kept tense by not getting it.

II

She had been a warehouse girl in Adams's lace factory before she was married. Sam Adams was her employer. He was a bachelor of forty, growing stout, a man well dressed and florid, with a large brown moustache and thin hair. From the rest of his well-groomed, showy appearance, it was evident his baldness was a chagrin to him. He had a good presence, and some Irish blood in his veins.

His fondness for the girls, or the fondness of the girls for him, was notorious. And Elsie, quick, pretty, almost witty little thing—see *seemed* witty, although, when her sayings were repeated, they were entirely trivial—she had a great attraction for him. He would come into the warehouse dressed in a rather sporting reefer coat, of fawn colour, and trousers of fine black-and-white check, a cap with a big peak and scarlet carnation in his button-hole, to impress her. She was only half impressed. He was too loud for her good taste. Instinctively perceiving this, he sobered down to navy blue. Then a well-built man, florid, with large brown whiskers, smart navy blue suit, fashionable boots, and manly hat, he was the irreproachable. Elsie was impressed.

But meanwhile Whiston was courting her, and she made splendid little gestures, before her bedroom mirror, of the constant-and-true sort.

"True, true till death——"

That was her song. Whiston was made that way, so there was no need to take thought for him.

Every Christmas Sam Adams gave a party at his house, to which he invited his superior work-people—not factory hands and labourers, but those above. He was a generous man in his way, with a real warm feeling for giving pleasure.

Two years ago Elsie had attended this Christmas-party for the last time. Whiston had accompanied her. At that time he worked for Sam Adams.

She had been very proud of herself, in her close-fitting, full-skirted dress of blue silk. Whiston called for her. Then she tripped beside him, holding her large cashmere shawl across her breast. He strode with long strides, his trousers handsomely strapped under his boots, and her silk shoes bulging the pocket of his full-skirted overcoat.

They passed through the park gates, and her spirits rose. Above them the Castle Rock loomed grandly in the night, the naked trees stood still and dark in the frost, along the boulevard.

They were rather late. Agitated with anticipation, in the cloak-room she gave up her shawl, donned her silk shoes, and looked at herself in the mirror. The loose bunches of curls on either side her face danced prettily, her mouth smiled.

She hung a moment in the door of the brilliantly lighted room. Many people were moving within the blaze of lamps, under the crystal chandeliers, the full skirts of the women balancing and floating, the side-whiskers and white cravats of the men bowing above. Then she entered the light.

In an instant Sam Adams was coming forward, lifting both his arms in boisterous welcome. There was a constant red laugh on his face.

"Come late, would you," he shouted, "like royalty."

He seized her hands and led her forward. He opened his mouth wide when he spoke, and the effect of the warm, dark opening behind the brown whiskers was disturbing. But she was floating into the throng on his arm. He was very gallant.

"Now then," he said, taking her card to write down the dances, "I've got *carte blanche*, haven't I?"

"Mr. Whiston doesn't dance," she said.

"I am a lucky man!" he said, scribbling his initials. "I was born with an *amourette* in my mouth."

He wrote on, quietly. She blushed and laughed, not knowing what it meant.

"Why, what is that?" she said.

"It's you, even littler than you are, dressed in little wings," he said.

"I should have to be pretty small to get in your mouth," she said.

"You think you're too big, do you!" he said easily.

He handed her her card, with a bow.

"Now I'm set up, my darling, for this evening," he said.

Then, quick, always at his ease, he looked over the room. She waited in front of him. He was ready. Catching the eye of the band, he nodded. In a moment, the music began. He seemed to relax, giving himself up.

"Now then, Elsie," he said, with a curious caress in his voice that seemed to lap the outside of her body in a warm glow, delicious. She gave herself to it. She liked it.

He was an excellent dancer. He seemed to draw her close in to him by some male warmth of attraction, so that she became all soft and pliant to him, flowing to his form, whilst he united her with him and they lapsed along in one movement. She was just carried in a kind of strong, warm flood, her feet moved of themselves, and only the music threw her away from him, threw her back to him, to his clasp, in his strong form moving against her, rhythmically, deliciously.

When it was over, he was pleased and his eyes had a curious gleam which thrilled her and yet had nothing to do with her. Yet it held her. He did not speak to her. He only looked straight into her eyes with a curious, gleaming look that disturbed her fearfully and deliciously. But also there was in his look some of the automatic irony of the *roué*. It left her partly cold. She was not carried away.

She went, driven by an opposite, heavier impulse, to Whiston. He stood looking gloomy, trying to admit that she had a perfect right to enjoy herself apart from him. He received her with rather grudging kindliness.

"Aren't you going to play whist?" she asked.

"Aye," he said. "Directly."

"I do wish you could dance."

"Well, I can't," he said. "So you enjoy yourself."

"But I should enjoy it better if I could dance with you."

"Nay, you're all right," he said. "I'm not made that way."

"Then you ought to be!" she cried.

"Well, it's my fault, not yours. You enjoy yourself," he bade her. Which she proceeded to do, a little bit irked.

She went with anticipation to the arms of Sam Adams, when the time came to dance with him. It *was* so gratifying, irrespective of the man. And she felt a little grudge against Whiston, soon forgotten when her host was holding her near to him, in a delicious embrace. And she watched his eyes, to meet the gleam in them, which gratified her.

She was getting warmed right through, the glow was penetrating into her, driving away everything else. Only in her heart was a little tightness, like conscience.

When she got a chance, she escaped from the dancing-room to the card-room. There in a cloud of smoke, she found Whiston playing cribbage. Radiant, roused, animated, she came up to him and greeted him. She was too strong, too vibrant a note in the quiet room. He lifted his head, and a frown knitted his gloomy forehead.

"Are you playing cribbage? Is it exciting? How are you getting on?" she chattered.

He looked at her. None of these questions needed answering, and he did not feel in touch with her. She turned to the cribbage-board.

"Are you white or red?" she asked.

"He's red," replied the partner.

"Then you're losing," she said, still to Whiston. And she lifted the red peg from the board. "One—two—three—four—five—six—seven—eight—— Right up there you ought to jump——"

"Now put it back in its right place," said Whiston.

"Where was it?" she asked gaily, knowing her transgression. He took the little red peg away from her and stuck it in its hole.

The cards were shuffled.

"What a shame you're losing," said Elsie.

"You'd better cut for him," said the partner.

She did so hastily. The cards were dealt. She put her hand on his shoulder, looking at his cards.

"It's good," she cried, "isn't it?"

He did not answer, but threw down two cards. It moved him more strongly than was comfortable, to have her hand on his shoulder, her curls dangling and touching his ears, whilst she was roused to another man. It made the blood flame over him.

At that moment Sam Adams appeared, florid and boisterous, intoxicated more with himself, with the dancing, than with wine. In his eye the curious, impersonal light gleamed.

"I thought I should find you here, Elsie," he cried boisterously, a disturbing, high note in his voice.

"What made you think so?" she replied, the mischief rousing in her.

The florid, well-built man narrowed his eyes to a smile.

"I should never look for you among the ladies," he said, with a kind of intimate, animal call to her. He laughed, bowed, and offered her his arm.

"Madam, the music waits."

She went almost helplessly, carried along with him, unwilling, yet delighted.

That dance was an intoxication to her. After the first few steps, she felt herself slipping away from herself. She almost knew she was going, she did not even want to go. Yet she must have chosen to go. She lay in the arm of the steady, close man with whom she was dancing, and she seemed to swim away out of contact with the room, into him. She had passed into another, denser element of him, an essential privacy. The room was all vague around her, like an atmosphere, like under sea, with a flow of ghostly, dumb movements. But she herself was held real against her partner, and it seemed she was connected with him, as if the movements of his body and limbs were her own movements, yet not her own movements—and oh, delicious! He also was given up, oblivious, concentrated, into the dance. His eye was unseeing. Only his large, voluptuous body gave off a subtle activity. His fingers seemed to search into her flesh. Every moment, and every moment, she felt she would give way, utterly, and sink molten: the fusion point was coming when she would fuse down into perfect unconsciousness at his feet and knees. But he bore her round the room in the dance, and he seemed to sustain all her body with his limbs, his body, and his warmth seemed to come closer into her, nearer, till it would fuse right through her, and she would be as liquid to him as an intoxication only.

It was exquisite. When it was over, she was dazed, and was scarcely breathing. She stood with him in the middle of the room as if she were alone in a remote place. He bent over her. She expected his lips on her bare shoulder, and waited. Yet they were not alone, they were not alone. It was cruel.

" 'Twas good, wasn't it, my darling?" he said to her, low and delighted. There was a strange impersonality about his low, exultant call that appealed to her irresistibly. Yet why was she aware of some part shut off in her? She pressed his arm, and he led her towards the door.

She was not aware of what she was doing, only a little grain of resistant trouble was in her. The man, possessed, yet with a superficial presence of mind, made way to the dining-room, as if to give her refreshment, cunningly working to his own escape with her. He was molten hot, filmed over with presence of mind, and bottomed with cold disbelief. In the dining-room was Whiston, carrying coffee to the plain, neglected ladies. Elsie saw him, but felt as if he could not see her. She was beyond his reach and ken. A sort of fusion existed between her and the large man at her side. She ate her custard, but an incomplete fusion all the while sustained and contained within the being of her employer.

But she was growing cooler. Whiston came up. She looked at him, and saw him with different eyes. She saw his slim, young man's figure real and enduring before her. That was he. But she was in the spell with the other man, fused with him, and she could not be taken away.

"Have you finished your cribbage?" she asked, with hasty evasion of him.

"Yes," he replied. "Aren't you getting tired of dancing?"

"Not a bit," she said.

"Not she," said Adams heartily. "No girl with any spirit gets tired of dancing. Have something else, Elsie. Come— sherry. Have a glass of sherry with us, Whiston."

Whilst they sipped the wine, Adams watched Whiston almost cunningly, to find his advantage.

"We'd better be getting back—there's the music," he said. "See the women get something to eat, Whiston, will you, there's a good chap."

And he began to draw away. Elsie was drifting helplessly with him. But Whiston put himself beside them, and went along with them. In silence they passed through to the dancing-room. There Adams hesitated, and looked round the room. It was as if he could not see.

A man came hurrying forward, claiming Elsie, and Adams went to his other partner. Whiston stood watching during the dance. She was conscious of him standing there observant of her, like a ghost, or a judgment, or a guardian angel. She was also conscious, must more intimately and personally, of the body of the other man moving somewhere in the room. She still belonged to him, but a feeling of distraction possessed her, and helplessness. Adams danced on, adhering to Elsie, waiting his time, with the persistence of cynicism.

The dance was over. Adams was detained. Elsie found herself beside Whiston. There was something shapely about him as he sat, about his knees and his distinct figure, that she clung to. It was as if he had enduring form. She put her hand on his knee.

"Are you enjoying yourself?" he asked.

"*Ever* so," she replied, with a fervent, yet detached tone.

"It's going on for one o'clock," he said.

"Is it?" she answered. It meant nothing to her.

"Should we be going?" he said.

She was silent. For the first time for an hour or more an inkling of her normal consciousness returned. She resented it.

"What for?" she said.

"I thought you might have had enough," he said.

A slight soberness came over her, an irritation at being frustrated of her illusion.

"Why?" she said.

"We've been here since nine," he said.

That was no answer, no reason. It conveyed nothing to her. She sat detached from him. Across the room Sam Adams glanced at her. She sat there exposed for him.

"You don't want to be too free with Sam Adams," said Whiston cautiously, suffering. "You know what he is."

"How, free?" she asked.

"Why—you don't want to have too much to do with him."

She sat silent. He was forcing her into consciousness of her position. But he could not get hold of her feelings, to change them. She had a curious, perverse desire that he should not.

"I like him," she said.

"What do you find to like in him?" he said, with a hot heart.

"I don't know—but I like him," she said.

She was immutable. He sat feeling heavy and dulled with rage. He was not clear as to what he felt. He sat there unliving whilst she danced. And she, distracted, lost to herself between the opposing forces of the two men, drifted. Between the dances, Whiston kept near to her. She was scarcely conscious. She glanced repeatedly at her card, to see when she would dance again with Adams, half in desire, half in dread. Sometimes she met his steady, glaucous eye as she passed him in the dance. Sometimes she saw the steadiness of his flank as he danced. And it was always as if she rested on his arm, were borne along, up-borne by him, away from herself. And always there was present the other's antagonism. She was divided.

The time came for her to dance with Adams. Oh, the delicious closing of contact with him, of his limbs touching her limbs, his arm supporting her. She seemed to resolve. Whiston had not made himself real to her. He was only a heavy place in her consciousness.

But she breathed heavily, beginning to suffer from the closeness of strain. She was nervous. Adams also was constrained. A tightness, a tension was coming over them all. And he was exasperated, feeling something counteracting physical magnetism, feeling a will stronger with her than his own, intervening in what was becoming a vital necessity to him.

Elsie was almost lost to her own control. As she went forward with him to take her place at the dance, she stooped for her pocket handkerchief. The music sounded for quadrilles. Everybody was ready. Adams stood with his body near her, exerting his attraction over her. He was tense and fighting. She stooped for her pocket handkerchief, and shook it as she rose. It shook out and fell from her hand. With agony, she saw she had taken a white stocking instead of a handkerchief. For a second it lay on the floor, a twist of white stocking. Then, in an instant, Adams picked it up, with a little, surprised laugh of triumph.

"That'll do for me," he whispered—seeming to take possession of her. And he stuffed the stocking in his trousers pocket, and quickly offered her his handkerchief.

The dance began. She felt weak and faint, as if her will were turned to water. A heavy sense of loss came over her. She could not help herself any more. But it was peace.

When the dance was over, Adams yielded her up. Whiston came to her.

"What was it as you dropped?" Whiston asked.

"I thought it was my handkerchief—I'd taken a stocking by mistake," she said, detached and muted.

"And he's got it?"

"Yes."

"What does he mean by that?"

She lifted her shoulders.

"Are you going to let him keep it?" he asked.

"I don't let him."

There was a long pause.

"Am I to go and have it out with him?" he asked, his face flushed, his blue eyes going hard with opposition.

"No," she said, pale.

"Why?"

"No—I don't want you to say anything about it."

He sat exasperated and nonplussed.

"You'll let him keep it, then?" he asked.

She sat silent and made no form of answer.

"What do you mean by it?" he said, dark with fury. And he started up.

"No!" she cried. "Ted!" And she caught hold of him, sharply detaining him.

It made him black with rage. "Why?" he said.

The something about her mouth was pitiful to him. He did not understand, but he felt she must have her reasons.

"Then I'm not stopping here," he said. "Are you coming with me?"

She rose mutely, and they went out of the room. Adams had not noticed.

In a few moments they were in the street.

"What the hell do you mean?" he said, in a black fury.

She went at his side, in silence, neutral.

"That great hog, an' all," he added.

Then they went a long time in silence through the frozen, deserted darkness of the town. She felt she could not go indoors. They were drawing near her house.

"I don't want to go home," she suddenly cried in distress and anguish. "I don't want to go home."

He looked at her.

"Why don't you?" he said.

"I don't want to go home," was all she could sob.

He heard somebody coming.

"Well, we can walk a bit farther," he said.

She was silent again. They passed out of the town into the fields. He held her by the arm—they could not speak.

"What's a-matter?" he asked at length, puzzled.

She began to cry again.

At last he took her in his arms, to soothe her. She sobbed by herself, almost unaware of him.

"Tell me what's a-matter, Elsie," he said. "Tell me what's a-matter—my dear—tell me, then——"

He kissed her wet face, and caressed her. She made no response. He was puzzled and tender and miserable.

At length she became quiet. Then he kissed her, and she put her arms round him, and clung to him very tight, as if for fear and anguish. He held her in his arms, wondering.

"Ted!" she whispered, frantic. "Ted!"

"What, my love?" he answered, becoming also afraid.

"Be good to me," she cried. "Don't be cruel to me."

"No, my pet," he said, amazed and grieved. "Why?"

"Oh, be good to me," she sobbed.

And he held her very safe, and his heart was white-hot with love for her. His mind was amazed. He could only hold her against his chest that was white-hot with love and belief in her. So she was restored at last.

III

She refused to go to her work at Adams's any more. Her father had to submit and she sent in her notice—she was not well. Sam Adams was ironical. But he had a curious patience. He did not fight.

In a few weeks, she and Whiston were married. She loved him with passion and worship, a fierce little abandon of love that moved him to the depths of his being, and gave him a permanent surety and sense of realness in himself. He did not trouble about himself any more: he felt he was fulfilled and now he had only the many things in the world to busy himself about. Whatever troubled him, at the bottom was surety. He had found himself in this love.

They spoke once or twice of the white stocking.

"Ah!" Whiston exclaimed. "What does it matter?"

He was impatient and angry, and could not bear to consider the matter. So it was left unresolved.

She was quite happy at first, carried away by her adoration of her husband. Then gradually she got used to him. He always was the ground of her happiness, but she got used to him, as to the air she breathed. He never got used to her in the same way.

Inside of marriage she found her liberty. She was rid of the responsibility of herself. Her husband must look after that. She was free to get what she could out of her time.

So that, when, after some months, she met Sam Adams, she was not quite as unkind to him as she might have been. With a young wife's new and exciting knowledge of men, she perceived he was in love with her, she knew he had always kept an unsatisfied desire for her. And, sportive, she could not help playing a little with this, though she cared not one jot for the man himself.

When Valentine's day came, which was near the first anniversary of her wedding day, there arrived a white stocking with a little amethyst brooch. Luckily Whiston did not see it, so she said nothing of it to him. She had not the faintest intention of having anything to do with Sam Adams, but once a little brooch was in her possession, it was hers, and she did not trouble her head for a moment how she had come by it. She kept it.

Now she had the pearl ear-rings. They were a more valuable and a more conspicuous present. She would have to ask her mother to give them to her, to explain their presence. She made a little plan in her head. And she was extraordinarily pleased. As for Sam Adams, even if he saw her wearing them, he would not give her away. What fun, if he saw her wearing his ear-rings! She would pretend she had inherited them from her grandmother, her mother's mother. She laughed to herself as she went down-town in the afternoon, the pretty drops dangling in front of her curls. But she saw no one of importance.

Whiston came home tired and depressed. All day the male in him had been uneasy, and this had fatigued him. She was curiously against him, inclined, as she sometimes was nowadays, to make mock of him and jeer at him and cut him off. He did not understand this, and it angered him deeply. She was uneasy before him.

She knew he was in a state of suppressed irritation. The veins stood out on the backs of his hands, his brow was drawn stiffly. Yet she could not help goading him.

"What did you do wi' that white stocking?" he asked, out of a gloomy silence, his voice strong and brutal.

"I put it in a drawer—why?" she replied flippantly.

"Why didn't you put it on the fire-back?" he said harshly. "What are you hoarding it up for?"

"I'm not hoarding it up," she said. "I've got a pair."

He relapsed into gloomy silence. She, unable to move him, ran away upstairs, leaving him smoking by the fire. Again she tried on the ear-rings. Then another little inspiration came to her. She drew on the white stockings, both of them.

Presently she came down in them. Her husband still sat immovable and glowering by the fire.

"Look!" she said. "They'll do beautifully."

And she picked up her skirts to her knees, and twisted round, looking at her pretty legs in the neat stockings.

He filled with unreasonable rage, and took the pipe from his mouth.

"Don't they look nice?" she said. "One from last year and one from this, they just do. Save you buying a pair."

And she looked over her shoulders at her pretty calves, and at the dangling frills of her knickers.

"Put your skirts down and don't make a fool of yourself," he said.

"Why a fool of myself?" she asked.

And she began to dance slowly round the room, kicking up her feet half reckless, half jeering, in ballet-dancer's fashion. Almost fearful, yet in defiance, she kicked up her legs at him, singing as she did so. She resented him.

"You little fool, ha' done with it," he said. "And you'll back-fire them stockings, I'm telling you." He was angry. His face flushed dark, he kept his head bent. She ceased to dance.

"I shan't," she said. "They'll come in very useful."

He lifted his head and watched her, with lighted, dangerous eyes.

"You'll put 'em on the fire-back, I tell you," he said.

It was a war now. She bent forward, in a ballet-dancer's fashion, and put her tongue between her teeth.

"I shan't back-fire them stockings," she sang, repeating his words, "I shan't, I shan't, I shan't."

And she danced round the room doing a high kick to the tune of her words. There was a real biting indifference in her behaviour.

"We'll see whether you will or not," he said, "trollops! You'd like Sam Adams to know you was wearing 'em, wouldn't you? That's what would please you."

"Yes, I'd like him to see how nicely they fit me, he might give me some more then."

And she looked down at her pretty legs.

He knew somehow that she *would* like Sam Adams to see how pretty her legs looked in the white stockings. It made his anger go deep, almost to hatred.

"Yer nasty trolley," he cried. "Put yer petticoats down, and stop being so foul-minded."

"I'm not foul-minded," she said. "My legs are my own. And why shouldn't Sam Adams think they're nice?"

There was a pause. He watched her with eyes glittering to a point.

"Have you been havin' owt to do with him?" he asked.

"I've just spoken to him when I've seen him," she said. "He's not as bad as you would make out."

"Isn't he?" he cried, a certain wakefulness in his voice. "Them who has anything to do wi' him is too bad for me, I tell you."

"Why, what are you frightened of him for?" she mocked.

She was rousing all his uncontrollable anger. He sat glowering. Every one of her sentences stirred him up like a red-hot iron. Soon it would be too much. And she was afraid herself; but she was neither conquered nor convinced.

A curious little grin of hate came on his face. He had a long score against her.

"What am I frightened of him for?" he repeated automatically. "What am I frightened of him for? Why, for you, you stray-running little bitch."

She flushed. The insult went deep into her, right home.

"Well, if you're so dull——" she said, lowering her eyelids, and speaking coldly, haughtily.

"If I'm so dull I'll break your neck the first word you speak to him," he said, tense.

"Pf!" she sneered. "Do you think I'm frightened of you?" She spoke coldly, detached.

She was frightened, for all that, white round the mouth.

His heart was getting hotter.

"You *will* be frightened of me, the next time you have anything to do with him," he said.

"Do you think *you'd* ever be told—ha!"

Her jeering scorn made him go white-hot, molten. He knew he was incoherent, scarcely responsible for what he might do. Slowly, unseeing, he rose and went out of doors, stifled, moved to kill her.

He stood leaning against the garden fence, unable either to see or hear. Below him, far off, fumed the lights of the town. He stood still, unconscious with a black storm of rage, his face lifted to the night.

Presently, still unconscious of what he was doing, he went indoors again. She stood, a small, stubborn figure with tight-pressed lips and big, sullen, childish eyes, watching him, white with fear. He went heavily across the floor and dropped into his chair.

There was a silence.

"*You're* not going to tell me everything I shall do, and everything I shan't," she broke out at last.

He lifted his head.

"I tell you *this*," he said, low and intense. "Have anything to do with Sam Adams, and I'll break your neck."

She laughed, shrill and false.

"How I hate your word 'break your neck'," she said, with a grimace of the mouth. "It sounds so common and beastly. Can't you say something else—"

There was a dead silence.

"And besides," she said, with a queer chirrup of mocking laughter, "what do you know about anything? He sent me an amethyst brooch and a pair of pearl ear-rings."

"He what?" said Whiston, in a suddenly normal voice. His eyes were fixed on her.

"Sent me a pair of pearl ear-rings, and an amethyst brooch," she repeated, mechanically, pale to the lips.

And her big, black, childish eyes watched him, fascinated, held in her spell.

He seemed to thrust his face and his eyes forward at her, as he rose slowly and came to her. She watched transfixed in terror. Her throat made a small sound, as she tried to scream.

Then, quick as lightning, the back of his hand struck her

with a crash across the mouth, and she was flung back blinded against the wall. The shock shook a queer sound out of her. And then she saw him still coming on, his eyes holding her, his fist drawn back, advancing slowly. At any instant the blow might crash into her.

Mad with terror, she raised her hands with a queer clawing movement to cover her eyes and her temples, opening her mouth in a dumb shriek. There was no sound. But the sight of her slowly arrested him. He hung before her, looking at her fixedly, as she stood crouched against the wall with open, bleeding mouth, and wide-staring eyes, and two hands clawing over her temples. And his lust to see her bleed, to break her and destroy her, rose from an old source against her. It carried him. He wanted satisfaction.

But he had seen her standing there, a piteous, horrified thing, and he turned his face aside in shame and nausea. He went and sat heavily in his chair, and a curious ease, almost like sleep, came over his brain.

She walked away from the wall towards the fire, dizzy, white to the lips, mechanically wiping her small, bleeding mouth. He sat motionless. Then, gradually, her breath began to hiss, she shook, and was sobbing silently, in grief for herself. Without looking, he saw. It made his mad desire to destroy her come back.

At length he lifted his head. His eyes were glowing again, fixed on her.

"And what did he give them you for?" he asked, in a steady, unyielding voice.

Her crying dried up in a second. She also was tense.

"They came as valentines," she replied, still not subjugated, even if beaten.

"When, to-day?"

"The pearl ear-rings to-day—the amethyst brooch last year."

"You've had it a year?"

"Yes."

She felt that now nothing would prevent him if he rose to kill her. She could not prevent him any more. She was yielded up to him. They both trembled in the balance, unconscious.

"What have you had to do with him?" he asked, in a barren voice.

"I've not had anything to do with him," she quavered.

"You just kept 'em because they were jewellery?" he said.

A weariness came over him. What was the worth of speaking any more of it? He did not care any more. He was dreary and sick.

She began to cry again, but he took no notice. She kept wiping her mouth on her handkerchief. He could see it, the blood-mark. It made him only more sick and tired of the responsibility of it, the violence, the shame.

When she began to move about again, he raised his head once more from his dead, motionless position.

"Where are the things?" he said.

"They are upstairs," she quavered. She knew the passion had gone down in him.

"Bring them down," he said.

"I won't," she wept with rage. "You're not going to bully me and hit me like that on the mouth."

And she sobbed again. He looked at her in contempt and compassion and in rising anger.

"Where are they?" he said.

"They're in the little drawer under the looking glass," she sobbed.

He went slowly upstairs, struck a match, and found the trinkets. He brought them downstairs in his hand.

"These?" he said, looking at them as they lay in his palm.

She looked at them without answering. She was not interested in them any more.

He looked at the little jewels. They were pretty.

"It's none of their fault," he said to himself.

And he searched round slowly, persistently, for a box. He tied the things up and addressed them to Sam Adams. Then he went out in his slippers to post the little package.

When he came back she was still sitting crying.

"You'd better go to bed," he said.

She paid no attention. He sat by the fire. She still cried.

"I'm sleeping down here," he said. "Go you to bed."

In a few moments she lifted her tear-stained, swollen face and looked at him with eyes all forlorn and pathetic. A great flash of anguish went over his body. He went over, slowly, and very gently took her in his hands. She let herself be taken. Then as she lay against his shoulder, she sobbed aloud:

"I never meant——"

"My love—my little love——" he cried, in anguish of spirit, holding her in his arms.

Odour of Chrysanthemums

I

THE SMALL locomotive engine, Number 4, came clanking, stumbling down from Selston with seven full wagons. It appeared round the corner with loud threats of speed, but the colt that it startled from among the gorse, which still flickered indistinctly in the raw afternoon, out-distanced it at a canter. A woman, walking up the railway line to Underwood, drew back into the hedge, held her basket aside, and watched the footplate of the engine advancing. The trucks thumped heavily past, one by one, with slow inevitable movement, as she stood insignificantly trapped between the jolting black wagons and the hedge; then they curved away towards the coppice where the withered oak leaves dropped noiselessly, while the birds, pulling at the scarlet hips beside the track, made off into the dusk that had already crept into the spinney. In the open, the smoke from the engine sank and cleaved to the rough grass. The fields were dreary and forsaken, and in the marshy strip that led to the whimsey, a reedy pit-pond, the fowls had already abandoned their run among the alders, to roost in the tarred fowl-house. The pit-bank loomed up behind the pond, flames like red sores licking its ashy sides, in the afternoon's stagnant light. Just beyond rose the tapering chimneys and the clumsy black headstocks of Brinsley Colliery. The two wheels were spinning fast up against the sky, and the winding engine rapped out its little spasms. The miners were being turned up.

The engine whistled as it came into the wide bay of railway lines beside the colliery, where rows of trucks stood in harbour.

Miners, single, trailing and in groups, passed like shadows diverging home. At the edge of the ribbed level of sidings squat a low cottage, three steps down from the cinder track. A large bony vine clutched at the house, as if to claw down the tiled roof. Round the bricked yard grew a few wintry primroses. Beyond, the long garden sloped down to a bush-covered brook course. There were some twiggy apple trees, winter-crack trees, and ragged cabbages. Beside the path hung dishevelled pink chrysanthemums, like pink cloths hung on bushes. A woman came stooping out of the felt-covered fowl-house, half-way down the garden. She closed and pad-locked the door, then drew herself erect, having brushed some bits from her white apron.

She was a tall woman of imperious mien, handsome, with definite black eyebrows. Her smooth black hair was parted exactly. For a few moments she stood steadily watching the miners as they passed along the railway: then she turned towards the brook course. Her face was calm and set, her mouth was closed with disillusionment. After a moment she called:

"John!" There was no answer. She waited, and then said distinctly:

"Where are you?"

"Here!" replied a child's sulky voice from among the bushes. The woman looked piercingly through the dusk.

"Are you at that brook?" she asked sternly.

For answer the child showed himself before the raspberry-canes that rose like whips. He was a small, sturdy boy of five. He stood quite still, defiantly.

"Oh!" said the mother, conciliated. "I thought you were down at that wet brook—and you remember what I told you——"

The boy did not move or answer.

"Come, come on in," she said more gently, "it's getting dark. There's your grandfather's engine coming down the line!"

The lad advanced slowly, with resentful, taciturn move-ment. He was dressed in trousers and waistcoat of cloth that was too thick and hard for the size of the garments. They were evidently cut down from a man's clothes.

As they went slowly towards the house he tore at the

ragged wisps of chrysanthemums and dropped the petals in handfuls among the path.

"Don't do that—it does look nasty," said his mother. He refrained, and she, suddenly pitiful, broke off a twig with three or four wan flowers and held them against her face. When mother and son reached the yard her hand hesitated, and instead of laying the flower aside, she pushed it in her apron-band. The mother and son stood at the foot of the three steps looking across the bay of lines at the passing home of the miners. The trundle of the small train was imminent. Suddenly the engine loomed past the house and came to a stop opposite the gate.

The engine-driver, a short man with round grey beard, leaned out of the cab high above the woman.

"Have you got a cup of tea?" he said in a cheery, hearty fashion.

It was her father. She went in, saying she would mash. Directly, she returned.

"I didn't come to see you on Sunday," began the little grey-bearded man.

"I didn't expect you," said his daughter.

The engine-driver winced; then, reassuming his cheery, airy manner, he said:

"Oh, have you heard then? Well, and what do you think?"

"I think it is soon enough," she replied.

At her brief censure the little man made an impatient gesture, and said coaxingly, yet with dangerous coldness:

"Well, what's a man to do? It's no sort of life for a man of my years, to sit at my own hearth like a stranger. And if I'm going to marry again it may as well be soon as late—what does it matter to anybody?"

The woman did not reply, but turned and went into the house. The man in the engine-cab stood assertive, till she returned with a cup of tea and a piece of bread and butter on a plate. She went up the steps and stood near the foot-plate of the hissing engine.

"You needn't 'a' brought me bread an' butter," said her father. "But a cup of tea"—he sipped appreciatively—"it's very nice." He sipped for a moment or two, then: "I hear as Walter's got another bout on," he said.

"When hasn't he?" said the woman bitterly.

"I heerd tell of him in the 'Lord Nelson' braggin' as he was going to spend that b—— afore he went: half a sovereign that was."

"When?" asked the woman.

"A' Sat'day night—I know that's true."

"Very likely," she laughed bitterly. "He gives me twenty-three shillings."

"Aye, it's a nice thing, when a man can do nothing with his money but make a beast of himself!" said the grey-whiskered man. The woman turned her head away. Her father swallowed the last of his tea and handed her the cup.

"Aye," he sighed, wiping his mouth. "It's a settler, it is——."

He put his hand on the lever. The little engine strained and groaned, and the train rumbled towards the crossing. The woman again looked across the metals. Darkness was settling over the spaces of the railway and tracks: the miners, in grey sombre groups, were still passing home. The winding engine pulsed hurriedly, with brief pauses. Elizabeth Bates looked at the dreary flow of men, then she went indoors. Her husband did not come.

The kitchen was small and full of firelight; red coals piled glowing up the chimney mouth. All the life of the room seemed in the white, warm hearth and the steel fender reflecting the red fire. The cloth was laid for tea; cups glinted in the shadows. At the back, where the lowest stairs protruded into the room, the boy sat struggling with a knife and a piece of white wood. He was almost hidden in the shadow. It was half-past four. They had but to await the father's coming to begin tea. As the mother watched her son's sullen little struggle with the wood, she saw herself in his silence and pertinacity; she saw the father in her child's indifference to all but himself. She seemed to be occupied by her husband. He had probably gone past his home, slunk past his own door, to drink before he came in, while his dinner spoiled and wasted in waiting. She glanced at the clock, then took the potatoes to strain them in the yard. The garden and fields beyond the brook were closed in uncertain darkness. When she rose with the saucepan, leaving the drain steaming into the night behind her, she saw the yellow lamps were lit along the high road that went up the hill away beyond the space of the railway lines and the field.

Then again she watched the men trooping home, fewer now and fewer.

Indoors the fire was sinking and the room was dark red. The woman put her saucepan on the hob, and set a batter-pudding near the mouth of the oven. Then she stood unmoving. Directly, gracefully, came quick young steps to the door. Someone hung on the latch a moment, then a little girl entered and began pulling off her outdoor things, dragging a mass of curls, just ripening from gold to brown, over her eyes with her hat.

Her mother chid her for coming late from school, and said she would have to keep her at home the dark winter days.

"Why, mother, it's hardly a bit dark yet. The lamp's not lighted, and my father's not home."

"No, he isn't. But it's a quarter to five! Did you see anything of him?"

The child became serious. She looked at her mother with large, wistful blue eyes.

"No, mother, I've never seen him. Why? Has he come up an' gone past, to Old Brinsley? He hasn't, mother, 'cos I never saw him."

"He'd watch that," said the mother bitterly, "he'd take care as you didn't see him. But you may depend upon it, he's seated in the 'Prince o' Wales.' He wouldn't be this late."

The girl looked at her mother piteously.

"Let's have our teas, mother, should we?" said she.

The mother called John to table. She opened the door once more and looked out across the darkness of the lines. All was deserted: she could not hear the winding-engines.

"Perhaps," she said to herself, "he's stopped to get some ripping done."

They sat down to tea. John, at the end of the table near the door, was almost lost in the darkness. Their faces were hidden from each other. The girl crouched against the fender slowly moving a thick piece of bread before the fire. The lad, his face a dusky mark on the shadow, sat watching her who was transfigured in the red glow.

"I do think it's beautiful to look in the fire," said the child.

"Do you?" said her mother. "Why?"

"It's so red, and full of little caves—and it feels so nice, and you can fair smell it."

"It'll want mending directly," replied her mother, "and then if your father comes he'll carry on and say there never is a fire when a man comes home sweating from the pit. A public-house is always warm enough."

There was silence till the boy said complainingly: "Make haste, our Annie."

"Well, I am doing! I can't make the fire do it no faster, can I?"

"She keeps wafflin' it about so's to make 'er slow," grumbled the boy.

"Don't have such an evil imagination, child," replied the mother.

Soon the room was busy in the darkness with the crisp sound of crunching. The mother ate very little. She drank her tea determinedly, and sat thinking. When she rose her anger was evident in the stern unbending of her head. She looked at the pudding in the fender, and broke out:

"It is a scandalous thing as a man can't even come home to his dinner! If it's crozzled up to a cinder I don't see why I should care. Past his very door he goes to get to a public-house, and here I sit with his dinner waiting for him——"

She went out. As she dropped piece after piece of coal on the red fire, the shadows fell on the walls, till the room was almost in total darkness.

"I canna see," grumbled the invisible John. In spite of herself, the mother laughed.

"You know the way to your mouth," she said. She set the dust-pan outside the door. When she came again like a shadow on the hearth, the lad repeated, complaining sulkily:

"I canna see."

"Good gracious!" cried the mother irritably, "you're as bad as your father if it's a bit dusk!"

Nevertheless, she took a paper spill from a sheaf on the mantelpiece and proceeded to light the lamp that hung from the ceiling in the middle of the room. As she reached up, her figure displayed itself just rounding with maternity.

"Oh, mother——!" exclaimed the girl.

"What?" said the woman, suspended in the act of putting the lamp-glass over the flame. The copper reflector shone handsomely on her, as she stood with uplifted arm, turning to face her daughter.

"You've got a flower in your apron!" said the child, in a little rapture at this unusual event.

"Goodness me!" exclaimed the woman, relieved. "One would think the house was afire." She replaced the glass and waited a moment before turning up the wick. A pale shadow was seen floating vaguely on the floor.

"Let me smell!" said the child, still rapturously, coming forward and putting her face to her mother's waist.

"Go along, silly!" said the mother, turning up the lamp. The light revealed their suspense so that the woman felt it almost unbearable. Annie was still bending at her waist. Irritably, the mother took the flowers out from her apron-band.

"Oh, mother—don't take them out!" Annie cried, catching her hand and trying to replace the sprig.

"Such nonsense!" said the mother, turning away. The child put the pale chrysanthemums to her lips, murmuring:

"Don't they smell beautiful!"

Her mother gave a short laugh.

"No," she said, "not to me. It was chrysanthemums when I married him, and chrysanthemums when you were born, and the first time they ever brought him home drunk, he'd got brown chrysanthemums in his button-hole."

She looked at the children. Their eyes and their parted lips were wondering. The mother sat rocking in silence for some time. Then she looked at the clock.

"Twenty minutes to six!" In a tone of fine bitter careless-ness she continued: "Eh, he'll not come now till they bring

him. There he'll stick! But he needn't come rolling in here in
his pit-dirt, for *I* won't wash him. He can lie on the floor——
Eh, what a fool I've been, what a fool! And this is what I
came here for, to this dirty hole, rats and all, for him to slink
past his very door. Twice last week—he's begun now——"

She silenced herself, and rose to clear the table.

While for an hour or more the children played, subduedly
intent, fertile of imagination, united in fear of the mother's
wrath, and in dread of their father's home-coming, Mrs.
Bates sat in her rocking-chair making a 'singlet' of thick
cream-coloured flannel, which gave a dull wounded sound as
she tore off the grey edge. She worked at her sewing with
energy, listening to the children, and her anger wearied itself,
lay down to rest, opening its eyes from time to time and
steadily watching, its ears raised to listen. Sometimes even
her anger quailed and shrank, and the mother suspended her
sewing, tracing the footsteps that thudded along the sleepers
outside; she would lift her head sharply to bid the children
'hush', but she recovered herself in time, and the footsteps
went past the gate, and the children were not flung out of
their play-world.

But at last Annie sighed, and gave in. She glanced at her
wagon of slippers, and loathed the game. She turned
plaintively to her mother.

"Mother!"—but she was inarticulate.

John crept out like a frog from under the sofa. His mother
glanced up.

"Yes," she said, "just look at those shirt-sleeves!"

The boy held them out to survey them, saying nothing.
Then somebody called in a hoarse voice away down the line,
and suspense bristled in the room, till two people had gone
by outside, talking.

"It is time for bed," said the mother.

"My father hasn't come," wailed Annie plaintively. But her
mother was primed with courage.

"Never mind. They'll bring him when he does come—like
a log." She meant there would be no scene. "And he may
sleep on the floor till he wakes himself. I know he'll not go to
work to-morrow after this!"

The children had their hands and faces wiped with a flannel. They were very quiet. When they had put on their nightdresses, they said their prayers, the boy mumbling. The mother looked down at them, at the brown silken bush of intertwining curls in the nape of the girl's neck, at the little black head of the lad, and her heart burst with anger at their father, who caused all three such distress. The children hid their faces in her skirts for comfort.

When Mrs. Bates came down, the room was strangely empty, with a tension of expectancy. She took up her sewing and stitched for some time without raising her head. Meantime her anger was tinged with fear.

II

The clock struck eight and she rose suddenly, dropping her sewing on her chair. She went to the stair-foot door, opened it, listening. Then she went out, locking the door behind her.

Something scuffled in the yard, and she started, though she knew it was only the rats with which the place was over-run. The night was very dark. In the great bay of railway lines, bulked with trucks, there was no trace of light, only away back she could see a few yellow lamps at the pit-top, and the red smear of the burning pit-bank on the night. She hurried along the edge of the track, then, crossing the converging lines, came to the stile by the white gates, whence she emerged on the road. Then the fear which had led her shrank. People were walking up to New Brinsley; she saw the lights in the houses; twenty yards farther on were the broad windows of the 'Prince of Wales', very warm and bright, and the loud voices of men could be heard distinctly. What a fool she had been to imagine that anything had happened to him! He was merely drinking over there at the 'Prince of Wales'. She faltered. She had never yet been to fetch him, and she never would go. So she continued her walk towards the long straggling line of houses, standing back on the highway. She entered a passage between the dwellings.

"Mr. Rigley?—Yes! Did you want him? No, he's not in at this minute."

The raw-boned woman leaned forward from her dark scullery and peered at the other, upon whom fell a dim light through the blind of the kitchen window.

"Is it Mrs. Bates?" she asked in a tone tinged with respect.

"Yes. I wondered if your Master was at home. Mine hasn't come yet."

" 'Asn't 'e! Oh, Jack's been 'ome an' 'ad 'is dinner an' gone out. 'E's just gone for 'alf an hour afore bed-time. Did you call at the 'Prince of Wales'?"

"No——"

"No, you don't like——! It's not very nice." The other woman was indulgent. There was an awkward pause. "Jack never said nothing about—about your Master," she said.

"No!—I expect he's stuck in there!"

Elizabeth Bates said this bitterly, and with recklessness. She knew that the woman across the yard was standing at her door listening, but she did not care. As she turned:

"Stop a minute! I'll just go an' ask Jack if 'e knows anythink," said Mrs. Rigley.

"Oh no—I wouldn't like to put——!"

"Yes, I will, if you'll just step inside an' see as th' childer doesn't come downstairs and set theirselves afire."

Elizabeth Bates, murmuring a remonstrance, stepped inside. The other woman apologised for the state of the room.

The kitchen needed apology. There were little frocks and trousers and childish undergarments on the squab and on the floor, and a litter of playthings everywhere. On the black American cloth of the table were pieces of bread and cake, crusts, slops, and a teapot with cold tea.

"Eh, ours is just as bad," said Elizabeth Bates, looking at the woman, not at the house. Mrs. Rigley put a shawl over her head and hurried out, saying:

"I shanna be a minute."

The other sat, noting with faint disapproval the general untidiness of the room. Then she fell to counting the shoes of various sizes scattered over the floor. There were twelve. She sighed and said to herself: "No wonder!"—glancing at the litter. There came the scratching of two pairs of feet on the yard, and the Rigleys entered. Elizabeth Bates rose. Rigley was a big man, with very large bones. His head looked particularly bony. Across his temple was a blue scar, caused by a wound got in the pit, a wound in which the coal-dust remained blue like tattooing.

" 'Asna 'e come whoam yit?" asked the man, without any form of greeting, but with deference and sympathy. "I could na say wheer he is—'e's non ower theer!"—he jerked his head to signify the 'Prince of Wales'.

" 'E's 'appen gone up to th' 'Yew'," said Mrs. Rigley.

There was another pause. Rigley had evidently something to get off his mind:

"Ah left 'im finishin' a stint," he began. "Loose-all 'ad bin gone about ten minutes when we com'n away, an' I shouted: 'Are ter comin', Walt?' an' 'e said: 'Go on, Ah shanna be but a'ef a minnit,' so we com'n ter th' bottom, me an' Bowers, thinkin' as 'e wor just behint, an' 'ud come up. i' th' next bantle——"

He stood perplexed, as if answering a charge of deserting his mate. Elizabeth Bates, now again certain of disaster, hastened to reassure him:

"I expect 'e's gone up to th' 'Yew Tree', as you say. It's not the first time. I've fretted myself into a fever before now. He'll come home when they carry him."

"Ay, isn't it too bad!" deplored the other woman.

"I'll just step up to Dick's an' see if 'e *is* theer," offered the man, afraid of appearing alarmed, afraid of taking liberties.

"Oh, I wouldn't think of bothering you that far," said Elizabeth Bates, with emphasis, but he knew she was glad of his offer.

As they stumbled up the entry, Elizabeth Bates heard Rigley's wife run across the yard and open her neighbour's door. At this, suddenly all the blood in her body seemed to switch away from her heart.

"Mind!" warned Rigley. "Ah've said many a time as Ah'd fill up them ruts in this entry, sumb'dy 'll be breakin' their legs yit."

She recovered herself and walked quietly along with the miner.

"I don't like leaving the children in bed, and nobody in the house," she said.

"No, you dunna!" he replied courteously. They were soon at the gate of the cottage.

"Well, I shanna be many minnits. Dunna you be frettin' now, 'e'll be all right," said the butty.

"Thank you very much, Mr. Rigley," she replied.

"You're welcome!" he stammered, moving away. "I shanna be many minnits."

The house was quiet. Elizabeth Bates took off her hat and shawl, and rolled back the rug. When she had finished, she sat down. It was a few minutes past nine. She was startled by the rapid chuff of the winding-engine at the pit, and the sharp whirr of the brakes on the rope as it descended. Again she felt the painful sweep of her blood, and she put her hand to her side, saying aloud: "Good gracious!—it's only the nine o'clock deputy going down," rebuking herself.

She sat still, listening. Half an hour of this, and she was wearied out.

"What am I working myself up like this for?" she said pitiably to herself, "I s'll only be doing myself some damage."

She took out her sewing again.

At a quarter to ten there were footsteps. One person! She watched for the door to open. It was an elderly woman, in a black bonnet and a black woollen shawl—his mother. She was about sixty years old, pale, with blue eyes, and her face all wrinkled and lamentable. She shut the door and turned to her daughter-in-law peevishly.

"Eh, Lizzie, whatever shall we do, whatever shall we do!" she cried.

Elizabeth drew back a little, sharply.

"What is it, mother?" she said.

The elder woman seated herself on the sofa.

"I don't know, child, I can't tell you!"—she shook her head slowly. Elizabeth sat watching her, anxious and vexed.

"I don't know," replied the grandmother, sighing very deeply. "There's no end to my troubles, there isn't. The things

I've gone through, I'm sure it's enough——!" She wept without wiping her eyes, the tears running.

"But, mother," interrupted Elizabeth, "what do you mean? What is it?"

The grandmother slowly wiped her eyes. The fountains of her tears were stopped by Elizabeth's directness. She wiped her eyes slowly.

"Poor child! Eh, you poor thing!" she moaned. "I don't know what we're going to do, I don't—and you as you are—it's a thing, it is indeed!"

Elizabeth waited.

"Is he dead?" she asked, and at the words her heart swung violently, though she felt a slight flush of shame at the ultimate extravagance of the question. Her words sufficiently frightened the old lady, almost brought her to herself.

"Don't say so, Elizabeth! We'll hope it's not as bad as that; no, may the Lord spare us that, Elizabeth. Jack Rigley came just as I was sittin' down to a glass afore going to bed, an' 'e said: ' 'Appen you'll go down th' line, Mrs. Bates. Walt's had an accident. 'Appen you'll go an' sit wi' 'er till we can get him home.' I hadn't time to ask him a word afore he was gone. An' I put my bonnet on an' come straight down, Lizzie. I thought to myself: 'Eh, that poor blessed child, if anybody should come an' tell her of a sudden, there's no knowin' what'll 'appen to 'er.' You mustn't let it upset you, Lizzie—or you know what to expect. How long is it, six months—or is it five, Lizzie? Ay!"—the old woman shook her head—"time slips on, it slips on! Ay!"

Elizabeth's thoughts were busy elsewhere. If he was killed—would she be able to manage on the little pension and what she could earn?—she counted up rapidly. If he was hurt—they wouldn't take him to the hospital—how tiresome he would be to nurse!—but perhaps she'd be able to get him away from the drink and his hateful ways. She would—while he was ill. The tears offered to come to her eyes at the picture. But what sentimental luxury was this she was beginning? She turned to consider the children. At any rate she was absolutely necessary for them. They were her business.

"Ay!" repeated the old woman, "it seems but a week or

two since he brought me his first wages. Ay—he was a good lad, Elizabeth, he was, in his way. I don't know why he got to be such a trouble, I don't. He was a happy lad at home, only full of spirits. But there's no mistake he's been a handful of trouble, he has! I hope the Lord'll spare him to mend his ways. I hope so, I hope so. You've had a sight o' trouble with him, Elizabeth, you have indeed. But he was a jolly enough lad wi' me, he was, I can assure you. I don't know how it is. . . ."

The old woman continued to muse aloud, a monotonous irritating sound, while Elizabeth thought concentratedly, startled once, when she heard the winding-engine chuff quickly. and the brakes skirr with a shriek. Then she heard the engine more slowly, and the brakes made no sound. The old woman did not notice. Elizabeth waited in suspense. The mother-in-law talked, with lapses into silence.

"But he wasn't your son, Lizzie, an' it makes a difference. Whatever he was, I remember him when he was little, an' I learned to understand him and to make allowances. You've got to make allowances for them——"

It was half-past ten, and the old woman was saying: "But it's trouble from beginning to end; you're never too old for trouble, never too old for that——" when the gate banged back, and there were heavy feet on the steps.

"I'll go, Lizzie, let me go," cried the old woman, rising. But Elizabeth was at the door. It was a man in pit-clothes.

"They're bringin' 'im, Missis," he said. Elizabeth's heart halted a moment. Then it surged on again, almost suffocating her.

"Is he—is it bad?" she asked.

The man turned away, looking at the darkness:

"The doctor says 'e'd been dead hours. 'E saw 'im i' th' lamp-cabin."

The old woman, who stood just behind Elizabeth, dropped into a chair, and folded her hands, crying: "Oh, my boy, my boy!"

"Hush!" said Elizabeth, with a sharp twitch of a frown. "Be still, mother, don't waken th' children: I wouldn't have them down for anything!"

The old woman moaned softly, rocking herself. The man was drawing away. Eilzabeth took a step forward.

"How was it?" she asked.

"Well, I couldn't say for sure," the man replied, very ill at ease. " 'E wor finishin' a stint an' th' butties 'ad gone, an' a lot o' stuff come down atop 'n 'im."

"And crushed him?" cried the widow, with a shudder.

"No," said the man, "it fell at th' back of 'im. 'E wor under th' face, an' it niver touched 'im. It shut 'im in. It seems 'e wor smothered."

Elizabeth shrank back. She heard the old woman behind her cry:

"What?—what did 'e say it was?"

The man replied, more loudly: " 'E wor smothered!"

Then the old woman wailed aloud, and this relieved Elizabeth.

"Oh, mother," she said, putting her hand on the old woman, "don't waken th' children, don't waken th' children."

She wept a little, unknowing, while the old mother rocked herself and moaned. Elizabeth remembered that they were bringing him home, and she must be ready. "They'll lay him in the parlour," she said to herself, standing a moment pale and perplexed.

Then she lighted a candle and went into the tiny room. The air was cold and damp, but she could not make a fire, there was no fireplace. She set down the candle and looked round. The candlelight glittered on the lustre-glasses, on the two vases that held some of the pink chrysanthemums, and on the dark mahogany. There was a cold, deathly smell of chrysanthemums in the room. Elizabeth stood looking at the flowers. She turned away, and calculated whether there would be room to lay him on the floor, between the couch and the chiffonier. She pushed the chairs aside. There would be room to lay him down and to step round him. Then she fetched the old red tablecloth, and another old cloth, spreading them down to save her bit of carpet. She shivered on leaving the parlour; so, from the dresser drawer she took a clean shirt and put it at the fire to air. All the time her mother-in-law was rocking herself in the chair and moaning.

"You'll have to move from here, mother," said Elizabeth. "They'll be bringing him in. Come in the rocker."

The old mother rose mechanically, and seated herself by the fire, continuing to lament. Elizabeth went into the pantry for another candle, and there, in the little pent-house under the naked tiles, she heard them coming. She stood still in the pantry doorway, listening. She heard them pass the end of the house, and come awkwardly down the three steps, a jumble of shuffling footsteps and muttering voices. The old woman was silent. The men were in the yard.

Then Elizabeth heard Matthews, the manager of the pit, say: "You go in first, Jim. Mind!"

The door came open, and the two women saw a collier backing into the room, holding one end of a stretcher, on which they could see the nailed pit-boots of the dead man. The two carriers halted, the man at the head stooping to the lintel of the door.

"Wheer will you have him?" asked the manager, a short, white-bearded man.

Elizabeth roused herself and came from the pantry carrying the unlighted candle.

"In the parlour," she said.

"In there, Jim!" pointed the manager, and the carriers backed round into the tiny room. The coat with which they had covered the body fell off as they awkwardly turned through the two doorways, and the women saw their man, naked to the waist, lying stripped for work. The old woman began to moan in a low voice of horror.

"Lay th' stretcher at th' side," snapped the manager, "an' put 'im on th' cloths. Mind now, mind! Look you now——!"

One of the men had knocked off a vase of chrysanthemums. He stared awkwardly, then they set down the stretcher. Elizabeth did not look at her husband. As soon as she could get in the room, she went and picked up the broken vase and the flowers.

"Wait a minute!" she said.

The three men waited in silence while she mopped up the water with a duster.

"Eh, what a job, what a job, to be sure!" the manager was

saying, rubbing his brow with trouble and perplexity. "Never knew such a thing in my life, never! He'd no business to ha' been left. I never knew such a thing in my life! Fell over him clean as a whistle, an' shut him in. Not four foot of space, there wasn't—yet it scarce bruised him."

He looked down at the dead man, lying prone, half naked, all grimed with coal-dust.

" ' 'Sphyxiated', the doctor said. It *is* the most terrible job I've ever known. Seems as if it was done o' purpose. Clean over him, an' shut 'im in, like a mouse-trap"—he made a sharp, descending gesture with his hand.

The colliers standing by jerked aside their heads in hopeless comment.

The horror of the thing bristled upon them all.

Then they heard the girl's voice upstairs calling shrilly: "Mother, mother—who is it? Mother, who is it?"

Elizabeth hurried to the foot of the stairs and opened the door:

"Go to sleep!" she commanded sharply. "What are you shouting about? Go to sleep at once—there's nothing——"

Then she began to mount the stairs. They could hear her on the boards, and on the plaster floor of the little bedroom. They could hear her distinctly:

"What's the matter now?—what's the matter with you, silly thing?"—her voice was much agitated, with an unreal gentleness.

"I thought it was some men come," said the plaintive voice of the child. "Has he come?"

"Yes, they've brought him. There's nothing to make a fuss about. Go to sleep now, like a good child."

They could hear her voice in the bedroom, they waited whilst she covered the children under the bedclothes.

"Is he drunk?" asked the girl, timidly, faintly.

"No! No—he's not! He—he's asleep."

"Is he asleep downstairs?"

"Yes—and don't make a noise."

There was a silence for a moment, then the men heard the frightened child again:

"What's that noise?"

"It's nothing, I tell you, what are you bothering for?"

The noise was the grandmother moaning. She was oblivious of everything, sitting on her chair rocking and moaning. The manager put his hand on her arm and bade her "Sh—sh!!"

The old woman opened her eyes and looked at him. She was shocked by this interruption, and seemed to wonder.

"What time is it?" the plaintive thin voice of the child, sinking back unhappily into sleep, asked this last question.

"Ten o'clock," answered the mother more softly. Then she must have bent down and kissed the children.

Matthews beckoned to the men to come away. They put on their caps and took up the stretcher. Stepping over the body, they tiptoed out of the house. None of them spoke till they were far from the wakeful children.

When Elizabeth came down she found her mother alone on the parlour floor, leaning over the dead man, the tears dropping on him.

"We must lay him out," the wife said. She put on the kettle, then returning knelt at the feet, and began to unfasten the knotted leather laces. The room was clammy and dim with only one candle, so that she had to bend her face almost to the floor. At last she got off the heavy boots and put them away.

"You must help me now," she whispered to the old woman. Together they stripped the man.

When they arose, saw him lying in the naïve dignity of death, the women stood arrested in fear and respect. For a few moments they remained still, looking down, the old mother whimpering. Elizabeth felt countermanded. She saw him, how utterly inviolable he lay in himself. She had nothing to do with him. She could not accept it. Stooping, she laid her hand on him, in claim. He was still warm, for the mine was hot where he had died. His mother had his face between her hands, and was murmuring incoherently. The old tears fell in succession as drops from wet leaves; the mother was not weeping, merely her tears flowed. Elizabeth embraced the body of her husband, with cheek and lips. She seemed to be listening, inquiring, trying to get some connection. But she could not. She was driven away. He was impregnable.

She rose, went into the kitchen, where she poured warm water into a bowl, brought soap and flannel and a soft towel.

"I must wash him," she said.

Then the old mother rose stiffly, and watched Elizabeth as she carefully washed his face, carefully brushing the big blond moustache from his mouth with the flannel. She was afraid with a bottomless fear, so she ministered to him. The old woman, jealous, said:

"Let me wipe him!"—and she kneeled on the other side drying slowly as Elizabeth washed, her big black bonnet sometimes brushing the dark head of her daughter-in-law. They worked thus in silence for a long time. They never forgot it was death, and the touch of the man's dead body gave them strange emotions, different in each of the women; a great dread possessed them both, the mother felt the lie was given to her womb, she was denied; the wife felt the utter isolation of the human soul, the child within her was a weight apart from her.

At last it was finished. He was a man of handsome body, and his face showed no traces of drink. He was blond, full-fleshed, with fine limbs. But he was dead.

"Bless him," whispered his mother, looking always at his face, and speaking out of sheer terror. "Dear lad—bless him!" She spoke in a faint, sibilant ecstasy of fear and mother love.

Elizabeth sank down again to the floor, and put her face against his neck, and trembled and shuddered. But she had to draw away again. He was dead, and her living flesh had no place against his. A great dread and weariness held her: she was so unavailing. Her life was gone like this.

"White as milk he is, clear as a twelve-month baby, bless him, the darling!" the old mother murmured to herself. "Not a mark on him, clear and clean and white, beautiful as ever a child was made," she murmured with pride. Elizabeth kept her face hidden.

"He went peaceful, Lizzie—peaceful as sleep. Isn't he beautiful, the lamb? Ay—he must ha' made his peace, Lizzie.

'Appen he made it all right, Lizzie, shut in there. He'd have time. He wouldn't look like this if he hadn't made his peace. The lamb, the dear lamb. Eh, but he had a hearty laugh. I loved to hear it. He had the heartiest laugh, Lizzie, as a lad——"

Elizabeth looked up. The man's mouth was fallen back, slightly open under the cover of the moustache. The eyes, half shut, did not show glazed in the obscurity. Life with its smoky burning gone from him, had left him apart and utterly alien to her. And she knew what a stranger he was to her. In her womb was ice of fear, because of this separate stranger with whom she had been living as one flesh. Was this what it all meant—utter, intact separateness, obscured by heat of living? In dread she turned her face away. The fact was too deadly. There had been nothing between them, and yet they had come together, exchanging their nakedness repeatedly. Each time he had taken her, they had been two isolated beings, far apart as now. He was no more responsible than she. The child was like ice in her womb. For as she looked at the dead man, her mind, cold and detached, said clearly: "Who am I? What have I been doing? I have been fighting a husband who did not exist. *He* existed all the time. What wrong have I done? What was that I have been living with? There lies the reality, this man." And her soul died in her for fear: she knew she had never seen him, he had never seen her, they had met in the dark and had fought in the dark, not knowing whom they met nor whom they fought. And now she saw, and turned silent in seeing. For she had been wrong. She had said he was something he was not; she had felt familiar with him. Whereas he was apart all the while, living as she never lived, feeling as she never felt.

In fear and shame she looked at his naked body, that she had known falsely. And he was the father of her children. Her soul was torn from her body and stood apart. She looked at his naked body and was ashamed, as if she had denied it. After all, it was itself. It seemed awful to her. She looked at his face, and she turned her own face to the wall. For his look was other than hers, his way was not her way. She had denied him what he was—she saw it now. She had refused him as himself. And this had been her life, and his life. She was grateful to death, which restored the truth. And she knew she was not dead.

And all the while her heart was bursting with grief and pity for him. What had he suffered? What stretch of horror for this helpless man! She was rigid with agony. She had not been able to help him. He had been cruelly injured, this naked man, this other being, and she could make no reparation. There were the children—but the children belonged to life. This dead man had nothing to do with them. He and she were only channels through which life had flowed to issue in the children. She was a mother—but how awful she knew it now to have been a wife. And he, dead now, how awful he must have felt it to be a husband. She felt that in the next world he would be a stranger to her. If they met there, in the beyond, they would only be ashamed of what had been before. The children had come, for some mysterious reason, out of both of them. But the children did not unite them. Now he was dead, she knew how eternally he was apart from her, how eternally he had nothing more to do with her. She saw this episode of her life closed. They had denied each other in life. Now he had withdrawn. An anguish came over her. It was finished then: it had become hopeless between them long before he died. Yet he had been her husband. But how little!

"Have you got his shirt, 'Lizabeth?"

Elizabeth turned without answering, though she strove to weep and behave as her mother-in-law expected. But she could not, she was silenced. She went into the kitchen and returned with the garment.

"It is aired," she said, grasping the cotton shirt here and there to try. She was almost ashamed to handle him; what right had she or anyone to lay hands on him; but her touch was humble on his body. It was hard work to clothe him. He was so heavy and inert. A terrible dread gripped her all the while: that he could be so heavy and utterly inert, unresponsive, apart. The horror of the distance between them was almost too much for her—it was so infinite a gap she must look across.

At last it was finished. They covered him with a sheet and left him lying, with his face bound. And she fastened the door of the little parlour, lest the children should see what was lying there. Then, with peace sunk heavy on her heart, she went about making tidy the kitchen. She knew she submitted to life, which was her immediate master. But from death, her ultimate master, she winced with fear and shame.

England, My England

HE WAS working on the edge of the common, beyond the small brook that ran in the dip at the bottom of the garden, carrying the garden path in continuation from the plank bridge on to the common. He had cut the rough turf and bracken, leaving the grey, dryish soil bare. But he was worried because he could not get the path straight, there was a pleat between his brows. He had set up his sticks, and taken the sights between the big pine trees, but for some reason everything seemed wrong. He looked again, straining his keen blue eyes, that had a touch of the Viking in them, through the shadowy pine trees as through a doorway, at the green-grassed garden path rising from the shadow of alders by the log bridge up to the sunlit flowers. Tall white and purple columbines, and the butt-end of the old Hampshire cottage that crouched near the earth amid flowers, blossoming in the bit of shaggy wildness round about.

There was a sound of children's voices calling and talking: high, childish, girlish voices, slightly didactic and tinged with domineering: "If you don't come quick, nurse, I shall run out there to where there are snakes." And nobody had the sang-froid to reply: "Run then, little fool." It was always: "No, darling. Very well, darling. In a moment, darling. Darling, you *must* be patient."

His heart was hard with disillusion: a continual gnawing and resistance. But he worked on. What was there to do but submit!

The sunlight blazed down upon the earth, there was a vividness of flamy vegetation, of fierce seclusion amid the savage peace of the commons. Strange how the savage England lingers in patches: as here, amid these shaggy gorse commons, and marshy, snake-infested places near the foot of the South Downs. The spirit of place lingering on primeval, as when the Saxons came, so long ago.

Ah, how he had loved it! The green garden path, the tufts of flowers, purple and white columbines, and great Oriental red poppies with their black chaps and mulleins tall and yellow: this flamy garden which had been a garden for a thousand years, scooped out in the little hollow among the snake-infested commons. He had made it flame with flowers, in a sun-cup under its hedges and trees. So old, so old a place! And yet he had re-created it.

The timbered cottage with its sloping, cloak-like roof was old and forgotten. It belonged to the old England of hamlets and yeomen. Lost all alone on the edge of the common, at the end of a wide, grassy, briar-entangled lane shaded with oak, it had never known the world of to-day. Not till Egbert came with his bride. And he had come to fill it with flowers.

The house was ancient and very uncomfortable. But he did not want to alter it. Ah, marvellous to sit there in the wide, black, time-old chimney, at night when the wind roared overhead, and the wood which he had chopped himself sputtered on the hearth! Himself on one side the angle, and Winifred on the other.

Ah, how he had wanted her: Winifred! She was young and beautiful and strong with life, like a flame in sunshine. She moved with a slow grace of energy like a blossoming, red-flowered bush in motion. She, too, seemed to come out of the old England, ruddy, strong, with a certain crude, passionate quiescence and a hawthorn robustness. And he, he was tall and slim and agile, like an English archer with his long supple legs and fine movements. Her hair was nut-brown and all in energic curls and tendrils. Her eyes were nut-brown, too, like a robin's for brightness. And he was white-skinned with fine, silky hair that had darkened from fair, and a slightly arched nose of an old country family. They were a beautiful couple.

The house was Winifred's. Her father was a man of energy, too. He had come from the north poor. Now he was moderately rich. He had bought this fair stretch of inexpensive land, down in Hampshire. Not far from the tiny church of the almost extinct hamlet stood his own house, a commodious old farmhouse standing back from the road across a bare grassed yard. On one side of this quadrangle was the long, long barn or shed which he had made into a cottage for his youngest daughter Priscilla. One saw little blue-and-white check curtains at the long windows, and inside, overhead, the grand old timbers of the high-pitched shed. This was Prissy's house. Fifty yards away was the pretty little new cottage which he had built for his daughter Magdalen, with the vegetable garden stretching away to the oak copse. And then away beyond the lawns and rose trees of the house-garden went the track across a shaggy, wild grass space, towards the ridge of tall black pines that grew on a dyke-bank, through the pines and above the sloping little bog, under the wide, desolate oak trees, till there was Winifred's cottage crouching unexpectedly in front, so much alone, and so primitive.

It was Winifred's own house, and the gardens and the bit of common and the boggy slope were hers: her tiny domain. She had married just at the time when her father had bought the estate, about ten years before the war, so she had been able to come to Egbert with this for a marriage portion. And who was more delighted, he or she, it would be hard to say. She was only twenty at the time, and he was only twenty-one. He had about a hundred and fifty pounds a year of his own—and nothing else but his very considerable personal attractions. He had no profession: he earned nothing. But he talked of literature and music, he had a passion for old folk-music, collecting folk-songs and folk-dances, studying the Morris-dance and the old customs. Of course, in time he would make money in these ways.

Meanwhile youth and health and passion and promise. Winifred's father was always generous: but still, he was a man from the north with a hard head and a hard skin too, having received a good many knocks. At home he kept the hard head out of sight, and played at poetry and romance with his literary wife and his sturdy, passionate girls. He was a man of courage, not given to complaining, bearing his burdens by himself. No, he did not let the world intrude far into his home. He had a delicate, sensitive wife whose poetry won some fame in the narrow world of letters. He himself, with his tough old barbarian fighting spirit, had an almost child-like delight in verse, in sweet poetry, and in the delightful game of a cultured home. His blood was strong even to coarseness. But that only made the home more vigorous, more robust and Christmassy. There was always a touch of Christmas about him, now he was well off. If there was poetry after dinner, there were also chocolates, and nuts, and good little out-of-the-way things to be munching.

Well then, into this family came Egbert. He was made of quite a different paste. The girls and the father were strong-limbed, thick-blooded people, true English, as holly trees and hawthorn are English. Their culture was grafted on to them, as one might perhaps graft a common pink rose on to a thorn stem. It flowered oddly enough, but it did not alter their blood.

And Egbert was a born rose. The age-long breeding had left him with a delightful spontaneous passion. He was not clever, nor even "literary". No, but the intonation of his voice, and the movement of his supple, handsome body, and the fine texture of his flesh and his hair, the slight arch of his nose, the quickness of his blue eyes would easily take the place of poetry. Winifred loved him, loved him, this southerner, as a higher being. A *higher* being, mind you. Not a deeper. And as for him, he loved her in passion with every fibre of him. She was the very warm stuff of life to him.

Wonderful then, those days at Crockham Cottage, the first days, all alone save for the woman who came to work in the mornings. Marvellous days, when she had all his tall, supple, fine-fleshed youth to herself, for herself, and he had her like a ruddy fire into which he could cast himself for rejuvenation. Ah, that it might never end, this passion, this marriage! The flame of their two bodies burnt again into that old cottage, that was haunted already by so much bygone, physical desire. You could not be in the dark room for an hour without the influences coming over you. The hot blood-desire of bygone yeomen, there in this old den where they had lusted and bred for so many generations. The silent house, dark, with thick, timbered walls, and the big black chimney-place, and the sense of secrecy. Dark, with low, little windows, sunk into the earth. Dark, like a lair where strong beasts had lurked and mated, lonely at night and lonely by day, left to themselves and their own intensity for so many generations. It seemed to cast a spell on the two young people. They became different. There was a curious secret glow about them, a certain slumbering flame hard to understand, that enveloped them both. They too felt they did not belong to the London world any more. Crockham had changed their blood: the sense of the snakes that lived and slept even in their own garden, in the sun, so that he, going forward with the spade, would see a curious coiled brownish pile on the black soil, which suddenly would start up, hiss, and dazzle rapidly away, hissing. One day Winifred heard the strangest scream from the flower-bed under the low window of the living-room: ah, the strangest scream, like the very soul of the dark past crying aloud. She ran out, and saw a long brown snake on the flower-bed, and in its flat mouth the one hind leg of a frog was striving to escape, and screaming its strange, tiny, bellowing scream. She looked at the snake, and from its sullen flat head it looked at her, obstinately. She gave a cry, and it released the frog and slid angrily away.

That was Crockham. The spear of modern invention had not passed through it, and it lay there secret, primitive, savage as when the Saxons first came. And Egbert and she were caught there, caught out of the world.

He was not idle, nor was she. There were plenty of things to be done, the house to be put into final repair after the workman had gone, cushions and curtains to sew, the paths to make, the water to fetch and attend to, and then the slope of the deep-soiled, neglected garden to level, to terrace with little terraces and paths, and to fill with flowers. He worked away, in his shirt-sleeves, worked all day intermittently doing this thing and the other. And she, quiet and rich in herself, seeing him stooping and labouring away by himself, would come to help him, to be near him. He of course was an amateur—a born amateur. He worked so hard, and did so little, and nothing he ever did would hold together for long.

If he terraced the garden, he held up the earth with a couple of long narrow planks that soon began to bend with the pressure from behind, and would not need many years to rot through and break and let the soil slither all down again in a heap towards the stream-bed. But there you are. He had not been brought up to come to grips with anything, and he thought it would do. Nay, he did not think there was anything else except little temporary contrivances possible, he who had such a passion for his old enduring cottage, and for the old enduring things of the bygone England. Curious that the sense of permanency in the past had such a hold over him, whilst in the present he was all amateurish and sketchy.

Winifred would not criticise him. Town-bred, everything seemed to her splendid, and the very digging and shovelling itself seemed romantic. But neither Egbert nor she realised the difference between work and romance.

Godfrey Marshall, her father, was at first perfectly pleased with the *ménage* down at Crockham Cottage. He thought Egbert was wonderful, the many things he accomplished, and he was gratified by the glow of physical passion between the two young people. To the man who in London still worked hard to keep steady his modest fortune, the thought of this young couple digging away and loving one another down at Crockham Cottage, buried deep among the commons and marshes, near the pale-showing bulk of the down, was like a chapter of living romance. And they drew the sustenance for their fire of passion from him, from the old man. It was he who fed their flame. He triumphed secretly in the thought. And it was to her father that Winifred still turned, as the one source of all surety and life and support. She loved Egbert with passion. But behind her was the power of her father. It was the power of her father she referred to, whenever she needed to refer. It never occurred to her to refer to Egbert, if she were in difficulty or doubt. No, in all the *serious* matters she depended on her father.

For Egbert had no intention of coming to grips with life. He had no ambition whatsoever. He came from a decent family from a pleasant country home, from delightful surroundings. He should, of course, have had a profession. He should have studied law or entered business in some way. But no—that fatal three pounds a week would keep him from starving as long as he lived, and he did not want to give himself into bondage. It was not that he was idle. He was always doing something, in his amateurish way. But he had no desire to give himself to the world, and still less had he any desire to fight his way in the world. No, no, the world wasn't worth it. He wanted to ignore it, to go his own way apart, like a casual pilgrim down the forsaken side-tracks. He loved his wife, his cottage and garden. He would make his life there, as a sort of epicurean hermit. He loved the past, the old music and dances and customs of old England. He would try and live in the spirit of these, not in the spirit of the world of business.

But often Winifred's father called her to London: for he loved to have his children round him. So Egbert and she must have a tiny flat in town, and the young couple must transfer themselves from time to time from the country to the city. In town Egbert had plenty of friends, of the same ineffectual sort as himself, tampering with the arts, literature, painting, sculpture, music. He was not bored.

Three pounds a week, however, would not pay for all this. Winifred's father paid. He liked paying. He made her only a very small allowance, but he often gave her ten pounds—or gave Egbert ten pounds. So they both looked on the old man as the mainstay. Egbert didn't mind being patronised and paid for. Only when he felt the family was a little *too* condescending, on account of money, he began to get huffy.

Then of course children came: a lovely little blonde daughter with a head of thistle-down. Everybody adored the child. It was the first exquisite blonde thing that had come into the family, a little mite with the white, slim, beautiful limbs of its father, and as it grew up the dancing, dainty movement of a wild little daisy-spirit. No wonder the Marshalls all loved the child: they called her Joyce. They themselves had their own grace, but it was slow, rather heavy. They had every one of them strong, heavy limbs and darkish skins, and they were short in stature. And now they had for one of their own this light little cowslip child. She was like a little poem in herself.

But nevertheless, she brought a new difficulty. Winifred must have a nurse for her. Yes, yes, there must be a nurse. It was the family decree. Who was to pay for the nurse? The grandfather—seeing the father himself earned no money. Yes, the grandfather would pay, as he had paid all the lying-in expenses. There came a slight sense of money-strain. Egbert was living on his father-in-law.

After the child was born, it was never quite the same between him and Winifred. The difference was at first hardly perceptible. But it was there. In the first place Winifred had a new centre of interest. She was not going to adore her child. But she had what the modern mother so often has in the place of spontaneous love: a profound sense of duty towards her child. Winifred appreciated her darling little girl, and felt a deep sense of duty towards her. Strange, that this sense of duty should go deeper than the love for her husband. But so it was. And so it often is. The responsibility of motherhood was the prime responsibility in Winifred's heart: the responsibility of wifehood came a long way second.

Her child seemed to link her up again in a circuit with her own family. Her father and mother, herself, and her child, that was the human trinity for her. Her husband——? Yes, she loved him still. But that was like play. She had an almost barbaric sense of duty and of family. Till she married, her first human duty had been towards her father: he was the pillar, the source of life, the everlasting support. Now another link was added to the chain of duty: her father, herself, and her child.

Egbert was out of it. Without anything happening, he was gradually, unconsciously excluded from the circle. His wife still loved him, physically. But, but—he was *almost* the unnecessary party in the affair. He could not complain of Winifred. She still did her duty towards him. She still had physical passion for him, that physical passion on which he had put all his life and soul. But—but——

It was for a long while an ever-recurring *but*. And then, after the second child, another blonde, winsome touching little thing, not so proud and flame-like as Joyce—after Annabel came, then Egbert began truly to realise how it was. His wife still loved him. But—and now the but had grown enormous—her physical love for him was of secondary importance to her. It became ever less important. After all, she had had it, this physical passion, for two years now. It was not this that one lived from. No, no—something sterner, realer.

She began to resent her own passion for Egbert—just a little she began to despise it. For after all there he was, he was charming, he was lovable, he was terribly desirable. But—but—oh, the awful looming cloud of that *but*!—he did not stand firm in the landscape of her life like a tower of strength, like a great pillar of significance. No, he was like a cat one has about the house, which will one day disappear and leave no trace. He was like a flower in the garden, trembling in the wind of life, and then gone, leaving nothing to show. As an adjunct, as an accessory, he was perfect. Many a woman would have adored to have him about her all her life, the most beautiful and desirable of all her possessions. But Winifred belonged to another school.

The years went by, and instead of coming more to grips with life, he relaxed more. He was of a subtle, sensitive, passionate nature. But he simply *would* not give himself to what Winifred called life, *Work*. No, he would not go into the world and work for money. No, he just would not. If Winifred liked to live beyond their small income—well, it was her look-out.

And Winifred did not really want him to go out into the world to work for money. Money became, alas, a word like a firebrand between them, setting them both aflame with anger. But that is because we must talk in symbols. Winifred did not really care about money. She did not care whether he earned or did not earn anything. Only she knew she was dependent on her father for three-fourths of the money spent for herself and her children, that she let that be the *casus belli*, the drawn weapon between herself and Egbert.

What did she want—what did she want? Her mother once said to her, with that characteristic touch of irony: "Well, dear, if it is your fate to consider the lilies, that toil not, neither do they spin, that is one destiny among many others, and perhaps not so unpleasant as most. Why do you take it amiss, my child?"

The mother was subtler than her children, they very rarely knew how to answer her. So Winifred was only more confused. It was not a question of lilies. At least, if it were a question of lilies, then her children were the little blossoms. They at least *grew*. Doesn't Jesus said: "Consider the lilies *how they grow*." Good then, she had her growing babies. But as for that other tall, handsome flower of a father of theirs, he was full grown already, so she did not want to spend her life considering him in the flower of his days.

No, it was not that he didn't earn money. It was not that he was idle. He was *not* idle. He was always doing something, always working away, down at Crockham, doing little jobs. But, oh dear, the little jobs—the garden paths—the gorgeous flowers—the chairs to mend, old chairs to mend!

It was that he stood for nothing. If he had done something unsuccessfully, and *lost* what money they had! If he had but striven with something. Nay, even if he had been wicked, a waster, she would have been more free. She would have had something to resist, at least. A waster stands for something, really. He says: "No, I will not aid and abet society in this business of increase and hanging together, I will upset the apple-cart as much as I can, in my small way." Or else he says: "No, I will *not* bother about others. I have lusts, they are my own, and I prefer them to other people's virtues." So, a waster, a scamp, takes a sort of stand. He exposes himself to opposition and final castigation: at any rate in story-books.

But Egbert! What are you to do with a man like Egbert? He had no vices. He was really kind, nay, generous. And he was not weak. If he had been weak Winifred could have been kind to him. But he did not even give her that consolation. He was not weak, and he did not want her consolation or her kindness. No, thank you. He was of a fine passionate temper, and of a rare steel than she. He knew it, and she knew it. Hence she was only the more baffled and maddened, poor thing. He, the higher, the finer, in his way the stronger, played with his garden, and his old folk-songs and Morris dances, just played, and let her support the pillars of the future on her own heart.

And he began to get bitter, and a wicked look began to come on his face. He did not give in to her: not he. There were seven devils inside his long, slim, white body. He was healthy, full of restrained life. Yes, even he himself had to lock up his own vivid life inside himself, now she would not take it from him. Or rather, now that she only took it occasionally. For she had to yield at times. She loved him so, she desired him so, he was so exquisite to her, the fine creature that he was, finer than herself. Yes, with a groan she had to give in to her own unquenched passion for him. And he came to her then—ah, terrible, ah, wonderful, sometimes she wondered how either of them could live after the terror of the passion that swept between them. It was to her as if pure lightning, flash after flash, went through every fibre of her, till extinction came.

But it is the fate of human beings to live on. And it is the fate of clouds that seem nothing but bits of vapour slowly to pile up, to pile up and fill the heavens and blacken the sun entirely.

So it was. The love came back, the lightning of passion flashed tremendously between them. And there was blue sky and gorgeousness for a little while. And then, as inevitably, as inevitably, slowly the clouds began to edge up again above the horizon, slowly, slowly to lurk about the heavens, throwing an occasional cold and hateful shadow: slowly, slowly to congregate, to fill the empyrean space.

And as the years passed, the lightning cleared the sky more and more rarely, less and less the blue showed. Gradually the grey lid sank down upon them, as if it would be permanent.

Why didn't Egbert do something, then? Why didn't he come to grips with life? Why wasn't he like Winifred's father, a pillar of society, even if a slender, exquisite column? Why didn't he go into harness of some sort? Why didn't he take *some* direction?

Well, you can bring an ass to the water, but you cannot

make him drink. The world was the water and Egbert was the ass. And he wasn't having any. He couldn't: he just couldn't. Since necessity did not force him to work for his bread and butter, he would not work for work's sake. You can't make the columbine flowers nod in January, nor make the cuckoo sing in England at Christmas. Why? It isn't his season. He doesn't want to. Nay, he *can't* want to.

And there it was with Egbert. He couldn't link up with the world's work, because the basic desire was absent from him. Nay, at the bottom of him he had an even stronger desire: to hold aloof. To hold aloof. To do nobody any damage. But to hold aloof. It was not his season.

Perhaps he should not have married and had children. But you can't stop the waters flowing.

Which held true for Winifred, too. She was not made to endure aloof. Her family tree was a robust vegetation that had to be stirring and believing. In one direction or another her life *had* to go. In her own home she had known nothing of this diffidence which she found in Egbert, and which she could not understand, and which threw her into such dismay. What was she to do, what was she to do, in face of this terrible diffidence?

It was all so different in her own home. Her father may have had his own misgivings, but he kept them to himself. Perhaps he had no very profound belief in this world of ours, this society which we have elaborated with so much effort, only to find ourselves elaborated to death at last. But Godfrey Marshall was of tough, rough fibre, not without a vein of healthy cunning through it all. It was for him a question of winning through, and leaving the rest to heaven. Without having many illusions to grace him, he still *did* believe in heaven. In a dark and unquestioning way, he had a sort of faith: an acrid faith like the sap of some not-to-be-exterminated tree. Just a blind acrid faith as sap is blind and acrid, and yet pushes on in growth and in faith. Perhaps he was unscrupulous, but only as a striving tree is unscrupulous, pushing its single way in a jungle of others.

In the end, it is only this robust, sap-like faith which keeps man going. He may live on for many generations inside the shelter of the social establishment which he has erected for himself, as pear trees and currant bushes would go on bearing fruit for many seasons, inside a walled garden, even if the race of man were suddenly exterminated. But bit by bit the wall fruit trees would gradually pull down the very walls that sustained them. Bit by bit every establishment collapses, unless it is renewed or restored by living hands, all the while.

Egbert could not bring himself to any more of this restoring or renewing business. He was not aware of the fact: but awareness doesn't help much, anyhow. He just couldn't. He had the stoic and epicurean quality of his old, fine breeding. His father-in-law, however, though he was not one bit more of a fool than Egbert, realised that since we are here we may as well live. And so he applied himself to his own tiny section of the social work, and to doing the best for his family, and to leaving the rest to the ultimate will of heaven. A certain robustness of blood made him able to go on. But sometimes even from him spurted a sudden gall of bitterness against the world and its make-up. And yet—he had his own will-to-succeed, and this carried him through. He refused to ask himself what the success would amount to. It amounted to the estate down in Hampshire, and his children lacking for nothing, and himself of some importance in the world: *and basta!*—Basta! Basta!

Nevertheless, do not let us imagine that he was a common pusher. He was not. He knew as well as Egbert what disillusion meant. Perhaps in his soul he had the same estimation of success. But he had a certain acrid courage, and a certain will-to-power. In his own small circle he would emanate power, the single power of his own blind self. With all his spoiling of his children, he was still the father of the old English type. He was too wise to make laws and to domineer in the abstract. But he had kept, and all honour to him, a certain primitive dominion over the souls of his children, the old, almost magic prestige of paternity. There it was, still burning in him, the old smoky torch of paternal godhead.

And in the sacred glare of this torch his children had been brought up. He had given the girls every liberty, at last. But he had never really let them go beyond his power. And they, venturing out into the hard white light of our fatherless world, learned to see with the eyes of the world. They learned to criticise their father, even, from some effulgence of worldly white light, to see him as inferior. But this was all very well in the head. The moment they forgot their tricks of criticism, the old red glow of his authority came over them again. He was not to be quenched.

Let the psycho-analyst talk about father complex. It is just a word invented. Here was a man who had kept alive the old red flame of fatherhood, fatherhood that had even the right to sacrifice the child to God, like Isaac. Fatherhood that had life-and-death authority over the children: a great natural power. And till his children could be brought under some other great authority as girls; or could arrive at manhood and became themselves centres of the same power, continuing the same male mystery as men; until such time, willynilly, Godfrey Marshall would keep his children.

It had seemed as if he might lose Winifred. Winifred had *adored* her husband, and looked up to him as to something wonderful. Perhaps she had expected in him another great wonderful, a male authority greater, finer than her father's. For having once known the glow of male power, she would not easily turn to the cold white light of feminine independence. She would hunger, hunger all her life for the warmth and shelter of true male strength.

And hunger she might, for Egbert's power lay in the abnegation of power. He was himself the living negative of power. Even of responsibility. For the negation of power at last means the negation of responsibility. As far as these things went, he would confine himself to himself. He would try to confine his own *influence* even to himself. He would try, as far as possible, to abstain from influencing his children by assuming any responsibility for them. "A little child shall lead them——" His child should lead, then. He would try not to make it go in any direction whatever. He would abstain from influencing it. Liberty!——

Poor Winifred was like a fish out of water in this liberty, gasping for the denser element which should contain her. Till her child came. And then she knew that she must be responsible for it, that she must have authority over it.

But here Egbert, silently and negatively, stepped in. Silently, negatively, but fatally he neutralised her authority over her children.

There was a third little girl born. And after this Winifred wanted no more children. Her soul was turning to salt.

So she had charge of the children, they were her responsibility. The money for them had come from her father. She would do her very best for them, and have command over their life and death. But no! Egbert would not take the responsibility. He would not even provide the money. But he would not let her have her way. Her dark, silent, passionate authority he would not allow. It was a battle between them, the battle between liberty and the old blood-power. And of course he won. The little girls loved him and adored him. "Daddy! Daddy!" They could do as they liked with him. Their mother would have ruled them. She would have ruled them passionately, with indulgence, with the old dark magic of parental authority, something looming and unquestioned and, after all, divine: if we believe in divine authority. The Marshalls did, being Catholic.

And Egbert, he turned her old dark, Catholic blood-authority into a sort of tyranny. He would not leave her her children. He stole them from her, and yet without assuming responsibility for them. He stole them from her, in emotion and spirit, and left her only to command their behaviour. A thankless lot for a mother. And her children adored him, adored him, little knowing the empty bitterness they were preparing for themselves when they too grew up to have husbands: husbands such as Egbert, adorable and null.

Joyce, the eldest, was still his favourite. She was now a quicksilver little thing of six years old. Barbara, the youngest, was a toddler of two years. They spent most of the time down at Crockham, because he wanted to be there. And even Winifred loved the place really. But now, in her frustrated and blinded state, it was full of menace for her children. The adders, the poison-berries, the brook, the marsh, the water that might not be pure—one thing and another. From mother and nurse it was a guerilla gunfire of commands, and blithe, quicksilver disobedience from the three blonde, never-still little girls. Behind the girls was the father, against mother and nurse. And so it was.

"If you don't come quick, nurse, I shall run out there to where there are snakes."

"Joyce, you *must* be patient. I'm just changing Annabel!"

There you are. There it was: always the same. Working away on the common across the brook he heard it. And he worked on, just the same.

Suddenly he heard a shriek, and he flung the spade from him and started for the bridge, looking up like a startled deer. Ah, there was Winifred—Joyce had hurt herself. He went on up the garden.

"What is it?"

The child was still screaming—now it was—"Daddy! Daddy! Oh—oh, Daddy!" And the mother was saying:

"Don't be frightened, darling. Let mother look."

But the child only cried:

"Oh, Daddy, Daddy, Daddy!"

She was terrified by the sight of the blood running from her own knee. Winifred crouched down, with her child of six in her lap, to examine the knee. Egbert bent over also.

"Don't make such a noise, Joyce," he said irritably. "How did she do it?"

"She fell on that sickle thing which you left lying about after cutting the grass," said Winifred, looking into his face with bitter accusation as he bent near.

He had taken his handkerchief and tied it round the knee. Then he lifted the still sobbing child in his arms, and carried her into the house and upstairs to her bed. In his arms she became quiet. But his heart was burning with pain and with guilt. He had left the sickle there lying on the edge of the grass, and so his first-born child whom he loved so dearly had come to hurt. But then it was an accident—it was an accident. Why should he feel guilty? It would probably be nothing, better in two or three days. Why take it to heart, why worry? He put it aside.

The child lay on the bed in her little summer frock, her

face very white now after the shock. Nurse had come carrying the youngest child: and little Annabel stood holding her skirt. Winifred, terribly serious and wooden-seeming, was bending over the knee, from which she had taken his blood-soaked handkerchief. Egbert bent forward, too, keeping more sang-froid in his face than in his heart. Winifred went all of a lump of seriousness, so he had to keep some reserve. The child moaned and whimpered.

The knee was still bleeding profusely—it was a deep cut right in the joint.

"You'd better go for the doctor, Egbert," said Winifred bitterly.

"Oh no! Oh no!" cried Joyce in a panic.

"Joyce, my darling, don't cry!" said Winifred, suddenly catching the little girl to her breast in a strange tragic anguish, the *Mater Dolorata*. Even the child was frightened into silence. Egbert looked at the tragic figure of his wife with the child at her breast, and turned away. Only Annabel started suddenly to cry: "Joycey, Joycey, don't have your leg bleeding!"

Egbert rode four miles to the village for the doctor. He could not help feeling that Winifred was laying it on rather. Surely the knee itself wasn't hurt! Surely not. It was only a surface cut.

The doctor was out. Egbert left the message and came cycling swiftly home, his heart pinched with anxiety. He dropped sweating off his bicycle and went into the house, looking rather small, like a man who is at fault. Winifred was upstairs sitting by Joyce, who was looking pale and important in bed, and was eating some tapioca pudding. The pale, small, scared face of his child went to Egbert's heart.

"Doctor Wing was out. He'll be here about half-past two," said Egbert.

"I don't want him to come," whimpered Joyce.

"Joyce, dear, you must be patient and quiet," said Winifred. "He won't hurt you. But he will tell us what to do to make your knee better quickly. That is why he must come."

Winifred always explained carefully to her little girls: and it always took the words off their lips for the moment.

"Does it bleed yet?" said Egbert.

Winifred moved the bedclothes carefully aside.

"I think not," she said.

Egbert stooped also to look.

"No, it doesn't," he said. Then he stood up with a relieved look on his face. He turned to the child.

"Eat your pudding, Joyce," he said. "It won't be anything. You've only got to keep still for a few days."

"You haven't had your dinner, have you, Daddy?"

"Not yet."

"Nurse will give it to you," said Winifred.

"You'll be all right, Joyce," he said, smiling to the child and pushing the blonde hair aside off her brow. She smiled back winsomely into his face.

He went downstairs and ate his meal alone. Nurse served him. She liked waiting on him. All women liked him and liked to do things for him.

The doctor came—a fat country practitioner, pleasant and kind.

"What, little girl, been tumbling down, have you? There's a thing to be doing, for a smart little lady like you! What! And cutting your knee! Tut-tut-tut! That *wasn't* clever of you, now was it? Never mind, never mind, soon be better. Let us look at it. Won't hurt you. Not the least in life. Bring a bowl with a little warm water, nurse. Soon have it all right again, soon have it all right."

Joyce smiled at him with a pale smile of faint superiority. This was *not* the way in which she was used to being talked to.

He bent down, carefully looking at the little, thin, wounded knee of the child. Egbert bent over him.

"Oh, dead, oh, dear! Quite a deep little cut. Nasty little cut. Nasty little cut. But, never mind. Never mind, little lady. What's your name?"

"My name is Joyce," said the child distinctly.

"Oh, really!" he replied. "Oh, really! Well, that's a fine name too, in my opinion. Joyce, eh?—And how old might Miss Joyce be? Can she tell me that?"

"I'm six," said the child, slightly amused and very condescending.

"Six! There now. Add up and count as far as six, can you? Well, that's a clever little girl, a clever little girl. And if she has to drink a spoonful of medicine, she won't make a murmur, I'll be bound. Not like *some* little girls. What? Eh?"

"I take it if mother wishes me to," said Joyce.

"Ah, there now! That's the style! That's what I like to hear from a little lady in bed because she's cut her knee. That's the style——"

The comfortable and prolix doctor dressed and bandaged the knee and recommended bed and a light diet for the little lady. He thought a week or a fortnight would put it right. No bones or ligatures damaged—fortunately. Only a flesh cut. He would come again in a day or two.

So Joyce was reassured and stayed in bed and had all her toys up. Her father often played with her. The doctor came the third day. He was fairly pleased with the knee. It was healing. It was healing—yes—yes. Let the child continue in bed. He came again after a day or two. Winifred was a trifle uneasy. The wound seemed to be healing on the top, but it hurt the child too much. It didn't look quite right. She said so to Egbert.

"Egbert, I'm sure Joyce's knee isn't healing properly."

"I think it is," he said. "I think it's all right."

"I'd rather Doctor Wing came again—I don't feel satisfied."

"Aren't you trying to imagine it worse than it really is?"

"You would say so, of course. But I shall write a post-card to Doctor Wing now."

The doctor came next day. He examined the knee. Yes there was inflammation. Yes, there *might* be a little septic poisoning—there might. There might. Was the child feverish?

So a fortnight passed by, and the child *was* feverish, and the knee was more inflamed and grew worse and was painful, painful. She cried in the night, and her mother had to sit up with her. Egbert still insisted it was nothing, really—it would pass. But in his heart he was anxious.

Winifred wrote again to her father. On Saturday the elderly man appeared. And no sooner did Winifred see the thick, rather short figure in its grey suit than a great yearning came over her.

"Father, I'm not satisfied with Joyce. I'm not satisfied with Doctor Wing."

"Well, Winnie, dear, if you're not satisfied we must have further advice, that is all."

The sturdy, powerful, elderly man went upstairs, his voice sounding rather grating through the house, as if it cut upon the tense atmosphere.

"How are you, Joyce, darling?" he said to the child. "Does your knee hurt you? Does it hurt you, dear?"

"It does sometimes." The child was shy of him, cold towards him.

"Well, dear, I'm sorry for that. I hope you try to bear it, and not trouble mother too much."

There was no answer. He looked at the knee. It was red and stiff.

"Of course," he said, "I think we must have another doctor's opinion. And if we're going to have it, we had better have it at once. Egbert, do you think you might cycle in to Bingham for Doctor Wayne? I found him *very* satisfactory for Winnie's mother."

"I can go if you think it necessary," said Egbert.

"Certainly I think it necessary. Even if there *is* nothing, we can have peace of mind. Certainly I think it necessary. I should like Doctor Wayne to come this evening if possible."

So Egbert set off on his bicycle through the wind, like a boy sent on an errand, leaving his father-in-law a pillar of assurance, with Winifred.

Doctor Wayne came, and looked grave. Yes, the knee was certainly taking the wrong way. The child might be lame for life.

Up went the fire of fear and anger in every heart. Doctor Wayne came again the next day for a proper examination. And, yes, the knee had really taken bad ways. It should be X-rayed. It was very important.

Godfrey Marshall walked up and down the lane with the doctor, beside the standing motor-car: up and down, up and down in one of those consultations of which he had had so many in his life.

As a result he came indoors to Winifred.

"Well, Winnie, dear, the best thing to do is to take Joyce up to London, to a nursing home where she can have proper treatment. Of course this knee has been allowed to go wrong. And apparently there is a risk that the child may even lose her leg. What do you think, dear? You agree to our taking her up to town and putting her under the best care?"

"Oh, father, you *know* I would do anything on earth for her."

"I know you would, Winnie darling. The pity is that there has been this unfortunate delay already. I can't think what Doctor Wing was doing. Apparently the child is in danger of losing her leg. Well then, if you will have everything ready, we will take her up to town to-morrow. I will order the large car from Denley's to be here at ten. Egbert, will you take a telegram at once to Doctor Jackson? It is a small nursing home for children and for surgical cases, not far from Baker Street. I'm sure Joyce will be all right there."

"Oh, father, can't I nurse her myself?"

"Well, darling, if she is to have proper treatment, she had best be in a home. The X-ray treatment, and the electric treatment, and whatever is necessary."

"It will cost a great deal——" said Winifred.

"We can't think of cost, if the child's leg is in danger—or even her life. No use speaking of cost," said the elder man impatiently.

And so it was. Poor Joyce, stretched out on a bed in the big closed motor-car—the mother sitting by her head, the grandfather in his short grey beard and a bowler hat, sitting by her feet, thick, and implacable in his responsibility—they rolled slowly away from Crockham, and from Egbert, who stood there bareheaded and a little ignominious, left behind. He was to shut up the house and bring the rest of the family back to town, by train, the next day.

Followed a dark and bitter time. The poor child. The poor, poor child, how she suffered, an agony and a long crucifixion in that nursing home. It was a bitter six weeks which changed the soul of Winifred for ever. As she sat by the bed of her poor, tortured little child, tortured with the agony of the knee, and the still worse agony of these diabolic, but perhaps necessary modern treatments, she felt her heart killed and going cold in her breast. Her little Joyce, her frail, brave, wonderful, little Joyce, frail and small and pale as a white flower! Ah, how had she, Winifred, dared to be so wicked, so wicked, so careless, so sensual.

"Let my heart die! Let my woman's heart of flesh die! Saviour, let my heart die. And save my child. Let my heart die from the world and from the flesh. Oh, destroy my heart that is so wayward. Let my heart of pride die. Let my heart die."

She prayed beside the bed of her child. And like the Mother with the seven swords in her breast, slowly her heart of pride and passion died in her breast, bleeding away. Slowly it died, bleeding away, and she turned to the Church for comfort, to Jesus, to the Mother of God, but most of all, to that great and enduring institution, the Roman Catholic Church. She withdrew into the shadow of the Church. She was a mother with three children. But in her soul she died, her heart of pride and passion and desire bled to death, her soul belonged to her Church, her body belonged to her duty as a mother.

Her duty as a wife did not enter. As a wife she had no sense of duty: only a certain bitterness towards the man with whom she had known such sensuality and distraction. She was purely the *Mater Dolorata*. To the man she was closed as a tomb.

Egbert came to see his child. But Winifred seemed to be always seated there, like the tomb of his manhood and his fatherhood. Poor Winifred: she was still young, still strong and ruddy and beautiful like a ruddy hard flower of the field. Strange—her ruddy, healthy face, so sombre, and her strong, heavy, full-blooded body, so still. She, a nun! Never. And yet the gates of her heart and soul had shut in his face with a slow, resonant clang, shutting him out for ever. There was no need for her to go into a convent. Her will had done it.

And between this young mother and this young father lay

the crippled child, like a bit of pale silk floss on the pillow, and a little white pain-quenched face. He could not bear it. He just could not bear it. He turned aside. There was nothing to do but to turn aside. He turned aside, and went hither and thither, desultory. He was still attractive and desirable. But there was a little frown between his brow as if he had been cleft there with a hatchet: cleft right in, for ever, and that was the stigma.

The child's leg was saved: but the knee was locked stiff. The fear now was lest the lower leg should wither, or cease to grow. There must be long-continued massage and treatment, daily treatment, even when the child left the nursing home. And the whole of the expense was borne by the grandfather.

Egbert now had no real home. Winifred with the children and nurse was tied to the little flat in London. He could not live there: he could not contain himself. The cottage was shut up—or lent to friends. He went down sometimes to work in his garden and keep the place in order. Then with the empty house around him at night, all the empty rooms, he felt his heart go wicked. The sense of frustration and futility, like some slow, torpid snake, slowly bit right through his heart. Futility, futility, futility: the horrible marsh-poison went through his veins and killed him.

As he worked in the garden in the silence of day he would listen for a sound. No sound. No sound of Winifred from the dark inside of the cottage: no sound of children's voices from the air, from the common, from the near distance. No sound, nothing but the old dark marsh-venomous atmosphere of the place. So he worked spasmodically through the day, and at night made a fire and cooked some food alone.

He was alone. He himself cleaned the cottage and made his bed. But his mending he did not do. His shirts were slit on the shoulders, when he had been working, and the white flesh showed through. He would feel the air and the spots of rain on his exposed flesh. And he would look again across the common, where the dark, tufted gorse was dying to seed, and the bits of cat-heather were coming pink in tufts, like a sprinkling of sacrificial blood.

His heart went back to the savage old spirit of the place: the desire for old gods, old, lost passions, the passion of the cold-blooded, darting snakes that hissed and shot away from him, the mystery of blood-sacrifices, all the lost, intense sensations of the primeval people of the place, whose passions seethed in the air still, from those long days before the Romans came. The seethe of a lost, dark passion in the air. The presence of unseen snakes.

A queer, baffled, half-wicked look came on his face. He could not stay long at the cottage. Suddenly he must swing on to his bicycle and go—anywhere. Anywhere, away from the place. He would stay a few days with his mother in the old home. His mother adored him and grieved as a mother would. But the little, baffled, half-wicked smile curled on his face, and he swung away from his mother's solicitude as from everything else.

Always moving on—from place to place, friend to friend: and always swinging away from sympathy. As soon as sympathy, like a soft hand, was reached out to touch him, away he swerved, instinctively, as a harmless snake swerves and swerves and swerves away from an outstretched hand. Away he must go. And periodically he went back to Winifred.

He was terrible to her now, like a temptation. She had devoted herself to her children and her Church. Joyce was once more on her feet; but, alas! lame, with iron supports to her leg, and a little crutch. It was strange how she had grown into a long, pallid, wild little thing. Strange that the pain had not made her soft and docile, but had brought out a wild, almost mænad temper in the child. She was seven, and long and white and thin, but by no means subdued. Her blonde hair was darkening. She still had long sufferings to face, and, in her own childish consciousness, the stigma of her lameness to bear.

And she bore it. An almost mænad courage seemed to possess her, as if she were a long, thin, young weapon of life. She acknowledged all her mother's care. She would stand by her mother for ever. But some of her father's fine-tempered desperation flashed in her.

When Egbert saw his little girl limping horribly—not only

limping but lurching horribly in crippled, childish way, his heart again hardened with chagrin, like steel that is tempered again. There was a tacit understanding between him and his little girl: not what we would call love, but a weapon-like kinship. There was a tiny touch of irony in his manner towards her, contrasting sharply with Winifred's heavy, unleavened solicitude and care. The child flickered back to him with an answering little smile of irony and recklessness: an odd flippancy which made Winifred only the more sombre and earnest.

The Marshalls took endless thought and trouble for the child, searching out every means to save her limb and her active freedom. They spared no effort and no money, they spared no strength of will. With all their slow, heavy power of will they willed that Joyce should have her liberty of movement, should win back her wild, free grace. Even if it took a long time to recover, it should be recovered.

So the situation stood. And Joyce submitted, week after week, month after month, to the tyranny and pain of the treatment. She acknowledged the honourable effort on her behalf. But her flamy reckless spirit was her father's. It was he who had all the glamour for her. He and she were like members of some forbidden secret society who know one another but may not recognise one another. Knowledge they had in common, the same secret of life, the father and the child. But the child stayed in the camp of her mother, honourably, and the father wandered outside like Ishmael, only coming sometimes to sit in the home for an hour or two, an evening or two beside the camp-fire, like Ishmael, in a curious silence and tension, with the mocking answer of the desert speaking out of his silence, and annulling the whole convention of the domestic home.

His presence was almost an anguish to Winifred. She prayed against it. That little cleft between his brow, that flickering, wicked little smile that seemed to haunt his face, and above all, the triumphant loneliness, the Ishmael quality. And then the erectness of his supple body, like a symbol. The very way he stood, so quiet, so insidious, like an erect, supple symbol of life, the living body, confronting her downcast soul, was torture to her. He was like a supple living idol moving before her eyes, and she felt if she watched him she was damned.

And he came and made himself at home in her little home. When he was there, moving in his own quiet way, she felt as if the whole great law of sacrifice, by which she had elected to live, were annulled. He annulled by his very presence the laws of her life. And what did he substitute? Ah, against that question she hardened herself in recoil.

It was awful to her to have to have him about—moving about in his shirt-sleeves, speaking in his tenor, throaty voice to the children. Annabel simply adored him, and he teased the little girl. The baby, Barbara, was not sure of him. She had been born a stranger to him. But even the nurse, when she saw his white shoulder of flesh through the slits of his torn shirt, thought it a shame.

Winifred felt it was only another weapon of his against her.

"You have other shirts—why do you wear that old one that is all torn, Egbert?" she said.

"I may as well wear it out," he said subtly.

He knew she would not offer to mend it for him. She *could* not. And no, she would not. Had she not her own gods to honour? And could she betray them, submitting to his Baal and Ashtaroth? And it was terrible to her, his unsheathed presence, that seemed to annul her and her faith, like another revelation. Like a gleaming idol evoked against her, a vivid life-idol that might triumph.

He came and he went—and she persisted. And then the Great War broke out. He was a man who could not go to the dogs. He could not dissipate himself. He was pure-bred in his Englishness, and even when he would have liked to be vicious, he could not.

So when the war broke out his whole instinct was against it: against war. He had not the faintest desire to overcome any foreigners or to help in their death. He had no conception of Imperial England, and Rule Britannia was just a joke to him. He was a pure-blooded Englishman, perfect in his race, and when he was truly himself he could no more have been aggressive on the score of his Englishness than a rose can be aggressive on the score of its rosiness.

No, he had no desire to defy Germany and to exalt England. The distinction between German and English was not for him the distinction between good and bad. It was the distinction between blue water-flowers and red or white bush-blossoms: just difference. The difference between the wild boar and the wild bear. And a man was good or bad according to his nature, not according to his nationality.

Egbert was well-bred, and this was part of his natural understanding. It was merely unnatural to him to hate a nation *en bloc*. Certain individuals he disliked, and others he liked, and the mass he knew nothing about. Certain deeds he disliked, certain deeds seemed natural to him, and about most deeds he had no particular feeling.

He had, however, the one deepest pure-bred instinct. He recoiled inevitably from having his feelings dictated to him by the mass feeling. His feelings were his own, his understanding was his own, and he would never go back on either, willingly. Shall a man become inferior to his own true knowledge and self, just because the mob expects it of him?

What Egbert felt subtly and without question, his father-in-law felt also in a rough, more combative way. Different as the two men were, they were two real Englishmen, and their instincts were almost the same.

And Godfrey Marshall had the world to reckon with. There was German military aggression, and the English non-military idea of liberty and the 'conquests of peace'—meaning industrialism. Even if the choice between militarism and industrialism were a choice of evils, the elderly man asserted his choice of the latter, perforce. He whose soul was quick with the instinct of power.

Egbert just refused to reckon with the world. He just refused even to decide between German militarism and British industrialism. He chose neither. As for atrocities, he despised the people who committed them, as inferior criminal types. There was nothing national about crime.

And yet, war! War! Just war! Not right or wrong, but just war itself. Should he join? Should he give himself over to war? The question was in his mind for some weeks. Not because he thought England was right and Germany wrong. Probably Germany was wrong, but he refused to make a choice. Not because he felt inspired. No. But just—war.

The deterrent was the giving himself over into the power of other men, and into the power of the mob-spirit of a democratic army. Should he give himself over? Should he make over his own life and body to the control of something which he *knew* was inferior, in spirit, to his own self? Should he commit himself into the power of an inferior control? Should he? Should he betray himself?

He was going to put himself into the power of his inferiors, and he knew it. He was going to subjugate himself. He was going to be ordered about by petty *canaille* of non-commissioned officers—and even commissioned officers. He who was born and bred free. Should he do it?

He went to his wife, to speak to her.

"Shall I join up, Winifred?"

She was silent. Her instinct also was dead against it. And yet a certain profound resentment made her answer:

"You have three children dependent on you. I don't know whether you have thought of that."

It was still only the third month of the war, and the old pre-war ideas were still alive.

"Of course. But it won't make much difference to them. I shall be earning a shilling a day, at least."

"You'd better speak to father, I think," she replied heavily.

Egbert went to his father-in-law. The elderly man's heart was full of resentment.

"I should say," he said rather sourly, "it is the best thing you could do."

Egbert went and joined up immediately, as a private soldier. He was drafted into the light artillery.

Winifred now had a new duty towards him: the duty of a wife towards a husband who is himself performing his duty towards the world. She loved him still. She would always love him, as far as earthly love went. But it was duty she now lived by. When he came back to her in khaki, a soldier, she submitted to him as a wife. It was her duty. But to his passion she could never again fully submit. Something prevented her, for ever: even her own deepest choice.

He went back again to camp. It did not suit him to be a modern soldier. In the thick, gritty, hideous khaki his subtle physique was extinguished as if he had been killed. In the ugly intimacy of the camp his thoroughbred sensibilities were just degraded. But he had chosen, so he accepted. An ugly little look came on to his face, of a man who has accepted his own degradation.

In the early spring Winifred went down to Crockham to be there when primroses were out, and the tassels hanging on the hazel-bushes. She felt something like a reconciliation towards Egbert, now he was a prisoner in camp most of his days. Joyce was wild with delight at seeing the garden and the common again, after the eight or nine months of London and misery. She was still lame. She still had the irons up her leg. But she lurched about with a wild, crippled agility.

Egbert came for a week-end, in his gritty, thick, sandpaper khaki and puttees and the hideous cap. Nay, he looked terrible. And on his face a slightly impure look, a little sore on his lip, as if he had eaten too much or drunk too much or let his blood become a little unclean. He was almost uglily healthy, with the camp life. It did not suit him.

Winifred waited for him in a little passion of duty and sacrifice, willing to serve the soldier, if not the man. It only made him feel a little more ugly inside. The week-end was torment to him: the memory of the camp, the knowledge of the life he led there; even the sight of his own legs in that abhorrent khaki. He felt as if the hideous cloth went into his blood and made it gritty and dirty. Then Winifred so ready to serve the *soldier,* when she repudiated the man. And this made the grit worse between his teeth. And the children running around praying and calling in the rather mincing fashion of children who have nurses and governesses and literature in the family. And Joyce so lame! It had all become unreal to him, after the camp. It only set his soul on edge. He left at dawn on the Monday morning, glad to get back to the realness and vulgarity of the camp.

Winifred would never meet him again at the cottage—only

in London, where the world was with them. But sometimes he came alone to Crockham, perhaps when friends were staying there. And then he would work a while in his garden. This summer still it would flame with blue anchusas and big red poppies, the mulleins would sway their soft, downy erections in the air: he loved mulleins: and the honeysuckle would stream out scent like memory, when the owl was whooing. Then he sat by the fire with the friends and with Winifred's sisters, and they sang the folk-songs. He put on thin civilian clothes and his charm and his beauty and the supple dominancy of his body glowed out again. But Winifred was not there.

At the end of the summer he went to Flanders, into action. He seemed already to have gone out of life, beyond the pale of life. He hardly remembered his life any more, being like a man who is going to take a jump from a height, and is only looking to where he must land.

He was twice slightly wounded, in two months. But not enough to put him off duty for more than a day or two. They were retiring again, holding the enemy back. He was in the rear—three machine-guns. The country was all pleasant, war had not yet trampled it. Only the air seemed shattered, and the land awaiting death. It was a small, unimportant action in which he was engaged.

The guns were stationed on a little bushy hillock just outside a village. But occasionally, it was difficult to say from which direction came the sharp crackle of rifle-fire, and beyond, the far-off thud of cannon. The afternoon was wintry and cold.

A lieutenant stood on a little iron platform at the top of the ladders, taking the sights and giving the aim, calling in a high, tense, mechanical voice. Out of the sky came the sharp cry of the directions, then the warning numbers, then "Fire!" The shot went, the piston of the gun sprang back, there was a sharp explosion, and a very faint film of smoke in the air. Then the other two guns fired, and there was a lull. The officer was uncertain of the enemy's position. The thick clump of horse-chestnut trees below was without change. Only in the far distance the sound of heavy firing continued, so far off as to give a sense of peace.

The gorse bushes on either hand were dark, but a few sparks of flowers showed yellow. He noticed them almost unconsciously as he waited in the lull. He was in his shirt-sleeves, and the air came chill on his arms. Again his shirt was slit on the shoulders, and the flesh showed through. He was dirty and unkempt. But his face was quiet. So many things go out of consciousness before we come to the end of consciousness.

Before him, below, was the highroad, running between high banks of grass and gorse. He saw the whitish, muddy tracks and deep scores in the road, where the part of the regiment had retired. Now all was still. Sounds that came, came from the outside. The place where he stood was still silent, chill, serene: the white church among the trees beyond seemed like a thought only.

He moved into a lightning-like mechanical response at the sharp cry from the officer overhead. Mechanism, the pure mechanical action of obedience at the guns. Pure mechanical action at the guns. It left the soul unburdened, brooding in dark nakedness. In the end, the soul is alone, brooding on the face of the uncreated flux, as a bird on a dark sea.

Nothing could be seen but the road, and a crucifix knocked slanting and the dark, autumnal fields and woods. There appeared three horsemen on a little eminence, very small, on the crest of a ploughed field. They were our own men. Of the enemy, nothing.

The lull continued. Then suddenly came sharp orders, and a new direction of the guns, and an intense, exciting activity. Yet at the centre the soul remained dark and aloof, alone.

But even so, it was the soul that heard the new sound: the new, deep 'papp!' of a gun that seemed to touch right upon the soul. He kept up the rapid activity at the machine-gun, sweating. But in his soul was the echo of the new, deep sound, deeper than life.

And in confirmation came the awful faint whistling of a shell, advancing almost suddenly into a piercing, tearing shriek that would tear through the membrane of life. He heard it in his ears, but he heard it also in his soul, in tension. There was relief when the thing had swung by and struck, away beyond. He heard the hoarseness of its explosion, and the voice of the soldier calling to the horses. But he did not turn round to look. He only noticed a twig of holly with red berries fall like a gift on to the road below.

Not this time, not this time. Whither thou goest I will go. Did he say it to the shell, or to whom? Whither thou goest I will go. Then, the faint whistling of another shell dawned, and his blood became small and still to receive it. It drew nearer, like some horrible blast of wind; his blood lost consciousness. But in the second of suspension he saw the heavy shell swoop to earth, into the rocky bushes on the right, and earth and stones poured up into the sky. It was as if he heard no sound. The earth and stones and fragments of bush fell to earth again, and there was the same unchanging peace. The Germans had got the aim.

Would they move now? Would they retire? Yes. The officer was giving the last lightning-rapid orders to fire before withdrawing. A shell passed unnoticed in the rapidity of action. And then, into the silence, into the suspense where the soul brooded, finally crashed a noise and a darkness and a moment's flaming agony and horror. Ah, he had seen the dark bird flying towards him, flying home this time. In one instant life and eternity went up in a conflagration of agony, then there was a weight of darkness.

When faintly something began to struggle in the darkness, a consciousness of himself, he was aware of a great load and a clanging sound. To have known the moment of death! And to be forced, before dying, to review it. So, fate, even in death.

There was a resounding of pain. It seemed to sound from the outside of his consciousness: like a loud bell clanging very near. Yet he knew it was himself. He must associate himself with it. After a lapse and a new effort, he identified a pain in his head, a large pain that clanged and resounded. So far he could identify himself with himself. Then there was a lapse.

After a time he seemed to wake up again, and waking, to

know that he was at the front, and that he was killed. He did not open his eyes. Light was not yet his. The clanging pain in his head rang out the rest of his consciousness. So he lapsed away from consciousness, in unutterable sick abandon of life.

Bit by bit, like a doom, came the necessity to know. He was hit in the head. It was only a vague surmise at first. But in the swinging of the pendulum of pain, swinging ever nearer and nearer, to touch him into an agony of consciousness and a consciousness of agony, gradually the knowledge emerged—he must be hit in the head—hit on the left brow; if so, there would be blood—was there blood?—could he feel blood in his left eye? Then the clanging seemed to burst the membrane of his brain, like death-madness.

Was there blood on his face? Was hot blood flowing? Or was it dry blood congealing down his cheek? It took him hours even to ask the question: time being no more than an agony in darkness, without measurement.

A long time after he had opened his eyes he realised he was seeing something—something, something, but the effort to recall what was too great. No, no; no recall!

Were they the stars in the dark sky? Was it possible it was stars in the dark sky? Stars? The world? Ah, no, he could not know it! Stars and the world were gone for him, he closed his eyes. No stars, no sky, no world. No, no! The thick darkness of blood alone. It should be one great lapse into the thick darkness of blood in agony.

Death, oh, death! The world all blood, and the blood all writhing with death. The soul like the tiniest little light out on a dark sea, the sea of blood. And the light guttering, beating, pulsing in a windless storm, wishing it could go out, yet unable.

There had been life. There had been Winifred and his children. But the frail death-agony effort to catch at straws of memory, straws of life from the past, brought on too great a nausea. No, no! No Winifred, no children. No world, no people. Better the agony of dissolution ahead than the nausea of the effort backwards. Better the terrible work should go forward, the dissolving into the black sea of death, in the extremity of dissolution, than that there should be any reaching back towards life. To forget! To forget! Utterly, utterly to forget, in the great forgetting of death. To break the core and the unit of life, and to lapse out on the great darkness. Only that. To break the clue, and mingle and commingle with the one darkness, without afterwards or forwards. Let the black sea of death itself solve the problem of futurity. Let the will of man break and give up.

What was that? A light! A terrible light! Was it figures? Was it legs of a horse colossal—colossal above him: huge, huge?

The Germans heard a slight noise, and started. Then, in the glare of a light-bomb, by the side of the heap of earth thrown up by the shell, they saw the dead face.

Tickets, Please

THERE IS in the Midlands a single-line tramway system which boldly leaves the county town and plunges off into the black, industrial country-side, up hill and down dale, through the long ugly villages of workmen's houses, over canals and railways, past churches perched high and nobly over the smoke and shadows, through stark, grimy cold little market-places, tilting away in a rush past cinemas and shops down to the hollow where the collieries are, then up again, past a little rural church, under the ash trees, on in a rush to the terminus, the last little ugly place of industry, the cold little town that shivers on the edge of the wild, gloomy country beyond. There the green and creamy coloured tram-car seems to pause and purr with curious satisfaction. But in a few minutes—the clock on the turret of the Co-operative Wholesale Society's shops gives the time—away it starts once more on the adventure. Again there are the reckless swoops downhill, bouncing the loops: again the chilly wait in the hill-top market-place: again the breathless slithering round the precipitous drop under the church: again the patient halts at the loops, waiting for the outcoming car: so on and on, for two long hours, till at last the city looms beyond the fat gas-works, the narrow factories draw near, we are in the sordid streets of the great town, once more we sidle to a standstill at our terminus, abashed by the great crimson and cream-coloured city cars, but still perky, jaunty, somewhat dare-devil, green as a jaunty sprig of parsley out of a black colliery garden.

To ride on these cars is always an adventure. Since we are in war-time, the drivers are men unfit for active service: cripples and hunchbacks. So they have the spirit of the devil in them. The ride becomes a steeplechase. Hurray! we have leapt in a clear jump over the canal bridge—now for the four-lane corner. With a shriek and a trail of sparks we are clear again. To be sure, a tram often leaps the rails—but what matter! It sits in a ditch till other trams come to haul it out. It is quite common for a car, packed with one solid mass of living people, to come to a dead halt in the midst of unbroken blackness, the heart of nowhere on a dark night, and for the driver and the girl conductor to call: "All get off—car's on fire!" Instead, however, of rushing out in a panic, the passengers stolidly reply: "Get on—get on! We're not coming out. We're stopping where we are. Push on, George." So till flames actually appear.

The reason for this reluctance to dismount is that the nights are howlingly cold, black, and windswept, and a car is a haven of refuge. From village to village the miners travel, for a change of cinema, of girl, of pub. The trams are desperately packed. Who is going to risk himself in the black gulf outside, to wait perhaps an hour for another tram, then to see the forlorn notice 'Depot Only', because there is something wrong! Or to greet a unit of three bright cars all so tight with people that they sail past with a howl of derision. Trams that pass in the night.

This, the most dangerous tram-service in England, as the authorities themselves declare, with pride, is entirely conducted by girls, and driven by rash young men, a little crippled, or by delicate young men, who creep forward in terror. The girls are fearless young hussies. In their ugly blue uniform, skirts up to their knees, shapeless old peaked caps on their heads, they have all the *sang-froid* of an old non-commissioned officer. With a tram packed with howling colliers, roaring hymns downstairs and a sort of antiphony of obscenities upstairs, the lasses are perfectly at their ease. They pounce on the youths who try to evade their ticket-machine. They push off the men at the end of their distance. They are not going to be done in the eye—not they. They fear nobody—and everybody fears them.

"Hello, Annie!"

"Hello, Ted!"

"Oh, mind my corn, Miss Stone. It's my belief you've got a heart of stone, for you've trod on it again."

"You should keep it in your pocket,' replies Miss Stone, and she goes sturdily upstairs in her high boots.

"Tickets, please."

She is peremptory, suspicious, and ready to hit first. She can hold her own against ten thousand. The step of that tram-car is her Thermopylæ.

Therefore, there is a certain wild romance aboard these cars—and in the sturdy bosom of Annie herself. The time for soft romance is in the morning, between ten o'clock and one, when things are rather slack: that is, except market-day and Saturday. Thus Annie has time to look about her. Then she often hops off her car and into a shop where she has spied something, while the driver chats in the main road. There is very good feeling between the girls and the drivers. Are they not companions in peril, shipmates aboard this careering vessel of a tram-car, for ever rocking on the waves of a stormy land.

Then, also, during the easy hours, the inspectors are most in evidence. For some reason, everybody employed in this tram-service is young: there are no grey heads. It would not do. Therefore the inspectors are of the right age, and one, the chief, is also good-looking. See him stand on a wet, gloomy morning, in his long oilskin, his peaked cap well down over his eyes, waiting to board a car. His face ruddy, his small brown moustache is weathered, he has a faint impudent smile. Fairly tall and agile, even in his waterproof, he springs aboard a car and greets Annie.

"Hello, Annie! Keeping the wet out?"

"Trying to.'

There are only two people in the car. Inspecting is soon over. Then for a long and impudent chat on the foot-board, a good, easy, twelve-mile chat.

The inspector's name is John Thomas Raynor—always called John Thomas, except sometimes, in malice, Coddy. His face sets in fury when he is addressed, from a distance, with this abbreviation. There is considerable scandal about John Thomas in half a dozen villages. He flirts with the girl conductors in the morning, and walks out with them in the dark night, when they leave their tram-car at the depôt. Of course, the girls quit the service frequently. Then he flirts and walks out with the newcomer: always providing she is sufficiently attractive, and that she will consent to walk. It is remarkable, however, that most of the girls are quite comely, they are all young, and this roving life aboard the car gives them a sailor's dash and recklessness. What matter how they behave when the ship is in port? To-morrow they will be aboard again.

Annie, however, was something of a Tartar, and her sharp tongue had kept John Thomas at arm's length for many months. Perhaps, therefore, she liked him all the more: for he always came up smiling, with impudence. She watched him vanquish one girl, then another. She could tell by the movement of his mouth and eyes, when he flirted with her in the morning, that he had been walking out with this lass, or the other, the night before. A fine cock-of-the-walk he was. She could sum him up pretty well.

In this subtle antagonism they knew each other like old friends, they were as shrewd with one another almost as man and wife. But Annie had always kept him sufficiently at arm's length. Besides, she had a boy of her own.

The Statutes fair, however, came in November, at Bestwood. It happened that Annie had the Monday night off. It was a drizzling ugly night, yet she dressed herself up and went to the fair-ground. She was alone, but she expected soon to find a pal of some sort.

The roundabouts were veering round and grinding out their music, the side-shows were making as much commotion as possible. In the coconut shies there were no coconuts, but artificial war-time substitutes, which the lads declared were fastened into the irons. There was a sad decline in brilliance and luxury. None the less, the ground was muddy as ever, there was the same crush, the press of faces lighted up by the flares and the electric lights, the same smell of naphtha and a few potatoes, and of electricity.

Who should be the first to greet Miss Annie on the show-ground but John Thomas. He had a black overcoat buttoned up to his chin, and a tweed cap pulled down over his brows, his face between was ruddy and smiling and handy as ever. She knew so well the way his mouth moved.

She was very glad to have a 'boy'. To be at the Statutes without a fellow was no fun. Instantly, like the gallant he was, he took her on the Dragons, grim-toothed, roundabout switchbacks. It was not nearly so exciting as a tram-car actually. But, then, to be seated in a shaking, green dragon, uplifted above the sea of bubble faces, careering in a rickety fashion in the lower heavens, whilst John Thomas leaned over her, his cigarette in his mouth, was after all the right style. She was a plump, quick, alive little creature. So she was quite excited and happy.

John Thomas made her stay on for the next round. And therefore she could hardly for shame repulse him when he put his arm round her and drew her a little nearer to him, in a very warm and cuddly manner. Besides, he was fairly discreet, he kept his movement as hidden as possible. She looked down, and saw that his red, clean hand was out of sight of the crowd. And they knew each other so well. So they warmed up to the fair.

After the dragons they went on the horses. John Thomas paid each time, so she could but be complaisant. He, of course, sat astride on the outer horse—named 'Black Bess'— and she sat sideways, towards him, on the inner horse— named 'Wildfire'. But of course John Thomas was not going to sit discreetly on 'Black Bess', holding the brass bar. Round they spun and heaved, in the light. And round he swung on his wooden steed, flinging one leg across her mount, and perilously tipping up and down, across the space, half lying back, laughing at her. He was perfectly happy; she was afraid her hat was on one side, but she was excited.

He threw quoits on a table, and won for her two large, pale·blue hat-pins. And then, hearing the noise of the cinemas, announcing another performance, they climbed the boards and went in.

Of course, during these performances pitch darkness falls from time to time, when the machine goes wrong. Then there is a wild whooping, and a loud smacking of simulated kisses.

In these moments John Thomas drew Anne towards him. After all, he had a wonderfully warm, cosy way of holding a girl with his arm, he seemed to make such a nice fit. And, after all, it was pleasant to be so held: so very comforting and cosy and nice. He leaned over her and she felt his breath on her hair; she knew he wanted to kiss her on the lips. And, after all, he was so warm and she fitted in to him so softly. After all, she wanted him to touch her lips.

But the light sprang up; she also started electrically, and put her hat straight. He left his arm lying nonchalantly behind her. Well, it was fun, it was exciting to be at the Statutes with John Thomas.

When the cinema was over they went for a walk across the dark, damp fields. He had all the arts of love-making. He was especially good at holding a girl, when he sat with her on a stile in the black, drizzling darkness. He seemed to be holding her in space, against his own warmth and gratification. And his kisses were soft and slow and searching.

So Annie walked out with John Thomas, though she kept her own boy dangling in the distance. Some of the tram-girls chose to be huffy. But there, you must take things as you find them, in this life.

There was no mistake about it, Annie liked John Thomas a good deal. She felt so rich and warm in herself whenever he was near. And John Thomas really liked Annie, more than usual. The soft, melting way in which she could flow into a fellow, as if she melted into his very bones, was something rare and good. He fully appreciated this.

But with a developing acquaintance there began a developing intimacy. Annie wanted to consider him a person, a man: she wanted to take an intelligent interest in him, and to have an intelligent response. She did not want a mere nocturnal presence, which was what he was so far. And she prided herself that he could not leave her.

Here she made a mistake. John Thomas intended to remain a nocturnal presence; he had no idea of becoming an all-round individual to her. When she started to take an intelligent interest in him and his life and his character, he sheered off. He hated intelligent interest. And he knew that the only way to stop it was to avoid it. The possessive female was aroused in Annie. So he left her.

It is no use saying she was not surprised. She was at first startled, thrown out of her count. For she had been so *very* sure of holding him. For a while she was staggered, and everything became uncertain to her. Then she wept with fury, indignation, desolation, and misery. Then she had a spasm of despair. And then, when he came, still impudently, on to her car, still familiar, but letting her see by the movement of his head that he had gone away to somebody else for the time being, and was enjoying pastures new, then she determined to have her own back.

She had a very shrewd idea what girls John Thomas had taken out. She went to Nora Purdy. Nora was a tall, rather pale, but well-built girl, with beautiful yellow hair. She was rather secretive.

"Hey!" said Annie, accosting her; then softly: "Who's John Thomas on with now?"

"I don't know," said Nora.

"Why, tha does," said Annie, ironically lapsing into dialect. "Tha knows as well as I do."

"Well, I do, then," said Nora. "It isn't me, so don't bother."

"It's Cissy Meakin, isn't it?"

"It is, for all I know."

"Hasn't he got a face on him!" said Annie. "I don't half like his cheek. I could knock him off the foot-board when he comes round at me."

"He'll get dropped on one of these days," said Nora.

"Ay, he will, when somebody makes up their mind to drop it on him. I should like to see him taken down a peg or two, shouldn't you?"

"I shouldn't mind," said Nora.

"You've got quite as much cause to as I have," said Annie. "But we'll drop on him one of these days, my girl. What? Don't you want to?"

"I don't mind," said Nora.

But as a matter of fact, Nora was much more vindictive than Annie.

One by one Annie went the round of the old flames. It so happened that Cissy Meakin left the tramway service in quite a short time. Her mother made her leave. Then John Thomas was on the *qui vive*. He cast his eyes over his old flock. And his eyes lighted on Annie. He thought she would be safe now. Besides, he liked her.

She arranged to walk home with him on Sunday night. It so happened that her car would be in the depôt at half-past nine: the last car would come in at 10.15. So John Thomas was to wait for her there.

At the depôt the girls had a little waiting-room of their own. It was quite rough, but cosy, with a fire and an oven and a mirror, and table and wooden chairs. The half-dozen girls who knew John Thomas only too well had arranged to take service this Sunday afternoon. So, as the cars began to come in, early, the girls dropped into the waiting-room. And instead of hurrying off home, they sat around the fire and had a cup of tea. Outside was the darkness and lawlessness of war-time.

John Thomas came on the car after Annie, at about a quarter to ten. He poked his head easily into the girls' waiting-room.

"Prayer-meeting?" he asked.

"Ay," said Laura Sharp. "Ladies only."

"That's me!" said John Thomas. It was one of his favourite exclamations.

"Shut the door, boy," said Muriel Baggaley.

"Oh, which side of me?" said John Thomas.

"Which tha likes," said Polly Birkin.

He had come in and closed the door behind him. The girls moved in their circle, to make a place for him near the fire. He took off his great-coat and pushed back his hat.

"Who handles the teapot?" he said.

Nora Purdy silently poured him out a cup of tea.

"Want a bit o' my bread and drippin'?" said Muriel Baggaley to him.

"Ay, give us a bit."

And he began to eat his piece of bread.

"There's no place like home, girls," he said.

They all looked at him as he uttered this piece of impudence. He seemed to be sunning himself in the presence of so many damsels.

"Especially if you're not afraid to go home in the dark," said Laura Sharp.

"Me! By myself I am."

They sat till they heard the last tram come in. In a few minutes Emma Houselay entered.

"Come on, my old duck!" cried Polly Birkin.

"It *is* perishing," said Emma, holding her fingers to the fire.

"But—I'm afraid to, go home in, the dark," sang Laura Sharp, the tune having got into her mind.

"Who're you going with to-night, John Thomas?" asked Muriel Baggaley coolly.

"To-night?" said John Thomas. "Oh, I'm going home by myself to-night—all on my lonely-o."

"That's me!" said Nora Purdy, using his own ejaculation.

The girls laughed shrilly.

"Me as well, Nora," said John Thomas.

"Don't know what you mean," said Laura.

"Yes, I'm toddling," said he, rising and reaching for his overcoat.

"Nay," said Polly. "We're all here waiting for you."

"We've got to be up in good time in the morning," he said, in the benevolent official manner.

They all laughed.

"Nay," said Muriel. "Don't leave us all lonely, John Thomas. Take one!"

"I'll take the lot, if you like," he responded gallantly.

"That you won't, either," said Muriel. "Two's company; seven's too much of a good thing."

"Nay—take one," said Laura. "Fair and square, all above board and say which."

"Ay," cried Annie, speaking for the first time. "Pick, John Thomas; let's hear thee."

"Nay," he said. "I'm going home quiet to-night. Feeling good, for once."

"Whereabouts?" said Annie. "Take a good 'un, then. But tha's got to take one of us!"

"Nay, how can I take one," he said, laughing uneasily. "I don't want to make enemies."

"You'd only make *one*," said Annie.

"The chosen *one*," added Laura.

"Oh, my! Who said girls!" exclaimed John Thomas, again turning, as if to escape. "Well—good-night."

"Nay, you've got to make your pick," said Muriel. "Turn your face to the wall, and say which one touches you. Go on—we shall only just touch your back—one of us. Go on—turn your face to the wall, and don't look, and say which one touches you."

He was uneasy, mistrusting them. Yet he had not the courage to break away. They pushed him to a wall and stood him there with his face to it. Behind his back they all grimaced, tittering. He looked so comical. He looked around uneasily.

"Go on!" he cried.

"You're looking—you're looking!" they shouted.

He turned his head away. And suddenly, with a movement like a swift cat, Annie went forward and fetched him a box on the side of the head that sent his cap flying and himself staggering. He started round.

But at Annie's signal they all flew at him, slapping him, pinching him, pulling his hair, though more in fun than in spite or anger. He, however, saw red. His blue eyes flamed with strange fear as well as fury, and he butted through the girls to the door. It was locked. He wrenched at it. Roused, alert, the girls stood round and looked at him. He faced them, at bay. At that moment they were rather horrifying to him, as they stood in their short uniforms. He was distinctly afraid.

"Come on, John Thomas! Come on! Choose!" said Annie.

"What are you after? Open the door," he said.

"We shan't—not till you've chosen!" said Muriel.

"Chosen what?" he said.

"Chosen the one you're going to marry," she replied.

He hesitated a moment.

"Open the blasted door," he said, "and get back to your senses." He spoke with official authority.

"You've got to choose!" cried the girls.

"Come on!" cried Annie, looking him in the eye. "Come on! Come on!"

He went forward, rather vaguely. She had taken off her belt, and swinging it, she fetched him a sharp blow over the head with the buckle end. He sprang and seized her. But immediately the other girls rushed upon him, pulling and tearing and beating him. Their blood was now thoroughly up. He was their sport now. They were going to have their own back, out of him. Strange, wild creatures, they hung on him and rushed at him to bear him down. His tunic was torn right up the back, Nora had hold at the back of his collar, and was actually strangling him. Luckily the button burst. He struggled in a wild frenzy of fury and terror, almost mad terror. His tunic was simply torn off his back, his shirt-sleeves were torn away, his arms were naked. The girls rushed at him, clenched their hands on him and pulled at him: or they rushed at him and pushed him, butted him with all their might: or they struck him wild blows. He ducked and cringed and struck sideways. They became more intense.

At last he was down. They rushed on him, kneeling on him. He had neither breath nor strength to move. His face was bleeding with a long scratch, his brow was bruised.

Annie knelt on him, the other girls knelt and hung on to him. Their faces were flushed, their hair wild, their eyes were all glittering strangely. He lay at last quite still, with face averted, as an animal lies when it is defeated and at the mercy of the captor. Sometimes his eye glanced back at the wild faces of the girls. His breast rose heavily, his wrists were torn.

"Now, then, my fellow!" gasped Annie at length. "Now then—now——"

At the sound of her terrifying, cold triumph, he suddenly started to struggle as an animal might, but the girls threw themselves upon him with unnatural strength and power, forcing him down.

"Yes—now, then!" gasped Annie at length.

And there was a dead silence, in which the thud of heart-beating was to be heard. It was a suspense of pure silence in every soul.

"Now you know where you are," said Annie.

The sight of his white, bare arm maddened the girls. He lay in a kind of trance of fear and antagonism. They felt themselves filled with supernatural strength.

Suddenly Polly started to laugh—to giggle wildly—helplessly—and Emma and Muriel joined in. But Annie and Nora and Laura remained the same, tense, watchful, with gleaming eyes. He winced away from these eyes.

"Yes," said Annie, in a curious low tone, secret and deadly. "Yes! You've got it now. You know what you've done, don't you? You know what you've done."

He made no sound nor sign, but lay with bright, averted eyes, and averted, bleeding face.

"You ought to be *killed,* that's what you ought," said Annie, tensely. "You ought to be *killed.*" And there was a terrifying lust in her voice.

Polly was ceasing to laugh, and giving long-drawn Oh-h-hs and sighs as she came to herself.

"He's got to choose," she said vaguely.

"Oh, yes, he has," said Laura, with vindictive decision.

"Do you hear—do you hear?" said Annie. And with a sharp movement, that made him wince, she turned his face to her.

"Do you hear?" she repeated, shaking him.

But he was quite dumb. She fetched him a sharp slap on the face. He started, and his eyes widened. Then his face darkened with defiance, after all.

"Do you hear?" she repeated.

He only looked at her with hostile eyes.

"Speak!" she said, putting her face devilishly near his.

"What?" he said, almost overcome.

"You've got to *choose!*" she cried, as if it were some terrible menace, and as if it hurt her that she could not exact more.

"What?" he said, in fear.

"Choose your girl, Coddy. You've got to choose her now.

And you'll get your neck broken if you play any more of your tricks, my boy. You're settled now."

There was a pause. Again he averted his face. He was cunning in his overthrow. He did not give in to them really— no, not if they tore him to bits.

"All right, then," he said, "I choose Annie." His voice was strange and full of malice. Annie let go of him as if he had been a hot coal.

"He's chosen Annie!" said the girls in chorus.

"Me!" cried Annie. She was still kneeling, but away from him. He was still lying prostrate, with averted face. The girls grouped uneasily around.

"Me!" repeated Annie, with a terrible bitter accent.

Then she got up, drawing away from him with strange disgust and bitterness.

"I wouldn't touch him," she said.

But her face quivered with a kind of agony, she seemed as if she would fall. The other girls turned aside. He remained lying on the floor, with his torn clothes and bleeding, averted face.

"Oh, if he's chosen——" said Polly.

"I don't want him—he can choose again," said Annie, with the same rather bitter hopelessness.

"Get up," said Polly, lifting his shoulder. "Get up."

He rose slowly, a strange, ragged, dazed creature. The girls eyed him from a distance, curiously, furtively, dangerously.

"Who wants him?" cried Laura, roughly.

"Nobody," they answered, with contempt. Yet each one of them waited for him to look at her, hoped he would look at her. All except Annie, and something was broken in her.

He, however, kept his face closed and averted from them all. There was a silence of the end. He picked up the torn pieces of his tunic, without knowing what to do with them. The girls stood about uneasily, flushed, panting, tidying their hair and their dress unconsciously, and watching him. He looked at none of them. He espied his cap in a corner, and went and picked it up. He put it on his head, and one of the girls burst into a shrill, hysteric laugh at the sight he presented. He, however, took no heed, but went straight to where his overcoat hung on a peg. The girls moved away from contact with him as if he had been an electric wire. He put on his coat and buttoned it down. Then he rolled his tunic-rags into a bundle, and stood before the locked door, dumbly.

"Open the door, somebody," said Laura.

"Annie's got the key," said one.

Annie silently offered the key to the girls. Nora unlocked the door.

"Tit for tat, old man," she said, "Show yourself a man, and don't bear a grudge."

But without a word or sign he had opened the door and gone, his face closed, his head dropped.

"That'll learn him," said Laura.

"Coddy!" said Nora.

"Shut up, for God's sake!" cried Annie fiercely, as if in torture.

"Well, I'm about ready to go, Polly. Look sharp!" said Muriel.

The girls were all anxious to be off. They were tidying themselves hurriedly, with mute, stupefied faces.

The Blind Man

ISABEL PERVIN was listening for two sounds—for the sound of wheels on the drive outside and for the noise of her husband's footsteps in the hall. Her dearest and oldest friend, a man who seemed almost indispensable to her living, would drive up in the rainy dusk of the closing November day. The trap had gone to fetch him from the station. And her husband, who had been blinded in Flanders, and who had a disfiguring mark on his brow, would be coming in from the out-houses.

He had been home for a year now. He was totally blind. Yet they had been very happy. The Grange was Maurice's own place. The back was a farmstead, and the Wernhams, who occupied the rear premises, acted as farmers. Isabel lived with her husband in the handsome rooms in front. She and he had been almost entirely alone together since he was wounded. They talked and sang and read together in a wonderful and unspeakable intimacy. Then she reviewed books for a Scottish newspaper, carrying on her old interest, and he occupied himself a good deal with the farm. Sightless, he could still discuss everything with Wernham, and he could also do a good deal of work about the place—menial work, it is true, but it gave him satisfaction. He milked the cows, carried in the pails, turned the separator, attended to the pigs and horses. Life was still very full and strangely serene for the blind man, peaceful with the almost incomprehensible peace of immediate contact in darkness. With his wife he had a whole world, rich and real and invisible.

They were newly and remotely happy. He did not even regret the loss of his sight in these times of dark, palpable joy. A certain exultance swelled his soul.

But as time wore on, sometimes the rich glamour would leave them. Sometimes, after months of this intensity, a sense of burden overcame Isabel, a weariness, a terrible ennui, in that silent house approached between a colonnade of tall-shafted pines. Then she felt she would go mad, for she could not bear it. And sometimes he had devastating fits of depression, which seemed to lay waste his whole being. It was worse than depression—a black misery, when his own life was a torture to him, and when his presence was unbearable to his wife. The dread went down to the roots of her soul as these black days recurred. In a kind of panic she tried to wrap herself up still further in her husband. She forced the old spontaneous cheerfulness and joy to continue. But the effort it cost her was almost too much. She knew she could not keep it up. She felt she would scream with the strain, and would give anything, anything, to escape. She longed to possess her husband utterly; it gave her inordinate joy to have him entirely to herself. And yet, when again he was gone in a black and massive misery, she could not bear him, she could not bear herself; she wished she could be snatched away off the earth altogether, anything rather than live at this cost.

Dazed, she schemed for a way out. She invited friends, she tried to give him some further connection with the outer world. But it was no good. After all their joy and suffering, after their dark, great year of blindness and solitude and unspeakable nearness, other people seemed to them both shallow, prattling, rather impertinent. Shallow prattle seemed presumptuous. He became impatient and irritated, she was wearied. And so they lapsed into their solitude again. For they preferred it.

But now, in a few weeks' time, her second baby would be born. The first had died, an infant, when her husband first went out to France. She looked with joy and relief to the coming of the second. It would be her salvation. But also she felt some anxiety. She was thirty years old, her husband was a year younger. They both wanted the child very much. Yet she could not help feeling afraid. She had her husband on her hands, a terrible joy to her, and a terrifying burden. The child would occupy her love and attention. And then, what of Maurice? What would he do? If only she could feel that he, too, would be at peace and happy when the child came! She did so want to luxuriate in a rich, physical satisfaction of maternity. But the man, what would he do? How could she provide for him, how avert those shattering black moods of his, which destroyed them both?

She sighed with fear. But at this time Bertie Reid wrote to Isabel. He was her old friend, a second or third cousin, a Scotsman, as she was a Scotswoman. They had been brought up near to one another, and all her life he had been her friend, like a brother, but better than her own brothers. She loved him—through not in the marrying sense. There was a sort of kinship between them, an affinity. They understood one another instinctively. But Isabel would never have thought of marrying Bertie. It would have seemed like marrying in her own family.

Bertie was a barrister and a man of letters, a Scotsman of the intellectual type, quick, ironical, sentimental, and on his knees before the women he adored but did not want to marry. Maurice Pervin was different. He came of a good old country family—the Grange was not a very great distance from Oxford. He was passionate, sensitive, perhaps over-sensitive, wincing—a big fellow with heavy limbs and a forehead that flushed painfully. For his mind was slow, as if drugged by the strong provincial blood that beat in his veins. He was very sensitive to his own mental slowness, his feelings being quick and acute. So that he was just the opposite to Bertie, whose mind was much quicker than his emotions, which were not so very fine.

From the first the two men did not like each other. Isabel felt that they *ought* to get on together. But they did not. She felt that if only each could have the clue to the other there would be such a rare understanding between them. It did not come off, however. Bertie adopted a slightly ironical attitude, very offensive to Maurice, who returned the Scotch irony with English resentment, a resentment which deepened sometimes into stupid hatred.

This was a little puzzling to Isabel. However, she accepted

it in the course of things. Men were made freakish and unreasonable. Therefore, when Maurice was going out to France for the second time, she felt that, for her husband's sake, she must discontinue her friendship with Bertie. She wrote to the barrister to this effect. Bertram Reid simply replied that in this, as in all other matters, he must obey her wishes, if these were indeed her wishes.

For nearly two years nothing had passed between the two friends. Isabel rather gloried in the fact; she had no compunction. She had one great article of faith, which was, that husband and wife should be so important to one another, that the rest of the world simply did not count. She and Maurice were husband and wife. They loved one another. They would have children. Then let everybody and everything else fade into insignificance outside this connubial felicity. She professed herself quite happy and ready to receive Maurice's friend. She was happy and ready: the happy life, the ready woman in possession. Without knowing why, the friends retired abashed, and came no more. Maurice, of course, took as much satisfaction in this connubial absorption as Isabel did.

He shared in Isabel's literary activities, she cultivated a real interest in agriculture and cattle-raising. For she, being at heart perhaps an emotional enthusiast, always cultivated the practical side of life, and prided herself on her mastery of practical affairs. Thus the husband and wife had spent the five years of their married life. The last had been one of blindness and unspeakable intimacy. And now Isabel felt a great indifference coming over her, a sort of lethargy. She wanted to be allowed to bear her child in peace, to nod by the fire and drift vaguely, physically, from day to day. Maurice was like an ominous thunder-cloud. She had to keep waking up to remember him.

When a little note came from Bertie, asking if he were to put up a tombstone to their dead friendship, and speaking of the real pain he felt on account of her husband's loss of sight, she felt a pang, a fluttering agitation of re-awakening. And she read the letter to Maurice.

"Ask him to come down," he said.

"Ask Bertie to come here!" she re-echoed.

"Yes—if he wants to."

Isabel paused for a few moments.

"I know he wants to—he'd only be too glad," she replied. "But what about you, Maurice? How would you like it?"

"I should like it."

"Well—in that case—— But I thought you didn't care for him——"

"Oh, I don't know. I might think differently of him now," the blind man replied. It was rather abstruse to Isabel.

"Well, dear," she said, "if you're quite sure——"

"I'm sure enough. Let him come," said Maurice.

So Bertie was coming, coming this evening, in the November rain and darkness. Isabel was agitated, racked with her old restlessness and indecision. She had always suffered from this pain of doubt, just an agonising sense of uncertainty. It had begun to pass off, in the lethargy of maternity. Now it returned, and she resented it. She struggled as usual to maintain her calm, composed, friendly bearing, a sort of mask she wore over all her body.

A woman had lighted a tall lamp beside the table, and spread the cloth. The long dining-room was dim, with its elegant but rather severe pieces of old furniture. Only the round table glowed softly under the light. It had a rich, beautiful effect. The white cloth glistened and dropped its heavy, pointed lace corners almost to the carpet, the china was old and handsome, creamy-yellow, with a blotched pattern of harsh red and deep blue, the cups large and bell-shaped, the teapot gallant. Isabel looked at it with superficial appreciation.

Her nerves were hurting her. She looked automatically again at the high, uncurtained windows. In the last dusk she could just perceive outside a huge fir tree swaying its boughs: it was as if she thought it rather than saw it. The rain came flying on the window panes. Ah, why had she no peace? These two men, why did they tear at her? Why did they not come—why was there this suspense?

She sat in a lassitude that was really suspense and irritation. Maurice, at least, might come in—there was nothing to

keep him out. She rose to her feet. Catching sight of her
reflection in a mirror, she glanced at herself with a slight
smile of recognition, as if she were an old friend to herself.
Her face was oval and calm, her nose a little arched. Her
neck made a beautiful line down to her shoulder. With hair
knotted loosely behind, she had something of a warm, maternal look. Thinking this of herself, she arched her eyebrows
and her rather heavy eyelids, with a little flicker of a smile,
and for a moment her grey eyes looked amused and wicked,
a little sardonic, out of her transfigured Madonna face.

Then, resuming her air of womanly patience—she was
really fatally self-determined—she went with a little jerk
towards the door. Her eyes were slightly reddened.

She passed down the wide hall, and through a door at the
end. Then she was in the farm premises. The scent of dairy,
and of farm-kitchen, and of farmyard and of leather almost
overcame her: but particularly the scent of dairy. They had
been scalding out the pans. The flagged passage in front of
her was dark, puddled and wet. Light came out from the
open kitchen door. She went forward and stood in the doorway. The farm-people were at tea, seated at a little distance
from her, round a long, narrow table, in the centre of which
stood a white lamp. Ruddy faces, ruddy hands holding food,
red mouths working, heads bent over the tea-cups: men,
land-girls, boys: it was tea-time, feeding-time. Some faces
caught sight of her. Mrs. Wernham, going round behind the
chairs with a large black teapot, halting slightly in her walk,
was not aware of her for a moment. Then she turned
suddenly.

"Oh, is it Madame!" she exclaimed. "Come in, then, come
in! We're at tea." And she dragged forward a chair.

"No, I won't come in," said Isabel. "I'm afraid I interrupt
your meal."

"No—no—not likely, Madame, not likely."

"Hasn't Mr. Pervin come in, do you know?"

"I'm sure I couldn't say! Missed him, have you, Madame?"

"No, I only wanted him to come in," laughed Isabel, as if
shyly.

"Wanted him, did ye? Get up, boy—get up, now——"

Mrs. Wernham knocked one of the boys on the shoulder. He began to scrape to his feet, chewing largely.

"I believe he's in top stable," said another face from the table.

"Ah! No, don't get up. I'm going myself," said Isabel.

"Don't you go out of a dirty night like this. Let the lad go. Get along wi' ye, boy," said Mrs. Wernham.

"No, no," said Isabel, with a decision that was always obeyed. "Go on with your tea, Tom. I'd like to go across to the stable, Mrs. Wernham."

"Did ever you hear tell!" exclaimed the woman.

"Isn't the trap late?" asked Isabel.

"Why, no," said Mrs. Wernham, peering into the distance at the tall, dim clock. "No, Madame—we can give it another quarter or twenty minutes yet, good—yes, every bit of a quarter."

"Ah! It seems late when darkness falls so early," said Isabel.

"It do, that it do. Bother the days, that they draw in so," answered Mrs. Wernham. "Proper miserable!"

"They are," said Isabel, withdrawing.

She pulled on her over-shoes, wrapped a large tartan shawl around her, put on a man's felt hat, and ventured out along the causeways of the first yard. It was very dark. The wind was roaring in the great elms behind the out-houses. When she came to the second yard the darkness seemed deeper. She was unsure of her footing. She wished she had brought a lantern. Rain blew against her. Half she liked it, half she felt unwilling to battle.

She reached at last the just visible door of the stable. There was no sign of a light anywhere. Opening the upper half, she looked in: Into a simple well of darkness. The smell of horses, ammonia, and of warmth was startling to her, in that full night. She listened with all her ears, but could hear nothing save the night, and the stirring of a horse.

"Maurice!" she called, softly and musically, though she was afraid. "Maurice—are you there?"

Nothing came from the darkness. She knew the rain and wind blew in upon the horses, the hot animal life. Feeling it wrong, she entered the stable, and drew the lower half of the door shut, holding the upper part close. She did not stir, because she was aware of the presence of the dark hind-quarters of the horses, though she could not see them, and she was afraid. Something wild stirred in her heart.

She listened intensely. Then she heard a small noise in the distance—far away, it seemed—the chink of a pan, and a man's voice speaking a brief word. It would be Maurice, in the other part of the stable. She stood motionless, waiting for him to come through the partition door. The horses were so terrifyingly near to her, in the invisible.

The loud jarring of the inner door-latch made her start; the door was opened. She could hear and feel her husband entering and invisibly passing among the horses near her, in darkness as they were, actively intermingled. The rather low sound of his voice as he spoke to the horses came velvety to her nerves. How near he was, and how invisible! The darkness seemed to be in a strange swirl of violent life, just upon her. She turned giddy.

Her presence of mind made her call, quietly and musically:

"Maurice! Maurice—dea-ar!"

"Yes," he answered. "Isabel?"

She saw nothing, and the sound of his voice seemed to touch her.

"Hello!" she answered cheerfully, straining her eyes to see him. He was still busy, attending to the horses near her, but she saw only darkness. It made her almost desperate.

"Won't you come in, dear?" she said.

"Yes, I'm coming. Just half a minute. *Stand over—now!* Trap's not come, has it?"

"Not yet," said Isabel.

His voice was pleasant and ordinary, but it had a slight suggestion of the stable to her. She wished he would come away. While he was so utterly invisible she was afraid of him.

"How's the time?" he asked.

"Not yet six," she replied. She disliked to answer into the

dark. Presently he came very near to her, and she retreated out of doors.

"The weather blows in here," he said, coming steadily forward, feeling for the doors. She shrank away. At last she could dimly see him.

"Bertie won't have much of a drive," he said, as he closed the doors.

"He won't indeed!" said Isabel calmly, watching the dark shape at the door.

"Give me your arm, dear," she said.

She pressed his arm close to her, as she went. But she longed to see him, to look at him. She was nervous. He walked erect, with face rather lifted, but with a curious tentative movement of his powerful, muscular legs. She could feel the clever, careful, strong contact of his feet with the earth, as she balanced against him. For a moment he was a tower of darkness to her, as if he rose out of the earth.

In the house-passage he wavered, and went cautiously, with a curious look of silence about him as he felt for the bench. Then he sat down heavily. He was a man with rather sloping shoulders, but with heavy limbs, powerful legs that seemed to know the earth. His head was small, usually carried high and light. As he bent down to unfasten his gaiters and boots he did not look blind. His hair was brown and crisp, his hands were large, reddish, intelligent, the veins stood out in the wrists; and his thighs and knees seemed massive. When he stood up his face and neck were sur-charged with blood, the veins stood out on his temples. She did not look at his blindness.

Isabel was always glad when they had passed through the dividing door into their own regions of repose and beauty. She was a little afraid of him, out there in the animal grossness of the back. His bearing also changed, as he smelt the familiar, indefinable odour that pervaded his wife's sur-roundings, a delicate, refined scent, very faintly spicy. Per-haps it came from the pot-pourri bowls.

He stood at the foot of the stairs, arrested, listening. She watched him, and her heart sickened. He seemed to be listening to fate.

"He's not here yet," he said. "I'll go up and change."

"Maurice," she said, "you're not wishing he wouldn't come, are you?"

"I couldn't quite say," he answered. "I feel myself rather on the *qui vive*."

"I can see you are," she answered. And she reached up and kissed his cheek. She saw his mouth relax into a slow smile.

"What are you laughing at?" she said roguishly.

"You consoling me," he answered.

"Nay," she answered. "Why should I console you? You know we love each other—you know *how* married we are! What does anything else matter?"

"Nothing at all, my dear."

He felt for her face, and touched it, smiling.

"*You're* all right, aren't you?" he asked, anxiously.

"I'm wonderfully all right, love," she answered. "It's you I am a little troubled about, at times."

"Why me?" he said, touching her cheeks delicately with the tips of his fingers. The touch had an almost hypnotising effect on her.

He went away upstairs. She saw him mount into the darkness, unseeing and unchanging. He did not know that the lamps on the upper corridor were unlighted. He went on into the darkness with unchanging step. She heard him in the bathroom.

Pervin moved about almost unconsciously in his familiar surroundings, dark though everything was. He seemed to know the presence of objects before he touched them. It was a pleasure to him to rock thus through a world of things, carried on the flood in a sort of blood-prescience. He did not think much or trouble much. So long as he kept this sheer immediacy of blood-contact with the substantial world he was happy, he wanted no intervention of visual consciousness. In this state there was a certain rich positivity, bordering sometimes on rapture. Life seemed to move in him like a tide lapping, lapping, and advancing, enveloping all things darkly. It was a pleasure to stretch forth the hand and meet the unseen object, clasp it, and possess it in pure contact. He did not try to remember, to visualise. He did not want to. The new way of consciousness substituted itself in him.

The rich suffusion of this state generally kept him happy, reaching its culmination in the consuming passion for his wife. But at times the flow would seem to be checked and thrown back. Then it would beat inside him like a tangled sea, and he was tortured in the shattered chaos of his own blood. He grew to dread this arrest, this throw-back, this chaos inside himself, when he seemed merely at the mercy of his own powerful and conflicting elements. How to get some measure of control or surety, this was the question. And when the question rose maddening in him, he would clench his fists as if he would *compel* the whole universe to submit to him. But it was in vain. He could not even compel himself.

To-night, however, he was still serene, though little tremors of unreasonable exasperation ran through him. He had to handle the razor very carefully, as he shaved, for it was not at one with him, he was afraid of it. His hearing also was too much sharpened. He heard the woman lighting the lamps on the corridor, and attending to the fire in the visitor's room. And then, as he went to his room he heard the trap arrive. Then came Isabel's voice, lifted and calling, like a bell ringing:

"Is it you, Bertie? Have you come?"

And a man's voice answered out of the wind:

"Hello, Isabel! There you are."

"Have you had a miserable drive? I'm so sorry we couldn't send a closed carriage. I can't see you at all, you know."

"I'm coming. No, I liked the drive—it was like Perthshire. Well, how are you? You're looking fit as ever, as far as I can see."

"Oh, yes," said Isabel. "I'm wonderfully well. How are you? Rather thin, I think——"

"Worked to death—everybody's old cry. But I'm all right, Ciss. How's Pervin?—isn't he here?"

"Oh, yes, he's upstairs changing. Yes, he's awfully well. Take off your wet things; I'll send them to be dried."

"And how are you both, in spirits? He doesn't fret?"

"No—no, not at all. No, on the contrary, really. We've been wonderfully happy, incredibly. It's more than I can understand—so wonderful: the nearness, and the peace——"

"Ah! Well, that's awfully good news——"

They moved away. Pervin heard no more. But a childish sense of desolation had come over him, as he heard their brisk voices. He seemed shut out—like a child that is left out. He was aimless and excluded, he did not know what to do with himself. The helpless desolation came over him. He fumbled nervously as he dressed himself, in a state almost of childishness. He disliked the Scotch accent in Bertie's speech, and the slight response it found on Isabel's tongue. He disliked the slight purr of complacency in the Scottish speech. He disliked intensely the glib way in which Isabel spoke of their happiness and nearness. It made him recoil. He was fretful and beside himself like a child, he had almost a childish nostalgia to be included in the life circle. And at the same time he was a man, dark and powerful and infuriated by his own weakness. By some fatal flaw, he could not be by himself, he had to depend on the support of another. And this very dependence enraged him. He hated Bertie Reid, and at the same time he knew the hatred was nonsense, he knew it was the outcome of his own weakness.

He went downstairs. Isabel was alone in the dining-room. She watched him enter, head erect, his feet tentative. He looked so strong-blooded and healthy, and, at the same time, cancelled. Cancelled—that was the word that flew across her mind. Perhaps it was his scars suggested it.

"You heard Bertie come, Maurice?" she said.

"Yes—isn't he here?"

"He's in his room. He looks very thin and worn."

"I suppose he works himself to death."

A woman came in with a tray—and after a few minutes Bertie came down. He was a little dark man, with a very big forehead, thin, wispy hair, and sad, large eyes. His expression was inordinately sad—almost funny. He had odd, short legs.

Isabel watched him hesitate under the door, and glance nervously at her husband. Pervin heard him and turned.

"Here you are, now," said Isabel. "Come, let us eat."

Bertie went across to Maurice.

"How are you, Pervin?" he said, as he advanced.

The blind man stuck his hand out into space, and Bertie took it.

"Very fit. Glad you've come," said Maurice.

Isabel glanced at them, and glanced away, as if she could not bear to see them.

"Come," she said. "Come to table. Aren't you both awfully hungry? I am, tremendously."

"I'm afraid you waited for me," said Bertie, as they sat down.

Maurice had a curious monolithic way of sitting in a chair, erect and distant. Isabel's heart always beat when she caught sight of him thus.

"No," she replied to Bertie. "We're very little later than usual. We're having a sort of high tea, not dinner. Do you mind? It gives us such a nice long evening uninterrupted."

"I like it," said Bertie.

Maurice was feeling, with curious little movements, almost like a cat kneading her bed, for his place, his knife and fork, his napkin. He was getting the whole geography of his cover into his consciousness. He sat erect and inscrutable, remote-seeming. Bertie watched the static figure of the blind man, the delicate tactile discernment of the large, ruddy hands, and the curious mindless silence of the brow, above the scar. With difficulty he looked away, and without knowing what he did, picked up a little crystal bowl of violets from the table, and held them to his nose.

"They are sweet-scented," he said. "Where do they come from?"

"From the garden—under the windows," said Isabel.

"So late in the year—and so fragrant! Do you remember the violets under Aunt Bell's south wall?"

The two friends looked at each other and exchanged a smile, Isabel's eyes lighting up.

"Don't I?" she replied. "*Wasn't* she queer!"

"A curious old girl," laughed Bertie. "There's a streak of freakishness in the family, Isabel."

"Ah—but not in you and me, Bertie," said Isabel. "Give

them to Maurice, will you?" she added, as Bertie was putting down the flowers. "Have you smelled the violets, dear? Do!— they are so scented."

Maurice held out his hand, and Bertie placed the tiny bowl against his large, warm-looking fingers. Maurice's hand closed over the thin white fingers of the barrister. Bertie carefully extricated himself. Then the two watched the blind man smelling the violets. He bent his head and seemed to be thinking. Isabel waited.

"Aren't they sweet, Maurice?" she said at last, anxiously.

"Very," he said. And he held out the bowl. Bertie took it. Both he and Isabel were a little afraid, and deeply disturbed.

The meal continued. Isabel and Bertie chatted spasmodically. The blind man was silent. He touched his food repeatedly, with quick, delicate touches of his knife-point, then cut irregular bits. He could not bear to be helped. Both Isabel and Bertie suffered: Isabel wondered why. She did not suffer when he was alone with Maurice. Bertie made her conscious of a strangeness.

After the meal the three drew their chairs to the fire, and sat down to talk. The decanters were put on a table near at hand. Isabel knocked the logs on the fire, and clouds of brilliant sparks went up the chimney. Bertie noticed a slight weariness in her bearing.

"You will be glad when your child comes now, Isabel?" he said.

She looked up to him with a quick wan smile.

"Yes, I shall be glad," she answered. "It begins to seem long. Yes, I shall be very glad. So will you, Maurice, won't you?" she added.

"Yes, I shall," replied her husband.

"We are both looking forward so much to having it," she said.

"Yes, of course," said Bertie.

He was a bachelor, three or four years older than Isabel. He lived in beautiful rooms overlooking the river, guarded by a faithful Scottish manservant. And he had his friends among the fair sex—not lovers, friends. So long as he could avoid any danger of courtship or marriage, he adored a few good women with constant and unfailing homage, and he was chivalrously fond of quite a number. But if they seemed to encroach on him, he withdrew and detested them.

Isabel knew him very well, knew his beautiful constancy, and kindness, also his incurable weakness, which made him unable ever to enter into close contact of any sort. He was ashamed of himself, because he could not marry, could not approach women physically. He wanted to do so. But he could not. At the centre of him he was afraid, helplessly and even brutally afraid. He had given up hope, had ceased to expect any more that he could escape his own weakness. Hence he was a brilliant and successful barrister, also *littérateur* of high repute, a rich man, and a great social success. At the centre he felt himself neuter, nothing.

Isabel knew him well. She despised him even while she admired him. She looked at his sad face, his little short legs, and felt contempt of him. She looked at his dark grey eyes, with their uncanny, almost child-like intuition, and she loved him. He understood amazingly—but she had no fear of his understanding. As a man she patronised him.

And she turned to the impassive, silent figure of her husband. He sat leaning back, with folded arms, and face a little up-tilted. His knees were straight and massive. She sighed, picked up the poker, and again began to prod the fire, to rouse the clouds of soft, brilliant sparks.

"Isabel tells me," Bertie began suddenly, "that you have not suffered unbearably from the loss of sight."

Maurice straightened himself to attend, but kept his arms folded.

"No," he said, "not unbearably. Now and again one struggles against it, you know. But there are compensations."

"They say it is much worse to be stone deaf," said Isabel.

"I believe it is," said Bertie. "Are there compensations?" he added, to Maurice.

"Yes. You cease to bother about a great many things." Again Maurice stretched his figure, stretched the strong muscles of his back, and leaned backwards, with uplifted face.

"And that is a relief," said Bertie. "But what is there in place of the bothering? What replaces the activity?"

There was a pause. At length the blind man replied, as out of a negligent, unattentive thinking:

"Oh, I don't know. There's a good deal when you're not active."

"Is there?" said Bertie. "What, exactly? It always seems to me that when there is no thought and no action, there is nothing."

Again Maurice was slow in replying.

"There is something," he replied. "I couldn't tell you what it is."

And the talk lapsed once more, Isabel and Bertie chatting gossip and reminiscence, the blind man silent.

At length Maurice rose restlessly, a big, obtrusive figure. He felt tight and hampered. He wanted to go away.

"Do you mind," he said, "if I go and speak to Wernham?"

"No—go along, dear," said Isabel.

And he went out. A silence came over the two friends. At length Bertie said:

"Nevertheless, it is a great deprivation, Cissie."

"It is, Bertie. I know it is."

"Something lacking all the time," said Bertie.

"Yes, I know. And yet—and yet—Maurice is right. There is something else, something *there,* which you never knew was there, and which you can't express."

"What is there?" asked Bertie.

"I don't know—it's awfully hard to define it—but something strong and immediate. There's something strange in Maurice's presence—indefinable—but I couldn't do without it. I agree that it seems to put one's mind to sleep. But when we're alone I miss nothing; it seems awfully rich, almost splendid, you know."

"I'm afraid I don't follow," said Bertie.

They talked desultorily. The wind blew loudly outside, rain chattered on the window-panes, making a sharp drum-sound, because of the closed, mellow-golden shutters inside. The logs burned slowly, with hot, almost invisible small flames. Bertie seemed uneasy, there were dark circles round his eyes. Isabel, rich with her approaching maternity, leaned looking into the fire. Her hair curled in old, loose strands, very pleasing to the man. But she had a curious feeling of old woe in her heart, old, timeless night-woe.

"I suppose we're all deficient somewhere," said Bertie.

"I suppose so," said Isabel wearily.

"Damned, sooner or later."

"I don't know," she said, rousing herself. "I feel quite all right, you know. The child coming seems to make me indifferent to everything, just placid. I can't feel that there's anything to trouble about, you know."

"A good thing, I should say," he replied slowly.

"Well, there it is. I suppose it's just Nature. If only I felt I needn't trouble about Maurice, I should be perfectly content ———"

"But you feel you must trouble about him?"

"Well—I don't know——" She even resented this much effort.

The evening passed slowly. Isabel looked at the clock. "I say," she said. "It's nearly ten o'clock. Where can Maurice be? I'm sure they're all in bed at the back. Excuse me a moment."

She went out, returning almost immediately.

"It's all shut up and in darkness," she said. "I wonder where he is. He must have gone out to the farm——"

Bertie looked at her.

"I suppose he'll come in," he said.

"I suppose so," she said. "But it's unusual for him to be out now."

"Would you like me to go out and see?"

"Well—if you wouldn't mind. I'd go, but——" She did not want to make the physical effort.

Bertie put on an old overcoat and took a lantern. He went out from the side door. He shrank from the wet and roaring night. Such weather had a nervous effect on him: too much moisture everywhere made him feel almost imbecile. Unwilling, he went through it all. A dog barked violently at him. He peered in all the buildings. At last, as he opened the upper door of a sort of intermediate barn, he heard a grinding noise, and looking in, holding up his lantern, saw Maurice, in his shirt-sleeves, standing listening, holding the handle of a turnip-pulper. He had been pulping sweet roots, a pile of which lay dimly heaped in a corner behind him.

"That you, Wernham," said Maurice, listening.

"No, it's me," said Bertie.

A large, half-wild grey cat was rubbing at Maurice's leg. The blind man stooped to rub its sides. Bertie watched the scene, then unconsciously entered and shut the door behind him. He was in a high sort of barn-place, from which, right and left, ran off the corridors in front of the stalled cattle. He watched the slow, stooping motion of the other man, as he caressed the great cat.

Maurice straightened himself.

"You came to look for me?" he said.

"Isabel was a little uneasy," said Bertie.

"I'll come in. I like messing about doing these jobs."

The cat had reared her sinister, feline length against his leg, clawing at his thigh affectionately. He lifted her claws out of his flesh.

"I hope I'm not in your way at all at the Grange here," said Bertie, rather shy and stiff.

"My way? No, not a bit. I'm glad Isabel has somebody to talk to. I'm afraid it's I who am in the way. I know I'm not very lively company. Isabel's all right, don't you think? She's not unhappy, is she?"

"I don't think so."

"What does she say?"

"She says she's very content—only a little troubled about you."

"Why me?"

"Perhaps afraid that you might brood," said Bertie cautiously.

"She needn't be afraid of that." He continued to caress the flattened grey head of the cat with his fingers. "What I am a bit afraid of," he resumed, "is that she'll find me a dead weight, always alone with me down here."

"I don't think you need think that," said Bertie, though this was what he feared himself.

"I don't know," said Maurice. "Sometimes I feel it isn't fair that she's saddled with me." Then he dropped his voice curiously. "I say," he asked, secretly struggling, "is my face much disfigured? Do you mind telling me?"

"There is the scar," said Bertie, wondering. "Yes, it is a disfigurement. But more pitiable than shocking."

"A pretty bad scar, though," said Maurice.

"Oh yes."

There was a pause.

"Sometimes I feel I am horrible," said Maurice, in a low voice, talking as if to himself. And Bertie actually felt a quiver of horror.

"That's nonsense," he said.

Maurice again straightened himself, leaving the cat.

"There's no telling," he said. Then again, in an odd tone, he added: "I don't really know you, do I?"

"Probably not," said Bertie.

"Do you mind if I touch you?"

The lawyer shrank away instinctively. And yet, out of very philanthropy, he said, in a small voice: "Not at all."

But he suffered as the blind man stretched out a strong, naked hand to him. Maurice accidentally knocked off Bertie's hat.

"I thought you were taller," he said, starting. Then he laid his hand on Bertie Reid's head, closing the dome of the skull in a soft, firm grasp, gathering it, as it were; then, shifting his grasp and softly closing again, with a fine, close pressure, till he had covered the skull and the face of the smaller man, tracing the brows, and touching the full, closed eyes, touching the small nose and the nostrils, the rough, short moustache, the mouth, the rather strong chin. The hand of the blind man grasped the shoulder, the arm, the hand of the other man. He seemed to take him, in the soft, travelling grasp.

"You seem young," he said quietly, at last.

The lawyer stood almost annihilated, unable to answer.

"Your head seems tender, as if you were young," Maurice repeated. "So do your hands. Touch my eyes, will you?— touch my scar."

Now Bertie quivered with revulsion. Yet he was under the power of the blind man, as if hypnotised. He lifted his hand, and laid the fingers on the scar, on the scarred eyes. Maurice suddenly covered them with his own hand, pressed the fingers of the other man upon his disfigured eye-sockets, trembling in every fibre, and rocking slightly, slowly, from side to side. He remained thus for a minute or more, whilst Bertie stood as if in a swoon, unconscious, imprisoned.

Then suddenly Maurice removed the hand of the other man from his brow, and stood holding it in his own.

"Oh, my God," he said, "we shall know each other now, shan't we? We shall know each other now."

Bertie could not answer. He gazed mute and terror-struck, overcome by his own weakness. He knew he could not answer. He had an unreasonable fear, lest the other man should suddenly destroy him. Whereas Maurice was actually filled with hot, poignant love, the passion of friendship. Perhaps it was this very passion of friendship which Bertie shrank from most.

"We're all right together now, aren't we?" said Maurice. "It's all right now, as long as we live, so far as we're concerned."

"Yes," said Bertie, trying by any means to escape.

Maurice stood with head lifted, as if listening. The new delicate fulfilment of mortal friendship had come as a revelation and surprise to him, something exquisite and unhoped-for. He seemed to be listening to hear if it were real.

Then he turned for his coat.

"Come," he said, "we'll go to Isabel."

Bertie took the lantern and opened the door. The cat disappeared. The two men went in silence along the causeways. Isabel, as they came, thought their footsteps sounded strange. She looked up pathetically and anxiously for their entrance. There seemed a curious elation about Maurice. Bertie was haggard, with sunken eyes.

"What is it?" she asked.

"We've become friends," said Maurice, standing with his feet apart, like a strange colossus.

"Friends!" re-echoed Isabel. And she looked again at Bertie. He met her eyes with a furtive, haggard look; his eyes were as if glazed with misery.

"I'm so glad," she said, in sheer perplexity.

"Yes," said Maurice.

He was indeed so glad. Isabel took his hand with both hers, and held it fast.

"You'll be happier now, dear," she said.

But she was watching Bertie. She knew that he had one desire—to escape from this intimacy, this friendship, which had been thrust upon him. He could not bear it that he had been touched by the blind man, his insane reserve broken in. He was like a mollusc whose shell is broken.

Monkey Nuts

AT FIRST Joe thought the job O.K. He was loading hay on the trucks, along with Albert, the corporal. The two men were pleasantly billeted in a cottage not far from the station: they were their own masters, for Joe never thought of Albert as a master. And the little siding of the tiny village station was as pleasant a place as you could wish for. On one side, beyond the line, stretched the woods: on the other, the near side, across a green smooth field, red houses were dotted among flowering apple trees. The weather being sunny, work being easy, Albert, a real good pal, what life could be better! After Flanders, it was heaven itself.

Albert, the corporal, was a clean-shaven, shrewd-looking fellow of about forty. He seemed to think his one aim in life was to be full of fun and nonsense. In repose, his face looked a little withered, old. He was a very good pal to Joe, steady decent and grave under all his 'mischief'; for his mischief was only his laborious way of skirting his own ennui.

Joe was much younger than Albert—only twenty-three. He was a tallish, quiet youth, pleasant-looking. He was of a slightly better class than his corporal, more personable. Careful about his appearance, he shaved every day. "I haven't got much of a face," said Albert. "If I was to shave every day like you, Joe, I should have none."

There was plenty of life in the little goods-yard: three porter youths, a continual come and go of farm wagons bringing hay, wagons with timber from the woods, coal-carts loading at the trucks. The black coal seemed to make the place sleepier, hotter. Round the big white gate the station-master's children played and his white chickens walked, whilst the station-master himself, a young man getting too

264

fat, helped his wife to peg out the washing on the clothes-line in the meadow.

The great boat-shaped wagons came up from Playcross with the hay. At first the farm-men wagoned it. On the third day one of the land-girls appeared with the first load, drawing to a standstill easily at the head of her two great horses. She was a buxom girl, young, in linen overalls and gaiters. Her face was ruddy, she had large blue eyes.

"Now that's the wagoner for us, boys," said the corporal loudly.

"Whoa!" she said to her horses; and then to the corporal: "Which boys do you mean?"

"We are the pick of the bunch. That's Joe, my pal. Don't you let on that my name's Albert," said the corporal to his private. "I'm the corporal."

"And I'm Miss Stokes," said the land-girl coolly, "if that's all the boys you are."

"You know you couldn't want more, Miss Stokes," said Albert politely. Joe, who was bare-headed, whose grey flannel sleeves were rolled up to the elbow, and whose shirt was open at the breast, looked modestly aside as if he had no part in the affair.

"Are you on this job regular then?" said the corporal to Miss Stokes.

"I don't know for sure," she said, pushing a piece of hair under her hat, and attending to her splendid horses.

"Oh, make it a certainty," said Albert.

She did not reply. She turned and looked over the two men coolly. She was pretty, moderately blonde, with crisp hair, a good skin, and large blue eyes. She was strong, too, and the work went on leisurely and easily.

"Now!" said the corporal, stopping as usual to look round, "pleasant company makes work a pleasure—don't hurry it, boys." He stood on the truck surveying the world. That was one of his great and absorbing occupations: to stand and look out on things in general. Joe, also standing on the truck, also turned round to look what was to be seen. But he could not become blankly absorbed, as Albert could.

Miss Stokes watched the two men from under her broad

felt hat. She had seen hundreds of Alberts, khaki soldiers standing in loose attitudes, absorbed in watching nothing in particular. She had seen also a good many Joes, quiet, good-looking young soldiers with half-averted faces. But there was something in the turn of Joe's head, and something in his quiet, tender-looking form, young and fresh—which attracted her eye. As she watched him closely from below, he turned as if he felt her, and his dark-blue eye met her straight, light-blue gaze. He faltered and turned aside again and looked as if he were going to fall off the truck. A slight flush mounted under the girl's full, ruddy face. She liked him.

Always, after this, when she came in the sidings with her team, it was Joe she looked for. She acknowledged to herself that she was sweet on him. But Albert did all the talking. He was so full of fun and nonsense. Joe was a very shy bird, very brief and remote in his answers. Miss Stokes was driven to indulge in repartee with Albert, but she fixed her magnetic attention on the younger fellow. Joe would talk with Albert, and laugh at his jokes. But Miss Stokes could get little out of him. She had to depend on her silent forces. They were more effective than might be imagined.

Suddenly, on Saturday afternoon, at about two o'clock, Joe received a bolt from the blue—a telegram: "Meet me Belbury Station 6.00 p.m. to-day. M.S." He knew at once who M.S. was. His heart melted, he felt weak as if he had had a blow.

"What's the trouble, boy?" asked Albert anxiously.

"No—no trouble—it's to meet somebody." Joe lifted his dark, blue eyes in confusion towards his corporal.

"Meet somebody!" repeated the corporal, watching his young pal with keen blue eyes. "It's all right, then; nothing wrong?"

"No—nothing wrong. I'm not going," said Joe.

Albert was old and shrewd enough to see that nothing more should be said before the housewife. He also saw that Joe did not want to take him into confidence. So he held his peace, though he was piqued.

The two soldiers went into town, smartened up. Albert knew a fair number of the boys round about; there would be plenty of gossip in the market-place, plenty of lounging in groups on the Bath Road, watching the Saturday evening shoppers. Then a modest drink or two, and the movies. They passed an agreeable, casual, nothing-in-particular evening, with which Joe was quite satisfied. He thought of Belbury Station, and of M.S. waiting there. He had not the faintest intention of meeting her. And he had not the faintest intention of telling Albert.

And yet, when the two men were in their bedroom, half undressed, Joe suddenly held out the telegram to his corporal, saying: "What d'you think of that?"

Albert was just unbuttoning his braces. He desisted, took the telegram form, and turned towards the candle to read it.

"Meet me Belbury Station 6:00 p.m. to-day. M.S.," he read, *sotto voce*. His face took on its fun-and-nonsense look.

"Who's M.S.?" he asked, looking shrewdly at Joe.

"You know as well as I do," said Joe, non-committal.

"M.S.," repeated Albert. "Blamed if I know, boy. Is it a woman?"

The conversation was carried on in tiny voices, for fear of disturbing the householders.

"I don't know," said Joe, turning. He looked full at Albert, the two men looked straight into each other's eyes. There was a lurking grin in each of them.

"Well, I'm—*blamed!*" said Albert at last, throwing the telegram down emphatically on the bed.

"Wha—at?" said Joe, grinning rather sheepishly, his eyes clouded, none the less.

Albert sat on the bed and proceeded to undress, nodding his head with mock gravity all the while. Joe watched him foolishly.

"What?" he repeated faintly.

Albert looked up at him with a knowing look.

"If that isn't coming it quick, boy!" he said. "What the blazes! What ha' you bin doing?"

"Nothing!" said Joe.

Albert slowly shook his head as he sat on the side of the bed.

"Don't happen to me when *I've* bin doin' nothing," he said. And he proceeded to pull off his stockings.

Joe turned away, looking at himself in the mirror as he unbuttoned his tunic.

"You didn't want to keep the appointment?" Albert asked, in a changed voice, from the bedside.

Joe did not answer for a moment. Then he said:

"I made no appointment."

"I'm not saying you did, boy. Don't be nasty about it. I mean you didn't want to answer the—unknown person's summons—shall I put it that way?"

"No," said Joe.

"What was the deterring motive?" asked Albert, who was now lying on his back in bed.

"Oh," said Joe, suddenly looking round rather haughtily. "I didn't want to." He had a well-balanced head, and could take on a sudden distant bearing.

"Didn't want to—didn't cotton on, like. Well—*they be artful, the women——*" he mimicked his landlord. "Come on into bed, boy. Don't loiter about as if you'd lost something."

Albert turned over, to sleep.

On Monday Miss Stokes turned up as usual, striding beside her team. Her 'whoa!' was resonant and challenging, she looked up at the truck as her steeds came to a standstill. Joe had turned aside, and had his face averted from her. She glanced him over—save for his slender succulent tenderness she would have despised him. She sized him up in a steady look. Then she turned to Albert, who was looking down at her and smiling in his mischievous turn. She knew his aspects by now. She looked straight back at him, though her eyes were hot. He saluted her.

"Beautiful morning, Miss Stokes."

"Very!" she replied.

"Handsome is as handsome looks," said Albert.

Which produced no reponse.

"Now, Joe, come on here," said the corporal. "Don't keep the ladies waiting—it's the sign of a weak heart."

Joe turned and the work began. Nothing more was said for the time being. As the week went on all parties became more comfortable. Joe remained silent, averted, neutral, a little on his dignity. Miss Stokes was off-hand and masterful. Albert was full of mischief.

The great theme was a circus, which was coming to the market town on the following Saturday.

"You'll go to the circus, Miss Stokes?" said Albert.

"I may go. Are you going?"

"Certainly. Give us the pleasure of escorting you."

"No thanks."

"That's what I call a flat refusal—what, Joe? You don't mean that you have no liking for our company, Miss Stokes?"

"Oh, I don't know," said Miss Stokes. "How many are there of you?"

"Only me and Joe."

"Oh, is that all?" she said satirically.

Albert was a little nonplussed.

"Isn't that enough for you?" he asked.

"Too many by half," blurted out Joe, jeeringly, in a sudden fit of uncouth rudeness that made both the others stare.

"Oh, I'll stand out of the way, boy, if that's it," said Albert to Joe. Then he turned mischievously to Miss Stokes. "He wants to know what M. stands for," he said confidentially.

"Monkeys," she replied, turning to her horses.

"What's M.S.?" said Albert.

"Monkey-nuts," she retorted, leading off her team.

Albert looked after her a little discomfited. Joe had flushed dark, and cursed Albert in his heart.

On the Saturday afternoon the two soldiers took the train into town. They would have to walk home. They had tea at six o'clock, and lounged about till half-past seven. The circus was in a meadow near the river—a great red-and-white striped tent. Caravans stood at the side. A great crowd of people was gathered round the ticket-caravan.

Inside the tent the lamps were lighted, shining on a ring of faces, a great circular bank of faces round the green grassy centre. Along with some comrades, the two soldiers packed themselves on a thin plank seat, rather high. They were delighted with the flaring lights, the wild effect. But the circus performance did not affect them deeply. They admired the lady in black velvet with rose-purple legs who leapt so neatly on to the galloping horse; they watched the feats of strength, and laughed at the clown. But they felt a little patronising, they missed the sensational drama of the cinema.

Half-way through the performance Joe was electrified to see the face of Miss Stokes not very far from him. There she was, in her khaki and her felt hat, as usual; he pretended not to see her. She was laughing at the clown; she also pretended not to see him. It was a blow to him, and it made him angry. He would not even mention it to Albert. Least said, soonest mended. He liked to believe she had not seen him. But he knew, fatally, that she had.

When they came out it was nearly eleven o'clock; a lovely night, with a moon and tall, dark, noble trees: a magnificent May night. Joe and Albert laughed and chaffed with the boys. Joe looked round frequently to see if he were safe from Miss Stokes. It seemed so.

But there were six miles to walk home. At last the two soldiers set off, swinging their canes. The road was white between tall hedges, other stragglers were passing out of the town towards the villages; the air was full of pleased excitement.

They were drawing near to the village when they saw a dark figure ahead. Joe's heart sank with pure fear. It was a figure wheeling a bicycle; a land-girl; Miss Stokes. Albert was ready with his nonsense. Miss Stokes had a puncture.

"Let me wheel the rattler," said Albert.

"Thank you," said Miss Stokes. "You *are* kind."

"Oh, I'd be kinder than that, if you'd show me how," said Albert.

"Are you sure?" said Miss Stokes.

"Doubt my words?" said Albert. "That's cruel of you, Miss Stokes."

Miss Stokes walked between them, close to Joe.

"Have you been to the circus?" she asked him.

"Yes," he replied mildly.

"Have *you* been?" Albert asked her.

"Yes. I didn't see you," she replied.

"What!—you say so! Didn't see us! Didn't think us worth looking at," began Albert. "Aren't I as handsome as the clown, now? And you didn't as much as glance in our direction? I call it a downright oversight."

"I never *saw* you," reiterated Miss Stokes. "I didn't know you saw me."

"That makes it worse," said Albert.

The road passed through a belt of dark pine-wood. The village, and the branch road, was very near. Miss Stokes put out her fingers and felt for Joe's hand as it swung at his side. To say he was staggered is to put it mildly. Yet he allowed her softly to clasp his fingers for a few moments. But he was a mortified youth.

At the cross-road they stopped—Miss Stokes should turn off. She had another mile to go.

"You'll let us see you home," said Albert.

"Do me a kindness," she said. "Put my bike in your shed, and take it to Baker's on Monday, will you?"

"I'll sit up all night and mend it for you, if you like."

"No, thanks. And Joe and I'll walk on."

"Oh—ho! Oh—ho!" sang Albert. "Joe! Joe! What do you say to that, boy? Aren't you in luck's way? And I get the bloomin' old bike for my pal. Consider it again, Miss Stokes."

Joe turned aside his face, and did not speak.

"Oh, well! I wheel the grid, do I? I leave you, boy——"

"I'm not keen on going any farther," barked out Joe, in an uncouth voice. "She bain't my choice."

The girl stood silent, and watched the two men.

"There now!" said Albert. "Think o' that! If it was *me* now——" But he was uncomfortable. "Well, Miss Stokes, have me," he added.

Miss Stokes stood quite still, neither moved nor spoke. And so the three remained for some time at the lane end. At last Joe began kicking the ground—then he suddenly lifted his face. At that moment Miss Stokes was at his side. She put her arm delicately round his waist.

"Seems I'm the one extra, don't you think?" Albert inquired of the high bland moon.

Joe had dropped his head and did not answer. Miss Stokes stood with her arm lightly round his waist. Albert bowed,

saluted, and bade good night. He walked away, leaving the
two standing.

Miss Stokes put a light pressure on Joe's waist, and drew
him down the road. They walked in silence. The night was
full of scent—wild cherry, the first bluebells. Still they walked
in silence. A nightingale was singing. They approached nearer
and nearer, till they stood close by his dark bush. The
powerful notes sounded from the cover, almost like flashes of
light—then the interval of silence—then the moaning notes,
almost like a dog faintly howling, followed by the long, rich
trill, and flashing notes. Then a short silence again.

Miss Stokes turned at last to Joe. She looked up at him,
and in the moonlight he saw her faintly smiling. He felt
maddened, but helpless. Her arm was round his waist, she
drew him closely to her with a soft pressure that made all his
bones rotten.

Meanwhile Albert was waiting at home. He put on his
overcoat, for the fire was out, and he had had malarial fever.
He looked fitfully at the *Daily Morror* and the *Daily Sketch,*
but he saw nothing. It seemed a long time. He began to yawn
widely, even to nod. At last Joe came in.

Albert looked at him keenly. The young man's brow was
black, his face sullen.

"All right, boy?" asked Albert.

Joe merely grunted for a reply. There was nothing more to
be got out of him. So they went to bed.

Next day Joe was silent, sullen. Albert could make nothing
of him. He proposed a walk after tea.

"I'm going somewhere," said Joe.

"Where—Monkey-nuts?" asked the corporal. But Joe's
brow only became darker.

So the days went by. Almost every evening Joe went off
alone, returning late. He was sullen, taciturn and had a
hangdog look, a curious way of dropping his head and
looking dangerously from under his brows. And he and
Albert did not get on so well any more with one another. For
all his fun and nonsense, Albert was really irritable, soon
made angry. And Joe's stand-offish sulkiness and complete
lack of confidence riled him, got on his nerves. His fun and

nonsense took a biting, sarcastic turn, at which Joe's eyes glittered occasionally, though the young man turned unheeding aside. Then again Joe would be full of odd, whimsical fun, out-shining Albert himself.

Miss Stokes still came to the station with the wain: Monkey-nuts, Albert called her, though not to her face. For she was very clean and good-looking, almost she seemed to gleam. And Albert was a tiny bit afraid of her. She very rarely addressed Joe whilst the hay-loading was going on, and that young man always turned his back to her. He seemed thinner, and his limber figure looked more slouching. But still it had the tender, attractive appearance, especially from behind. His tanned face, a little thinned and darkened, took a handsome, slightly sinister look.

"Come on, Joe!" the corporal urged sharply one day. "What're you going, boy? Looking for beetles on the bank?"

Joe turned round swiftly, almost menacing, to work.

"He's a different fellow these days, Miss Stokes," said Albert to the young woman. "What's got him? Is it Monkey-nuts that don't suit him, do you think?"

"Choked with chaff, more like," she retorted. "It's as bad as feeding a threshing machine, to have to listen to some folks."

"As bad as what?" said Albert. "You don't mean *me*, do you, Miss Stokes?"

"No," she cried. "I don't mean you."

Joe's face became dark red during these sallies, but he said nothing. He would eye the young woman curiously, as she swung so easily at the work, and he had some of the look of a dog which is going to bite.

Albert, with his nerves on edge, began to find the strain rather severe. The next Saturday evening, when Joe came in more black-browed than ever, he watched him, determined to have it out with him.

When the boy went upstairs to bed, the corporal followed him. He closed the door behind him carefully, sat on the bed and watched the younger man undressing. And for once he spoke in a natural voice, neither chaffing nor commanding.

"What's gone wrong, boy?"

Joe stopped a moment as if he had been shot. Then he went on unwinding his puttees, and did not answer or look up.

"You can hear, can't you?" said Albert, nettled.

"Yes, I can hear," said Joe, stooping over his puttees till his face was purple.

"Then why don't you answer?"

Joe sat up. He gave a long, sideways look at the corporal. Then he lifted his eyes and stared at a crack in the ceiling.

The corporal watched these movements shrewdly.

"And *then* what?" he asked ironically.

Again Joe turned and stared him in the face. The corporal smiled very slightly, but kindly.

"There'll be murder done one of these days," said Joe, in a quiet, unimpassioned voice.

"So long as it's by daylight——" replied Albert. Then he went over, sat down by Joe, put his hand on his shoulder affectionately, and continued: "What is it, boy? What's gone wrong? You can trust me, can't you?"

Joe turned and looked curiously at the face so near to his.

"It's nothing, that's all," he said laconically.

Albert frowned.

"Then who's going to be murdered?—and who's going to do the murdering?—me or you—which is it, boy?" He smiled gently at the stupid youth, looking straight at him all the while, into his eyes. Gradually the stupid, hunted, glowering look died out of Joe's eyes. He turned his head aside, gently, as one rousing from a spell.

"I don't want her," he said, with fierce resentment.

"Then you needn't have her," said Albert. "What do you go for, boy?"

But it wasn't as simple as all that. Joe made no remark.

"She's a smart-looking girl. What's wrong with her, my boy? I should have thought you were a lucky chap, myself."

"I don't want 'er," Joe barked, with ferocity and resentment.

"Then tell her so and have done," said Albert. He waited a while. There was no response. "Why don't you?" he added.

"Because I don't," confessed Joe sulkily.

Albert pondered—rubbed his head.

"You're too soft-hearted, that's where it is, boy. You want your mettle dipping in cold water, to temper it. You're too soft-hearted——"

He laid his arm affectionately across the shoulders of the younger man. Joe seemed to yield a little towards him.

"When are you going to see her again?" Albert asked. For a long time there was no answer.

"When is it, boy?" persisted the softened voice of the corporal.

"To-morrow," confessed Joe.

"Then let me go," said Albert. "Let me go, will you?"

The morrow was Sunday, a sunny day, but a cold evening. The sky was grey, the new foliage very green, but the air was chill and depressing. Albert walked briskly down the white road towards Beeley. He crossed a larch plantation, and followed a narrow by-road, where blue speedwell flowers fell from the banks into the dust. He walked swinging his cane, with mixed sensations. Then having gone a certain length, he turned and began to walk in the opposite direction.

So he saw a young woman approaching him. She was wearing a wide hat of grey straw, and a loose, swinging dress of nigger-grey velvet. She walked with slow inevitability. Albert faltered a little as he approached her. Then he saluted her, and his roguish, slightly withered skin flushed. She was staring straight into his face.

He fell in by her side, saying impudently:

"Not so nice for a walk as it was, is it?"

She only stared at him. He looked back at her.

"You've seen me before, you know," he said, grinning slightly. "Perhaps you never noticed me. Oh, I'm quite nice-looking, in a quiet way, you know. What——?"

But Miss Stokes did not speak: she only stared with large, icy blue eyes at him. He became self-conscious, lifted up his chin, walked with his nose in the air, and whistled at random. So they went down the quiet, deserted grey lane. He was whistling the air: "I'm Gilbert, the filbert, the colonel of the nuts."

At last she found her voice:

"Where's Joe?"

"He thought you'd like a change: they say variety's the salt of life—that's why I'm mostly in pickle."

"Where is he?"

"Am I my brother's keeper? He's gone his own ways."

"Where?"

"Nay, how am I to know? Not so far but he'll be back for supper."

She stopped in the middle of the lane. He stopped facing her.

"Where's Joe?" she asked.

He struck a careless attitude, looked down the road this way and that, lifted his eyebrows, pushed his khaki cap on one side, and answered:

"He is not conducting the service to-night: he asked me if I'd officiate."

"Why hasn't he come?"

"Didn't want to, I expect. *I* wanted to."

She stared him up and down, and he felt uncomfortable in his spine, but maintained his air of nonchalance. Then she turned slowly on her heel, and started to walk back. The corporal went at her side.

"You're not going back, are you?" he pleaded. "Why, me and you, we should get on like a house on fire."

She took no need, but walked on. He went uncomfortably at her side, making his funny remarks from time to time. But she was as if stone deaf. He glanced at her, and to his dismay saw the tears running down her cheeks. He stopped suddenly, and pushed back his cap.

"I say, you know——" he began.

But she was walking on like an automaton, and he had to hurry after her.

She never spoke to him. At the gate of her farm she walked straight in, as if he were not there. He watched her disappear. Then he turned on his heel, cursing silently, puzzled, lifting off his cap to scratch his head.

That night, when they were in bed, he remarked:

"Say, Joe, boy; strikes me you're well off without Monkey-nuts. Gord love us, beans ain't in it."

So they slept in amity. But they waited with some anxiety for the morrow.

It was a cold morning, a grey sky shifting in a cold wind, and threatening rain. They watched the wagon come up the road and through the yard gates. Miss Stokes was with her team as usual; her "Whoa!" rang out like a war-whoop.

She faced up at the truck where the two men stood.

"Joe!" she called, to the averted figure which stood up in the wind.

"What?" he turned unwillingly.

She made a queer movement, lifting her head slightly in a sipping, half-inviting, half-commanding gesture. And Joe was crouching already to jump off the truck to obey her, when Albert put his hand on his shoulder.

"Half a minute, boy! Where are you off? Work's work, and nuts is nuts. You stop here."

Joe slowly straightened himself.

"Joe?" came the woman's clear call from below.

Again Joe looked at her. But Albert's hand was on his shoulder, detaining him. He stood half averted, with his tail between his legs.

"Take your hand off him, you!" said Miss Stokes.

"Yes, Major," retorted Albert satirically.

She stood and watched.

"Joe!" Her voice rang for the third time.

Joe turned and looked at her, and a slow, jeering smile gathered on his face.

"Monkey-nuts!" he replied, in a tone mocking her call.

She turned white—dead white. The men thought she would fall. Albert began yelling to the porters up the line to come and help with the load. He could yell like any non-commissioned officer upon occasion.

Some way or other the wagon was unloaded, the girl was gone. Joe and his corporal looked at one another and smiled slowly. But they had a weight on their minds, they were afraid.

They were reassured, however, when they found that Miss Stokes came no more with the hay. As far as they were concerned, she had vanished into oblivion. And Joe felt more relieved even than he had felt when he heard the firing cease, after the news had come that the armistice was signed.

You Touched Me

THE POTTERY HOUSE was a square, ugly, brick house girt in by the wall that enclosed the whole grounds of the pottery itself. To be sure, a privet hedge partly masked the house and its ground from the pottery-yard and works: but only partly. Through the hedge could be seen the desolate yard, and the many-windowed, factory-like pottery, over the hedge could be seen the chimneys and the out-houses. But inside the hedge, a pleasant garden and lawn sloped down to a willow pool, which had once supplied the works.

The Pottery itself was now closed, the great doors of the yard permanently shut. No more the great crates with yellow straw showing through stood in stacks by the packing-shed. No more the drays drawn by great horses rolled down the hill with a high load. No more the pottery-lasses in their clay-coloured overalls, their faces and hair splashed with grey fine mud, shrieked and larked with the men. All that was over.

"We like it much better—oh, much better—quieter," said Matilda Rockley.

"Oh, yes," assented Emmie Rockley, her sister.

"I'm sure you do," agreed the visitor.

But whether the two Rockley girls really liked it better, or whether they only imagined they did, is a question. Certainly their lives were much more grey and dreary now that the grey clay had ceased to spatter its mud and silt its dust over the premises. They did not quite realise how they missed the shrieking, shouting lasses, whom they had known all their lives and disliked so much.

Matilda and Emmie were already old maids. In a thorough industrial district, it is not easy for the girls who have expectations above the common to find husbands. The ugly industrial town was full of men, young men who were ready to marry. But they were all colliers or pottery-hands, mere workmen. The Rockley girls would have about ten thousand pounds each when their father died: ten thousand pounds' worth of profitable house-property. It was not to be sneezed at: they felt so themselves, and refrained from sneezing away such a fortune on any mere member of the proletariat. Consequently, bank-clerks or non-conformist clergymen or even school-teachers having failed to come forward, Matilda had begun to give up all idea of ever leaving the Pottery House.

Matilda was a tall, thin, graceful, fair girl, with a rather large nose. She was the Mary to Emmie's Martha: that is, Matilda loved painting and music, and read a good many novels, whilst Emmie looked after the housekeeping. Emmie was shorter, plumper than her sister, and she had no accomplishments. She looked up to Matilda, whose mind was naturally refined and sensible.

In their quiet, melancholy way, the two girls were happy. Their mother was dead. Their father was ill also. He was an intelligent man who had had some education, but preferred to remain as if he were one with the rest of the working people. He had a passion for music and played the violin pretty well. But now he was getting old, he was very ill, dying of a kidney disease. He had been rather a heavy whisky-drinker.

This quiet household, with one servant-maid, lived on year after year in the Pottery House. Friends came in, the girls went out, the father drank himself more and more ill. Outside in the street there was a continual racket of the colliers and their dogs and children. But inside the pottery wall was a deserted quiet.

In all this ointment there was one little fly. Ted Rockley, the father of the girls, had had four daughters, and no son. As his girls grew, he felt angry at finding himself always in a household of women. He went off to London and adopted a boy out of a Charity Institution. Emmie was fourteen years old, and Matilda sixteen, when their father arrived home with his prodigy, the boy of six, Hadrian.

Hadrian was just an ordinary boy from a Charity Home, with ordinary brownish hair and ordinary bluish eyes and of ordinary rather Cockney speech. The Rockley girls—there were three at home at the time of his arrival—had resented his being sprung on them. He, with his watchful, charity-institution instinct, knew this at once. Though he was only six years old, Hadrian had a subtle, jeering look on his face when he regarded the three young women. They insisted he should address them as Cousin: Cousin Flora, Cousin Matilda, Cousin Emmie. He complied, but there seemed a mockery in his tone.

The girls, however, were kind-hearted by nature. Flora married and left home. Hadrian did very much as he pleased with Matilda and Emmie, though they had certain strictnesses. He grew up in the Pottery House and about the Pottery premises, went to an elementary school, and was invariably called Hadrian Rockley. He regarded Cousin Matilda and Cousin Emmie with a certain laconic indifference, was quiet and reticent in his ways. The girls called him sly, but that was unjust. He was merely cautious, and without frankness. His uncle, Ted Rockley, understood him tacitly, their natures were somewhat akin. Hadrian and the elderly man had a real but unemotional regard for one another.

When he was thirteen years old the boy was sent to a High School in the County town. He did not like it. His Cousin Matilda had longed to make a little gentleman of him, but he refused to be made. He would give a little contemptuous curve to his lip, and take on a shy, charity-boy grin, when refinement was thrust upon him. He played truant from the High School, sold his books, his cap with its badge, even his very scarf and pocket-handkerchief, to his school-fellows, and went raking off heaven knows where with the money. So he spent two very unsatisfactory years.

When he was fifteen he announced that he wanted to leave England to go to the Colonies. He had kept touch with the Home. The Rockleys knew that, when Hadrian made a declaration, in his quiet, half-jeering manner, it was worse than useless to oppose him. So at last the boy departed, going to Canada under the protection of the Institution to which he

had belonged. He said good-bye to the Rockleys, without a
word of thanks, and parted, it seemed, without a pang.
Matilda and Emmie wept often to think of how he left them:
even on their father's face a queer look came. But Hadrian
wrote fairly regularly from Canada. He had entered some
electricity works near Montreal, and was doing well.

At last, however, the war came. In his turn, Hadrian
joined up and came to Europe. The Rockleys saw nothing of
him. They lived on, just the same, in the Pottery House. Ted
Rockley was dying of a sort of dropsy, and in his heart he
wanted to see the boy. When the Armistice was signed,
Hadrian had a long leave, and wrote that he was coming
home to the Pottery House.

The girls were terribly fluttered. To tell the truth, they
were a little afraid of Hadrian. Matilda, tall and thin, was
frail in her health, both girls were worn with nursing their
father. To have Hadrian, a young man of twenty-one, in the
house with them, after he had left them so coldly five years
before, was a trying circumstance.

They were in a flutter. Emmie persuaded her father to
have his bed made finally in the morning-room downstairs,
whilst his room upstairs was prepared for Hadrian. This was
done, and preparations were going on for the arrival, when,
at ten o'clock in the morning, the young man suddenly turned
up, quite unexpectedly. Cousin Emmie, with her hair bobbed
up in absurd little bobs round her forehead, was busily pol-
ishing the stair-rods, while Cousin Matilda was in the kitchen
washing the drawing-room ornaments in a lather, her sleeves
rolled back on her thin arms, and her head tied up oddly and
coquettishly in a duster.

Cousin Matilda blushed deep with mortification when the
self-possessed young man walked in with his kit-bag, and put
his cap on the sewing-machine. He was little and self-
confident, with a curious neatness about him that still suggested the Charity Institution. His face was brown, he had a
small moustache, he was vigorous enough in his smallness.

"*Well,* is it Hadrian!" exclaimed Cousin Matilda, wringing
the lather off her hand. "We didn't expect you till
to-morrow."

"I got off Monday night," said Hadrian, glancing round the room.

"Fancy!" said Cousin Matilda. Then, having dried her hands, she went forward, held out her hand, and said:

"How are you?"

"Quite well, thank you," said Hadrian.

"You're quite a man," said Cousin Matilda.

Hadrian glanced at her. She did not look her best: so thin, so large-nosed, with that pink-and-white checked duster tied round her head. She felt her disadvantage. But she had had a good deal of suffering and sorrow, she did not mind any more.

The servant entered—one that did not know Hadrian.

"Come and see my father," said Cousin Matilda.

In the hall they roused Cousin Emmie like a partridge from cover. She was on the stairs pushing the bright stair-rods into place. Instinctively her hand went to the little knobs, her front hair bobbed on her forehead.

"Why!" she exclaimed, crossly. "What have you come today for?"

"I got off a day earlier," said Hadrian, and his man's voice so deep and unexpected was like a blow to Cousin Emmie.

"Well, you've caught us in the midst of it," she said, with resentment. Then all three went into the middle room.

Mr. Rockley was dressed—that is, he had on his trousers and socks—but he was resting on the bed, propped up just under the window, from whence he could see his beloved and resplendent garden, where tulips and apple trees were ablaze. He did not look as ill as he was, for the water puffed him up, and his face kept its colour. His stomach was much swollen.

He glanced round swiftly, turning his eyes without turning his head. He was the wreck of a handsome, well-built man.

Seeing Hadrian, a queer, unwilling smile went over his face. The young man greeted him sheepishly.

"You wouldn't make a life-guardsman," he said. "Do you want something to eat?"

Hadrian looked round—as if for the meal.

"I don't mind," he said.

"What shall you have—egg and bacon?" asked Emmie shortly.

"Yes, I don't mind," said Hadrian.

The sisters went down to the kitchen, and sent the servant to finish the stairs.

"Isn't he *altered?*" said Matilda, *sotto voce*.

"Isn't he!" said Cousin Emmie. "*What* a little man!"

They both made a grimace, and laughed nervously.

"Get the frying-pan," said Emmie to Matilda.

"But he's as cocky as ever," said Matilda, narrowing her eyes and shaking her head knowingly, as she handed the frying-pan.

"Mannie!" said Emmie sarcastically. Hadrian's new-fledged, cocksure manliness evidently found no favour in her eyes.

"Oh, he's not bad," said Matilda. "You don't want to be prejudiced against him."

"I'm not prejudiced against him, I think he's all right for looks," said Emmie, "but there's too much of the little mannie about him."

"Fancy catching us like this," said Matilda.

"They've no thought for anything," said Emmie with contempt. "You go up and get dressed, our Matilda. I don't care about him. I can see to things, and you can talk to him. I shan't."

"He'll talk to my father," said Matilda, meaningful.

"*Sly——!*" exclaimed Emmie, with a grimace.

The sisters believed that Hadrian had come hoping to get something out of their father—hoping for a legacy. And they were not at all sure he would not get it.

Matilda went upstairs to change. She had thought it all out how she would receive Hadrian, and impress him. And he had caught her with her head tied up in a duster, and her thin arms in a basin of lather. But she did not care. She now dressed herself most scrupulously, carefully folded her long, beautiful, blonde hair, touched her pallor with a little rouge, and put her long string of exquisite crystal beads over her soft green dress. Now she looked elegant, like a heroine in a magazine illustration, and almost as unreal.

She found Hadrian and her father talking away. The young man was short of speech as a rule, but he could find his tongue with his 'uncle'. They were both sipping a glass of brandy, and smoking, and chatting like a pair of old cronies. Hadrian was telling about Canada. He was going back there when his leave was up.

"You wouldn't like to stop in England, then?" said Mr. Rockley.

"No, I wouldn't stop in England," said Hadrian.

"How's that? There's plenty of electricians here," said Mr. Rockley.

"Yes. But there's too much difference between the men and the employers over here—too much of that for me," said Hadrian.

The sick man looked at him narrowly, with oddly smiling eyes.

"That's it, is it?" he replied.

Matilda heard and understood. "So that's your big idea, is it, my little man," she said to herself. She had always said of Hadrian that he had no proper *respect* for anybody or anything, that he was sly and *common*. She went down to the kitchen for a *sotto voce* confab with Emmie.

"He thinks a rare lot of himself!" she whispered.

"He's somebody, he is!" said Emmie with contempt.

"He thinks there's too much difference between masters and men over here," said Matilda.

"Is it any different in Canada?" asked Emmie.

"Oh yes—democratic," replied Matilda. "He thinks they're all on a level over there."

"Ay, well, he's over here now," said Emmie dryly, "so he can keep his place."

As they talked they saw the young man sauntering down the garden, looking casually at the flowers. He had his hands in his pockets, and his soldier's cap neatly on his head. He looked quite at his ease, as if in possession. The two women, fluttered, watched him through the window.

"We know what he's come for," said Emmie, churlishly. Matilda looked a long time at the neat khaki figure. It had something of the charity-box about it still; but it was a man's figure, laconic, charged with plebeian energy. She thought of a derisive passion in his voice as he had declaimed against the propertied classes, to her father.

"You don't know, Emmie. Perhaps he's not come for that," she rebuked her sister. They were both thinking of the money.

They were still watching the young soldier. He stood away at the bottom of the garden, with his back to hem, his hands in his pockets, looking into the water of the willow pond. Matilda's dark blue eyes had a strange, full look in them, the lids, with the faint blue veins showing, dropped rather low. She carried her head light and high, but she had a look of pain. The young man at the bottom of the garden turned and looked up the path. Perhaps he saw them through the window. Matilda moved into shadow.

That afternoon their father seemed weak and ill. He was easily exhausted. The doctor came, and told Matilda that the sick man might die suddenly at any moment—but then he might not. They must be prepared.

So the day passed, and the next. Hadrian made himself at home. He went about in the morning in his brownish jersey and his khaki trousers, collarless, his bare neck showing. He explored the pottery premises, as if he had some secret purpose in so doing, he talked with Mr. Rockley, when the sick man had strength. The two girls were always angry when the two men sat talking together like cronies. Yet it was chiefly a kind of politics they talked.

On the second day after Hadrian's arrival, Matilda sat with her father in the evening. She was drawing a picture which she wanted to copy. It was very still, Hadrian was gone out somewhere, no one knew where, and Emmie was busy. Mr. Rockley reclined on his bed, looking out in silence over his evening-sunny garden.

"If anything happens to me, Matilda," he said, "you won't sell this house—you'll stop here——"

Matilda's eyes took their slightly haggard look as she stared at her father.

"Well, we couldn't do anything else," she said.

"You don't know what you might do," he said. "Everything is left to you and Emmie, equally. You do as you like with it—only don't sell this house, don't part with it."

"No," she said.

"And give Hadrian my watch and chain, and a hundred pounds out of what's in the bank—and help him if he ever wants helping. I haven't put his name in the will."

"Your watch and chain, and a hundred pounds—yes. But you'll be here when he goes back to Canada, father."

"You never know what'll happen," said her father.

Matilda sat and watched him, with her full, haggard eyes, for a long time, as if tranced. She saw that he knew he must go soon—she saw like a clairvoyant.

Later on she told Emmie what her father had said about the watch and chain and the money.

"What right has *he*"—he—meaning Hadrian—"to my father's watch and chain—what has it to do with him? Let him have the money, and get off," said Emmie. She loved her father.

That night Matilda sat late in her room. Her heart was anxious and breaking, her mind seemed entranced. She was too much entranced even to weep, and all the time she thought of her father, only her father. At last she felt she must go to him.

It was near midnight. She went along the passage and to his room. There was a faint light from the moon outside. She listened at his door. Then she softly opened and entered. The room was faintly dark. She heard a movement on the bed.

"Are you asleep?" she said softly, advancing to the side of the bed.

"Are you asleep?" she repeated gently, as she stood at the side of the bed. And she reached her hand in the darkness to touch his forehead. Delicately, her fingers met the nose and the eyebrows, she laid her fine, delicate hand on his brow. It seemed fresh and smooth—very fresh and smooth. A sort of surprise stirred her, in her entranced state. But it could not waken her. Gently, she leaned over the bed and stirred her fingers over the low-growing hair on his brow.

"Can't you sleep to-night?" she said.

There was a quick stirring in the bed. "Yes, I can," a voice answered. It was Hadrian's voice. She started away. Instantly she was wakened from her late-at-night trance. She remembered that her father was downstairs, that Hadrian had his room. She stood in the darkness as if stung.

"Is it you, Hadrian?" she said. "I thought it was my father." She was so startled, so shocked, that she could not move. The young man gave an uncomfortable laugh, and turned in his bed.

At last she got out of the room. When she was back in her own room, in the light, and her door was closed, she stood holding up her hand that had touched him, as if it were hurt. She was almost too shocked, she could not endure.

"Well," said her calm and weary mind, "it was only a mistake, why take any notice of it."

But she could not reason her feelings so easily. She suffered, feeling herself in a false position. Her right hand, which she had laid so gently on his face, on his fresh skin, ached now, as if it were really injured. She could not forgive Hadrian for the mistake: it made her dislike him deeply.

Hadrian too slept badly. He had been awakened by the opening of the door, and had not realised what the question meant. But the soft, straying tenderness of her hand on his face startled something out of his soul. He was a charity boy, aloof and more or less at bay. The fragile exquisiteness of her caress startled him most, revealed unknown things to him.

In the morning she could feel the consciousness in his eyes, when she came downstairs. She tried to bear herself as if nothing at all had happened, and she succeeded. She had the calm self-control, self-indifference, of one who has suffered and borne her suffering. She looked at him from her darkish, almost drugged blue eyes, she met the spark of consciousness in his eyes, and quenched it. And with her long, fine hand she put the sugar in his coffee.

But she could not control him as she thought she could. He had a keen memory stinging his mind, a new set of sensations working in his consciousness. Something new was alert in him. At the back of his reticent, guarded mind he kept his secret alive and vivid. She was at his mercy, for he was unscrupulous, his standard was not her standard.

He looked at her curiously. She was not beautiful, her nose was too large, her chin was too small, her neck was too thin. But her skin was clear and fine, she had a high-bred sensitiveness. This queer, brave, high-bred quality she shared with her father. The charity boy could see it in her tapering fingers, which were white and ringed. The same glamour that he knew in the elderly man he now saw in the woman. And he wanted to possess himself of it, he wanted to make himself master of it. As he went about through the old pottery-yard, his secretive mind schemed and worked. To be master of that strange soft delicacy such as he had felt in her hand upon his face—this was what he set himself towards. He was secretly plotting.

He watched Matilda as she went about, and she became aware of his attention, as of some shadow following her. But her pride made her ignore it. When he sauntered near her, his hands in his pockets, she received him with that same commonplace kindliness which mastered him more than any contempt. Her superior breeding seemed to control him. She made herself feel towards him exactly as she had always felt: he was a young boy who lived in the house with them, but was a stranger. Only, she dared not remember his face under her hand. When she remembered that, she was bewildered. Her hand had offended her, she wanted to cut it off. And she wanted, fiercely, to cut off the memory in him. She assumed she had done so.

One day, when he sat talking with his 'uncle', he looked straight into the eyes of the sick man, and said:

"But I shouldn't like to live and die here in Rawsley."

"No—well—you needn't," said the sick man.

"Do you think Cousin Matilda likes it?"

"I should think so."

"I don't call it much of a life," said the youth. "How much older is she than me, Uncle?"

The sick man looked at the young soldier.

"A good bit," he said.

"Over thirty?" said Hadrian.

"Well, not so much. She's thirty-two."

Hadrian considered a while.

"She doesn't look it," he said.

Again the sick father looked at him.

"Do you think she'd like to leave here?" said Hadrian.

"Nay, I don't know," replied the father, restive.

Hadrian sat still, having his own thoughts. Then in a small, quiet voice, as if he were speaking from inside himself, he said:

"I'd marry her if you wanted me to."

The sick man raised his eyes suddenly and stared. He stared for a long time. The youth looked inscrutably out of the window.

"You!" said the sick man, mocking, with some contempt. Hadrian turned and met his eyes. The two men had an inexplicable understanding.

"If you wasn't against it," said Hadrian.

"Nay," said the father, turning aside, "I don't think I'm against it. I've never thought of it. But—but Emmie's the youngest."

He had flushed, and looked suddenly more alive. Secretly he loved the boy.

"You might ask her," said Hadrian.

The elder man considered.

"Hadn't you better ask her yourself?" he said.

"She'd take more notice of you," said Hadrian.

They were both silent. Then Emmie came in.

For two days Mr. Rockley was excited and thoughtful. Hadrian went about quietly, secretly, unquestioning. At last the father and daughter were alone together. It was very early morning, the father had been in much pain. As the pain abated, he lay still thinking.

"Matilda!" he said suddenly, looking at his daughter.

"Yes, I'm here," she said.

"Ay! I want you to do something——"

She rose in anticipation.

"Nay, sit still. I want you to marry Hadrian——"

She thought he was raving. She rose, bewildered and frightened.

"Nay, sit you still, sit you still. You hear what I tell you."

"But you don't know what you're saying, father."

"Ay, I know well enough. I want you to marry Hadrian, I tell you."

She was dumfounded. He was a man of few words.

"You'll do what I tell you," he said.

She looked at him slowly.

"What put such an idea in your mind?" she said proudly.

"He did."

Matilda almost looked her father down, her pride was so offended.

"Why, it's disgraceful," she said.

"Why?"

She watched him slowly.

"What do you ask me for?" she said. "It's disgusting."

"The lad's sound enough," he replied testily.

"You'd better tell him to clear out," she said coldly.

He turned and looked out of the window. She sat flushed and erect for a long time. At length her father turned to her, looking really malevolent.

"If you won't," he said, "you're a fool, and I'll make you pay for your foolishness, do you see?"

Suddenly a cold fear gripped her. She could not believe her senses. She was terrified and bewildered. She stared at her father, believing him to be delirious, or mad, or drunk. What could she do?

"I tell you," he said. "I'll send for Whittle to-morrow if you don't. You shall neither of you have anything of mine."

Whittle was the solicitor. She understood her father well enough: he would send for his solicitor, and make a will leaving all his property to Hadrian: neither she nor Emmie should have anything. It was too much. She rose and went out of the room, up to her own room, where she locked herself in.

She did not come out for some hours. At last, late at night, she confided in Emmie.

"The sliving demon, he wants the money," said Emmie. "My father's out of his mind."

The thought that Hadrian merely wanted the money was

another blow to Matilda. She did not love the impossible youth—but she had not yet learned to think of him as a thing of evil. He now became hideous to her mind.

Emmie had a little scene with her father next day.

"You don't mean what you said to our Matilda yesterday, do you, father?" she asked aggressively.

"Yes," he replied.

"What, that you'll alter your will?"

"Yes."

"You won't," said his angry daughter.

But he looked at her with a malevolent little smile.

"Annie!" he shouted. "Annie!"

He had still power to make his voice carry. The servant maid came in from the kitchen.

"Put your things on, and go down to Whittle's office, and say I want to see Mr. Whittle as soon as he can, and will he bring a will-form."

The sick man lay back a little—he could not lie down. His daughter sat as if she had been struck. Then she left the room.

Hadrian was pottering about in the garden. She went straight down to him.

"Here," she said. "You'd better get off. You'd better take your things and go from here, quick."

Hadrian looked slowly at the infuriated girl.

"Who says so?" he asked.

"*We* say so—get off, you've done enough mischief and damage."

"Does Uncle say so?"

"Yes, he does."

"I'll go and ask him."

But like a fury Emmie barred his way.

"No, you needn't. You needn't ask him nothing at all. We don't want you, so you can go."

"Uncle's boss here."

"A man that's dying, and you crawling round and working on him for his money!—you're not fit to live."

"Oh!" he said. "Who says I'm working for his money?"

"I say. But my father told our Matilda, and *she* knows what you are. *She* knows what you're after. So you might as well clear out, for all you'll get—guttersnipe!"

He turned his back on her, to think. It had not occurred to him that they would think he was after the money. He *did* want the money—badly. He badly wanted to be an employer himself, not one of the employed. But he knew, in his subtle, calculating way, that it was not for money he wanted Matilda. He wanted both the money and Matilda. But he told himself the two desires were separate, not one. He could not do with Matilda, *without* the money. But he did not want her *for* the money.

When he got this clear in his mind, he sought for an opportunity to tell it to her, lurking and watching. But she avoided him. In the evening the lawyer came. Mr. Rockley seemed to have a new access of strength—a will was drawn up, making the previous arrangements wholly conditional. The old will held good, if Matilda would consent to marry Hadrian. If she refused then at the end of six months the whole property passed to Hadrian.

Mr. Rockley told this to the young man, with malevolent satisfaction. He seemed to have a strange desire, quite unreasonable, for revenge upon the women who had surrounded him for so long, and served him so carefully.

"Tell her in front of me," said Hadrian.

So. Mr. Rockley sent for his daughters.

At last they came, pale, mute, stubborn. Matilda seemed to have retired far off, Emmie seemed like a fighter ready to fight to the death. The sick man reclined on the bed, his eyes bright, his puffed hand trembling. But his face had again some of its old, bright handsomeness. Hadrian sat quiet, a little aside: the indomitable, dangerous charity boy.

"There's the will," said their father, pointing them to the paper.

The two women sat mute and immovable, they took no notice.

"Either you marry Hadrian, or he has everything," said the father with satisfaction.

"Then let him have everything," said Matilda coldly.

"He's not! He's not!" cried Emmie fiercely. "He's not going to have it. The guttersnipe!"

An amused look came on her father's face.

"You hear that, Hadrian," he said.

"I didn't offer to marry Cousin Matilda for the money," said Hadrian, flushing and moving on his seat.

Matilda looked at him slowly, with her dark blue, drugged eyes. He seemed a strange little monster to her.

"Why, you liar, you know you did," cried Emmie.

The sick man laughed. Matilda continued to gaze strangely at the young man.

"She knows I didn't," said Hadrian.

He too had his courage, as a rat has indomitable courage in the end. Hadrian had some of the neatness, the reserve, the underground quality of the rat. But he had perhaps the ultimate courage, the most unquenched courage of all.

Emmie looked at her sister.

"Oh, well," she said. "Matilda—don't you bother. Let him have everything, we can look after ourselves."

"I know he'll take everything," said Matilda, abstractedly.

Hadrian did not answer. He knew in fact that if Matilda refused him he would take everything, and go off with it.

"A clever little mannie——!" said Emmie, with a jeering grimace.

The father laughed noiselessly to himself. But he was tired. . . .

"Go on, then," he said. "Go on, let me be quiet."

Emmie turned and looked at him.

"You deserve what you've got," she said to her father bluntly.

"Go on," he answered mildly. "Go on."

Another night passed—a night nurse sat up with Mr. Rockley. Another day came. Hadrian was there as ever, in his woollen jersey and coarse khaki trousers and bare neck. Matilda went about, frail and distant, Emmie black-browed in spite of her blondness. They were all quiet, for they did not intend the mystified servant to learn anything.

Mr. Rockley had very bad attacks of pain, he could not breathe. The end seemed near. They all went about quiet and stoical, all unyielding. Hadrian pondered within himself. If he did not marry Matilda he would go to Canada with twenty thousand pounds. This was itself a very satisfactory prospect. If Matilda consented he would have nothing—she would have her own money.

Emmie was the one to act. She went off in search of the solicitor and brought him home with her. There was an interview, and Whittle tried to frighten the youth into withdrawal—but without avail. The clergyman and relatives were summoned—but Hadrian stared at them and took no notice, It made him angry, however.

He wanted to catch Matilda alone. Many days went by, and he was not successful: she avoided him. At last, lurking, he surprised her one day as she came to pick gooseberries, and he cut off her retreat. He came to the point at once.

"You don't want me, then?" he said, in his subtle, insinuating voice.

"I don't want to speak to you," she said, averting her face.

"You put your hand on me, though," he said. "You shouldn't have done that, and then I should never have thought of it. You shouldn't have touched me."

"If you were anything decent, you'd know that was a mistake, and forget it," she said.

"I know it was a mistake—but I shan't forget it. If you wake a man up, he can't go to sleep again because he's told to."

"If you had any decent feeling in you, you'd have gone away," she replied.

"I didn't want to," he replied.

She looked away into the distance. At last she asked:

"What do you persecute me for, if it isn't for the money? I'm old enough to be your mother. In a way I've been your mother."

"Doesn't matter," he said. "You've been no mother to me. Let us marry and go out to Canada—you might as well— you've touched me."

She was white and trembling. Suddenly she flushed with anger.

"It's so *indecent,*" she said.

"How?" he retorted. "You touched me."

But she walked away from him. She felt as if he had trapped her. He was angry and depressed, he felt again despised.

That same evening she went into her father's room.

"Yes," she said suddenly. "I'll marry him."

Her father looked up at her. He was in pain, and very ill.

"You like him now, do you?" he said, with a faint smile.

She looked down into his face, and saw death not far off. She turned and went coldly out of the room.

The solicitor was sent for, preparations were hastily made. In all the interval Matilda did not speak to Hadrian, never answered him if he addressed her. He approached her in the morning.

"You've come round to it, then?" he said, giving her a pleasant look from his twinking, almost kindly eyes. She looked down at him and turned aside. She looked down on him both literally and figuratively. Still he persisted, and triumphed.

Emmie raved and wept, the secret flew abroad. But Matilda was silent and unmoved, Hadrian was quiet and satisfied, and nipped with fear also. But he held out against his fear. Mr. Rockley was very ill, but unchanged.

On the third day the marriage took place. Matilda and Hadrian drove straight home from the registrar, and went straight into the room of the dying man. His face lit up with a clear twinkling smile.

"Hadrian—you've got her?" he said, a little hoarsely.

"Yes," said Hadrian, who was pale round the gills.

"Ay, my lad, I'm glad you're mine," replied the dying man. Then he turned his eyes closely on Matilda.

"Let's look at you, Matilda," he said. Then his voice went strange and unrecognisable. "Kiss me," he said.

She stooped and kissed him. She had never kissed him before, not since she was a tiny child. But she was quiet, very still.

"Kiss him," the dying man said.

Obediently, Matilda put forward her mouth and kissed the young husband.

"That's right! That's right!" murmured the dying man.

Samson and Delilah

A MAN got down from the motor-omnibus that runs from
Penzance to St. Just-in-Penwith, and turned northwards,
uphill towards the Polestar. It was only half-past six, but
already the stars were out, a cold little wind was blowing
from the sea, and the crystalline, three-pulse flash of the
lighthouse below the cliffs beat rhythmically in the first
darkness.

The man was alone. He went his way unhesitating, but
looked from side to side with cautious curiosity. Tall, ruined
power-houses of tin-mines loomed in the darkness from time
to time, like remnants of some by-gone civilisation. The lights
of many miners' cottages scattered on the hilly darkness
twinkled desolate in their disorder, yet twinkled with the
lonely homeliness of the Celtic night.

He tramped steadily on, always watchful with curiosity. He
was a tall, well-built man, apparently in the prime of life. His
shoulders were square and rather stiff, he leaned forwards a
little as he went, from the hips, like a man who must stoop to
lower his height. But he did not stoop his shoulders: he bent
his straight back from the hips.

Now and again short, stump, thick-legged figures of Cornish miners passed him, and he invariably gave them good
night, as if to insist that he was on his own ground. He spoke
with the West Cornish intonation. And as he went along the
dreary road, looking now at the lights of the dwellings on
land, now at the lights away to sea, vessels veering round in
sight of the Longships Lighthouse, the whole of the Atlantic
Ocean in darkness and space between him and America, he
seemed a little excited and pleased with himself, watchful,

thrilled, veering along in a sense of mastery and of power in conflict.

The houses began to close on the road, he was entering the straggling, formless, desolate mining village, that he knew of old. On the left was a little space set back from the road, and cosy lights of an inn. There it was. He peered up at the sign: 'The Tinners' Rest'. But he could not make out the name of the proprietor. He listened. There was excited talking and laughing, a woman's voice laughing shrilly among the men's.

Stooping a little, he entered the warmly-lit bar. The lamp was burning, a buxom woman rose from the white-scrubbed deal table where the black and white and red cards were scattered, and several men, miners, lifted their faces from the game.

The stranger went to the counter, averting his face. His cap was pulled down over his brow.

"Good evening!" said the landlady, in her rather ingratiating voice.

"Good evening. A glass of ale."

"A glass of ale," repeated the landlady suavely. "Cold night—but bright."

"Yes," the man assented, laconically. Then he added, when nobody expected him to say any more: "Seasonable weather."

"Quite seasonable, quite," said the landlady. "Thank you."

The man lifted his glass straight to his lips, and emptied it. He put it down again on the zinc counter with a click.

"Let's have another," he said.

The woman drew the beer, and the man went away with his glass to the second table, near the fire. The woman, after a moment's hesitation, took her seat again at the table with the card-players. She had noticed the man: a big fine fellow, well dressed, a stranger.

But he spoke with that Cornish–Yankee accent she accepted as the natural twang among the miners.

The stranger put his foot on the fender and looked into the fire. He was handsome, well coloured, with well-drawn Cornish eyebrows, and the usual dark, bright, mindless Cornish eyes. He seemed abstracted in thought. Then he watched the card-party.

The woman was buxom and healthy, with dark hair and small, quick brown eyes. She was bursting with life and vigour, the energy she threw into the game of cards excited all the men, they shouted, and laughed, and the woman held her breast, shrieking with laughter.

"Oh, my, it'll be the death o' me," she panted. "Now, come on, Mr. Trevorrow, play fair. Play fair, I say, or I s'll put the cards down."

"Play fair! Why, who's played unfair?" ejaculated Mr. Trevorrow. "Do you mean t'accuse me, as I haven't played fair, Mrs. Nankervis?"

"I do. I say it, and I mean it. Haven't you got the Queen of Spades? Now, come on, no dodging round me. I know you've got that Queen, as well as I know my name's Alice."

"Well, if your name's Alice, you'll have to have it——"

"Ay, now—what did I say? Did ever you see such a man? My word, but your missus must be easy took in, by the looks of things."

And off she went into peals of laughter. She was interrupted by the entrance of four men in khaki, a short, stumpy sergeant of middle age, a young corporal, and two young privates. The woman leaned back in her chair.

"Oh, my!" she cried. "If there isn't the boys back: looking perished, I believe——"

"Perished, Ma!" exclaimed the sergeant. "Not yet."

"Near enough," said a young private uncouthly.

The woman got up.

"I'm sure you are, my dears. You'll be wanting your suppers, I'll be bound."

"We could do with 'em."

"Let's have a wet first," said the sergeant.

The woman bustled about getting the drinks. The soldiers moved to the fire, spreading out their hands.

"Have your suppers in here, will you?" she said. "Or in the kitchen?"

"Let's have it here," said the sergeant. "More cosier—*if* you don't mind."

"You shall have it where you like, boys, where you like."

She disappeared. In a minute a girl of about sixteen came

in. She was tall and fresh, with dark, young, expressionless eyes, and well-drawn brows, and the immature softness and mindlessness of the sensuous Celtic type.

"Ho, Maryann! Evenin', Maryann! How's Maryann, now?" came the multiple greeting.

She replied to everybody in a soft voice, a strange, soft aplomb that was very attractive. And she moved round with rather mechanical, attractive movements, as if her thoughts were elsewhere, but she had always this dim far-awayness in her bearing: a sort of modesty. The strange man by the fire watched her curiously. There was an alert, inquisitive, mindless curiosity on his well-coloured face.

"I'll have a bit of supper with you, if I might," he said.

She looked at him with her clear, unreasoning eyes, just like the eyes of some non-human creature.

"I'll ask mother," she said. Her voice was soft-breathing, gently sing-song.

When she came in again:

"Yes," she said, almost whispering. "What will you have?"

"What have you got?" he said, looking up into her face.

"There's cold meat——"

"That's for me, then."

The stranger sat at the end of the table, and ate with the tired, quiet soldiers. Now the landlady was interested in him. Her brow was knit rather tense, there was a look of panic in her large, healthy face, but her small brown eyes were fixed most dangerously. She was a big woman, but her eyes were small and tense. She drew near the stranger. She wore a rather loud-patterned flannelette blouse and a dark skirt.

"What will you have to drink with your supper?" she asked, and there was a new, dangerous note in her voice.

He moved uneasily.

"Oh, I'll go on with ale."

She drew him another glass. Then she sat down on the bench at the table with him and the soldiers, and fixed him with her attention.

"You've come from St. Just, have you?" she said.

He looked at her with those clear, dark, inscrutable Cornish eyes, and answered at length:

"No, from Penzance."

"Penzance!—but you're not thinking of going back there to-night?"

"No—no."

He still looked at her with those wide, clear eyes that seemed like very bright agate. Her anger began to rise. It was seen on her brow. Yet her voice was still suave and deprecating.

"I *thought* not—but you're not living in these parts, are you?"

"No—no, I'm not living here." He was always slow in answering, as if something intervened between him and any outside question.

"Oh, I see," she said. "You've got relations down here."

Again he looked straight into her eyes, as if looking her into silence.

"Yes," he said.

He did not say any more. She rose with a flounce. The anger was tight on her brow. There was no more laughing and card-playing that evening, though she kept up her motherly, suave, good-humoured way with the men. But they knew her, they were all afraid of her.

The supper was finished, the table cleared, the stranger did not go. Two of the young soldiers went off to bed, with their cheery:

"Good night, Ma. Good night, Maryann."

The stranger talked a little to the sergeant about the war, which was in its first year, about the new army, a fragment of which was quartered in this district, about America.

The landlady darted looks at him from her small eyes, minute by minute the electric storm welled in her bosom, as still he did not go. She was quivering with suppressed, violent passion, something frightening and abnormal. She could not sit still for a moment. Her heavy form seemed to flash with sudden, involuntary movements as the minutes passed by, and still he sat there, and the tension on her heart grew unbearable. She watched the hands of the clock move on. Three of the soldiers had gone to bed, only the crop-headed, terrier-like old sergeant remained.

The landlady sat behind the bar fidgeting spasmodically with the newspaper. She looked again at the clock. At last it was five minutes to ten.

"Gentlemen—the enemy!" she said in her diminished, furious voice. "Time, please. Time, my dears. And good night, all!"

The men began to drop out, with a brief good night. It was a minute to ten. The landlady rose.

"Come," she said. "I'm shutting the door."

The last of the miners passed out. She stood, stout and menacing, holding the door. Still the stranger sat on by the fire, his black overcoat opened, smoking.

"We're closed now, sir," came the perilous, narrowed voice of the landlady.

The little, dog-like, hard-headed sergeant touched the arm of the stranger.

"Closing time," he said.

The stranger turned round in his seat, and his quick-moving, dark, jewel-like eyes went from the sergeant to the landlady.

"I'm stopping here to-night," he said, in his laconic Cornish–Yankee accent.

The landlady seemed to tower. Her eyes lifted strangely, frightening.

"Oh, indeed!" she cried. "Oh, indeed! And whose orders are those, may I ask?"

He looked at her again.

"My orders," he said.

Involuntarily she shut the door, and advanced like a great, dangerous bird. Her voice rose, there was a touch of hoarseness in it.

"And what might *your* orders be, if you please?" she cried. "Who might *you* be, to give orders, in the house?"

He sat still, watching her.

"You know who I am," he said. "At least, I know who you are."

"Oh, do you? Oh, do you? And who am *I* then, if you'll be so good as to tell me?"

He stared at her with his bright, dark eyes.

"You're my Missis, you are," he said. "And you know it, as well as I do."

She started as if something had exploded in her.

Her eyes lifted and flared madly.

"*Do* I know it, indeed!" she cried. "I know no such thing! I know no such thing! Do you think a man's going to walk into this bar, and tell me off-hand I'm his Missis, and I'm going to believe him? I say to you, whoever you may be, you're mistaken. I know myself for no Missis of yours, and I'll thank you to go out of this house, this minute, before I get those that will put you out."

The man rose to his feet, stretching his head towards her a little. He was a handsomely built Cornishman in the prime of life.

"What you say, eh? You don't know me?" he said in his sing-song voice, emotionless, but rather smothered and pressing: it reminded one of the girl's. "I should know you anywhere, you see. I should! I shouldn't have to look twice to know you, you see. You see, now, don't you?"

The woman was baffled.

"So you may say," she replied, staccato. "So you may say. That's easy enough. My name's known, and respected, by most people for ten miles round. But I don't know *you.*"

Her voice ran to sarcasm. "I can't say I know *you.* You're a *perfect* stranger to me, and I don't believe I've ever set eyes on you before to-night."

Her voice was very flexible and sarcastic.

"Yes, you have," replied the man, in his reasonable way. "Yes, you have. Your name's my name, and that girl Mary-ann is my girl; she's my daughter. You're my Missis right enough. As sure as I'm Willie Nankervis."

He spoke as if it were an accepted fact. His face was handsome, with a strange, watchful alertness and a fundamental fixity of intention that maddened her.

"You villain!" she cried. "You villain, to come to this house and dare to speak to me. You villain, you downright rascal!"

He looked at her.

"Ay," he said, unmoved. "All that." He was uneasy before

her. Only he was not afraid of her. There was something impenetrable about him, like his eyes, which were as bright as agate.

She towered, and drew near to him menacingly.

"You're going out of this house, aren't you?" She stamped her foot in sudden madness. *"This minute!"*

He watched her. He knew she wanted to strike him.

"No," he said, with suppressed emphasis. "I've told you, I'm stopping here."

He was afraid of her personality, but it did not alter him. She wavered. Her small, tawny-brown eyes concentrated in a point of vivid, sightless fury, like a tiger's. The man was wincing, but he stood his ground. Then she bethought herself. She would gather her forces.

"We'll see whether you're stopping here," she said. And she turned, with a curious, frightening lifting of her eyes, and surged out of the room. The man, listening, heard her go upstairs, heard her tapping at a bedroom door, heard her saying: "Do you mind coming down a minute, boys? I want you. I'm in trouble."

The man in the bar took off his cap and his black overcoat, and threw them on the seat behind him. His black hair was short and touched with grey at the temples. He wore a well-cut, well-fitting suit of dark grey, American in style, and a turn-down collar. He looked well-to-do, a fine, solid figure of a man. The rather rigid look of the shoulders came from his having had his collar-bone twice broken in the mines.

The little terrier of a sergeant, in dirty khaki, looked at him furtively.

"She's your Missis?" he asked, jerking his head in the direction of the departed woman.

"Yes, she is," barked the man. "She's that, sure enough."

"Not seen her for a long time, haven't ye?"

"Sixteen years come March month."

"Hm!"

The sergeant laconically resumed his smoking.

The landlady was coming back, followed by the three young soldiers, who entered rather sheepishly, in trousers and shirt and stocking-feet. The woman stood histrionically at the end of the bar, and exclaimed:

"That man refuses to leave the house, claims he's stopping the night here. You know very well I have no bed, don't you? And this house doesn't accommodate travellers. Yet he's going to stop in spite of all! But not while I've a drop of blood in my body, that I declare with my dying breath. And not if you men are worth the name of men, and will help a woman as has no one to help her."

Her eyes sparkled, her face was flushed pink. She was drawn up like an Amazon.

The young soldiers did not quite know what to do. They looked at the man, they looked at the sergeant, one of them looked down and fastened his braces on the second button.

"What say, sergeant?" asked one whose face twinkled for a little devilment.

"Man says he's husband to Mrs. Nankervis," said the sergeant.

"He's no husband of mine. I declare I never set eyes on him before this night. It's a dirty trick, nothing else, it's a dirty trick."

"Why, you're a liar, saying you never set eyes on me before," barked the man near the hearth. "You're married to me, and that girl Maryann you had by me—well enough you know it."

The young soldier looked on in delight, the sergeant smoked imperturbed.

"Yes," sang the landlady, slowly shaking her head in supreme sarcasm, "it sounds very pretty, doesn't it? But you see we don't believe a word of it, and *how* are you going to prove it?" She smiled nastily.

The man watched in silence for a moment, then he said:

"It wants no proof."

"Oh, yes, but it does! Oh, yes, but it does, sir, it wants a lot of proving!" sang the lady's sarcasm. "We're not such gulls as all that, to swallow your words whole."

But he stood unmoved near the fire. She stood with one hand resting on the zinc-covered bar, the sergeant sat with legs crossed, smoking, on the seat half-way between them, the three young soldiers in their shirts and braces stood wavering in the gloom behind the bar. There was silence.

"Do you know anything of the whereabouts of your husband, Mrs. Nankervis? Is he still living?" asked the sergeant, in his judicious fashion.

Suddenly the landlady began to cry, great scalding tears, that left the young men aghast.

"I know nothing of him," she sobbed, feeling for her pocket handkerchief. "He left me when Maryann was a baby, went mining to America, and after about six months never wrote a line nor sent me a penny bit. I can't say whether he's alive or dead, the villain. All I've heard of him's the bad—and I've heard nothing for years an' all, now." She sobbed violently.

The golden-skinned, handsome man near the fire watched her as she wept. He was frightened, he was troubled, he was bewildered, but none of his emotions altered him underneath.

There was no sound in the room but the violent sobbing of the landlady. The men, one and all, were overcome.

"Don't you think as you'd better go, for to-night?" said the sergeant to the man, with sweet reasonableness. "You'd better leave it a bit, and arrange something between you. You can't have much claim on a woman, I should imagine, if it's how she says. And you've come down on her a bit too sudden-like."

The landlady sobbed heart-brokenly. The man watched her large breasts shaken. They seemed to cast a spell over his mind.

"How I've treated her, that's no matter," he replied. "I've come back, and I'm going to stop in my own home—for a bit, anyhow. There you've got it."

"A dirty action," said the sergeant, his face flushing dark. "A dirty action, to come, after deserting a woman for that number of years, and want to force yourself on her! A dirty action—as isn't allowed by the law."

The landlady wiped her eyes.

"Never you mind about law nor nothing," cried the man, in a strange, strong voice. "I'm not moving out of this public to-night."

The woman turned to the soldiers behind her, and said in a wheedling, sarcastic tone:

"Are we going to stand it, boys? Are we going to be done like this, Sergeant Thomas, by a scoundrel and a bully as has led a life beyond *mention* in those American mining-camps, and then wants to come back and make havoc of a poor woman's life and savings, after having left her with a baby in arms to struggle as best she might? It's a crying shame if nobody will stand up for me—a crying shame——!"

The soldiers and the little sergeant were bristling. The woman stooped and rummaged under the counter for a minute. Then, unseen to the man away near the fire, she threw out a plaited grass rope, such as is used for binding bales, and left it lying near the feet of the young soldiers, in the gloom at the back of the bar.

Then she rose and fronted the situation.

"Come now," she said to the man, in a reasonable, coldly-coaxing tone, "put your coat on and leave us alone. Be a man, and not worse than a brute of a German. You can get a bed easy enough in St. Just, and if you've nothing to pay for it, sergeant would lend you a couple of shillings, I'm sure he would."

All eyes were fixed on the man. He was looking down at the woman like a creature spell-bound or possessed by some devil's own intention.

"I've got money of my own," he said. "Don't you be frightened for your money, I've plenty of that, for the time."

"Well, then," she coaxed, in a cold, almost sneering propitiation, "put your coat on and go where you're wanted—be a *man,* not a brute of a German."

She had drawn quite near to him, in her challenging coaxing intentness. He looked down at her with his bewitched face.

"No, I shan't," he said. "I shan't do no such thing. *You'll* put me up for to-night."

"Shall I?" she cried. And suddenly she flung her arms round him, hung on to him with all her powerful weight, calling to the soldiers: "Get the rope, boys, and fasten him up. Alfred—John, quick now——"

The man reared, looked round with maddened eyes, and heaved his powerful body. But the woman was powerful also, and very heavy, and was clenched with the determination of death. Her face, with its exulting, horribly vindictive look, was turned up to him from his own breast; he reached back his head frantically, to get away from it. Meanwhile the young soldiers, after having watched this frightful Laocoon swaying for a moment, stirred, and the malicious one darted swiftly with the rope. It was tangled a little.

"Give me the end here," cried the sergeant.

Meanwhile the big man heaved and struggled, swung the woman round against the seat and the table, in his convulsive effort to get free. But she pinned down his arms like a cuttlefish wreathed heavily upon him. And he heaved and swayed, and they crashed about the room, the soldiers hopping, the furniture bumping.

The young soldier had got the rope once round, the brisk sergeant helping him. The woman sank heavily lower, they got the rope round several times. In the struggle the victim fell over against the table. The ropes tightened till they cut his arms. The woman clung to his knees. Another soldier ran in a flash of genius, and fastened the strange man's feet with the pair of braces. Seats had crashed over, the table was thrown against the wall, but the man was bound, his arms pinned against his sides, his feet tied. He lay half-fallen, sunk against the table, still for a moment.

The woman rose, and sank, faint, on to the seat against the wall. Her breast heaved, she could not speak, she thought she was going to die. The bound man lay against the overturned table, his coat all twisted and pulled up beneath the ropes, leaving the loins exposed. The soldiers stood around, a little dazed, but excited with the row.

The man began to struggle again, heaving instinctively against the ropes, taking great, deep breaths. His face, with its golden skin, flushed dark and surcharged. He heaved again. The great veins in his neck stood out. But it was no good, he went relaxed. Then again, suddenly, he jerked his feet.

"Another pair of braces, William," cried the excited soldier. He threw himself on the legs of the bound man, and managed to fasten the knees. Then again there was stillness. They could hear the clock tick.

The woman looked at the prostrate figure, the strong, straight limbs, the strong back bound in subjection, the wide-eyed face that reminded her of a calf tied in a sack in a cart, only its head stretched dumbly backwards. And she triumphed.

The bound-up body began to struggle again. She watched fascinated the muscles working, the shoulders, the hips, the large, clean thighs. Even now he might break the ropes. She was afraid. But the lively young soldier sat on the shoulders of the bound man, and after a few perilous moments, there was stillness again.

"Now," said the judicious sergeant to the bound man, "if we untie you, will you promise to go off and make no more trouble?"

"You'll not untie him in here," cried the woman. "I wouldn't trust him as far as I could blow him."

There was silence.

"We might carry him outside, and undo him there," said the soldier. "Then we could get the policeman, if he made any more bother."

"Yes," said the sergeant. "We could do that." Then again, in an altered, almost severe tone, to the prisoner: "If we undo you outside, will you take your coat and go without creating any more disturbance?"

But the prisoner would not answer, he only lay with wide, dark, bright eyes, like a bound animal. There was a space of perplexed silence.

"Well, then, do as you say," said the woman irritably. "Carry him out amongst you, and let us shut up the house."

They did so. Picking up the bound man, the four soldiers staggered clumsily into the silent square in front of the inn, the woman following with the cap and the overcoat. The young soldiers quickly unfastened the braces from the prisoner's legs, and they hopped indoors. They were in their stocking-feet, and outside the stars flashed cold. They stood in the doorway watching. The man lay quite still on the cold ground.

"Now," said the sergeant, in a subdued voice, "I'll loosen the knot, and he can work himself free, if you go in, Missis."

She gave a last look at the dishevelled, bound man, as he sat on the ground. Then she went indoors, followed quickly by the sergeant. Then they were heard locking and barring the door.

The man seated on the ground outside worked and strained at the rope. But it was not so easy to undo himself even now. So, with hands bound, making an effort, he got on his feet, and went and worked the cord against the rough edge of an old wall. The rope, being of a kind of plaited grass, soon frayed and broke, and he freed himself. He had various contusions. His arms were hurt and bruised from the bonds. He rubbed them slowly. Then he pulled his clothes straight, stooped, put on his cap, struggled into his overcoat, and walked away.

The stars were very brilliant. Clear as crystal, the beam from the lighthouse under the cliffs struck rhythmically on the night. Dazed, the man walked along the road past the churchyard. Then he stood leaning up against a wall, for a long time.

He was roused because his feet were so cold. So he pulled himself together, and turned again in the silent night, back towards the inn.

The bar was in darkness. But there was a light in the kitchen. He hesitated. Then very quietly he tried the door.

He was surprised to find it open. He entered, and quietly closed it behind him. Then he went down the step past the bar-counter, and through to the lighted doorway of the kitchen. There sat his wife, planted in front of the range, where a furze fire was burning. She sat in a chair full in front of the range, her knees wide apart on the fender. She looked over her shoulder at him as he entered, but she did not speak. Then she stared in the fire again.

It was a small, narrow kitchen. He dropped his cap on the table that was covered with yellowish American cloth, and took a seat with his back to the wall, near the oven. His wife still sat with her knees apart, her feet on the steel fender and stared into the fire, motionless. Her skin was smooth and rosy in the firelight. Everything in the house was very clean and bright. The man sat silent, too, his head dropped. And thus they remained.

It was a question who would speak first. The woman leaned forward and poked the ends of the sticks in between the bars of the range. He lifted his head and looked at her.

"Others gone to bed, have they?" he asked.

But she remained closed in silence.

" 'S a cold night out," he said, as if to himself.

And he laid his large, yet well-shapen workman's hand on the top of the stove, that was polished black and smooth as velvet. She would not look at him, yet she glanced out of the corners of her eyes.

His eyes were fixed brightly on her, the pupils large and electric like those of a cat.

"I should have picked you out among thousands," he said. "Though you're bigger than I'd have believed. Fine flesh you've made."

She was silent for some time. Then she turned in her chair upon him.

"What do you think of yourself," she said, "coming back on me like this after over fifteen years? You don't think I've not heard of you, neither, in Butte City and elsewhere?"

He was watching her with his clear, translucent, unchallenged eyes.

"Yes," he said. "Chaps comes an' goes—I've heard tell of you from time to time."

She drew herself up.

"And what lies have you heard about me?" she demanded superbly.

"I dunno as I've heard any lies at all—'cept as you was getting on very well, like."

His voice ran warily and detached. Her anger stirred again in her violently. But she subdued it, because of the danger there was in him, and more, perhaps, because of the beauty of his head and his level drawn brows, which she could not bear to forfeit.

"That's more than I can say of *you*," she said. "I've heard more harm than good about *you*."

"Ay, I dessay," he said looking in the fire. It was a long time since he had seen the furze burning, he said to himself. There was a silence, during which she watched his face.

"Do you call yourself a *man*?" she said, more in contemptuous reproach than in anger. "Leave a woman as you've left me, you don't care to what!—and then to turn up in *this* fashion, without a word to say for yourself."

He stirred in his chair, planted his feet apart, and resting his arms on his knees, looked steadily into the fire without answering. So near to her was his head, and the close black hair, she could scarcely refrain from starting away, as if it would bite her.

"Do you call that the action of a *man*?" she repeated.

"No," he said, reaching and poking the bits of wood into the fire with his fingers. "I didn't call it anything, as I know of. It's no good calling things by any names whatsoever, as I know of."

She watched him in his actions. There was a longer and longer pause between each speech, though neither knew it.

"I *wonder* what you think of yourself!" she exclaimed with vexed emphasis. "I *wonder* what sort of a fellow you take yourself to be!" She was really perplexed as well as angry.

"Well," he said, lifting his head to look at her, "I guess I'll answer for my own faults, if everybody else'll answer for theirs."

Her heart beat fiery hot as he lifted his face to her. She breathed heavily, averting her face, almost losing her self-control.

"And what do you take *me* to be?" she cried, in real helplessness.

His face was lifted, watching her soft, averted face. And the softly heaving mass of her breasts.

"I take you," he said, with that laconic truthfulness which exercised such power over her, "to be the deuce of a fine woman—darn me if you're not as fine a built woman as I've seen, handsome with it as well. I shouldn't have expected you to put on such handsome flesh: 'struth I shouldn't."

Her heart beat fiery hot, as he watched her with those bright agate eyes, fixedly.

"Been very handsome to *you*, for fifteen years, my sakes!" she replied.

He made no answer to this, but sat with his bright, quick eyes upon her.

Then he rose. She started involuntarily. But he only said, in his laconic, measured way:

"It's warm in here now."

And he pulled off his overcoat, throwing it on the table. She sat as if slightly cowed, whilst he did so.

"Them ropes has given my arms something, by Ga-ard," he drawled, feeling his arms with his hands.

Still she sat in her chair before him, slightly cowed.

"You was sharp, wasn't you, to catch me like that, eh?" he smiled slowly. "By Ga-ard, you had me fixed proper, proper you had. Darn me, you fixed me up proper—proper, you did."

He leaned forwards in his chair towards her.

"I don't think no worse of you for it, no, darned if I do. Fine pluck in a woman's what I admire. That I do, indeed."

She only gazed into the fire.

"We fet from the start, we did. And, my word, you begin again quick the minute you see me, you did. Darn me, you was too sharp for me. A darn fine woman, puts up a darn good fight. Darn me if I could find a woman in all the darn States as could get me down like that. Wonderful fine woman you be, truth to say, at this minute."

She only sat glowering into the fire.

"As grand a pluck as a man could wish to find in a woman, true as I'm here," he said, reaching forward his hand and tentatively touching her between her full, warm breasts, quietly.

She started, and seemed to shudder. But his hand insinuated itself between her breasts, as she continued to gaze in the fire.

"And don't you think I've come back here a-begging," he said. "I've more than *one* thousand pounds to my name, I have. And a bit of a fight for a how-de-do pleases me, that it do. But that doesn't mean as you're going to deny as you're my Missis . . ."

The Horse Dealer's Daughter

"WELL, MABEL, and what are you going to do with yourself?"
asked Joe, with foolish flippancy. He felt quite safe himself.
Without listening for an answer, he turned aside, worked a
grain of tobacco to the tip of his tongue, and spat it out. He
did not care about anything, since he felt safe himself.

The three brothers and the sister sat round the desolate
breakfast-table, attempting some sort of desultory consultation. The morning's post had given the final tap to the family
fortunes, and all was over. The dreary dining-room itself,
with its heavy mahogany furniture, looked as if it were
waiting to be done away with.

But the consultation amounted to nothing. There was a
strange air of ineffectuality about the three men, as they
sprawled at table, smoking and reflecting vaguely on their
own condition. The girl was alone, a rather short, sullen-
looking young woman of twenty-seven. She did not share the
same life as her brothers. She would have been good-looking,
save for the impressive fixity of her face, 'bull-dog', as her
brothers called it.

There was a confused tramping of horses' feet outside. The
three men all sprawled round in their chairs to watch. Beyond the dark holly bushes that separated the strip of lawn
from the high-road, they could see a cavalcade of shire
horses swinging out of their own yard, being taken for
exercise. This was the last time. These were the last horses
that would go through their hands. The young men watched
with critical, callous look. They were all frightened at the
collapse of their lives, and the sense of disaster in which they
were involved left them no inner freedom.

Yet they were three fine, well-set fellows enough. Joe, the

eldest, was a man of thirty-three, broad and handsome in a hot, flushed way. His face was red, he twisted his black moustache over a thick finger, his eyes were shallow and restless. He had a sensual way of uncovering his teeth when he laughed, and his bearing was stupid. Now he watched the horses with a glazed look of helplessness in his eyes, a certain stupor of downfall.

The great draught-horses swung past. They were tied head to tail, four of them, and they heaved along to where a lane branched off from the high-road, planting their great hoofs floutingly in the fine black mud, swinging their great rounded haunches sumptuously, and trotting a few sudden steps as they were led into the lane, round the corner. Every movement showed a massive, slumbrous strength, and a stupidity which held them in subjection. The groom at the head looked back, jerking the leading rope. And the cavalcade moved out of sight up the lane, the tail of the last horse, bobbed up tight and stiff, held out taut from the swinging great haunches as they rocked behind the hedges in a motion-like sleep.

Joe watched with glazed hopeless eyes. The horses were almost like his own body to him. He felt he was done for now. Luckily he was engaged to a woman as old as himself, and therefore her father, who was steward of a neighbouring estate, would provide him with a job. He would marry and go into harness. His life was over, he would be a subject animal now.

He turned uneasily aside, the retreating steps of the horses echoing in his ears. Then, with foolish restlessness, he reached for the scraps of bacon-rind from the plates, and making a faint whistling sound, flung them to the terrier that lay against the fender. He watched the dog swallow them, and waited till the creature looked into his eyes. Then a faint grin came on his face, and in a high, foolish voice he said:

"You won't get much more bacon, shall you, you little b——?"

The dog faintly and dismally wagged its tail, then lowered its haunches, circled round, and lay down again.

There was another helpless silence at the table. Joe sprawled uneasily in his seat, not willing to go till the family conclave was dissolved. Fred Henry, the second brother, was erect, clean-limbered, alert. He had watched the passing of the horses with more *sang-froid.* If he was an animal, like Joe, he was an animal which controls, not one which is controlled. He was master of any horse, and he carried himself with a well-tempered air of mastery. But he was not master of the situations of life. He pushed his coarse brown moustache upwards, off his lip, and glanced irritably at his sister, who sat impassive and inscrutable.

"You'll go and stop with Lucy for a bit, shan't you?" he asked. The girl did not answer.

"I don't see what else you can do," persisted Fred Henry.

"Go as a skivvy," Joe interpolated laconically.

The girl did not move a muscle.

"If I was her, I should go in for training for a nurse," said Malcolm, the youngest of them all. He was the baby of the family, a young man of twenty-two, with a fresh, jaunty *museau.*

But Mabel did not take any notice of him. They had talked at her and round her for so many years, that she hardly heard them at all.

The marble clock on the mantelpiece softly chimed the half-hour, the dog rose uneasily from the hearth-rug and looked at the party at the breakfast-table. But still they sat on in ineffectual conclave.

"Oh, all right," said Joe suddenly, apropos of nothing. "I'll get a move on."

He pushed back his chair, straddled his knees with a downward jerk, to get them free, in horsey fashion, and went to the fire. Still he did not go out of the room; he was curious to know what the others would do or say. He began to charge his pipe, looking down at the dog and saying in a high, affected voice:

"Going wi' me? Going wi' me are ter? Tha'rt goin' further than tha counts on just now, dost hear?"

The dog faintly wagged its tail, the man stuck out his jaw and covered his pipe with his hands, and puffed intently, losing himself in the tobacco, looking down all the while at the dog with an absent brown eye. The dog looked up at him in mournful distrust. Joe stood with his knees stuck out, in real horsey fashion.

"Have you had a letter from Lucy?" Fred Henry asked of his sister.

"Last week," came the neutral reply.

"And what does she say?"

There was no answer.

"Does she *ask* you to go and stop there?" persisted Fred Henry.

"She says I can if I like."

"Well, then, you'd better. Tell her you'll come on Monday."

This was received in silence.

"That's what you'll do then, is it?" said Fred Henry, in some exasperation.

But she made no answer. There was silence of futility and irritation in the room. Malcolm grinned fatuously.

"You'll have to make up your mind between now and next Wednesday," said Joe loudly, "or else find yourself lodgings on the kerbstone."

The face of the young woman darkened, but she sat on immutable.

"Here's Jack Ferguson!" exclaimed Malcolm, who was looking aimlessly out of the window.

"Where?" exclaimed Joe loudly.

"Just gone past."

"Coming in?"

Malcolm craned his neck to see the gate.

"Yes," he said.

There was a silence. Mabel sat on like one condemned, at the head of the table. Then a whistle was heard from the kitchen. The dog got up and barked sharply. Joe opened the door and shouted:

"Come on."

After a moment a young man entered. He was muffled up in overcoat and a purple woollen scarf, and his tweed cap, which he did not remove, was pulled down on his head. He was of medium height, his face was rather long and pale, his eyes looked tired.

"Hello, Jack! Well, Jack!" exclaimed Malcolm and Joe. Fred Henry merely said: "Jack."

"What's doing?" asked the newcomer, evidently addressing Fred Henry.

"Same. We've got to be out by Wednesday. Got a cold?"

"I have—got it bad, too."

"Why don't you stop in?"

"Me stop in? When I can't stand on my legs, perhaps I shall have a chance." The young man spoke huskily. He had a slight Scotch accent.

"It's a knock-out, isn't it," said Joe, boisterously, "if a doctor goes round croaking with a cold. Looks bad for the patients, doesn't it?"

The young doctor looked at him slowly.

"Anything the matter with *you,* then?" he asked sarcastically.

"Not as I know of. Damn your eyes, I hope not. Why?"

"I thought you were very concerned about the patients, wondered if you might be one yourself."

"Damn it, no, I've never been patient to no flaming doctor, and hope I never shall be," returned Joe.

At this point Mabel rose from the table, and they all seemed to become aware of her existence. She began putting the dishes together. The young doctor looked at her, but did not address her. He had not greeted her. She went out of the room with the tray, her face impassive and unchanged.

"When are you off then, all of you?" asked the doctor.

"I'm catching the eleven-forty," replied Malcolm. "Are you goin' down wi' th' trap, Joe?"

"Yes, I've told you I'm going down wi' th' trap, haven't I?"

"We'd better be getting her in then. So long, Jack, if I don't see you before I go," said Malcolm, shaking hands.

He went out, followed by Joe, who seemed to have his tail between his legs.

"Well, this is the devil's own," exclaimed the doctor, when he was left alone with Fred Henry. "Going before Wednesday, are you?"

"That's the orders," replied the other.

"Where, to Northampton?"

"That's it."

"The devil!" exclaimed Ferguson, with quiet chagrin.

And there was silence between the two.

"All settled up, are you?" asked Ferguson.

There was another pause.

"Well, I shall miss yer, Freddy, boy," said the young doctor.

"And I shall miss thee, Jack," returned the other.

"Miss you like hell," mused the doctor.

Fred Henry turned aside. There was nothing to say. Mabel came in again, to finish clearing the table.

"What are *you* going to do, then, Miss Pervin?" asked Ferguson. "Going to your sister's, are you?"

Mabel looked at him with her steady, dangerous eyes, that always made him uncomfortable, unsettling his superficial ease.

"No," she said.

"Well, what in the name of fortune *are* you going to do? Say what you mean to do," cried Fred Henry, with futile intensity.

But she only averted her head, and continued her work. She folded the white table-cloth, and put on the chenille cloth.

"The sulkiest bitch that ever trod!" muttered her brother.

But she finished her task with perfectly impassive face, the young doctor watching her interestedly all the while. Then she went out.

Fred Henry stared after her, clenching his lips, his blue eyes fixing in sharp antagonism, as he made a grimace of sour exasperation.

"You could bray her into bits, and that's all you'd get out of her," he said, in a small, narrowed tone.

The doctor smiled faintly.

"What's she *going* to do, then?" he asked.

"Strike me if *I* know!" returned the other.

There was a pause. Then the doctor stirred.

"I'll be seeing you to-night, shall I?" he said to his friend.

"Ay—where's it to be? Are we going over to Jessdale?"

"I don't know. I've got such a cold on me. I'll come round to the 'Moon and Stars', anyway."

"Let Lizzie and May miss their night for once, eh?"

"That's it—if I feel as I do now."

"All's one——"

The two young men went through the passage and down to the back door together. The house was large, but it was servantless now, and desolate. At the back was a small bricked houseyard and beyond that a big square, gravelled fine and red, and having stables on two sides. Sloping, dank, winter-dark fields stretched away on the open sides.

But the stables were empty. Joseph Pervin, the father of the family, had been a man of no education, who had become a fairly large horse dealer. The stables had been full of horses, there was a great turmoil and come-and-go of horses and of dealers and grooms. Then the kitchen was full of servants. But of late things had declined. The old man had married a second time, to retrieve his fortunes. Now he was dead and everything was gone to the dogs, there was nothing but debt and threatening.

For months, Mabel had been servantless in the big house, keeping the home together in penury for her ineffectual brothers. She had kept house for ten years. But previously it was with unstinted means. Then, however brutal and coarse everything was, the sense of money had kept her proud, confident. The men might be foul-mouthed, the women in the kitchen might have bad reputations, her brothers might have illegitimate children. But so long as there was money, the girl felt herself established, and brutally proud, reserved.

No company came to the house, save dealers and coarse men. Mabel had no associates of her own sex, after her sister went away. But she did not mind. She went regularly to church, she attended to her father. And she lived in the memory of her mother, who had died when she was fourteen, and whom she had loved. She had loved her father, too, in a different way, depending upon him, and feeling secure in him, until at the age of fifty-four he married again. And then she had set hard against him. Now he had died and left them all hopelessly in debt.

She had suffered badly during the period of poverty. Nothing, however, could shake the curious, sullen, animal pride that dominated each member of the family. Now, for Mabel, the end had come. Still she would not cast about her. She would follow her own way just the same. She would always hold the keys of her own situation. Mindless and persistent, she endured from day to day. Why should she think? Why should she answer anybody? It was enough that this was the end, and there was no way out. She need not pass any more darkly along the main street of the small town, avoiding every eye. She need not demean herself any more, going into the shops and buying the cheapest food. This was at an end. She thought of nobody, not even of herself. Mindless and persistent, she seemed in a sort of ecstasy to be coming nearer to her fulfilment, her own glorification, approaching her dead mother, who was glorified.

In the afternoon she took a little bag, with shears and sponge and a small scrubbing-brush, and went out. It was a grey, wintry day, with saddened, dark green fields and an atmosphere blackened by the smoke of foundries not far off. She went quickly, darkly along the causeway, heeding nobody, through the town to the churchyard.

There, she always felt secure, as if no one could see her, although as a matter of fact she was exposed to the stare of everyone who passed along under the churchyard wall. Nevertheless, once under the shadow of the great looming church, among the graves, she felt immune from the world, reserved within the thick churchyard wall as in another country.

Carefully she clipped the grass from the grave, and arranged the pinky white, small chrysanthemums in the tin cross. When this was done, she took an empty jar from a neighbouring grave, brought water, and carefully, most scrupulously sponged the marble headstone and the coping-stone.

It gave her sincere satisfaction to do this. She felt in immediate contact with the world of her mother: She took minute pains, went through the park in a state bordering on pure happiness, as if in performing this task she came into a subtle, intimate connection with her mother. For the life she

followed here in the world was far less real than the world of
death she inherited from her mother.

The doctor's house was just by the church. Ferguson,
being a mere hired assistant, was slave to the country-side.
As he hurried now to attend to the out-patients in the
surgery, glancing across the graveyard with his quick eye, he
saw the girl at her task at the grave. She seemed so intent
and remote, it was like looking into another world. Some
mystical element was touched in him. He slowed down as he
walked, watching her as if spellbound.

She lifted her eyes, feeling him looking. Their eyes met.
And each looked again at once, each feeling, in some way,
found out by the other. He lifted his cap and passed on down
the road. There remained distinct in consciousness, like a
vision, the memory of her face, lifted from the tombstone in
the churchyard, and looking at him with slow, large, portentous eyes. It *was* portentous, her face. It seemed to mesmer-
ise him. There was a heavy power in her eyes which laid hold
of his whole being, as if he had drunk some powerful drug.
He had been feeling weak and done before. Now the life
came back into him, he felt delivered from his own fretted,
daily self.

He finished his duties at the surgery as quickly as might
be, hastily filling up the bottles of the waiting people with
cheap drugs. Then, in perpetual haste, he set off again to visit
several cases in another part of his round, before tea-time.
At all times he preferred to walk if he could, but particularly
when he was not well. He fancied the motion restored him.

The afternoon was falling. It was grey, deadened, and
wintry, with a slow, moist, heavy coldness sinking in and
deadening all the faculties. But why should he think or
notice? He hastily climbed the hill and turned across the dark
green fields, following the black cinder-track. In the distance,
across a shallow dip in the country, the small town was
clustered like smouldering ash, a tower, a spire, a heap of
low, raw, extinct houses. And on the nearest fringe of the
town, sloping into the dip, was Oldmeadow, the Pervins'
house. He could see the stables and the outbuildings distinctly, as they lay towards him on the slope. Well, he would not

go there many more times! Another resource would be lost to him, another place gone: the only company he cared for in the alien, ugly little town he was losing. Nothing but work, drudgery, constant hastening from dwelling to dwelling among the colliers and the iron-workers. It wore him out, but at the same time he had a craving for it. It was a stimulant to him to be in the homes of the working people, moving, as it were, through the innermost body of their life. His nerves were excited and gratified. He could come so near, into the very lives of the rough, inarticulate, powerfully emotional men and women. He grumbled, he said he hated the hellish hole. But as a matter of fact it excited him, the contact with the rough, strongly-feeling people was a stimulant applied direct to his nerves.

Below Oldmeadow, in the green, shallow, soddened hollow of fields, lay a square, deep pond. Roving across the land-scape, the doctor's quick eye detected a figure in black passing through the gate of the field, down towards the pond. He looked again. It would be Mabel Pervin. His mind sud-denly became alive and attentive.

Why was she going down there? He pulled up on the path on the slope above, and stood staring. He could just make sure of the small black figure moving in the hollow of the failing day. He seemed to see her in the midst of such obscurity, that he was like a clairvoyant, seeing rather with the mind's eye than with ordinary sight. Yet he could see her positively enough, whilst he kept his eye attentive. He felt, if he looked away from her, in the thick, ugly falling dusk, he would lose her altogether.

He followed her minutely as she moved, direct and intent, like something transmitted rather than stirring in voluntary activity, straight down the field toward the pond. There she stood on the bank for a moment. She never raised her head. Then she waded slowly into the water.

He stood motionless as the small black figure walked slowly and deliberately towards the centre of the pond, very slowly, gradually moving deeper into the motionless water, and still moving forward as the water got up to her breast.

Then he could see her no more in the dusk of the dead afternoon.

"There!" he exclaimed. "Would you believe it?"

And he hastened straight down, running over the wet, soddened fields, pushing through the hedges, down into the depression of callous wintry obscurity. It took him several minutes to come to the pond. He stood on the bank, breathing heavily. He could see nothing. His eyes seemed to penetrate the dead water. Yes, perhaps that was the dark shadow of her black clothing beneath the surface of the water.

He slowly ventured into the pond. The bottom was deep, soft clay, he sank in, and the water clasped dead cold round his legs. As he stirred he could smell the cold, rotten clay that fouled up into the water. It was objectionable in his lungs. Still, repelled and yet not heeding, he moved deeper into the pond. The cold water rose over his thighs, over his loins, upon his abdomen. The lower part of his body was all sunk in the hideous cold element. And the bottom was so deeply soft and uncertain, he was afraid of pitching with his mouth underneath. He could not swim, and was afraid.

He crouched, a little, spreading his hands under the water and moving them round, trying to feel for her. The dead cold pond swayed upon his chest. He moved again, a little deeper, and again, with his hands underneath, he felt all around under the water. And he touched her clothing. But it evaded his fingers. He made a desperate effort to grasp it.

And so doing he lost his balance and went under, horribly, suffocating in the foul earthy water, struggling madly for a few moments. At last, after what seemed an eternity, he got his footing, rose again into the air and looked around. He gasped, and knew he was in the world. Then he looked at the water. She had risen near him. He grasped her clothing, and drawing her nearer, turned to take his way to land again.

He went very slowly, carefully, absorbed in the slow progress. He rose higher, climbing out of the pond. The water was now only about his legs; he was thankful, full of relief to be out of the clutches of the pond. He lifted her and staggered on to the bank, out of the horror of wet, grey clay.

He laid her down on the bank. She was quite unconscious and running with water. He made the water come from her mouth, he worked to restore her. He did not have to work very long before he could feel the breathing begin again in her; she was breathing naturally. He worked a little longer. He could feel her live beneath his hands; she was coming back. He wiped her face, wrapped her in his overcoat, looked round into the dim, dark grey world, then lifted her and staggered down the bank and across the fields.

It seemed an unthinkably long way, and his burden so heavy he felt he would never get to the house. But at last he was in the stable-yard, and then in the house-yard. He opened the door and went into the house. In the kitchen he laid her down on the hearth-rug and called. The house was empty. But the fire was burning in the grate.

Then again he kneeled to attend to her. She was breathing regularly, her eyes were wide open and as if conscious, but there seemed something missing in her look. She was conscious in herself, but unconscious of her surroundings.

He ran upstairs, took blankets from a bed, and put them before the fire to warm. Then he removed her saturated, earthy-smelling clothing, rubbed her dry with a towel, and wrapped her naked in the blankets. Then he went into the dining-room, to look for spirits. There was a little whisky. He drank a gulp himself, and put some into her mouth.

The effect was instantaneous. She looked full into his face, as if she had been seeing him for some time, and yet had only just become conscious of him.

"Dr. Ferguson?" she said.

"What?" he answered.

He was divesting himself of his coat, intending to find some dry clothing upstairs. He could not bear the smell of the dead, clayey water, and he was mortally afraid for his own health.

"What did I do?" she asked.

"Walked into the pond," he replied. He had begun to shudder like one sick, and could hardly attend to her. Her eyes remained full on him, he seemed to be going dark in his mind, looking back at her helplessly. The shuddering became quieter in him, his life came back to him, dark and unknowing, but strong again.

"Was I out of my mind?" she asked, while her eyes were fixed on him all the time.

"Maybe, for the moment," he replied. He felt quiet, because his strength had come back. The strange fretful strain had left him.

"Am I out of my mind now?" she asked.

"Are you?" he reflected a moment. "No," he answered truthfully, "I don't see that you are." He turned his face aside. He was afraid now, because he felt dazed, and felt dimly that her power was stronger than his, in this issue. And she continued to look at him fixedly all the time. "Can you tell me where I shall find some dry things to put on?" he asked.

"Did you dive into the pond for me?" she asked.

"No," he answered. "I walked in. But I went in overhead as well."

There was silence for a moment. He hesitated. He very much wanted to go upstairs to get into dry clothing. But there was another desire in him. And she seemed to hold him. His will seemed to have gone to sleep, and left him, standing there slack before her. But he felt warm inside himself. He did not shudder at all, though his clothes were sodden on him.

"Why did you?" she asked.

"Because I didn't want you to do such a foolish thing," he said.

"It wasn't foolish," she said, still gazing at him as she lay on the floor, with a sofa cushion under her head. "It was the right thing to do. *I* knew best, then."

"I'll go and shift these wet things," he said. But still he had not the power to move out of her presence, until she sent him. It was as if she had the life of his body in her hands, and he could not extricate himself. Or perhaps he did not want to.

Suddenly she sat up. The she became aware of her own immediate condition. She felt the blankets about her, she knew her own limbs. For a moment it seemed as if her reason were going. She looked round, with wild eyes, as if seeking something. He stood still with fear. She saw her clothing lying scattered.

"Who undressed me?" she asked, her eyes resting full and inevitable on his face.

"I did," he replied, "to bring you round."

For some moments she sat and gazed at him awfully, her lips parted.

"Do you love me, then?" she asked.

He only stood and stared at her, fascinated. His soul seemed to melt.

She shuffled forward on her knees, and put her arms round him, round his legs, as he stood there, pressing her breasts against his knees and thighs, clutching him with strange, convulsive certainty, pressing his thighs against her, drawing him to her face, her throat, as she looked up at him with flaring, humble eyes of transfiguration, triumphant in first possession.

"You love me," she murmured, in strange transport, yearning and triumphant and confident. "You love me. I know you love me, I know."

And she was passionately kissing his knees, through the wet clothing, passionately and indiscriminately kissing his knees, his legs, as if unaware of everything.

He looked down at the tangled wet hair, the wild, bare, animal shoulders. He was amazed, bewildered, and afraid. He had never thought of loving her. He had never wanted to love her. When he rescued her and restored her, he was a doctor, and she was a patient. He had had no single personal thought of her. Nay, this introduction of the personal element was very distasteful to him, a violation of his professional honour. It was horrible to have her there embracing his knees. It was horrible. He revolted from it, violently. And yet—and yet—he had not the power to break away.

She looked at him again, with the same supplication of powerful love, and that same transcendent, frightening light of triumph. In view of the delicate flame which seemed to come from her face like a light, he was powerless. And yet he had never intended to love her. He had never intended. And something stubborn in him could not give way.

"You love me," she repeated, in a murmur of deep, rhapsodic assurance. "You love me."

Her hands were drawing him, drawing him down to her. He was afraid, even a little horrified. For he had, really, no intention of loving her. Yet her hands were drawing him towards her. He put out his hand quickly to steady himself, and grasped her bare shoulder. A flame seemed to burn the hand that grasped her soft shoulder. He had no intention of loving her: his whole will was against his yielding. It was horrible. And yet wonderful was the touch of her shoulders, beautiful the shining of her face. Was she perhaps mad? He had a horror of yielding to her. Yet something in him ached also.

He had been staring away at the door, away from her. But his hand remained on her shoulder. She had gone suddenly very still. He looked down at her. Her eyes were now wide with fear, with doubt, the light was dying from her face, a shadow of terrible greyness was returning. He could not bear the touch of her eyes' question upon him, and the look of death behind the question.

With an inward groan he gave way, and let his heart yield towards her. A sudden gentle smile came on his face. And her eyes, which never left his face, slowly, slowly filled with tears. He watched the strange water rise in her eyes, like some slow fountain coming up. And his heart seemed to burn and melt away in his breast.

He could not bear to look at her any more. He dropped on his knees and caught her head with his arms and pressed her face against his throat. She was very still. His heart, which seemed to have broken, was burning with a kind of agony in his breast. And he felt her slow, hot tears wetting his throat. But he could not move.

He felt the hot tears wet his neck and the hollows of his neck, and he remained motionless, suspended through one of man's eternities. Only now it had become indispensable to him to have her face pressed close to him; he could never let her go again. He could never let her head go away from the close clutch of his arm. He wanted to remain like that for ever, with his heart hurting him in a pain that was also life to him. Without knowing, he was looking down on her damp, soft brown hair.

Then, as it were suddenly, he smelt the horrid stagnant smell of that water. And at the same moment she drew away from him and looked at him. Her eyes were wistful and unfathomable. He was afraid of them, and he fell to kissing her, not knowing what he was doing. He wanted her eyes not to have that terrible, wistful, unfathomable look.

When she turned her face to him again, a faint delicate flush was glowing, and there was again dawning that terrible shining of joy in her eyes, which really terrified him, and yet which he now wanted to see, because he feared the look of doubt still more.

"You love me?" she said, rather faltering.

"Yes." The word cost him a painful effort. Not because it wasn't true. But because it was too newly true, the *saying* seemed to tear open again his newly-torn heart. And he hardly wanted it to be true, even now.

She lifted her face to him, and he bent forward and kissed her on the mouth, gently, with the one kiss that is an eternal pledge. And as he kissed her his heart strained again in his breast. He never intended to love her. But now it was over. He had crossed over the gulf to her, and all that he had left behind had shrivelled and become void.

After the kiss, her eyes again slowly filled with tears. She sat still, away from him, with her face drooped aside, and her hands folded in her lap. The tears fell very slowly. There was complete silence. He too sat there motionless and silent on the hearth-rug. The strange pain of his heart that was broken seemed to consume him. That he should love her? That this was love! That he should be ripped open in this way! Him, a doctor! How they would all jeer if they knew! It was agony to him to think they might know.

In the curious naked pain of the thought he looked again to her. She was sitting there drooped into a muse. He saw a tear fall, and his heart flared hot. He saw for the first time that one of her shoulders was quite uncovered, one arm bare, he could see one of her small breasts; dimly, because it had become almost dark in the room.

"Why are you crying?" he asked, in an altered voice.

She looked up at him, and behind her tears the consciousness of her situation for the first time brought a dark look of shame to her eyes.

"I'm not crying, really," she said, watching him, half frightened.

He reached his hand, and softly closed it on her bare arm.

"I love you! I love you!" he said in a soft, low vibrating voice, unlike himself.

She shrank, and dropped her head. The soft, penetrating grip of his hand on her arm distressed her. She looked up at him.

"I want to go," she said. "I want to go and get you some dry things."

"Why?" he said. "I'm all right."

"But I want to go," she said. "And I want you to change your things."

He released her arm, and she wrapped herself in the blanket, looking at him rather frightened. And still she did not rise.

"Kiss me," she said wistfully.

He kissed her, but briefly, half in anger.

Then, after a second, she rose nervously, all mixed up in the blanket. He watched her in her confusion as she tried to extricate herself and wrap herself up so that she could walk. He watched her relentlessly, as she knew. And as she went, the blanket trailing, and as he saw a glimpse of her feet and her white leg, he tried to remember her as she was when he had wrapped her in the blanket. But then he didn't want to remember, because she had been nothing to him then, and his nature revolted from remembering her as she was when she was nothing to him.

A tumbling, muffled noise from within the dark house startled him. Then he heard her voice: "There are clothes." He rose and went to the foot of the stairs, and gathered up the garments she had thrown down. Then he came back to the fire, to rub himself down and dress. He grinned at his own appearance when he had finished.

The fire was sinking, so he put on coal. The house was now quite dark, save for the light of a street-lamp that shone in faintly from beyond the holly trees. He lit the gas with matches he found on the mantelpiece. Then he emptied the pockets of his own clothes, and threw all his wet things in a heap into the scullery. After which he gathered up her sodden clothes, gently, and put them in a separate heap on the copper-top in the scullery.

It was six o'clock on the clock. His own watch had stopped. He ought to go back to the surgery. He waited, and still she did not come down. So he went to the foot of the stairs and called:

"I shall have to go."

Almost immediately he heard her coming down. She had on her best dress of black voile, and her hair was tidy, but still damp. She looked at him—and in spite of herself, smiled.

"I don't like you in those clothes," she said.

"Do I look a sight?" he answered.

They were shy of one another.

"I'll make you some tea," she said.

"No, I must go."

"Must you?" And she looked at him again with the wide, strained, doubtful eyes. And again, from the pain of his breast, he knew how he loved her. He went and bent to kiss her, gently, passionately, with his heart's painful kiss.

"And my hair smells so horrible," she murmured in distraction. "And I'm so awful, I'm so awful! Oh no, I'm too awful." And she broke into bitter, heart-broken sobbing. "You can't want to love me, I'm horrible."

"Don't be silly, don't be silly," he said, trying to comfort her, kissing her, holding her in his arms. "I want you, I want to marry you, we're going to be married, quickly, quickly—to-morrow if I can."

But she only sobbed terribly, and cried:

"I feel awful. I feel awful. I feel I'm horrible to you."

"No, I want you, I want you," was all he answered, blindly, with that terrible intonation which frightened her almost more than her horror lest he should *not* want her.

The Princess

To HER father, she was The Princess. To her Boston aunts and uncles she was just *Dollie Urquhart, poor little thing*.

Colin Urquhart was just a bit mad. He was of an old Scottish family, and he claimed royal blood. The blood of Scottish kings flowed in his veins. On this point, his American relatives said, he was just a bit "off". They could not bear any more to be told *which* royal blood of Scotland blued his veins. The whole thing was rather ridiculous, and a sore point. The only fact they remembered was that it was not Stuart.

He was a handsome man, with a wide-open blue eye that seemed sometimes to be looking at nothing, soft black hair brushed rather low on his low, broad brow, and a very attractive body. Add to this a most beautiful speaking voice, usually rather hushed and diffident, but sometimes resonant and powerful like bronze, and you have the sum of his charms. He looked like some old Celtic hero. He looked as if he should have worn a greyish kilt and a sporran, and shown his knees. His voice came direct out of the hushed Ossianic past.

For the rest, he was one of those gentlemen of sufficient but not excessive means who fifty years ago wandered vaguely about, never arriving anywhere, never doing anything, and never definitely being anything, yet well received in the good society of more than one country.

He did not marry till he was nearly forty, and then it was a wealthy Miss Prescott, from New England. Hannah Prescott at twenty-two was fascinated by the man with the soft black hair not yet touched by grey, and the wide, rather vague blue eyes. Many women had been fascinated before

335

her. But Colin Urquhart, by his very vagueness, had avoided any decisive connection.

Mrs. Urquhart lived three years in the mist and glamour of her husband's presence. And then it broke her. It was like living with a fascinating spectre. About most things he was completely, even ghostly oblivious. He was always charming, courteous, perfectly gracious in that hushed, musical voice of his. But absent. When all came to all, he just wasn't there. "Not all there," as the vulgar say.

He was the father of the little girl she bore at the end of the first year. But this did not substantiate him the more. His very beauty and his haunting musical quality became dreadful to her after the first few months. The strange echo: he was like a living echo! His very flesh, when you touched it, did not seem quite the flesh of a real man.

Perhaps it was that he was a little bit mad. She thought it definitely the night her baby was born.

"Ah, so my little princess has come at last!" he said, in his throaty, singing Celtic voice, like a glad chant, swaying absorbed.

It was a tiny, frail baby, with wide, amazed blue eyes. They christened it Mary Henrietta. She called the little thing *My Dollie*. He called it always *My Princess*.

It was useless to fly at him. He just opened his wide blue eyes wider, and took a child-like, silent dignity there was no getting past.

Hannah Prescott had never been robust. She had no great desire to live. So when the baby was two years old she suddenly died.

The Prescotts felt a deep but unadmitted resentment against Colin Urquhart. They said he was selfish. Therefore they discontinued Hannah's income, a month after her burial in Florence, after they had urged the father to give the child over to them, and he had courteously, musically, but quite finally refused. He treated the Prescotts as if they were not of his world, not realities to him: just casual phenomena, or gramophones, talking-machines that had to be answered. He answered them. But of their actual existence he was never once aware.

They debated having him certified unsuitable to be guardian of his own child. But that would have created a scandal. So they did the simplest thing, after all—washed their hands of him. But they wrote scrupulously to the child, and sent her modest presents of money at Christmas, and on the anniversary of the death of her mother.

To The Princess her Boston relatives were for many years just a nominal reality. She lived with her father, and he travelled continually, though in a modest way, living on his moderate income. And never going to America. The child changed nurses all the time. In Italy it was a contadina; in India she had an ayah; in Germany she had a yellow-haired peasant girl.

Father and child were inseparable. He was not a recluse. Wherever he went he was to be seen paying formal calls going out to luncheon or to tea, rarely to dinner. And always with the child. People called her Princess Urquhart, as if that were her christened name.

She was a quick, dainty little thing with dark gold hair that went a soft brown, and wide, slightly prominent blue eyes that were at once so candid and so knowing. She was always grown up; she never really grew up. Always strangely wise, and always childish.

It was her father's fault.

"My little Princess must never take too much notice of people and the things they say and do," he repeated to her. "People don't know what they are doing and saying. They chatter-chatter, and they hurt one another, and they hurt themselves very often, till they cry. But don't take any notice, my little Princess. Because it is all nothing. Inside everybody there is another creature, a demon which doesn't care at all. You peel away all the things they say and do and feel, as cook peels away the outside of the onions. And in the middle of everybody there is a green demon which you can't peel away. And this green demon never changes, and it doesn't care at all about all the things that happen to the outside leaves of the person, all the chatter-chatter, and all the husbands and wives and children, and trouble and fusses. You peel everything away from people, and there is a green, upright demon in every man and woman; and this demon is a man's real self, and a woman's real self. It doesn't really care about anybody, it belongs to the demons and the primitive fairies, who never care. But, even so, there are big demons and mean demons, and splendid demonish fairies, and vulgar ones. But there are no royal fairy women left. Only you, my little Princess. You are the last of the royal race of the old people; the last, my Princess. There are no others. You and I are the last. When I am dead there will be only you. And that is why, darling, you will never care for any of the people in the world very much. Because their demons are all dwindled and vulgar. They are not royal. Only you are royal, after me. Always remember that. And always remember, it is a *great secret*. If you tell people, they will try to kill you, because they will envy you for being a Princess. It is our great secret, darling. I am a prince, and you a princess, of the old, old blood. And we keep our secret between us, all alone. And so, darling, you must treat all people very politely, because *noblesse oblige*. But you must never forget that you alone are the last of Princesses, and that all other are less than you are, less noble, more vulgar. Treat them politely and gently and kindly, darling. But you are the Princess, and they are commoners. Never try to think of them, as if they were like you. They are not. You will find, always, that they are lacking, lacking in the royal touch, which only you have——"

The Princess learned her lesson early—the first lesson, of absolute reticence, the impossibility of intimacy with any other than her father; the second lesson, of naïve, slightly benevolent politeness. As a small child, something crystallised in her character, making her clear and finished, and as impervious as crystal.

"Dear child!" her hostesses said of her. "She is so quaint and old-fashioned; such a lady, poor little mite!"

She was erect, and very dainty. Always small, nearly tiny in physique, she seemed like a changeling beside her big, handsome, slightly mad father. She dressed very simply, usually in blue or delicate greys, with little collars of old Milan point, or very finely-worked linen. She had exquisite little hands, that made the piano sound like a spinet when she played. She was rather given to wearing cloaks and capes, instead of coats, out of doors, and little eighteenth-century sort of hats. Her complexion was pure apple-blossom.

She looked as if she had stepped out of a picture. But no one, to her dying day, ever knew exactly the strange picture her father had framed her in and from which she never stepped.

Her grandfather and grandmother and her Aunt Maud demanded twice to see her, once in Rome and once in Paris. Each time they were charmed, piqued, and annoyed. She was so exquisite and such a little virgin. At the same time so knowing and so oddly assured. That odd, assured touch of condescension, and the inward coldness, infuriated her American relations.

Only she really fascinated her grandfather. He was spellbound; in a way, in love with the little faultless thing. His wife would catch him brooding, musing over his grandchild, long months after the meeting, and craving to see her again. He cherished to the end the fond hope that she might come to live with him and her grandmother.

"Thank you so much, grandfather. You are so very kind. But Papa and I are such an old couple, you see, such a crochety old couple, living in a world of our own."

Her father let her see the world—from the outside. And he let her read. When she was in her teens she read Zola and Maupassant, and with the eyes of Zola and Maupassant she looked on Paris. A little later she read Tolstoi and Dostoevsky. The latter confused her. The others, she seemed to understand with a very shrewd, canny understanding, just as she understood the Decameron stories as she read them in their old Italian, or the Nibelung poems. Strange and *uncanny*, she seemed to understand things in a cold light perfectly, with all the flush of fire absent. She was something like a changeling, not quite human.

This earned her, also, strange antipathies. Cabmen and railway porters, especially in Paris and Rome, would suddenly treat her with brutal rudeness, when she was alone. They seemed to look on her with sudden violent antipathy. They sensed in her curious impertinence, an easy, sterile impertinence towards the things *they* felt most. She was so assured, and her flower of maidenhood was so scentless. She could look at a lusty, sensual Roman cabman as if he were a sort of grotesque, to make her smile. She knew all about him, in Zola. And the peculiar condescension with which she would give him her order, as if she, frail, beautiful thing, were the only reality, and he, coarse monster, was a sort of Caliban floundering in the mud on the margin of the pool of the perfect lotus, would suddenly enrage the fellow, the real Mediterranean who prided himself on his *beauté male,* and to whom the phallic mystery was still the only mystery. And he would turn a terrible face on her, bully her in a brutal, coarse fashion—hideous. For to him she had only the blasphemous impertinence of her own sterility.

Encounters like these made her tremble, and made her know she must have support from the outside. The power of her spirit did not extend to these low people, and they had all the physical power. She realised an implacability of hatred in their turning on her. But she did not lose her head. She quietly paid out money and turned away.

Those were dangerous moments, though, and she learned to be prepared for them. The Princess she was, and the fairy from the North, and could never understand the volcanic phallic rage with which coarse people could turn on her in a paroxysm of hatred. They never turned on her father like that. And quite early she decided it was the New England mother in her whom they hated. Never for one minute could she see with the old Roman eyes, see herself as sterility, the barren flower taking on airs and an intolerable impertinence. This was what the Roman cabman saw in her. And he longed to crush the barren blossom. Its sexless beauty and its authority put him in a passion of brutal revolt.

When she was nineteen her grandfather died, leaving her a considerable fortune in the safe hands of responsible trustees. They would deliver her her income, but only on condition that she resided for six months in the year in the United States.

"Why should they make me conditions?" she said to her

father. "I refuse to be imprisoned six months in the year in the United States. We will tell them to keep their money."

"Let us be wise, my little Princess, let us be wise. No, we are almost poor, and we are never safe from rudeness. I cannot allow anybody to be rude to me. I hate it, I hate it!" His eyes flamed as he said it. "I could kill any man or woman who is rude to me. But we are in exile in the world. We are powerless. If we were really poor, we should be quite powerless, and then I should die. No, my Princess. Let us take their money, then they will not dare to be rude to us. Let us take it, as we put on clothes, to cover ourselves from their aggressions."

There began a new phase, when the father and daughter spent their summers on the Great Lakes or in California, or in the South-West. The father was something of a poet, the daughter something of a painter. He wrote poems about the lakes or the redwood trees, and she made dainty drawings. He was physically a strong man, and he loved the out-of-doors. He would go off with her for days, paddling in a canoe and sleeping by a camp-fire. Frail little Princess, she was always undaunted, always undaunted. She would ride with him on horseback over the mountain trails till she was so tired she was nothing but a bodiless consciousness sitting astride her pony. But she never gave in. And at night he folded her in her blanket on a bed of balsam pine twigs, and she lay and looked at the stars unmurmuring. She was fulfilling her rôle.

People said to her as the years passed, and she was a woman of twenty-five, then a woman of thirty, and always the same virgin dainty Princess, 'knowing' in a dispassionate way, like an old woman, and utterly intact:

"Don't you ever think what you will do when your father is no longer with you?"

She looked at her interlocutor with that cold, elfin detachment of hers:

"No, I never think of it," she said.

She had a tiny, but exquisite little house in London, and another small, perfect house in Connecticut, each with a faithful housekeeper. Two homes, if she chose. And she knew many interesting literary and artistic people. What more?

So the years passed imperceptibly. And she had that quality of the sexless fairies, she did not change. At thirty-three she looked twenty-three.

Her father, however, was ageing, and becoming more and more queer. It was now her task to be his guardian in his private madness. He spent the last three years of life in the house in Connecticut. He was very much estranged, sometimes had fits of violence which almost killed the little Princess. Physical violence was horrible to her; it seemed to shatter her heart. But she found a woman a few years younger than herself, well-educated and sensitive, to be a sort of nurse-companion to the mad old man. So the fact of madness was never openly admitted. Miss Cummins, the companion, had a passionate loyalty to the Princess, and a curious affection, tinged with love, for the handsome, white-haired courteous old man, who was never at all aware of his fits of violence once they had passed.

The Princess was thirty-eight years old when her father died. And quite unchanged. She was still tiny, and like a dignified, scentless flower. Her soft brownish hair, almost the colour of beaver fur, was bobbed, and fluffed softly round her apple-blossom face, that was modelled with an arched nose like a proud old Florentine portrait. In her voice, manner and bearing she was exceedingly still, like a flower that has blossomed in a shadowy place. And from her blue eyes looked out the Princess's eternal laconic challenge, that grew almost sardonic as the years passed. She was the Princess, and sardonically she looked out on a princeless world.

She was relieved when her father died, and at the same time, it was as if everything had evaporated around her. She had lived in a sort of hot-house, in the aura of her father's madness. Suddenly the hot-house had been removed from around her, and she was in the raw, vast, vulgar open air.

Quoi faire? What was she to do? She seemed faced with absolute nothingness. Only she had Miss Cummins, who shared with her the secret, and almost the passion for her father. In fact, the Princess felt that her passion for her mad father had in some curious way transferred itself largely to Charlotte Cummins during the last years. And now Miss Cummins was the vessel that held the passion for the dead man. She herself, the Princess, was an empty vessel.

An empty vessel in the enormous warehouse of the world.

Quoi faire? What was she to do? She felt that, since she could not evaporate into nothingness, like alcohol from an unstoppered bottle, she must *do* something. Never before in her life had she felt the incumbency. Never, never had she felt she must *do* anything. That was left to the vulgar.

Now her father was dead, she found herself on the *fringe* of the vulgar crowd, sharing their necessity to *do* something. It was a little humiliating. She felt herself becoming vulgarised. At the same time she found herself looking at men with a shrewder eye: an eye to marriage. Not that she felt any sudden interest in men, or attraction towards them. No. She was still neither interested nor attracted towards men vitally. But *marriage,* that peculiar abstraction, had imposed a sort of spell on her. She thought that *marriage,* in the blank abstract, was the thing she ought to *do.* That *marriage* implied a man she also knew. She knew all the facts. But the man seemed a property of her own mind rather than a thing in himself, another thing.

His father died in the summer, the month after her thirty-eighth birthday. When all was over, the obvious thing to do, of course, was to travel. With Miss Cummins. The two women knew each other intimately, but they were always Miss Urquhart and Miss Cummins to one another, and a certain distance was instinctively maintained. Miss Cummins, from Philadelphia, of scholastic stock, and intelligent but untravelled, four years younger than the Princess, felt herself immensely the junior of her 'lady'. She had a sort of passionate veneration for the Princess, who seemed to her ageless, timeless. She could not see the rows of tiny, dainty, exquisite shoes in the Princess's cupboard without feeling a stab at the heart, a stab of tenderness and reverence, almost of awe.

Miss Cummins also was virginal, but with a look of puzzled surprise in her brown eyes. Her skin was pale and clear, her features well modelled, but there was a certain blankness in her expression, where the Princess had an odd touch of Renaissance grandeur. Miss Cummins's voice was also hushed almost to a whisper; it was the inevitable effect of Colin Urquhart's room. But the hushedness had a hoarse quality.

The Princess did not want to go to Europe. Her face seemed turned west. Now her father was gone, she felt she would go west, westwards, as if for ever. Following, no doubt, the March of Empire, which is brought up rather short on the Pacific coast, among swarms of wallowing bathers.

No, not the Pacific coast. She would stop short of that. The South-West was less vulgar. She would go to New Mexico.

She and Miss Cummins arrived at the Rancho del Cerro Gordo towards the end of August, when the crowd was beginning to drift back east. The ranch lay by a stream on the desert some four miles from the foot of the mountains, a mile away from the Indian pueblo of San Cristobal. It was a ranch for the rich; the Princess paid thirty dollars a day for herself and Miss Cummins. But then she had a little cottage to herself, among the apple trees of the orchard, with an excellent cook. She and Miss Cummins, however, took dinner at evening in the large guest-house. For the Princess still entertained the idea of *marriage*.

The guests at the Rancho del Cerro Gordo were of all sorts, except the poor sort. They were practically all rich, and many were romantic. Some were charming, others were vulgar, some were movie people, quite quaint and not unattractive in their vulgarity, and many were Jews. The Princess did not care for Jews, though they were usually the most interesting to *talk* to. So she talked a good deal with the Jews, and painted with the artists, and rode with the young men from college, and had altogether quite a good time. And yet she felt something of a fish out of water, or a bird in the wrong forest. And *marriage* remained still completely in the abstract. No connecting it with any of these young men, even the nice ones.

The Princess looked just twenty-five. The freshness of her mouth, the hushed, delicate-complexioned virginity of her face gave her not a day more. Only a certain laconic look in her eyes was disconcerting. When she was *forced* to write her age, she put twenty-eight, making the figure *two* rather badly, so that it just avoided being a three.

Men hinted marriage at her. Especially boys from college suggested it from a distance. But they all failed before the look of sardonic ridicule in the Princess's eyes. It always seemed to her rather preposterous, quite ridiculous, and a tiny bit impertinent on their part.

The only man that intrigued her at all was one of the guides, a man called Romero—Domingo Romero. It was he who had sold the ranch itself to the Wilkiesons, ten years before, for two thousand dollars. He had gone away, then reappeared at the old place. For he was the son of the old Romero, the last of the Spanish family that had owned miles of land around San Cristobal. But the coming of the white man and the failure of the vast flocks of sheep, and the fatal inertia which overcomes all men, at last, on the desert near the mountains, had finished the Romero family. The last descendants were just Mexican peasants.

Domingo, the heir, had spent his two thousand dollars, and was working for white people. He was now about thirty years old, a tall, silent fellow, with a heavy closed mouth and black eyes that looked across at one almost sullenly. From behind he was handsome, with a strong, natural body, and the back of his neck very dark and well-shapen, strong with life. But his dark face was long and heavy, almost sinister, with that peculiar heavy meaninglessness in it, characteristic of the Mexicans of his own locality. They are strong, they seem healthy. They laugh and joke with one another. But their physique and their natures seem static, as if there were nowhere, nowhere at all for their energies to go, and their faces, degenerating to misshapen heaviness, seem to have no *raison d'être*, no radical meaning. Waiting either to die or to be aroused into passion and hope. In some of the black eyes a queer, haunting mystic quality, sombre and a bit gruesome, the skull-and-cross-bones look of the Penitentes. They had found their *raison d'être* in self-torture and death-worship. Unable to wrest a *positive* significance for themselves from the vast, beautiful, but vindictive landscape they were born into, they turned on their own selves, and worshipped death through self-torture. The mystic gloom of this showed in their eyes.

But as a rule the dark eyes of the Mexicans were heavy and half alive, sometimes hostile, sometimes kindly, often with the fatal Indian glaze on them, or the fatal Indian glint.

Domingo Romero was *almost* a typical Mexican to look at, with the typical heavy, dark, long face, clean-shaven, with an almost brutally heavy mouth. His eyes were black and Indian-looking. Only, at the centre of their hopelessness was a spark of pride, or self-confidence, or dauntlessness. Just a spark in the midst of the blackness of static despair.

But this spark was the difference between him and the mass of men. It gave a certain alert sensitiveness to his bearing and a certain beauty to his appearance. He wore a low-crowned black hat, instead of the ponderous headgear of the usual Mexican, and his clothes were thinnish and graceful. Silent, aloof, almost imperceptible in the landscape, he was an admirable guide, with a startling quick intelligence that anticipated difficulties about to rise. He could cook, too, crouching over the camp-fire and moving his lean deft brown hands. The only fault he had was that he was not forthcoming, he wasn't chatty and cosy.

"Oh, don't send Romero with us," the Jews would say. "One can't get any response from him."

Tourists come and go, but they rarely *see* anything, inwardly. None of them ever saw the spark at the middle of Romero's eye; they were not alive enough to see it.

The Princess caught it one day, when she had him for a guide. She was fishing for trout in the canyon. Miss Cummins was reading a book, the horses were tied under the trees, Romero was fixing a proper fly on her line. He fixed the fly and handed her the line, looking up at her. And at that moment she caught the spark in his eye. And instantly she knew that he was a gentleman, that his 'demon', as her father would have said, was a fine demon. And instantly her manner towards him changed.

He had perched her on a rock over a quiet pool, beyond

the cotton-wood trees. It was early September, and the canyon already cool, but the leaves of the cottonwoods were still green. The Princess stood on her rock, a small but perfectly formed figure, wearing a soft, close grey sweater and neatly-cut grey riding-breeches, with tall black boots, her fluffy brown hair straggling from under a little grey felt hat. A woman? Not quite. A changeling of some sort, perched in outline there on the rock, in the bristling wild canyon. She knew perfectly well how to handle a line. Her father had made a fisherman of her.

Romero, in a black shirt and with loose black trousers pushed into wide black riding-boots, was fishing a little farther down. He had put his hat on a rock behind him; his dark head was bent a little forward, watching the water. He had caught three trout. From time to time he glanced up-stream at the Princess, perched there so daintily. He saw she had caught nothing.

Soon he quietly drew in his line and came up to her. His keen eye watched her line, watched her position. Then, quietly, he suggested certain changes to her, putting his sensitive brown hand before her. And he withdrew a little, and stood in silence, leaning against a tree, watching her. He was helping her across the distance. She knew it, and thrilled. And in a moment she had a bite. In two minutes she landed a good trout. She looked round at him quickly, her eyes sparkling, the colour heightened in her cheeks. And as she met his eyes a smile of greeting went over his dark face, very sudden, with an odd sweetness.

She knew he was helping her. And she felt in his presence a subtle, insidious male *kindliness* she had never known before waiting upon her. Her cheek flushed, and her blue eyes darkened.

After this, she always looked for him, and for that curious dark beam of a man's kindliness which he could give her, as it were, from his chest, from his heart. It was something she had never known before.

A vague, unspoken intimacy grew up between them. She liked his voice, his appearance, his presence. His natural language was Spanish; he spoke English like a foreign language, rather slow, with a slight hesitation, but with a sad, plangent sonority lingering over from his Spanish. There was a certain subtle correctness in his appearance; he was always perfectly shaved; his hair was thick and rather long on top, but always carefully groomed behind. And his fine black cashmere shirt, his wide leather belt, his well-cut, wide black trousers going into the embroidered cowboy boots had a certain inextinguishable elegance. He wore no silver rings or buckles. Only his boots were embroidered and decorated at the top with an inlay of white *suède*. He seemed elegant, slender, yet he was very strong.

And at the same time, curiously, he gave her the feeling that death was not far from him. Perhaps he too was half in love with death. However that may be, the sense she had that death was not far from him made him 'possible' to her.

Small as she was, she was quite a good horsewoman. They gave her at the ranch a sorrel mare, very lovely in colour, and well-made, with a powerful broad neck and the hollow back that betokens a swift runner. Tansy, she was called. Her only fault was the usual mare's failing, she was inclined to be hysterical.

So that every day the Princess set off with Miss Cummins and Romero, on horseback, riding into the mountains. Once they went camping for several days, with two more friends in the party.

"I think I like it better," the Princess said to Romero, "when we three go alone."

And he gave her one of his quick, transfiguring smiles.

It was curious no white man had ever showed her this capacity for subtle gentleness, this power to *help* her in silence across a distance, if she were fishing without success, or tired of her horse, or if Tansy suddenly got scared. It was as if Romero could send her *from his heart* a dark beam of succour and sustaining. She had never known this before, and it was very thrilling.

Then the smile that suddenly creased his dark face, showing the strong white teeth. It creased his face almost into a savage grotesque. And at the same time there was in it something so warm, such a dark flame of kindliness for her, she was elated into her true Princess self.

Then that vivid, latent spark in his eye, which she had seen, and which she knew he was aware she had seen. It made an inter-recognition between them, silent and delicate. Here he was delicate as a woman in this subtle inter-recognition.

And yet his presence only put to flight in her the *idée fixe* of 'marriage'. For some reason, in her strange little brain, the idea of *marrying* him could not enter. Not for any definite reason. He was in himself a gentleman, and she had plenty of money for two. There was no actual obstacle. Nor was she conventional.

No, now she came down to it, it was as if their two 'dæmons' could marry, were perhaps married. Only their two *selves,* Miss Urquhart and Señor Domingo Romero, were for some reason incompatible. There was a peculiar subtle intimacy of inter-recognition between them. But she did not see in the least how it would lead to marriage. Almost she could more easily marry one of the nice boys from Harvard or Yale.

The time passed, and she let it pass. The end of September came, with aspens going yellow on the mountain heights, and oak-scrub going red. But as yet the cottonwoods in the valley and canyons had not changed.

"When will you go away?" Romero asked her, looking at her fixedly, with a blank black eye.

"By the end of October," she said. "I have promised to be in Santa Barbara at the beginning of November."

He was hiding the spark in his eye from her. But she saw the peculiar sullen thickening of his heavy mouth.

She had complained to him many times that one never saw any wild animals, except chipmunks and squirrels, and perhaps a skunk and a porcupine. Never a deer, or a bear, or a mountain lion.

"Are these no bigger animals in these mountains?" she asked, dissatisfied.

"Yes," he said. "There are deer—I see their tracks. And I saw the tracks of a bear."

"But why can one never see the animals themselves?" She looked dissatisfied and wistful like a child.

"Why, it's pretty hard for you to see them. They won't let you come close. You have to keep still, in a place where they come. Or else you have to follow their tracks a long way."

"I can't bear to go away till I've seen them: a bear, or a deer——"

The smile came suddenly on his face, indulgent.

"Well, what do you want? Do you want to go up into the mountains to some place, to wait till they come?"

"Yes," she said, looking up at him with a sudden naïve impulse of recklessness.

And immediately his face became sombre again, responsible.

"Well," he said, with slight irony, a touch of mockery of her. "You will have to find a house. It's very cold at night now. You would have to stay all night in a house."

"And there are no houses up there?" she said.

"Yes," he replied. "There is a little shack that belongs to me, that a miner built a long time ago, looking for gold. You can go there and stay one night, and maybe you see something. Maybe! I don't know. Maybe nothing come."

"How much chance is there?"

"Well, I don't know. Last time when I was there I see three deer come down to drink at the water, and I shot two raccoons. But maybe this time we don't see anything."

"Is there water there?" she asked.

"Yes, there is a little round pond, you know, below the spruce trees. And the water from the snow runs into it."

"Is it far away?" she asked.

"Yes, pretty far. You see that ridge there"—and turning to the mountains he lifted his arm in the gesture which is somehow so moving, out in the West, pointing to the distance—"that ridge where there are no trees, only rock"—his black eyes were focussed on the distance, his face impassive, but as if in pain—"you go round that ridge, and along, then you come down through the spruce trees to where that cabin is. My father bought that placer claim from a miner who was broke, but nobody ever found any gold or anything, and nobody ever goes there. Too lonesome!"

The Princess watched the massive, heavy-sitting, beautiful bulk of the Rocky Mountains. It was early in October, and the aspens were already losing their gold leaves; high up, the spruce and pine seemed to be growing darker; the great flat patches of oak scrub on the heights were red like gore.

"Can I go over there?" she asked, turning to him and meeting the spark in his eye.

His face was heavy with responsibility.

"Yes," he said, "you can go. But there'll be snow over the ridge, and it's awful cold, and awful lonesome."

"I should like to go," she said, persistent.

"All right," he said. "You can go if you want to."

She doubted, though, if the Wilkiesons would let her go; at least alone with Romero and Miss Cummins.

Yet an obstinacy characteristic of her nature, an obstinacy tinged perhaps with madness, had taken hold of her. She wanted to look over the mountains into their secret heart. she wanted to descend to the cabin below the spruce trees, near the tarn of bright green water. She wanted to see the wild animals move about in their wild unconsciousness.

"Let us say to the Wilkiesons that we want to make the trip round the Frijoles canyon," she said.

The trip round the Frijoles canyon was a usual thing. It would not be strenuous, nor cold, nor lonely; they could sleep in the log house that was called an hotel.

Romero looked at her quickly.

"If you want to say that," he replied, "you can tell Mrs. Wilkieson. Only I know she'll be mad with me if I take you up in the mountains to that place. And I've got to go there first with a pack-horse, to take lots of blankets and some bread. Maybe Miss Cummins can't stand it. Maybe not. It's a hard trip."

He was speaking, and thinking, in the heavy, disconnected Mexican fashion.

"Never mind!" The Princess was suddenly very decisive and stiff with authority. "I want to do it. I will arrange with Mrs. Wilkieson. And we'll go on Saturday."

He shook his head slowly.

"I've got to go up on Sunday with a pack-horse and blankets," he said. "Can't do it before."

"Very well!" she said, rather piqued. "Then we'll start on Monday."

She hated being thwarted even the tiniest bit.

He knew that if he started with the pack on Sunday at dawn he would not be back until late at night. But he consented that they should start on Monday morning at seven. The obedient Miss Cummins was told to prepare for the Frijoles trip. On Sunday Romero had his day off. He had not put in an appearance when the Princess retired on Sunday night, but on Monday morning, as she was dressing, she saw him bringing in the three horses from the corral. She was in high spirits.

The night had been cold. There was ice at the edges of the irrigation ditch, and the chipmunks crawled into the sun and lay with wide, dumb, anxious eyes, almost too numb to run.

"We may be away two or three days," said the Princess.

"Very well. We won't begin to be anxious about you before Thursday, then," said Mrs. Wilkieson, who was young and capable: from Chicago. "Anyway," she added, "Romero will see you through. He's so trustworthy."

The sun was already on the desert as they set off towards the mountains, making the greasewood and the sage pale as pale-grey sands, luminous the great level around them. To the right glinted the shadows of the adobe pueblo, flat and almost invisible on the plain, earth of its earth. Behind lay the ranch and the tufts of tall, plumy cottonwoods, whose summits were yellowing under the perfect blue sky.

Autumn breaking into colour in the great spaces of the South-West.

But the three trotted gently along the trail, towards the sun that sparkled yellow just above the dark bulk of the ponderous mountains. Side-slopes were already gleaming yellow, flaming with a second light, under coldish blue of the pale sky. The front slopes were in shadow, with submerged lustre of red oak scrub and dull-gold aspens, blue-black pines and grey-blue rock. While the canyon was full of a deep blueness.

They rode single file, Romero first, on a black horse. Himself in black, made a flickering black spot in the delicate pallor of the great landscape, where even pine trees at a distance take a film of blue paler than their green. Romero rode on in silence past the tufts of furry greasewood. The Princess came next, on her sorrel mare. And Miss Cummins, who was not quite happy on horseback, came last, in the pale dust that the others kicked up. Sometimes her horse sneezed, and she started.

But on they went at a gentle trot. Romero never looked round. He could hear the sound of the hoofs following, and that was all he wanted.

For the rest, he held ahead. And the Princess, with that black, unheeding figure always travelling away from her, felt strangely helpless, withal elated.

They neared the pale, round foot-hills, dotted with the round dark piñon and cedar shrubs. The horses clinked and trotted among the stones. Occasionally a big round greasewood held out fleecy tufts of flowers, pure gold. They wound into blue shadow, then up a steep stony slope, with the world lying pallid away behind and below. Then they dropped into the shadow of the San Cristobal canyon.

The stream was running full and swift. Occasionally the horses snatched at a tuft of grass. The trail narrowed and became rocky; the rocks closed in; it was dark and cool as the horses climbed and climbed upwards, and the tree trunks crowded in the shadowy, silent tightness of the canyon. They were among cottonwood trees that ran straight up and smooth and round to an extraordinary height. Above, the tips were gold, and it was sun. But away below, where the horses struggled up the rocks and wound among the trunks, there was still blue shadow by the sound of waters and an occasional grey festoon of old man's beard, and here and there a pale, dripping crane's-bill flower among the tangle and the débris of the virgin place. And again the chill entered the Princess's heart as she realised what a tangle of decay and despair lay in the virgin forests.

They scramble downwards, splashed across stream, up rocks and along the trail of the other side. Romero's black horse stopped, looked down quizzically at the fallen trees, then stepped over lightly. The Princess's sorrel followed, carefully. But Miss Cummins's buckskin made a fuss, and had to be got round.

In the same silence, save for the clinking of the horses and the splashing as the trail crossed stream, they worked their way upwards in the tight, tangled shadow of the canyon. Sometimes, crossing stream, the Princess would glance upwards, and then always her heart caught in her breast. For high up, away in heaven, the mountain heights shone yellow, dappled with dark spruce firs, clear almost as speckled daffodils against the pale turquoise blue lying high and serene above the dark-blue shadow where the Princess was. And she would snatch at the blood-red leaves of the oak as her horse crossed a more open slope, not knowing what she felt.

They were getting fairly high, occasionally lifted above the canyon itself, in the low groove below the speckled, gold-sparkling heights which towered beyond. Then again they dipped and crossed stream, the horses stepping gingerly across a tangle of fallen, frail aspen stems, then suddenly floundering in a mass of rocks. The black emerged ahead, his black tail waving. The Princess let her mare find her own footing; then she too emerged from the clatter. She rode on after the black. Then came a great frantic rattle of the buckskin behind. The Princess was aware of Romero's dark face looking round, with a strange, demon-like watchfulness, before she herself looked round, to see the buckskin scrambling rather lamely beyond the rocks, with one of his pale buff knees already red with blood.

"He almost went down!" called Miss Cummins.

But Romero was already out of the saddle and hastening down the path. He made quiet little noises to the buckskin, and began examining the cut knee.

"Is he hurt?" cried Miss Cummins anxiously, and she climbed hastily down.

"Oh, my goodness!" she cried, as she saw the blood running down the slender buff leg of the horse in a thin trickle. "Isn't that *awful*?" She spoke in a stricken voice, and her face was white.

Romero was still carefully feeling the knee of the buckskin. Then he made him walk a few paces. And at last he stood up straight and shook his head.

"Not very bad!" he said. "Nothing broken."

Again he bent and worked at the knees. Then he looked up at the Princess.

"He can go on," he said. "It's not bad."

The Princess looked down at the dark face in silence.

"What, go on right up here?" cried Miss Cummins. "How many hours?"

"About five!" said Romero simply.

"Five hours!" cried Miss Cummins. "A horse with a lame knee! And a steep mountain! Why-y!"

"Yes, it's pretty steep up there," said Romero, pushing back his hat and staring fixedly at the bleeding knee. The buckskin stood in a stricken sort of dejection. "But I think he'll make it all right," the man added.

"Oh!" cried Miss Cummins, her eyes bright with sudden passion of unshed tears. "I wouldn't think of it. I wouldn't ride him up there, not for any money."

"Why wouldn't you?" asked Romero.

"It *hurts* him."

Romero bent down again to the horse's knee.

"Maybe it hurts him a little," he said. "But he can make it all right, and his leg won't get stiff."

"What! Ride him five hours up the steep mountain?" cried Miss Cummins. "I couldn't. I just couldn't do it. I'll lead him a little way and see if he can go. But I *couldn't* ride him again. I couldn't. Let me walk."

"But Miss Cummins, dear, if Romero says he'll be all right?" said the Princess.

"I know it hurts him. Oh, I just couldn't bear it."

There was no doing anything with Miss Cummins. The thought of a hurt animal always put her into a sort of hysterics.

They walked forward a little, leading the buckskin. He limped rather badly. Miss Cummins sat on a rock.

"Why, it's agony to see him!" she cried. "It's *cruel*!"

"He won't limp after a bit, if you take no notice of him,"

said Romero. "Now he plays up, and limps very much, because he wants to make you see."

"I don't think there can be much playing up," said Miss Cummins bitterly. "We can *see* how it must hurt him."

"It don't hurt much," said Romero.

But now Miss Cummins was silent wtih antipathy.

It was a deadlock. The party remained motionless on the trail, the Princess in the saddle, Miss Cummins seated on a rock, Romero standing black and remote near the drooping buckskin.

"Well!" said the man suddenly at last. "I guess we go back, then."

And he looked up swiftly at his horse, which was cropping at the mountain herbage and treading on the trailing reins.

"No!" cried the Princess. "Oh no!" Her voice rang with a great wail of disappointment and anger. Then she checked herself.

Miss Cummins rose with energy.

"Let me lead the buckskin home," she said, with cold dignity, "and you two go on."

This was received in silence. The Princess was looking down at her with a sardonic, almost cruel gaze.

"We've only come about two hours," said Miss Cummins. "I don't mind a bit leading him home. But I *couldn't* ride him. I *couldn't* have him ridden with that knee."

This again was received in dead silence. Romero remained impassive, almost inert.

"Very well, then," said the Princess. "You lead him home. You'll be quite all right. Nothing can happen to you, possibly. And say to them that we have gone on and shall be home tomorrow—or the day after."

She spoke coldly and distinctly. For she could not bear to be thwarted.

"Better all go back, and come again another day," said Romero—non-committal.

"There will never *be* another day," cried the Princess. "I want to go on."

She looked at him square in the eyes, and met the spark in his eye.

He raised his shoulders slightly.

"If you want it," he said. "I'll go on with you. But Miss Cummins can ride my horse to the end of the canyon, and I lead the buckskin. Then I can come back to you."

It was arranged so. Miss Cummins had her saddle put on Romero's black horse, Romero took the buckskin's bridle, and they started back. The Princess rode very slowly on, upwards, alone. She was at first so angry with Miss Cummins that she was blind to everything else. She just let her mare follow her own inclinations.

The peculiar spell of anger carried the Princess on, almost unconscious, for an hour or so. And by this time she was beginning to climb pretty high. Her horse walked steadily all the time. They emerged on a bare slope, and the trail wound through frail aspen stems. Here a wind swept, and some of the aspens were already bare. Others were fluttering their discs of pure, solid yellow leaves, so *nearly* like petals, while the slope ahead was one soft, glowing fleece of daffodil yellow; fleecy like a golden foxskin, and yellow as daffodils alive in the wind and the high mountain sun.

She paused and looked back. The near great slopes were mottled with gold and the dark hue of spruce, like some unsinged eagle, and the light lay gleaming upon them. Away through the gap of the canyon she could see the pale blue of the egg-like desert, with the crumpled dark crack of the Rio Grande Canyon. And far, far off, the blue mountains like a fence of angels on the horizon.

And she thought of her adventure. She was going on alone with Romero. But then she was very sure of herself, and Romero was not the kind of man to do anything to her against her will. This was her first thought. And she just had a fixed desire to go over the brim of the mountain, to look into the inner chaos of the Rockies. And she wanted to go with Romero, because he had some peculiar kinship with her; there was some peculiar link between the two of them. Miss Cummins anyhow would have been only a discordant note.

She rode on, and emerged at length in the lap of the summit. Beyond her was a great concave of stone and stark, dead-grey trees, where the mountain ended against the sky.

But nearer was the dense black, bristling spruce, and at her feet was a lap of the summit, a flat little valley of sere grass and quiet-standing yellow aspens, the stream trickling like a thread across.

It was a little valley or shell from which the stream was gently poured into the lower rocks and trees of the canyon. Around her was fairy-like gentleness, the delicate sere grass, the groves of delicate-stemmed aspens dropping their flakes of bright yellow. And the delicate, quick little stream threading through the wild, sere grass.

Here one might expect deer and fawns and wild things, as in a little paradise. Here she was to wait for Romero, and they were to have lunch.

She unfastened her saddle and pulled it to the ground with a crash, letting her horse wander with a long rope. How beautiful Tansy looked, sorrel, among the yellow leaves that lay like a patina on the sere ground. The Princess herself wore a fleecy sweater of a pale, sere buff, like the grass, and riding-breeches of a pure orange-tawny colour. She felt quite in the picture.

From her saddle-pouches she took the packages of lunch, spread a little cloth, and sat to wait for Romero. Then she made a little fire. Then she ate a devilled egg. Then she ran after Tansy, who was straying across-stream. Then she sat in the sun, in the stillness near the aspens, and waited.

The sky was blue. Her little alp was soft and delicate as fairy-land. But beyond and up jutted the great slopes, dark with the pointed feathers of spruce, bristling with grey dead trees among grey rock, or dappled with dark and gold. The beautiful, but fierce, heavy cruel mountains, with their moments of tenderness.

She saw Tansy start, and begin to run. Two ghost-like figures on horseback emerged from the black of the spruce across the stream. It was two Indians on horseback, swathed like seated mummies in their pale-grey cotton blankets. Their guns jutted beyond the saddles. They rode straight towards her, to her thread of smoke.

As they came near, they unswathed themselves and greeted her, looking at her curiously from their dark eyes. Their black hair was somewhat untidy, the long rolled plaits on their shoulders were soiled. They looked tired.

They got down from their horses near her little fire—a camp was a camp—swathed their blankets round their hips, pulled the saddles from their ponies and turned them loose, then sat down. One was a young Indian whom she had met before, the other was an older man.

"You all alone?" said the younger man.

"Romero will be here in a minute," she said, glancing back along the trail.

"Ah, Romero! You with him? Where are you going?"

"Round the ridge," she said. "Where are you going?"

"We going down to Pueblo."

"Been out hunting? How long have you been out?"

"Yes. Been out five days." The young Indian gave a little meaningless laugh.

"Got anything?"

"No. We see tracks of two deer—but not got nothing."

The Princess noticed a suspicious-looking bulk under one of the saddles—surely a folded-up deer. But she said nothing.

"You must have been cold," she said.

"Yes, very cold in the night. And hungry. Got nothing to eat since yesterday. Eat it all up." And again he laughed his little meaningless laugh. Under their dark skins, the two men looked peaked and hungry. The Princess rummaged for food among the saddle-bags. There was a lump of bacon—the regular stand-back—and some bread. She gave them this, and they began toasting slices of it on long sticks at the fire. Such was the little camp Romero saw as he rode down the slope: the Princess in her orange breeches, her head tied in a blue-and-brown silk kerchief, sitting opposite the two dark-headed Indians across the camp-fire, while one of the Indians was leaning forward toasting bacon, his two plaits of braid-hair dangling as if wearily.

Romero rode up, his face expressionless. The Indians greeted him in Spanish. He unsaddled his horse, took food from the bags, and sat down at the camp to eat. The Princess went to the stream for water, and to wash her hands.

"Got coffee?" asked the Indians.

"No coffee this outfit," said Romero.

They lingered an hour or more in the warm midday sun. Then Romero saddled the horses. The Indians still squatted by the fire. Romero and the Princess rode away, calling *Adios!* to the Indians over the stream and into the dense spruce whence two strange figures had emerged.

When they were alone, Romero turned and looked at her curiously, in a way she could not understand, with such a hard glint in his eyes. And for the first time she wondered if she was rash.

"I hope you don't mind going alone with me," she said.

"If you want it," he replied.

They emerged at the foot of the great bare slope of rocky summit, where dead spruce trees stood spare and bristling like bristles on a grey dead hog. Romero said the Mexicans, twenty years back, had fired the mountains, to drive out the whites. This grey concave slope of summit was corpse-like.

The trail was almost invisible. Romero watched for the trees which the Forest Service had blazed. And they climbed the stark corpse slope, among dead spruce, fallen and ash-grey, into the wind. The wind came rushing from the west, up the funnel of the canyon, from the desert. And there was the desert, like a vast mirage tilting slowly upwards towards the west, immense and pallid, away beyond the funnel of the canyon. The Princess could hardly look.

For an hour their horses rushed the slope, hastening with a great working of the haunches upwards, and halting to breathe, scrambling again, and rowing their way up length by length, on the livid, slanting wall. While the wind blew like some vast machine.

After an hour they were working their way on the incline, no longer forcing straight up. All was grey and dead around them; the horses picked their way over the silver-grey corpses of the spruce. But they were near the top, near the ridge.

Even the horses made a rush for the last bit. They had worked round to a scrap of spruce forest near the very top. They hurried in, out of the huge, monstrous, mechanical wind, that whistled inhumanly and was palely cold. So, stepping through the dark screen of trees, they emerged over the crest.

In front now was nothing but mountains, ponderous, massive, down-sitting mountains, in a huge and intricate knot, empty of life or soul. Under the bristling black feathers of spruce near-by lay patches of white snow. The lifeless valleys were concaves of rock and spruce, the rounded summits and the hog-backed summits of grey rock crowded one behind the other like some monstrous herd in arrest.

It frightened the Princess, it was *so* inhuman. She had not thought it could be so inhuman, so, as it were, anti-life. And yet now one of her desires was fulfilled. She had seen it, the massive, gruesome, repellent core of the Rockies. She saw it there beneath her eyes in its gigantic, heavy gruesomeness.

And she wanted to go back. At this moment she wanted to turn back. She had looked down into the intestinal knot of these mountains. She was frightened. She wanted to go back.

But Romero was riding on, on the lee side of the spruce forest, above the concaves of the inner mountains. He turned round to her and pointed at the slope with a dark hand.

"Here a miner has been trying for gold," he said. It was a grey, scratched-out heap near a hole—like a great badger hole. And it looked quite fresh.

"Quite lately?" said the Princess.

"No, long ago—twenty, thirty years." He had reined in his horse and was looking at the mountains. "Look!" he said. "There goes the Forest Service trail—along those ridges, on the top, way over there till it comes to Lucytown, where is the Government road. We go down there—no trail—see behind that mountain—you see the top, no trees, and some grass?"

His arm was lifted, his brown hand pointing, his dark eyes piercing into the distance, as he sat on his black horse twisting round to her. Strange and ominous, only the demon of himself, he seemed to her. She was dazed and a little sick, at that height, and she could not see any more. Only she saw an eagle turning in the air beyond, and the light from the west showed the pattern on him underneath.

"Shall I ever be able to go so far?" asked the Princess faintly, petulantly.

"Oh yes! All easy now. No more hard places."

They worked along the ridge, up and down, keeping on the lee side, the inner side, in the dark shadow. It was cold. Then the trail laddered up again, and they emerged on a narrow ridge-track, with the mountain slipping away enormously on either side. The Princess was afraid. For one moment she looked out, and saw the desert, the desert ridges, more desert, more blue ridges, shining pale and very vast, far below, vastly palely tilting to the western horizon. It was ethereal and terrifying in its gleaming, pale, half-burnished immensity, tilted at the west. She could not bear it. To the left was the ponderous, involved mass of mountains all kneeling heavily.

She closed her eyes and let her consciousness evaporate away. The mare followed the trail. So on and on, in the wind again.

They turned their backs to the wind, facing inwards to the mountains. She thought they had left the trail; it was quite invisible.

"No," he said, lifting his hand and pointing. "Don't you see the blazed trees?"

And making an effort of consciousness, she was able to perceive on a pale-grey dead spruce stem the old marks where an axe had chipped a piece away. But with the height, the cold, the wind, her brain was numb.

They turned again and began to descend; he told her they had left the trail. The horses slithered in the loose stones, picking their way downward. It was afternoon, the sun stood obtrusive and gleaming in the lower heavens—about four o'clock. The horses went steadily, slowly, but obstinately onwards. The air was getting colder. They were in among the lumpish peaks and steep concave valleys. She was barely conscious at all of Romero.

He dismounted and came to help her from her saddle. She tottered, but would not betray her feebleness.

"We must slide down here," he said. "I can lead the horses."

They were on a ridge, and facing a steep bare slope of pallid, tawny mountain grass on which the western sun shone full. It was steep and concave. The Princess felt she might start slipping, and go down like a toboggan into the great hollow.

But she pulled herself together. Her eyes blazed up again with excitement and determination. A wind rushed past her; she could hear the shriek of spruce trees far below. Bright spots came on her cheeks as her hair blew across. She looked a wild, fairy-like little thing.

"No," she said. "I will take my horse."

"Then mind she doesn't slip down on top of you," said Romero. And away he went, nimbly dropping down the pale, steep incline, making from rock to rock, down the grass, and following any little slanting groove. His horse hopped and slithered after him, and sometimes stopped dead, with fore-feet pressed back, refusing to go farther. He, below his horse, looked up and pulled the reins gently, and encouraged the creature. Then the horse once more dropped his forefeet with a jerk, and the descent continued.

The Princess set off in blind, reckless pursuit, tottering and yet nimble. And Romero, looking constantly back to see how she was faring, saw her fluttering down like some queer little bird, her orange breeches twinkling like the legs of some duck, and her head, tied in the blue and buff kerchief, bound round and round like the head of some blue-topped bird. The sorrel mare rocked and slipped behind her. But down came the Princess in a reckless intensity, a tiny, vivid spot on the great hollow flank of the tawny mountain. So tiny! Tiny as a frail bird's egg. It made Romero's mind go blank with wonder.

But they had to get down, out of that cold and dragging wind. The spruce trees stood below, where a tiny stream emerged in stones. Away plunged Romero, zigzagging down. And away behind, up the slope, fluttered the tiny, bright-coloured Princess, holding the end of the long reins, and leading the lumbering, four-footed, sliding mare.

At last they were down. Romero sat in the sun, below the wind, beside some squaw-berry bushes. The Princess came near, the colour flaming in her cheeks, her eyes dark blue, much darker than the kerchief on her head, and glowing unnaturally.

"We make it," said Romero.

"Yes," said the princess, dropping the reins and subsiding on to the grass, unable to speak, unable to think.

But, thank heaven, they were out of the wind and in the sun.

In a few minutes her consciousness and her control began to come back. She drank a little water. Romero was attending to the saddles. Then they set off again, leading the horses still a little farther down the tiny stream-bed. Then they could mount.

They rode down a bank and into a valley grove dense with aspens. Winding through the thin, crowding, pale-smooth stems, the sun shone flickering beyond them, and the disc-like aspen leaves, waving queer mechanical signals, seemed to be splashing the gold light before her eyes. She rode on in a splashing dazzle of gold.

Then they entered shadow and the dark, resinous spruce trees. The fierce boughs always wanted to sweep her off her horse. She had to twist and squirm past.

But there was a semblance of an old trail. And all at once they emerged in the sun on the edge of the spruce grove, and there was a little cabin, and the bottom of a small, naked valley with grey rock and heaps of stones, and a round pool of intense green water, dark green. The sun was just about to leave it.

Indeed, as she stood, the shadow came over the cabin and over herself; they were in the lower gloom, a twilight. Above, the heights still blazed.

It was a little hole of a cabin, near the spruce trees, with an earthen floor and an unhinged door. There was a wooden bedbunk, three old sawed-off log-lengths to sit on as stools, and a sort of fireplace; no room for anything else. The little hole would hardly contain two people. The roof had gone—but Romero had laid on thick spruce boughs.

The strange squalor of the primitive forest pervaded the place, the squalor of animals and their droppings, the squalor of the wild. The Princess knew the peculiar repulsiveness of it. She was tired and faint.

Romero hastily got a handful of twigs, set a little fire going in the stove grate, and went out to attend to the horses. The Princess vaguely, mechanically, put sticks on the fire, in a sort of stupor, watching the blaze, stupefied and fascinated. She could not make much fire—it would set the whole cabin alight. And smoke oozed out of the dilapidated mud-and-stone chimney.

When Romero came in with the saddle-pouches and saddles, hanging the saddles on the wall, there sat the little Princess on her stump of wood in front of the dilapidated fire-grate, warming her tiny hands at the blaze, while her orange breeches glowed almost like another fire. She was in a sort of stupor.

"You have some whisky now, or some tea? Or wait for some soup?" he asked.

She rose and looked at him with bright, dazed eyes, half comprehending; the colour glowing hectic in her cheeks.

"Some tea," she said, "with a little whisky in it. Where's the kettle?"

"Wait," he said. "I'll bring the things."

She took her cloak from the back of her saddle, and followed him into the open. It was a deep cup of shadow. But above the sky was still shining, and the heights of the mountains were blazing with aspen like fire blazing.

Their horses were cropping the grass among the stones. Romero clambered up a heap of grey stones and began lifting away logs and rocks, till he had opened the mouth of one of the miner's little old workings. This was his cache. He brought out bundles of blankets, pans for cooking, a little petrol camp-stove, an axe, the regular camp outfit. He seemed so quick and energetic and full of force. This quick force dismayed the Princess a little.

She took a saucepan and went down the stones to the water. It was very still and mysterious, and of a deep green colour, yet pure, transparent as glass. How cold the place was! How mysterious and fearful.

She crouched in her dark cloak by the water, rinsing the

saucepan, feeling the cold heavy above her, the shadow like a vast weight upon her, bowing her down. The sun was leaving the mountain-tops, departing, leaving her under profound shadow. Soon it would crush her down completely.

Sparks? Or eyes looking at her across the water? She gazed, hypnotised. And with her sharp eyes she made out in the dusk the pale form of a bob-cat crouching by the water's edge, pale as the stones amongst which it crouched, opposite. And it was watching her with cold, electric eyes of strange intentness, a sort of cold, icy wonder and fearlessness. She saw its *museau* pushed forward, its tufted ears pricking intensely up. It was watching her with cold, animal curiosity, something demonish and conscienceless.

She made a swift movement, spilling her water. And in a flash the creature was gone, leaping like a cat that is escaping; but strange and soft in its motion, with its little bob-tail. Rather fascinating. Yet that cold, intent, demonish watching! She shivered with cold and fear. She knew well enough the dread and repulsiveness of the wild.

Romero carried in the bundles of bedding and the camp outfit. The windowless cabin was already dark inside. He lit a lantern, and then went out again with the axe. She heard him chopping wood as she fed sticks to the fire under her water. When he came in with an armful of oak-scrub faggots, she had just thrown the tea into the water.

"Sit down," she said, "and drink tea."

He poured a little bootleg whisky into the enamel cups, and in the silence the two sat on the log-ends, sipping the hot liquid and coughing occasionally from the smoke.

"We burn these oak sticks," he said. "They don't make hardly any smoke."

Curious and remote he was, saying nothing except what had to be said. And she, for her part, was as remote from him. They seemed far, far apart, worlds apart, now they were so near.

He unwrapped one bundle of bedding, and spread the blankets and the sheepskin in the wooden bunk.

"You lie down and rest," he said, "and I make the supper."

She decided to do so. Wrapping her cloak round her, she lay down in the bunk, turning her face to the wall. She could hear him preparing supper over the little petrol stove. Soon she could smell the soup he was heating; and soon she heard the hissing of fried chicken in a pan.

"You eat your supper now?" he said.

With a jerky, despairing movement, she sat up in the bunk, tossing back her hair. She felt cornered.

"Give it me here," she said.

He handed her first the cupful of soup. She sat among the blankets, eating it slowly. She was hungry. Then he gave her an enamel plate with pieces of fried chicken and currant jelly, butter and bread. It was very good. As they ate the chicken he made the coffee. She said never a word. A certain resentment filled her. She was cornered.

When supper was over he washed the dishes, dried them, and put everything away carefully, else there would have been no room to move in the hole of a cabin. The oak-wood gave out a good bright heat.

He stood for a few moments at a loss. Then he asked her: "You want to go to bed soon?"

"Soon," she said. "Where are you going to sleep?"

"I make my bed here——" he pointed to the floor along the wall. "Too cold out of doors."

"Yes," she said. "I suppose it is."

She sat immobile, her cheeks hot, full of conflicting thoughts. And she watched him while he folded the blankets on the floor, a sheepskin underneath. Then she went out into night.

The stars were big. Mars sat on the edge of a mountain, for all the world like the blazing eye of a crouching mountain lion. But she herself was deep, deep below in a pit of shadow. In the intense silence she seemed to hear the spruce forest crackling with electricity and cold. Strange, foreign stars floated on that unmoving water. The night was going to freeze. Over the hills came the far sobbing-singing howling of the coyotes. She wondered how the horses would be.

Shuddering a little, she turned to the cabin. Warm light

showed through its chinks. She pushed at the rickety, half-opened door.

"What about the horses?" she said.

"My black, he won't go away. And your mare will stay with him. You want to go to bed now?"

"I think I do."

"All right. I feed the horses some oats."

And he went out into the night.

He did not come back for some time. She was lying wrapped up tight in the bunk.

He blew out the lantern, and sat down on his bedding to take off his clothes. She lay with her back turned. And soon, in the silence, she was asleep.

She dreamed it was snowing, and the snow was falling on her through the roof, softly, softly, helplessly and she was going to be buried alive. She was growing colder and colder, the snow was weighing down on her. The snow as going to absorb her.

She awoke with a sudden convulsion, like pain. She was really very cold; perhaps the heavy blankets had numbed her. Her heart seemed unable to beat, she felt she could not move.

With another convulsion she sat up. It was intensely dark. There was not even a spark of fire, the light wood had burned right away. She sat in thick oblivious darkness. Only through a chink she could see a star.

What did she want? Oh, what did she want? She sat in bed and rocked herself woefully. She could hear the steady breathing of the sleeping man. She was shivering with cold; her heart seemed as if it could not beat. She wanted warmth, protection, she wanted to be taken away from herself. And at the same time, perhaps more deeply than anything, she wanted to keep herself intact, intact, untouched, that no one should have any power over her, or rights to her. It was a wild necessity in her that no one, particularly no man, should have any rights or power over her, that no one and nothing should possess her.

Yet that other thing! And she was so cold, so shivering,

and her heart could not beat. Oh, would not someone help her heart to beat?

She tried to speak, and could not. Then she cleared her throat.

"Romero," she said strangely, "it is so cold."

Where did her voice come from, and whose voice was it, in the dark?

She heard him at once sit up, and his voice, startled, with a resonance that seemed to vibrate against her, saying:

"You want me to make you warm?"

"Yes."

As soon as he had lifted her in his arms, she wanted to scream to him not to touch her. She stiffened herself. Yet she was dumb.

And he was warm, but with a terrible animal warmth that seemed to annihilate her. He panted like an animal with desire. And she was given over to this thing.

She had never, never wanted to be given over to this. But she had *willed* that it should happen to her. And according to her will, she lay and let it happen. But she never wanted it. She never wanted to be thus assailed and handled, and mauled. She wanted to keep herself to herself.

However, she had willed it to happen, and it had happened. She panted with relief when it was over.

Yet even now she had to lie within the hard, powerful clasp of this other creature, this man. She dreaded to struggle to go away. She dreaded almost too much the icy cold of that other bunk.

"Do you want to go away from me?" asked his strange voice. Oh, if it could only have been a thousand miles away from her! Yet she had willed to have it thus close.

"No," she said.

And she could feel a curious joy and pride surging up again in him: at her expense. Because he had got her. She felt like a victim there. And he was exulting in his power over her, his possession, his pleasure.

When dawn came, he was fast asleep. She sat up suddenly.

"I want a fire," she said.

He opened his brown eyes wide, and smiled with a curious tender luxuriousness.

"I want you to make a fire," she said.

He glanced at the chinks of light. His brown face hardened to the day.

"All right," he said. "I'll make it."

She did her face while he dressed. She could not bear to look at him. He was so suffused with pride and luxury. She hid her face almost in despair. But feeling the cold blast of air as he opened the door, she wriggled down into the warm place where he had been. How soon the warmth ebbed, when he had gone!

He made a fire and went out, returning after a while with water.

"You stay in bed till the sun comes," he said. "It very cold."

"Hand me my cloak."

She wrapped the cloak fast round her, and sat up among the blankets. The warmth was already spreading from the fire.

"I suppose we will start back as soon as we've had breakfast?"

He was crouching at his camp-stove making scrambled eggs. He looked up suddenly, transfixed, and his brown eyes, so soft and luxuriously widened, looked straight at her.

"You want to?" he said.

"We'd better get back as soon as possible," she said, turning aside from his eyes.

"You want to get away from me?" he asked, repeating the question of the night in a sort of dread.

"I want to get away from here," she said decisively. And it was true. She wanted supremely to get away, back to the world of people.

He rose slowly to his feet, holding the aluminium frying-pan.

"Don't you like last night?" he asked.

"Not really," she said. "Why? Do you?"

He put down the frying-pan and stood staring at the wall. She could see she had given him a cruel blow. But she did not relent. She was getting her own back. She wanted to regain possession of all herself, and in some mysterious way she felt that he possessed some part of her still.

He looked round at her slowly, his face greyish and heavy.

"You Americans," he said, "you always want to do a man down."

"I am not American," she said. "I am British. And I don't want to do any man down. I only want to go back now."

"And what will you say about me, down there?"

"That you were very kind to me, and very good."

He crouched down again, and went on turning the eggs. He gave her her plate, and her coffee, and sat down to his own food.

But again he seemed not to be able to swallow. He looked up at her.

"You don't like last night?" he asked.

"Not really," she said, though with some difficulty. "I don't care for that kind of thing."

A blank sort of wonder spread over his face at these words, followed immediately by a black look of anger, and then a stony, sinister despair.

"You don't?" he said, looking her in the eyes.

"Not really," she replied, looking back with steady hostility into his eyes.

Then a dark flame seemed to come from his face.

"I make you," he said, as if to himself.

He rose and reached her clothes, that hung on a peg: the fine linen underwear, the orange breeches, the fleecy jumper, the blue-and-brown kerchief; then he took up her riding-boots and her bead moccasins. Crushing everything in his arms, he opened the door. Sitting up, she saw him stride down to the dark-green pool in the frozen shadow of that deep cut of a valley. He tossed the clothing and the boots out on the pool. Ice had formed. And on the pure, dark green mirror, in the slaty shadow, the Princess saw her things lying, the white linen, the orange breeches, the black boots, the blue moccasins, a tangled heap of colour. Romero picked up rocks and heaved them out at the ice, till the surface broke and the fluttering clothing disappeared in the rattling water, while the valley echoed and shouted again with the sound.

She sat in despair among the blankets, hugging tight her pale-blue cloak. Romero strode straight back to the cabin.

"Now you stay here with me," he said.

She was furious. Her blue eyes met his. They were like two demons watching one another. In his face, beyond a sort of unrelieved gloom, was a demonish desire for death.

He saw her looking round the cabin, scheming. He saw her eyes on his rifle. He took the gun and went out with it. Returning, he pulled out her saddle, carried it to the tarn, and threw it in. Then he fetched his own saddle, and did the same.

"Now will you go away?" he said, looking at her with a smile.

She debated within herself whether to coax him and wheedle him. But she knew he was already beyond it. She sat among her blankets in a frozen sort of despair, hard as hard ice with anger.

He did the chores, and disappeared with the gun. She got up in her blue pyjamas, huddled in her cloak, and stood in the doorway. The dark-green pool was motionless again, the stone slopes were pallid and frozen. Shadow still lay, like an after-death, deep in this valley. Always in the distance she saw the horses feeding. If she could catch one! The brilliant yellow sun was half-way down the mountain. It was nine o'clock.

All day she was alone, and she was frightened. What she was frightened of she didn't know. Perhaps the crackling in the dark spruce wood. Perhaps just the savage, heartless wildness of the mountains. But all day she sat in the sun in the doorway of the cabin, watching, watching for hope. And all the time her bowels were cramped with fear.

She saw a dark spot that probably was a bear, roving across the pale grassy slope in the far distance, in the sun.

When, in the afternoon, she saw Romero approaching, with silent suddenness, carrying his gun and a dead deer, the cramp in her bowels relaxed, then became colder. She dreaded him with a cold dread.

"There is deer-meat," he said, throwing the dead doe at her feet.

"You don't want to go away from here," he said. "This is a nice place."

She shrank into the cabin.

"Come into the sun," he said, following her. She looked up at him with hostile, frightened eyes.

"Come into the sun," he repeated, taking her gently by the arm, in a powerful grasp.

She knew it was useless to rebel. Quietly he led her out, and seated himself in the doorway, holding her still by the arm.

"In the sun it is warm," he said. "Look, this is a nice place. You are such a pretty white woman, why do you want to act mean to me? Isn't this a nice place? Come! Come here! It is sure warm here."

He drew her to him, and in spite of her stony resistance, he took her cloak from her, holding her in her thin blue pyjamas.

"You sure are a pretty little white woman, small and pretty," he said. "You sure won't act mean to me—you don't want to, I know you don't."

She, stony and powerless, had to submit to him. The sun shone on her white, delicate skin.

"I sure don't mind hell fire," he said. "After this."

A queer, luxurious good humour seemed to possess him again. But though outwardly she was powerless, inwardly she resisted him, absolutely and stonily.

When later he was leaving her again, she said to him suddenly:

"You think you can conquer me this way. But you can't. You can never conquer me."

He stood arrested, looking back at her, with many emotions conflicting in his face—wonder, surprise, a touch of horror, and an unconscious pain that crumpled his face till it was like a mask. Then he went out without saying a word, hung the dead deer on a bough, and started to flay it. While he was at this butcher's work, the sun sank and cold night came on again.

"You see," he said to her as he crouched, cooking the supper, "I ain't going to let you go. I reckon you called to me in the night, and I've some right. If you want to fix it up right now with me, and say you want to be with me, we'll fix it up now and go down to the ranch to-morrow and get married or whatever you want. But you've got to say you want to be with me. Else I shall stay right here, till something happens."

She waited a while before she answered:

"I don't want to be with anybody against my will. I don't dislike you; at least, I didn't, till you tried to put your will over mine. I won't have anybody's will put over me. You can't succeed. Nobody could. You can never get me under your will. And you won't have long to try, because soon they will send someone to look for me."

He pondered this last, and she regretted having said it. Then, sombre, he bent to the cooking again.

He could not conquer her, however much he violated her. Because her spirit was hard and flawless as a diamond. But he could shatter her. This she knew. Much more, and she would be shattered.

In a sombre, violent excess he tried to expend his desire for her. And she was racked with agony, and felt each time she would die. Because, in some peculiar way, he had got hold of her, some unrealised part of her which she never wished to realise. Racked with a burning, tearing anguish, she felt that the thread of her being would break, and she would die. The burning heat that racked her inwardly.

If only, only she could be alone again, cool and intact! If only she could recover herself again, cool and intact! Would she ever, ever, ever be able to bear herself again?

Even now she did not hate him. It was beyond that. Like some racking, hot doom. Personally he hardly existed.

The next day he would not let her have any fire, because of attracting attention with the smoke. It was a grey day, and she was cold. He stayed round, and heated soup on the petrol stove. She lay motionless in the blankets.

And in the afternoon she pulled the clothes over her head and broke into tears. She had never really cried in her life.

He dragged the blankets away and looked to see what was shaking her. She sobbed in helpless hysterics. He covered her over again and went outside, looking at the mountains, where clouds were dragging and leaving a little snow. It was a violent, windy, horrible day, the evil of winter rushing down.

She cried for hours. And after this a great silence came between them. They were two people who had died. He did not touch her any more. In the night she lay and shivered like a dying dog. She felt that her very shivering would rupture something in her body, and she would die.

At last she had to speak.

"Could you make a fire? I am so cold," she said, with chattering teeth.

"Want to come over here?" came his voice.

"I would rather you made me a fire," she said, her teeth knocking together and chopping the words in two.

He got up and kindled a fire. At last the warmth spread, and she could sleep.

The next day was still chilly, with some wind. But the sun shone. He went about in silence, with a dead-looking face. It was now so dreary and so like death she wished he would do anything rather than continue in this negation. If now he asked her to go down with him to the world and marry him, she would do it. What did it matter? Nothing mattered any more.

But he would not ask her. His desire was dead and heavy like ice within him. He kept watch around the house.

On the fourth day as she sat huddled in the doorway in the sun, hugged in a blanket, she saw two horsemen come over the crest of the grassy slope—small figures. She gave a cry. He looked up quickly and saw the figures. The men had dismounted. They were looking for the trail.

"They are looking for me," she said.

"Muy bien," he answered in Spanish.

He went and fetched his gun, and sat with it across his knees.

"Oh!" she said. "Don't shoot!"

He looked across at her.

"Why?" he said. "You like staying with me?"

"No," she said. "But don't shoot."

"I ain't going to Pen," he said.

"You won't have to go to Pen," she said. "Don't shoot!"

"I'm going to shoot," he muttered.

And straightaway he kneeled and took very careful aim. The Princess sat on in an agony of helplessness and hopelessness.

The shot rang out. In an instant she saw one of the horses on the pale grassy slope rear and go rolling down. The man had dropped in the grass, and was invisible. The second man clambered on his horse, and on that precipitous place went at a gallop in a long swerve towards the nearest spruce tree cover. Bang! Bang! went Romero's shots. But each time he missed, and the running horse leaped like a kangaroo towards cover.

It was hidden. Romero now got behind a rock; tense silence, in the brilliant sunshine. The Princess sat on the bunk inside the cabin, crouched, paralysed. For hours, it seemed, Romero knelt behind this rock, in his black shirt, bareheaded, watching. He had a beautiful, alert figure. The Princess wondered why she did not feel sorry for him. But her spirit was hard and cold, her heart could not melt. Though now she would have called him to her, with love.

But no, she did not love him. She would never love any man. Never! It was fixed and sealed in her, almost vindictively.

Suddenly she was so startled she almost fell from the bunk. A shot rang out quite close from behind the cabin. Romero leaped straight into the air, his arms fell outstretched, turning as he leaped. And even while he was in the air, a second shot rang out, and he fell with a crash, squirming, his hands clutching the earth towards the cabin door.

The Princess sat absolutely motionless, transfixed, staring at the prostrate figure. In a few moments the figure of a man in the Forest Service appeared close to the house; a young man in a broad-brimmed Stetson hat, dark flannel shirt, and riding-boots, carrying a gun. He strode over to the prostrate figure.

"Got you, Romero!" he said aloud. And he turned the

dead man over. There was already a little pool of blood where Romero's breast had been.

"H'm!" said the Forest Service man. "Guess I got you nearer than I thought."

And he squatted there, staring at the dead man.

The distant calling of his comrade aroused him. He stood up.

"Hullo, Bill!" he shouted. "Yep! Got him! Yep! Done him in, apparently."

The second man rode out of the forest on a grey horse. He had a ruddy, kind face, and round brown eyes, dilated with dismay.

"He's not passed out?" he asked anxiously.

"Looks like it," said the first young man coolly.

The second dismounted and bent over the body. Then he stood up again, and nodded.

"Yea-a!" he said. "He's done in all right. It's him all right, boy! It's Domingo Romero."

"Yep! I know it!" replied the other.

Then in perplexity he turned and looked into the cabin, where the Princess squatted, staring with big owl eyes from her red blanket.

"Hello!" he said, coming towards the hut. And he took his hat off. Oh, the sense of ridicule she felt! Though he did not mean any.

But she could not speak, no matter what she felt.

"What'd this man start firing for?" he asked.

She fumbled for words, with numb lips.

"He had gone out of his mind!" she said, with solemn, stammering conviction.

"Good Lord! You mean to say he'd gone out of his mind? Whew! That's pretty awful! That explains it then. H'm!"

He accepted the explanation without more ado.

With some difficulty they succeeded in getting the Princess down to the ranch. But she, too, was not a little mad.

"I'm not quite sure where I am," she said to Mrs. Wilkieson, as she lay in bed. "Do you mind explaining?"

Mrs. Wilkieson explained tactfully.

"Oh yes!" said the Princess. "I remember. And I had an

accident in the mountains, didn't I? Didn't we meet a man who'd gone mad, and who shot my horse from under me?"

"Yes, you met a man who had gone out of his mind."

The real affair was hushed up. The Princess departed east in a fortnight's time, in Miss Cummins's care. Apparently she had recovered herself entirely. She was the Princess, and a virgin intact.

But her bobbed hair was grey at the temples, and her eyes were a little mad. She was slightly crazy.

"Since my accident in the mountains, when a man went mad and shot my horse from under me, and my guide had to shoot him dead, I have never felt quite myself."

So she put it.

Later, she married an elderly man, and seemed pleased.

Sun
—————

"TAKE HER away, into the sun," the doctors said.

She herself was sceptical of the sun, but she permitted herself to be carried away, with her child, and a nurse, and her mother, over the sea.

The ship sailed at midnight. And for two hours her husband stayed with her, while the child was put to bed, and the passengers came on board. It was a black night, the Hudson swayed with heavy blackness, shaken over with spilled dribbles of light. She leaned on the rail, and looking down thought: This is the sea; it is deeper than one imagines, and fuller of memories. At that moment the sea seemed to heave like the serpent of chaos that has lived for ever.

"These partings are no good, you know," her husband was saying, at her side. "They're no good, I don't like them."

His tone was full of apprehension, misgiving, and there was a certain note of clinging to the last straw of hope.

"No, neither do I," she responded in a flat voice.

She remembered how bitterly they had wanted to get away from one another, he and she. The emotion of parting gave a slight tug at her emotions, but only caused the iron that had gone into her soul to gore deeper.

So, they looked at their sleeping son, and the father's eyes were wet. But it is not the wetting of the eyes which counts, it is the deep iron rhythm of habit, the year-long, life-long habits; the deep-set stroke of power.

And in their two lives the stroke of power was hostile, his and hers. Like two engines running at variance, they shattered one another.

"All ashore! All ashore!"

"Maurice, you must go!"

And she thought to herself: For him it is *All ashore!* For
me it is *Out to sea!*

Well, he waved his hanky on the midnight dreariness of the
pier as the boat inched away; one among a crowd. One among
a crowd! *C'est ça!*

The ferry-boats, like great dishes piled with rows of lights,
were still slanting across the Hudson. That black mouth must
be the Lackawanna Station.

The ship ebbed on, the Hudson seemed interminable. But
at last they were round the bend, and there was the poor
harvest of lights at the Battery. Liberty flung up her torch in
a tantrum. There was the wash of the sea.

And though the Atlantic was grey as lava, she did come at
last into the sun. Even she had a house above the bluest of
seas, with a vast garden, or vineyard, all vines and olives
steeply, terrace after terrace, to the strip of coast-plain; and
the garden full of secret places, deep groves of lemon far
down in the cleft of the earth, and hidden, pure green
reservoirs of water; then a spring issuing out of a little
cavern, where the old Sicules had drunk before the Greeks
came; and a grey goat bleating, stabled in an ancient tomb,
with all the niches empty. There was the scent of mimosa,
and beyond, the snow of the volcano.

She saw it all, and in a measure it was soothing. But it was
all external. She didn't really care about it. She was herself,
just the same, with all her anger and frustration inside her,
and her incapacity to feel anything real. The child irritated
her, and preyed on her peace of mind. She felt so horribly,
ghastly responsible for him: as if she must be responsible for
every breath he drew. And that was torture to her, to the
child, and to everybody else concerned.

"You know, Juliet, the doctor told you to lie in the sun,
without your clothes. Why don't you?" said the mother.

"When I am fit to do so, I will. Do you want to kill me?"
Juliet flew at her.

"To kill you, no! Only to do you good."

"For God's sake, leave off wanting to do me good."

The mother at last was so hurt and incensed, she departed.

The sea went white—and then invisible. Pouring rain fell. It was cold, in the house built for the sun.

Again a morning when the sun lifted himself naked and molten, sparkling over the sea's rim. The house faced southwest. Juliet lay in her bed and watched him rise. It was as if she had never seen the sun rise before. She had never seen the naked sun stand up pure upon the sea-line, shaking the night off himself.

So the desire sprang secretly in her to go naked in the sun. She cherished her desire like a secret.

But she wanted to go away from the house—away from people. And it is not easy, in a country where every olive tree has eyes, and every slope is seen from afar, to go hidden.

But she found a place: a rocky bluff, shoved out to the sea and sun and overgrown with large cactus, the flat-leaved cactus called prickly pear. Out of this blue-grey knoll of cactus rose one cypress tree, with a pallid, thick trunk, and a tip that leaned over, flexible, up in the blue. It stood like a guardian looking to sea; or a low, silvery candle whose huge flame was darkness against light: earth sending up her proud tongue of gloom.

Juliet sat down by the cypress trees and took off her clothes. The contorted cactus made a forest, hideous yet fascinating, about her. She sat and offered her bosom to the sun, sighing, even now, with a certain hard pain, against the cruelty of having to give herself.

But the sun marched in blue heaven and sent down his rays as he went. She felt the soft air of the sea on her breasts, that seemed as if they would never ripen. But she hardly felt the sun. Fruits that would wither and not mature, her breasts.

Soon, however she felt the sun inside them, warmer than ever love had been, warmer than milk or the hands of her baby. At last, at last her breasts were like long white grapes in the hot sun.

She slid off all her clothes and lay naked in the sun, and as she lay she looked up through her fingers at the central sun, his blue pulsing roundness, whose outer edges streamed brilliance. Pulsing with marvelous blue, and alive, and streaming white fire from his edges, the sun! He faced down to her with his look of blue fire, and enveloped her breasts and her face, her throat, her tired belly, her knees, her thighs and her feet.

She lay with shut eyes, the colour of rosy flame through her lids. It was too much. She reached and put leaves over her eyes. Then she lay again, like a long white gourd in the sun, that must ripen to gold.

She could feel the sun penetrating even into her bones; nay, farther, even into her emotions and her thoughts. The dark tensions of her emotion began to give way, the cold dark clots of her thoughts began to dissolve. She was beginning to feel warm right through. Turning over, she let her shoulders dissolve in the sun, her loins, the backs of her thighs, even her heels. And she lay half stunned with wonder at the thing that was happening to her. Her weary, chilled heart was melting, and, in melting, evaporating.

When she was dressed again she lay once more and looked up at the cypress tree, whose crest, a flexible filament, fell this way and that in the breeze. Meanwhile, she was conscious of the great sun roaming in heaven.

So, dazed, she went home, only half-seeing, sun-blinded and sun-dazed. And her blindness was like a richness to her, and her dim, warm, heavy half-consciousness was like wealth.

"Mummy! Mummy!" her child came running towards her, calling in that peculiar bird-like little anguish of want, always wanting her. She was surprised that her drowsed heart for once felt none of the anxious love-anguish in return. She caught the child up in her arms, but she thought: He should not be such a lump! If he were in he sun, he would spring up.

She resented, rather, his little hands clutching at her, especially at her neck. She pulled her throat away. She did not want to be touched. She put the child gently down.

"Run!" she said. "Run in the sun!"

And there and then she took off his clothes and set him naked on the warm terrace.

"Play in the sun!" she said.

He was frightened and wanted to cry. But she, in the

warm indolence of her body, and the complete indifference
of her heart, rolled him an orange across the red tiles, and
with his soft, unformed little body he toddled after it. Then
immediately he had it, he dropped it because it felt strange
against his flesh. And he looked back at her, querulous,
wrinkling his face to cry, frightened because he was stark.

"Bring me the orange," she said, amazed at her own deep
indifference to his trepidation. "Bring Mummy the orange."

"He shall not grow up like his father," she said to herself.
"Like a worm that the sun has never seen."

II

She had had the child so much on her mind, in a torment
of responsibility, as if, having borne him, she had to answer
for his whole existence. Even if his nose were running, it had
been repulsive and a goad in her vitals, as if she must say to
herself: Look at the thing you brought forth!

Now a change took place. She was no longer vitally
interested in the child, she took the strain of her anxiety and
her will from off him. And he thrived all the more for it.

She was thinking inside herself, of the sun in his splendour,
and her mating with him. Her life was now a whole ritual.
She lay always awake, before dawn, watching for the grey to
colour to pale gold, to know if cloud lay on the sea's edge.
Her joy was when he rose all molten in his nakedness, and
threw off blue-white fire, into the tender heaven.

But sometimes he came ruddy, like a big, shy creature.
And sometimes slow and crimson red, with a look of anger,
slowly pushing and shouldering. Sometimes again she could
not see him, only the level cloud threw down gold and scarlet
from above, as he moved behind the wall.

She was fortunate. Weeks went by, and though the dawn
was sometimes clouded, and afternoon was sometimes grey,
never a day passed sunless, and most days, winter though it
was, streamed radiant. Then thin little wild crocuses came up
mauve and striped, the wild narcissi hung their winter stars.

Every day she went down to the cypress tree, among the
cactus grove on the knoll with yellowish cliffs at the foot. She

was wiser and subtler now, wearing only a dove-grey wrapper, and sandals. So that in an instant, in any hidden niche, she was naked to the sun. And the moment she was covered again she was grey and invisible.

Every day, in the morning towards noon, she lay at the foot of the powerful, silver-pawed cypress tree, while the sun rode jovial in heaven. By now she knew the sun in every thread of her body, there was not a cold shadow left. And her heart, that anxious, straining heart, had disappeared altogether, like a flower that falls in the sun, and leaves only a ripe seed-case.

She knew the sun in heaven, blue-molten with his white fire edges, throwing off fire. And though he shone on all the world, when she lay unclothed he focussed on her. It was one of the wonders of the sun, he could shine on a million people and still be the radiant, splendid, unique sun, focussed on her alone.

With her knowledge of the sun, and her conviction that the sun *knew* her, in the cosmic carnal sense of the word, came over her a feeling of detachment from people, and a certain contempt for human beings altogether. They were so unelemental, so unsunned. They were so like graveyard worms.

Even the peasants passing up the rocky, ancient little road with their donkeys, sun-blackened as they were, were not sunned right through. There was a little soft white core of fear, like a snail in a shell, where the soul of the men cowered in fear of death, and in fear of the natural blaze of life. He dared not quite emerge; always innerly cowed. All men were like that.

Why admit men!

With her indifference to people, to men, she was not now so cautious about being unseen. She had told Marinina, who went shopping for her in the village, that the doctor had ordered sun-baths. Let that suffice.

Marinina was a woman over sixty, tall, thin, erect, with curling dark grey hair, and dark grey eyes that had the shrewdness of thousands of years in them, with the laugh that underlies all long experience. Tragedy is lack of experience.

"It must be beautiful to go unclothed in the sun," said

Marinina, with a shrewd laugh in her eyes, as she looked keenly at the other woman. Juliet's fair, bobbed hair curled in a little cloud at her temple. Marinina was a woman of Magna Græcia, and had far memories. She looked again at Juliet. "But you have to be beautiful yourself, if you're not going to give offence to the sun? Isn't it so?" she added, with that queer, breathless little laugh of the women of the past.

"Who knows if I am beautiful!" said Juliet.

But beautiful or not, she felt that by the sun she was appreciated. Which is the same.

When, out of the sun at noon, sometimes she stole down over the rocks and past the cliff-edge, down to the deep gully where the lemons hung in cool eternal shadow, and in the silence slipped off her wrapper to wash herself quickly at one of the deep, clear green basins, she would notice, in the bare green twilight under the lemon leaves, that all her body was rosy, rosy and turning to gold. She was like another person. She was another person.

So she remembered that the Greeks had said, a white, unsunned body was fishy and unhealthy.

And she would rub a little olive oil in her skin, and wander a moment in the dark underworld of the lemons, balancing a lemon flower in her navel, laughing to herself. There was just a chance some peasant might see her. But if he did he would be more afraid of her than she of him. She knew the white core of fear in the clothed bodies of men.

She knew it even in her little son. How he mistrusted her, now that she laughed at him, with the sun in her face! She insisted on his toddling naked in the sunshine every day. And now his little body was pink, too, his blond hair was pushed thick from his brow, his cheeks had a pomegranate scarlet, in the delicate gold of the sunny skin. He was bonny and healthy, and the servants, loving his red and gold and blue, called him an angel from heaven.

But he mistrusted his mother: she laughed at him. And she saw in his wide blue eyes, under the little frown, that centre of fear, misgiving, which she believed was at the centre of all male eyes now. She called it fear of the sun.

"He fears the sun," she would say to herself, looking down into the eyes of the child.

And as she watched him toddling, swaying, tumbling in the sunshine, making his little, bird-like noises, she saw that he held himself tight and hidden from the sun, inside himself. His spirit was like a snail in a shell, in a damp, cold crevice inside himself. It made her think of his father. She wished she could make him come forth, break out in a gesture of recklessness and salutation.

She determined to take him with her, down to the cypress tree among the cactus. She would have to watch him, because of the thorns. But surely in that place he would come forth from that little shell, deep inside him. That little civilised tension would disappear off his brow.

She spread a rug for him and sat him down. Then she slid off her wrapper and lay down herself, watching a hawk high in the blue, and the tip of the cypress hanging over.

The boy played with stones on the rug. When he got up to toddle away, she sat up too. He turned and looked at her. Almost, from his blue eyes, it was the challenging, warm look of the true male. And he was handsome, with the scarlet in the golden blond of his skin. He was not really white. His skin was gold-dusky.

"Mind the thorns, darling," she said.

"Thorns!" re-echoed the child, in a birdy chirp, still looking at her over his shoulder, like some naked cherub in a picture, doubtful.

"Nasty prickly thorns."

" 'Ickly thorns!"

He staggered in his little sandals over the stones, pulling at the dry, wild mint. She was quick as a serpent, leaping to him, when he was going to fall against the prickles. It surprised even herself. "What a wild cat I am, really!" she said to herself.

She brought him every day, when the sun shone, to the cypress tree.

"Come!" she said. "Let us go to the cypress tree."

And if there was a cloudy day, with the tramontana

blowing, so that she could not go down, the child would chirp incessantly: "Cypress tree! Cypress tree!"

He missed it as much as she did.

It was not just taking sunbaths. It was much more than that. Something deep inside her unfolded and relaxed, and she was given. By some mysterious power inside her, deeper than her known consciousness and will, she was put into connection with the sun, and the stream flowed of itself, from her womb. She herself, her conscious self, was secondary, a secondary person, almost an onlooker. The true Juliet was this dark flow from her deep body to the sun.

She had always been mistress of herself, aware of what she was doing, and held tense for her own power. Now she felt inside her quite another sort of power, something greater than herself, flowing by itself. Now she was vague, but she had a power beyond herself.

III

The end of February was suddenly very hot. Almond blossom was falling like pink snow, in the touch of the smallest breeze. The mauve, silky little anemones were out, the asphodels tall in bud, and the sea was cornflower blue.

Juliet had ceased to trouble about anything. Now, most of the day, she and the child were naked in the sun, and it was all she wanted. Sometimes she went down to the sea to bathe: often she wandered in the gullies where the sun shone in, and she was out of sight. Sometimes she saw a peasant with an ass, and he saw her. But she went so simply and quietly with her child; and the fame of the sun's healing power, for the soul as well as for the body, had already spread among the people; so that there was no excitement.

The child and she were now both tanned with a rosy-golden tan all over. "I am another being!" she said to herself, as she looked at her red-gold breasts and thighs.

The child, too, was another creature, with a peculiar, quiet, sun-darkened absorption. Now he played by himself in silence, and she hardly need notice him. He seemed no longer to know when he was alone.

There was a breeze, and the sea was ultramarine. She sat by the great silver paw of the cypress tree, drowsed in the sun, but her breasts alert, full of sap. She was becoming aware that an activity was rousing in her, an activity which would carry her into a new way of life. Still she did not want to be aware. She knew well enough the vast cold apparatus of civilisation, so difficult to evade.

The child had gone a few yards down the rocky path, round the great sprawling of a cactus. She had seen him, a real gold-brown infant of the winds, with burnt gold hair and red cheeks, collecting the speckled pitcher-flowers and laying them in rows. He could balance now, and was quick for his own emergencies, like an absorbed young animal playing silent.

Suddenly she heard him speaking: *"Look, Mummy! Mummy, look!"* A note in his bird-like voice made her lean forward sharply.

Her heart stood still. He was looking over his naked little shoulder at her, and pointing with a loose little hand at a snake which had reared itself up a yard away from him, and was opening its mouth so that its forked, soft tongue flickered black like a shadow, uttering a short hiss.

"Look, Mummy!"

"Yes, darling, it's a snake!" came the slow, deep voice.

He looked at her, his wide blue eyes uncertain whether to be afraid or not. Some stillness of the sun in her reassured him.

"Snake!" he chirped.

"Yes, darling! Don't touch it, it can bite."

The snake had sunk down, and was reaching away from the coils in which it had been basking asleep, and slowly was easing its long, gold-brown body into the rocks, with slow curves. The boy turned and watched it in silence. Then he said:

"Snake going!"

"Yes! Let it go. It likes to be alone."

He still watched the slow, easing length as the creature drew itself apathetic out of sight.

"Snake gone back," he said.

"Yes, it's gone back. Come to Mummy a moment."

He came and sat with his plump, naked little body on her naked lap, and she smoothed his burnt, bright hair. She said nothing, feeling that everything was passed. The curious soothing power of the sun filled her, filled the whole place like a charm, and the snake was part of the place, along with her and the child.

Another day, in the dry stone wall of one of the olive terraces, she saw a black snake horizontally creeping.

"Marinina," she said, "I saw a black snake. Are they harmful?"

"Ah, the black snakes, no! But the yellow ones, yes! If the yellow ones bite you, you die. But they frighten me, they frighten me, even the black ones, when I see one."

Juliet still went to the cypress tree with the child. But she always looked carefully round before she sat down, examining everywhere where the child might go. Then she would lie and turn to the sun again, her tanned, pear-shaped breasts pointing up. She would take no thought for the morrow. She refused to think outside her garden, and she could not write letters. She would tell the nurse to write.

IV

It was March, and the sun was growing very powerful. In the hot hours she would lie in the shade of the trees, or she would even go down to the depths of the cool lemon grove. The child ran in the distance, like a young animal absorbed in life.

One day she was sitting in the sun on the steep slope of the gully, having bathed in one of the great tanks. Below, under the lemons, the child was wading among the yellow oxalis flowers of the shadow, gathering fallen lemons, passing with his tanned little body into flecks of light, moving all dappled.

Suddenly, high over the land's edge, against the full-lit pale blue sky, Marinina appeared, a black cloth tied round her head, calling quietly: *"Signora! Signora Giulietta!"*

Juliet faced round, standing up, Marinina paused a moment, seeing the naked woman standing alert, her sun-faded fair hair in a little cloud. Then the swift old woman came on down the slant of the steep track.

She stood a few steps, erect, in front of the sun-coloured woman, and eyed her shrewdly.

"But how beautiful you are, you!" she said coolly, almost cynically. "There is your husband."

"My husband!" cried Juliet.

The old woman gave a shrewd bark of a little laugh, the mockery of the women of the past.

"Haven't you got one, a husband, you?" she taunted.

"But where is he?" cried Juliet.

The old woman glanced over her shoulder.

"He was following me," she said. "But he will not have found the path." And she gave another little bark of a laugh.

The paths were all grown high with grass and flowers and nepitella, till they were like bird-trails in an eternally wild place. Strange, the vivid wildness of the old places of civilisation, a wildness that is not gaunt.

Juliet looked at her serving-woman with meditating eyes.

"Oh, very well!" she said at last. "Let him come."

"Let him come here? Now?" asked Marinina, her laughing, smoke-grey eyes looking with mockery into Juliet's. Then she gave a little jerk of her shoulders.

"All right, as you wish. But for him it is a rare one."

She opened her mouth in a laugh of noiseless joy. Then she pointed down to the child, who was heaping lemons against his little chest. "Look how beautiful the child is! That, certainly, will please him, poor thing. Then I'll bring him."

"Bring him," said Juliet.

The old woman scrambled rapidly up the track again. Maurice was standing grey-faced, in his grey felt hat and his dark grey suit, at a loss among the vine terraces. He looked pathetically out of place, in that resplendent sunshine and the grace of the old Greek world; like a blot of ink on the pale, sun-glowing slope.

"Come!" said Marinina to him. "She is down here."

And swiftly she led the way, striding with a rapid stride, making her way through the grasses. Suddenly she stopped on the brow of the slope. The tops of the lemon trees were dark, away below.

"You, you go down here," she said to him, and he thanked her, looking up at her swiftly.

He was a man of forty, clean-shaven, grey-faced, very quiet and really shy. He managed his own business carefully, without startling success, but efficiently. And he confided in nobody. The old woman of Magna Græcia saw him at a glance: he is good, she said to herself, but not a man, poor thing.

"Down there is the Signora!" said Marinina, pointing like one of the Fates.

And again he said "Thank you! Thank you!" without a twinkle, and stepped carefully into the track. Marinina lifted her chin with a joyful wickedness. Then she strode off towards the house.

Maurice was watching his step through the tangle of Mediterranean herbage, so he did not catch sight of his wife till he came round a little bend, quite near her. She was standing erect and nude by the jutting rock, glistening with the sun and with warm life. Her breasts seemed to be lifting up, alert, to listen, her thighs looked brown and fleet. Her glance on him, as he came like ink on blotting-paper, was swift and nervous.

Maurice, poor fellow, hesitated, and glanced away from her. He turned his face aside.

"Hello, Julie!" he said, with a little nervous cough—"Splendid! Splendid!"

He advanced with his face averted, shooting further glances at her, as she stood with the peculiar satiny gleam of the sun on her tanned skin. Somehow she did not seem so terribly naked. It was the golden-rose tan of the sun that clothed her.

"Hello, Maurice!" she said, hanging back from him. "I wasn't expecting you so soon."

"No," he said. "No! I managed to slip away a little earlier."

And again he coughed awkwardly.

They stood several yards away from one another, and there was silence.

"Well!" he said, "er—this is splendid, splendid! You are—er—splendid! Where is the boy?"

"There he is," she said, pointing down to where a naked urchin in the deep shade was piling fallen lemons together.

The father gave an odd little laugh.

"Ah, yes, there he is! So there's the little man! Fine!" he said. He really was thrilled in his suppressed nervous soul. "Hello, Johnny!" he called, and it sounded rather feeble. "Hello, Johnny!"

The child looked up, spilling lemons from his chubby arms, but did not respond.

"I guess we'll go down to him," said Juliet, as she turned and went striding down the path. Her husband followed, watching the rosy, fleet-looking lifting and sinking of her quick hips, as she swayed a little in the socket of her waist. He was dazed with admiration, but also, at a deadly loss. What should he do with himself? He was utterly out of the picture, in his dark grey suit and pale grey hat, and his grey, monastic face of a shy business man.

"He looks all right, doesn't he," said Juliet, as they came through the deep sea of yellow-flowering oxalis, under the lemon trees.

"Ah!—yes! yes! Splendid! Splendid! Hello, Johnny! Do you know Daddy? Do you know Daddy, Johnny?"

He crouched down and held out his hands.

"Lemons!" said the child, birdily chirping. "Two lemons!"

"Two lemons!" replied the father. "Lots of lemons."

The infant came and put a lemon in each of his father's open hands. Then he stood back to look.

"Two lemons!" repeated the father. "Come, Johnny! Come and say 'Hello' to Daddy."

"Daddy going back?" said the child.

"Going back? Well—well—not to-day."

And he gathered his son in his arms.

"Take a coat off! Daddy take a coat off!" said the boy, squirming debonair away from the cloth.

"All right, son! Daddy take a coat off!"

He took off his coat and laid it carefully aside, then again took his son in his arms. The naked woman looked down at the naked infant in the arms of the man in his shirt-sleeves. The boy had pulled off the father's hat, and Juliet looked at the sleek, black-and-grey hair of her husband, not a hair out of place. And utterly, utterly indoors. She was silent for a long time, while the father talked to the child, who was fond of his Daddy.

"What are you going to do about it, Maurice?" she said suddenly.

He looked at her swiftly, sideways.

"Er—about what, Julie?"

"Oh, everything! About this! I can't go back into East Forty-Seventh."

"Er——" he hesitated, "no, I suppose not—not just now at least."

"Never," she said, and there was a silence.

"Well—er—I don't know," he said.

"Do you think you can come out here?" she said.

"Yes, I can stay for a month. I think I can manage a month," he hesitated. Then he ventured a complicated, shy peep at her, and hid his face again.

She looked down at him, her alert breasts lifted with a sigh, as if a breeze of impatience shook them.

"I can't go back," she said slowly. "I can't go back on this sun. If you can't come here——"

She ended on an open note. He glanced at her again and again, furtively, but with growing admiration and lessening confusion.

"No!" he said. "This kind of thing suits you. You are splendid! No, I don't think you can go back."

He was thinking of her in the New York flat, pale, silent, oppressing him terribly. He was the soul of gentle timidity, in his human relations, and her silent, awful hostility after the baby was born, had frightened him deeply. Because he had realised she couldn't help it. Women were like that. Their feelings took a reverse direction, even against their own selves, and it was awful—awful! Awful, awful to live in the house with a woman like that, whose feelings were reversed even against herself! He had felt himself ground down under the millstone of her helpless enmity. She had ground even herself down to the quick, and the child as well. No, anything rather than that.

"But what about *you*?" she asked.

"I? Oh, I! I can carry on the business, and—er—come over here for the holidays—as long as you like to stay. You stay as long as you wish." He looked a long time down at the earth, then glanced up at her with a touch of supplication in his uneasy eyes.

"Even for ever?"

"Well—er—yes, if you like. For ever is a long time. One can't set a date."

"And I can do anything I like?" She looked him straight in the eyes, challenging. And he was powerless against her rosy, wind-hardened nakedness.

"Er—yes! I suppose so! So long as you don't make yourself unhappy—or the boy."

Again he looked up at her with a complicated, uneasy appeal—thinking of the child, but hoping for himself.

"I won't," she said quickly.

"No!" he said. "No! I don't think you will."

There was a pause. The bells of the village were hastily clanging midday. That meant lunch.

She slipped into her grey crêpe kimono, and fastened a broad green sash round her waist. Then she slipped a little blue shirt over the boy's head, and they went up to the house.

At table she watched her husband, his grey city face, his fixed, black-grey hair, his very precise table manners, and his extreme moderation in eating and drinking. Sometimes he glanced at her, furtively, from under his black lashes. He had the gold-grey eyes of an animal that has been caught young, and reared completely in captivity.

They went on to the balcony for coffee. Below, beyond, on the next podere across the steep little gully, a peasant and his wife were sitting under an almond tree, near the green wheat, eating their midday meal from a little white cloth spread on the ground. There was a huge piece of bread, and glasses with dark wine.

Juliet put her husband with his back to this picture; she sat facing. Because, the woment she and Maurice had come out on the balcony, the peasant had glanced up.

V

She knew him, in the distance, perfectly. He was a rather fat, very broad fellow of about thirty-five, and he chewed large mouthfuls of bread. His wife was stiff and dark-faced, handsome, somber. They had no children. So much Juliet had learned.

The peasant worked a great deal alone, on the opposite podere. His clothes were always very clean and cared-for, white trousers and a coloured shirt, and an old straw hat. Both he and his wife had that air of quiet superiority which belongs to individuals, not to a class.

His attraction was in his vitality, the peculiar quick energy which gave a charm to his movements, stout and broad as he was. In the early days before she took to the sun, Juliet had met him suddenly, among the rocks, when she had scrambled over to the next podere. He had been aware of her before she saw him, so that when she did look up, he took off his hat, gazing at her with shyness and pride, from his big blue eyes. His face was broad, sunburnt, he had a cropped brown moustache, and thick brown eyebrows, nearly as thick as his moustache, meeting under his low, wide brow.

"Oh!" she said. "Can I walk here?"

"Surely!" he replied, with that peculiar hot haste which characterised his movement. "My padrone would wish you to walk wherever you like on his land."

And he pressed back his head in the quick, vivid, shy generosity of his nature. She had gone on quickly. But instantly she had recognised the violent generosity of his blood, and the equally violent *farouche* shyness.

Since then she had seen him in the distance every day, and she came to realise that he was one who lived a good deal to himself, like a quick animal, and that his wife loved him intensely, with a jealousy that was almost hate; because, probably, he wanted to give himself still, still further, beyond where she could take him.

One day, when a group of peasants sat under a tree, she had seen him dancing quick and gay with a child—his wife watching darkly.

Gradually Juliet and he had become intimate, across the distance. They were aware of one another. She knew, in the morning, the moment he arrived with his ass. And the moment she went out on the balcony he turned to look. But they never saluted. Yet she missed him when he did not come to work on the podere.

Once, in the hot morning when she had been walking naked, deep in the gully between the two estates, she had came upon him, as he was bending down, with his powerful shoulders, picking up wood to pile on his motionless, waiting donkey. He saw her as he lifted his flushed face, and she was backing away. A flame went over his eyes, and a flame flew over her body, melting her bones. But she backed away behind the bushes, silently, and retreated whence she had come. And she wondered a little resentfully over the silence in which he could work, hidden in the bushy places. He had that wild animal faculty.

Since then there had been a definite pain of consciousness in the body of each of them, though neither would admit it, and they gave no sign of recognition. But the man's wife was instinctively aware.

And Juliet had thought: Why shouldn't I meet this man for an hour, and bear his child? Why should I have to identify my life with a man's life? Why not meet him for an hour, as long as the desire lasts, and no more? There is already the spark between us.

But she had never made any sign. And now she saw him looking up, from where he sat by the white cloth, opposite his black-clad wife, looking up at Maurice. The wife turned and looked, too, saturnine.

And Juliet felt a grudge come over her. She would have to bear Maurice's child again. She had seen it in her husband's

eyes. And she knew it from his answer, when she spoke to
him.

"Will you walk about in the sun, too, without your
clothes?" she asked him.

"Why—er—yes! Yes, I should like to, while I'm here—I
suppose it's quite private?"

There was a gleam in his eyes, a desperate kind of courage
of his desire, and a glance at the alert lifting of her breasts in
her wrapper. In this way, he was a man, too, he faced the
world and was not entirely quenched in his male courage. He
would dare to walk in the sun, even ridiculously.

But he smelled of the world, and all its fetters and its
mongrel cowering. He was branded with the brand that is not
a hall-mark.

Ripe now, and brown-rosy all over with the sun, and with
a heart like a fallen rose, she had wanted to go down to the
hot, shy peasant and bear his child. Her sentiments had fallen
like petals. She had seen the flushed blood in the burnt face,
and the flame in the southern blue eyes, and the answer in
her had been a gush of fire. He would have been a pro-
creative sun-bath to her, and she wanted it.

Nevertheless, her next child would be Maurice's. The fatal
chain of continuity would cause it.

The Woman Who Rode Away

I

SHE HAD thought that this marriage, of all marriages, would be an adventure. Not that the man himself was exactly magical to her. A little, wiry, twisted fellow, twenty years older than herself, with brown eyes and greying hair, who had come to America a scrap of a wastrel, from Holland, years ago, as a tiny boy, and from the gold-mines of the west had been kicked south into Mexico, and now was more or less rich, owning silver-mines in the wilds of the Sierra Madre: it was obvious that the adventure lay in his circumstances, rather than his person. But he was still a little dynamo of energy, in spite of accidents survived, and what he had accomplished he had accomplished alone. One of those human oddments there is no accounting for.

When she actually *saw* what he had accomplished, her heart quailed. Great green-covered, unbroken mountain-hills, and in the midst of the lifeless isolation, the sharp pinkish mounds of the dried mud from the silver-works. Under the nakedness of the works, the walled-in, one-storey adobe house, with its garden inside, and its deep inner veranda with tropical climbers on the sides. And when you looked up from this shut-in flowered patio, you saw the huge pink cone of the silver-mud refuse, and the machinery of the extracting plant against heaven above. No more.

To be sure, the great wooden doors were often open. And then she could stand outside, in the vast open world. And see great, void, tree-clad hills piling behind one another, from nowhere into nowhere. They were green in autumn-time. For the rest, pinkish, stark dry and abstract.

And in his battered Ford car her husband would take her into the dead, thrice-dead little Spanish town forgotten among the mountains. The great, sun-dried dead church, the dead portales, the hopeless covered market-place, where, the first time she went, she saw a dead dog lying between the meat-stalls and the vegetable array, stretched out as if for ever, nobody troubling to throw it away. Deadness within deadness.

Everybody feebly talking silver, and showing bits of ore. But silver was at a standstill. The great war came and went. Silver was a dead market. Her husband's mines were closed down. But she and he lived on in the adobe house under the works, among the flowers that were never very flowery to her.

She had two children, a boy and a girl. And her eldest, the boy, was nearly ten years old before she aroused from her stupor of subjected amazement. She was now thirty-three, a large, blue-eyed, dazed woman, beginning to grow stout. Her little, wiry, tough, twisted, brown-eyed husband was fifty-three, a man as tough as wire, tenacious as wire, still full of energy, but dimmed by the lapse of silver from the market, and by some curious inaccessibility on his wife's part.

He was a man of principles, and a good husband. In a way, he doted on her. He never quite got over his dazzled admiration of her. But essentially, he was still a bachelor. He had been thrown out on the world, a little bachelor, at the age of ten. When he married he was over forty, and had enough money to marry on. But his capital was all a bachelor's. He was boss of his own works, and marriage was the last and most intimate bit of his own works.

He admired his wife to extinction, he admired her body, all her points. And she was to him always the rather dazzling Californian girl from Berkeley, whom he had first known. Like any sheikh, he kept her guarded among those mountains of Chihuahua. He was jealous of her as he was of his silver-mine: and that is saying a lot.

At thirty-three she really was still the girl from Berkeley, in all but physique. Her conscious development had stopped mysteriously with her marriage, completely arrested. Her husband had never become real to her, neither mentally nor physically. In spite of his late sort of passion for her, he never meant anything to her, physically. Only morally he swayed her, downed her, kept her in an invincible slavery.

So the years went by, in the adobe house strung round the sunny patio, with the silver-works overhead. Her husband was never still. When the silver went dead, he ran a ranch lower down, some twenty miles away, and raised pure-bred hogs, splendid creatures. At the same time, he hated pigs. He was a squeamish waif of an idealist, and really hated the physical side of life. He loved work, work, work, and making things. His marriage, his children, were something he was making, part of his business, but with a sentimental income this time.

Gradually her nerves began to go wrong: she must get out. She must get out. So he took her to El Paso for three months. And at least it was the United States.

But he kept his spell over her. The three months ended: back she was, just the same, in her adobe house among those eternal green or pinky-brown hills, void as only the undiscovered is void. She taught her children, she supervised the Mexican boys who were her servants. And sometimes her husband brought visitors, Spaniards or Mexicans or occasionally white men.

He really loved to have white men staying on the place. Yet he had not a moment's peace when they were there. It was as if his wife were some peculiar secret vein of ore in his mines, which no one must be aware of except himself. And she was fascinated by the young gentlemen, mining engineers, who were his guests at times. He, too, was fascinated by a real gentleman. But he was an old-timer miner with a wife, and if a gentleman looked at his wife, he felt as if his mine were being looted, the secrets of it pried out.

It was one of these young gentlemen who put the idea into her mind. They were all standing outside the great wooden doors of the patio, looking at the outer world. The eternal, motionless hills were all green, it was September, after the rains. There was no sign of anything, save the deserted mine, the deserted works, and a bunch of half-deserted miners' dwellings.

"I wonder," said the young man, "what there is behind those great blank hills."

"More hills," said Lederman. "If you go that way, Sonora and the coast. This way is the desert—you came from there—and the other way, hills and mountains."

"Yes, but what *lives* in the hills and the mountains? *Surely* there is something wonderful? It looks *so* like nowhere on earth: like being on the moon."

"There's plenty of game, if you want to shoot. And Indians, if you call *them* wonderful."

"Wild ones?"

"Wild enough."

"But friendly?"

"It depends. Some of them are quite wild, and they don't let anybody near. They kill a missionary at sight. And where a missionary can't get, nobody can."

"But what does the government say?"

"They're so far from everywhere, the government leaves 'em alone. And they're wily; if they think there'll be trouble, they send a delegation to Chihuahua and make a formal submission. The government is glad to leave it at that."

"And do they live quite wild, with their own savage customs and religion?"

"Oh yes. They use nothing but bows and arrows. I've seen them in town, in the Plaza, with funny sort of hats with flowers round them, and a bow in one hand, quite naked except for a sort of shirt, even in cold weather—striding round with their savage's bare legs."

"But don't you suppose it's wonderful, up there in their secret villages?"

"No. What would there be wonderful about it? Savages are savages, and all savages behave more or less alike: rather low-down and dirty, unsanitary, with a few cunning tricks, and struggling to get enough to eat."

"But surely they have old, old religions and mysteries—it *must* be wonderful, surely it must."

"I don't know about mysteries—howling and heathen practices, more or less indecent. No, I see nothing wonderful in that kind of stuff. And I wonder that you should, when you have lived in London or Paris or New York——"

"Ah, *everybody* lives in London or Paris or New York"—said the young man, as if this were an argument.

And this particular vague enthusiasm for unknown Indians found a full echo in the woman's heart. She was overcome by a foolish romanticism more unreal than a girl's. She felt it was her destiny to wander into the secret haunts of these timeless, mysterious, marvellous Indians of the mountains.

She kept her secret. The young man was departing, her husband was going with him down to Torreon, on business: would be away for some days. But before the departure, she made her husband talk about the Indians: about the wandering tribes, resembling the Navajo, who were still wandering free; and the Yaquis of Sonora: and the different groups in the different valley of Chihuahua State.

There was supposed to be one tribe, the Chilchuis, living in a high valley to the south, who were the sacred tribe of all the Indians. The descendants of Montezuma and the old Aztec or Totonac kings still lived among them, and the old priests still kept up the ancient religion, and offered human sacrifices—so it was said. Some scientists had been to the Chilchui country, and had come back gaunt and exhausted with hunger and bitter privation, bringing various curious, barbaric objects of worship, but having seen nothing extraordinary in the hungry, stark village of savages.

Though Lederman talked in this off-hand way, it was obvious he felt some of the vulgar excitement at the idea of ancient and mysterious savages.

"How far away are they?" she asked.

"Oh—three days on horseback—past Cuchitee and a little lake there is up there."

Her husband and the young man departed. The woman made her crazy plans. Of late, to break the monotony of her life, she had harassed her husband into letting her go riding with him, occasionally, on horseback. She was never allowed to go out alone. The country truly was not safe, lawless and crude.

But she had her own horse, and she dreamed of being free as she had been as a girl, among the hills of California.

Her daughter, nine years old, was now in a tiny convent in the little half-deserted Spanish mining-town five miles away.

"Manuel," said the woman to her house-servant, "I'm going to ride to the convent to see Margarita, and take her a few things. Perhaps I shall stay the night in the convent. You look after Freddy and see everything is all right till I come back."

"Shall I ride with you on the master's horse, or shall Juan?" asked the servant.

"Neither of you. I shall go alone."

The young man looked her in the eyes, in protest. Absolutely impossible that the woman should ride alone!

"I shall go alone," repeated the large, placid-seeming, fair-complexioned woman, with peculiar overbearing emphasis. And the man silently, unhappily yielded.

"Why are you going alone, mother?" asked her son, as she made up parcels of food.

"Am I *never* to be let alone? Not one moment of my life?" she cried, with sudden explosion of energy. And the child, like the servant, shrank into silence.

She set off without a qualm, riding astride on her strong roan horse, and wearing a riding-suit of coarse linen, a riding-skirt over her linen breeches, a scarlet neck-tie over her white blouse, and a black felt hat on her head. She had food in her saddle-bags, an army canteen with water, and a large, native blanket tied on behind the saddle. Peering into the distance, she set off from her home. Manuel and the little boy stood in the gateway to watch her go. She did not even turn to wave them farewell.

But when she had ridden about a mile, she left the wild road and took a small trail to the right, that led into another valley, over steep places and past great trees, and through another deserted mining settlement. It was September, the water was running freely in the little stream that had fed the now-abandoned mine. She got down to drink, and let the horse drink too.

She saw natives coming through the trees, away up the

slope. They had seen her, and were watching her closely. She watched in turn. The three people, two women and a youth, were making a wide detour, so as not to come too close to her. She did not care. Mounting, she trotted ahead up the silent valley, beyond the silver-works, beyond any trace of mining. There was still a rough trail that led over rocks and loose stones into the valley beyond. This trail she had already ridden, with her husband. Beyond that she knew she must go south.

Curiously she was not afraid, although it was a frightening country, the silent, fatal-seeming mountain slopes, the occasional distant, suspicious, elusive natives among the trees, the great carrion birds occasionally hovering, like great flies, in the distance, over some carrion or some ranch-house or some group of huts.

As she climbed, the trees shrank and the trail ran through a thorny scrub, that was trailed over with blue convolvulus and an occasional pink creeper. Then these flowers lapsed. She was nearing the pine trees.

She was over the crest, and before her another silent, void, green-clad valley. It was past midday. Her horse turned to a little runlet of water, so she got down to eat her midday meal. She sat in silence looking at the motionless unliving valley, and at the sharp-peaked hills, rising higher to rock and pine trees, southwards. She rested two hours in the heat of the day, while the horse cropped around her.

Curious that she was neither afraid nor lonely. Indeed, the loneliness was like a drink of cold water to one who is very thirsty. And a strange elation sustained her from within.

She travelled on, and camped at night in a valley beside a stream, deep among the bushes. She had seen cattle and had crossed several trails. There must be a ranch not far off. She heard the strange wailing shriek of a mountain-lion, and the answer of dogs. But she sat by her small camp-fire in a secret hollow place and was not really afraid. She was buoyed up always by the curious, bubbling elation within her.

It was very cold before dawn. She lay wrapped in her blanket looking at the stars, listening to her horse shivering, and feeling like a woman who has died and passed beyond.

She was not sure that she had not heard, during the night, a great crash at the centre of herself, which was the crash of her own death. Or else it was a crash at the centre of the earth, and meant something big and mysterious.

With the first peep of light she got up, numb with cold, and made a fire. She ate hastily, gave her horse some pieces of oil-seed cake, and set off again. She avoided any meeting—and since she met nobody, it was evident that she in turn was avoided. She came at last in sight of the village of Cuchitee, with its black houses with their reddish roofs, a sombre, dreary little cluster below another silent, long-abandoned mine. And beyond, a long, great mountain-side, rising up green and light to the darker, shaggier green of pine trees. And beyond the pine trees stretches of naked rock against the sky, rock slashed already and brindled with white stripes of snow. High up, the new snow had already begun to fall.

And now, as she neared, more or less, her destination, she began to go vague and disheartened. She had passed the little lake among the yellowing aspen trees whose white trunks were round and suave like the white round arms of some woman. What a lovely place! In California she would have raved about it. But here she looked and saw that it was lovely, but she didn't care. She was weary and spent with her two nights in the open, afraid of the coming night. She didn't know where she was going, or what she was going for. Her horse plodded dejectedly on, towards that immense and forbidding mountain-slope, following a stony little trail. And if she had had any will of her own left, she would have turned back, to the village, to be protected and sent home to her husband.

But she had no will of her own. Her horse splashed through a brook, and turned up a valley, under immense yellowing cottonwood trees. She must have been near nine thousand feet above sea-level, and her head was light with the altitude and with weariness. Beyond the cottonwood trees she could see, on each side, the steep sides of mountain-slopes hemming her in, sharp-plumaged with overlapping aspen, and, higher up, with sprouting, pointed spruce and pine tree.

Her horse went on automatically. In this tight valley, on this slight trail, there was nowhere to go but ahead, climbing.

Suddenly her horse jumped, and three men in dark blankets were on the trail before her.

"Adios!" came the greeting, in the full, restrained Indian voice.

"Adios!" she replied, in her assured, American woman's voice.

"Where are you going?" came the quiet question, in Spanish.

The men in the dark sarapes had come closer, and were looking up at her.

"On ahead," she replied coolly, in her hard, Saxon Spanish.

These were just natives to her: dark-faced, strongly-built men in dark sarapes and straw hats. They would have been the same as the men who worked for her husband, except, strangely, for the long black hair that fell over their shoulders. She noted this long black hair with a certain distaste. These must be the wild Indians she had come to see.

"Where do you come from?" the same man asked. It was always the one man who spoke. He was young, with quick, large, bright black eyes that glanced sideways at her. He had a soft black moustache on his dark face, and a sparse tuft of beard, loose hairs on his chin. His long black hair, full of life, hung unrestrained on his shoulders. Dark as he was, he did not look as if he had washed lately.

His two companions were the same, but older men, powerful and silent. One had a thin black line of moustache, but was beardless. The other had the smooth cheeks and the sparse dark hairs marking the lines of his chin with the beard characteristic of the Indians.

"I come from far away," she replied, with half-jocular evasion.

This was received in silence.

"But where do you live?" asked the young man, with that same quiet insistence.

"In the north," she replied airily.

Again there was a moment's silence. The young man conversed quietly, in Indian, with his two companions.

"Where do you want to go, up this way?" he asked suddenly, with challenge and authority, pointing briefly up the trail.

"To the Chilchui Indians," answered the woman laconically.

The young man looked at her. His eyes were quick and black, and inhuman. He saw, in the full evening light, the faint sub-smile of assurance on her rather large, calm, fresh-complexioned face; the weary, bluish lines under her large blue eyes; and in her eyes, as she looked down at him, a half-childish, half-arrogant confidence in her own female power. But in her eyes also, a curious look of trance.

"*Usted es Señora?* You are a lady?" the Indian asked her.

"Yes, I am a lady," she replied complacently.

"With a family?"

"With a husband and two children, boy and girl," she said.

The Indian turned to his companion and translated, in the low, gurgling speech, like hidden water running. They were evidently at a loss.

"Where is your husband?" asked the young man.

"Who knows?" she replied airily. "He has gone away on business for a week."

The black eyes watched her shrewdly. She, for all her weariness, smiled faintly in the pride of her own adventure and the assurance of her own womanhood, and the spell of the madness that was on her.

"And what do *you* want to do?" the Indian asked her.

"I want to visit the Chilchui Indians—to see their houses and to know their gods," she replied.

The young man turned and translated quickly, and there was a silence almost of consternation. The grave elder men were glancing at her sideways, with strange looks, from under their decorated hats. And they said something to the young man, in deep chest voices.

The latter still hesitated. Then he turned to the woman.

"Good!" he said. "Let us go. But we cannot arrive until to-morrow. We shall have to make a camp to-night."

"Good!" she said. "I can make a camp."

Without more ado, they set off at a good speed up the

stony trail. The young Indian ran alongside her horse's head, the other two ran behind. One of them had taken a thick stick, and occasionally he struck her horse a resounding blow on the haunch, to urge him forward. This made the horse jump, and thew her back in the saddle, which, tired as she was, made her angry.

"Don't do that!" she cried, looking round angrily at the fellow. She met his black, large, bright eyes, and for the first time her spirit really quailed. The man's eyes were not human to her, and they did not see her as a beautiful white woman. He looked at her with a black, bright inhuman look, and saw no woman in her at all. As if she were some strange, unaccountable *thing,* incomprehensible to him, but inimical. She sat in her saddle in wonder, feeling once more as if she had died. And again he struck her horse, and jerked her badly in the saddle.

All the passionate anger of the spoilt white woman rose in her. She pulled her horse to a standstill, and turned with blazing eyes to the man at her bridle.

"Tell that fellow not to touch my horse again," she cried.

She met the eyes of the young man, and in their bright black inscrutability she saw a fine spark, as in a snake's eye, of derision. He spoke to his companion in the rear, in the low tones of the Indian. The man with the stick listened without looking. Then, giving a strange low cry to the horse, he struck it again on the rear, so that it leaped forward spasmodically up the stony trail, scattering the stones, pitching the weary woman in her seat.

The anger flew like a madness into her eyes, she went white at the gills. Fiercely she reined in her horse. But before she could turn, the young Indian had caught the reins under the horse's throat, jerked them forward, and was trotting ahead rapidly, leading the horse.

The woman was powerless. And along with her supreme anger there came a slight thrill of exultation. She knew she was dead.

The sun was setting, a great yellow light flooded the last of the aspens, flared on the trunks of the pine trees, the pine needles bristled and stood out with dark lustre, the rocks glowed with unearthly glamour. And through the effulgence the Indian at her horse's head trotted unweariedly on, his dark blanket swinging, his bare legs glowing with a strange transfigured ruddiness in the powerful light, and his straw hat with its half-absurd decorations of flowers and feathers shining showily above his river of long black hair. At times he would utter a low call to the horse, and then the other Indian, behind, would fetch the beast a whack with the stick.

The wonder-light faded off the mountains, the world began to grow dark, a cold air breathed down. In the sky, half a moon was struggling against the glow in the west. Huge shadows came down from steep rocky slopes. Water was rushing. The woman was conscious only of her fatigue, her unspeakable fatigue, and the cold wind from the heights. She was not aware how moonlight replaced daylight. It happened while she travelled unconscious with weariness.

For some hours they travelled by moonlight. Then suddenly they came to a standstill. The men conversed in low tones for a moment.

"We camp here," said the young man.

She waited for him to help her down. He merely stood holding the horse's bridle. She almost fell from the saddle, so fatigued.

They had chosen a place at the foot of rocks that still gave off a little warmth of the sun. One man cut pine boughs, another erected little screens of pine boughs against the rock for shelter, and put boughs of balsam pine for beds. The third made a small fire, to heat tortillas. They worked in silence.

The woman drank water. She did not want to eat—only to lie down.

"Where do I sleep?" she asked.

The young man pointed to one of the shelters. She crept in and lay inert. She did not care what happened to her, she was so weary, and so beyond everything. Through the twigs of spruce she could see the three men squatting round the fire on their hams, chewing the tortillas they picked from the ashes with their dark fingers, and drinking water from a gourd. They talked in low, muttering tones, with long intervals of silence. Her saddle and saddle-bags lay not far from the fire, unopened, untouched. The men were not interested in her nor her belongings. There they squatted with their hats on their heads, eating, eating mechanically, like animals, the dark sarape with its fringe falling to the ground before and behind, the powerful dark legs naked and squatting like an animal's showing the dirty white shirt and the sort of loin-cloth which was the only other garment, underneath. And they showed no more sign of interest in her than if she had been a piece of venison they were bringing home from the hunt, and had hung inside a shelter.

After a while they carefully extinguished the fire, and went inside their own shelter. Watching through the screen of boughs, she had a moment's thrill of fear and anxiety, seeing the dark forms cross and pass silently in the moonlight. Would they attack her now?

But no! They were as if oblivious to her. Her horse was hobbled; she could hear it hopping wearily. All was silent, mountain-silent, cold, deathly. She slept and woke and slept in a semi-conscious numbness of cold and fatigue. A long, long night, icy and eternal, and she aware that she had died.

II

Yet when there was a stirring, and a clink of flint and steel, and the form of a man crouching like a dog over a bone, at a red splutter of fire, and she knew it was morning coming, it seemed to her the night had passed too soon.

When the fire was going, she came out of her shelter with one real desire left: for coffee. The men were warming more tortillas.

"Can we make coffee?" she asked.

The young man looked at her, and she imagined the same faint spark of derision in his eyes. He shook his head.

"We don't take it," he said. "There is no time."

And the elder men, squatting on their haunches, looked up at her in the terrible paling dawn, and there was not even derision in their eyes. Only that intense, yet remote, inhuman glitter which was terrible to her. They were inaccessible.

They could not see her as a woman at all. As if she *were* not a woman. As if, perhaps, her whiteness took away all her womanhood, and left her as some giant, female white ant. That was all they could see in her.

Before the sun was up, she was in the saddle again, and they were climbing steeply, in the icy air. The sun came, and soon she was very hot, exposed to the glare in the bare places. It seemed to her they were climbing to the roof of the world. Beyond against heaven were slashes of snow.

During the course of the morning, they came to a place where the horse could not go farther. They rested for a time with a great slant of living rock in front of them, like the glossy breast of some earth-beast. Across this rock, along a wavering crack, they had to go. It seemed to her that for hours she went in torment, on her hands and knees, from crack to crevice, along the slanting face of this pure rock-mountain. An Indian in front and an Indian behind walked slowly erect, shod with sandals of braided leather. But she in her riding-boots dared not stand erect.

Yet what she wondered, all the time, was why she persisted in clinging and crawling along these mile-long sheets of rock. Why she did not hurl herself down, and have done! The world was below her.

When they emerged at last on a stony slope, she looked back, and saw the third Indian coming carrying her saddle and saddle-bags on his back, the whole hung from a band across his forehead. And he had his hat in his hand, as he stepped slowly, with the slow, soft, heavy tread of the Indian, unwavering in the chinks of rock, as if along a scratch in the mountain's iron shield.

The stony slope led downwards. The Indians seemed to grow excited. One ran ahead at a slow trot, disappearing round the curve of stones. And the track curved round and down, till at last in the full blaze of the mid-morning sun, they could see a valley below them, between walls of rock, as in a great wide chasm let in the mountains. A green valley, with a river, and trees, and clusters of low flat sparkling houses. It was all tiny and perfect, three thousand feet below. Even the flat bridge over the stream, and the square with the houses around it, the bigger buildings piled up at opposite ends of the square, the tall cottonwood trees, the pastures and stretches of yellow-sere maize, the patches of brown sheep or goats in the distance, on the slopes, the railed enclosures by the stream-side. There it was, all small and perfect, looking magical, as any place will look magical, seen from the mountains above. The unusual thing was that the low houses glittered white, white-washed, looking like crystals of salt, or silver. This frightened her.

They began the long, winding descent at the head of the barranca, following the stream that rushed and fell. At first it was all rocks; then the pine trees began, and soon, the silver-limbed aspens. The flowers of autumn, big daisy-like flowers, and white ones, and many yellow flowers, were in profusion. But she had to sit down and rest, she was so weary. And she saw the bright flowers shadowily, as pale shadows hovering, as one who is dead must see them.

At length came grass and pasture-slopes between mingled aspen and pine trees. A shepherd, naked in the sun save for his hat and his cotton loin-cloth, was driving his brown sheep away. In a grove of trees they sat and waited, she and the young Indian. The one with the saddle had also gone forward.

They heard a sound of someone coming. It was three men, in fine sarapes of red and orange and yellow and black, and with brilliant feather head-dresses. The oldest had his grey hair braided with fur, and his red and orange-yellow sarape was covered with curious black markings, like a leopard-skin. The other two were not grey-haired, but they were elders too. Their blankets were in stripes, and their head-dresses not so elaborate.

The young Indian addressed the elders in a few quiet words. They listened without answering or looking at him or at the woman, keeping their faces averted and their eyes turned to the ground, only listening. And at length they turned and looked at the woman.

The old chief, or medicine-man, whatever he was, had a deeply wrinkled and lined face of dark bronze, with a few sparse grey hairs round the mouth. Two long braids of grey hair, braided with fur and coloured feather, hung on his shoulders. And yet, it was only his eyes that mattered. They were black and of extraordinary piercing strength, without a qualm of misgiving in their demonish, dauntless power. He looked into the eyes of the white woman with a long piercing look, seeking she knew not what. She summoned all her strength to meet his eyes and keep up her guard. But it was no good. He was not looking at her as one human being looks at another. He never even perceived her resistance or her challenge, but looked past them both, into she knew not what.

She could see it was hopeless to expect an human communication with this old being.

He turned and said a few words to the young Indian.

"He asks what do you seek here?" said the young man in Spanish.

"I? Nothing! I only came to see what it was like."

This was again translated, and the old man turned his eyes on her once more. Then he spoke again, in his low muttering tone, to the young Indian.

"He says, why does she leave her house with the white men? Does she want to bring the white man's God to the Chilchui?"

"No," she replied, foolhardy. "I came away from the white man's God myself. I came to look for the God of the Chilchui."

Profound silence followed, when this was translated. Then the old man spoke again, in a small voice almost of weariness.

"Does the white woman seek the gods of the Chilchui because she is weary of her own God?" came the question.

"Yes, she does. She is tired of the white man's God," she replied, thinking that was what they wanted her to say. She would like to serve the gods of the Chilchui.

She was aware of an extraordinary thrill of triumph and exultance passing through the Indians, in the tense silence that followed when this was translated. Then they all looked at her with piercing black eyes, in which a steely covetous intent glittered incomprehensible. She was the more puzzled, as there was nothing sensual or sexual in the look. It had a terrible glittering purity that was beyond her. She was afraid, she would have been paralysed with fear, had not something died within her, leaving her with a cold, watchful wonder only.

The elders talked a little while, then the two went away, leaving her with the young man and the oldest chief. The old man now looked at her with a certain solicitude.

"He says are you tired?" asked the young man.

"Very tired," she said.

"The men will bring you a carriage," said the young Indian.

The carriage, when it came, proved to be a litter consisting of a sort of hammock of dark woollen frieze, slung on to a pole which was borne on the shoulders of two long-haired Indians. The woollen hammock was spread on the ground, she sat down on it, and the two men raised the pole to their shoulders. Swinging rather as if she were in a sack, she was carried out of the grove of trees, following the old chief, whose leopard-spotted blanket moved curiously in the sunlight.

They had emerged in the valley-head. Just in front were the maize-fields, with ripe ears of maize. The corn was not very tall, in this high altitude. The well-worn path went between it, and all she could see was the erect form of the old chief in the flame and black sarape, stepping soft and heavy and swift, his head forward, looking neither to right nor left. Her bearers followed, stepping rhythmically, the long blue-black hair glistening like a river down the naked shoulders of the man in front.

They passed the maize, and came to a big wall or earthwork made of earth and adobe bricks. The wooden doors were open. Passing on, they were in a network of small gardens, full of flowers and herbs and fruit trees, each garden watered by a tiny ditch of running water. Among each cluster of trees and flowers was a small, glittering white house, windowless, and with closed door. The place was a network of little paths, small streams, and little bridges among square, flowering gardens.

Following the broadest path—a soft narrow track between leaves and grass, a path worn smooth by centuries of human feet, no hoof of horse nor any wheel to disfigure it—they came to the little river of swift bright water, and crossed on a log bridge. Everything was silent—there was not a human being anywhere. The road went on under magnificent cotton-wood trees. It emerged suddenly outside the central plaza or square of the village.

This was a long oblong of low white houses with flat roofs, and two bigger buildings, having as it were little square huts piled on top of bigger long huts, stood at either end of the oblong, facing each other rather askew. Every little house was a dazzling white, save for the great round beam-ends which projected under the flat eaves, and for the flat roofs. Round each of the bigger buildings, on the outside of the square, was a stockyard fence, inside which was garden with trees and flowers, and various small houses.

Not a soul was in sight. They passed silently between the houses into the central square. This was quite bare and arid, the earth trodden smooth by endless generations of passing feet, passing across from door to door. All the doors of the windowless houses gave on to this blank square, but all doors were closed. The firewood lay near the threshold, a clay oven was still smoking, but there was no sign of moving life.

The old man walked straight across the square to the big house at the end, where the two upper storeys, as in a house of toy bricks, stood each one smaller than the lower one. A stone staircase, outside, led up to the roof of the first storey.

At the foot of this staircase the litter-bearers stood still, and lowered the woman to the ground.

"You will come up," said the young Indian who spoke Spanish.

She mounted the stone stairs to the earthen roof of the first house, which formed a platform round the wall of the second storey. She followed around this platform to the back of the big house. There they descended again, into a garden at the rear.

So far they had seen no one. But now two men appeared, bare-headed, with long braided hair, and wearing a sort of white shirt gathered into a loin-cloth. These went along with the three newcomers, across the garden where red flowers and yellow flowers were blooming, to a long, low white house. There they entered without knocking.

It was dark inside. There was a low murmur of men's voices. Several men were present, their white shirts showing in the gloom, their dark faces invisible. They were sitting on a great log of smooth old wood, that lay along the far wall. And save for this log, the room seemed empty. But no, in the dark at one end was a couch, a sort of bed, and someone lying there, covered with furs.

The old Indian in the spotted sarape, who had accompanied the women, now took off his hat and his blanket and his sandals. Laying them aside, he approached the couch, and spoke in a low voice. For some moments there was no answer. Then an old man with the snow-white hair hanging round his darkly-visible face, roused himself like a vision, and leaned on one elbow, looking vaguely at the company, in tense silence.

The grey-haired Indian spoke again, and then the young Indian, taking the woman's hand, led her forward. In her linen riding-habit, and black boots and hat, and her pathetic bit of a red tie, she stood there beside the fur-covered bed of the old, old man, who sat reared up, leaning on one elbow, remote as a ghost, his white hair streaming in disorder, his face almost black, yet with a far-off intentness, not of this world, leaning forward to look at her.

His face was so old, it was like dark glass, and the few curling hairs that sprang white from his lips and chin were quite incredible. The long white locks fell unbraided and disorderly on either side of the glassy dark face. And under a faint powder of white eyebrows, the black eyes of the old chief looked at her as if from the far, far dead, seeing something that was never to be seen.

At last he spoke a few deep, hollow words, as if to the dark air.

"He says, do you bring your heart to the god of the Chilchui?" translated the young Indian.

"Tell him yes," she said, automatically.

There was a pause. The old Indian spoke again, as if to the air. One of the men present went out. There was a silence as if of eternity in the dim room that was lighted only through the open door.

The woman looked round. Four old men with grey hair sat on the log by the wall facing the door. Two other men, powerful and impassive, stood near the door. They all had long hair, and wore white shirts gathered into a loin-cloth. Their powerful legs were naked and dark. There was a silence like eternity.

At length the man returned, with white and dark clothing on his arm. The young Indian took them, and holding them in front of the woman, said:

"You must take off your clothes, and put these on."

"If all you men will go out," she said.

"No one will hurt you," he said quietly.

"Not while you men are here," she said.

He looked at the two men by the door. They came quickly forward, and suddenly gripped her arms as she stood, without hurting her, but with great power. Then two of the old men came, and with curious skill slit her boots down with keen knives, and drew them off, and slit her clothing so that it came away from her. In a few moments she stood there white and uncovered. The old man on the bed spoke, and they turned her round for him to see. He spoke again, and the young Indian deftly took the pins and comb from her fair hair, so that it fell over her shoulders in a bunchy tangle.

Then the old man spoke again. The Indian led her to the bedside. The white-haired, glassy-dark old man moistened his finger-tips at his mouth, and most delicately touched her on the breasts and on the body, then on the back. And she winced strangely each time, as the finger-tips drew along her skin, as if Death itself were touching her.

And she wondered, almost sadly, why she did not feel shamed in her nakedness. She only felt sad and lost. Because nobody felt ashamed. The elder men were all dark and tense with some other deep, gloomy, incomprehensible emotion, which suspended all her agitation, while the young Indian had a strange look of ecstasy on his face. And she, she was only utterly strange and beyond herself, as if her body were not her own.

They gave her the new clothing: a long white cotton shift, that came to her knees: then a tunic of thick blue woollen stuff, embroidered with scarlet and green flowers. It was fastened over one shoulder only, and belted with a braid sash of scarlet and black wool.

When she was thus dressed, they took her away, barefoot, to a little house in the stockaded garden. The young Indian told her she might have what she wanted. She asked for water to wash herself. He brought it in a jar, together with a long wooden bowl. Then he fastened the gate-door of her house, and left her a prisoner. She could see through the bars of the gate-door of her house, the red flowers of the garden, and a humming-bird. Then from the roof of the big house she heard the long, heavy sound of a drum, unearthly to her in its summons, and an uplifted voice calling from the house-top in a strange language, with a far-away emotionless intonation, delivering some speech or message. And she listened as if from the dead.

But she was very tired. She lay down on a couch of skins, pulling over her the blanket of dark wool, and she slept, giving up everything.

When she woke it was late afternoon, and the young Indian was entering with a basket-tray containing food, tortillas, and corn-mush with bits of meat, probably mutton, and a drink made of honey, and some fresh plums. He brought her also a long garland of red and yellow flowers with knots of blue buds at the end. He sprinkled the garland with water from a jar, then offered it to her, with a smile. He seemed very gentle and thoughtful, and on his face and in his dark eyes was a curious look of triumph and ecstasy, that frightened her a little. The glitter had gone from the black eyes, with their curving dark lashes, and he would look at her with this strange soft glow of ecstasy that was not quite human, and terribly impersonal, and which made her uneasy.

"Is there anything you want?" he said, in his low, slow, melodious voice, that always seemed withheld, as if he were

speaking aside to somebody else, or as if he did not want to
let the sound come out to her.

"Am I going to be kept a prisoner here?" she asked.

"No, you can walk in the garden to-morrow," he said
softly. Always this curious solicitude.

"Do you like that drink?" he said, offering her a little
earthenware cup. "It is very refreshing."

She sipped the liquor curiously. It was made with herbs
and sweetened with honey, and had a strange, lingering
flavour. The young man watched her with gratification.

"It has a peculiar taste," she said.

"It is very refreshing," he replied, his black eyes resting on
her always with that look of gratified ecstasy. Then he went
away. And presently she began to be sick, and to vomit
violently, as if she had no control over herself.

Afterwards she felt a great soothing languor steal over
her, her limbs felt strong and loose and full of languor, and
she lay on her couch listening to the sounds of the village,
watching the yellowing sky, smelling the scent of burning
cedar wood, or pine wood. So distinctly she heard the yap-
ping of tiny dogs, the shuffle of far-off feet, the murmur of
voices, so keenly she detected the smell of smoke, and flowers, and evening falling, so vividly she saw the one bright star
infinitely remote, stirring above the sunset, that she felt as if
all her senses were diffused on the air, that she could distinguish the sound of evening flowers unfolding, and the actual
crystal sound of the heavens, as the vast belts of the world-
atmosphere slid past one another, and as if the moisture
ascending and the moisture descending in the air resounded
like some harp in the cosmos.

She was a prisoner in her house, and in the stockaded
garden, but she scarcely minded. And it was days before she
realised that she never saw another woman. Only the men,
the elderly men of the big house, that she imagined must be
some sort of temple, and the men priests of some sort. For
they always had the same colours, red, orange, yellow, and
black, and the same grave, abstracted demeanour.

Sometimes an old man would come and sit in her room
with her, in absolute silence. None spoke any language but

Indian, save the one younger man. The older men would smile at her, and sit with her for an hour at a time, sometimes smiling at her when she spoke in Spanish, but never answering save with this slow, benevolent-seeming smile. And they gave off a feeling of almost fatherly solicitude. Yet their dark eyes, brooding over her, had something away in their depths that was awesomely ferocious and relentless. They would cover it with a smile, at once, if they felt her looking. But she had seen it.

Always they treated her with this curious impersonal solicitude, this utterly impersonal gentleness, as an old man treats a child. But underneath it she felt there was something else, something terrible. When her old visitor had gone away, in his silent, insidious, fatherly fashion, a shock of fear would come over her; though of what she knew not.

The young Indian would sit and talk with her freely, as if with great candour. But with him, too, she felt that everything real was unsaid. Perhaps it was unspeakable. His big dark eyes would rest on her almost cherishingly, touched with ecstasy, and his beautiful, slow, languorous voice would trail out its simple, ungrammatical Spanish. He told her he was the grandson of the old, old man, son of the man in the spotted sarape: and they were caciques, kings from the old, old days, before even the Spaniards came. But he himself had been in Mexico City, and also in the United States. He had worked as a labourer, building the roads in Los Angeles. He had travelled as far as Chicago.

"Don't you speak English, then?" she asked.

His eyes rested on her with a curious look of duplicity and conflict, and he mutely shook his head.

"What did you do with your long hair, when you were in the United States?" she asked. "Did you cut it off?"

Again, with the look of torment in his eyes, he shook his head.

"No," he said, in a low, subdued voice, "I wore a hat, and a handkerchief tied round my head."

And he relapsed into silence, as if of tormented memories.

"Are you the only man of your prople who has been to the United States?" she asked him.

"Yes. I am the only one who has been away from here for a long time. The others come back soon, in one week. They don't stay away. The old men don't let them."

"And why did you go?"

"The old men want me to go—because I shall be the cacique——"

He talked always with the same naïveté, and almost childish candour. But she felt that this was perhaps just the effect of his Spanish. Or perhaps speech altogether was unreal to him. Anyhow, she felt that all the real things were kept back.

He came and sat with her a good deal—sometimes more than she wished—as if he wanted to be near her. She asked him if he was married. He said he was—with two children.

"I should like to see your children," she said.

But he answered, only with that smile, a sweet, almost ecstatic smile, above which the dark eyes hardly changed from their enigmatic abstraction.

It was curious, he would sit with her by the hour, without ever making her self-conscious, or sex-conscious. He seemed to have no sex, as he sat there so still and gentle and apparently submissive with his head bent a little forward, and the river of glistening black hair streaming maidenly over his shoulders.

Yet when she looked again, she saw his shoulders broad and powerful, his eyebrows black and level, the short, curved, obstinate black lashes over his lowered eyes, the small, fur-like line of moustache above his blackish, heavy lips, and the strong chin, and she knew that in some other mysterious way he was darkly and powerfully male. And he, feeling her watching him, would glance up at her swiftly with a dark lurking look in his eyes, which immediately he veiled with that half-sad smile.

The days and the weeks went by, in a vague kind of contentment. She was uneasy sometimes, feeling she had lost the power over herself. She was not in her own power, she was under the spell of some other control. And at times she had moments of terror and horror. But then these Indians would come and sit with her, casting their insidious spell over her by their very silent presence, their silent, sexless, powerful physical presence. As they sat they seemed to take her will away, and leaving her will-less and victim to her own indifference. And the young man would bring her sweetened drink, often the same emetic drink, but sometimes other kinds. And after drinking, the languor filled her heavy limbs, her senses seemed to float in the air, listening, hearing. They had brought her a little female dog, which she called Flora. And once, in the trance of her senses, she felt she *heard* the little dog conceive, in her tiny womb, and begin to be complex, with young. And another day she could hear the vast sound of the earth going round, like some immense arrow-string booming.

But as the days grew shorter and colder, when she was cold, she would get a sudden revival of her will, and a desire to go out, to go away. And she insisted to the young man, she wanted to go out.

So one day, they let her climb to the topmost roof of the big house where she was, and look down the square. It was the day of the big dance, but not everybody was dancing. Women with babies in their arms stood in their doorways, watching. Opposite, at the other end of the square, there was a throng before the other big house, and a small, brilliant group on the terrace roof of the first storey, in front of wide open doors of the upper storey. Through these wide open doors she could see fire glinting in darkness and priests in head-dresses of black and yellow and scarlet feathers, wearing robe-like blankets of black and red and yellow, with long green fringes, were moving about. A big drum was beating slowly and regularly, in the dense, Indian silence. The crowd below waited.

Then a drum started on a high beat, and there came the deep, powerful burst of men singing a heavy, savage music, like a wind roaring in some timeless forest, many mature men singing in one breath, like the wind; and long lines of dancers walked out from under the big house. Men with naked, golden-bronze bodies and streaming black hair, tufts of red and yellow feathers on their arms, and kilts of white frieze with a bar of heavy red and black and green embroidery round their waists, bending slightly forward and stamping the earth in their absorbed, monotonous stamp of the dance, a fox-fur, hung by the nose from their belt behind, swaying with the sumptuous swaying of a beautiful fox-fur, the tip of the tail writhing above the dancer's heels. And after each man, a woman with a strange elaborate head-dress of feathers and sea-shells, and wearing a short black tunic, moving erect, holding up tufts of feathers in each hand, swaying her wrists rhythmically and subtly beating the earth with her bare feet.

So, the long line of the dance unfurling from the big house opposite. And from the big house beneath her, strange scent of incense, strange tense silence, then the answering burst of inhuman male singing, and the long line of the dance unfurling.

It went on all day, the insistence of the drum, the cavernous, roaring, storm-like sound of male singing, the incessant swinging of the fox-skins behind the powerful, gold-bronze, stamping legs of the men, the autumn sun from a perfect blue heaven pouring on the rivers of black hair, men's and woman's, the valley all still, the walls of rock beyond, the awful huge bulking of the mountain against the pure sky, its snow seething with sheer whiteness.

For hours and hours she watched, spellbound, and as if drugged. And in all the terrible persistence of the drumming and the primeval, rushing deep singing, and the endless stamping of the dance of the fox-tailed men, the tread of heavy, bird-erect women in their black tunics, she seemed at last to feel her own death; her own obliteration. As if she were to be obliterated from the field of life again. In the strange towering symbols on the heads of the changeless, absorbed women she seemed to read once more the *Mene Mene Tekel Upharsin*. Her kind of womanhood, intensely personal and individual, was to be obliterated again, and the great primeval symbols were to tower once more over the fallen individual independence of woman. The sharpness and the quivering nervous consciousness of the high-bred white woman was to be destroyed again, womanhood was to be cast once more into the great stream of impersonal sex and impersonal passion. Strangely, as if clairvoyant, she saw the immense sacrifice prepared. And she went back to her little house in a trance of agony.

After this, there was always a certain agony when she heard the drums at evening, and the strange uplifted savage sound of men singing round the drum, like wild creatures howling to the invisible gods of the moon and the vanished sun. Something of the chuckling, sobbing cry of the coyote, something of the exultant bark of the fox, the far-off wild melancholy exultance of the howling wolf, the torment of the puma's scream, and the insistence of the ancient fierce human male, with his lapses of tenderness and his abiding ferocity.

Sometimes she would climb the high roof after nightfall, and listen to the dim cluster of young men round the drum on the bridge just beyond the square, singing by the hour. Sometimes there would be a fire, and in the fire-glow, men in their white shirts or naked save for a loin-cloth, would be dancing and stamping like spectres, hour after hour in the dark cold air, within the fire-glow, for ever dancing and stamping like turkeys, or dropping squatting by the fire to rest, throwing their blankets round them.

"Why do you all have the same colours?" she asked the young Indian. "Why do you all have red and yellow and black, over your white shirts? And the women have black tunics?"

He looked into her eyes, curiously, and the faint, evasive smile came on to his face. Behind the smile lay a soft, strange malignancy.

"Because our men are the fire and the day-time, and our women are the spaces between the stars at night," he said.

"Aren't the women even stars?" she said.

"No. We say they are the spaces between the stars, that keep the stars apart."

He looked at her oddly, and again the touch of derision came into his eyes.

"White people," he said, "they know nothing. They are like children, always with toys. We know the sun, and we know the moon. And we say, when a white woman sacrifice herself to our gods, then our gods will begin to make the world again, and the white man's gods will fall to pieces."

"How sacrifice herself?" she asked quickly.

And he, as quickly covered, covered himself with a subtle smile.

"She sacrifice her own gods and come to our gods, I mean that," he said soothingly.

But she was not reassured. An icy pang of fear and certainty was at her heart.

"The sun he is alive at one end of the sky," he continued, "and the moon lives at the other end. And the man all the time have to keep the sun happy in his side of the sky, and the woman have to keep the moon quiet at her side of the sky. All the time she have to work at this. And the sun can't ever go into the house of the moon, and the moon can't ever go into the house of the sun, in the sky. So the woman, she asks the moon to come into her cave, inside her. And the man, he draws the sun down till he has the power of the sun. All the time he do this. Then when the man gets a woman, the sun goes into the cave of the moon, and that is how everything in the world starts."

She listened, watching him closely, as one enemy watches another who is speaking with double meaning.

"Then," she said, "why aren't you Indians masters of the white men?"

"Because," he said, "the Indian got weak, and lost his power with the sun, so the white men stole the sun. But they can't keep him—they don't know how. They got him, but they don't know what to do with him, like a boy who catch a big grizzly bear, and can't kill him, and can't run away from him. The grizzly bear eats the boy that catch him, when he want to run away from him. White men don't know what they are doing with the sun, and white women don't know what they do with the moon. The moon she got angry with white women, like a puma when someone kills her little ones. The moon, she bites white women—here inside," and he pressed his side. "The moon, she is angry in a white woman's cave. The Indian can see it. And soon," he added, "the Indian women get the moon back and keep her quiet in their house. And the Indian men get the sun, and the power over all the world. White men don't know what the sun is. They never know."

He subsided into a curious exultant silence.

"But," she faltered, "why do you hate us so? Why do you hate me?"

He looked up suddenly with a light on his face, and a startling flame of a smile.

"No, we don't hate," he said softly, looking with a curious glitter into her face.

"You do," she said, forlorn and hopeless.

And after a moment's silence, he rose and went away.

III

Winter had now come, in the high valley, with snow that melted in the day's sun, and nights that were bitter cold. She lived on, in a kind of daze, feeling her power ebbing more and more away from her, as if her will were leaving her. She felt always in the same relaxed, confused, victimised state, unless the sweetened herb drink would numb her mind altogether, and release her senses into a sort of heightened, mystic acuteness and a feeling as if she were diffusing out deliciously into the harmony of things. This at length became the only state of consciousness she really recognised: this exquisite sense of bleeding out into the higher beauty and harmony of things. Then she could actually hear the great stars in heaven, which she saw through her door, speaking from their motion and brightness, saying things perfectly to the cosmos, as they trod in perfect ripples, like bells on the floor of heaven, passing one another and grouping in the timeless dance, with the spaces of dark between. And she could hear the snow on a cold, cloudy day twittering and faintly whistling in the sky, like birds that flock and fly away in autumn, suddenly calling farewell to the invisible moon, and slipping out of the plains of the air, releasing peaceful warmth. She herself would call to the arrested snow to fall from the upper air. She would call to the unseen moon to cease to be angry, to make peace again with the unseen sun like a woman who ceases to be angry in her house. And she would smell the sweetness of the moon relaxing to the sun in the wintry heaven, when the snow fell in a faint, cold-perfumed relaxation, as the peace of the sun mingled again in a sort of unison with the peace of the moon.

She was aware too of the sort of shadow that was on the Indians of the valley, a deep stoical disconsolation, almost religious in its depth.

"We have lost our power over the sun, and we are trying to get him back. But he is wild with us, and shy like a horse that has got away. We have to go through a lot." So the young Indian said to her, looking into her eyes with a strained meaning. And she, as if bewitched, replied:

"I hope you will get him back."

The smile of triumph flew over his face.

"Do you hope it?" he said.

"I do," she answered fatally.

"Then all right," he said, "We shall get him."

And he went away in exultance.

She felt she was drifting on some consummation, which she had no will to avoid, yet which seemed heavy and finally terrible to her.

It must have been almost December, for the days were short when she was taken again before the aged man, and stripped of her clothing, and touched with the old finger-tips.

The aged cacique looked her in the eyes, with his eyes of lonely, far-off, black intentness, and murmured something to her.

"He wants you to make the sign of peace," the young man translated, showing her the gesture. "Peace and farewell to him."

She was fascinated by the black, glass-like, intent eyes of the old cacique, that watched her without blinking, like a basilisk's, overpowering her. In their depths also she saw a certain fatherly compassion, and pleading. She put her hand before her face, in the required manner, making the sign of peace and farewell. He made the sign of peace back again to her, then sank among his furs. She thought he was going to die, and that he knew it.

There followed a day of ceremonial, when she was brought out before all the people, in a blue blanket with white fringe, and holding blue feathers in her hands. Before an altar of one house she was perfumed with incense and sprinkled with ash. Before the altar of the opposite house she was fumigated again with incense by the gorgeous, terrifying priests in yellow and scarlet and black, their faces painted with scarlet paint. And then they threw water on her. Meanwhile she was faintly aware of the fire on the altar, the heavy, heavy sound of a drum, the heavy sound of men beginning powerfully, deeply, savagely to sing, the swaying of the crowd of faces in the plaza below, and the formation for a sacred dance.

But at this time her commonplace consciousness was numb, she was aware of her immediate surroundings as shadows, almost immaterial. With refined and heightened senses she could hear the sound of the earth winging on its journey, like a shot arrow, the ripple-rustling of the air, and the boom of the great arrow-string. And it seemed to her there were two great influences in the upper air, one golden towards the sun, and one invisible silver; the first travelling like rain ascending to the gold presence sunwards, the second like rain silverily descending the ladders of space towards the hovering, lurking clouds over the snowy mountain-top. Then between them, another presence, waiting to shake himself free of moisture, of heavy white snow that had mysteriously collected about him. And in summer, like a scorched eagle, he would wait to shake himself clear of the weight of heavy sunbeams. And he was coloured like fire. And he was always shaking himself clear, of snow or of heavy heat, like an eagle rustling.

Then there was a still stranger presence, standing watching from the blue distance, always watching. Sometimes running in upon the wind, or shimmering in the heat-waves. The blue wind itself, rushing, as it were, out of the holes into the sky, rushing out of the sky down upon the earth. The blue wind, the go-between, the invisible ghost that belonged to two worlds, that played upon the ascending and the descending chords of the rains.

More and more her ordinary personal consciousness had

left her, she had gone into that other state of passional cosmic consciousness, like one who is drugged. The Indians, with their heavily religious natures, had made her succumb to their vision.

Only one personal question she asked the young Indian:

"Why am I the only one that wears blue?"

"It is the colour of the wind. It is the colour of what goes away and is never coming back, but which is always here, waiting like death among us. It is the colour of the dead. And it is the colour that stands away off, looking at us from the distance, that cannot come near to us. When we go near, it goes farther. It can't be near. We are all brown and yellow and black hair, and white teeth and red blood. We are the ones that are here. You with blue eyes, you are the messengers from the far-away, you cannot stay, and now it is time for you to go back."

"Where to?" she asked.

"To the way-off things like the sun and the blue mother of rain, and tell them that we are the people on the world again, and we can bring the sun to the moon again, like a red horse to a blue mare; we are the people. The white women have driven back the moon in the sky, won't let her come to the sun. So the sun is angry. And the Indian must give the moon to the sun."

"How?" she said.

"The white woman got to die and go like a wind to the sun, tell him the Indians will open the gate to him. And the Indian women will open the gate to the moon. The white women don't let the moon come down out of the blue coral. The moon used to come down among the Indian women, like a white goat among the flowers. And the sun want to come down to the Indian men, like an eagle to the pine trees. The sun, he is shut out behind the white man, and the moon she is shut out behind the white woman, and they can't get away. They are angry, everything in the world gets angrier. The Indian says he will give the white woman to the sun, so the sun will leap over the white man and come to the Indian again. And the moon will be surprised, she will see the gate open, and she not know which way to go. But the Indian woman will call to the moon: *Come! Come! Come back into my grasslands. The wicked white woman can't harm you any more.* Then the sun will look over the heads of the white men, and see the moon in the pastures of our women, with the Red Men standing around like pine trees. Then he will leap over the heads of the white men, and come running past to the Indians through the spruce trees. And we, who are red and black and yellow, we who stay, we shall have the sun on our right hand and the moon on our left. So we can bring the rain down out of the blue meadows, and up out of the black; and we can call the wind that tells the corn to grow, when we ask him, and we shall make the clouds to break, and the sheep to have twin lambs. And we shall be full of power, like a spring day. But the white people will be a hard winter, without snow——"

"But," said the white woman, "I don't shut out the moon—how can I?"

"Yes," he said, "you shut the gate, and then laugh, think you have it all your own way."

She could never quite understand the way he looked at her. He was always so curiously gentle, and his smile was so soft. Yet there was such a glitter in his eyes, and an unrelenting sort of hate came out of his words, a strange, profound, impersonal hate. Personally he liked her, she was sure. He was gentle with her, attracted by her in some strange, soft, passionless way. But impersonally he hated her with a mystic hatred. He would smile at her, winningly. Yet if, the next moment, she glanced round at him unawares, she would catch that gleam of pure after-hate in his eyes.

"Have I got to die and be given to the sun?" she asked.

"Some time," he said, laughing evasively. "Some time we all die."

They were gentle with her, and very considerate with her. Strange men, the old priests and the young cacique alike, they watched over her and cared for her like women. In their soft, insidious understanding, there was something womanly. Yet their eyes, with that strange glitter, and their dark, shut mouths that would open to the broad jaw, the small, strong, white teeth, had something very primitively male and cruel.

One wintry day, when snow was falling, they took her to a great dark chamber in the big house. The fire was burning in a corner on a high raised dais under a sort of hood or canopy of adobe-work. She saw in the fire-glow the glowing bodies of the almost naked priests, and strange symbols on the roof and walls of the chamber. There was no door or window in the chamber, they had descended by a ladder, from the roof. And the fire of pinewood danced continually, showing walls painted with strange devices, which she could not understand, and a ceiling of poles making a curious pattern of black and red and yellow, and alcoves or niches in which were curious objects she could not discern.

The older priests were going through some ceremony near the fire, in silence, intense Indian silence. She was seated on a low projection of the wall, opposite the fire, two men seated beside her. Presently they gave her a drink from a cup, which she took gladly, because of the semi-trance it would induce.

In the darkness and in the silence she was accurately aware of everything that happened to her: how they took off her clothes, and, standing her before a great, weird device on the wall, coloured blue and white and black, washed her all over with water and the amole infusion; washed even her hair, softly, carefully, and dried it on white cloths, till it was soft and glistening. Then they laid her on a couch under another great indecipherable image of red and black and yellow, and now rubbed all her body with sweet-scented oil, and massaged all her limbs, and her back, and her sides, with a long, strange, hypnotic massage. Their dark hands were incredibly powerful, yet soft with a watery softness she could not understand. And the dark faces, leaning near her white body, she saw were darkened with red pigment, with lines of yellow round the cheeks. And the dark eyes glittered absorbed, as the hands worked upon the soft white body of the woman.

They were so impersonal, absorbed in something that was beyond her. They never saw her as a personal woman: she could tell that. She was some mystic object to them, some vehicle of passions too remote for her to grasp. Herself in a state of trance, she watched their faces bending over her,

dark, strangely glistening with the transparent red paint, and
lined with bars of yellow. And in this weird, luminous-dark
mask of living face, the eyes were fixed with an unchanging
steadfast gleam, and the purplish-pigmented lips were closed
in a full, sinister, sad grimness. The immense fundamental
sadness, the grimness of ultimate decision, the fixity of revenge, and the nascent exultance of those that are going to
triumph—these things she could read in their faces, as she lay
and was rubbed into a misty glow by their uncanny dark
hands. Her limbs, her flesh, her very bones at last seemed to
be diffusing into a roseate sort of mist, in which her consciousness hovered like some sun-gleam in a flushed cloud.

She knew the gleam would fade, the cloud would go grey.
But at present she did not believe it. She knew she was a
victim; that all this elaborate work upon her was the work of
victimising her. But she did not mind. She wanted it.

Later, they put a short blue tunic on her and took her to
the upper terrace, and presented her to the people. She saw
the plaza below her full of dark faces and of glittering eyes.
There was no pity: only the curious hard exultance. The
people gave a subdued cry when they saw her, and she
shuddered. But she hardly cared.

Next day was the last. She slept in a chamber of the big
house. At dawn they put on her a big blue blanket with a
fringe, and led her out into the plaza, among the throng of
silent, dark-blanketed people. There was pure white snow on
the ground, and the dark people in their dark-brown blankets
looked like inhabitants of another world.

A large drum was slowly pounding, and an old priest was
declaiming from a house-top. But it was not till noon that a
litter came forth, and the people gave that low, animal cry
which was so moving. In the sack-like litter sat the old, old
cacique, his white hair braided with black braid and large
turquoise stones. His face was like a piece of obsidian. He
lifted his hand in token, and the litter stopped in front of her.
Fixing her with his cold eyes, he spoke to her for a few
moments, in his hollow voice. No one translated.

Another litter came, and she was placed in it. Four priests
moved ahead, in their scarlet and yellow and black, with

plumed head-dresses. Then came the litter of the old cacique. Then the light drums began, and two groups of singers burst simultaneously into song, male and wild. And the golden-red, almost naked men, adorned with ceremonial feathers and kilts, the rivers of black hair down their backs, formed into two files and began to tread the dance. So they threaded out of the snowy plaza, in two long, sumptuous lines of dark red-gold and black and fur, swaying with a faint tinkle of bits of shell and flint, winding over the snow between the two bee-clusters of men who sang around the drums.

Slowly they moved out, and her litter, with its attendance of feathered, lurid dancing priests, moved after. Everybody danced the thread of the dance-step, even, subtly, the litter-bearers. And out of the plaza they went, past smoking ovens, on the trail to the great cottonwood trees, that stood like grey-silver lace against the blue sky, bare and exquisite above the snow. The river, diminished, rushed among fangs of ice. The chequer-squares of gardens within fences were all snowy, and the white houses now looked yellowish.

The whole valley glittered intolerably with pure snow, away to the walls of the standing rock. And across the flat cradle of snow-bed wound the long thread of the dance, shaking slowly and sumptuously in its orange and black motion. The high drums thudded quickly, and on the crystal-line frozen air the swell and roar of the chant of savages was like an obsession.

She sat looking out of her litter with big, transfixed blue eyes, under which were the wan markings of her drugged weariness. She knew she was going to die, among the glisten of this snow, at the hands of this savage, sumptuous people. And as she stared at the blaze of the blue sky above the slashed and ponderous mountain, she thought: "I am dead already. What difference does it make, the transition from the dead I am to the dead I shall be, very soon!" Yet her soul sickened and felt wan.

The strange procession trailed on, in perpetual dance, slowly across the plain of snow, and then entered the slopes between the pine trees. She saw the copper-dark men dancing the dance-tread, onwards, between the copper-pale tree trunks. And at last, she, too, in her swaying litter, entered the pine trees.

They were travelling on and on, upwards, across the snow under the trees, past superb shafts of pale, flaked copper, the rustle and shake and tread of the threading dance, penetrating into the forest, into the mountain. They were following a stream-bed: but the stream was dry, like summer, dried up by the frozenness of the head-waters. There were dark, red-bronze willow bushes with wattles like wild hair, and pallid aspen trees looking cold flesh again the snow. Then jutting dark rocks.

At last she could tell that the dancers were moving forward no more. Nearer and nearer she came upon the drums, as to a lair of mysterious animals. Then through the bushes she emerged into a strange amphitheatre. Facing was a great wall of hollow rock, down the front of which hung a great, dripping, fang-like spoke of ice. The ice came pouring over the rock from the precipice above, and then stood arrested, dripping out of high heaven, almost down to the hollow stones where the stream-pool should be below. But the pool was dry.

On either side the dry pool the lines of dancers had formed, and the dance was continuing without intermission, against a background of bushes.

But what she felt was that fanged inverted pinnacle of ice, hanging from the lip of the dark precipice above. And behind the great rope of ice she saw the leopard-like figures of priests climbing the hollow cliff face, to the cave that like a dark socket bored a cavity, an orifice, half-way up the crag.

Before she could realise, her litter-bearers were staggering in the footholds, climbing the rock. She, too, was behind the ice. There it hung, like a curtain that is not spread, but hangs like a great fang. And near above her was the orifice of the cave sinking dark into the rock. She watched it as she swayed upwards.

On the platform of the cave stood the priests, waiting in all their gorgeousness of feathers and fringed robes, watching her ascent. Two of them stooped to help her litter-bearer. And at length she was on the platform of the cave, far in behind the shaft of ice, above the hollow amphitheatre among the bushes below, where men were dancing, and the whole populace of the village was clustered in silence.

The sun was sloping down the afternoon sky, on the left. She knew that this was the shortest day of the year, and the last day of her life. They stood her facing the iridescent column of ice, which fell down marvellously arrested, away in front of her.

Some signal was given, and the dance below stopped. There was now absolute silence. She was given a little to drink, then two priests took off her mantle and her tunic, and in her strange pallor she stood there, between the lurid robes of the priests, beyond the pillar of ice, beyond and above the dark-faced people. The throng below gave the low, wild cry. Then the priest turned her round, so she stood with her back to the open world, her long blonde hair to the people below. And they cried again.

She was facing the cave, inwards. A fire was burning and flickering in the depths. Four priests had taken off their robes, and were almost as naked as she was. They were powerful men in the prime of life, and they kept their dark, painted faces lowered.

From the fire came the old, old priest, with an incense-pan. He was naked and in a state of barbaric ecstasy. He fumigated his victim, reciting at the same time in a hollow voice. Behind him came another robeless priest, with two flint knives.

When she was fumigated, they laid her on a large flat stone, the four powerful men holding her by the outstretched arms and legs. Behind stood the aged man, like a skeleton covered with dark glass, holding a knife and transfixedly watching the sun; and behind him again was another naked priest, with a knife.

She felt little sensation, though she knew all that was happening. Turning to the sky, she looked at the yellow sun. It was sinking. The shaft of ice was like a shadow between her and it. And she realised that the yellow rays were filling half the cave, though they had not reached the altar where the fire was, at the far end of the funnel-shaped cavity.

Yes, the rays were creeping round slowly. As they grew ruddier, they penetrated farther. When the red sun was about to sink, he would shine full through the shaft of ice deep into the hollow of the cave, to the innermost.

She understood now that this was what the men were waiting for. Even those that held her down were bent and twisted round, their black eyes watching the sun with a glittering eagerness, and awe, and craving. The black eyes of the aged cacique were fixed like black mirrors on the sun, as if sightless, yet containing some terrible answer to the reddening winter planet. And all the eyes of the priests were fixed and glittering on the sinking orb, in the reddening, icy silence of the winter afternoon.

They were anxious, terribly anxious, and fierce. Their ferocity wanted something, and they were waiting the moment. And their ferocity was ready to leap out into a mystic exultance, of triumph. But they were anxious.

Only the eyes of the oldest man were not anxious. Black, and fixed, and as if sightless, they watched the sun, seeing beyond the sun. And in their black, empty concentration there was power, power intensely abstract and remote, but deep, deep to the heart of the earth, and the heart of the sun. In absolute motionlessness he watched till the red sun should send his ray through the column of ice. Then the old man would strike, and strike home, accomplish the sacrifice and achieve the power.

The mastery that man must hold, and that passes from race to race.

The Lovely Lady

AT SEVENTY-TWO, Pauline Attenborough could still sometimes be mistaken, in the half-light, for thirty. She really was a wonderfully preserved woman, of perfect *chic*. Of course, it helps a great deal to have the right frame. She would be an exquisite skeleton, and her skull would be an exquisite skull, like that of some Etruscan woman, with feminine charm still in the swerve of the bone and the pretty naïve teeth.

Mrs. Attenborough's face was of the perfect oval, and slightly flat type that wears best. There is no flesh to sag. Her nose rode serenely, in its finely bridged curve. Only her big grey eyes were a tiny bit prominent on the surface of her face, and they gave her away most. The bluish lids were heavy, as if they ached sometimes with the strain of keeping the eyes beneath them arch and bright; and at the corners of the eyes were fine little wrinkles which would slacken with haggardness, then be pulled up tense again, to that bright, gay look like a Leonardo woman who really could laugh outright.

Her niece Cecilia was perhaps the only person in the world who was aware of the invisible little wire which connected Pauline's eye-wrinkles with Pauline's will-power. Only Cecilia *consciously* watched the eyes go haggard and old and tired, and remain so, for hours; until Robert came home. Then ping!—the mysterious little wire that worked between Pauline's will and her face went taut, the weary, haggard, prominent eyes suddenly began to gleam, the eyelids arched, the queer curved eyebrows which floated in such frail arches on Pauline's forehead began to gather a mocking significance, and you had the *real* lovely lady, in all her charm.

She really had the secret of everlasting youth; that is to

say, she could don her youth again like an eagle. But she was sparing of it. She was wise enough not to try being young for too many people. Her son Robert, in the evenings, and Sir Wilfred Knipe sometimes in the afternoon to tea: then occasional visitors on Sunday, when Robert was home: for these she was her lovely and changeless self, that age could not wither, nor custom stale: so bright and kindly and yet subtly mocking, like Mona Lisa, who knew a thing or two. But Pauline knew more, so she needn't be smug at all, she could laugh that lovely mocking Bacchante laugh of hers, which was at the same time never malicious, always good-naturedly tolerant, both of virtues and vices. The former, of course, taking much more tolerating. So she suggested, roguishly.

Only with her niece Cecilia she did not trouble to keep up the glamour. Ciss was not very observant, anyhow: and more than that, she was plain: more still, she was in love with Robert: and most of all, she was thirty, and dependent on her Aunt Pauline. Oh, Cecilia! Why make music for her!

Cecilia, called by her aunt and by her cousin Robert just Ciss, like a cat spitting, was a big dark-complexioned, pug-faced young woman who very rarely spoke, and when she did, couldn't get it out. She was the daughter of a poor Congregational minister who had been, while he lived, brother to Ronald, Aunt Pauline's husband. Ronald and the Congregational minister were both well dead, and Aunt Pauline had had charge of Ciss for the last five years.

They lived all together in a quite exquisite though rather small Queen Anne house some twenty-five miles out of town, secluded in a little dale, and surrounded by small but very quaint and pleasant grounds. It was an ideal place and an ideal life for Aunt Pauline, at the age of seventy-two. When the kingfishers flashed up the little stream in the garden, going under the alders, something still flashed in her heart. She was that kind of woman.

Robert, who was two years older than Ciss, went every day to town, to his chambers in one of the Inns. He was a barrister, and, to his secret but very deep mortification, he earned about a hundred pounds a year. He simply *couldn't* get above that figure, though it was rather easy to get below it. Of course, it didn't matter. Pauline had money. But then what was Pauline's was Pauline's, and though she could give almost lavishly, still, one was always aware of having a *lovely* and *undeserved* present made to one: presents are so much nicer when they are undeserved, Aunt Pauline would say.

Robert too was plain, and almost speechless. He was medium-sized, rather broad and stout, though not fat. Only his creamy, clean-shaven face was rather fat, and sometimes suggestive of an Italian priest, in its silence and its secrecy. But he had grey eyes like his mother, but very shy and uneasy, not bold like hers. Perhaps Ciss was the only person who fathomed his awful shyness and *malaise,* his habitual feeling that he was in the wrong place: almost like a soul that has got into the wrong body. But he never did anything about it. He went up to his chambers and read law. It was, however, all the weird old processes that interested him. He had, unknown to everybody but his mother, a quite extraordinary collection of old Mexican legal documents, reports of processes and trials, pleas, accusations, the weird and awful mixture of ecclesiastical law and common law in seventeenth-century Mexico. He had started a study in this direction through coming across a report of a trial of two English sailors, for murder, in Mexico in 1620, and he had gone on, when the next document was an accusation against a Don Miguel Estrada for seducing one of the nuns of the Sacred Heart Convent in Oaxaca in 1680.

Pauline and her son Robert had wonderful evenings with these old papers. The lovely lady knew a little Spanish. She even looked a trifle Spanish herself, with a high comb and a marvellous dark brown shawl embroidered in thick silvery silk embroidery. So she would sit at the perfect old table, soft as velvet in its deep brown surface, a high comb in her hair, ear-rings with dropping pendants in her ears, her arms bare and still beautiful, a few strings of pearls round her throat, a puce velvet dress on and this or another beautiful shawl, and by candle-light she looked, yes, a Spanish high-bred beauty of thirty-two or three. She set the candles to give her face just the chiaroscuro she knew suited her; her high chair that rose behind her face was done in old green brocade, against which her face emerged like a Christmas rose.

They were always three at table; and they always drank a bottle of champagne: Pauline two glasses, Ciss two glasses, Robert the rest. The lovely lady sparkled and was radiant. Ciss, her black hair bobbed, her broad shoulders in a very nice and becoming dress that Aunt Pauline had helped her to make, stared from her aunt to her cousin and back again, with rather confused, mute, hazel eyes, and played the part of an audience suitably impressed. She *was* impressed, some-where, all the time. And even rendered speechless by Pauline's brilliancy, even after five years. But at the bottom of her consciousness were the data of as weird a document as Robert ever studied: all the things she knew about her aunt and cousin.

Robert was always a gentleman, with an old-fashioned punctilious courtesy that covered his shyness quite complete-ly. He was, and Ciss knew it, more confused than shy. He was worse than she was. Cecilia's own confusion dated from only five years back—Robert's must have started before he was born. In the lovely lady's womb he must have felt *very* confused.

He paid all his attention to his mother, drawn to her as a humble flower to the sun. And yet, priest-like, he was all the time aware, with the tail of his consciousness, that Ciss was there, and that she was a bit shut out of it, and that something wasn't right. He was aware of the third conscious-ness in the room. Whereas to Pauline, her niece Cecilia was an appropriate part of her own setting, rather than a distinct consciousness.

Robert took coffee with his mother and Ciss in the warm drawing-room, where all the furniture was so lovely, all collectors' pieces—Mrs. Attenborough had made her own money, dealing privately in pictures and furniture and rare things from barbaric countries—and the three talked desulto-rily till about eight or half-past. It was very pleasant, very cosy, very homely even: Pauline made a real home cosiness out of much elegant material. The chat was simple, and nearly always bright. Pauline was her *real* self, emanating a friendly mockery and an odd, ironic gaiety. Till there came a little pause.

At which Ciss always rose and said good night and carried out the coffee-tray, to prevent Burnett from intruding any more.

And then! Oh, then, the lovely glowing intimacy of the evening, between mother and son, when they deciphered manuscripts, and discussed points, Pauline with that eagerness of a girl, for which she was famous. And it was quite genuine. In some mysterious way she had *saved up* her power for being thrilled, in connection with a man. Robert, solid, rather quiet and subdued, seemed like the elder of the two: almost like a priest with a young girl pupil. And that was rather how he felt.

Ciss had a flat for herself just across the courtyard, over the old coach-house and stables. There were no horses. Robert kept his car in the coach-house. Ciss had three very nice rooms up there, stretching along in a row one after another, and she had got used to the ticking of the stable clock.

But sometimes she did not go up to her rooms. In the summer she would sit on the lawn, and from the open window of the drawing-room upstairs she would hear Pauline's wonderful heart-searching laugh. And in the winter the young woman would put on a thick coat and walk slowly to the little balustraded bridge over the stream, and then look back at the three lighted windows of that drawing-room where mother and son were so happy together.

Ciss loved Robert, and she believed that Pauline intended the two of them to marry: when she was dead. But poor Robert, he was so convulsed with shyness already, with man or woman. What would he be when his mother was dead—in a dozen more years? He would be just a shell, the shell of a man who had never lived.

The strange unspoken sympathy of the young with one another, when they are overshadowed by the old, was one of the bonds between Robert and Ciss. But another bond, which Ciss did not know how to draw tight, was the bond of passion. Poor Robert, was by nature a passionate man. His silence and his agonised, though hidden, shyness were both the result of a secret physical passionateness. And how Pauline could play on this! Ah, Ciss was not blind to the eyes which he fixed on his mother, eyes fascinated yet humiliated, full of shame. He was ashamed that he was not a man. And he did not love his mother. He was fascinated by her. Competely fascinated. And for the rest, paralysed in a life-long confusion.

Ciss stayed in the garden till the lights leapt up in Pauline's bedroom—about ten o'clock. The lovely lady had retired. Robert would now stay another hour or so, alone. Then he too would retire. Ciss, in the dark outside, sometimes wished she could creep up to him and say: "Oh, Robert! It's all wrong!" But Aunt Pauline would hear. And, anyhow, Ciss couldn't do it. She went off to her own rooms once more, and so for ever.

In the morning coffee was brought up on a tray to each of the three relatives. Ciss had to be at Sir Wilfred Knipe's at nine o'clock, to give two hours' lessons to his little granddaughter. It was her sole serious occupation, except that she played the piano for the love of it. Robert set off to town about nine. And, as a rule, Aunt Pauline appeared at lunch, though sometimes not until tea-time. When she appeared, she looked fresh and young. But she was inclined to fade rather quickly, like a flower without water, in the day-time. Her hour was the candle hour.

So she always rested in the afternoon. When the sun shone, if possible she took a sun-bath. This was one of her secrets. Her lunch was very light, she could take her sun-and-air-bath before noon or after, as it pleased her. Often it was in the afternoon, when the sun shone very warmly into a queer little yew-welled square just behind the stables. Here Ciss stretched out the lying-chair and rugs, and put the light parasol in the silent little enclosure of thick dark yew hedges beyond the red walls of the unused stables. And hither came the lovely lady with her book. Ciss then had to be on guard in one of her own rooms, should her aunt, who was very keen-eared, hear a footstep.

One afternoon it occurred to Cecilia that she herself might while away this rather long afternoon by taking a sun-bath.

She was growing restive. The thought of the flat roof of the stable buildings, to which she could climb from a loft at the end, started her on a new adventure. She often went on to the roof: she had to, to wind up the stable clock, which was a job she had assumed to herself. Now she took a rug, climbed out under the heavens, looked at the sky and the great elm-tops, looked at the sun, then took off her things and lay down perfectly serenely, in a corner of the roof under the parapet, full in the sun.

It was rather lovely, to bask all one's length like this in warm sun and air. Yes, it was very lovely! It even seemed to melt some of the hard bitterness of her heart, some of that core of unspoken resentment which never dissolved. Luxuriously, she spread herself, so that the sun should touch her limbs fully, fully. If she had no other lover, she should have the sun! She rolled voluptuously. And suddenly her heart stood still in her body, and her hair almost rose on end as a voice said very softly, musingly in her ear:

"No, Henry dear! It was not my fault you died instead of marrying that Claudia. No, darling. I was quite, quite willing for you to marry her, unsuitable though she was."

Cecilia sank down on her rug powerless and perspiring with dread. That awful voice, so soft, so musing, yet so unnatural. Not a human voice at all. Yet there must, there must be someone on the roof! Oh! how unspeakably awful!

She lifted her weak head and peeped across the sloping leads. Nobody! The chimneys were far too narrow to shelter anybody. There was nobody on the roof. Then it must be someone in the trees, in the elms. Either that, or terror unspeakable, a bodiless voice! She reared her head a little higher.

And as she did so, came the voice again:

"No, darling! I told you you would tire of her in six months. And you see, it was true, dear. It was true, true, true! I wanted to spare you that. So it wasn't I who made you feel weak and disabled, wanting that very silly Claudia; poor thing, she looked so woebegone afterwards! Wanting her and not wanting her, you got *yourself* into that perplexity, my dear. I only warned you. What else could I do? And you lost your spirit and died without ever knowing me again. It was bitter, bitter——"

The voice faded away. Cecilia subsided weakly on to her rug, after the anguished tension of listening. Oh, it was awful. The sun shone, the sky was blue, all seemed so lovely and afternoony and summery. And yet, oh, horror!—she was going to be forced to believe in the supernatural! And she loathed the supernatural, ghosts and voices and rappings and all the rest.

But that awful creepy bodiless voice, with its rusty sort of whisper of an overtone! It had something so fearfully familiar in it too! and yet was so utterly uncanny. Poor Cecilia could only lie there unclothed, and so all the more agonisingly helpless, inert, collapsed in sheer dread.

And then she heard the thing sigh! A deep sigh that seemed weirdly familiar, yet was not human. "Ah, well; ah, well, the heart must bleed! Better it should bleed than break. It is grief, grief! But it wasn't my fault, dear. And Robert could marry our poor dull Ciss to-morrow, if he wanted her. But he doesn't care about it, so why force him into anything!" The sounds were very uneven, sometimes only a husky sort of whisper. Listen! Listen!

Cecilia was about to give vent to loud and piercing screams of hysteria, when the last two sentences arrested her. All her caution and her cunning sprang alert. It was Aunt Pauline! It must be Aunt Pauline, practising ventriloquism or something like that! What a devil she was!

Where was she? She must be lying down there, right below where Cecilia herself was lying. And it was either some fiend's trick of ventriloquism, or else thought transference that conveyed itself like sound. The sounds were very uneven. Sometimes quite inaudible, sometimes only a brushing sort of noise. Ciss listened intently. No, it could not be ventriloquism. It was worse, some form of thought transference. Some horror of that sort. Cecilia still lay weak and inert, terrified to move, but she was growing calmer with suspicion. It was some diabolic trick of that unnatural woman.

But *what a devil* of a woman! She even knew that she,

Cecilia, had mentally accused her of killing her son Henry. Poor Henry was Robert's elder brother, twelve years older than Robert. He had died suddenly when he was twenty-two, after an awful struggle with himself, because he was passionately in love with a young and very good-looking actress, and his mother had humorously despised him for the attachment. So he had caught some sudden ordinary disease, but the poison had gone to his brain and killed him before he ever regained consciousness. Ciss knew the few facts from her own father. And lately she had been thinking that Pauline was going to kill Robert as she had killed Henry. It was clear murder: a mother murdering her sensitive sons, who were fascinated by her: the Circe!

"I suppose I may as well get up," murmured the dim, unbreaking voice. "Too much sun is as bad as too little. Enough sun, enough love thrill, enough proper food, and not too much of any of them, and a woman might live for ever. I verily believe for ever. If she absorbs as much vitality as she expends! Or perhaps a trifle more!"

It was certainly Aunt Pauline! How, how horrible! She, Ciss, was hearing Aunt Pauline's thoughts. Oh, how ghastly! Aunt Pauline was sending out her thoughts in a sort of radio, and she, Ciss, had to *hear* what her aunt was thinking. How ghastly! How insufferable! One of them would surely have to die.

She twisted and she lay inert and crumpled, staring vacantly in front of her. Vacantly! Vacantly! And her eyes were staring almost into a hole. She was staring into it unseeing, a hole going down in the corner from the lead gutter. It meant nothing to her. Only it frightened her a little more.

When suddenly out of the hole came a sigh and a last whisper. "Ah, well! Pauline! Get up, it's enough for to-day!" Good God! Out of the hole of the rain-pipe! The rain-pipe was acting as a speaking-tube! Impossible! No, quite possible. She had read of it even in some book. And Aunt Pauline, like the old and guilty woman she was, talked aloud to herself. That was it!

A sullen exultance sprang into Ciss's breast. *That* was why she would never have anybody, not even Robert, in her bedroom. That was why she never dozed in a chair, never sat absent-minded anywhere, but went to her room, and kept to her room, except when she roused herself to be alert. When she slackened off, she talked to herself! She talked in a soft little crazy voice to herself. But she was not crazy. It was only her thoughts murmuring themselves aloud.

So she had qualms about poor Henry! Well she might have! Ciss believed that Aunt Pauline had loved her big, handsome, brilliant first-born much more than she loved Robert, and that his death had been a terrible blow and a chagrin to her. Poor Robert had been only ten years old when Henry died. Since then he had been the substitute.

Ah, how awful!

But Aunt Pauline was a strange woman. She had left her husband when Henry was a small child, some years even before Robert was born. There was no quarrel. Sometimes she saw her husband again, quite amicably, but a little mockingly. And she even gave him money.

For Pauline earned all her own. Her father had been a consul in the East and in Naples: and a devoted collector of beautiful and exotic things. When he died, soon after his grandson Henry was born, he left his collection of treasures to his daughter. And Pauline, who had really a passion and a genius for loveliness, whether in texture or form or colour, had laid the basis of her fortune on her father's collection. She had gone on collecting, buying where she could, and selling to collectors and to museums. She was one of the first to sell old, weird African wooden figures to the museums, and ivory carvings from New Guinea. She bought Renoir as soon as she saw his pictures. But not Rousseau. And all by herself she made a fortune.

After her husband died, she had not married again. She was not even *known* to have had lovers. If she did have lovers, it was not among the men who admired her most and paid her devout and open attendance. To these she was a 'friend'.

Cecilia slipped on her clothes and caught up her rug, hastened carefully down the ladder to the loft. As she descended she heard the ringing musical call: "All right, Ciss!"

which meant that the lovely lady was finished, and returning to the house. Even her voice was marvellously young and sonorous, beautifully balanced and self-possessed. So different from the little voice in which she talked to herself. *That* was much more the voice of an old woman.

Ciss hastened round to the yew enclosure, where lay the comfortable chaise-longue with the various delicate rugs. Everything Pauline had was choice, to the fine straw mat on the floor. The great yew walls were beginning to cast long shadows. Only in the corner, where the rugs tumbled their delicate colours, was there hot, still sunshine.

The rugs folded up, the chair lifted away, Cecilia stooped to look at the mouth of the rain-pipe. There it was, in the corner, under a little hood of masonry and just projecting from the thick leaves of the creeper on the wall. If Pauline, lying there, turned her face towards the wall, she would speak into the very mouth of the hole. Cecilia was reassured. She had heard her aunt's thoughts indeed, but by no uncanny agency.

That evening, as if aware of something, Pauline was a little quicker than usual, though she looked her own serene, rather mysterious self. And after coffee she said to Robert and Ciss: "I'm so sleepy. The sun has made me so sleepy. I feel full of sunshine like a bee. I shall go to bed, if you don't mind. You two sit and have a talk."

Cecilia looked quickly at her cousin.

"Perhaps you would rather be alone," she said to him.

"No, no," he replied. "Do keep me company for a while, if it doesn't bore you."

The windows were open, the scent of the honeysuckle wafted in with the sound of an owl. Robert smoked in silence. There was a sort of despair in the motionless, rather squat body. He looked like a caryatid bearing a weight.

"Do you remember Cousin Henry?" Cecilia asked him suddenly.

He looked up in surprise.

"Yes, very well," he said.

"What did he look like?" she said, glancing into her cousin's big, secret-troubled eyes, in which there was so much frustration.

"Oh, he was handsome: tall and fresh-coloured, with mother's soft brown hair." As a matter of fact, Pauline's hair was grey. "The ladies admired him very much; he was at all the dances."

"And what kind of character had he?"

"Oh, very good-natured and jolly. He liked to be amused. He was rather quick and clever, like mother, and very good company."

"And did he love your mother?"

"Very much. She loved him too—better than she does me, as a matter of fact. He was so much more nearly her idea of a man."

"Why was he more her idea of a man?"

"Tall—handsome—attractive, and very good company— and would, I believe, have been very successful at law. I'm afraid I am merely negative in all those respects."

Ciss looked at him attentively, with her slow-thinking hazel eyes. Under his impassive mask, she knew he suffered.

"Do you think you are so much more negative than he?" she said.

He did not lift his face. But after a few moments he replied:

"My life, certainly, is a negative affair."

She hesitated before she dared ask him:

"And do you mind?"

He did not answer her at all. Her heart sank.

"You see, I am afraid my life is as negative as yours is," she said. "And I'm beginning to mind bitterly. I'm thirsty."

She saw his creamy, well-bred hand tremble.

"I suppose," he said, without looking at her, "one will rebel when it is too late."

That was queer, from him.

"Robert," she said, "do you like me at all?"

She saw his dusky, creamy face, so changeless in its folds, go pale. "I am very fond of you," he murmured.

"Won't you kiss me? Nobody ever kisses me," she said pathetically.

He looked at her, his eyes strange with fear and a certain haughtiness. Then he rose and came softly over to her and kissed her gently on the cheek.

"It's an awful shame, Ciss!" he said softly.

She caught his hand and pressed it to her breast.

"And sit with me some time in the garden," she said, murmuring with difficulty. "Won't you?"

He looked at her anxiously and searchingly.

"What about mother!" he said.

Ciss smiled a funny little smile, and looked into his eyes. He suddenly flushed crimson, turning aside his face. It was a painful sight.

"I know," he said, "I am no lover of women."

He spoke with sarcastic stoicism against himself, but even she did not know the shame it was to him.

"You never try to be!" she said.

Again his eyes changed uncannily.

"Does one have to try?" he said.

"Why, yes! One never does anything if one doesn't try."

He went pale again.

"Perhaps you are right," he said.

In a few minutes she left him and went to her room. At least, she had tried to take off the everlasting lid from things.

The weather continued sunny, Pauline continued her sun-baths, and Ciss lay on the roof eavesdropping in the literal sense of the word. But Pauline was not to be heard. No sound came up the pipe. She must be lying with her face away into the open. Ciss listened with all her might. She could just detect the faintest, faintest murmur away below, but no audible syllable.

And at night, under the stars, Cecilia sat and waited in silence, on the seat which kept in view the drawing-room windows and the side door into the garden. She saw the light go up in her aunt's room. She saw the lights at last go out in the drawing-room. And she waited. But he did not come. She stayed on in the darkness half the night, while the owl hooted. But she stayed alone.

Two days she heard nothing, her aunt's thoughts were not revealed and at evening nothing happened. Then the second night, as she sat with heavy, helpless persistence in the garden, suddenly she started. He had come out. She rose and went softly over the grass to him.

"Don't speak," he murmured.

And in silence, in the dark, they walked down the garden and over the little bridge to the paddock, where the hay, cut very late, was in cock. There they stood disconsolate under the stars.

"You see," he said, "how can I ask for love, if I don't feel any love in myself. You know I have a real regard for you——"

"How can you feel any love, when you never feel anything?" she said.

"That is true," he replied.

And she waited for what next.

"And how can I marry?" he said. "I am a failure even at making money. I can't ask my mother for money."

She sighed deeply.

"Then don't bother yet about marrying," she said. "Only love me a little. Won't you?"

He gave a short laugh.

"It sounds so atrocious, to say it is hard to begin," he said.

She sighed again. He was so stiff to move.

"Shall we sit down a minute," she said. And then as they sat on the hay, she added: "May I touch you? Do you mind?"

"Yes, I mind! But do as you wish," he replied, with that mixture of shyness and queer candour which made him a little ridiculous, as he knew quite well. But in his heart there was almost murder.

She touched his black, always tidy hair with her fingers.

"I suppose I shall rebel one day," he said again, suddenly.

They sat some time, till it grew chilly. And he held her hand fast, but he never put his arms round her. At last she rose and went indoors, saying good night.

The next day, as Cecilia lay stunned and angry on the roof, taking her sun-bath, and becoming hot and fierce with sunshine, suddenly she started. A terror seized her in spite of herself. It was the voice.

"Caro, caro, tu non l hai visto!" it was murmuring away, in a language Cecilia did not understand. She lay and writhed her limbs in the sun, listening intently to words she could not follow. Softly, whisperingly, with infinite caressiveness and yet with that subtle, insidious arrogance under its velvet, came the voice, murmuring in Italian: *"Bravo, si molto bravo, poverino, ma uomo come te non lo sara mai, mai, mai!"* Oh, especially in Italian Cecilia heard the poisonous charm of the voice, so caressive, so soft and flexible, yet so utterly egoistic. She hated it with intensity as it sighed and whispered out of nowhere. Why, why should it be so delicate, so subtle and flexible and beautifully controlled, while she herself was so clumsy! Oh, poor Cecilia, she writhed in the afternoon sun, knowing her own clownish clumsiness and lack of suavity, in comparison.

"No, Robert dear, you will never be the man your father was, though you have some of his looks. He was a marvellous lover, soft as a flower, yet piercing as a humming-bird. No, Robert dear, you will never know how to serve a woman as Monsignor Mauro did. *Cara, cara mia bellissima, ti ho aspettato come l'agonizzante aspetta la morte, morte deliziosa, quasi quasi troppo deliziosa per un' anima humana*—Soft as a flower, yet probing like a humming-bird. He gave himself to a woman as he gave himself to God. Mauro! Mauro! How you loved me!"

The voice ceased in reverie, and Cecilia knew what she had guessed before, that Robert was not the son of her Uncle Ronald, but of some Italian.

"I am disappointed in you, Robert. There is no poignancy in you. Your father was a Jesuit, but he was the most perfect and poignant lover in the world. You are a Jesuit like a fish in a tank. And that Ciss of yours is the cat fishing for you. It is less edifying even than poor Henry."

Cecilia suddenly bent her mouth down to the tube, and said in a deep voice:

"Leave Robert alone! Don't kill him as well."

There was a dead silence, in the hot July afternoon that was lowering for thunder. Cecilia lay prostrate, her heart beating in great thumps. She was listening as if her whole soul were an ear. At last she caught the whisper:

"Did someone speak?"

She leaned again to the mouth of the tube.

"Don't kill Robert as you killed me," she said with slow enunciation, and a deep but small voice.

"Ah," came the sharp little cry. "Who is that speaking?"

"Henry!" said the deep voice.

There was a dead silence. Poor Cecilia lay with all the use gone out of her. And there was dead silence. Till at last came the whisper:

"I didn't kill Henry. No, NO! Henry, surely you can't blame me! I loved you, dearest. I only wanted to help you."

"You killed me!" came the deep, artificial, accusing voice. "Now, let Robert live. Let him go! Let him marry!"

There was a pause.

"How very, very awful!" mused the whispering voice. "Is it possible, Henry, you are a spirit, and you condemn me?"

"Yes! I condemn you!"

Cecilia felt all her pent-up rage going down that rain-pipe. At the same time, she almost laughed. It was awful.

She lay and listened and listened. No sound! As if time had ceased, she lay inert in the weakening sun. The sky was yellowing. Quickly she dressed herself, went down, and out to the corner of the stables.

"Aunt Pauline!" she called discreetly. "Did you hear thunder?"

"Yes! I am going in. Don't wait," came a feeble voice.

Cecilia retired, and from the loft watched, spying as the figure of the lovely lady, wrapped in a lovely wrap of old blue silk, went rather totteringly to the house.

The sky gradually darkened, Cecilia hastened in with the rugs. Then the storm broke. Aunt Pauline did not appear to tea. She found the thunder trying. Robert also did not arrive till after tea, in the pouring rain. Cecilia went down the covered passage to her own house, and dressed carefully for dinner, putting some white columbines at her breast.

The drawing-room was lit with a softly-shaded lamp. Robert, dressed, was waiting, listening to the rain. He too seemed strangely cracking and on edge. Cecilia came in with the white flowers nodding at her breast. Robert was watching her curiously, a new look on his face. Cecilia went to the bookshelves near the door, and was peering for something, listening acutely. She heard a rustle, then the door softly opening. And as it opened, Ciss suddenly switched on the strong electric light by the door.

Her aunt, in a dress of black lace over ivory colour, stood in the doorway. Her face was made up, but haggard with a look of unspeakable irritability, as if years of suppressed exasperation and dislike of her fellow-men had suddenly crumpled her into an old witch.

"Oh, aunt!" cried Cecilia.

"Why, mother, you're a little old lady!" came the astounded voice of Robert: like an astonished boy: as if it were a joke.

"Have you only just found it out?" snapped the old woman venomously.

"Yes! Why, I thought——" his voice tailed out in misgiving.

The haggard, old Pauline, in a frenzy of exasperation, said:

"Aren't we going down?"

She had never even noticed the excess of light, a thing she shunned. And she went downstairs almost tottering.

At table she sat with her face like a crumpled mask of unspeakable irritability. She looked old, very old, and like a witch. Robert and Cecilia fetched furtive glances at her. And Ciss, watching Robert, saw that he was so astonished and repelled by his mother's looks, that he was another man.

"What kind of a drive home did you have?" snapped Pauline, with an almost gibbering irritability.

"It rained, of course," he said.

"How clever of you to have found that out!" said his mother, with the grisly grin of malice that had succeeded her arch smirk.

"I don't understand," he said with quiet suavity.

"It's apparent," said his mother, rapidly and sloppily eating her food.

She rushed through the meal like a crazy dog, to the utter consternation of the servant. And the moment it was over, she darted in a queer, crab-like way upstairs. Robert and Cecilia followed her, thunderstruck, like two conspirators.

"You pour the coffee. I loathe it! I'm going! Good night!" said the old woman, in a succession of sharp shots. And she scrambled out of the room.

There was a dead silence. At last he said:

"I'm afraid mother isn't well. I must persuade her to see a doctor."

"Yes!" said Cecilia.

The evening passed in silence. Robert and Ciss stayed on in the drawing-room, having lit a fire. Outside was cold rain. Each pretended to read. They did not want to separate. The evening passed with ominous mysteriousness, yet quickly.

At about ten o'clock, the door suddenly opened, and Pauline appeared in a blue wrap. She shut the door behind her, and came to the fire. Then she looked at the two young people in hate, real hate.

"You two had better get married quickly," she said in an ugly voice. "It would look more decent; such a passionate pair of lovers!"

Robert looked up at her quietly.

"I thought you believed that cousins should not marry, mother," he said.

"I do! But you're not cousins. Your father was an Italian priest." Pauline held her daintily-slippered foot to the fire, in an old coquettish gesture. Her body tried to repeat all the old graceful gestures. But the nerve had snapped, so it was a rather dreadful caricature.

"Is that really true, mother?" he asked.

"True! What do you think? He was a distinguished man, or he wouldn't have been my lover. He was far too distinguished a man to have had you for a son. But that joy fell to me."

"How unfortunate all round," he said slowly.

"Unfortunate for you? *You* were lucky. It was *my* misfortune," she said acidly to him.

She was really a dreadful sight, like a piece of lovely

Venetian glass that has been dropped, and gathered up again in horrible, sharp-edged fragments.

Suddenly she left the room again.

For a week it went on. She did not recover. It was as if every nerve in her body had suddenly started screaming in an insanity of discordance. The doctor came, and gave her sedatives, for she never slept. Without drugs, she never slept at all, only paced back and forth in her room, looking hideous and evil, reeking with malevolence. She could not bear to see either her son or her niece. Only when either of them came, she asked in pure malice:

"Well! When's the wedding! Have you celebrated the nuptials yet?"

At first Cecilia was stunned by what she had done. She realised vaguely that her aunt, once a definite thrust of condemnation had penetrated her beautiful armour, had just collapsed squirming inside her shell. It was too terrible. Ciss was almost terrified into repentance. Then she thought: This is what she always was. Now let her live the rest of her days in her true colours.

But Pauline would not live long. She was literally shrivelling away. She kept to her room, and saw no one. She had her mirrors taken away.

Robert and Cecilia sat a good deal together. The jeering of the mad Pauline had not driven them apart, as she had hoped. But Cecilia dared not confess to him what she had done.

"Do you think your mother ever loved anybody?" Ciss asked him tentatively, rather wistfully, one evening.

He looked at her fixedly.

"Herself!" he said at last.

"She didn't even *love* herself," said Ciss. "It was something else—what was it?" She lifted a troubled, utterly puzzled face to him.

"Power!" he said curtly.

"But what power?" she asked. "I don't understand."

"Power to feed on other lives," he said bitterly. "She was beautiful, and she fed on life. She has fed on me as she fed on Henry. She put a sucker into one's soul and sucked up one's essential life."

"And don't you forgive her?"

"No."

"Poor Aunt Pauline!"

But even Ciss did not mean it. She was only aghast.

"I *know* I've got a heart," he said, passionately striking his breast. "But it's almost sucked dry. I *know* people who want power over others."

Ciss was silent; what was there to say?

And two days later, Pauline was found dead in her bed, having taken too much veronal, for her heart was weakened. From the grave even she hit back at her son and her niece. She left Robert the noble sum of one thousand pounds; and Ciss one hundred. All the rest, with the nucleus of her valuable antiques, went to form the 'Pauline Attenborough Museum'.

Rawdon's Roof

RAWDON WAS the sort of man who said, privately, to his men friends, over a glass of wine after dinner: "No woman shall sleep again under my roof!"

He said it with pride, rather vaunting, pursing his lips. "Even my housekeeper goes home to sleep."

But the housekeeper was a gentle old thing of about sixty, so it seemed a little fantastic. Moreover, the man had a wife, of whom he was secretly rather proud, as a piece of fine property, and with whom he kept up a very witty correspondence, epistolary, and whom he treated with humorous gallantry when they occasionally met for half an hour. Also he had a love affair going on. At least, if it wasn't a love affair, what was it? However!

"No, I've come to the determination that no woman shall ever sleep under my roof again—not even a female cat!"

One looked at the roof, and wondered what it had done amiss. Besides, it wasn't his roof. He only rented the house. What does a man mean, anyhow, when he says "my roof"? *My* roof! The only roof I am conscious of having, myself, is the top of my head. However, he hardly can have meant that no woman should sleep under the elegant dome of his skull. Though there's no telling. You see the top of a sleek head through a window, and you say: "By Jove, what a pretty girl's head!" And after all, when the individual comes out, it's in trousers.

The point, however, is that Rawdon said so emphatically— no, not emphatically, succinctly: "No woman shall ever again sleep under my roof." It was a case of futurity. No doubt he had had his ceilings whitewashed, and their memories put out. Or rather, repainted, for it was a handsome wooden

457

ceiling. Anyhow, if ceilings have eyes, as walls have ears, then Rawdon had given his ceilings a new outlook, with a new coat of paint, and all memory of any woman's having slept under them—for after all, in decent circumstances we sleep under ceilings, not under roofs—was wiped out for ever.

"And will you neither sleep under any woman's roof?"

That pulled him up rather short. He was not prepared to sauce his gander as he had sauced his goose. Even I could see the thought flitting through his mind, that some of his pleasantest holidays depended on the charm of his hostess. Even some of the nicest hotels were run by women.

"Ah! Well! That's not quite the same thing, you know. When one leaves one's own house one gives up the keys of circumstance, so to speak. But, as far as possible, I make it a rule not to sleep under a roof that is openly, and obviously, and obtrusively a woman's roof!"

"Quite!" said I with a shudder. "So do I!"

Now I understood his mysterious love affair less than ever. He was never known to speak of this love affair: he did not even write about it to his wife. The lady—for she was a lady—lived only five minutes' walk from Rawdon. She had a husband, but he was in diplomatic service or something like that, which kept him occupied in the sufficiently-far distance. Yes, far enough. And, as a husband, he was a complete diplomat. A balance of power. If he was entitled to occupy the wide field of the world, she, the other and contrasting power, might concentrate and consolidate her position at home.

She was a charming woman, too, and even a beautiful woman. She had two charming children, long-legged, stalky, clove-pink-half-opened sort of children. But really charming. And she was a woman with a certain mystery. She never talked. She never said anything about herself. Perhaps she suffered; perhaps she was frightfully happy, and made *that* her cause for silence. Perhaps she was wise enough to be beautifully silent about her happiness. Certainly she never mentioned her sufferings, or even her trials: and certainly she must have a fair handful of the latter, for Alec Drummond sometimes fled home in the teeth of a gale of debts. He simply got through his own money and through hers, and, third and fatal stride, through other people's as well. Then something had to be done about it. And Janet, dear soul, had to put her hat on and take journeys. But she never said anything of it. At least, she did just hint that Alec didn't *quite* make enough money to meet expenses. But after all, we don't go about with our eyes shut, and Alec Drummond, whatever else he did, didn't hide his prowess under a bushel.

Rawdon and he were quite friendly, but really! None of them ever talked. Drummond didn't talk, he just went off and behaved in his own way. And though Rawdon would chat away till the small hours, *he* never 'talked'. Not to his nearest male friend did he ever mention Janet save as a very pleasant woman and his neighbour: he admitted he adored her children. They often came to see him.

And one felt about Rawdon, he was making a mystery of something. And that was rather irritating. He went every day to see Janet, and of course we saw him going: going or coming. How can one help but see? But he always went in the morning, at about eleven, and did not stay for lunch: or he went in the afternoon, and came home to dinner. Apparently he was never there in the evening. Poor Janet, she lived like a widow.

Very well, if Rawdon wanted to make it so blatantly obvious that it was only platonic, purely platonic, why wasn't he natural? Why didn't he say simply: "I'm very fond of Janet Drummond, she is my very dear friend?" Why did he sort of curl up at the very mention of her name, and curdle into silence: or else say rather forcedly: "Yes, she is a charming woman. I see a good deal of her, but chiefly for the children's sake. I'm devoted to the children!" Then he would look at one in such a curious way, as if he were hiding something. And after all, what was there to hide? If he was the woman's friend, why not? It could be a charming friendship. And if he were her lover, why, heaven bless me, he ought to have been proud of it, and showed just a glint, just an honest man's glint.

But no, never a glint of pride or pleasure in the relation

either way. Instead of that, this rather theatrical reserve. Janet, it is true, was just as reserved. If she could, she avoided mentioning his name. Yet one knew, sure as houses, she felt something. One suspected her of being more in love with Rawdon than ever she had been with Alec. And one felt that there was a hush put upon it all. She had had a hush put upon her. By whom? By both the men? Or by Rawdon only? Or by Drummond? Was it for her husband's sake? Impossible! For her children's? But why! Her children were devoted to Rawdon.

It now had become the custom for them to go to him three times a week, for music. I don't mean he taught them the piano. Rawdon was a very refined musical amateur. He had them sing, in their delicate girlish voices, delicate little songs, and really he succeeded wonderfully with them; he made them so true, which children rarely are, musically, and so pure and effortless, like little flamelets of sound. It really was rather beautiful, and sweet of him. And he taught them *music*, the delicacy of the feel of it. They had a regular teacher for the practice.

Even the little girls, in their young little ways, were in love with Rawdon! So if their mother were in love too, in her ripened womanhood, why not?

Poor Janet! She was so still, and so elusive: the hush upon her! She was rather like a half-opened rose that somebody had tied a string round, so that it couldn't open any more. But why? Why? In her there was a real touch of mystery. One could never *ask* her, because one knew her heart was too keenly involved: or her pride.

Whereas there was, really, no mystery about Rawdon, refined and handsome and subtle as he was. He *had* no mystery: at least, to a man. What *he* wrapped himself up in was a certain amount of mystification.

Who wouldn't be irritated to hear a fellow saying, when for months and months he has been paying a daily visit to a lonely and very attractive woman—nay, lately even a twice-daily visit, even if always before sundown—to hear him say, pursing his lips after a sip of his own very moderate port:

"I've taken a vow that no woman shall sleep under my roof again!"

I almost snapped out! "Oh, what the hell! And what about your Janet?" But I remembered in time, it was not *my* affair, and if he wanted to have his mystifications, let him have them.

If he meant he wouldn't have his wife sleep under his roof again, that one could understand. They were really very witty with one another, he and she, but fatally and damnably married.

Yet neither wanted a divorce. And neither put the slightest claim to any control over the other's behaviour. He said: "Women live on the moon, men on the earth." And she said: "I don't mind in the least if he loves Janet Drummond, poor thing. It would be a change for him, from loving himself. And a change for her, if somebody loved her———"

Poor Janet! But he wouldn't have her sleep under his roof, no, not for any money. And apparently he never slept under hers—if she could be said to have one. So what the deuce?

Of course, if they were friends, just friends, all right! But then in that case, why start talking about not having a woman sleep under your roof? Pure mystification!

The cat never came out of the bag. But one evening I distinctly heard it mewing inside its sack, and I even believe I saw a claw through the canvas.

It was in November—everything much as usual—myself pricking my ears to hear if the rain had stopped, and I could go home, because I was just a little bored about 'cornemuse' music. I had been having dinner with Rawdon, and listening to him ever since on his favourite topic: not, of course, women, and why they shouldn't sleep under his roof, but fourteenth-century melody and windbag accompaniment.

It was not late—not yet ten o'clock—but I was restless, and wanted to go home. There was no longer any sound of rain. And Rawdon was perhaps going to make a pause in his monologue.

Suddenly there was a tap at the door, and Rawdon's man, Hawken, edged in. Rawdon, who had been a major in some fantastic capacity during the war, had brought Hawken back with him. This fresh-faced man of about thirty-five appeared in the doorway with an intensely blank and bewildered look on his face. He was really an extraordinarily good actor.

"A lady, sir!" he said, with a look of utter blankness.

"A what?" snapped Rawdon.

"A lady!"—then with a most discreet drop in his voice: "Mrs. Drummond, sir!" He looked modestly down at his feet.

Rawdon went deathly white, and his lips quivered.

"Mrs. Drummond! Where?"

Hawken lifted his eyes to his master in a fleeting glance.

"I showed her into the dining-room, there being no fire in the drawing-room."

Rawdon got to his feet and took two or three agitated strides. He could not make up his mind. At last he said, his lips working with agitation:

"Bring her in here."

Then he turned with a theatrical gesture to me.

"What this is all about, I *don't* know," he said.

"Let me clear out," said I, making for the door.

He caught me by the arm.

"No, for God's sake! For God's sake, stop and see me through!"

He gripped my arm till it really hurt, and his eyes were quite wild. I did not know my Olympic Rawdon.

Hastily I backed away to the side of the fire—we were in Rawdon's room, where the books and piano were—and Mrs. Drummond appeared in the doorway. She was much paler than usual, being a rather warm-coloured woman, and she glanced at me with big reproachful eyes, as much as to say: You intruder! You interloper! For my part, I could do nothing but stare. She wore a black wrap, which I knew quite well, over her black dinner-dress.

"Rawdon!" she said, turning to him and blotting out my existence from her consciousness. Hawken softly closed the door, and I could *feel* him standing on the threshold outside, listening keen as a hawk.

"Sit down, Janet," said Rawdon, with a grimace of a sour smile, which he could not get rid of once he had started it, so that his face looked very odd indeed, like a mask which he was unable either to fit on or take off. He had several conflicting expressions all at once, and they had all stuck.

She let her wrap slip back on her shoulders, and knitted her white fingers against her skirt, pressing down her arms, and gazing at him with a terrible gaze. I began to creep to the door.

Rawdon started after me.

"No, don't go! Don't go! I specially want you not to go," he said in extreme agitation.

I looked at her. She was looking at him with a heavy, sombre kind of stare. Me she absolutely ignored. Not for a second could she forgive me for existing on the earth. I slunk back to my post behind the leather arm-chair, as if hiding.

"Do sit down, Janet," he said to her again. "And have a smoke. What will you drink?"

"No, thanks!" she said, as if it were one word slurred out. "No, thanks."

And she proceeded again to fix him with that heavy, portentous stare.

He offered her a cigarette, his hand trembling as he held out the silver box.

"Nothanks," she slurred out again, not even looking at the box, but keeping him fixed with that dark and heavy stare.

He turned away, making a great delay lighting a cigarette, with his back to her, to get out of the stream of that stare. He carefully went for an ash-tray, and put it carefully within reach—all the time trying not to be swept away on that stare. And she stood with her fingers locked, her straight, plump, handsome arms pressed downwards against her skirt, and she gazed at him.

He leaned his elbow on the mantelpiece abstractedly for a moment—then he started suddenly, and rang the bell. She turned her eyes from him for a moment, to watch his middle finger pressing the bell button. Then there was a tension of waiting, an interruption in the previous tension. We waited. Nobody came. Rawdon rang again.

"That's very curious!" he murmured to himself. Hawken was usually so prompt. Hawken, not being a woman, slept under the roof, so there was no excuse for his not answering the bell. The tension in the room had now changed quality, owing to this new suspense. Poor Janet's sombre stare became gradually loosened, so to speak. Attention was divided. Where was Hawken? Rawdon rang the bell a third time, a long peal. And now Janet was no longer the centre of suspense. Where was Hawken? The question loomed large over every other.

"I'll just look in the kitchen," said I, making for the door.

"No, no. I'll go," said Rawdon.

But I was in the passage—and Rawdon was on my heels.

The kitchen was very tidy and cheerful, but empty; only a bottle of beer and two glasses stood on the table. To Rawdon the kitchen was as strange a world as to me—he never entered the servants' quarters. But to me it was curious that the bottle of beer was empty, and both the glasses had been used. I knew Rawdon wouldn't notice.

"That's very curious!" said Rawdon: meaning the absence of his man.

At that moment we heard a step on the servants' stairs, and Rawdon opened the door, to reveal Hawken descending with an armful of sheets and things.

"What are you doing?"

"Why!——" and a pause. "I was airing the clean laundry, like—not to waste the fire last thing."

Hawken descended into the kitchen with a very flushed face and very bright eyes and rather ruffled hair, and proceeded to spread the linen on chairs before the fire.

"I hope I've not done wrong, sir," he said in his most winning manner. "Was you ringing?"

"Three times! Leave that linen and bring a bottle of the fizz."

"I'm sorry, sir. You can't hear the bell from the front, sir."

It was perfectly true. The house was small, but it had been built for a very nervous author, and the servants' quarters were shut off, padded off from the rest of the house.

Rawdon said no more about the sheets and things, but he looked more peaked than ever.

We went back to the music-room. Janet had gone to the

hearth, and stood with her hand on the mantel. She looked round at us, baffled.

"We're having a bottle of fizz," said Rawdon. "Do let me take your wrap."

"And where was Hawken?" she asked satirically.

"Oh, busy somewhere upstairs."

"He's a busy young man, that!" she said sardonically. And she sat uncomfortably on the edge of the chair where I had been sitting.

When Hawken came with the tray, she said:

"I'm not going to drink."

Rawdon appealed to me, so I took a glass. She looked inquiringly at the flushed and bright-eyed Hawken, as if she understood something.

The manservant left the room. We drank our wine, and the awkwardness returned.

"Rawdon!" she said suddenly, as if she were firing a revolver at him. "Alec came home to-night in a bigger mess than ever, and wanted to make love to me to get it off his mind. I can't stand it any more. I'm in love with you, and I simply can't stand Alec getting too near to me. He's dangerous when he's crossed—and when he's worked up. So I just came here. I didn't see what else I could do."

She left off as suddenly as a machine-gun leaves off firing. We were just dazed.

"You are quite right," Rawdon began, in a vague and neutral tone. . . .

"I am, am I not?" she said eagerly.

"I'll tell you what I'll do," he said. "I'll go round to the hotel to-night, and you can stay here."

"Under the kindly protection of Hawken, you mean!" she said, with quiet sarcasm.

"Why!—I could send Mrs. Betts, I suppose," he said.

Mrs. Betts was his housekeeper.

"You couldn't stay and protect me yourself?" she said quietly.

"I! I! Why, I've made a vow—haven't I, Joe?"—he turned to me—"not to have any woman sleep under my roof again."—He got the mixed sour smile on his face.

She looked up at the ceiling for a moment, then lapsed into silence. Then she said:

"Sort of monastery, so to speak!"

And she rose and reached for her wrap, adding:

"I'd better go, then."

"Joe will see you home," he said.

She faced round on me.

"Do you mind *not* seeing me home, Mr. Bradley?" she said, gazing at me.

"Not if you don't want me," said I.

"Hawken will drive you," said Rawdon.

"Oh, no, he won't!" she said. "I'll walk. Good night."

"I'll get my hat," stammered Rawdon, in an agony. "Wait! Wait! The gate will be locked."

"It was open when I came," she said.

He rang for Hawken to unlock the iron doors at the end of the short drive, whilst he himself huddled into a greatcoat and scarf, fumbling for a flashlight.

"You won't go till I come back, will you?" he pleaded to me. "I'd be awfully glad if you'd stay the night. The sheets *will* be aired."

I had to promise—and he set off with an umbrella, in the rain, at the same time asking Hawken to take a flashlight and go in front. So that was how they went, in single file along the path over the fields to Mrs. Drummond's house, Hawken in front, with flashlight and umbrella, curving round to light up in front of Mrs. Drummond, who, with umbrella only, walked isolated between two lights, Rawdon shining his flashlight on her from the rear from under his umbrella. I turned indoors.

So that was over! At least, for the moment!

I thought I would go upstairs and see how damp the bed in the guest-chamber was before I actually stayed the night with Rawdon. He never had guests—perferred to go away himself.

The guest-chamber was a good room across a passage and round a corner from Rawdon's room—its door just opposite the padded service-door. This latter service-door stood open, and a light shone through. I went into the spare bedroom, switching on the light.

To my surprise, the bed looked as if it had just been left—the sheets tumbled, the pillows pressed. I put in my hands under the bedclothes, and it was warm. Very curious!

As I stood looking round in mild wonder, I heard a voice call softly: "Joe!"

"Yes!" said I instinctively, and, though startled, strode at once out of the room and through the servants' door, towards the voice. Light shone from the open doorway of one of the servants' rooms.

There was a muffled little shriek, and I was standing looking into what was probably Hawken's bedroom, and seeing a soft and pretty white leg and a very pretty feminine posterior very thinly dimmed in a rather short night-dress, just in the act of climbing into a narrow little bed, and, then arrested, the owner of the pretty posterior burying her face in the bedclothes, to be invisible, like the ostrich in the sand.

I discreetly withdrew, went downstairs and poured myself a glass of wine. And very shortly Rawdon returned looking like Hamlet in the last act.

He said nothing, neither did I. We sat and merely smoked. Only as he was seeing me upstairs to bed, in the now immaculate bedroom, he said pathetically:

"Why aren't women content to be what a man wants them to be?"

"Why aren't they!" said I wearily.

"I thought I had made everything clear," he said.

"You start at the wrong end," said I.

And as I said it, the picture came into my mind of the pretty feminine butt-end in Hawken's bedroom. Yes, Hawken made better starts, wherever he ended.

When he brought me my cup of tea in the morning, he was was very soft and cat-like. I asked him what sort of day it was, and he asked me if I'd had a good night, and was I comfortable.

"Very comfortable!" said I. "But I turned you out, I'm afraid."

"Me, sir?" He turned on me a face of utter bewilderment.

But I looked him in the eye.

"Is your name Joe?" I asked him.

"You're right, sir."

"So is mine," said I. "However, I didn't see her face, so it's all right. I suppose you *were* a bit tight, in that little bed!"

"Well, sir!" and he flashed me a smile of amazing impudence, and lowered his tone to utter confidence. "This is the best bed in the house, this is." And he touched it softly.

"You've not tried them all, surely?"

A look of indignant horror on his face!

"No, sir, indeed I haven't."

That day, Rawdon left for London, on his way to Tunis, and Hawken was to follow him. The roof of his house looked just the same.

The Drummonds moved too—went away somewhere, and left a lot of unsatisfied tradespeople behind.

The Rocking-Horse Winner

THERE WAS a woman who was beautiful, who started with all the advantages, yet she had no luck. She married for love, and the love turned to dust. She had bonny children, yet she felt they had been thrust upon her, and she could not love them. They looked at her coldly, as if they were finding fault with her. And hurriedly she felt she must cover up some fault in herself. Yet what it was that she must cover up she never knew. Nevertheless, when her children were present, she always felt the centre of her heart go hard. This troubled her, and in her manner she was all the more gentle and anxious for her children, as if she loved them very much. Only she herself knew that at the centre of her heart was a hard little place that could not feel love, no, not for anybody. Everybody else said of her: "She is such a good mother. She adores her children." Only she herself, and her children themselves, knew it was not so. They read it in each other's eyes.

There were a boy and two little girls. They lived in a pleasant house, with a garden, and they had discreet servants, and felt themselves superior to anyone in the neighbourhood.

Although they lived in style, they felt always an anxiety in the house. There was never enough money. The mother had a small income, and the father had a small income, but not nearly enough for the social position which they had to keep up. The father went into town to some office. But though he had good prospects, these prospects never materialised. There was always the grinding sense of the shortage of money, though the style was always kept up.

At last the mother said: "I will see if *I* can't make something." But she did not know where to begin. She racked her brains, and tried this thing and the other, but could not find anything successful. The failure made deep lines come into her face. Her children were growing up, they would have to go to school. There must be more money, there must be more money. The father, who was always very handsome and expensive in his tastes, seemed as if he never would be able to do anything worth doing. And the mother, who had a great belief in herself, did not succeed any better, and her tastes were just as expensive.

And so the house came to be haunted by the unspoken phrase: *There must be more money! There must be more money!* The children could hear it all the time, though nobody said it aloud. They heard it at Christmas, when the expensive and splendid toys filled the nursery. Behind the shining modern rocking-horse, behind the smart doll's house, a voice would start whispering: "There *must* be more money! There *must* be more money!" And the children would stop playing, to listen for a moment. They would look into each other's eyes, to see if they had all heard. And each one saw in the eyes of the other two that they too had heard. "There *must* be more money! There *must* be more money!"

It came whispering from the springs of the still-swaying rocking-horse, and even the horse, bending his wooden, champing head, heard it. The big doll, sitting so pink and smirking in her new pram, could hear it quite plainly, and seemed to be smirking all the more self-consciously because of it. The foolish puppy, too, that took the place of the teddy-bear, he was looking so extraordinarily foolish for no other reason but that he heard the secret whisper all over the house: "There *must* be more money!"

Yet nobody ever said it aloud. The whisper was everywhere, and therefore no one spoke it. Just as no one ever says: "We are breathing!" in spite of the fact that breath is coming and going all the time.

"Mother," said the boy Paul one day, "why don't we keep a car of our own? Why do we always use uncle's, or else a taxi?"

"Because we're the poor members of the family," said the mother.

"But why *are* we, mother?"

"Well—I suppose," she said slowly and bitterly, "it's because your father has no luck."

The boy was silent for some time.

"Is luck money, mother?" he asked, rather timidly.

"No, Paul. Not quite. It's what causes you to have money."

"Oh!" said Paul vaguely. "I thought when Uncle Oscar said *filthy lucker,* it meant money."

"*Filthy lucre* does mean money," said the mother. "But it's lucre, not luck."

"Oh!" said the boy. "Then what *is* luck, mother?"

"It's what causes you to have money. If you're lucky you have money. That's why it's better to be born lucky than rich. If you're rich, you may lose your money. But if you're lucky, you will always get more money."

"Oh! Will you? And is father not lucky?"

"Very unlucky, I should say," she said bitterly.

The boy watched her with unsure eyes.

"Why?" he asked.

"I don't know. Nobody ever knows why one person is lucky and another unlucky."

"Don't they? Nobody at all? Does *nobody* know?"

"Perhaps God. But He never tells."

"He ought to, then. And aren't you lucky either, mother?"

"I can't be, if I married an unlucky husband."

"But by yourself, aren't you?"

"I used to think I was, before I married. Now I think I am very unlucky indeed."

"Why?"

"Well—never mind! Perhaps I'm not really," she said.

The child looked at her to see if she meant it. But he saw, by the lines of her mouth, that she was only trying to hide something from him.

"Well, anyhow," he said stoutly, "I'm a lucky person."

"Why?" said his mother, with a sudden laugh.

He stared at her. He didn't even know why he had said it.

"God told me," he asserted, brazening it out.

"I hope He did, dear!" she said, again with a laugh, but rather bitter.

"He did, mother!"

"Excellent!" said the mother, using one of her husband's exclamations.

The boy saw she did not believe him; or rather, that she paid no attention to his assertion. This angered him somewhere, and made him want to compel her attention.

He went off by himself, vaguely, in a childish way, seeking for the clue to 'luck'. Absorbed, taking no heed of other people, he went about with a sort of stealth, seeking inwardly for luck. He wanted luck, he wanted it, he wanted it. When the two girls were playing dolls in the nursery, he would sit on his big rocking-horse, charging madly into space, with a frenzy that made the little girls peer at him uneasily. Wildly the horse careered, the waving dark hair of the boy tossed, his eyes had a strange glare in them. The little girls dared not speak to him.

When he had ridden to the end of his mad little journey, he climbed down and stood in front of his rocking-horse, staring fixedly into its lowered face. Its red mouth was slightly open, its big eye was wide and glassy-bright.

"Now!" he would silently command the snorting steed. "Now, take me to where there is luck! Now take me!"

And he would slash the horse on the neck with the little whip he had asked Uncle Oscar for. He *knew* the horse could take him to where there was luck, if only he forced it. So he would mount again and start on his furious ride, hoping at last to get there. He knew he could get there.

"You'll break your horse, Paul!" said the nurse.

"He's always riding like that! I wish he'd leave off!" said his elder sister Joan.

But he only glared down on them in silence. Nurse gave him up. She could make nothing of him. Anyhow, he was growing beyond her.

One day his mother and his Uncle Oscar came in when he was on one of his furious rides. He did not speak to them.

"Hallo, you young jockey! Riding a winner?" said his uncle.

"Aren't you growing too big for a rocking-horse? You're not a very little boy any longer, you know," said his mother.

But Paul only gave a blue glare from his big, rather close-set eyes. He would speak to nobody when he was in full tilt. His mother watched him with an anxious expression on her face.

At last he suddenly stopped forcing his horse into the mechanical gallop and slid down.

"Well, I got there!" he announced fiercely, his blue eyes still flaring, and his sturdy long legs straddling apart.

"Where did you get to?" asked his mother.

"Where I wanted to go," he flared back at her.

"That's right, son!" said Uncle Oscar. "Don't you stop till you get there. What's the horse's name?"

"He doesn't have a name," said the boy.

"Gets on without all right?" asked the uncle.

"Well, he has different names. He was called Sansovino last week."

"Sansovino, eh? Won the Ascot. How did you know this name?"

"He always talks about horse-races with Bassett," said Joan.

The uncle was delighted to find that his small nephew was posted with all the racing news. Bassett, the young gardener, who had been wounded in the left foot in the war and had got his present job through Oscar Cresswell, whose batman he had been, was a perfect blade of the 'turf'. He lived in the racing events, and the small boy lived with him.

Oscar Cresswell got it all from Bassett.

"Master Paul comes and asks me, so I can't do more than tell him, sir," said Bassett, his face terribly serious, as if he were speaking of religious matters.

"And does he ever put anything on a horse he fancies?"

"Well—I don't want to give him away—he's a young sport, a fine sport, sir. Would you mind asking him himself? He sort of takes a pleasure in it, and perhaps he'd feel I was giving him away, sir, if you don't mind."

Bassett was serious as a church.

The uncle went back to his nephew and took him off for a ride in the car.

"Say, Paul, old man, do you ever put anything on a horse?" the uncle asked.

The boy watched the handsome man closely.

"Why, do you think I oughtn't to?" he parried.

"Not a bit of it! I thought perhaps you might give me a tip for the Lincoln."

The car sped on into the country, going down to Uncle Oscar's place in Hampshire.

"Honour bright?" said the nephew.

"Honour bright, son!" said the uncle.

"Well, then, Daffodil."

"Daffodil! I doubt it, sonny. What about Mirza?"

"I only know the winner," said the boy. "That's Daffodil."

"Daffodil, eh?"

There was a pause. Daffodil was an obscure horse comparatively.

"Uncle!"

"Yes, son?"

"You won't let it go any further, will you? I promised Bassett."

"Bassett be damned, old man! What's he got to do with it?"

"We're partners. We've been partners from the first. Uncle, he lent me my first five shillings, which I lost. I promised him, honour bright, it was only between me and him; only you gave me that ten-shilling note I started winning with, so I thought you were lucky. You won't let it go any further, will you?"

The boy gazed at his uncle from those big, hot, blue eyes, set rather close together. The uncle stirred and laughed uneasily.

"Right you are, son! I'll keep your tip private. Daffodil, eh? How much are you putting on him?"

"All except twenty pounds," said the boy. "I keep that in reserve."

The uncle thought it a good joke.

"You keep twenty pounds in reserve, do you, you young romancer? What are you betting, then?"

"I'm betting three hundred," said the boy gravely. "But it's between you and me, Uncle Oscar! Honour bright?"

The uncle burst into a roar of laughter.

"It's between you and me all right, you young Nat Gould," he said, laughing. "But where's your three hundred?"

"Bassett keeps it for me. We're partners."

"You are, are you! And what is Bassett putting on Daffodil?"

"He won't go quite as high as I do, I expect. Perhaps he'll go a hundred and fifty."

"What, pennies?" laughed the uncle.

"Pounds," said the child, with a surprised look at his uncle. "Bassett keeps a bigger reserve than I do."

Between wonder and amusement Uncle Oscar was silent. He pursued the matter no further, but he determined to take his nephew with him to the Lincoln races.

"Now, son," he said, "I'm putting twenty on Mirza, and I'll put five on for you on any horse you fancy. What's your pick?"

"Daffodil, uncle."

"No, not the fiver on Daffodil!"

"I should if it was my own fiver," said the child.

"Good! Good! Right you are! A fiver for me and a fiver for you on Daffodil."

The child had never been to a race-meeting before, and his eyes were blue fire. He pursed his mouth tight and watched. A Frenchman just in front had put his money on Lancelot. Wild with excitement, he flayed his arms up and down, yelling "Lancelot! Lancelot!" in his French accent.

Daffodil came in first, Lancelot second, Mirza third. The child, flushed and with eyes blazing, was curiously serene. His uncle brought him four five-pound notes, four to one.

"What am I to do with these?" he cried, waving them before the boy's eyes.

"I suppose we'll talk to Bassett," said the boy. "I expect I have fifteen hundred now; and twenty in reserve; and this twenty."

His uncle studied him for some moments.

"Look here, son!" he said. "You're not serious about Bassett and that fifteen hundred, are you?"

"Yes, I am. But it's between you and me, uncle. Honour bright?"

"Honour bright all right, son! But I must talk to Bassett."

"If you'd like to be a partner, uncle, with Bassett and me, we could all be partners. Only, you'd have to promise, honour bright, uncle, not to let it go beyond us three. Bassett and I are lucky, and you must be lucky, because it was your ten shillings I started winning with. . . ."

Uncle Oscar took both Bassett and Paul into Richmond Park for an afternoon, and there they talked.

"It's like this, you see, sir," Bassett said. "Master Paul would get me talking about racing events, spinning yarns, you know, sir. And he was always keen on knowing if I'd made or if I'd lost. It's about a year since, now, that I put five shillings on Blush of Dawn for him: and we lost. Then the luck turned, with that ten shillings he had from you: that we put on Singhalese. And since that time, it's been pretty steady, all things considering. What do you say, Master Paul?"

"We're all right when we're sure," said Paul. "It's when we're not quite sure that we go down."

"Oh, but we're careful then," said Bassett.

"But when are you *sure?*" smiled Uncle Oscar.

"It's Master Paul, sir," said Bassett in a secret, religious voice. "It's as if he had it from heaven. Like Daffodil, now, for the Lincoln. That was as sure as eggs."

"Did you put anything on Daffodil?" asked Oscar Cresswell.

"Yes, sir. I made my bit."

"And my nephew?"

Bassett was obstinately-silent, looking at Paul.

"I made twelve hundred, didn't I, Bassett? I told uncle I was putting three hundred on Daffodil."

"That's right," said Bassett, nodding.

"But where's the money?" asked the uncle.

"I keep it safe locked up, sir. Master Paul he can have it any minute he likes to ask for it."

"What, fifteen hundred pounds?"

"And twenty! And *forty*, that is, with the twenty he made on the course."

"It's amazing!" said the uncle.

"If Master Paul offers you to be partners, sir, I would, if I were you: if you'll excuse me," said Bassett.

Oscar Cresswell thought about it.

"I'll see the money," he said.

They drove home again, and, sure enough, Bassett came round to the garden-house with fifteen hundred pounds in notes. The twenty pounds reserve was left with Joe Glee, in the Turf Commission deposit.

"You see, it's all right, uncle, when I'm *sure!* Then we go strong, for all we're worth. Don't we, Bassett?"

"We do that, Master Paul."

"And when are you sure?" said the uncle, laughing.

"Oh, well, sometimes I'm *absolutely* sure, like about Daffodil," said the boy; "and sometimes I have an idea; and sometimes I haven't even an idea, have I, Bassett? Then we're careful, because we mostly go down."

"You do, do you! And when you're sure, like about Daffodil, what makes you sure, sonny?"

"Oh, well, I don't know," said the boy uneasily. "I'm sure, you know, uncle; that's all."

"It's as if he had it from heaven, sir," Bassett reiterated.

"I should say so!" said the uncle.

But he became a partner. And when the Leger was coming on Paul was 'sure' about Lively Spark, which was a quite inconsiderable horse. The boy insisted on putting a thousand on the horse, Bassett went for five hundred, and Oscar Cresswell two hundred. Lively Spark came in first, and the betting had been ten to one against him. Paul had made ten thousand.

"You see," he said, "I was absolutely sure of him."

Even Oscar Cresswell had cleared two thousand.

"Look here, son," he said, "this sort of thing makes me nervous."

"It needn't, uncle! Perhaps I shan't be sure again for a long time."

"But what are you going to do with your money?" asked the uncle.

"Of course," said the boy, "I started it for mother. She said she had no luck, because father is unlucky, so I thought if *I* was lucky, it might stop whispering."

"What might stop whispering?"

"Our house. I *hate* our house for whispering."

"What does it whisper?"

"Why—why"—the boy fidgeted—"why, I don't know. But it's always short of money, you know, uncle."

"I know it, son, I know it."

"You know people send mother writs, don't you, uncle?"

"I'm afraid I do," said the uncle.

"And then the house whispers, like people laughing at you behind your back. It's awful, that is! I thought if I was lucky——"

"You might stop it," added the uncle.

The boy watched him with big blue eyes, that had an uncanny cold fire in them, and he said never a word.

"Well, then!" said the uncle. "What are we doing?"

"I shouldn't like mother to know I was lucky," said the boy.

"Why not, son?"

"She'd stop me."

"I don't think she would."

"Oh!"—and the boy writhed in an odd way—"I *don't* want her to know, uncle."

"All right, son! We'll manage it without her knowing."

They managed it very easily. Paul, at the other's suggestion, handed over five thousand pounds to his uncle, who deposited it with the family lawyer, who was then to inform Paul's mother that a relative had put five thousand pounds into his hands, which sum was to be paid out a thousand pounds at a time, on the mother's birthday, for the next five years.

"So she'll have a birthday present of a thousand pounds for five successive years," said Uncle Oscar. "I hope it won't make it all the harder for her later."

Paul's mother had her birthday in November. The house had been 'whispering' worse than ever lately, and, even in spite of his luck, Paul could not bear up against it. He was very anxious to see the effect of the birthday letter, telling his mother about the thousand pounds.

When there were no visitors, Paul now took his meals with his parents, as he was beyond the nursery control. His mother went into town nearly every day. She had discovered that she had an odd knack of sketching furs and dress materials, so she worked secretly in the studio of a friend who was the chief 'artist' for the leading drapers. She drew the figures of ladies in furs and ladies in silk and sequins for the newspaper advertisements. This young woman artist earned several thousand pounds a year, but Paul's mother only made several hundreds, and she was again dissatisfied. She so wanted to be first in something, and she did not succeed, even in making sketches for drapery advertisements.

She was down to breakfast on the morning of her birthday. Paul watched her face as she read her letters. He knew the lawyer's letter. As his mother read it, her face hardened and became more expressionless. Then a cold, determined look came on her mouth. She hid the letter under the pile of others, and said not a word about it.

"Didn't you have anything nice in the post for your birthday, mother?" said Paul.

"Quite moderately nice," she said, her voice cold and absent.

She went away to town without saying more.

But in the afternoon Uncle Oscar appeared. He said Paul's mother had had a long interview with the lawyer, asking if the whole five thousand could not be advanced at once, as she was in debt.

"What do you think, uncle?" said the boy.

"I leave it to you, son."

"Oh, let her have it, then! We can get some more with the other," said the boy.

"A bird in the hand is worth two in the bush, laddie!" said Uncle Oscar.

"But I'm sure to *know* for the Grand National; or the Lincolnshire; or else the Derby. I'm sure to know for *one* of them," said Paul.

So Uncle Oscar signed the agreement, and Paul's mother touched the whole five thousand. Then something very curious happened. The voices in the house suddenly went mad, like a chorus of frogs on a spring evening. There were certain new furnishings, and Paul had a tutor. He was *really* going to Eton, his father's school, in the following autumn. There were flowers in the winter, and a blossoming of the luxury Paul's mother had been used to. And yet the voices in the house, behind the sprays of mimosa and almond-blossom, and from under the piles of iridescent cushions, simply trilled and screamed in a sort of ecstasy: "There *must* be more money! Oh-h-h; there *must* be more money. Oh, now, now-w! Now-w-w—there *must* be more money!—more than ever! More than ever!"

It frightened Paul terribly. He studied away at his Latin and Greek with his tutor. But his intense hours were spent with Bassett. The Grand National had gone by: he had not 'known', and had lost a hundred pounds. Summer was at hand. He was in agony for the Lincoln. But even for the Lincoln he didn't 'know', and he lost fifty pounds. He became wild-eyed and strange, as if something were going to explode in him.

"Let it alone, son! Don't you bother about it!" urged Uncle Oscar. But it was as if the boy couldn't really hear what his uncle was saying.

"I've got to know for the Derby! I've got to know for the Derby!" the child reiterated, his big blue eyes blazing with a sort of madness.

His mother noticed how overwrought he was.

"You'd better go to the seaside. Wouldn't you like to go now to the seaside, instead of waiting? I think you'd better," she said, looking down at him anxiously, her heart curiously heavy because of him.

But the child lifted his uncanny blue eyes.

"I couldn't possibly go before the Derby, mother!" he said. "I couldn't possibly!"

"Why not?" she said, her voice becoming heavy when she was opposed. "Why not? You can still go from the seaside to see the Derby with your Uncle Oscar, if that's what you wish. No need for you to wait here. Besides, I think you care too much about these races. It's a bad sign. My family has been a gambling family, and you won't know till you grow up how much damage it has done. But it has done damage. I shall have to send Bassett away, and ask Uncle Oscar not to talk racing to you, unless you promise to be reasonable about it: go away to the seaside and forget it. You're all nerves!"

"I'll do what you like, mother, so long as you don't send me away till after the Derby," the boy said.

"Send you away from where? Just from this house?"

"Yes," he said, gazing at her.

"Why, you curious child, what makes you care about this house so much, suddenly? I never knew you loved it."

He gazed at her without speaking. He had a secret within a secret, something he had not divulged, even to Bassett or to his Uncle Oscar.

But his mother, after standing undecided and a little bit sullen for some moments, said:

"Very well, then! Don't go to the seaside till after the Derby, if you don't wish it. But promise me you won't let your nerves go to pieces. Promise you won't think so much about horse-racing and *events,* as you call them!"

"Oh no," said the boy casually. "I won't think much about them, mother. You needn't worry. I wouldn't worry, mother, if I were you."

"If you were me and I were you," said his mother, "I wonder what we *should* do!"

"But you know you needn't worry, mother, don't you?" the boy repeated.

"I should be awfully glad to know it," she said wearily.

"Oh, well, you *can,* you know. I mean, you *ought* to know you needn't worry," he insisted.

"Ought I? Then I'll see about it," she said.

Paul's secret of secrets was his wooden horse, that which had no name. Since he was emancipated from a nurse and a nursery-governess, he had had his rocking-horse removed to his own bedroom at the top of the house.

"Surely you're too big for a rocking-horse!" his mother had remonstrated.

"Well, you see, mother, till I can have a *real* horse, I like to have *some* sort of animal about," had been his quaint answer.

"Do you feel he keeps you company?" she laughed.

"Oh yes! He's very good, he always keeps me company, when I'm there," said Paul.

So the horse, rather shabby, stood in an arrested prance in the boy's bedroom.

The Derby was drawing near, and the boy grew more and more tense. He hardly heard what was spoken to him, he was very frail, and his eyes were really uncanny. His mother had sudden strange seizures of uneasiness about him. Sometimes, for half an hour, she would feel a sudden anxiety about him that was almost anguish. She wanted to rush to him at once, and know he was safe.

Two nights before the Derby, she was at a big party in town, when one of her rushes of anxiety about her boy, her first-born, gripped her heart till she could hardly speak. She fought with the feeling, might and main, for she believed in common sense. But it was too strong. She had to leave the dance and go downstairs to telephone to the country. The children's nursery-governess was terribly surprised and startled at being rung up in the night.

"Are the children all right, Miss Wilmot?"

"Oh yes, they are quite all right."

"Master Paul? Is he all right?"

"He went to bed as right as a trivet. Shall I run up and look at him?"

"No," said Paul's mother reluctantly. "No! Don't trouble. It's all right. Don't sit up. We shall be home fairly soon." She did not want her son's privacy intruded upon.

"Very good," said the governess.

It was about one o'clock when Paul's mother and father drove up to their house. All was still. Paul's mother went to her room and slipped off her white fur cloak. She had told her maid not to wait up for her. She heard her husband downstairs, mixing a whisky and soda.

And then, because of the strange anxiety at her heart, she

stole upstairs to her son's room. Noiselessly she went along the upper corridor. Was there a faint noise? What was it?

She stood, with arrested muscles, outside his door, listening. There was a strange, heavy, and yet not loud noise. Her heart stood still. It was a soundless noise, yet rushing and powerful. Something huge, in violent, hushed motion. What was it? What in God's name was it? She ought to know. She felt that she knew the noise. She knew what it was.

Yet she could not place it. She couldn't say what it was. And on and on it went, like a madness.

Softly, frozen with anxiety and fear, she turned the door-handle.

The room was dark. Yet in the space near the window, she heard and saw something plunging to and fro. She gazed in fear and amazement.

Then suddenly she switched on the light, and saw her son, in his green pyjamas, madly surging on the rocking-horse. The blaze of light suddenly lit him up, as he urged the wooden horse, and lit her up, as she stood, blonde, in her dress of pale green and crystal, in the doorway.

"Paul!" she cried. "Whatever are you doing?"

"It's Malabar!" he screamed in a powerful, strange voice. "It's Malabar!"

His eyes blazed at her for one strange and senseless second, as he ceased urging his wooden horse. Then he fell with a crash to the ground, and she, all her tormented motherhood flooding upon her, rushed to gather him up.

But he was unconscious, and unconscious he remained, with some brain-fever. He talked and tossed, and his mother sat stonily by his side.

"Malabar! It's Malabar! Bassett, Bassett, I *know*! It's Malabar!"

So the child cried, trying to get up and urge the rocking-horse that gave him his inspiration.

"What does he mean by Malabar?" asked the heart-frozen mother.

"I don't know," said the father stonily.

"What does he mean by Malabar?" she asked her brother Oscar.

"It's one of the horses running for the Derby," was the answer.

And, in spite of himself, Oscar Cresswell spoke to Bassett, and himself put a thousand on Malabar: at fourteen to one.

The third day of the illness was critical: they were waiting for a change. The boy, with his rather long, curly hair, was tossing ceaselessly on the pillow. He neither slept nor regained consciousness, and his eyes were like blue stones. His mother sat, feeling her heart had gone, turned actually into a stone.

In the evening, Oscar Cresswell did not come, but Bassett sent a message, saying could he come up for one moment, just one moment? Paul's mother was very angry at the intrusion, but on second thoughts she agreed. The boy was the same. Perhaps Bassett might bring him to consciousness.

The gardener, a shortish fellow with a little brown moustache and sharp little brown eyes, tiptoed into the room, touched his imaginary cap to Paul's mother, and stole to the bedside, staring with glittering, smallish eyes at the tossing, dying child.

"Master Paul!" he whispered. "Master Paul! Malabar came in first all right, a clean win. I did as you told me. You've made over seventy thousand pounds, you have; you've got over eighty thousand. Malabar came in all right, Master Paul."

"Malabar! Malabar! Did I say Malabar, mother? Did I say Malabar? Do you think I'm lucky, mother? I knew Malabar, didn't I? Over eighty thousand pounds! I call that lucky, don't you, mother? Over eighty thousand pounds! I knew, didn't I know I knew? Malabar came in all right. If I ride my horse till I'm sure, then I tell you, Bassett, you can go as high as you like. Did you go for all you were worth, Bassett?"

"I went a thousand on it, Master Paul."

"I never told you, mother, that if I can ride my horse, and *get there,* then I'm absolutely sure—oh, absolutely! Mother, did I ever tell you? I *am* lucky!"

"No, you never did," said his mother.

But the boy died in the night.

And even as he lay dead, his mother heard her brother's

voice saying to her: "My God, Hester, you're eighty-odd thousand to the good, and a poor devil of a son to the bad. But, poor devil, poor devil, he's best gone out of a life where he rides his rocking-horse to find a winner."

The Blue Moccasins

THE FASHION in women changes nowadays even faster than women's fashions. At twenty, Lina M'Leod was almost painfully modern. At sixty, almost obsolete!

She started off in life to be really independent. In that remote day, forty years ago, when a woman said she was going to be independent, it meant she was having no nonsense with men. She was kicking over the masculine traces, and living her own life, manless.

To-day, when a girl says she is going to be independent, it means she is going to devote her attentions almost exclusively to men; though not necessarily to 'a man'.

Miss M'Leod had an income from her mother. Therefore, at the age of twenty, she turned her back on that image of tyranny, her father, and went to Paris to study art. Art having been studied, she turned her attention to the globe of earth. Being terribly independent, she soon made Africa look small: she dallied energetically with vast hinterlands of China: and she knew the Rocky Mountains and the deserts of Arizona as if she had been married to them. All this, to escape mere man.

It was in New Mexico she purchased the blue moccasins, blue bead moccasins, from an Indian who was her guide and her subordinate. In her independence she made use of men, of course, but merely as servants, subordinates.

When the war broke out she came home. She was then forty-five, and already going grey. Her brother, two years older than herself, but a bachelor, went off to the war; she stayed at home in the small family mansion in the country, and did what she could. She was small and erect and brief in her speech, her face was like pale ivory, her skin like a very delicate parchment, and her eyes were very blue. There was no nonsense about her, though she did paint pictures. She never even touched her delicately parchment face with pigment. She was good enough as she was, honest-to-God, and the country town had a tremendous respect for her.

In her various activities she came pretty often into contact with Percy Barlow, the clerk at the bank. He was only twenty-two when she first set eyes on him in 1914, and she immediately liked him. He was a stranger in the town, his father being a poor country vicar in Yorkshire. But he was of the confiding sort. He soon confided in Miss M'Leod, for whom he had a towering respect, how he disliked his stepmother, how he feared his father, was but as wax in the hands of that downright woman, and how, in consequence, he was homeless. Wrath shone in his pleasant features, but somehow it was an amusing wrath; at least to Miss M'Leod.

He was distinctly a good-looking boy, with stiff dark hair and odd, twinkling grey eyes under thick dark brows, and a rather full mouth and a queer, deep voice that had a caressing touch of hoarseness. It was his voice that somehow got behind Miss M'Leod's reserve. Not that he had the faintest intention of so doing. He looked up to her immensely: "She's miles above me."

When she watched him playing tennis, letting himself go a bit too much, hitting too hard, running too fast, being too nice to his partner, her heart yearned over him. The orphan in him! Why should he go and be shot? She kept him at home as long as possible, working with her at all kinds of war-work. He was so absolutely willing to do everything she wanted: devoted to her.

But at last the time came when he must go. He was now twenty-four and she forty-seven. He came to say good-bye, in his awkward fashion. She suddenly turned away, leaned her forehead against the wall, and burst into bitter tears. He was frightened out of his wits. Before he knew what was happening he had his arm in front of his face and was sobbing too.

She came to comfort him. "Don't cry, dear, don't! It will all be all right."

At last he wiped his face on his sleeve and looked at her

sheepishly. "It was you crying as did me in," he said. Her blue eyes were brilliant with tears. She suddenly kissed him.

"You are such a dear!" she said wistfully. Then she added, flushing suddenly vivid pink under her transparent parchment skin: "It wouldn't be right for you to marry an old thing like me, would it?"

He looked at her dumbfounded.

"No, I'm too old," she added hastily.

"Don't talk about old! You're not old!" he said hotly.

"At least I'm too old for *that*," she said sadly.

"Not as far as I'm concerned," he said. "You're younger than me, in most ways, I'm hanged if you're not!"

"Are you hanged if I'm not?" she teased wistfully.

"I am," he said. "And if I thought you wanted me, I'd be jolly proud if you married me. I would, I assure you."

"Would you?" she said, still teasing him.

Nevertheless, the next time he was home on leave she married him, very quietly, but very definitely. He was a young lieutenant. They stayed in her family home, Twybit Hall, for the honeymoon. It was her house now, her brother being dead. And they had a strangely happy month. She had made a strange discovery: a man.

He went off to Gallipoli, and became a captain. He came home in 1919, still green with malaria, but otherwise sound. She was in her fiftieth year. And she was almost white-haired; long, thick, white hair, done perfectly, and perfectly creamy, colourless face, with very blue eyes.

He had been true to her, not being very forward with women. But he was a bit startled by her white hair. However, he shut his eyes to it, and loved her. And she, though frightened and somewhat bewildered, was happy. But she was bewildered. It always seemed awkward to her, that he should come wandering into her room in his pyjamas when she was half dressed, and brushing her hair. And he would sit there silent, watching her brush the long swinging river of silver, of her white hair, the bare, ivory-white, slender arm working with a strange mechanical motion, sharp and forcible, brushing down the long silvery stream of hair. He would sit as if mesmerised, just gazing. And she would at last glance round sharply, and he would rise, saying some little casual thing to her and smiling to her oddly with his eyes. Then he would go out, his thin cotton pyjamas hitching up over his hips, for he was a rather big-built fellow. And she would feel dazed, as if she did not quite know her own self any more. And the queer, ducking motion of his silently going out of her door impressed her ominously, his curious cat head, his big hips and limbs.

They were alone in the house, save for the servants. He had no work. They lived modestly, for a good deal of her money had been lost during the war. But she still painted pictures. Marriage had only stimulated her to this. She painted canvases of flowers, beautiful flowers that thrilled her soul. And he would sit, pipe in first, silent, and watch her. He had nothing to do. He just sat and watched her small, neat figure and her concentrated movements as she painted. Then he knocked out his pipe and filled it again.

She said that at last she was perfectly happy. And he said that he was perfectly happy. They were always together. He hardly went out, save riding in the lanes. And practically nobody came to the house.

But still, they were very silent with one another. The old chatter had died out. And he did not read much. He just sat still, and smoked, and was silent. It got on her nerves sometimes, and she would think as she had thought in the past, that the highest bliss a human being can experience is perhaps the bliss of being quite alone, quite, quite alone.

His bank firm offered to make him manager of the local branch, and, at her advice, he accepted. Now he went out of the house every morning and came home every evening, which was much more agreeable. The rector begged him to sing again in the church choir: and again she advised him to accept. These were the old grooves in which his bachelor life had run. He felt more like himself.

He was popular: a nice, harmless fellow, everyone said of him. Some of the men secretly pitied him. They made rather much of him, took him home to luncheon, and let him loose with their daughters. He was popular among the daughters too: naturally, for if a girl expressed a wish, he would instinctively say: "What! Would you like it? I'll get it for you." And if he were not in a position to satisfy the desire, he would say: "I only wish I could do it for you. I'd do it like a shot." All of which he meant.

At the same time, though he got on so well with the maidens of the town, there was no coming forward about him. He was, in some way, not wakened up. Good-looking, and big, and serviceable, he was inwardly remote, without self-confidence, almost without a self at all.

The rector's daughter took upon herself to wake him up. She was exactly as old as he was, a smallish, rather sharp-faced young woman who had lost her husband in the war, and it had been a grief to her. But she took the stoic attitude of the young: You've got to live, so you may as well do it! She was a kindly soul, in spite of her sharpness. And she had a very perky little red-brown Pomeranian Dog that she had bought in Florence in the street, but which had turned out a handsome little fellow. Miss M'Leod looked down a bit on Alice Howells and her pom, so Mrs. Howells felt no special love for Miss M'Leod—"Mrs. Barlow, that is!" she would add sharply. "For it's quite impossible to think of her as anything but Miss M'Leod!"

Percy was really more at ease at the rectory, where the pom yapped and Mrs. Howells changed her dress three or four times a day, and looked it, than in the semi-cloisteral atmosphere of Twybit Hall, where Miss M'Leod wore tweeds and a natural knitted jumper, her skirts rather long, her hair done up pure silver, and painted her wonderful flower pictures in the deepening silence of the daytime. At evening she would go up to-change, after he came home. And though it thrilled her to have a man coming into her room as he dressed, snapping his collar-stud, to tell her something trivial as she stood bare-armed in her silk slip, rapidly coiling up the rope of silver hair behind her head, still, it worried her. When he was there, he couldn't keep away from her. And he would watch her, watch her, watch her as if she was the ultimate revelation. Sometimes it made her irritable. She was so absolutely used to her own privacy. What was he looking at? She never watched *him*. Rather she looked the other way.

His watching tried her nerves. She was turned fifty. And his great silent body loomed almost dreadful.

He was quite happy playing tennis or croquet with Alice Howells and the rest. Alice was choir-mistress, a bossy little person outwardly, inwardly rather forlorn and affectionate, and not very sure that life hadn't let her down for good. She was now over thirty—and had no one but the pom and her father and the parish—nothing in her really intimate life. But she was very cheerful, busy, even gay, with her choir and school work, her dancing, and flirting, and dressmaking.

She was intrigued by Percy Barlow. "How *can* a man be so nice to *everybody?*" she asked him, a little exasperated. "Well, why not?" he replied, with the odd smile of his eyes. "It's not why he shouldn't, but how he manages to do it! How can you have so much good-nature? I *have* to be catty to some people, but you're nice to *everybody*."

"Oh, am I!" he said ominously.

He was like a man in a dream, or in a cloud. He was quite a good bank-manager, in fact very intelligent. Even in appearance, his great charm was his beautifully-shaped head. He had plenty of brains, really. But in his will, in his body, he was asleep. And sometimes this lethargy, or coma made him look haggard. And sometimes it made his body seem inert and despicable, meaningless.

Alice Howells longed to ask him about his wife. *"Do* you love her? *Can* you really care for her?" But she daren't. She daren't ask him one word about his wife. Another thing she couldn't do, she couldn't persuade him to dance. Never, not once. But in everything else he was pliable as wax.

Mrs. Barlow—Miss M'Leod—stayed out at Twybit all the time. She did not even come in to church on Sunday. She had shaken off church, among other things. And she watched Percy depart, and felt just a little humiliated. He was going to sing in the choir! Yes, marriage was also a humiliation to her. She had distinctly married beneath her.

The years had gone by: she was now fifty-seven, Percy was thirty-four. He was still, in many ways, a boy. But in his curious silence, he was ageless. She managed him with perfect ease. If she expressed a wish, he acquiesced at once. So now it was agreed he should not come to her room any more. And he never did. But sometimes she went to him in his room, and was winsome in a pathetic, heart-breaking way.

She twisted him round her little finger, as the saying goes. And yet secretly she was afraid of him. In the early years he had displayed a clumsy but violent sort of passion, from which she had shrunk away. She felt it had nothing to do with her. It was just his indiscriminating desire for Woman, and for his own satisfaction. Whereas she was not just unidentified Woman, to give him his general satisfaction. So she had recoiled, and withdrawn herself. She had put him off. She had regained the absolute privacy of her room.

He was perfectly sweet about it. Yet she was uneasy with him now. She was afraid of him; or rather, not of him, but of a mysterious something in him. She was not a bit afraid of *him*, oh no! And when she went to him now, to be nice to him, in her pathetic winsomeness of an unused woman of fifty-seven, she found him sweet-natured as ever, but really indifferent. He saw her pathos and her winsomeness. In some way, the mystery of her, her thick white hair, her vivid blue eyes, her ladylike refinement still fascinated him. But his bodily desire for her had gone, utterly gone. And secretly, she was rather glad. But as he looked at her, looked at her, as he lay there so silent, she was afraid, as if some finger were pointed at her. Yet she knew, the moment she spoke to him, he would twist his eyes to that good-natured and 'kindly' smile of his.

It was in the late, dark months of this year that she missed the blue moccasins. She had hung them on a nail in his room. Not that he ever wore them: they were too small. Nor did she: they were too big. Moccasins are male footwear, among the Indians, not female. But they were of a lovely turquoise-blue colour, made all of little turquoise beads, with little forked flames of dead-white and dark-green. When, at the beginning of their marriage, he had exclaimed over them, she had said: "Yes! Aren't they a lovely colour! So blue!" And he had replied: "Not as blue as your eyes, even then."

So, naturally, she had hung them up on the wall in his room, and there they had stayed. Till, one November day, when there were no flowers, and she was pining to paint a still-life with something blue in it—oh, so blue, like delphiniums!—she had gone to his room for the moccasins. And they were not there. And though she hunted, she could not find them. Nor did the maids know anything of them.

So she asked him: "Percy, do you know where those blue moccasins are, which hung in your room?" There was a moment's dead silence. Then he looked at her with his good-naturedly twinkling eyes, and said: "No, *I* know nothing of them." There was another dead pause. She did not believe him. But being a perfect lady, she only said, as she turned away: "Well then, how curious it is!" And there was another dead pause. Out of which he asked her what she wanted them for, and she told him. Whereon the matter lapsed.

It was November, and Percy was out in the evening fairly often now. He was rehearsing for a 'play' which was to be given in the church schoolroom at Christmas. He had asked her about it. "Do you think it's a bit *infra dig,* if I play one of the characters?" She had looked at him mildly, disguising her real feeling. "If you don't feel *personally* humiliated," she said, "then there's nothing else to consider." And he had answered: "Oh, it doesn't upset *me* at all." So she mildly said: "Then do it, by all means." Adding at the back of her mind: If it amuses you, child!—but she thought, a change had indeed come over the world, when the master of Twybit Hall, or even, for that matter, the manager of the dignified Stubbs' Bank, should perform in public on a schoolroom stage in amateur theatricals. And she kept calmly aloof, preferring not to know any details. She had a world of her own.

When he had said to Alice Howells: "You don't think other folk'll mind—clients of the bank and so forth—think it beneath my dignity?" she had cried, looking up into his twinkling eyes: "Oh, you don't have to keep *your* dignity on ice, Percy—any more than I do mine."

The play was to be performed for the first time on Christmas Eve: and after the play, there was the midnight service in church. Percy therefore told his wife not to expect him home till the small hours, at least. So he drove himself off in the car.

As night fell, and rain, Miss M'Leod felt a little forlorn. She was left out of everything. Life was slipping past her. It was Christmas Eve, and she was more alone than she had ever been. Percy only seemed to intensify her aloneness, leaving her in this fashion.

She decided not to be left out. She would go to the play too. It was past six o'clock, and she had worked herself into a highly nervous state. Outside was darkness and rain: inside was silence, forlornness. She went to the telephone and rang up the garage in Shewbury. It was with great difficulty she got them to promise to send a car for her: Mr. Slater would have to fetch her himself in the two-seater runabout: everything else was out.

She dressed nervously, in a dark-green dress with a few modest jewels. Looking at herself in the mirror, she still thought herself slim, young looking and distinguished. She did not see how old-fashioned she was, with her uncompromising erectness, her glistening knob of silver hair sticking out behind, and her long dress.

It was a three-mile drive in the rain, to the small country town. She sat next to old Slater, who was used to driving horses and was nervous and clumsy with a car, without saying a word. He thankfully deposited her at the gate of St. Barnabas' School.

It was almost half-past seven. The schoolroom was packed and buzzing with excitement. "I'm afraid we haven't a seat left, Mrs. Barlow!" said Jackson, one of the church sidesmen, who was standing guard in the school porch, where people were still fighting to get in. He faced her in consternation. She faced him in consternation. "Well, I shall have to stay somewhere, till Mr. Barlow can drive me home," she said. "Couldn't you put me a chair somewhere?"

Worried and flustered, he went worrying and flustering the other people in charge. The schoolroom was simply packed solid. But Mr. Simmons, the leading grocer, gave up his chair in the front row to Mrs. Barlow, whilst he sat in a chair right under the stage, where he couldn't see a thing. But he could see Mrs. Barlow seated between his wife and daughter, speaking a word or two to them occasionally, and that was enough.

The lights went down: *The Shoes of Shagput* was about to begin. The amateur curtains were drawn back, disclosing the little amateur stage with a white amateur back-cloth daubed to represent a Moorish courtyard. In stalked Percy, dressed as a Moor, his face darkened. He looked quite handsome, his pale grey eyes queer and startling in his dark face. But he was afraid of the audience—he spoke away from them, stalking around clumsily. After a certain amount of would-be funny dialogue, in tripped the heroine, Alice Howells, of course. She was an Eastern houri, in white gauze Turkish trousers, silver veil, and—the blue moccasins. The whole stage was white, save for her blue moccasins, Percy's dark-green sash, and a negro boy's red fez.

When Mrs. Barlow saw the blue moccasins, a little bomb of rage exploded in her. This, of all places! The blue moccasins that she had bought in the western desert! The blue moccasins that were not so blue as her own eyes! *Her* blue moccasins! On the feet of that creature, Mrs. Howells.

Alice Howells was not afraid of the audience. She looked full at them, lifting her silver veil. And of course she saw Mrs. Barlow, sitting there like the Ancient of Days in judgment, in the front row. And a bomb of rage exploded in *her* breast too.

In the play, Alice was the wife of the grey-bearded old Caliph, but she captured the love of the young Ali, otherwise Percy, and the whole business was the attempt of these two to evade Caliph and negro-eunuchs and ancient crones, and get into each other's arms. The blue shoes were very important: for while the sweet Leila wore them, the gallant Ali was to know there was danger. But when she took them off, he might approach her.

It was all quite childish, and everybody loved it and Miss M'Leod might have been quite complacent about it all, had not Alice Howells got her monkey up, so to speak. Alice with a lot of make-up, looked boldly handsome. And sudden-ly bold she was, bold as the devil. All these years the poor

young widow has been 'good', slaving in the parish, and only
even flirting just to cheer things up, never going very far and
knowing she could never get anything out of it, but determined never to mope.

Now the sight of Miss M'Leod sitting there so erect, so
coolly 'higher plane', and calmly superior, suddenly let loose
a devil in Alice Howells. All her limbs went suave and
molten, as her young sex, long pent up, flooded to her
finger-tips. Her voice was strange, even to herself, with its
long, plaintive notes. She felt all her movements soft and
fluid, she felt herself like living liquid. And it was lovely.
Underneath it all was the sting of malice against Miss
M'Leod, sitting there so erect, with her great knob of white
hair.

Alice's business, as the lovely Leila, was to be seductive to
the rather heavy Percy. And seductive she was. In two
minutes, she had him spellbound. He saw nothing of the
audience. A faint, fascinated grin came on to his face, as he
acted up to the young woman in the Turkish trousers. His
rather full, hoarse voice changed and became clear, with a
new, naked clang in it. When the two sang together, in the
simple banal duets of the play, it was with a most fascinating
intimacy. And when, at the end of Act One, the lovely Leila
kicked off the blue moccasins, saying: "Away, shoes of bondage, shoes of sorrow!" and danced a little dance all alone,
barefoot, in her Turkish trousers, in front of her fascinated
hero, his smile was so spellbound that everybody else was
spellbound too.

Miss M'Leod's indignation knew no bounds. When the blue
moccasins were kicked across the stage by the brazen Alice,
with the words: "Away, shoes of bondage, shoes of sorrow!"
the older woman grew pink with fury, and it was all she
could do not to rise and snatch the moccasins from the stage,
and bear them away. She sat in speechless indignation during
the brief curtain between Act One and Act Two. Her moccasins! Her blue moccasins! Of the sacred blue colour, the
turquoise of heaven.

But there they were, in Act Two, on the feet of the bold
Alice. It was becoming too much. And the love-scenes be-

tween Percy and the young woman were becoming nakedly shameful. Alice grew worse and worse. She was worked up now, caught in her own spell, and unconscious of everything save of him, and the sting of that other woman, who presumed to own him. Own him? Ha-ha! For he was fascinated. The queer smile on his face, the concentrated gleam of his eyes, the queer way he leaned forward from his loins towards her, the new reckless, throaty twang in his voice—the audience had before their eyes a man spellbound and lost in passion.

Miss M'Leod sat in shame and torment, as if her chair was red-hot. She too was fast losing her normal consciousness, in the spell of rage. She was outraged. The second Act was working to its climax. The climax came. The lovely Leila kicked off the blue shoes: "Away, shoes of bondage, away!" and flew barefoot to the enraptured Ali, flinging herself into his arms. And if ever a man was gone in sheer desire, it was Percy, as he pressed the woman's lithe form against his body, and seemed unconsciously to envelop her, unaware of everything else. While she, blissful in his spell, but still aware of the audience and of the superior Miss M'Leod, let herself be wrapped closer and closer.

Miss M'Leod rose to her feet and looked towards the door. But the way out was packed with people standing holding their breath as the two on the stage remained wrapped in each other's arms, and the three fiddles and the flute softly woke up. Miss M'Leod could not bear it. She was on her feet, and beside herself. She could not get out. She could not sit down again.

"Percy!" she said, in a low clear voice. "Will you hand me my moccasins?"

He lifted his face like a man startled in a dream, lifted his face from the shoulder of his Leila. His gold-grey eyes were like softly-startled flames. He looked in sheer horrified wonder at the little white-haired woman standing below.

"Eh!" he said, purely dazed.

"Will you please hand me my moccasins!"—and she pointed to where they lay on the stage.

Alice had stepped away from him, and was gazing at the

risen viper of the little elderly woman on the tip of the audience. Then she watched him move across the stage, bending forward from the loins in his queer mesmerized way, pick up the blue moccasins, and stoop down to hand them over the edge of the stage to his wife, who reached up for them.

"Thank you!" said Miss M'Leod, seating herself with the blue moccasins in her lap.

Alice recovered her composure, gave a sign to the little orchestra, and began to sing at once, strong and assured, to sing her part in the duet that closed the Act. She knew she could command public opinion in her favour.

He too recovered at once, the little smile came back on his face, he calmly forgot his wife again as he sang his share in the duet. It was finished. The curtains were pulled to. There was immense cheering. The curtains opened, and Alice and Percy bowed to the audience, smiling both of them their peculiar secret smile, while Miss M'Leod sat with the blue moccasins in her lap.

The curtains were closed, it was the long interval. After a few moments of hesitation, Mrs. Barlow rose with dignity, gathered her wrap over her arm, and with the blue moccasins in her hand, moved towards the door. Way was respectfully made for her.

"I should like to speak to Mr. Barlow," she said to Jackson, who had anxiously ushered her in, and now would anxiously usher her out.

"Yes, Mrs. Barlow."

He led her round to the smaller class-room at the back, that acted as dressing-room. The amateur actors were drinking lemonade, and chattering freely. Mrs. Howells came forward, and Jackson whispered the news to her. She turned to Percy.

"Percy, Mrs. Barlow wants to speak to you. Shall I come with you?"

"Speak to me? Aye, come on with me."

The two followed the anxious Jackson into the other half-lighted class-room, where Mrs. Barlow stood in her wrap, holding the moccasins. She was very pale, and she watched the two butter-muslin Turkish figures enter, as if they could not possibly be real. She ignored Mrs. Howells entirely.

"Percy," she said, "I want you to drive me home."

"Drive you home!" he echoed.

"Yes, please!"

"Why—when?" he said, with vague bluntness.

"Now—if you don't mind——"

"What—in this get-up?" He looked at himself.

"I could wait while you changed."

There was a pause. He turned and looked at Alice Howells, and Alice Howells looked at him. The two women saw each other out of the corners of their eyes: but it was beneath notice. He turned to his wife, his black face ludicrously blank, his eyebrows cocked.

"Well, you see," he said, "it's rather awkward. I can hardly hold up the third Act while I've taken you home and got back here again, can I?"

"So you intend to play in the third Act?" she asked with cold ferocity.

"Why, I must, mustn't I?" he said blankly.

"Do you *wish* to?" she said, in all her intensity.

"I do, naturally. I want to finish the thing up properly," he replied, in the utter innocence of his head; about his heart he knew nothing.

She turned sharply away.

"Very well!" she said. And she called to Jackson, who was standing dejectedly by the door: "Mr. Jackson, will you please find some car or conveyance to take me home?"

"Aye! I say, Mr. Jackson," called Percy in his strong, democratic voice, going forward to the man. "Ask Tom Lomas if he'll do me a good turn and get my car out of the rectory garage, to drive Mrs. Barlow home. Aye, ask Tom Lomas! And if not him, ask Mr. Pilkington—Leonard. The key's there. You don't mind, do you? I'm ever so much obliged——"

The three were left awkwardly alone again.

"I expect you've had enough with two acts," said Percy soothingly to his wife. "These things aren't up to your mark.

I know it. They're only child's play. But, you see, they please the people. We've got a packed house, haven't we?"

His wife had nothing to answer. He looked so ludicrous, with his dark-brown face and butter-muslin bloomers. And his mind was so ludicrously innocent. His body, however, was not so ridiculously innocent as his mind, as she knew when he turned to the other woman.

"You and I, we're more on the nonsense level, aren't we?" he said, with the new, throaty clang of naked intimacy in his voice. His wife shivered.

"Absolutely on the nonsense level," said Alice, with easy assurance.

She looked into his eyes, then she looked at the blue moccasins in the hand of the other woman. He gave a little start, as if realising something for himself.

At that moment Tom Lomas looked in, saying heartily: "Right you are, Percy! I'll have my car here in half a tick. I'm more handy with it than yours."

"Thanks, old man! You're a Christian."

"Try to be—especially when you turn Turk! Well——" He disappeared.

"I say, Lina," said Percy in his most amiable democratic way, "would you mind leaving the moccasins for the next act? We s'll be in a bit of a hole without them."

Miss M'Leod faced him and stared at him with the full blast of her forget-me-not blue eyes, from her white face.

"Will you pardon me if I don't?" she said.

"What!" he exclaimed. "Why? Why not? It's nothing but play, to amuse the people. I can't see how it can hurt the *moccasins.* I understand you don't quite like seeing me make a fool of myself. But, anyhow, I'm a bit of a born fool. What?"—and his blackened face laughed with a Turkish laugh. "Oh, yes, you have to realise I rather enjoy playing the fool," he resumed. "And, after all, it doesn't really hurt *you,* now does it? Shan't you leave us those moccasins for the last act?"

She looked at him, then at the moccasins in her hand. No, it was useless to yield to so ludicrous a person. The vulgarity of his wheedling, the commonness of the whole performance!

It was useless to yield even the moccasins. It would be treachery to herself.

"I'm sorry," she said. "But I'd so much rather they weren't used for this kind of thing. I never intended them to be." She stood with her face averted from the ridiculous couple.

He changed as if she had slapped his face. He sat down on top of the low pupils' desk and gazed with glazed interest round the class-room. Alice sat beside him, in her white gauze and her bedizened face. They were like two rebuked sparrows on one twig, he with his great, easy, intimate limbs, she so light and alert. And as he sat he sank into an unconscious physical sympathy with her. Miss M'Leod walked towards the door.

"You'll have to think of something as'll do instead," he muttered to Alice in a low voice, meaning the blue moccasins. And leaning down, he drew off one of the grey shoes she had on, caressing her foot with the slip of his hand over its slim, bare shape. She hastily put the bare foot behind her other, shod foot.

Tom Lomas poked in his head, his overcoat collar turned up to his ears.

"Car's here," he said.

"Right-o! Tom! I'll chalk it up to thee, lad!" said Percy with heavy breeziness. Then, making a great effort with himself, he rose heavily and went across to the door, to his wife, saying to her, in the safe stiff voice of false heartiness:

"You'll be as right as rain with Tom. You won't mind if I don't come out? No! I'd better not show myself to the audience. Well—I'm glad you came, if only for a while. Good-bye then! I'll be home after the service—but I shan't disturb you. Good-bye! Don't get wet now——" And his voice, falsely cheerful, stiff with anger, ended in a clang of indignation.

Alice Howells sat on the infants' bench in silence. She was ignored. And she was unhappy, uneasy, because of the scene.

Percy closed the door after his wife. Then he turned with a looming slowness to Alice, and said in a hoarse whisper: "Think o' that, now!"

She looked up at him anxiously. His face, in its dark

pigment, was transfigured with indignant anger. His yellow-grey eyes blazed, and a great rush of anger seemed to be surging up volcanic in him. For a second his eyes rested on her upturned, troubled, dark-blue eyes, then glanced away as if he didn't want to look at her in his anger. Even so, she felt a touch of tenderness in his glance.

"And that's all she's ever cared about—her own things and her own way," he said, in the same hoarse whisper, hoarse with suddenly-released rage. Alice Howells hung her head in silence.

"Not another damned thing, but what's her own, her own—and her own holy way—damned holy-holy-holy, all to herself." His voice shook with hoarse, whispering rage, burst out at last.

Alice Howells looked up at him in distress.

"Oh, don't say it," she said. "I'm sure she's fond of you."

"Fond of me!" Fond of *me!"* he blazed with a grin of transcendent irony. "It makes her sick to look at me. I am a hairy brute, I own it. Why, she's never once touched me to be fond of me—never once—though she pretends sometimes. But a man knows——" and he made a grimace of contempt. "He knows when a woman's just stroking him, good doggie!— and when she's really a bit woman-fond of him. That woman's never been real fond of anybody or anything, all her life—she couldn't, for all her show of kindness. She's limited to herself, that woman is; and I've looked up to her as if she was God. More fool me! If God's not good-natured and good-hearted, then what is He——?"

Alice sat with her head dropped, realising once more that men aren't really fooled. She was upset, shaken by his rage, and frightened, as if she too were guilty. He had sat down blankly beside her. She glanced up at him.

"Never mind!" she said soothingly. "You'll like her again to-morrow."

He looked down at her with a grin, a grey sort of grin. "Are you going to stroke me 'good doggie!' as well?" he said.

"Why?" she asked, blank.

But he did not answer. Then after a while he resumed: "Wouldn't even leave the moccasins! And she's hung them up

in my room, left them there for years—any man'd consider
they were his. And I did want this show to-night to be a
success! What are you going to do about it?"

"I've sent over for a pair of pale-blue satin bed-slippers of
mine—they'll do just as well," she replied.

"Aye! For all that, it's done me in."

"You'll get over it."

"Happen so! She's curdled my inside, for all that. I don't
know how I'm going to be civil to her."

"Perhaps you'd better stay at the rectory to-night," she
said softly.

He looked into her eyes. And in that look, he transferred
his allegiance.

"*You* don't want to be drawn in, do you?" he asked, with
troubled tenderness.

But she only gazed with wide, darkened eyes into his eyes,
so she was like an open, dark doorway to him. His heart beat
thick, and the faint, breathless smile of passion came into his
eyes again.

"You'll have to go on, Mrs. Howells. We can't keep them
waiting any longer."

It was Jim Stokes, who was directing the show. They heard
the clapping and stamping of the impatient audience.

"Goodness!" cried Alice Howells, darting to the door.

Things

─ ─ ─ ─ ─ ─ ─

THEY WERE true idealists from New England. But this is some time ago: before the war. Several years before the war, they met and married; he a tall, keen-eyed young man from Connecticut, she a smallish, demure, Puritan-looking young woman from Massachusetts. They both had a little money. Not much, however. Even added together, it didn't make three thousand dollars a year. Still—they were free. Free!

Ah! Freedom! To be free to live one's own life! To be twenty-five and twenty-seven, a pair of true idealists with a mutual love of beauty, and an inclination towards 'Indian thought'—meaning, alas, Mrs. Besant—and an income a little under three thousand dollars a year! But what is money? All one wishes to do is to live a full and beautiful life. In Europe, of course, right at the fountain-head of tradition. It might possibly be done in America: in New England, for example. But at a forfeiture of a certain amount of 'beauty'. True beauty takes a long time to mature. The baroque is only half-beautiful, half-matured. No, the real silver bloom, the real golden-sweet bouquet of beauty had its roots in the Renaissance, not in any later or shallower period.

Therefore the two idealists, who were married in New Haven, sailed at once to Paris: Paris of the old days. They had a studio apartment on the Boulevard Montparnasse, and they became real Parisians, in the old, delightful sense, not in the modern, vulgar. It was the shimmer of the pure impressionists, Monet and his followers, the world seen in terms of pure light, light broken and unbroken. How lovely! How lovely the nights, the river, the mornings in the old streets and by the flower-stalls and the book-stalls, the afternoons up on Montmartre or in the Tuileries, the evenings on the boulevards!

They both painted, but not desperately. Art had not taken them by the throat, and they did not take Art by the throat. They painted: that's all. They knew people—nice people, if possible, though one had to take them mixed. And they were happy.

Yet it seems as if human beings must set their claws in *something*. To be 'free', to be 'living a full and beautiful life', you must, alas, be attached to something. A 'full and beautiful life' means a tight attachment to *something*—at least, it is so for all idealists—or else a certain boredom supervenes; there is a certain waving of loose ends upon the air, like the waving, yearning tendrils of the vine that spread and rotate, seeking something to clutch, something up which to climb towards the necessary sun. Finding nothing, the vine can only trail, half-fulfilled, upon the ground. Such is freedom!—a clutching of the right pole. And human beings are all vines. But especially the idealist. He is a vine, and he needs to clutch and climb. And he despises the man who is a mere *potato*, or turnip, or lump of wood.

Our idealists were frightfully happy, but they were all the time reaching out for something to cotton on to. At first, Paris was enough. They explored Paris *thoroughly*. And they learned French till they almost felt like French people, they could speak it so glibly.

Still, you know, you never talk French with your *soul*. It can't be done. And though it's very thrilling, at first, talking in French to clever Frenchmen—they seem *so* much cleverer than oneself—still, in the long run, it is not satisfying. The endlessly clever *materialism* of the French leaves you cold, in the end, gives a sense of barrenness and incompatibility with true New England depth. So our two idealists felt.

They turned away from France—but ever so gently. France had disappointed them. "We've loved it, and we've got a great deal out of it. But after a while, after a considerable while, several years, in fact, Paris leaves one feeling disappointed. It hasn't quite got what one wants."

"But Paris isn't France."

"No, perhaps not. France is quite different from Paris. And France is lovely—quite lovely. But *to us,* though we love it, it doesn't say a great deal."

So, when the war came, the idealists moved to Italy. And they loved Italy. They found it beautiful, and more poignant than France. It seemed much nearer to the New England conception of beauty: something pure, and full of sympathy, without the *materialism* and the *cynicism* of the French. The two idealists seemed to breathe their own true air in Italy.

And in Italy, much more than in Paris, they felt they could thrill to the teachings of the Buddha. They entered the swelling stream of modern Buddhistic emotion, and they read the books, and they practised meditation, and they deliberately set themselves to eliminate from their own souls greed, pain, and sorrow. They did not realise—yet—that Buddha's very eagerness to free himself from pain and sorrow is in itself a sort of greed. No, they dreamed of a perfect world, from which all greed, and nearly all pain, and a great deal of sorrow, were eliminated.

But America entered the war, so the two idealists had to help. They did hospital work. And though their experience made them realise more than ever that greed, pain, and sorrow *should* be eliminated from the world, nevertheless the Buddhism, or the theosophy, didn't emerge very triumphant from the long crisis. Somehow, somewhere, in some part of themselves, they felt that greed, pain, and sorrow would never be eliminated, because most people don't care about eliminating them, and never will care. Our idealists were far too Western to think of abandoning all the world to damnation, while they saved their two selves. They were far too unselfish to sit tight under a bho tree and reach Nirvana in a mere couple.

It was more than that, though. They simply hadn't enough *Sitzfleisch* to squat under a bho tree and get to Nirvana by contemplating anything, least of all their own navel. If the whole wide world was not going to be saved, they, personally, were not so very keen on being saved just by themselves. No, it would be so lonesome. They were New Englanders, so it must be all or nothing. Greed, pain, and sorrow must either be eliminated from *all the world,* or else, what was the use of eliminating them from oneself? No use at all! One was just a victim.

And so, although they still *loved* 'Indian thought', and felt very tender about it: well, to go back to our metaphor, the pole up which the green and anxious vines had clambered so far now proved dry-rotten. It snapped, and the vines came slowly subsiding to earth again. There was no crack and crash. The vines held themselves up by their own foliage, for a while. But they subsided. The beanstalk of 'Indian thought' had given way before Jack and Jill had climbed off the tip of it to a further world.

They subsided with a slow rustle back to earth again. But they made no outcry. They were again 'disappointed'. But they never admitted it. 'Indian thought' had let them down. But they never complained. Even to one another, they never said a word. They were disappointed, faintly but deeply disillusioned, and they both knew it. But the knowledge was tacit.

And they still had so much in their lives. They still had Italy—dear Italy. And they still had freedom, the priceless treasure. And they still had so much 'beauty'. About the fullness of their lives they were not quite so sure. They had one little boy, whom they loved as parents should love their children, but whom they wisely refrained from fastening upon, to build their lives on him. No, no, they must live their own lives! They still had strength of mind to know that.

But they were now no longer very young. Twenty-five and twenty-seven had become thirty-five and thirty-seven. And though they had had a very wonderful time in Europe, and though they still loved Italy—dear Italy!—yet: they were disappointed. They had got a lot out of it: oh, a very great deal indeed! Still, it hadn't given them quite, not *quite,* what they had expected. Europe was lovely, but it was dead. Living in Europe, you were living on the past. And Europeans, with all their superficial charm, were not *really* charming. They were materialistic, they had no *real* soul. They just did not understand the inner urge of the spirit, because the inner urge was dead in them, they were all survivals. There, that was the truth about Europeans: they were survivals, with no more getting ahead in them.

It was another bean-pole, another vine-support crumbled under the green life of the vine. And very bitter it was, this time. For up the old tree-trunk of Europe the green vine had been clambering silently for more than ten years, ten hugely important years, the years of real living. The two idealists had *lived* in Europe, lived on Europe and on European life and European things as vines in an everlasting vineyard.

They had made their home here: a home such as you could never make in America. Their watchword had been 'beauty'. They had rented, the last four years, the second floor of an old palazzo on the Arno, and here they had all their 'things'. And they derived a profound, profound satisfaction from their apartment: the lofty, silent, ancient rooms with windows on the river, with glistening, dark-red floors, and the beautiful furniture that the idealists had 'picked up'.

Yes, unknown to themselves, the lives of the idealists had been running with a fierce swiftness horizontally, all the time. They had become tense, fierce, hunters of 'things' for their home. While their souls were climbing up to the sun of old European culture or old Indian thought, their passions were running horizontally, clutching at 'things'. Of course they did not buy the things for the things' sakes, but for the sake of 'beauty'. They looked upon their home as a place entirely furnished by loveliness, not by 'things' at all. Valerie had some very lovely curtains at the windows of the long *salotto*, looking on the river: curtains of queer ancient material that looked like finely-knitted silk, most beautifully faded down from vermilion and orange, and gold, and black, down to a sheer soft glow. Valerie hardly ever came into the *salotto* without mentally falling on her knees before the curtains. "Chartres!" she said. "To me they are Chartres!" And Melville never turned and looked at his sixteenth-century Venetian bookcase, with its two or three dozen of choice books, without feeling his marrow stir in his bones. The holy of holies!

The child silently, almost sinisterly, avoided any rude contact with these ancient monuments of furniture, as if they

had been nests of sleeping cobras, or that 'thing' most perilous to the touch, the Ark of the Covenant. His childish awe
was silent and cold, but final.

Still, a couple of New England idealists cannot live merely
on the bygone glory of their furniture. At least, one couple
could not. They got used to the marvellous Bologna cupboard, they got used to the wonderful Venetian bookcase,
and the books, and the Siena curtains and bronzes, and the
lovely sofas and side-tables and chairs they had 'picked up' in
Paris. Oh, they had been picking things up since the first day
they landed in Europe. And they were still at it. It is the last
interest Europe can offer to an outsider: or to an insider
either.

When people came, and were thrilled by the Melville
interior, then Valerie and Erasmus felt they had not lived in
vain: that they still were living. But in the long mornings,
when Erasmus was desultorily working at Renaissance Florentine literature, and Valerie was attending to the apartment: and in the long hours after lunch; and in the long,
usually very cold and oppressive evenings in the ancient
palazzo: then the halo died from around the furniture, and
the things became things, lumps of matter that just stood
there or hung there, *ad infinitum*, and said nothing; and
Valerie and Erasmus almost hated them. The glow of beauty,
like every other glow, dies down unless it is fed. The idealists
still dearly loved their things. But they had got them. And the
sad fact is, things that glow vividly while you're getting them,
go almost quite cold after a year or two. Unless, of course,
people envy them very much, and the museums are pining
for them. And the Melvilles' 'things', though very good, were
not quite so good as that.

So, the glow gradually went out of everything, out of
Europe, out of Italy—"the Italians are *dears*"—even out of
that marvellous apartment on the Arno. "Why, if I had this
apartment, I'd never, never even want to go out of doors! It's
too lovely and perfect." That was something, of course—to
hear that.

And yet Valerie and Erasmus went out of doors: they
even went out to get away from its ancient, cold-floored,

stone-heavy silence and dead dignity. "We're living on the past, you know, Dick," said Valerie to her husband. She called him Dick.

They were grimly hanging on. They did not like to give in. They did not like to own up that they were through. For twelve years, now, they had been 'free' people living a 'full and beautiful life'. And America for twelve years had been their anathema, the Sodom and Gomorrah of industrial materialism.

It wasn't easy to own that you were 'through'. They hated to admit that they wanted to go back. But at last, reluctantly, they decided to go, "for the boy's sake".—"We can't *bear* to leave Europe. But Peter is an American, so he had better look at America while he's young." The Melvilles had an entirely English accent and manner; almost; a little Italian and French here and there.

They left Europe behind, but they took as much of it along with them as possible. Several van-loads, as a matter of fact. All those adorable and irreplaceable 'things'. And all arrived in New York, idealists, child, and the huge bulk of Europe they had lugged along.

Valerie had dreamed of a pleasant apartment, perhaps on Riverside Drive, where it was not so expensive as east of Fifth Avenue, and where all their wonderful things would look marvellous. She and Erasmus house-hunted. But alas! their income was quite under three thousand dollars a year. They found—well, everybody knows what they found. Two small rooms and a kitchenette, and don't let us unpack a *thing!*

The chunk of Europe which they had bitten off went into a warehouse, at fifty dollars a month. And they sat in two small rooms and a kitchenette, and wondered why they'd done it.

Erasmus, of course, ought to get a job. This was what was written on the wall, and what they both pretended not to see. But it had been the strange, vague threat that the Statue of Liberty had always held over them: "Thou shalt get a job!" Erasmus had the tickets, as they say. A scholastic career was still possible for him. He had taken his exams brilliantly at

Yale, and had kept up his 'researches' all the time he had been in Europe.

But both he and Valerie shuddered. A scholastic career! The scholastic world! The *American* scholastic world! Shudder upon shudder! Give up their freedom, their full and beautiful life? Never! Never! Erasmus would be forty next birthday.

The 'things' remained in warehouse. Valerie went to look at them. It cost her a dollar an hour, and horrid pangs. The 'things', poor things, looked a bit shabby and wretched, in that warehouse.

However, New York was not all America. There was the great clean West. So the Melvilles went West, with Peter, but without the things. They tried living the simple life, in the mountains. But doing their own chores became almost a nightmare. 'Things' are all very well to look at, but it's awful handling them, even when they're beautiful. To be the slave of hideous things, to keep a stove going, cook meals, wash dishes, carry water and clean floors: pure horror of sordid anti-life!

In the cabin on the mountains, Valerie dreamed of Florence, the lost apartment; and her Bologna cupboard and Louis-Quinze chairs, above all, her 'Chartres' curtains, stood in New York and costing fifty dollars a month.

A millionaire friend came to the rescue, offering them a cottage on the Californian coast—California! Where the new soul is to be born in man. With joy the idealists moved a little farther west, catching at new vine-props of hope.

And finding them straws! The millionaire cottage was perfectly equipped. It was perhaps as labour-savingly perfect as is possible: electric heating and cooking, a white-and-pearl-enamelled kitchen, nothing to make dirt except the human being himself. In an hour or so the idealists had got through their chores. They were 'free'—free to hear the great Pacific pounding the coast, and to feel a new soul filling their bodies.

Alas! the Pacific pounded the coast with hideous brutality, brute force itself! And the new soul, instead of sweetly stealing into their bodies, seemed only meanly to gnaw the old soul out of their bodies. To feel you are under the fist of the most blind and crunching brute force: to feel that your cherished idealist's soul is being gnawed out of you, and only irritation left in place of it: well, it isn't good enough.

After about nine months, the idealists departed from the Californian west. It had been a great experience, they were glad to have had it. But, in the long run, the West was not the place for them, and they knew it. No, the people who wanted new souls had better get them. They, Valerie and Erasmus Melville, would like to develop the old soul a little further. Anyway, they had not felt any influx of new soul on the Californian coast. On the contrary.

So, with a slight hole in their material capital, they returned to Massachusetts and paid a visit to Valerie's parents, taking the boy along. The grandparents welcomed the child— poor expatriated boy—and were rather cold to Valerie, but really cold to Erasmus. Valerie's mother definitely said to Valerie, one day, that Erasmus ought to take a job, so that Valerie could live decently. Valerie haughtily reminded her mother of the beautiful apartment on the Arno, and the 'wonderful' things in store in New York, and of the 'marvellous and satisfying life' she and Erasmus had led. Valerie's mother said that she didn't think her daughter's life looked so very marvellous at present: homeless, with a husband idle at the age of forty, a child to educate, and a dwindling capital: looked the reverse of marvellous to *her*. Let Erasmus take some post in one of the universities.

"What post? What university?" interrupted Valerie.

"That could be found, considering your father's connections and Erasmus's qualifications," replied Valerie's mother. "And you could get all your valuable things out of store, and have a really lovely home, which everybody in America would be proud to visit. As it is, your furniture is eating up your income, and you are living like rats in a hole, with nowhere to go to."

This was very true. Valerie was beginning to pine for a home, with her 'things'. Of course, she could have sold her furniture for a substantial sum. But nothing would have induced her to. Whatever else passed away, religions, cultures, continents, and hopes, Valerie would *never* part from the 'things' which she and Erasmus had collected with such passion. To these she was nailed.

But she and Erasmus still would not give up that freedom, that full and beautiful life they had so believed in. Erasmus cursed America. He did not *want* to earn a living. He panted for Europe.

Leaving the boy in charge of Valerie's parents, the two idealists once more set off for Europe. In New York they paid two dollars and looked for a brief, bitter hour at their 'things'. They sailed 'student class'—that is, third. Their income now was less than two thousand dollars instead of three. And they made straight for Paris—cheap Paris.

They found Europe, this time, a complete failure. "We have returned like dogs to our vomit," said Erasmus; "but the vomit has staled in the meantime." He found he couldn't stand Europe. It irritated every nerve in his body. He hated America too. But America at least was a darn sight better than this miserable, dirt-eating continent; which was by no means cheap any more, either.

Valerie, with her heart on her things—she had really burned to get them out of that warehouse, where they had stood now for three years, eating up two thousand dollars—wrote to her mother she thought Erasmus would come back if he could get some suitable work in America. Erasmus, in a state of frustration bordering on rage and insanity, just went round Italy in a poverty-stricken fashion, his coat-cuffs frayed, hating everything with intensity. And when a post was found for him in Cleveland University, to teach French, Italian, and Spanish literature, his eyes grew more beady, and his long, queer face grew sharper and more rat-like with utter baffled fury. He was forty, and the job was upon him.

"I think you'd better accept, dear. You don't care for Europe any longer. As you say, it's dead and finished. They offer us a house on the college lot, and mother says there's room in it for all our things. I think we'd better cable 'Accept'."

He glowered at her like a cornered rat. One almost expected to see rat's whiskers twitching at the sides of the sharp nose.

"Shall I send the cablegram?" she asked.

"Send it!" he blurted.

And she went out and sent it.

He was a changed man, quieter, much less irritable. A load was off him. He was inside the cage.

But when he looked at the furnaces of Cleveland, vast and like the greatest of black forests, with red and white-hot cascades of gushing metal, and tiny gnomes of men, and terrific noises, gigantic, he said to Valerie:

"Say what you like, Valerie, this is the biggest thing the modern world has to show."

And when they were in their up-to-date little house on the college lot of Cleveland University, and that woebegone débris of Europe: Bologna cupboard, Venice book-shelves, Ravenna bishop's chair, Louis-Quinze side-tables, 'Chartres' curtains, Siena bronze lamps, all were arrayed, and all looked perfectly out of keeping, and therefore very impressive; and when the idealists had had a bunch of gaping people in, and Erasmus had showed off in his best European manner, but still quite cordial and American; and Valerie had been most ladylike, but for all that, "we prefer America"; then Erasmus said, looking at her with queer, sharp eyes of a rat:

"Europe's the mayonnaise all right, but America supplies the good old lobster—what?"

"Every time!" she said, with satisfaction.

And he peered at her. He was in the cage: but it was safe inside. And she, evidently, was her real self at last. She had got the goods. Yet round his nose was a queer, evil scholastic look of pure scepticism. But he liked lobster.

About the Author

D[AVID] H[ERBERT] LAWRENCE was born in 1885 in a coal mining village in England. His first novel, published in 1911, *The White Peacock*, was followed by others, among them *Sons and Lovers* (1913), *The Rainbow* (1915), *Women in Love* (1920), *The Plumed Serpent* (1926), and *Lady Chatterly's Lover* (1928). At his death in 1930 Lawrence left behind him close to fifty volumes of his novels, long and short stories, plays, poems, essays, and travels journals, as well as an extensive personal correspondence and a mass of material that has been published posthumously.

More Ballantine Books
You Will Enjoy

THE CROWD, Gustave Le Bon   **$.95**
The famous classic on crowd behavior, with a new fore-
word for this edition by the author of *The Money Game*,
"Adam Smith."

**THE CLOSED CORPORATION: American Universities in
Crisis, James Ridgeway**   **$.95**
The explosive, documented report on how America's
largest universities are controlled by government and
big business. Every word of the new Random House
Bestseller!

**RED FLAG/BLACK FLAG, Patrick Seale and Maureen
McConville**   **$.95**
Eye-witness account of the student activist revolution
that almost overturned the government of France. A
close-up of the New Left in action.

GOTHIC POLITICS IN THE DEEP SOUTH, Robert Sherrill
$.95
A devastating scrutiny of George Wallace, Orval Faubus,
Lester Maddox and other Southern leaders, by the
author of *The Accidental President*. Revised and en-
larged.

THE POLITICS OF EXPERIENCE, R. D. Laing   **$.95**
A young British psychiatrist challenges the Establishment conception of "normality" in a key work that com-
pares with Norman O. Brown's *Life Against Death*.